Dedicated to my grandson James,
to his future siblings and cousins,
and to those who follow even them.
The future is yours!

Printed in the United States of America
First Edition Printing, 2017

Published by Greyfox Press
Graphic Design by Inkwell Book Co.
Cover Art by Sarah Lapallo Beck
Author Photo by Eric Dobbs

ISBN-13 978-0-9833982-2-6
Library of Congress Control Number 2017903192

www.InkwellBookCompany.com
www.ConnieLapallo.com

Praise for the *Jamestown Sky* Series

As a past National Governor of the Jamestowne Society and husband of a Colonial Dame, I am of the opinion that Connie's books truly capture the inner being, strength, and fortitude of the women and children at Jamestown.

—Aubrey R. "Bunky" Bowles, III

A magnificent work/trilogy. And a work of tremendous labor and restraint. Not historical fiction but rather the writing of history in the form of a novel. Boxed in by the few and scattered records we have of a remote time, this author has spent twenty years meeting the challenge of getting the tale to flow out of the actual facts, to move our hearts. Doubtless it would take her another book this size to explain how she did it.

—Edward Wright Haile, author of *Jamestown Narratives: Eyewitness Accounts of the Virginia Colony* and *John Smith in the Chesapeake*

I couldn't put it down! A wonderful series that makes you feel as if you're living in colonial Virginia.

—Dick Cheatham, Founder and Director, Living History Associates, Ltd.

From the very first page, the reader is aware of Lapallo's personal investment in making the story both historically accurate and beautiful.

—Tidewater Review

The description of the tempest 'hurican' the fleet of ships encounters off Bermuda is itself alone worth the read.

—Pleasant Living Magazine

The mention of the Jamestown colony brings to mind the work and the history of its men. Yet, Lapallo is helping to change that.

—Suffolk News-Herald

Lapallo has given the women that settled this colony a voice, and it's a powerful one.

—Sharon Baldacci, author of *A Sundog Moment*

Rich characters appear against the brutal background of the Starving Time.

—Northern Neck News

My dad and I had fun discussing your book. I'm glad you stuck to the facts, and didn't just make up most of it. That way, I could get it straight in my head, instead of thinking, "Wait! I learned something completely different in school!"

—Christina Cox, 13 years old

The Sun is but a
Morning Star

Based on the True Story of the Women & Children at Jamestown

BOOK THREE IN THE JAMESTOWN SKY SERIES
1621 — 1652

To Dolores,

Godspeed to you
in all your journeys.

C. Lapallo
2017

CONNIE LAPALLO

 Greyfox Press

Only that day dawns to which we are awake.
The sun is but a morning star.
> —Henry David Thoreau

Marking Her Fortieth Year in the Colony

August 1649
Mulberry Island, Virginia

Each night the Moon kisses secretly the Lover who counts the stars.
—Rumi

The sun is still low, a candle in Virginia's dusty blue sky, as it peeks over the river. The moon has hidden itself; the morning star has nearly vanished. But the sun breaks the day, changing the colors of the river as if to say, "See, I am the sun. I can do this."

Miss Joan is sitting beside me, her weathered hand tucked into mine. Her once dark hair has whitened to the color of dogwood tree blossoms. She has swept it behind her in a bun, her coif tucked over it. She is, just now, staring at the river and at the shore beyond. Her eyes are distant, and I notice they are rich and blue. Blue like the river, deep as the sky.

She is not speaking, only looking. She's tired, I know. At an age near seventy, she has remarkable vigor. She most loves to speak about her garden, to show you its blooms, and to tell you what it will become—if it is not yet.

I'm a stranger here on Mulberry Island. I've come to visit my cousin Joan. I believe we're related for my grandmother's mother was a Phippen from Dorset. Like everyone here in Virginia, we call ourselves cousins if we so much as believe ourselves to be cousins with one another's cousins. That's enough. Further bloodlines than that we simply call our kinsmen.

Blood in Virginia runs deep. Lines connect like the silvery threads of the great spider's web, the spider which builds so boldly in our doorways.

Soon the heat will bear down on us, as it always does in Virginia in August. So much hotter than ever the weather must get in the English fens and countryside. At least, I hear it to be so. In a Virginia summer, you stay inside except when the sun is low, be it coming up or going down.

We wait as if in vigil as the sun rises, a carved walnut bench our pew.

Above and around our seat, grapevines wriggle and wind like ribbon on the latticework. The vines give some coolness, especially when the breeze wafts through, tickling the leaves. Overhanging the pergola are mulberry branches, providing their shade and rich purple berries.

Above my head, a crow makes his scratchy call, and I can hear an osprey, too. I listen to these early morning birds as a peregrine falcon circles high aloft. "Peregrine" means "pilgrim" or "traveler," and it seems a fitting bird to punctuate our time together.

I glance at Miss Joan. She remembers England—a place I've never seen but hope to see someday. A place everyone speaks of as the old country. It is older than we are, surely.

The English roots dig deep into the ground like an ancient oak. I smile, picturing the flood of acorns at the base of such a tree. I remember Miss Joan's story about how she, with Lady Yeardley and Miss Maggie, collected those acorns. They then ground the acorns in secret and hid the meal. They knew that having a food—any food—in a Starving Time was fraught with danger.

Miss Joan did not wish to tell me more about the old days, this I suspect. She indulged me after first refusing. I'm not sure why the indulgence, but I do surmise the cause of refusal. She has relived much of the pain of her life, much of the triumph, and so, so many tears. She cannot speak of Temperance, Lady Yeardley, without fresh tears, I notice.

Tempie remained Miss Joan's dearest friend until death separated them. I should call her Dame Temperance, Lady Yeardley. But though I never met her, she has become Tempie to me as she is to Miss Joan. I suppose Tempie, from what I know of her, wouldn't mind. *Listen to my friend's stories, and call me anything you wish!* she might say.

Tempie has been on the other side, waiting for Miss Joan, lo, these past twenty years, as I reckon.

Miss Joan always grows misty when speaking of Maggie, too. Her love for this friend endures many years past Maggie's death. Perhaps Miss Joan feels she owes Maggie a debt she cannot repay. After all, Miss Maggie helped her prepare for great hardship, abandonment, and impending starvation. Maggie had a plan, Miss Joan said. "She made us face the grimness of our coming winter in Virginia. Maggie made us know that we would have to accept ourselves as widows and get on with it. We could not help our husbands then, nor could they help us," Miss Joan said. Maggie forced her two friends to face the harshness of the coming winter one day in the James Town church. "What we have, we have," Maggie had told them.

If only we could have saved her. Miss Joan doesn't say this, but I can read it as an unspoken undertone. A dear wish.

Yesterday, Miss Joan said to me, "Maggie helped us understand we couldn't change our circumstances. We could only change ourselves and what we did. We must, Maggie said, therefore help one another, strive together."

With that, Miss Joan twisted a handkerchief and was silent as her eyes drifted once more to the river.

Acorn flour. Manna from heaven, Miss Joan said they called it. Well, when you've got nothing else to eat, acorns do look mighty good. Anything looks good, in fact.

Miss Joan remembered the time they found a perished chickadee right outside their door. That little bird gave them hope that God hadn't forgotten them in the remote fort in the furthest reaches of the ocean. And she still recalls the chickadee as making the best pottage she ever had.

To think this little woman with the small frame and lined face once endured a hurricane at sea! I shake my head, letting Miss Joan keep her pensive watch of the river. What is she watching for? Or is she just thinking?

After a while, the servant girl brings us some tea, cool as the water from the well and sweet as the Bermudian sugar cane can make it. This drink is so welcome, so new to the colony. Miss Joan said she felt blessed that she had the means to purchase some and had lived to see it. The Indians of India drink it. Now here it is, having made its way from the East Indians to the East India Company, to England, and now on to us. I look at my tea and realize it has taken more journeys than have I.

What would it be like to outlive all your friends, I wonder.

Well, Miss Joan hasn't outlived Goody Laydon—Annie, Miss Joan calls her. Annie lives at the mouth of the Warwick River where it branches from the James, not far from Miss Joan's home on Mulberry Island. But both ladies being much older now, they don't chance the shallop voyage much and so do not see one another often. But they do send letters to one another upon the little vessels traveling between and beyond. Miss Joan chides many a harried captain not to forget to deliver Annie's letter. Only then might they sail down the James River.

The captains smile and tip their caps to the old woman. "Good day, Widow Peirce. Yes, indeed."

"You do commit thyself to do so?" she asks sharply with a pointed finger.

They indulge her with a "Yes, mistress, I do so promise."

And then she relaxes.

Miss Joan is the grand old dame of this part of the river, and she knows it not. But you don't have to be here long to see it.

"I am almost old enough to be Annie's mother, but when I arrived, 'twas Annie who taught me most about Virginia. She had been here ten or eleven months—a lifetime in this New World," Miss Joan told me. "No one knows now, no one remembers, except us few ... we of the early days, I mean."

When she said it, her eyes took on a distant look. And then in the eddies and swirls of the river, the passing clouds, she sees far more than I do. I'm certain of it. She sees the past. It is alive to her, and she has made it alive to me.

Annie, Miss Joan told me, can neither read nor write, but her daughters can. Annie is proud—fiercely proud—of this. And her daughters scribe the letters for Annie as she tells them what to put down. It amazes me that after almost forty years, Miss Joan is still indignant about Annie's whipping. Still sorrowful about the lost baby because of the lashes. Miss Joan's voice had risen in anger, and her cheeks flushed when she described it.

And she still laughed as she recalled the crusty midwife, Mistress Wright. Miss Joan said that Goody Wright had the blue eyes, as she herself did. But Goody Wright also had the left-handedness and the gift of foresight, all traits of witchery. Someone having so many oddities ought to hush up and not let on to the neighbors. Shouldn't Goody Wright have known that predicting deaths frightened folks? I suspect the neighbors thought Goody wasn't predicting fates but laying curses on them. Goody Wright said she'd just speak her mind, especially to folks who abused her. And the devil be hanged!

Babies born in Virginia, Pocahontas a captive, martial law and Captain Argall's piracy—all these Miss Joan related to me. Her eyes were sometimes misty, often distant, and occasionally fierce with old battles recalled.

Miss Joan spoke of Christmas 1620, after the African Angelo's arrival and Will's departure for England. Pocahontas's wedding to John Rolfe had brought peace with the Indians. But what would happen after both the Indian princess and her father King Powhatan died? My cousin alluded to worse—and I as every Virginian did—knew what that worse was. And I also know she does not wish to tell me about it. And yet I suspect she will.

Why? I am not sure. Perhaps because so few living can remember the first massacre and even fewer the Starving Time. Miss Joan called herself a relict of an earlier day. "I reckon God has forgotten I'm still here," she mused. "He's come for most everyone else. Why not me?" She seemed genuinely perplexed. "I would say He can't find us here in Virginia, but then He most surely can as He has found so many others before me." Her voice trailed off as she said it.

Of her parents, she speaks most often of her father. She remembers his sun-browned skin, etched with lines like an old sailor's map. His eyes were both kind and lively with adventure. How she loved him! How he loved her. This is plain to see. She awaited his stories of the sea; she pondered the riddles he had left behind for her. What was the journey which was neither Catholic nor Protestant, but one which we all took? What would happen if all the sea instruments failed? Why, when her father felt lost, was he then found? Captain Phippen, her father, had left these questions as gifts to her, she said. And from her mother, she learned the love and knowledge of herbs. "My mother was the best herbalist in Melcombe Regis, or so everyone said," she told me, pride seeping into her voice.

Now, this bright morning, I hesitate. Yesterday, I asked her few questions as she spoke. Oh, I have questions, surely. But I sense that if I interrupt her, if I remove her from the reveries and remembrances, she might not return to her story. She might say that was enough for one visit. And so I just listened. At times, I felt tears welling in my eyes or stifled laughter as she walked down this old lane, or that old path, of her memories. This story wasn't truly for me, I supposed. She just wanted to see all these events again—even the painful ones—and I was a welcome reason to do so.

And so we sit in silence as the river slips by.

Miss Joan suddenly speaks once more.

"No, Sir George Yeardley couldn't be with us that Christmas we held our flagons up in toast. I can still hear the wolves howling, can still feel Maggie's voice rising in song with us as if she had yet been alive. I don't suppose you want to carry on this old woman's long tale. Let's dispense here and ..."

"Oh, no, ma'am! I do wish to hear it. I am wondering how Captain Peirce fared in London, and if ... if ..." I pause. I cannot say the word "massacre." She will have to do that. "Just if," I finish. My gaze drops to my lap. Is it unfair to expect an old woman to relive such a day as that one was?

I lift my eyes once more to see her staring hard at me. What is she thinking? Our eyes meet for a moment. And then, with her gaze still locked on mine, I understand it is no longer me she sees. No, she is seeing something else. Something long ago.

The peregrines return on the higher winds, flying deeper into the distant blue. Miss Joan steals a glance at them and then draws a full breath while I hold mine.

She is going to tell me. I wait and listen, and she begins.

A Joy of Earth

February 8, 1621

James Town, Virginia

A Letter is a Joy of Earth—
It is denied the Gods.
        —Emily Dickinson

I bequeath all my goods to my kinsman Hamond Claxton of Gray's Inn, co.
Middlesex esquire ... for the better maintenance of my mother, so that no part
comes into the hands of her husband my father in law [stepfather] Captain
Godfrey Garrett.
        —From Stanley Flowerdieu's will, 10 May 1620,
        Scottow, County Norfolk, England

Tempie strode to my home, folded paper in her hands.

"Hello!" I called cheerfully, always happy to see her. "Is the baby down for a nap?"

"He is. Susanna is tending him, but I truly can't stay long."

Susanna was a servant girl of the Yeardleys. She'd been with Tempie for almost two years, and during that time, Tempie had come to think of her as an elder daughter. This was especially so since Susanna had come to her an orphan, her parents having been friends with Sir George's brother in London. Now twelve, Susanna was both mature and kind to the Yeardley children who ranged in age between the infant Francis and six-year-old Elizabeth.

"I have for you a letter from Will!" she said. "The *Supply of Bristol* is lying at anchor. Master Felgate's men just brought a trunk filled with letters to my home." Then her smile faded somewhat. "I received one, too, but I haven't opened it yet." She handed me Will's letter and clutched her own.

Letters from our old home, England.

It took months for such a letter to travel the ocean. Sometimes those who had written them died before the letter even reached our hands. Letters brought good news and bad news; some brought surprising news. One never knew what was going on across the sea. And since we might wait months before another ship arrived, we savored each letter.

Hearing from Will lifted my spirits. I already knew he'd survived the voyage to England. The *Swan of Barnstaple*, eight months before, had brought his only letter.

Yet I understood the slowness of sending news from so far away. To write me, Will must deliver the letter to the Virginia Company. Then the Company hired the next Virginia ship to carry its cluster of letters safely tucked away in a trunk, a voyage taking several months.

Upon landing, the ship's master would deliver the trunk of letters to the governor.

For letters bound upriver or downriver, the governor might send his own shallop or find a vessel headed out with a captain he trusted. If those from distant settlements heard a ship had arrived, they came seeking their posts. This made a fine time to deliver their own letters, to buy goods off ship, or to arrange tobacco sales, before the ship departed back to England.

Being close to the governor's wife had its privileges, and receiving my letter directly and at once was one.

The mere presence of Will's letter itself was good news. At least he'd been well enough to write. I turned over the folded paper and touched the writing with my name and *James Town* scrawled beneath it.

As much as we tried to change the name from James Town to James Cittie, the old name lingered. I supposed one could argue that the little group of homes here inside and around the old fort were James Town proper. James Cittie stretched further into the island and just beyond.

"Who's your letter from, and why do you worry?" I asked Tempie, patting a chair so she'd sit. I asked even though I knew it must be from her mother. These always upset her.

Tempie sat, still seeming troubled, so I added, "The last ship in brought Gloucester perry, and I bought me some. How about a dram on a cold day?" We didn't yet have pear trees here in Virginia, but we hoped to one day. Nothing like pear wine to warm a body. "And sit thee close to the fire," I said. The grey February skies threatened snow.

Tempie pulled off her cloak. "Perry would be lovely, Joan."

She sat, drawing a deep breath as the fire warmed her shoes. The flames crackled and spat.

I tapped the half firkin on the cupboard and poured some pear wine for each of us. The golden perry dancing in the firelight was itself cheerful on a dreary day.

Tempie lifted her glass and clinked it against mine. "Dearest friends keep one warm, howe'er bitter the weather. And the perry helps, too."

I laughed. Then we each took a sip. Without speaking, we let the perry and the brisk fire warm us. She would open her letter soon enough, and so would I. But we savored the moment first. We'd been friends for many years, so we could sit in silence for a long while and be comfortable.

At last, Tempie said, "The letter is from my mother. Each time she writes me, I fear the news. Seems it's all bad, somehow."

She and her mother had quarreled before Tempie sailed for Virginia in 1609. But on Tempie's return to England three years ago, the two had made amends. That had been Tempie's only visit to England in all her dozen years here. I myself had never been back at all, and I'd been in Virginia as long as she had.

One day, I thought. *One day, I'll return to England to visit my old home in Dorset.* But the longer I stayed here, the more I'd begun to dread sea travel. Well, no matter now.

Tempie had told me the reason for the quarrel. Tempie's mother, Mrs. Garrett, had thought the wilds of Virginia unbefitting for her daughter. After all, Tempie's family had close connections to much English nobility. The family heritage included Stanleys, Flowerdieus, and Appleyards.

Sir George had started life as a merchant tailor's son. In England, no one would have ever considered George Yeardley a fitting match for someone like Tempie.

Tempie's mother remained a bit unsure about Sir George, knighthood or not.

We'd grown up in such different worlds, Tempie and I. Tempie had been a child of privilege while my father had been a sea captain and trader. He had owned a few ships, but we weren't wealthy.

Properly, I should have referred to Tempie as Dame Temperance or Lady Yeardley, but Tempie would not hear it. James Town, Tempie had said, made us all but one class. Oh, not completely, but it certainly evened things out some.

Colonists here advanced by being expert in the strangeness of Virginia, not by wealth or family names alone.

Sir George was a perfect example. He'd become a knight and a governor.

He earned his high position here because of his understanding of Virginia, loyal service, and his military experience in the Lowlands.

In English society, the knighting of Sir George was unusual. The king had listened to the urgings of Virginia Company men like Sir Edwin Sandys and the new treasurer, the Earl of Southampton. Knighting a commoner imbued a faraway governor with needed authority.

Sir George was a survivor—a strong Company supporter.

Surviving helped those in Virginia to rise in prominence. Just keep on living, and see where you land! So many had died. Those of us who survived with any talent rose in this strange country. Our ability to survive became our currency to succeed.

And here was where Mrs. Garrett struggled.

Earning one's way did not often happen in England. There, birth alone counted, breeding brought benefits and position.

So some in London still thought Sir George's honors undeserved. Much dissension had ensued in the Virginia Company courts over Sir George being governor. The call went up: *We need noble blood in such a position!*

"Why don't we read your letter together then?" I asked, hoping to encourage her. We kept each other heartened as best we could—not always an easy task in Virginia.

Tempie and I were like the two friends in the Bible verse. *Two are better than one; because they have a good reward for their labor. For if they fall, the one will lift up his fellow: but woe to him that is alone when he falleth, for he hath not another to help him up.*

This verse also said a threefold cord was strongest. Tempie and I with Maggie had once been a threefold cord. Since Maggie had died during the Starving Time, Tempie and I had been as strong as we might as a cord of two.

Tempie reluctantly unfolded the letter and looked it over.

"Oh, Joan," she sighed. Her eyes filled with tears. "Stanley died last May of ague. My brother, I mean," she added. She said he'd only been in his early thirties, unmarried and without heirs. "My mother writes that Stanley hated our stepfather Garrett. So before his death, Stanley asked a kinsman to sell his estate and use the funds to care for our mother. Stanley had been adamant that no part of his estate should fall into Captain Garrett's hands."

Tempie's eyes betrayed her pain as she folded the letter back up.

"Our family is all muddled, Joan. I do agree with my brother. We can't trust Captain Garrett to look after our mother's best interests. And now Stanley's death leaves my mother alone with the captain."

Tempie's sister Marie had died eleven years before, leaving her son

Edmund as her only heir. Tempie's nephew Edmund Rossingham was even now in Virginia, living out at Flowerdieu Hundred, the Yeardleys' property. Sir George had hired Edmund to help manage his lands and tobacco shipping. Tempie felt Edmund had a selfish streak, but she was still glad Sir George had his help.

"Father, sister, brother ... all gone. And then a rift, besides." Tempie sat weeping. "And here am I, an ocean away. And Edmund here, too." She lifted her eyes, which were helpless and red. "No wonder my mother resents Virginia. We can do nothing for her so far away."

Little remained for Tempie but to write her mother, which I suggested she do quickly before the *Supply* departed.

"Still, you're blessed with a delightful new family here," I offered.

Tempie smiled a little. Elizabeth was six, Argall three and a half, Francis just an infant.

I saw my friend make an effort to push the gloom away. "What does Will say?" she asked with unfeigned eagerness. We shared all news, good or bad. Now we could hope Will had sent better tidings than had Mrs. Garrett.

Indeed, Will wrote that he had enlisted servants, both men and women, and was arranging passage. The Virginia Company was conferring to select our new governor, Will had added.

"Oh, praise the Lord!" Tempie cried. That was good news for her, too. Sir George had petitioned the Virginia Company to serve only his three-year term before returning to his private affairs and plantations. His holdings were extensive.

Virginia exacted a price from its past governors, and none had been here as long as Sir George. "George probably has a letter in the trunk from the Company, but now I've heard the news first!" She beamed. "What else does Will write?"

"He says he took young Tom to the Tobacco Exchange, that he feels it's never too soon for our son to begin learning 'the business.' He and Tom visited the school, and his cousin in London is happy to have Tom stay with him. 'He's a Virginia Company investor and eager to hear of things here.' I'm staying with him now, too, until I sail,' he writes."

Young Tom, I'll miss thee. At the same time, knowing he was settled at school made me happy.

What could we do but accept the things, like Stanley's death, that we could not change? Tempie's lifted spirits lifted mine further.

"Now, Tempie, let's hope that Will is on the next ship that arrives!"

Whenever we wished a loved one to be on a ship, we also prayed for good fortune and God's blessing on that ship. With Turkish pirates and Spanish enemies and hurricanes and leaky planks? Spoiled food and bad beer and contagions on board?

So sometimes for good measure, we crossed our fingers for luck. I crossed my second finger over my first and held it up to her.

"I hope Will is on that next ship, Joan. I do." Tempie's smile was sincere. She crossed her fingers and held them up to me, too. "And may it bring the new governor, as well!"

Tempie and I couldn't know that even as we crossed our fingers before the fire, a Virginia-bound ship was weighing anchor in the Thames. Nor could we know that this ship, the *Margaret and John,* was one I'd never want Will to be on.

With Plentie and Varietie

*The Land [Virginia] is stored with plentie and varietie of wild Beasts, Lions,
Beares, Deere of all sorts ... Beavers, Otters, Foxes, Racounes, almost as bigge
as a Foxe, as good meate as a Lambe, Hares, wild Cats, Muske Rats, Squirrels
flying ... Apossumes. ... Of each of these beasts, the Lion excepted, my selfe
have many times eaten, and can testifie that they are not onely tastefull, but
also wholsome and nourishing food.*
        —Ralph Hamor, 1614

*... wee have found a waie to make soe good drinke of Indian corne as I protest
I have divers times refused to drinke good stronge Englishe beare and chosen to
drinke that.*
        —George Thorpe, 1620, possibly the beginning of
            bourbon whiskey. A later inventory of Thorpe's estate
            included "a copper still, old."

Seasons in Virginia swung on the planting. Now we plant, now we harvest—as if the earth were a great clock chiming upon what we were to
do. Tobacco and corn, tobacco and corn. A life in Virginia made itself
on tobacco and corn.

Still, planting was a fair thing compared to what we'd endured. Those
here the longest had seen much hardship. Starvation and the summer
sicknesses. Indian wars and drought, bloody flux and siege, hurricane and
shipwreck, martial law and a dreadful fiery comet. We'd swung between near
abandonment and overcrowding and worked as if we were prisoners under
martial law. Why, not until 1617 were we even allowed to leave Virginia at
all.

Now in 1621, I'd reckon scarce one in five—perhaps one in ten!—of those who had come to Virginia were still living. We'd lost Maggie to the disease and starving and Maria Bucke to childbirth and so many others to maladies, poor food, or Indian arrow.

We'd seen so much and hoped so little for so long that at last, if planting were the thing to concern ourselves with, that was not so much. The Company had finally abolished martial law two years ago.

The Company had now granted us land—great plots of land—because the Company was near bankrupt. They could not afford to pay us pounds and shillings for our venture and work here. But land—land in Virginia stretched as far as the eye could see and farther behind that into realms no Englishman even knew.

West beyond the lands of the Powhatan lived their enemies the Monacan. North were the Anacostan and Patawomeck—sometimes allies of the Powhatan. Even further north and west lived the Susquehannock, known for their fur trade.

So the Company, still with empty coffers and afraid we might rebel without *something* for our years of trouble, granted us land.

Deserts and plains and grasslands, blue mountains and mountains of great rock. So said the Indians who lived near us. Their messengers talked with those from other tribes, who talked with others even further west, south, north. Certainly another ocean brushed against this land somewhere, but we knew not how far away that could be. *Vast.*

I sighed. We were at peace with the Indians, and no great contagions wracked the settlements. Still, we'd lost many over the past year. But we had hope that the days of so many falling at once were behind us, even if just barely so.

The days were growing warmer. The early planting had begun. This spring, *this one,* I hoped that so much misery lay behind us and none before us.

I was not alone in such dreams. All the settlements seemed to work with a fresh feeling of promise and cheer. God, see, gives one only so much to bear, metes a just amount and then no more. The scales had tilted to the outrageously difficult for far too long. The coming years would bring the promised prosperity at last. They had to. Gone the famines, gone the trials. *Yea, surely, Lord. Amen!*

It was a pleasant dream, even if it was not to be.

A morning in March found me at the river, scanning the horizon for a ship—the ship that would bring Will home to me. But when?

How many times have I stood, watching the river and waiting? Not that I had so much time to wait, of course. Much work there always was to do. But just watching the river gave me hope.

Will's letter had carried the same sense of promise that we all felt here in Virginia. He would be bringing with him silkworm seed, he said, for trials of silk. He also planned to try making wine from the wild grapes abounding. The Company must find a prosperous commodity beyond tobacco.

Will held that hope, even as he had grown, harvested, cured, casked, and shipped as much tobacco as anybody. Tobacco was a successful crop while nothing else anyone had produced had been.

But Will didn't favor the tobacco. The king, Will said, hated the smoky weed. But iron and glass, salt and silk and wine? Those the king could embrace.

Silk and wine. The French were far ahead of England in both these. Hopeful English eyes watched Virginia. We had good weather, mulberry trees as silkworm food, and native grapes for winemaking.

While plying other commodities, Will still knew he must keep growing tobacco. We had few coins in Virginia, few shillings or pounds or pence. What we had, and had aplenty, was tobacco. And so all our trade, all we bought and sold, was in weight of tobacco.

How much tobacco for those planks? Four and a half pounds at three shillings per pound of tobacco.

How much tobacco will ye charge for the Indian corn? Six pounds four.

How much tobacco for your ironwork, Mister? Five pounds one-half. But give it to Captain Ewens on my behalf, for I owe him my ship's passage.

I smiled as I remembered John Rolfe bringing me his tiny dark brown seeds ten years ago. *I am going to have a trial of tobacco plants,* he had said. *Look it up in your book, Joan! What does it say about Spanish tobacco? For I have procured it from Trinidad in secret.* The Spanish had punished with death those found buying their tobacco seeds, but John had been fearless. I could still remember the excitement in his eyes.

Tiny seeds, so dangerous to come by and so much prosperity had wrought.

Who could have known that John's tobacco trials would be that thing which brought Virginia the most prosperity?

For all our efforts, only tobacco and sassafras had brought us a sure way to earn money here. Our tobacco grew fine and strong. Spanish tobacco was a different, sweeter variety than the Indians' tobacco. Now our crops rivaled those of the Spanish as we shipped to England and to the Low Countries.

Everywhere, men and women clamored for this New World discovery, tobacco.

Tobacco, please. More tobacco! Even as the king scorned tobacco's black stinking fume.

Indian corn and tobacco. We could not have imagined when we came here twelve years before that these words would be the rhythms we slept to. Our English corn was barley and wheat, oats and millet. But none of these grew as well here as a crop with kernels the Indians beat into meal. We called it our Indian corn. Or just "corn."

From the Indians, we'd learned to make their corn *pone, pone* being the Indian word for bread. Like so many other Indian words, *pone* stuck. We English wives labored and admired our corn pone much as the Indian women did theirs.

The Indians showed us, too, how many ways we could use corn in cooking. We also made hoe cakes and thick corn porridge. The Indians called this porridge *uskatahomen* or sometimes just *hominy*. So we called it *hominy*, too, or sometimes *hominy grits*. We made a sweet corn pudding, and we all loved buttery *suppone*, an Indian corn porridge. While the Indians scooped the *suppone* with shells, we used spoons. We called it *suppone bread*, which newcomers heard as "spoonbread." Every good Virginian could tell *suppone* bread apart from corn pudding and *hominy*. The bafflement of newcomers at these odd meals did amuse us much.

How many ways can ye make the Indian's corn, Mary?

Three score and ten, Barbara. And more when I'm a mind to. And then to prove it, we'd offer them corn liquor!

Aye, not a person in Virginia wasn't eating corn or dreaming of tobacco.

It has come to this, I thought.

Yet I couldn't be unhappy about it. For so long, we'd had little to eat and had lived in complete poverty. We'd come, many of us, from nice homes in the English West Country or from London itself. From Dorset and Devon, Kent and Surrey. From the Midlands, the South—even from Wales. We'd come with dreams of hope. Instead, we'd found ourselves wearing rags, eating moldy peas and rancid wheat from England.

Corn and tobacco had changed all that.

How little the people in England understood us! Eating peculiar foods and living in a strange land. All the while, we were coming to love the Virginia forests and wide rivers. At times, Will had brought home raccoon or 'possum, beaver or fox. Sometimes he brought us bear or muskrat, and once even two flying squirrels. The Indians had taught us that these meats were tasty and nourishing. I'd learned to cook them all.

And so feasting on 'possum pottage and *suppone* bread seemed strange to those in England. We were something different. Not Indians, but not quite English either with our Indian words and meals. We ate wild victuals they in England had never even seen, much less served as meat!

In England, I thought, *they do not even know what a raccoon or 'possum looks like. And English squirrels, small things, they scamper or scurry.* Here we had squirrels as big as hares, and some did fly. Fly! Lions we hadn't eaten but had seen the claws. The Indians told us that west toward the mountains these lions flourished. And Captain Argall had once seen the wild cattle *búfalo* while traveling north and west with Indian friends.

One couldn't live in Virginia without feeling how tame, how staid, how ancient was England. Virginia was like her wild younger sister, hair flying, strangeness in all her ways.

I pulled Will's letter from the pocket tied about my waist, letting the linen page flap open as I did so. *Come home, Will.*

Today, the river was quiet. No ships on the horizon. Just the men working at the bridge and the sounds of the settlement. A few homes and buildings were growing east from the old fort into a place we called the New Towne.

We'd had peace with the Indians since Pocahontas had married John Rolfe. Now with Pocahontas gone, lo, these four years, John had married my daughter Jane. A wife and mother now, she was no longer my little Janey.

The truce between our peoples had endured even after the deaths of Pocahontas and her father, Chief Powhatan. These two had been the peacemakers.

Opitchapam had succeeded his older brother Powhatan, but we understood Opitchapam to be decrepit and lame. The true power rested with Opechancanough, another younger brother, a powerful and inspiring figure.

Opechancanough had promised us a lasting peace. Could we believe him? We thought so. We'd become friendlier with those from the various tribes. Some of the Indians even moved into our homes. Master Perry, who lived at my friend Isabella's plantation, had an Indian boy he thought of as a son. This story ran up and down the river: Indians were friends.

Still, Will had a cautious nature. One thing he'd taught me long ago was how to fire his snaphaunce pistol. "I don't want to affright you," he'd said. "But while the Indians are peaceful, the Spanish are unpredictable."

I had never needed to use it.

Peace! Praise God for it at long last. Even during the time of Sir Thomas Dale, the warrior Chacrow—some called him Chauco—had lived with Lieutenant Sharpe, Ensign Powell, and my Will. Governor Sir Thomas Dale had seen no harm in letting the men teach Chacrow to use a firearm. Sir George Yeardley, though, never did care much for the practice.

As for the Spanish, the spy Don Diego de Molina had attempted to attack the colony a few years before. And our ship the *Treasurer* had gone rogue under Governor Argall and pirated a Spanish ship. We'd heard nothing from the Spanish since those events. Will insisted that the sea made us vulnerable. Yet things had been otherwise quiet.

We were overcrowded, it was true. Hordes of settlers tended to disembark in the heat of summer. The time of year being unhealthful, many new arrivals died. But we had peace, coming prosperity, and most of all, hope.

Peace on the river, peace with the Indians, peace with the Spanish.

Or so I thought as I surveyed the serene river that morning.

But somewhere in the Southern Atlantic, two Spanish warships had other ideas.

Perils at Sea

March 14 – 15, 1621
On the *Margaret and John* in the West Indies

... the dangers of wars, and perils at sea, by storms, by tempests, shipwrecks,
encounters with pirates, meeting with enemies, cross winds, long voyages,
unknown shores, barbarous nations, and an hundred inconveniences ...
—Capt. John Smith, *Generall Historie*

Sir George had recommended the northern route to the Virginia Company for ships sailing both east and west during the summer months. The northern route sailed south of Newfoundland. The hot southern sailing routes caused many on ship to fall ill or die of the calenture. Already weakened by the heat, many died in Virginia's broiling summer.

The seas were friendlier up north, too.

After leaving England, ships traveled first through our fishing waters in Canada. From there, they sailed past a new English colony called Plymouth in North Virginia.

True, ships going this way sometimes encountered French squatters in Canada—North Virginia. But the French were less likely to attack than a Spanish ship might.

Sir George had argued that the abundant fish on the northern route provided ready food if a ship ran low on victuals during the long, tedious voyage. Newfoundland was a wonderful, and mostly safe, place to stop and refresh if needed.

We in Virginia had fished around Martha's Vineyard since the early days of Virginia's discovery. In fact, Captain Gosnold had long ago named Martha's Vineyard for his baby daughter. That was twenty years ago and Gosnold long dead.

"Arrive in the fall, please, and by the northern route!" Sir George had pleaded with the Company. He was not alone in this feeling; all the leaders here in Virginia agreed. But as with so many things, the Virginia Company scarcely understood our challenges here.

Some ships' masters still preferred the southern route during winter. They could catch the trades winds from England down past the islands of the Carib Indians. Ships' masters liked the lemons and oranges to help stave off scurvy. Ships could stop to water and refresh, then make for Virginia. If their ships were leaving a cold, dismal English winter, why could they not sail into the warm Caribbean? Such was the case with the little *Margaret and John*, who had sailed down the Narrow Seas toward the Caribbean islands in early February.

The danger, though, sailing the trades winds to the South, was that the Spanish didn't take kindly to English ships in waters they claimed. The kings of England and France disputed these claims, but no matter. When the Spaniards sighted foreign ships, they suspected us of spying or theft or perhaps worse. An English ship filled with goods and settlers, though, is not armed for warfare, neither to strike nor to defend.

Soon all on board the *Margaret and John* would understand the risks of entering the Spanish lair.

The little *Margaret and John* carried about eighty settlers. Of these, a quarter were apothecaries and chirurgeons. We had dire need of these. One man on board was even a doctor, Dr. Bohun—long associated with Virginia—who ranked, of course, much higher than these others. This one ship brought us more men skilled in healing arts than we'd had before in all our years in Virginia combined.

The little ship was weary by early March, beset by calms and storms. They'd been at sea nearly eleven weeks! Desiring to water and refresh among the islands of the Indies, the ship found itself some twenty leagues off the French island of Matalina.

Captain Anthony Chester was no coward, but he'd avoided a fight where he could. Especially when carrying colonists. The *Margaret and John* was crowded; she was not a man-of-war. God willing, no pirates or Spanish would attack, something every good ship's captain remained wary of. *The trials of the sea are many.*

Now, the ship's sails filled as the trades winds pushed her along to Guadeloupe. She cut through the rich, warm, blue water and a surge of relief filled the captain.

Land, fresh water, fruits to allay the scurvy. All was well.

He had not been at anchor long when to his surprise, he saw they were not alone.

A ragged castaway came over to his ship and gestured for permission to board. The captain granted it.

The foreigner began speaking in *lingua franca*, a choppy mix of Italian, French, Greek, Arabic, and Spanish.

Captain Chester held up a finger.

"Wait, please." The captain called for Thomas Hothersall, his interpreter.

Hothersall appeared on deck.

"Do you speak French? I believe these are Frenchman."

Hothersall nodded.

The Frenchman explained that sixteen months ago, he and five others had shipwrecked here. They had, he said, been doing their best to survive on the island.

They'd seen a few Carib Indians but had tried to stay hidden from them. And just this past week, they'd espied a Spanish man-of-war. Once again, they managed to keep from sight when the Spanish paused to water. The castaways were certain the Spaniards would have captured and enslaved them. Their hatred and fear of the Spanish was palpable, Chester noted.

"On that we can agree then," Captain Chester said affably. "Come aboard. I'm bound for Virginia. I can put you off there if you'd like."

"*Oui*, aye-aye, Monsieur," said the Frenchman. He called to the rest of his surviving crew, and they all came onto the ship. The castaways explained that they preferred the English of Virginia to Spanish or the Caribs.

Captain Chester wished to learn more about the warship these men had seen. He asked his cook to bring the Frenchmen some dried pork and peas along with sea biscuits. He carried dried fish as well, but suspected they'd had enough fish for one lifetime!

"A man-of-war? Here in this sea, you say?" Captain Chester asked through Hothersall.

One of the Frenchmen nodded. The ship had been awaiting its consort, another man-of-war, apparently. Once the other ship had arrived, both had sailed away. These castaways, hungrily filling their mouths with peas, could offer nothing more. The ships had been here, the men said, only seven days before.

This news relieved Chester. Seven days was enough that they should have no chance encounter.

Afterward, Dr. Bohun came aboveboard and tended to a wound on one of the men.

The next day, after departing Guadeloupe, the *Margaret and John* approached Nevis. Captain Chester anchored near two tall ships flying Dutch colors.

As soon as the English ship had dropped anchor, Chester ordered a boat to go to greet the ships. "Row over, men," he said to his son-in-law Mr. Mennes, the interpreter Hothersall, and a Mr. Jorland. "Send a friendly hail to these Hollanders."

As the three men approached the ships, they noticed one of the vessels sending boats ashore. A great many of the strangers were running toward those boats, and they didn't appear to be Hollanders.

"Spaniards!" Mr. Hothersall whispered. "We must row back and warn the captain."

But Captain Chester was angry at the hasty retreat. "Why did you not hail them as I ordered? Row back, I say, and hail them!" Unbeknownst to the three frightened men, the captain was stalling for time to prepare the ship in case of battle.

The three men followed orders, rowing to the ship and calling, "Ship ahoy! Who are you?"

"Come aboard!" ordered a man, who appeared to be the captain, in a thick Spanish accent.

Obeying this command would be tantamount to surrender. The three now hastened to row away from the ship. As they did so, small shot began to assault them, splitting and breaking their oars, striking their boat, and even hitting their clothes. Yet, remarkably, the three were not hurt.

As the Englishmen were within a musket shot of the *Margaret and John*, Spanish cannon fired upon the boat, and the Spaniards hoisted sail.

Captain Chester's heart fell to the deck. The hoisted sail and cannon fire meant the Spanish were attacking.

The perils of the sea were many. Now the men, women, and children on the little *Margaret and John* realized their ship was in trouble. Deep, deep trouble. The passage had exhausted them, and they had sore need of refreshment and water on shore. They were, after all, a ship carrying colonists— tradesmen and apothecaries. How could these spar with the soldiers of a man-of-war?

The tall Spanish ships were three hundred tons each to the *Margaret and John's* meager one hundred sixty tons.

Chester had counted thirty-eight ordnance pieces on the Spanish ships. The little English ship had only eight big guns and a falcon. And to that, four of the ordnance pieces were useless, blocked by fardels and bundles, trunks and crates, and had only scant ball and powder.

This would not only be less than a fair fight, it would be a wholesale slaughter. Enslavement, capture, or death came into view for all.

David was going to have to fight two Goliaths with far more fighting men and ten times the firepower.

The Scuppers Ran with Bloud

Early April 1621
James Town, Virginia

I am bound to Virginia and come here for water. The kings, our masters, are friends. We intend no wrong, neither will we take any.
    —Captain Chester's call to the Spanish warships, 1621

I am sure we saw many [Spanish] lie slaine on the Decke, and more cast over-boord in the fight, besides the Scuppers ran with bloud, and the very Sea in their quarter was coloured with a Scarlet hue, and looked fearfully upon us all.
    —Samuel Purchas, quoting a passenger on board the *Margaret and John*, 1621

A small but battered and bloody ship arrived at James Town early in April. The ragged survivors stumbled into James Fort from the *Margaret and John*. We didn't know exactly what had happened, but it appeared some enemy had fired upon the ship, maybe even engaged it in a sea fight.

I looked from my window, saw the condition of those coming off ship, and thought, *Dear God.* I was almost afraid to learn more. What if Will had been on board? I considered. He'd sent the letter in September. The ship before me likely departed England around February. Will could indeed have been on this ship.

"Spanish attack at Nevis!" I heard several men calling out. "Lost some, aye, but yet bested the Spanish curs!"

I was afraid to know, afraid to ask. A battle had ensued? I knew exactly which man would be the first on deck with a musket or a sword.

My Will.

In a moment, too quickly, Tempie was at my door. "We have to find out if Will was on this ship, Joan. Let's go together." She took my arm and steadied me.

I said nothing, but I sensed she knew I was grateful for the support. I drew a deep breath and gathered my courage.

"Let's go then," I croaked.

As we were trying to make sense of the crowd, we saw a boy of about ten or twelve who appeared bemused and lost.

Tempie waved to get his attention. "Say, were you on that ship?"

He nodded, eyes wide.

"What is your name, then?" Tempie asked kindly.

"I am Wood, mistress, Abraham Wood. I seen the battle, mistress. I fought it, e'en! It were right awful, but we showed 'em what the English could do, all right. They had ten times our firepower, mistress! We repelled them when they boarded us, these *two* warships which surprised us off Nevis."

The boy's clothes were but rags, and he had the odor all did after leaving a confined ship. He was paltry thin. But excitement still lit his face.

"Do you know, son, if a Lieutenant Peirce is on board?" Tempie asked.

He shrugged. "I know not, mistress. We lost our doctor, Dr. Bohun. This I do know. The Spanish killed more than just him, though. They come at us in Nevis, tried to board us. Our ship's carpenter's mate turned the tide by firing a falcon gun onto the deck of the Spanish ship! It rained a hail of iron on the Spanish, missus. The mate forced those Spanish below right quick." Abraham grinned despite his bewilderment.

Once he began to talk, the story poured out of him. "He forced them off, he did. We seen their scuppers running with blood, turning the sea round their ships a terrible red. It colored the sea, so it did. I swears me." He crossed his heart. "It were a fearful thing."

"I believe you. Well, I'm Temperance, Lady Yeardley, and I ..."

His eyes widened in surprise and fear. "I begs your pardon, mistress, er, Lady Yeardley," he said hastily, bowing his head respectfully. "I knew not when you come to me that you were a knight's dame. I swears again, mis— Lady Yeardley. You are the governor's wife?"

He must know the Yeardley name, I thought.

"Aye, 'tis so. Do not apologize, especially since you fought to help save our ship and passengers," she said. "Come with me to the barracks. Indeed, my husband is the governor, and I reckon him to be over there already. He'll need to meet with all on board and learn the story in case there remains danger of Spanish attack here."

Tempie turned her attention to me. 'Twas then I noticed I was trembling.

"Abraham," she said, "this is Mistress Peirce, who seeks to know if her husband is on the ship. Let's all retire to the barracks and learn more. We also must get thee some food."

Tempie's gentleness to one in distress reminded me for a moment of the Starving Time. I remembered when she suggested we take in old Grace after Grace's husband accused her of being a witch. Tempie knew the man to be mad with hunger and sensed he might harm the helpless older woman. She urged that we take her in, though I had been mostly unwilling to share food my daughter would need. But Tempie's pleading eyes had won, and since then I'd always been glad we did help Grace.

"You carry yourself like a true dame, indeed," I murmured to her as we made our way to the barracks. "Sometimes, I can see your nobility. I suppose the word 'gentility' comes from such gentleness."

She smiled. Then brushing aside the compliment, she said, "I doubt that Will was on board. Had he been, 'twould have been *Will* firing from the cabin, not the carpenter's mate!"

This broke the tension. It was true, too. "Aye, you speak truth! I hope you're right on that."

Several men speaking what sounded like French walked past.

"Castaways," the boy said, following our gaze. "They asked passage of us on Guadeloupe where they were shipwrecked and stranded."

What an odd story this was shaping up to be.

A strange trio, we strode toward the largest building, the barracks. We must find Governor Sir George and learn what had happened on this ship. More importantly, we needed to know *who* was on board when the Spanish struck.

The Natural Fool of Fortune

Early to Mid-April 1621
James Town, Virginia

*By reason of the Spaniards behaviour towards Captaine Chester wee have
some reason to doute wee maie alsoe heare of them in this place. I praie
therefore ... wee maie have some Pikes sent us wch weapon the maner of our
peoples for fightinge ye wth the natives hath worne quite out of use but if shall
have to do with the Spaniard we must fight with him in his treanches wch hee
that cann doe wth a Pike is a better Soldier then I.*
—George Thorpe, 15 May 1621

I am even the natural fool of fortune. Use me well.
—William Shakespeare

Over at the barracks, Sir George had arrived to hear the story and
welcome the captain. Then the governor looked directly at me.

"I've checked the ship's muster, Joan. Will wasn't on the *Margaret
and John*," Sir George said, holding a paper in his hand.

I was faint with relief. "Oh, thank you, Governor Sir George! Such
happy news."

Every corner of the colony would soon be telling how the little *Margaret
and John* had whipped the two Spanish men-of-war. We'd lost our doctor,
God bless him, but he had died nobly. Captain Chester said Dr. Bohun had
died in his arms, urging him to keep going.

All over, we were repeating Dr. Bohun's dying words: "Fight it out, brave
man! The cause is good, and the Lord receive my soul."

We could hear the mariners and passengers talking about scuppers filled
with blood turning the sea red, just as Abraham had said. The crew told of

Spanish soldiers boarding the *Margaret and John* and the need to repel her. Everyone praised Lucas, the carpenter's mate.

Englishmen would recount this battle across public houses and tavern tables for many years to come, I felt sure. One carpenter's mate had outwitted two Spanish warships! The story was just too good.

Still, that the sea battle occurred at all troubled us. My unease about Will's impending return to Virginia had grown knowing of the Spanish attack. My own fears of ever sailing again were growing along with it.

This didn't even touch the fears that I, and soon the rest of the settlement, had about a Spanish attack right here on land. Suppose those warships came here for revenge?

At least we worried little about the Indians these days, I thought.

"I just want him home, Tempie," I said. "And I want neither of us—none of us including you and Sir George—to go to sea again. If here is our home, let us here be." Worry knotted itself inside me.

She gave me a long look.

At last, she said, "I would wish it for you, too, except I think you're letting your fears grow and creep like a Virginia vine in summer. Fear is gnawing the corners of your soul. Let it not do so," she said firmly. "For what will worry gain you?" She put her arm around me. "Fight the battle when the battle it is." She pointed to the ship. "Like these men did."

A big sigh escaped me. "I see what you mean."

"Your worry changes nothing. Mr. Shakespeare said, 'I am the natural fool of fortune. Use me well!'" So it is with us in our little island here in the James. We're all fools of fortune in our way." Tempie looked thoughtful.

Then she added, "It doesn't mean I'm not sympathetic and concerned to see Will home. Just that you fretting does nothing to help you *or* him. Besides," she said, looking across the river, "one never knows what circumstances might call one to go to sea. As Dr. Bohun told the captain, 'Fight it out, brave man! The cause is good.' You must fight it out against your fears, Joan. As I keep fighting mine own, too," she added quietly.

I laughed. "So I should 'fight the battle when the battle it is' 'as the natural fool of fortune'?"

Now she also laughed. "We always have surprises here, don't we?"

"No more to come, I hope."

But the strange and the astonishing were part of our lives in Virginia. Hoping otherwise was to tempt fortune into making us his fools, sure.

Strange Shadows Fostered
of the Moon

Late June 1621
James Town, Virginia

There are strange shadows fostered of the moon,
More numerous than the clear-cut shade of day …
Go forth, when all the leaves whisper of June,
Into the dusk of swooping bats at play …
 —Arthur Davison Ficke

June was edging toward July.

A steady summer rain just passed, a peek of sun dropped low upon the waters. It always struck me as marvelous how the river could appear shades of plum late in a summer's day. In this purpling dusk, I saw two long, narrow canoes.

The Indians made canoes by burning out the centers of trees. These tree-boats glided through the water as the Indians paddled them smoothly with sticks. Canoes varied in size, from ones holding just a few men to the longest ones which could carry forty warriors.

The Indians often hid canoes near bodies of water. This way, on their journeys deep into the forests around them, water didn't hinder their travels. Once they had paddled to the other side, the Indians concealed the canoe again on the opposite bank.

Rivers, creeks, and runs cut all through the Virginia landscape, so canoes were useful. We sometimes purchased them from the natives ourselves.

We were at peace, so far as we knew, with all the tribes. Still, the first question when we saw canoes remained as ever, *Which tribe can it be?*

"Accomack!" was the whisper amongst those near the gate.

The six warriors landed the canoes and disembarked.

Even as skilled as the natives were with canoes, it still amazed us how far they could travel in one. These Indians would have paddled all the way across the Bay of the Chesapeakes from the Eastern Shore. The size of the body of water they had to cross probably explained the very long canoes they were in.

"*Chamay, wingapo!*" called the first warrior with a friendly gesture. *Greetings, friend.* I surprised myself sometimes with the Indian words I'd learned in my time here. *Chamay* was another Indian word we'd added to our language as we now sometimes called friends our *chums.*

Still, even friendly warriors betrayed little in their expressions. These braves wore a grimace, nearly a frown. Their faces they had smeared red with *puccoon* root, which they said kept at bay the insects swarming the woods and fields. Their hair, three feet long on the left, short on top. They plucked the hair on the right side so that it should not interfere with their bow string.

Animal claws dangled from one of the brave's ears. Another had a living yellow and green snake adorning his ears, which curled itself about the Indian's neck. The snake must have been half a yard in length.

Like almost all Indians, these men towered over us and moved quickly yet with great stealth.

The braves wore remarkably little clothing, much of it made from deer hides. We could understand them wearing so little in this heat. Yet even in the cooler months, Indians dressed much lighter than we did. Will said they wished to brave the cold as long as possible before donning matchcoats, feeling that it made them stronger.

I was forced to admit it probably did.

A time in the past there was when these fierce men with red faces, stone weapons, and unusual clothing had sent shivers through me. But with peace secured, I'd grown almost used to the Indians' appearance.

We never worried when it came to the Accomack. Their chief, Esmy Shichans, had a longstanding league of peace with us and we with him.

Living on the Eastern Shore, far beyond the ready grasp of Opechancanough and the Powhatan kingdom, Esmy knew diplomacy was his ally. He remained neutral, as cordial as possible with both sides, English and Powhatan. Officially, Esmy and Opechancanough were allies. As a practical matter, though, our mutual friendship with his tribe had survived through Indian wars.

Esmy had greeted the settlers upon their first arrival in '07 and remarkably, during all that time we'd had unbroken peace with his tribe.

In fact, no war had broken out with any Indians in the seven years since Pocahontas had first married John Rolfe. Pocahontas was Powhatan's favored daughter. The marriage between John and Pocahontas had seemed a good reason for a treaty.

King Powhatan had proclaimed to Ralph Hamor that too many men on both sides had died in these wars. How true that was.

By my occasion, there shall never be more. I, which have power to perform it, have said it. No, not though I should have just occasion offered, for I am now old and would gladly end my days in peace. So if the English offer me injury, my country is large enough. I will remove myself farther from you. That should satisfy my English brothers.

Powhatan's word was his bond. Since that time, all fighting between us had ceased even as we moved further west upriver.

Powhatan's successor, the war chief Opechancanough, whom we also called "Emperor," swore his utmost allegiance to the settlers. If anything, Opechancanough seemed much friendlier to the English than his brother had been. A few skirmishes had occurred, it was true, but nothing too severe. The peace was sure.

I pushed a memory of little Giles Fairfax and the sudden attack at James Town from my mind. Back when it happened, Opechancanough had called those murderous braves "renegadoes." He had sworn to punish them although we never heard if he had. That had been three years ago, and all had been quiet since.

And so we slept easy in our beds at night.

Now the Accomack braves, escorted by two soldiers, made their way to the governor's home. The Yeardleys lived just outside the fort in the heart of what would one day be New Towne.

Perhaps, I supposed, their visit meant nothing. Yet I couldn't remember seeing any of the Accomack here in a long while, if ever. That canoe paddle across the bay was a long one. I heard it was impossible to even see land from one side to the other. Whatever business they came on must be important.

Tempie was my spy at the governor's home, so I was sure I'd soon know why the warriors were here.

I did. The Accomack had come this far to discuss King Powhatan's bones and spotted cowbane. The reasons why I was soon to learn.

Poison Flowers

Late June to Late October 1621
James Town, Virginia

Dream at all of all the sorrows
That were ours,—
Bitter nights, more bitter morrows;
Poison flowers ...
—Philip Bourke Marston

My kitchen and herb gardens within the fort were small, but I was proud of them. Healing herbs such as chamomile and ginger I'd been able to grow here. The summer's strong sun beat down on the plants, so I'd drawn water from the town well to nourish them. As I poured, the warm, wet smell of the earth rose, and I knew the land here was good. A sense of contentment washed over me as the water washed over the seedlings.

That contentment would only last a few minutes.

I saw Tempie approaching, so I gave a wave, stood, and brushed off my apron. I made my way into the house to see if I had mulberry beer to offer her. We'd learned to make drinks for ourselves from all sorts of plants in Virginia. The heat of a summer here could wrap around a body like a warm woolen blanket. Like my little plants, she, too, would be parched.

A few moments later, Tempie slid into my house, her face rosy from the sun. She pushed the door shut behind her and dropped into a chair by the table.

"Oh, Joan." She let out a deep sigh, shaking her head in dismay. "Did you hear that the Accomack came to James Town last night?"

"I glimpsed them, aye," I replied. "What brought them here? Is our peace with the Accomack sure?"

"Yes, yes," she said, then paused to consider. "At least, I think so. They bring us peculiar news, though. I just came to think aloud, I suppose."

I placed a glass of beer before her and sat down, too. "Think aloud all you wish!" I said with a grin.

She drew a long swig and then mopped her brow, damp from the heat. "My, that's good, Joan," she said. She seemed to relax a little. "These braves come from Esmy Shichans, the Laughing King. He sent his messengers to warn us of Opechancanough's plot. It seems that while the water appears still, there may be turbulence beneath. Not long ago, Opechancanough sent half a dozen braves bearing gifts to Esmy at the Eastern Shore. In return, the braves requested that Esmy give them poisonous plants."

I frowned. "For the Powhatan to use against the Monacans?" Even as I said it, I knew such was not the case.

"No, Joan. To use against us."

I covered my mouth. "It can't be! Perhaps the Accomack are mistaken? What does Sir George think?"

"He knows not what to make of such news, but he'll be cautious. He'll have to be. The lives of many settlements depend on it."

The words *poisonous plants* hung in the air between us.

"Oh, my." This news left me speechless. "Poison?" As I said the word, an icy finger tickled my spine. *Poison.* "Might it be spotted cowbane?" I asked at last. "I believe it grows profusely on the land across the bay."

She nodded. "Aye, George thinks it may be cowbane, too. The braves described the plant to him."

Spotted cowbane, the dreaded water hemlock. A thimble's worth could kill a fully grown cow, I knew.

What did Gerard's *Herball* say about these plants, I wondered. I went over to the shelf and pulled down the unwieldy book. Dropping it to the table, I opened it to the back. I ran my finger down the page until I came to the listing for hemlocks.

"Here it is. Deadly poisonous, Mr. Gerard says. We knew that." I then read aloud, "*A very evil, dangerous, hurtful, and poisonous herb.* Gerard goes on to say, *He who takes it dies remediless.*" I looked at Tempie, who was listening intently. "The only remedy is drinking hot wine before the venom attacks the heart, he says. Once the poison attacks the heart, no cure can be. Gerard quotes Pliny the old Roman." I read again, "*But being drunk with wine, the poison is with greater speed carried to the heart, by reason whereof it killeth presently ...*"

I looked up to see Tempie's grave expression. She said, "Well, that's just it then, Joan."

I squinted, not understanding.

"Well, you know the time has come to take up Powhatan's bones. Three years have passed since the old king died," she went on.

I'd been in Virginia long enough that I knew the meaning of such things as "taking up of bones."

After the great *werowance* Powhatan had died, the Indians disemboweled his body and then placed it on a scaffold to allow it to decompose. Such an honor they reserved for their chiefs. His skin they had scraped and allowed to turn to dust. This they placed into pouches to wear as *memento mori*, as the old Romans called such things. A reminder of death.

Dust to dust, the Indians did take literally.

Now that three years had passed, time enough for the bones to dry thoroughly, the Indians would remove them and bundle them up.

During a great ceremony and feasting for the former high king, they would put his bones and jewelry into a bag. After that, the natives would place the bag in their temple at a sacred town called Uttamussack.

"Esmy claims the Powhatan had planned to invite our chiefest men to the ceremony," Tempie continued.

Upon its surface, inviting our men would have been a good thing, a wonderful cementing of the seven-year peace between our peoples. Nothing could have more commemorated the end of Powhatan's rule. That Opechancanough, now in full reign alongside his brother Opitchapam, wished to continue this peace.

She continued, "Do you see? The feasting! The invitation to George and our councilors to come for the celebration—the taking up of Powhatan's bones. Esmy believes Opechancanough planned to poison the wine at the friendship toast."

Suddenly, her meaning was clear. I gasped. "The tribes come from all around to feast and celebrate the life of the great Powhatan! And what better way to honor him than to distribute poison at that time. Did Esmy give the poison plants to Opechancanough's braves?" I reckoned not since he'd sent warning of it.

Tempie shook her head. "No, the Laughing King declined because of our constant peace. He and George have always gotten on well, too."

She ran her hand across the glass, staring into it as if it might give her answers. Then she dropped her face into her hands. The governorship had been hard on George—but hard, too, on Tempie. "Esmy believes that if our men had declined the invitation, Powhatan braves would have brought the poison to each settlement disguised as a gift," she finished dully.

"The news does sound credible," I said. *Sadly, too credible.*

"Aye, George thinks so, too. He's ordering us to prepare, but for what, we know not. He will himself travel to all the plantations and warn them to be on their guard against attack, to make sure they're well fortified. He'll put Captain Powell on alert here at James Town," she added.

Then a frightening thought jumped at me. *Cecily!* While Jane was safe here at James Town under Captain Powell, my oldest daughter and her husband Sam were in the outpost far upriver at Jordan's Journey. "Someone has to warn Sam and Cecily!" I cried.

Tempie nodded. "George will send a pinnace upriver in the next day or so. Write a letter and give it to me. I'll see that it goes aboard in safe hands."

One thing confused me. "But why should Opechancanough seek to begin another war?"

Another sip. A pause. Tempie set the cup down. "In fear, fear we'll displace them as the Spanish displaced the Carib Indians in the West Indies. So say the Accomack."

I understood. Our settlements spread further across the land with each new season.

"Will Sir George confront Opechancanough?" I asked. The icy finger had now become a hand, gripping my insides.

Tempie took a deep drink of mulberry beer. I could see the lines easing on her face.

"I don't know what George has decided to do. He probably *hasn't* decided, yet," she said, thinking aloud. "But even if he asks Opechancanough, I do suppose the Powhatan king will simply say Esmy is lying. And then the old chief will go after Esmy and his people. And then? Do we lose our best friends, the Accomack? Suppose Opechancanough kills the entire tribe as his brother did the Chesapeakes?" The Chesapeake Indians, after Powhatan's brutal hand, were now only a memory.

"Powhatan was a different kind of king, a wilier one," I put in thoughtfully.

The first great chief had once told us that the Roanoke Island settlers, abandoned by the English, had traveled up to live with the Chesapeakes. *And when I killed the Chesapeakes, these blue-eyed English were among them,* the king had said triumphantly in his language.

Still, Powhatan had promised permanent peace after John and Pocahontas had married. Marriages, we understood, often united Indian tribal enemies with one another.

I rested my chin in my palm as the many problems snaked into my head like the little green snakes I'd seen in the Indian's ears.

"We cannot repay Esmy's kindness by showing his hand to the Powhatans," I murmured.

Soon after this news, Sir George did send several men to meet with Opechancanough to ask if we still had a league of peace. The Indian emperor held his hands open wide. *Of course!* The chief seemed genuinely puzzled, Sir George's men reported. *Why do you ask?* The king had seemed befuddled by such a question.

Still, just to be secure, Sir George would go himself to each plantation as Tempie had thought he would. He planned to take a muster and to ask all to be on their guard, to be wary in case of surprise assault.

As Tempie had suggested, I gave her a letter for Cecily, which she said she'd ensure Sir George had in hand when he visited Jordan's Journey.

The shallop brought back a hearty response. *All is safe, mother. Sam has palisaded Jordan's Journey well. You know Sam! Vigilant he ever is on his guard. Cheerful news I have; I am expecting a child! Sam is delighted. Hope to see you and Jane, as well as John and little Elizabeth, soon.*

If Will could avoid the Spaniards on his return trip home ... If the Spaniards did attack here ... If Esmy had misunderstood the message ... If the peace we had, we could only keep.

Sir George had taken ill once more, this time being sick all of September. He'd hoped to go on an expedition seeking the Northwest Passage. Indians had told us that following the Patawomecks' river led to a great body of water. Perhaps at long last, the men could find the trade route through the continent to China!

Instead, Sir George's sickness prevented him going. So his wife's cousin John Pory, Lieutenant Perkinson, Ensign Savage, and some others would sail without him.

The hope, as it had always been on such voyages, was to find the head of the waters, the passage to the East Indies, the Orient. The Spanish, Dutch, and English were certain one of these rivers crossed to an ocean on the other side. So the men would be visiting tribes, seeking to know what the Indians knew of the northwestern waters.

"George is so disappointed," Tempie told me. "But 'tis clear he cannot go. And all agreed they should wait no longer than September with winter coming on."

Tempie paced and awaited the new governor as I awaited Will. *The worry over the poison has made him ill again,* Tempie said. His uncertain health had convinced her that he needed to hand over the governorship as soon as possible.

The months passed, and the Indians demonstrated their friendship at every turn. If anything, the peace seemed to deepen as more Indians came to settlements to visit fields, to discuss hunting, to stay overnight in our homes. It became more a partnership than it had ever been before. Perhaps Esmy had, indeed, been mistaken.

We saw no Spaniards in our waters either.

The *Abigail* and the *Elinor* came to port, but they held nothing for us but new settlers and some goods for trading. "No Spanish!" the captain of the *Abigail* reported cheerfully.

Still I awaited Will's ship. *Soon,* I told myself. *Soon.*

By October, the leaves in the treetops turned to a spectacle of oranges, reds, and golds; the nights were growing crisp.

Soon enough, the crops ripened with abundant corn and pumpions and squash. We'd had enough rain to make for a good harvest, and it was satisfying to see the amount of corn in our barrels grow.

My son-in-law John Rolfe came by to say that the corn and tobacco crops were especially fruitful out at Mulberry Island this year.

Famine, an event of the past. I was just so grateful for everything we could now enjoy.

This niggling fear of the Spanish I would, with effort, not dwell on. In fact, I kept all my worries at bay as the leaves began a silent march to their ends.

Jack of the Feather

Late October to November 1, 1621
James Town, Virginia

... Nemattanow, otherwise called Jack of the Feather, because hee commonly was most strangely adorned with them; and for his courage and policy, was accounted amongst the Salvages their chiefe Captaine, and immortall from any hurt could bee done him by the English.
    —Capt. John Smith, *Generall Historie*

I'd been walking toward the well when I caught a morsel of conversation behind me.

"So did you hear ol' Jack of the Feather met his fate?" I heard someone ask. I turned my head to peer over my shoulder. The man was a stranger to me, as was his companion.

"I heard something of it. You just come from upriver?" his friend asked.

"I did. Thorpe sent me down here to let the governor know. But first, a drink!" He laughed.

Does he mean Jack of the Feather has died? I thought.

Jack of the Feather was a boisterous warrior who boasted that English bullets couldn't kill him. Jack of the Feather had what Will would have called "bravado."

We heard Jack was one of Opechancanough's chief captains and that the Indian king relied on him heavily. In fact, Jack had been an important warrior going back to my first days here. He was Nemattanew to the Indians but "Jack of the Feather" to us, easily recognizable because of the enormous swan's wings sprawling from his shoulders. These wings spread so wide that the Indian looked as if he could fly away!

I paused and pretended to forget for a moment why I'd come. I stood near the men so that I could eavesdrop on the conversation. Maggie had taught me well: learn from those who know what you do not.

"And he told Thorpe's boys not to tell no one what killed him," said the first man.

What killed him? So Jack is dead. What of Master George Thorpe's boys? I wondered, leaning a little closer. I eyed the strangers casually. They were paying me no attention anyway.

The first soldier dipped a ladle of water from a barrel by the well. He drew a long drink.

As he did, the second man mused.

"Why would ol' Jack come from the forest with Morgan's cap on unless he did away with Morgan? Morgan ain't been seen since, neither. Trading expedition, huh?" The soldier grunted his skepticism. "Those boys done right. Jack moved their patience so as they had no choice but to shoot. What were they to do? Allow the Indian—be he a captain or not—to murder Morgan?"

I caught my breath. Opechancanough surely would not be happy about Jack's death.

Just then, a third soldier came over. I took my time adjusting the rope on my bucket. How glad I was I had not sent my servant Angelo or Esther for this water but had decided to come for it myself.

"You talking about Morgan's murder?" the third man asked. "'Swounds, Morgan ought never have believed the Indian when he offered to take him to Pamunkey to sell his baubles."

"We're at peace. Morgan had no reason to fear, not until it was too late." The first man took another sip of water. "Adam's ale, son, no finer!"

The three men laughed bitterly. We still struggled to keep enough spirits on hand, so sometimes circumstances forced the men to drink Adam's ale, that is, water.

"Peace or not, I myself never trusts an Indian," the third said.

Surely, Opechancancough would not threaten our peace over the loss of one captain, howe'er important he be. A chill ran through me, but I dismissed it. The weather was, after all, growing cold and damp.

The men turned to talking about some trapping they'd done, so I wandered away and over to Tempie's to see if she'd heard of this.

I gave her a hug, then wasted no time. "Did you hear about Jack of the Feather? Is it a problem, do you suppose?"

She didn't look surprised, but said, "We heard that Mr. Thorpe's boys shot Jack for murdering a man named Morgan. George doesn't seem too worried about it. Opechancanough assures him through messengers that Jack was out of favor with him lately. 'Bury me among your people that my people may not know,' he told the boys before he died."

Master Thorpe's word carried much weight in Virginia. He was a former gentleman of the king's Privy chamber, a military man, a councilor, and a great friend to Sir George Yeardley. A kinsman of Sir Thomas Dale, Mr. Thorpe was notably religious like Dale and wanted to clear Virginia of drunkenness.

"Master Thorpe? He is that rare man, virtuous *and* wise, a frame for our godly building," I heard Sir George say once. Everyone loved Master Thorpe. Even Master Pory, not easily impressed, called him an angel sent down from heaven.

Mr. Thorpe had become convinced of the spirit and intellect of the Indians through personal experience in London before he'd ever come to Virginia.

His wife's cousin, Sir Thomas Dale, had brought Princess Pocahontas, Rebecca Rolfe, back to England in 1616. Along with her had come a dozen or more Indians. Some had boarded ship to return with Pocahontas to Virginia, but not a few had stayed behind.

One of the natives had gone to live with Mr. Thorpe in St. Martin-in-the-Fields in London. This young man had learned to read and to write, even copying Mr. Thorpe's letters to Sir George.

But life in London had proved hard on the Indians who stayed behind as they fell ill to diseases new to them. One of those who survived only three years was Mr. Thorpe's adopted son, baptized and named George not long before he died. Young George had been buried in the church at St. Martin's with several of Mr. Thorpe's other children.

Mr. Thorpe's affection for his Indian son had left him with a zeal for the natives, a hope of missionary work to them and offering them an education. Besides commanding Berkeley Hundred, Mr. Thorpe was also in charge of the English college and Indian school upriver. We hoped to build these in the spring on ten thousand acres, a large tract to produce enough corn and tobacco for the schools to be self-supporting.

What the Indians thought of converting to English manners, we knew not. But a European education, learning to read and write, seemed inviting. To us, anyway.

These would be our first schools in Virginia.

Others at Berkeley were not so happy with the lengths Mr. Thorpe would go to in appealing to the natives. This anger increased when some watched Mr. Thorpe shoot their mastiffs after the Indians expressed fear of the large dogs. *See, they are mortal, too,* Mr. Thorpe had said to his Indian friends.

"He'd a-shot more mastiffs had we not raised up a loud hollering at him! We need our dogs of war. Plain and simple."

"Peace is worth more than your dogs, friends," Mr. Thorpe had replied. But nonetheless had agreed he'd kill no more of the mastiffs.

Mr. Thorpe, ever compassionate to his Indian friends, punished the boys who'd killed Jack. He then gave the Indian a burial place under an oak. Jack's grave on the College Lands adjoined those of the English buried nearby. The Indian captain had wished it not known that English bullets had, after all, killed him.

In the celebration of a ship's arrival, we had little time to consider Jack's death. Soon, we'd forgotten it.

Trumpets sounding and cannons firing announced the arrival of someone of importance. The new governor was here and Will with him!

Safe. No lives lost at sea, no pirates or Turks. Praise God.

Everything was, I was certain, going to be well after all. I could feel it.

My Sweet William

November 1, 1621
James Town, Virginia

All in the Downs the fleet was moor'd,
The streamers waving in the wind,
When Black-eyed Susan came aboard:—
'Oh! where shall I my true love find!
Tell me, ye jovial sailors! tell me true,
If my sweet William sails among the crew.'
—John Gay

The cheerful bulwarks of Mr. Wiseman's ship, green and gold, caught the sun. A feast of colors all around. Providence had brought the *George* to James Town on the first of November, All Saints' Day. Merriment saturated the air.

Sometimes I understood how far we'd come and how much joy was possible here, now that it seemed all the worst lay behind us.

Spirits were high, and why not? We'd had a plentiful harvest—barrels filled with Indian corn in kernels of orange, burnished red, yellow, and blue.

The Virginia trees were afire in colors of crimson and amber, cinnamon and bronze. The river, too, had turned its rich, dusky autumn hue, matching the skies dappled in clouds. What a stunning first look at James Town! Virginia had put on her finest for those arriving for the first time.

We were so proud of our little colony, how we'd withstood the challenges, even if worse for the wear. The promise of Virginia had never seemed brighter. Bright as the corn, the river, the leaves. Church bells pealed, and trumpets heralded the new governor.

On the dusty highway leading to the riverbank, folks clamored to welcome the newcomers.

Jane and John hurried over to me, and Jane wrapped her arm around my waist.

"Is he back? Is father on board?" Her eyes sparkled.

"Aye, I think this is the ship!" I cried, barely able to control my own excitement that the long wait was over.

John had a boyish grin on his face. He and Will were business partners and great friends as well as being related through John's marriage to Jane.

"You look as happy as I feel!" I said to him. Then with more concern, I asked, "And how do you feel?" He had been ill much of the fall.

"Almost recovered, I think," he said lightly. "Well, 'tis no easy feat to manage the Mulberry Island patent alone, I'll say that. Not to mention our properties over the water from James Town and on the Maine. And I've done so while sick. I need that gentleman, your husband, back here to do his share." He raised his brows in mock consternation.

I laughed. "You go tell the gentleman that!"

Could I just preserve this moment, this happiness, this relief, forever?

Another trumpet sounded as if we weren't already in a great state of eagerness.

Tempie and Sir George emerged from the governor's home, understanding the trumpet's meaning. Sir George smiled broadly. His letters to the Company had pressed for someone to take over as governor. He clearly hoped this ship brought this new man. He was still recovering from his September sickness.

A new governor? Tempie was as delighted as was her husband. Relieved of office, Sir George had many acres to plant and a sound trade in tobacco. He was intent on building an estate for his children.

"God willing," Tempie had told me recently, "George will never be governor again. Then he'll only sail to England if he chooses to, not because someone at the Virginia Company or the councilors here, ask ..." She paused. "Or order him to."

Now, down the plank came a man we'd soon learn to be Sir Francis Wyatt, new governor.

Behind Sir Francis and several other well-dressed men came Will. I surveyed my husband. Will looked tired but otherwise well. His hair had a few more flecks of grey than before. So did mine. But just a few.

My heart leapt, and I threw my arms around him and said, "Praise God, thou hast survived another ocean voyage!" The battle of the *Margaret and John* had reminded us that we could never take any sea journey for granted.

In all the ships that had ever arrived in James Town, rarely had any brought the delight this one did. The belief that Virginia would succeed, that the harshest times lay in the past, that our little colony would shine with prosperity.

Virginia, ho!

As these new arrivals stepped onto Virginia's rich soil, they wobbled ever so slightly. I could remember the feeling, though it had been so long ago.

Yet the newcomers' faces fairly glowed, even after such a strenuous journey.

I saw, too, that their faces were studying the landscape, the forests, the sweeping river. *So this is Virginia!* their awestruck expressions said.

Will himself was in fine spirits. He grabbed me and kissed me in front of all those assembled at the wharf, nearly scandalous.

"William!" I hissed, but not severely. His cheerfulness celebrated that he was home, no souls lost on voyage, no pirates or Spanish, and Virginia was in sound hands. I was soon to learn how much Will liked Sir Francis Wyatt.

As the gentlemen and travelers congregated on the dusty ground, Will whispered to John, Jane, and me who these new men were and something about each one. How glad I was to have him by my side again after so long!

"Here is Mr. George Sandys, brother of Sir Edwin Sandys, Company Treasurer. Mr. Sandys will be Treasurer here in Virginia. His duty is to oversee all commodities in Virginia. He's also a renowned poet, translator, and travel writer, quite well known in England," Will said in my ear. Mr. Sandys had a friendly face and curious eyes, I saw, as he waved amiably to Will.

Will whispered to me that Mr. Sandys had been a longtime bachelor since his only marriage had come apart abruptly and painfully, years before. "His parents and his bride's parents arranged the union, and the couple was incompatible from the start."

We'd also soon learn that Sir Francis often called Mr. Sandys "Uncle" because Sir Francis was married to Mr. Sandys's niece, Lady Margaret Sandys. She had remained at home in Kent, Will added.

"So you believe Sir Francis will be a good governor, not just that the Company chose him for his family connections?" I asked Will quietly, hoping no one could overhear me.

"I do," Will said. "I became friends with Sir Francis and Mr. Sandys on ship, and they earned my respect quickly. Sir Francis is young but intelligent. He comes from the ancient Wyatts of Kent. And Sir Edwin has such dreams for the Company, dreams his brother George seems to share," Will told me. I could hear the hope in his voice. "Mr. John Ferrar shares these dreams, too.

Ferrar is an able deputy of the Company, acting as Sir Edwin's primary help," he added.

Sir Francis was mild and temperate with a strong belief in Virginia's possibilities. Mr. Sandys brimmed with energy and enthusiasm.

"Tempie will be glad. She wishes Sir George to hand the reins to a new governor."

"The good knight has given his heart to Virginia, sure enough, which has taken due toll on his body," Will observed.

Bulbous and genial Dr. John Pott emerged from the ship as new Physician General of the colony. "His expertise is in the distilling of waters," Will remarked. Dr. Pott was to replace the unfortunate Dr. Bohun. We were desperate for a doctor in the colony. Dr. Pott brought along an attending apothecary, a Mr. Fitch.

Dr. Pott's wife Elizabeth held his arm and looked around with large eyes. She had a sweet face but looked exhausted.

Mr. William Claiborne, only twenty years old, would be Virginia's first surveyor. The Company had first selected a more experienced man named Norwood, but this appointment had fallen through somehow. Claiborne's face did not belie his eagerness to explore Virginia. "Claiborne is your friend Isabella's nephew," Will said to me. "Captain Roger Smith is his uncle."

"Oh." Such a strange procession was this!

Mr. John Pountis walked down the plank, brushing his clothing with his hands. Mr. Pountis was to be vice admiral, preventing fraud and abuses of ships.

A Mr. Bolton had signed on as clergyman and strode down behind Pountis. Mr. Bolton departed the ship talking to a man I would soon learn to be Mr. Christopher Davison, the new secretary.

Finally, a second clergyman, Pastor Haute Wyatt, the governor's brother, followed Mr. Bolton.

Sir William Newce and Mr. Lapworth, other new councilors, had arrived a few weeks before. Now it became clear that the Company thought a strong Council of State the way to govern Virginia.

Meanwhile, we in Virginia still had the privilege of electing our own General Assembly. Every settlement elected two members. The Assembly gave the settlers a voice, and we had every intention of keeping it. The advice of the Assembly joined that of the council and governor.

"Wow." That Indian word again. Sometimes it just seemed to suit a situation, and this was one. *Wow.* So many learned and honest gentlemen. Virginia's reputation at home must be improving at long last!

Then, even with so much good news, Will's face darkened just a bit.

Catching it, I asked, "What is it, Will?"

John and Jane were standing nearby. Will shook his head, indicating he would talk to me about it later.

Amongst the men and women on board were a dozen or more servants Will had hired.

Even the servants seemed hopeful and eager. Will had paid the cost of passage, and in return, the servants had agreed to work for Will for seven years. While the servants worked for him, Will would pay for all the servants' food, clothing, and shelter. The servants' duties were mostly to help farm corn and tobacco. This gave the servants ready work and provisions while they learned how to live in Virginia and grow these Virginia crops.

The Company would grant Will fifty acres for each servant whose passage he paid. We called these headrights, a right to land per servant.

After paying off their passage, the servants received their freedom and title to fifty acres—*fifty!* Now free men, these former servants might pay the passage of others. And so it all began again.

For folks who could have never owned land in England, this made Virginia seem once more like Canaan, the Promised Land of the Bible. Enticing indeed.

God had tested us beyond what we felt we could endure, and we had proven ourselves worthy of such a land. At last!

Fourteen years, I thought. Fourteen years had passed since James Town's founding, but at last we had this right. The ripening fruits from so many tears and years of trials were at last coming to harvest.

John and Jane offered to ferry the new servants to Mulberry Island this evening where housing awaited.

Will thanked them, and then suggested he and I return to the quiet of our home. "Where I can sleep for a long while," he murmured, taking my arm.

Once there, Will said wearily, "I'm sorry to say that Lady De La Warr has ordered John to return to England to account for her goods."

When the ill Baron De La Warr had departed Virginia suddenly, he'd placed these goods into John's care.

"Do you suppose that could wait until he improves?" I asked. "He's been sick much of this late summer and into fall. He's scarce recovered."

"Oh? I'm sorry indeed to hear that, but my Lady La Warr has grown impatient. After all, the baron invested a large amount of his estate in Virginia, leaving behind great debt and many children to support. No, John will have to go. He'll be hearing this from Sir Francis soon enough. I'll pull him aside first to let him know. But not today. Let him and Jane enjoy the festivities for a bit."

Just a few days later, the *Marmaduke* arrived. On it were Captain Norton and his Italian glassblowers and their families. Afterward, once in a while, my ears caught Italian words. Soon, the glassblowers would be settling at Glasshouse Point under Mr. Sandys's charge.

The next few months would bring many newcomers skilled in other commodities, all to be under Mr. Sandys's command.

We learned that a Mr. Berkeley, soon to be Captain Berkeley, planned to survey Falling Creek upriver. The Company had put him in charge of an ironworks. From what Berkeley had heard, Falling Creek could be an ideal location. He brought his young wife Joyce, who was expecting a child in the spring.

Two other gentlemen would be erecting saltworks for us, much needed, of course, for salting meats.

Will said, too, that the Company had plans to send over a Captain Barwick to be in charge of shipbuilding. Ships were yet another commodity we might be able to sell to replace tobacco. We had tall, strong trees as far as the eye could see. Besides, we needed ships, shallops, and pinnaces, too. The rivers and creeks of Virginia were its arteries, flowing like blood deep into the land. Will's excitement was palpable.

Meanwhile, a Mr. Gookin, an Englishman living in Ireland, brought a ship we called simply "the Irish ship," filled with kine and settlers. He planned to settle east of James Town.

Then, too, Will said some French Walloons had plans to come to Virginia. Their home, he said, was Flanders.

Suddenly, it was plain to see that Virginia's reputation had much improved both in England and abroad. The pleasant news rolled in like ocean waves, one following the other. We felt that we should almost burst with the coming prosperity. 'Twas all heady stuff.

Virginia, though, was like a maiden with two faces, dark and light. Whenever she showed us her bright side, her dark, cruel visage was soon to circle back to us.

But on this All Saints' Day, all was bright. We'd forgotten about her other face, a face even now moving toward us with eerie, stealthful steps.

Small Cheer and Great Welcome

November 8, 1621 to Early January 1622
James Town, Virginia

... the gentlemen you name in your letter are all dead except Mr Sandis who hath bin visited with long sicknes but now thankes be to god is well recovered, I doubt not but he will prove a worthy member. The people where he liveth take great liking to him, and I Assure you Sir he is most faythfully affected to his study, and doth deserve to be beloved ...
—Sir George Yeardley writing to Sir Edwin Sandys, about March 1622

Small cheer and great welcome makes a merry feast.
—William Shakespeare

Before us on this damp November evening was a table spread with the finest of dinners. The Yeardleys had butchered a hog for the occasion, a feast welcoming the incoming governor and councilors.

The table bulged beneath pork and a fat Virginia turkey. Some platters contained English roots like parsnips and beets. Others brimmed with native foods such as pumpion, squash, corn pone, corn pudding, and *suppone* bread.

A servant offered guests English or Virginia drinks. The Yeardleys had provided sack and apple cider. Most of the newcomers, though, desired to try the Virginia favorites of pumpion beer or Mr. Thorpe's distilled corn.

"They'll get used to corn soon enough," Tempie whispered to me with a half smile.

The Reverend Haute Wyatt offered a blessing.

Just as we were starting our meal, the Reverend Sam Macock and his young wife came to the house. "We've come down for a visit from Macock's

Divident!" the pastor announced.

Sir George stood and walked over to the Macocks, greeting them warmly. I knew from Tempie that Pastor Macock was one of Sir George's most loyal and reliable councilors. When Sir George had bouts of illness, Mr. Macock took over as he could.

"Sit, sit, please!" Sir George gestured the Macocks to the table. "We have a few more chairs."

Sir George had invited the Macocks, and here they were, having made an effort to come from their home upriver. Delight lit the governor's face, partly because he wanted to introduce Sam Macock to the incoming governor. Sir George was sure Mr. Macock would be as helpful to Sir Francis as he had been to him.

Virginia is filling up with good people, I thought, looking around the table.

As we passed platters of steaming victuals, noisy conversations followed.

Everyone seemed interested in the story of the *Margaret and John.* The new arrivals wanted to hear the story as it had come to us firsthand.

Dr. Bohun's loss was devastating to all, of course. What diseases might his plant trials have cured? His noble final words spoke well of him. "We shall remember them, I think," Sir George noted.

"And the castaways?" asked Mr. Sandys. "What of them?"

"They live in various settlements." Sir George shrugged. "The Indian thicket, Elizabeth Cittie, Martin's Hundred."

Sir George took the opportunity to mention his wife's cousin Pory and his Northwest Passage expedition.

"Let us wish Mr. Pory the best of fortune, then!" said Dr. Pott, holding up his glass.

Then Sir George and Tempie and those long here asked to know about London happenings. What had we missed?

The biggest news, we learned, was that the king had arrested the Earl of Southampton, our Company treasurer. "This happened in the middle of June. The dean of Westminster provided the care while Southampton was under arrest," Sir Francis said.

"My brother, Sir Edwin, arrested as well," said Mr. Sandys, rolling his eyes to show his displeasure.

"Arrested?" Tempie asked. A woman's place might be to sit quietly, but Tempie didn't care.

"The charges were mischievous intrigues with members of the Commons. The king released both a month later. But our Majesty doesn't like the good earl, I'm sorry to say," said Sir Francis, reaching for another piece of pork. "I fear me it bodes not well for the Company."

Mr. Sandys hastened to add, "But not before my brother suffered the indignity of having officials come to search his cabinet and boxes, forcing his wife to give over her keys to these men. She protested boldly to say, 'I only wish you had a key to my husband's heart, that you might see he has only loyalty inside!'"

Everyone was silent for a moment, taking that in.

"Other news?" Sir George asked at last.

"Well," Dr. Pott said, "Philip III, King of Spain, died peacefully in April. His son Philip succeeded him, being but seventeen years old."

We also learned that our king had ordered certain English apprentices whipped. The king said the boys had treated the Spanish ambassadors shamefully.

"Some of the members of the Lower House were unhappy that the king chose to send artillery to help Spain. But the king says he gave his word to the Spanish ambassador two years ago and must honor it," Sir Francis put in.

"Ambassador, bah!" cried Dr. Pott.

The king's inclination toward Spain troubled many. Most believed she was our enemy and a threat the English colonies.

As we passed the platters around the table, we learned that Thomas Hariot, the distinguished mathematician, had died.

"Well, small cheer and great welcome makes a merry feast, as Mr. Shakespeare hath written," Mr. Sandys volunteered. "I find great cheer as well as a great welcome here in Virginia!"

Mr. Sandys was an interesting guest. His book of his travels was among the most popular of its kind because of his thorough research and observations. Most well-bred Englishmen traveled only to Europe. But Mr. Sandys had traipsed to biblical lands. He'd seen Egypt, Turkey, Palestine, Constantinople, and Arabia. Mr. Sandys was the youngest of seven brothers and two sisters. His brother Sir Edwin was very much older. No wonder that Mr. Sandys and his niece's husband Sir Francis were so close. Mr. Sandys, in his early forties, was nearer in age to Sir Francis than to Sir Edwin.

Toward the end of dinner, Sir George beckoned to Will. "Lieutenant Peirce, I will wish to see you with the incoming governor tomorrow about an Indian matter. Captain Powell will also be present."

Will was second in military standing only to Captain Powell. I suspected that Sir George had two matters on his mind. First, Jack of the Feather's death. That had seemed to be of small importance to King Opechancanough.

The rumor about the poison also persisted. Sir George would tell them that he had been to each of the settlements and told them to keep watch. He'd found nothing to substantiate Esmy Shichans's assurances.

Tonight laughter and gossip and news rang from the Yeardley table. All had arrived safe and well provided. The *Margaret and John* had bested the Spanish. Clearly, we were riding a high tide.

Many times over the next year would I remember that evening, the abundant food and carefree laughter.

Mr. Sandys had moved in with us soon after his arrival. He had come eager with plans for prospering Virginia commodities. A long sickness came upon him, however. Soon his hands were full simply with surviving the Virginia winter, something most newcomers forgot to account for or to expect. The ague and a cough overcame him. I was well aware that these could take him from the world. Esther, Angelo, and I brought him herbs for the healing, warm possets, and chicken pottage each day.

"Mrs. Peirce, I do say you take better care of me than any new arrival might expect! And so my feeling of receiving a great welcome continues," he said. He had begun regaining his color, and only a slight lingering cough remained. That, too, had soon passed.

After that, he became a presence at our meals.

At first I was afraid he would make me feel uneducated. But he soon proved to be delightful as a home companion. Mr. Sandys's Company projects fascinated Will, and Will had many comments and observations from long years in the colony. Mr. Sandys was a scholar and was well traveled, but Will and I knew Virginia. This made Mr. Sandys as interested in us as we were in him as if we were travel specimens, delightful but travel specimens nonetheless. And this was all right.

We had some fascinating conversations over the supper table. Mr. Sandys enjoyed talking about such things as the canal streets of Venice, the grandeur of the pyramids, the desert lands of the Bible.

He had many questions for us. Had we met the Indian princess Pocahontas? Did we speak the Indian language? How did the little animal the Indians called *opossum* carry her young? He had heard it was a most unusual mammal.

He also had questions for Angelo, our servant from Angola. What was the climate in Angola? How did her people worship? What manner of clothing did they wear?

Angelo, who had learned much English in her time here, also spoke some

Portuguese as well as her native language. She shyly answered his questions and slipped back away as soon as she could.

And of course, the first question any newcomer asked once in the colony: "So how long have you been here?"

Mr. Sandys already knew that Will had been on the *Sea Venture*, marooned in the deserted Bermudas with all on the ship for nearly a year. But he wished to learn more details. Mr. Sandys savored the *suppone* as he wanted to know how strong the winds of the hurricane were, adding, "I hate a storm at sea, Lieutenant Peirce!"

"I have never seen such strong winds. I promise thee, sir, we could not tell if the rain came from the sky or the ocean. Seawater and rainwater mixed in the air!" Will said jovially. He was enjoying having Mr. Sandys with us. The hurricane and shipwreck were like an old war story to him, which I supposed they were.

"And Mistress Peirce, when did you arrive?" the poet asked.

Before I could answer, Will proudly told Mr. Sandys that I had been here almost a year before he arrived. He said I'd come on the *Blessing* through the hurricane and that I had survived the Starving Time by collecting and grinding acorns. "She hid acorn meal and rationed it throughout the winter with Lady Yeardley."

Mr. Sandys's eyes widened as he looked at me with, I thought, new respect.

I shrugged. "'Twas a long, long winter, sir. But those days are over, praise God!"

The poet nodded. He seemed to understand I didn't wish to remember it in more detail, and so he turned to the subject of lions. Had we *seen* any lions here in Virginia or just their claws? What about the Indians as sorcerers?

Our conversations were long and pleasant, and never did he treat us as less educated than himself. Although of course we were.

Meanwhile, the feeling of optimism in the colony seemed contagious.

Inspired by Tempie's mother owning a windmill, Sir George had completed one of his own at Flowerdieu Hundred. He was proud that his was the first windmill in Virginia and hoped that more would follow. He was already using the windmill to grind grain.

Mr. Sandys was working to build a watermill on his property. Such things were new here.

The ironworks far up at the falls of the river, our furthest settlement, expected to produce iron in the spring. Or so we heard from Mr. Berkeley, councilor and the one in charge of the works.

The saltworks were well underway. Sandys also felt there was hope for the glassworks, even though the Italians were not always cooperative.

Someone had sent a large contribution for an inn at James Town, the first guesthouse we'd ever had. Carpenters had already arrived to build it.

"Construction will begin in the spring," Mr. Sandys told us.

Iron, silk, grapes and vineyards, cordage and linen from native plants, pitch and tar, salt, sawmills, shipbuilding, and glass manufacture. Such hope and promise.

So many dreams.

A Caravan from China Comes

Late January 1622
James Town, Virginia

A caravan from China comes;
  For miles it sweetens all the air
With fragrant silks and dreaming gums,
  Attar and myrrh—
A caravan from China comes.

O merchant, tell me what you bring,
  With music sweet of camel bells;
How long have you been travelling
  With these sweet smells?
O merchant, tell me what you bring ...

The little moon my cargo is,
  About her neck the Pleiades
Clasp hands and sing; Hafiz, 't is this
  Perfumes the breeze—
The little moon my cargo is.
            —Richard Le Gallienne

I was at Tempie's home several months later when Mr. Pory returned from his voyage. He knocked enthusiastically on the Yeardleys' door.

"Well, good day, Cousin Pory," Tempie said, giving him an embrace. I admired Tempie, for though she didn't care much for her cousin, she never quite showed it. "Where is Sir George?" Mr. Pory cried with barely a greeting. "We bring news!"

At that moment, little Francis toddled around the corner. He had just started walking.

"Ah." Mr. Pory's face lightened. Strange how a small child can bring the joy out of even a serious man. John Pory said to the boy, "Young Master Yeardley, my newest cousin! Walking now, I see?" He smiled at Tempie, "I suppose a toast is in order, then?"

Ever so slightly, Tempie rolled her eyes at me. Mr. Pory had a bit of a reputation as a tippler.

Before Tempie could answer, Sir George emerged from the chamber.

Forgetting both baby and drink, Mr. Pory eagerly launched into his find. "Sir George! Good day, sir. And I do mean *a good day*. We've seen a China box at the Patawomeck king's house. We're near to discovering the Northwest Passage, I'm sure of it!"

Quietly, Tempie led little Francis to Susanna's waiting arms so that she could listen to what her cousin had to say. It was obvious to us both that it was important.

Sir George reached out and shook his guest's hand and then gestured to a chair. He sat himself, too.

Then Sir George leaned in. "Have you yet told Governor Sir Francis?"

"I will, sir, but you sent me on the mission. I felt it only right to inform you first."

"And you do conceive the Chinese to have made this box? Did the Indians say who gave it to them?" Sir George asked with interest. "What did the box look like?"

"It was a small casket. The people who crafted it used braided palmetto. The maker had painted the outside and lined the inside with blue taffeta as the Chinese do." Mr. Pory barely paused to breathe as he continued. "We, of course, asked the Patawomeck how they had come by the box. The Indian king said another nation, living thirty days journey from their tribe, sailed ships to the Patawomeck town. These people call their land *Acana Echinac*."

"*Acana Echinac*?" Sir George repeated slowly.

"The second word sounds much like 'China,' does it not, sir?" Pory asked. "Whoever these people be, they live but three or four days from the ocean. The king said the ships were like ours. He also described these men as being of small stature and having houses as we do, apparel like ours, and household stuff resembling ours, too. He also says they carry curved swords."

"How incredible. What a find, Pory!" Sir George exclaimed. "This news will astonish the governor and council and the Company in London as well."

Pory went on to say that the Patawomeck king offered to send his brother with them to find these people. "The king believes they live west at the head of the Seven Goodly Rivers. The rivers fall into a great bay and rise out of a ridge of hills ..."

Pory pointed into the distance of the Yeardleys' chamber as if, looking hard, we might see the ridge there. In fact, we all looked.

"These hills run all along the south and north. The Patawomeck believe we shall find this country but one hundred fifty miles from the falls of our own James River!"

This was the best clue we'd ever received that discovering the fabled Northwest Passage might be within our grasp. To find and claim the important trade route to the East Indies remained our single greatest goal. If the folks who had sailed to the Patawomeck were Chinese, then China was in reach! It meant we could reach China and Japan from a Virginia river, perhaps the river of the Patawomeck if not the James.

What fascinating news was this!

And on its heels, more news to come in the form of a pinnace, stripped and hobbling to Virginia.

The More Fantastic the World Becomes

Late January 1622
James Town, Virginia

The more we know, the more fantastic the world becomes and the profounder the surrounding darkness.
—Aldous Huxley

About this time, a curious sight entered the waters near James Town. A ship we would learn to be the *Concord*, towing a pinnace behind it. The pinnace had no sails and looked skeletal with only its rigging.

"Why would a pinnace leave England without sails?" I heard someone ask near my home.

"Pirates done taken them!" came the reply.

I threw on a cloak and went to see what it all was about. Outside, I saw Jane with Elizabeth by the hand and told her pirates may have attacked a pinnace.

"Pirates?" She shuddered. "John will be leaving soon on account of Lady De La Warr. I understood the passage from England to Virginia and back was free of pirates. Is it not so?"

"I don't know if any sea voyage is free from pirates completely. But I've never heard of pirates attacking any other ship coming or going from here."

We both wanted to learn more and found ourselves, as always, out by the wharf.

Vendors hawking their wares crowded the streets of London. I, not for the first time, thought wryly that someone selling cakes or poplin pears would do well if they but put themselves here by this James Town wharf.

The pinnace captain disembarked from the *Concord*. I recognized him. Gaunt and hollow-eyed, this was Captain Daniel Elfrith. Elfrith had piloted the *Treasurer* when it had captured a Spanish slaver sailing to Mexico three or four years before. Here stood the man who had stolen my African servant

Angelo from the Spanish. The Spanish had previously bought Angelo and others from the Portuguese, who had raided Angelo's Angolan town with the help of a neighboring tribe. The raiders had captured and enslaved the Christian villagers, including Angelo.

Angelo had lived through a painful ordeal, and this man Elfrith had taken part in it. Elfrith had been nothing but a pirate himself, sent out by then-Governor Sam Argall and the Earl of Warwick to rove the West Indian seas seeking Spanish booty. This rogue attack caused us to fear Spanish reprisals. Argall had seemed oblivious to that, escaping by a swift pinnace and leaving us to our own fates here in Virginia.

Back then, Sir George had turned away our own ship, the old *Treasurer* now a rotting hulk in a creek. The governor had no choice because Elfrith had stolen these Africans from the Spanish and brought them here. Pirating, robbing a Spanish ship, was against our laws and left us all in danger.

Now here was Elfrith again under strange circumstances.

Captain Elfrith enjoyed being the center of a story, so he didn't seem to mind telling those assembled of his adventures. He indeed had a harrowing tale.

Elfrith was a Warwickshire man, an ally of my Lord of Warwick just as Argall was. So, not surprisingly, his stripped pinnace had left England in consort with the ship *Warwick*. But the *Warwick* had arrived the month before. What had happened to this little ship?

"Well, now my pinnace the *Tyger* carried but forty passengers, we being but forty tons. Eight of our passengers were the maids the Virginia Company did wish me to deliver to Virginia," he began. "We in our little *Tyger* had a miserable early voyage such that headwinds and tempests blew my vessel to the North Cape," he began.

"The North Cape of Spain," I whispered to Jane. I suspected Elfrith's sailing ability might be part of the reason the storms had driven the ship.

"Well," the captain went on, "what should happen to us there, but being near the headlands we do spy two ships we believe to be Dutchmen. We bore up the helm to speak with them," he continued, warming to his story. "But, lo, these were but *captured* Flemish ships now in the hands of the Turks—Turkish pirates!"

About then, Tempie approached the wharf. "What have we here?" she asked, seeing the naked rigging.

"Pirates attacked the little *Tyger*," Jane exclaimed.

"Truly?" Tempie asked, eyebrows arched.

"Aye," I replied.

Captain Elfrith raised his voice. "What did the pirates do? Grappled us, came aboard, stealing most of our victuals and all our working sails, tackle, and anchors. They took all our sailing gear, down to our compass and hourglass! We were left adrift. Likely to starve to death at sea."

Tempie made a face. The seas near the Mediterranean were the lair of pirates, but a much rarer thing for them to come a-plundering near to England or the Spanish coast. Yet Elfrith said that's where the Turkish pirates had attacked him. It was a little frightening for us to hear that.

"By a miracle, the Turks captured none of us on board except we traded two English boys to them. They in return gave us two boys, one being French and the other Irish." He pointed toward two boys who were now disembarking. The boys had wide eyes and looked to be not more than ten years old. How had the Turks captured the boys, I wondered.

"Turks boarded your ship and left you to go on? How be it the pirates didn't enslave you?" a man near to the captain asked skeptically. A fair question. When pirates captured a ship, rarely did its occupants escape slavery.

"How be it, indeed? I know not," Elfrith said grandly. "Perhaps because our ship was so small, they did not want it for their piratical exploits. And we had nothing left to steal on board. I reckon they didn't find us fair booty for slaves, so they released us. But they had crippled the *Tyger* completely, leaving us with no way to sail her home or to Virginia."

The captain found himself with a growing crowd around him. He was tiring of his story, beginning to look fraught and exhausted. But now we all wished to know what happened.

"Here is the man to thank!" Elfrith proclaimed, gesturing to someone coming down the plank.

I also recognized this man, Mr. Delbridge. Richard Delbridge was a familiar sight in these waters. He came from a family of shrewd Devon traders. He was the son of John Delbridge, a prolific world trader of Devon, a former mayor, and sometime Member of Parliament. The Delbridges were prominent associates of my Earl of Southampton and Sir Edwin Sandys. This made the Delbridges enemies of my Lord of Warwick while Elfrith was a Warwick ally.

Fissures and cracks in the Virginia Company, a cauldron about to boil over.

Delbridge looked embarrassed. If I read his expression correctly, he might have wished to leave Elfrith behind for the Turks!

Now Elfrith resumed his story loudly. "We were adrift near the coast of Spain, hopeless. When what should happen? What in all the great and mighty ocean should occur? Where ships rarely meet? We espied another sail, that of Mr. Delbridge's *Concord*. Delbridge brought us on board and towed the *Tyger* across the entire ocean to Virginia. By way of Bermuda, the fabled Somers Isles, I might add."

Despite his fatigue, Elfrith had a sparkle in his eyes when he clapped the shoulder of the nearest man to him. "And that, son, is how God ransomed this ship! Now I needs me a good meal." With that, the tired seaman meandered over to the fort.

I had an odd notion, a feeling of something approaching. Our fortune had been so good. First, the *Margaret and John* had been the victor against two Spanish warships. Now this little ship had survived a pirate attack. Yet the pinnace had still arrived in Virginia and without starving.

How about the good fortune of those on board the *George*, who lost not a soul? Prosperity and promise indeed.

"So the pirate captain becomes now the pirated? How strange. Fantastical happenings, Tempie," I murmured, staring behind the captain as he walked away. "A China box and a Turk's ransom."

Under the Silver Moon

March 10 – 13, 1622
James Town, Virginia

Father will come to thee soon;
Father will come to his babe in the nest,
Silver sails all out of the west
Under the silver moon ...
  —Alfred, Lord Tennyson

During the time of his abode there [in Virginia], which draweth nigh upon
six years, no man hath labored more to his power by good example there and
worth encouragement until England by his letters than he has done.
  —Ralph Hamor, writing of John Rolfe, 1615

Sitting at our table, our son-in-law John looked pale, weak, nervous. Afraid.

The fire did little to chase March's dampness to the far corners of the chamber. Will stoked the fire, hoping it would help.

Jane's taut face said all that she was feeling. Her large eyes took in the scene around her, her hand she placed consolingly upon her husband's arm. Then she looked down at the little girl on her knee.

The two, with little Elizabeth, sat in our home enjoying a last meal together before John's departure in three days.

Oh, my Lord, how many fatherless children have there been in Virginia? I thought with a sudden rush of ... something. Something like foreboding, but with terror brushed through it. I'd been having these feelings for weeks, but said nothing lest I frighten my daughter even more. And worse, I'd been having dark dreams. Yet when I awoke in the mornings, I was never able to remember what in them had frightened me so.

Jane, I decided, should never know the fears I myself had. She carried enough of her own fears for us both anyway. She was a fair and strong young woman, only seventeen years old and quite the survivor herself.

Angelo brought ham and peas to the table. The corn pone steamed hot, and the butter was sure to melt onto the plate. All might have been well had not this journey loomed before us.

Journeys. Always another one behind this one.

Lady De La Warr's lawsuit was forcing John's hand. To England he must go. He had not left on the first magazine ship, the *George*, with cape merchant Abraham Peirsey. "A few weeks," John had mused. "A few weeks delay, and I'm sure to be well again."

But he was not.

John placed his head in his hands, pushing the furrows back from his brow.

"Will, I leave you in charge of my estate should anything ... happen." John's eyes darted from Will to Jane, to his daughter and to me. He always looked unsure of fate. He had, after all, endured a hurricane at sea and the birth and death of his first child as a castaway. His first wife had died soon after her arrival here, and Pocahontas, his second wife, had died in England at age twenty-one. Pocahontas, though longing to see Virginia once more, had not survived the return from England.

John and Pocahontas's young son Thomas, now aged about six, was in the care of John's brother Henry back in England. John had left the little boy behind upon Pocahontas's death in Gravesend.

Had he known Pocahontas would fall mortally ill, John might have left both mother and son behind in London rather than having them board ship. He'd placed the two at risk, as he later said, by obeying his orders to return to Virginia.

Their ship had made it only partway down the Thames before his Indian wife had become deathly ill. Little Thomas and other Indians on board were also ailing, perhaps from the time spent coming down the Thames in open barges to meet the ship. And so John had made the wrenching decision to leave Thomas behind, urged by Captain Argall.

"Leave him, and keep him. Bring him, and lose him. *Leave him,*" Argall had said. I didn't care much for Argall, but his words were true, and Sam Argall wasn't known for mincing them.

I knew John worried for his son, his only son. He wanted to be a presence in the boy's life, but doing so meant that John must bring him across the ocean. "I pray that I can get the boy a mite older before subjecting him to the perils at sea," he'd said once to me.

John had put off writing his will, but now the time for doing so was at an end. Everyone knew it was foolhardy to board a ship without one's last wishes left behind in writing, especially being ill as John was.

A sick feeling washed over me, but I tried to ignore it.

"Aye, of course." Will's voice sounded uncharacteristically gentle. "You're sure you don't want your brother Henry as administrator?"

John shook his head. "Henry strives to look after my interests with the Company. But he knows little of the actual business here on the island. And how could he?" John's voice rose a pitch. "Who could understand Virginia who hasn't been here? You know as well as I that there are two sorts of men—those who have been here and those who haven't."

Will agreed. "I do know. But, John, this I do know also. Things look to be the best they've ever been. Most everyone is healthy, and the winter mild. The trade with the Bermudas brings us much fresh fruit and other foods to keep us well. God willing, we'll soon grow Bermudian plants here ourselves. The peace with the Indians seems in place—thanks to your marriage with Pocahontas Rebecca. You leave us at a good time, friend. I'll see to our business while you're away, just as you've done for me. You have no worries about Jane or little Elizabeth. No worries, sir."

John's face, so grim with fatigue, relaxed. "No worries indeed." Then he mumbled, "At least, not over many." And his face creased once more.

"You'll get to see little Thomas again," I added in what I hoped was a cheerful tone.

At that, John smiled for the first time of the evening. "Little Thomas. How big he'll be now, how much he'll have grown. He had the beautiful rich eyes of his mother." Then, John added, "After supper, I'll show you the will. Then tomorrow, I'll get myself over to the Yeardleys and to Reverend Bucke to witness the signing."

Three days.

In three days, John would wave farewell to us from the deck of the *Concord* as it unmoored from the pines. He looked pale, but Will's assurances carried much weight with him.

Mr. Delbridge had shaken Will's hand before climbing aboard. Will trusted Delbridge, having shipped goods with him many times. It surprised Will not at all that Mr. Delbridge had rescued the *Tyger*. Knowing Delbridge's skill helped Will feel more comfortable sending his son-in-law, business partner, and friend away on the *Concord*.

John had completed his inventory of Lord La Warr's goods. The sailors had stowed the goods in the ship's hold, and John would escort the cargo back to England. He would testify before the chancery court about La Warr's belongings. Some of these goods were from 1611 and some from 1618. The first time, my Lord La Warr had left abruptly due to illness. The second time, the baron had never made it to Virginia, dying by the way.

God willing, John would be back here within a twelvemonth.

Jane's cheeks were tear-stained, but she stood tall. She had brought her little girl and herself to the wharf to see her husband off.

"John," she said to her husband just before he climbed aboard. "I have something for you. For luck."

Her husband raised his eyebrows. "A little luck on a sea voyage? I'll take it, missus!"

"Hold out your hand," she said.

He did so, and in it she placed a Spanish coin. "It's a *reale,* a bit. A sailor gave it to me many years ago. A kind mariner named Harrison who warned us of the hurricane. He said he'd plucked it from a Spanish galleon himself, that it had always brought him luck. He thought as a fatherless child, I might need some myself. God has blessed my family and me here. Keep my *reale* safe, John, and bring it back to me."

His eyes filled with tears as he clutched the coin. He gave her a kiss and said, "I will, darling."

At last, the ship loosed its moorings and left the shore.

John's face, looking toward his young wife and baby, grew smaller upon the tide taking him down the James, to sea.

Will and I each held a hand high as the ship grew smaller. We hoped John would see us from further away.

"Farewell, farewell, fare thee well," Jane whispered, taking little Elizabeth back to her home.

Standing there that day filled with March sunshine and spring hope, our worst fears were for John. Our course here, as we saw it, was secure.

For his part, John thought he was leaving his wife and child in plenty and peace. He would never know what was nigh to befall us in Virginia—the worst yet—in just nine days.

It would be the last time we saw Master John Rolfe.

Bright Scarlet Cloth, Beads, Buttons

March 19 – 21, 1622
James Town, Virginia

... as also in the Evening [of March 21], as in other dayes before, [Indians]
came unarmed into our howses, without Bows or Arrows or other Weapons,
with deere, Turkies, Fishe, furrs, and other Provisions to sell and truck with us,
for Glasse, Beades, and other Trifles ...
—Edward Waterhouse, 1622

Here are our wares for trading with the tribes;
Take something with thee for remembrance,
Bright scarlet cloth, beads, buttons, rosaries,
Ribbons and huswifes, scissors, looking-glasses ...
—John Hunter-Duvar

Despite our concerns about John sailing off, good news kept arriving from every corner, it seemed. The sense of prosperity and hope kept growing along the River of His Majesty James.

In early February, Tempie's cousin Pory had set out on another expedition, this time south to explore the Chowanoke's River. Captain Rayner had sailed down that way a few years before, but Mr. Pory would make an overland journey all the way to the old Roanoke colony. One of the missions of the James Town colony had always been to try to find the Roanoke settlers, missing now for over thirty years.

Mr. Pory had set off to see whether he could determine the fate of the colonists, what the Indians might tell him.

Upon returning, Mr. Pory joined his cousins at dinner. He had traveled sixty miles overland, past the great swamp, all the way to the River of the

Chowanoke tribe.

"I fear me none of the settlers of Ralegh's expedition survive unless they are with the Indian tribes. The Indians there tell me those English came north to join the Chesapeakes many years before. Their story is just as King Powhatan once told us," Pory had reported to those present.

Sir George sighed grimly. We'd all suspected those long ago lost colonists dead, but yet held out some hope for them. Pory's news extinguished that last ember.

Years ago, the old chief had said that he killed the English Roanoke colonists. We had never known whether this was bluster or fact. Now it seemed it might be true.

After relaying this sad news, Pory brightened. "Such a fruitful place it is south of us, though. The Indians there grow tall corn and reap it twice a year. They speak of pine forests fifteen miles wide which cover the land for sixty miles in length!"

Mr. Pory had leaned in and warmed to his topic. "These pines—tall and straight for masts of ships, excellent for pitch and tar as well. Much silkgrass there growing we could weave to rival the cotton and wool of the East Indies, certainly. And the Indians there have told me that just ten days march to the setting sun is a people who gather river sand, wash it in sieves, and melt it over the fire. Once melted, it becomes like unto our copper!"

Sir George was thrilled. "Do you wish to make an exploration to those people to find that copper sand?" he asked Mr. Pory.

"I do indeed. Give me men, and with Indian guides, we can make a discovery of this land."

"You shall have it then. I'm sure Governor Sir Francis will approve," Sir George told him.

Tempie had sighed in the retelling, a mischievous grin spreading across her face. "The River Chowanoke would be a good place for him to settle, thinkest thou not? Maybe even ten days west to the setting sun from there. So far away. So *very* far distant."

Still, Pory's news of fertile lands south only fueled the optimism we already felt. If prosperity were at last to be ours, we'd earned it. We had the scars—scars on our bodies and on our hearts—from years of wars, martial law, and privation to prove it.

Just as Pory was returning here, a bark from Bermuda arrived with gifts—two great chests filled with fruits and plants from our sister colony. One chest contained sugar cane, plantains, lemons, pomegranates, and oranges. The other was bursting with figs, potatoes, papayas, cassava roots, red pepper, and prickly pear.

Spring was but a few days away, and this year we expected to try growing these Bermuda plants. Mr. Sandys brought a sampling of them to our home. I would make trials of sowing some of these fruits, I decided.

Grateful to our Bermuda friends, we returned a ship filled with our own Virginia bounty. Our ship carried aqua vitae, sack and oil, bricks and limestone, ducks and turkeys. *Please send us more wonderful foods!* Sir Francis's note to the Bermuda governor said.

Trading with Bermuda was just the beginning. We were now hopeful of trading with Indians further north like the Susquehannock for furs. Our trade with the Powhatan Indians already flourished with good will.

In January, wanting to ensure that this peace was solid, Governor Sir Francis had sent Mr. Thorpe to Opechancanough with gifts. "Our new governor desires to keep the same peace as we've had—perhaps to enlarge it," Mr. Thorpe had assured the emperor.

It is well, Opechancanough replied. The Indians knew of the new governor and were certainly hoping the desired peace could continue. The Indian king pointed to the winter-blue Virginia sky. *The sky shall fall before our peace is broken,* the emperor had said.

The Indian king had requested a copy of the peace treaty. This we had done, stamping it in brass. The chief had nailed it to one of his large oaks. Meanwhile, George Thorpe had ordered some carpenters to build Opechancanough an English house with lock and key.

"He loves that new home!" Mr. Thorpe had exclaimed to the council. "He locks and unlocks the door a hundred times a day to see such a device."

So it was no surprise when near dusk on the first day of spring, March 21, twenty-two warriors approached James Town from the riverfront. Indians coming to trade were a common sight.

I paused to watch as the braves pulled their canoes to the shore. Three of these canoes carried five warriors, one of them seven. In typical fashion, one brave sat lookout in front, one watched from the back, and every other brave held a paddle.

I'd just left Tempie's new home by the causeway over the Pitch and Tar Swamp. I often wished the Yeardleys had not built their home across the swamp from the fort. Sir George preferred the quiet of the Back River. Yet the causeway was primitive and slippery, I not so surefooted.

As I continued back toward the old fort, I saw that most of the arriving Indians were headed toward the governor's home, the Country House. Little lay between Tempie's home on the Back River and the old fort except for the governor's home. It sat rather isolated east of the fort where we hoped to build a new town soon.

We called it the Country House because rather than belonging to any one person, it belonged to the country as a whole. Sir Thomas Gates had built it years before. At the time, most of us were still living upriver with Sir Thomas Dale.

Sir Thomas Dale. Even thinking of the old governor brought a shudder. We all tried to forget the days of martial law under his iron will and discipline. Two men could not have been more different than Governors Dale and Wyatt. Argall had stolen from us, and Dale had tried to kill us with martial law. How fortunate we were to have had Sir George and Sir Francis as governors afterward.

Governor Argall had later made the Country House his home when he moved the government back to James Town. Sir George had followed as the next governor to live there.

The Yeardleys, in turn, had moved out to allow the new governor, Sir Francis, to have it soon after the feast in the fall.

Sir Francis had made some improvements on the home. I glanced over and noticed one of his servants beating the laundry out back.

The braves greeted those they knew, some by name, who were working on the riverbank. They were probably seeking to trade down by the wharf, perhaps even to truck with the mariners on board the *Marmaduke* riding at anchor.

Evening made a good time to trade. The Indians understood when we English worked and when we rested. We'd been friends so long that this was true all up and down the river. I noticed men and even a woman walking over to them to see their wares, which looked to be small game.

Some of the natives were making their way toward the home of Governor Sir Francis.

One brave carried a large turkey. Others held a buck swinging between them on poles. A fourth had leather pouches filled, I imagined, with trade goods.

Last summer, the Accomack had been a curiosity, having rowed from across the Chesapeake Bay to visit. But the braves today were just local tribes, perhaps Pamunkey or Warrisquoyak. They visited often for trade and socializing.

Copper was most valuable to them. Their favorite English items were copper rings and bracelets. They also liked looking glasses, buttons, and glass beads. We traded axes and sometimes coats and caps. These items were but trifles to us, but the Indians valued them. We'd learned that of all the colors, they most preferred blue glass beads. Any of these goods they might in turn trade with other tribes further away from us.

I waved to the braves as they marched past, and they returned the gesture. One called, "*Chamay, wingapo!*" *Greetings friend.*

"*Chamay, wingapo!*" I said in return.

Opechancanough had indicated the sky. The peace, he'd said, was so firm that the sky would fall from the heavens before our peace dissolved.

In fact, the sky itself was a glorious blue, the first buds appearing on trees around the settlement.

I smiled. It looked like the sky would not be falling today.

Courage My Soul

March 22, 1622
James Town, Virginia

Courage my Soul, now learn to wield
The weight of thine immortal Shield.
Close on thy Head thy Helmet bright.
Ballance thy Sword against the Fight.
See where an Army, strong as fair,
With silken Banners spreads the air.
Now, if thou bee'st that thing Divine,
In this day's Combat let it shine:
And shew that Nature wants an Art
To conquer one resolved Heart.
　　　　—Andrew Marvell

Isabella's husband Richard set out with his own boat. This wouldn't have been unusual except that the sun had long been down. In fact, within just a few hours, cocks would begin to crow the sun's rising.

Yet here was Richard Pace, rowing frantically across the wide James River, over a mile across. His eyes scanned for the governor's house lit only by a moon near its third quarter.

Settlements both large and small, all along the water, had settled in for the night. This late, a few men and even women might be out carousing, but honest folk were in bed.

No one, however, was asleep at Pace's. There the men were busy, securing the homes and readying swords and muskets, while women sheltered the children. Isabella, for one, didn't think she'd ever been so frightened in all her years here.

The men and boys, you see, were readying for battle.

If only every settlement received the news that Richard Pace possessed.

If only ...

The moon, since rising this night, cast silver light on homes and farms who expected to wake to the sounds of a growing colony.

The moon tomorrow night would rise upon something very different.

At this moment, only those at Pace's had the alarm.

Pace grunted, pulling back on the oars with all his strength. Minutes counted.

If what Perry's young Indian boy had told him was true—and Pace had no reason to disbelieve it—a surprise attack was coming. The Indians would strike not long after sunrise tomorrow. Pace didn't think it was possible to warn all the river, unless each settlement sent a boat to the next ...

But no one would be prepared for this. Pace now understood the price the English would pay for their complacency. Each settlement would have to fight its own battles—a second price for disbursement too many miles up and down river.

What would the morning bring?

He didn't know. He only knew his hands were bleeding from blisters and that he thought the governor might owe those midnight carousers a debt of thanks. Due to their lamps burning past a decent hour, he could make out the largest part of the settlement.

The governor's home was off from the fort. Whatever else might happen, the men at James Town would have to protect Governor Sir Francis.

Richard Pace could still see the frightened, conflicted eyes of the young Indian boy. His elder brother lay asleep, and the young man had climbed from his bed to speak with Pace.

A gentle knock on his chamber door had awakened Richard although Isabella had continued to sleep. That is, until he himself arose.

"Do I betray my own people or save you and Mr. Perry, who hath well treated me? I fear me that whatever I do shall cause a great grief, either to the English or to my tribe."

Pace had struggled to make sense of the message, his heart thudding in his chest as the boy's words spilled out. Certain phrases stung his mind.

Morning ... tasked to murder you ... my brother must kill Mr. Perry ... cannot do it.

I Have Heard the Drums Beat

March 22, 1622
James Town, Virginia

And hurrying, stumbling through the street
Came the hurrying stumbling feet.
O I have heard the drums beat.
For war!
I have heard the townsfolk come,
I have heard the roll and thunder of the nearest drum
As the drummer stopped and cried, "Hear!
Be strong! The summons comes! Prepare!"
Closing he prayed us to be calm ...
　　　　　　　—Grace Fallow Norton

When Pace arrived at James Town, he was breathless. He pulled the canoe ashore and raced to knock on the governor's door.

Sir Francis's servant opened it a little and cautiously peered through the crack.

"I'm Richard Pace of Pace's Paines plantation. I must speak to the governor at once!"

The servant looked doubtful, but opened the door the rest of the way.

By now, the governor himself was awake and assured his servant that he knew Mr. Pace and would see him, despite the hour.

Pace didn't wait for greetings. Each moment brought daylight closer.

"Sir! Perry has an Indian boy who's like a son to him. The young man's brother came to stay this night. Perry welcomed him in, of course. The older boy told his brother that the two must attack Perry and me when the sun rises just over the horizon. Other Indians shall come in feigned friendship up and down river as they always do, but this time they'll use hidden weapons or weapons of those they visit." Mr. Pace paused to draw a shaky breath. "A massacre, sir! They plan a full-out surprise massacre upon all our settlements and all our people—in the morning!"

Sir Francis felt light-headed and dropped himself backward to a nearby chair.

"What shall I do, sir?" Pace clasped his hands nervously.

"You trust this boy?" Sir Francis knew the answer, but he must be certain.

"Absolutely, hearty trust! Perry is there now, ensuring that our men prepare to repel an ambush."

Sir Francis paused to give himself time to think clearly. His response, when he gave it, was deliberately measured.

"Cooke," he called to his servant. "Get thee to Captain Powell's house! Awake him at once." To another servant, the governor cried, "Sound the alarum bells, and rouse the drummer. Have all of James Cittie ready itself for attack!"

Sir Francis understood that settlements he could warn might repel the assault. In the settlements he could not, the number of deaths might be high. The Indians had lulled the colonists into complacency, a shrewd and devilish move. The English would have no idea that their friends would strike until too late. Sir Francis knew his choice of which settlements to warn in these few hours meant he would be deciding who lived and who died.

"Sir!" Mr. Pace said to his governor. "I'll hie to Captain Smith's home— Roger Smith. My wife's brother. I should like to warn him myself."

"Go then!" Sir Francis cried. "And tell Captain Smith to come to my home at once."

"Aye, sir!" Pace turned to leave.

Sir Francis called out, "Pace!"

The man, still breathing hard, turned.

"Well done."

Pace nodded his thanks and touched his cap. Then he sprinted through the darkness to Captain Smith's home without another word.

Captain Powell pounded on our door. Will startled awake. Not waiting for a servant, he bolted to the door. A soldier's instincts, perhaps.

Even as Will opened it, I heard a drummer sounding the alarum. *Pum. Pum. Pum-pum-pum!*

"Peirce, we must get to the governor's house posthaste! The Indians plan a massacre in every hundred near dawn. We must secure James Town and warn as many settlements as possible."

I had come forth, throwing a dressing gown over my nightgown, to stare at the scene before me.

"Sandys!" Will cried. But Mr. Sandys was already at the top of the stairs, looking perplexed. Then he, too, heard the drums.

Pum. Pum. Pum-pum-pum!

"Sandys, to the governor's house, now. Grab your sword!" Captain Powell bellowed.

Outside, the alarm bells were ringing furiously as well. The men in the town were stirring near my window. I could hear their voices.

"The men need a leader. You, Peirce!" Captain Powell barked. "Order them to the platforms, guns at the ready. Sandys, come with me. Peirce, as soon as the men have prepared for early morning battle, get thee to the governor's house for further orders."

"Aye, sir!" Will said. He turned to me. "Get dressed. Have the servants dress. Be ready to abandon James Town or to hold it. Prepare to hold the home as a fortress of defense if the Indians get onto the island. Be ready to move if we give the order." Then he did something he never had before. He reached for a pistol off the wall and handed it to me. "You remember what I taught you?"

"Aye," I said, my voice quaking.

"Just in case," he said, and then he was gone.

I fumbled the gun, and it nearly hit the floor, but I caught it. My heart hammered in my chest as confused servants gathered around me.

"Esther, can you shoot?"

She gaped at me, eyes wide.

"*Can you shoot?*" I nearly screamed at her.

She nodded.

"Prepare thyself, then. You'll be the one behind me if I should die. An Indian attacks, shoot! Understand?"

Still speechless, she just kept nodding.

Near Esther, Angelo crossed herself—a habit from her days in a Catholic African village. "*Aiué!*" she cried, a word she used in distressed fear or sorrow.

I gave Angelo Will's hunting knife. She looked down at it, then at me.

"If the Indians come into the house ..."

Angelo stared at me. "Yes, missus."

"Now, get dressed. Please!" They scurried up the stairs to the little rooms up top.

My little army, such that it was, prepared itself for battle.

A Breathing Statue

March 22, 1622
James Town, Virginia

... for certaine howres I seem'd a breathing Statue.
—Christopher Brooke, describing his reaction upon
learning that his two close friends, George Thorpe
and Thomas Sheffield, had been killed with 345
others as massacre news reached England

*The dayly feare that possest [the natives], that in time we by our growing
continually upon them, would dispossess them of this Country, as they had
been formerly of the West Indies by the Spaniards, produced this bloody Act.*
—Edward Waterhouse's account of the massacre, 1622

At first light, four Indian canoes paddled up toward the shore at
James Town.

These same braves had just been here the evening before, entering our homes and trading as friends. Now the soldiers met the natives with
muskets angled their way.

Quick as coneys in the woods, the warriors turned the canoes about and
paddled off in haste.

These Indians proved the truth Richard Pace had brought to the governor
the night before.

*One site saved. But what of the others? How many settlements had our men been able
to warn?*

Some men must stay to defend Virginia's little capital. Others had hurried away in shallops, and even the small ship *Tyger* had edged into the darkness upriver bearing stark warning.

By the time the soldiers had repelled the initial attack at James Town

Island, fear and nerves were setting in.

Within hours, the ashes of all we had done smoldered, literally and figuratively, around us. Smoke from hundreds of fires wafted into the sweet Virginia air.

We were at peace. Were we at peace? Was all this in retribution for Jack o' the Feather's death?

Tempie's words from last summer came rushing back to me, as they so often did. Last summer, I'd asked why Opechancanough would use poison. Why would he break the peace?

In fear, fear we will displace them as the Spanish displaced the Carib Indians in the West Indies. So say the Accomack, she'd said.

I recalled the friendly waves and greetings the braves had given just the evening before. They would have come ashore this morning with a greeting just as pleasant, just as harmless. It had been that way for years. No one would have suspected. Nine months or so had passed since Sir George had warned the settlements to fortify and be wary.

Hours gone by since those braves had come, and still, I sat.

I did not know, I could not know, but I could guess ... And guess I would, correctly.

The bones of so many now lay in fields and in homes. Their blood creeping and seeping into the earth, into the rivers and creeks, and even spreading across kitchen floors. The souls crying out, *avenge ye us.*

This was a day, amongst so many strange and brutal days, I knew I'd never forget. My body, too, tried to absorb the loss. My head throbbed, my heart fluttered, my blood coursed angrily through myself as if a weapon. Inside me, something pulled tight across my chest.

Our island was safe, but elsewhere ... Who was dead?

Faces of so many I hoped had survived flashed like lightning before my eyes. Driven by fear, I could not make the images stop, no matter how hard I tried. Thank God, Jane's home was here at James Town

But Cecily! The girls—Little Temp and Mary, Sam Jordan. All far upriver, very remote.

Tom and Alice Peirce. Their daughter, young Elizabeth.

Annie and Jack Laydon and their girls, living down at Kecoughtan.

Bright, earnest Mr. Macock and his sweet wife.

Young women striding off the ships of '20, heading to new lives.

Children who had survived the beating sea.

Young men newly married, marking their lands with cordage tied to trees.

The striving and the starving, the worrying and the battle, the hope and the promise.

And the death.

It was too much to bear on a sunny Tuesday in March. Too much.

How many?

I sat in a chair near my fireplace, afraid to imagine what was happening in other settlements. I stared straight ahead as I saw nothing, heard nothing, felt nothing. I was afraid to feel, afraid to wonder, afraid to remember. Nearby, Angelo and Esther huddled in fear. Neither spoke, but they rocked themselves in quiet weeping.

If only I could cease the images rampaging my mind.

The tomahawk and the firebrand.

The musket and the ax.

I felt so sick, so weak, so anguished I could not even move.

I would sit this way for, I later learned, nigh upon two hours, which passed as a single breath. A single heartbeat.

Nothing in Virginia would ever be the same after this. It could not be, could never be. Already the men were swearing revenge. "Extirpation, extermination!" and thus would be the end of Indian towns in Virginia, the soldiers said. They would see it so.

No more peace nor hope of peace.

Wars upon bloody wars would linger for years, surely. We would attack, they would attack; we would burn; they would burn. We'd starve them, they'd starve us.

Have we not been here before?

Extirpation. Move them out.

Extermination. Destroy them.

Entrenched in this land, the Indians said they'd been here many thousands of moons, many hundreds of generations. The Indians would not leave easily.

And so the fighting would wage on, would carry on, would be … unending.

The rivers sang merrily along to the sea, unable to sense our misery. The blood in the creeks and hopes and runs spilled into the river, and away it washed.

Bird cries filled the air.

If I could fly with them.

If I could sail down the river and out to sea …

If. If.

Spring was only one day old, and already it was horrible.

The Hande of God

March 22, 1622
James Town, Virginia

But amidst this happines was the Hande of God sett against us, in great part, no doubt, for the punishment of our ingratitude in not being thankefull but forgettfull that by his mercye we were delivered from such bondage and calamitie as before time we had suffered.
> —from "A Briefe Declaration … by the Ancient Planters nowe remaining alive in Virginia," 1624, reflecting on the causes of the massacre in the midst of hard sought prosperity

The sun was moving across the sky, a day like any other and yet like none other.

What has it all been for? Why are we here? We are not worthy. Again and again, life pushes us back.

I didn't want to do this anymore, wasn't sure I'd ever wanted to do it.

I just wanted to go home. *Dorset is my home, my only home!* I thought defiantly. Any sense that Virginia was home? It had all been an illusion, a dream with smoky apparitions and nothing more.

I'd felt this way as the Starving Time approached. I'd felt this way when I understood how brutal martial law would be. Now I felt this way again, and the dread dream was real. All too real.

The leaders and soldiers in James Town were counting hours as they had been since Pace's late night warning.

Shadows were lengthening, afternoon wearing on.

To Will, never had a day seemed so endless and so brief at the same time. He, Captains Powell and Smith, here on the island, had been awake the whole night long. So had the governor and council. Sir George, Mr. Sandys,

Mr. Davison, and Dr. Pott—all of whom lived in homes here on the island. None had slept since Pace's warning.

Fear, fortunately in this case, served as its own fuel. The councilors were trying hard to gain direction and momentum.

"We're going to Martin's Hundred!" Powell snapped at Will. "Their commander was here at the island when we presume the natives struck. A huge settlement and equally vulnerable. Need you with me. We're also to survey Mulberry Island and places downriver. You know Mulberry Island better than any here. We go to find survivors, aid the wounded," Captain Powell said curtly.

So they're sending us east of James Town? Along with his own people on Mulberry Island, Will's highest concern was for Jordan's Journey, Sam and Cecily and their children. But he was a military man, and he followed orders.

"Sir, aye, sir!" Will replied crisply. At that instant, Will conjured an image of himself, Powell, and Sharpe teaching Chacrow to use a musket. Will refused to let the thought linger. Were he and these two men, and men like them, partially to blame for the horror of this night and day? Teaching Indians to use English arms?

Dear God.

Chacrow had been a devoted friend to the three soldiers. At times, he'd even marched in formation with them. Will tried to imagine Chacrow using a weapon against the English. He just couldn't see his Indian friend doing that.

Had anyone warned his people at Mulberry Island? Jane and little Elizabeth were safe here at James Town but what about Sam and Cecily? *Impossible for any warnings to get that far upriver that quickly.*

I told Sam he should stay closer in. But Sam had fallen in love with the upriver bluffs and healthful air, the two great rivers meeting and dividing near his land that jutted far into the river as a point. That point was Jordan's Journey.

Will, that point, that's a strategic advantage. Just as you have your land sitting on a peninsula, I have mine in a point. You know that. Best locations on the river, mine and yours. You, friend, are fretting like an old woman.

Only Sam could call him an old woman and get away with it.

Will could still see Sam slapping him on the shoulder. *Stop your worrying, old man,* Sam had said.

But Will's heart was falling into his boots, not for the first time that day.

As a shallop readied, Will began seeking answers. Spying Sir George, Will called to him, "Sir, where do you go?"

"Up to Flowerdieu and nearby plantations," the knight replied, not pausing his rapid pace, musket and sword ready.

Then Will sighted Captain Roger Smith. *He's the one.* Captain Smith had long-standing military training in the Lowlands. The governor was likely sending him furthest upriver in case a battle raged there.

Will pulled the captain aside.

"Sir, might I ask a favor? Dost thou go upriver?"

"Aye, that I am. And make it quick, Peirce," replied the captain, but not in an unfriendly way. Captain Smith lived at James Town, so the two men knew each other, if not well. They had a certain mutual respect.

"I'm desperate to hear news of Jordan's Journey. My daughter and her husband, Sam Jordan, live there. Please, sir, let me know how they fare."

Smith gave Will a momentary, sympathetic look.

"I will."

Dust was billowing around the bridge as everyone seemed to have some-place to go, something to do, be it personal or an order.

Somehow through the clouds of dust, Will glimpsed one of Sir Francis's boys and hollered to him. "Please, son, I beg thee, to my home to let my wife know where I'm bound. Martin's Hundred and Mulberry Island, likely other places east. Mr. Sandys outbound as well but to return by nightfall. All are seeking survivors. A reward I promise thee later."

"Aye, Lieutenant Peirce!"

Will breathed a mite easier, and then hurried to the shallop taking them away to Martin's Hundred.

Will swallowed. The day of a thousand hours bore on.

And Martin's? God only knew what they'd find there.

The Stars Did Wander Darkling

March 22 – 23, 1622
James Town, Virginia

I had a dream, which was not all a dream.
The bright sun was extinguish'd, and the stars
Did wander darkling in the eternal space,
Rayless, and pathless; and the icy earth
Swung blind and blackening in the moonless air;
Morn came and went—and came, and brought no day,
And men forgot their passions in the dread
Of this their desolation; and all hearts
Were chill'd into a selfish prayer for light ...
Forests were set on fire—but hour by hour
They fell and faded—and the crackling trunks
Extinguish'd with a crash—and all was black.
　　　—Lord Byron

Dusk was approaching.

I'd sat and then paced, moving restlessly about the house. No one, not a single servant, had come looking for a meal.

No one was hungry.

The first waves of news made their way here. Boats, shallops, and canoes filled with refuge-seekers and tales of morning visits from Indians turning to bloody horror.

An eerie pall had fallen over the settlement. The earlier thudding of boots and shouts had given way to hushed voices. It seemed as if we thought speaking might wake the dead or disturb the restless souls. Or mayhap the survivors just couldn't bear to hear their own words, words of death and loss and injuries and fear.

A pounding brought me to my senses and caused me to tremble.

"Who's there?" I whimpered through the locked door.

"The governor's boy, mistress," he called back. "I bring word of your husband!"

I opened the door to see a breathless young man before it.

This started a new trembling, not my first of the day. Where was Will?

Before I could ask, the boy said, "I come from the lieutenant, Lieutenant Peirce. He says to tell ye that the governor is sending him to Martin's Hundred and to Mulberry Island and what other places, I know not. Mr. Sandys is also gone to survey the damages elsewhere, but he'll be back this night. They're looking for survivors."

Looking for survivors.

I didn't want to think about the losses we'd had or about Will's safety. I just chose not to think at all.

Night threw its cape of darkness over the town.

Will hadn't returned, and I realized that I still must see that the servants had victuals. Esther and Angelo and I began to boil some corn and prepare dried fish, fish Will had gotten in trade before it all went wrong.

We ate in silence, several of Will's men, the two women and I. Most of his men were out with him ... or somewhere someone had sent them. I knew not.

This was the beginning of confusing times.

I tried to force some food down, but it just didn't want to get to my belly. At last, I gave up.

Will's man Henry broke the silence by asking, "Where's Lieutenant Peirce, mistress?"

A question I wished not to think about.

"He probably sleeps on ship at Martin's Hundred or Mulberry Island tonight," I said in a dull tone.

Henry nodded, and we resumed our mortuarial meal.

The sun rose on a much different world than it had the day before.

Silence again pervaded the house and the settlement. I wondered how Tempie was, but each minded his own household. I was certain she did, too.

I could guess that Captains Powell, Smith, Tucker and Sir George would lead expeditions to settlements. Their aim would be to find survivors, aid the wounded, bury the dead. At least, they expected to find dead. They would gather any abandoned corn and bring it back to James Town.

Council members left behind took shifts guarding the governor. The governor's home had been a concern to the council. Sitting beyond the bounds of the fort where Sir Thomas Gates had built it perhaps nine years before, its remoteness now made it vulnerable. The council determined to keep watch by the house, muskets and swords poised, all through the night. Now, Mr. Davison. Later Mr. Pountis. Later still, Dr. Pott. At dawn, Mr. Treasurer Sandys. These were men who would have commanded respect in England. Now, they were but watchmen and sentinels.

Bitter dreams of darkness taunted my sleep. Had I not been so exhausted from the long night of wakefulness previously, I doubt not that I should have slept at all.

I awoke before dawn with my insides coiled. Thinking of Cecily and Sam terrified me. My only comfort lay in Cecily's note following the poison scare of last summer.

All is safe, mother. Sam has palisaded Jordan's Journey well. You know Sam! Vigilant he ever is on his guard.

Pray God Sam were indeed vigilant.

Sam! Oh, Sam. What did you do that morning, and how did you do it? I pictured Sam's reddish hair and friendly grin, such a contrast to the ambush he must have seen.

Unless, that is, he were at the ready.

Joan, cousin, you can trust old Sam. You know that, don't you? I seemed to hear him say. *Trust old Sam. Don't you fret.*

Tears filled my eyes and cascaded my cheeks, helplessness draping me in its cold web of despair. A thought unbidden came to me. *Work,* it said. *Keep thy hands busy, thy mind on thy tasks.*

I understood now that while my father had been at sea, my mother had not only cleaned for his sake, but for her own. Now I suspected she'd been striving to keep her fears at bay, fears that one day he would not return.

I must use my hands. Work. Plant what seeds I had saved from last fall. Clean our home.

I called Esther and Angelo to come down from their loft chamber at first light. Angelo would wake Esther and let her know that I had called them down. Esther's hearing, never good, seemed to be worsening. Angelo was learning to talk with Esther in such a way that Esther could follow. After all, Angelo had come here knowing little English but her native Angolan language with a smattering of Portuguese. Though I was sure she would rather be in her own land, Angelo had resolved to make the best of what she had.

In a few moments, both women stood before me.

I said, "Let's stay busy this day."

Angelo nodded, and Esther squinted. Angelo turned and motioned as if cleaning.

And so we scrubbed and swept and began preparing a small kitchen garden that first day after everything changed.

As I worked, I noticed my ears were burning, though. *Oh, dear. Is someone discussing me?* Every augur from the old Romans until the present claimed ears only burned for one reason. I shrugged it off.

Had I known why my ears burned, I might not have ignored it so flippantly.

Worthy, if Not Worthy

March 23, 1622
James Town, Virginia

Arms to have and to use them
And a soul to be made
Worthy, if not worthy;
If afraid, unafraid.
—Robert Nichols

Soon enough, someone rapped on the door. I opened it to see a servant of Sir Francis, not the boy from yesterday but a young man with blond hair.

"Mistress, the governor and council desire your presence in their meeting."

"I think you must be mistaken. They want to see my husband, Lieutenant Peirce. He's not here, though."

"No, mistress. 'Tis you I am to summon. With haste, please."

My thoughts raced. Had I done something wrong? Did they have bad news?

"Oh, my, Will? Is it Will?" I asked. At once I couldn't breathe, as if all the air had escaped out the door when the servant entered.

"Please come now. The council awaits."

Angelo gave me a concerned look and Esther a confused one. I didn't think either quite understood what was going on. How could they when I myself did not?

As I walked from the fort down the Back Street, I could just see the Country House up ahead. My knees buckled and shook. I forced deep, long breaths. *There is some other reasonable reason they have called you,* I told myself. I wished Tempie were here with me.

The servant led me inside the governor's home, and there I saw the council gathered about the table.

As I entered, they all stood. I searched their faces, looking for some sense of why they'd called me. Yet in the sorrow of the day following the massacre, everyone simply looked bereaved.

"Sirs?" I said, hearing my voice shake. I gave a slight bow.

Mr. Sandys stood and gestured me to his chair. "I'm the reason you're here, so I must offer you mine own seat." He smiled a little, and I relaxed just a bit.

"Mrs. Peirce," the governor said, kindly although wearily, "I hope we've not frightened you." He nodded to Mr. Sandys. "Mr. Treasurer has recommended you, and Dr. Pott and I also agree that you be fittest for the task at hand."

Bewildered, I looked from one man to the next and the next.

"Mistress Peirce," Mr. Sandys said, "you may not be aware that while some survivors have made their way here, we're bringing many more. James Town is the most protected location for people and goods and cattle."

"Aye, sir?" What this had to do with me was baffling.

Mr. Sandys continued. "And so comes the question of so many in the fort, how do we feed them? These are the multitudes of the Bible, the loaves and the fishes. Do you understand?"

I shook my head slowly. "No ... no, sir?"

Mr. Sandys went on, "We know that corn will be scarce, for how can we go into fields to plant and reap as dangerous as times now are? We'll recover some stored corn from abandoned settlements. Not Enough. Suddenly at war. So we'll have to ration what food we have. You are a Starving Time survivor." At once, he looked apologetic. "I beg thy pardon, mistress."

"'Tis all right. 'Tis true." I hoped they didn't mind my candor.

Mr. Sandys met my puzzled gaze directly. "We've decided to feed the survivors and stragglers in the barracks, letting it act as a great hall. We'll need the women of the fort to prepare and to serve the food and to give equal portions to all. I've told these gentlemen that having lived with you for four months, I've seen your ability to organize work. I know, too, that you are fair and industrious. We'd like you to choose the women to help you and for you to lead them as they serve each meal. You've been here near thirteen years and have much experience."

My face reddened. "I, sir? I ... I'm not ... I do not ..." Words were trying to escape from the vise on my throat. If I'd felt anxious before, this news had flustered me completely. Surely, they would see this was a mistake!

"We need you, Mrs. Peirce," said Sir Francis Wyatt. "I have as much confidence in you as I do in your husband. Can you go now to the barracks and begin selecting who in the settlement might help you?"

I turned my attention to each of the men. Sir Francis had aged ten years in a day. He'd probably not slept all night if one could believe the bags beneath his eyes. Mr. Sandys was putting on a brave front, but was undoubtedly worried for his nephew the governor and questioning his own abilities. Virginia was not a poem or a travel book!

Who could blame them if these new men were unsure? Virginia, as it had so many times, just toppled into a completely different world than what they—or anyone—had expected.

Dr. Pott would have his work before him when more injured settlers arrived.

I bowed my head. Outwardly, I said, "Of course, sirs. I'm honored." Inwardly, I cried, *Oh, no!*

The governor and council had misplaced their confidence. Where they'd lost it, I knew not, but they had certainly misplaced it somewhere.

Blessedness of Work

March 23, 1622
James Town, Virginia

*Charity has no limit; for the Love of God has been poured into our hearts
by His spirit dwelling in each one of us, calling us to a life of devotion and
inviting us to bloom in the garden where He has planted ...*
    —St. Francis de Sales

Ah, blessedness of work!
    —Louis James Block

I went straight to the hall and looked about.

It was a large building, the size of three houses built together. It served as the soldiers' barracks, so there were tables and benches. Maybe not enough, but we could get by.

Will had often told me I was as much a soldier as he, just of a different sort. Here, then, seemed the proof of that. The leaders had enlisted me as a soldier, a lieutenant this time like Will, I supposed. And I was going to have to find some foot soldiers.

I began to consider who might help me. Jane, of course. She also needed to keep busy while her husband was away at sea. Cecily lived too far upriver, but if the men brought her here ... *If she's still alive* ... I pushed the unwelcome thought from my mind as I had so many others.

I drew a deep if ragged breath and continued making a list.

Margaret Powell and Elizabeth Pott lived here. Annie Laydon and Isabella if they were brought here from their homes. Mrs. Hamor, Alice Davison, perhaps? I didn't know Alice well. She was a quiet sort. Could she handle these crowds? Could I? Could any of us for that matter? What if we couldn't provide enough food?

The loaves and the fishes. A slow panic was welling up through my body.

I could call in Esther and Angelo, but then again someone would have to keep our home secure and feed any men Will brought here from Mulberry Island. No, I dismissed that.

Finally, I thought, what of Tempie? She was a knight's wife, Dame Temperance Yeardley. It didn't seem appropriate to ask her to work. Besides, she had the large household as well as two small children and an infant.

I left the hall and went to the homes of those I'd chosen who lived around the fort.

"The governor and council have asked me to feed those who come here from other settlements, to cook and to serve the food fairly," I said to Mrs. Pott.

She nodded with wide eyes.

"Will you help?"

She kept nodding. I took that as *aye.*

At each house, it was the same. A quick discussion. In the end, all agreed to help.

Then I went back to the hall to sort the kettles and pots used to feed the soldiers.

After a while, Tempie came forth. I called to her from the hall.

She walked into the barracks and gave me a hug. We'd not seen each other since the terrible news from Isabella's husband, the night he'd rowed across the river.

I explained what the governor and council had asked of me.

She cast her eyes about the building then said, "And what do you want me to do?"

"Um, this seems not a task for you as Lady Yeardley."

She scowled. "I suppose the men conceive I'll get my dainty white hands dirty?"

I suppressed a smile. No matter the situation, Tempie was always Tempie.

Once she put her hands on her hips, I knew she was staying. She went on, "*Lady Yeardley* must be somewhere in England. Here you just have Tempie with her corn pone and *suppone*, and I'll work like the other wives. *Tempie* survived the Starving Time while *Dame Temperance* was having tea and cakes back in Scottow."

"Oh, thank you, Tempie!" I'd not realized how much I'd hoped for her help until then. "I'm not up to this. I'm not sure I'm the one to lead."

She gave me a steady gaze. "Who *but* you, Joan? And you *are* up to it. You can do this. You can do whatever you're called to do. This—" She gestured about the room. "This is healthful for us. We must keep our hands busy."

"Aye, 'tis so that. I thought the same this morning. Else we fall into despair."

"Yes."

As I began to survey the needed tasks, I understood: I had needed work to do, something to keep me occupied, and God had provided it.

He had not forgotten me after all. Even here. E'en with this great shadow over the land.

No, I did not feel worthy, did not feel capable, but somehow, I would find a way to feed those making their way to James Town, even now.

We set to work as the women started coming in to find their tasks.

Stragglers and strangers were already milling about. Boats, skiffs, and barks were landing. Even a few purchased canoes. If I thought feeding my household a challenge, I was about to see what feeding a crowd on little corn was like!

We'd decided we could stretch the scarce corn best by making thin porridge. Sailors often called it loblolly. We could break some fish or ham or other meats into the gruel if we could put our hands on some.

"Mrs. Peirce?" came a voice from the doorway. I turned to see. 'Twas Isabella's brother Captain Smith striding purposefully over to me. "Is your husband still away at other hundreds?"

"I ... I think so."

"Well, upriver I've been. I bring news to you of your daughter and her husband, Master Jordan."

I ceased breathing. The other women, overhearing, paused their work. Tempie was beside me in a heartbeat with her arm protectively around my shoulder.

I looked at her. My voice would not come.

"Mistress, fear you not. They are well. They are fine! Master Jordan had a sound palisade around Jordan's Journey. He lost *not a soul*. Unlike many, he hasn't allowed Indians at his table since last summer. Seems he's been, as he put it, vigilant since he learned of a poison plot. He sends word to you and Lieutenant Peirce to rest easy. Even now, he's gathering stragglers from settlements not faring ..." The captain's voice faltered, and I knew then he'd seen terrible things. "From settlements where many have died," he finished.

My knees buckled, too little sleep and too much fear.

Trust old Sam, Joan. Don't you fret.

The Gentlest to Suffer

March 23, 1622
James Town, Virginia

Endurance is the prerogative of woman, enabling the gentlest to suffer what would cause terror to manhood.
—Christoph Martin Wieland

I was still reeling from the news when Jane came into the barracks. I rushed over to her, threw my arms around her, and whispered, "Cecily and Sam are well! They survived."

As a family, we'd been so blessed for so long, just as Jane had said to John before he sailed.

Many years ago at the harbor in Melcombe Regis, I'd heard words assuring me I shouldn't worry. I'd even, once long ago in the Starving Time, thought strange old Grace was bestowing a blessing on Tempie and me.

Blessings be upon you both, and upon your children, she'd said not long before she died. Why came she into my mind just now? Except as stories of ambush began circling the fort, I knew God had been good to me. Even when it seemed He'd forgotten me, forgotten us all.

Jane broke the embrace. "I'm so grateful to hear the news, mother! Truly, I am, but ..." *Some are not as fortunate,* her eyes seemed to say.

Now, for the first time, I noticed that a wide-eyed woman accompanied Jane—Mrs. Macock. How peculiar that Mrs. Macock had come into my mind yesterday morning. She lived upriver near the Yeardleys' Flowerdieu Plantation.

Tempie whispered to me. "I need to talk to you." She gestured to the door.

What I was about to hear I would hear many more times, in various ways, over the next few weeks.

Reverend Samuel Macock had been a young man, educated at Cambridge and sorely needed here in Virginia. Some of the bright and promising Christian scholars like him felt the call to minister to the wandering sheep of Virginia.

We did have a lot of sheep that needed a good shepherd's crook.

Reverend Macock had been here about five years when the Indians rose up against us. He'd been friendly with the warriors of the nearby town and suspected no trouble. The Indians had approached with an innocent wave yesterday morning. A servant had let the natives in, and Reverend Macock had stood from his breakfast to greet them.

The pastor's wife was back in the bed chamber making the bed, door closed. She heard something—a chair?—knocked over. At first, Mrs. Macock felt confused. Then, she heard several men scuffling and shouting. One she knew to be her husband; several others cried out in the Indian tongue.

Treachery! She caught her breath, no time to think. She countered her instinct to grab a poker and rush to her husband's aid. She knew the Indians would overpower her easily. She'd have to hope for Sam's men in the field to hear and come running.

Save him, Lord! Save him! Save us, all of us. Her husband Samuel was a devoted minister to his people. Surely God would send an angel or two to rescue the couple. Maybe He'd even send those angels working the field.

Now she quickly and quietly dropped the latch on the door and climbed beneath the bed and behind a trunk. Somehow, she did not breathe or scream but kept herself small and quiet, even when something solid toppled hard into the door.

Mrs. Macock had not, then, seen the blows. The blood reached the floor, and a little trickled beneath the door sill, but she, mercifully, would not discover that until later.

Her heartbeat pounded so loud it threatened to give her away. It banged against her chest like Indian war drums. Then it thudded up into her throat and her head and everything throbbed with the sound of those drums. Beating and beating and beating.

But she never moved.

Shouts from behind the door, more distant, told her the fight was moving outside. Maybe the servants had heard after all.

She stayed beneath that bed, the tiny woman behind the trunk, for a full hour or more or maybe two.

Mrs. Macock, see, carried a secret, and that secret she was bound to protect for no one else could. That secret was due to arrive in about six months.

The governor and council were mapping locations to search for survivors.

They tried to assign men to their own plantations and environs. This was partly because each man fought panic, wondering in what state he'd find his property and servants. And partly because these men knew their own area of the river best.

But what to do next? The leaders' first priority was to help the injured. After that, to retrieve survivors, and then to save whatever corn or goods they might. They still had to bury the dead, too.

Sir George had been the one to survey Macock's. There among the dead, Sir George found the cowering woman. He helped her up and brought her and others back to James Town Island.

The Indians had already begun to loot and burn the homes and fields. Time was a-wasting.

"Sir George brought Mrs. Macock to me. I asked Jane to stay with her," Tempie said. "He so loved the pastor, relied on him heavily. George is in deep grief over the loss of his friend, and indeed, a great man."

"The baby lives, Tempie," I whispered. "We must cling ..."

"Cling to the good and holy, such as that?"

Had I said the wrong thing? I no longer knew what was comforting and what was crass.

Tempie touched her cheek to mine in a comforting move. "Aye, Joan. So true. I thank you for that thought. Oh, Joan!" Tempie said suddenly. "I forgot to tell you. Annie is well and fine as is her family. Kecoughtan succeeded in fighting off the Indians."

"I'm so glad, so grateful." I breathed the words rather than saying them. One by one, we learned of our losses and survivors. It was brutal.

After taking that moment to gather ourselves, we turned our attention to Jane and Mrs. Macock. Now, we both looked to the woman who shivered beneath her cloak. Her head drooped.

"Alack, poor soul to bear so much," I whispered.

Still gazing at the woman, Tempie added under her breath, "At Flowerdieu, nephew Edmund survived! He grabbed a musket and managed to scare off the Indians, but not until six servants there had already died. George and I mourn those, too. So Edmund is alive, though quite out of heart. A cruel time they had there although I know not the details."

I turned to embrace her. "I'm so sorry, Tempie."

She sniffled. Then said, "Let us help the living, though, for there's naught we can do for the dead."

Jane walked over to us right then, saying, "Mrs. Macock has the morning sickness from the child she carries."

"Oh, no."

Jane added, "She was on the shallop when Sir George visited Powle-Brook. Many killed there as well. She stayed on board and asked no questions, but she's in a bad way. If it be all right by you, I'll take her back to my house and let the others tend to the serving," Jane said. Her eyes were moist. "She'll be needing our help. I've offered her to live with me."

"That's kind of you, Jane. 'Twill fall to us to help such as we can," I said, eyeing the distraught woman.

Jane agreed. "It'll keep us from dwelling too much on the losses if we busy ourselves with the needy living."

We still had no idea how many needy living—or helpless dead—there even were.

Mother of Exiles

March 23, 1622
James Town, Virginia

Here at our sea-washed, sunset gates shall stand
A mighty woman with a torch, whose flame
Is the imprisoned lightning, and her name
Mother of Exiles.

Give me your tired, your poor,
Your huddled masses yearning to breathe free,
The wretched refuse of your teeming shore.
Send these, the homeless, tempest-tost to me ...
　　　　　—Emma Lazarus

And so they kept arriving. Homeless, cold, mourning, orphaned, widowed, hungry.

A chilling early spring drizzle made the cold colder.

"Stoke the fire!" I said to Isabella. She touched her forehead, almost as a salute. It would have amused me had I not been so dazed and horrified by this day.

The governor and council had ordered Pace's Paines abandoned, so I did indeed have Isabella's help. The harsh world of Virginia had tested her. Isabella had been a longtime friend, going back to the earlier days of the settlement. She, Richard, and their son George had moved in with her brother Captain Smith.

James Town, prosperous and optimistic just a mere two days before, now became a haunted place.

Hopes moldered as we heard story after story. Everyone arriving had one, it seemed.

Captain Smith brought along two small children, a boy and a girl. "I found them hiding beneath a shrub in the woods at the ironworks. They saw everything, but never moved." The old war captain's eyes were kind.

Jane had returned from her home, leaving Mrs. Macock to sleep. Seeing Jane, Captain Smith encouraged the children to go to her. As if in a trance, the orphans reached out their arms to my daughter.

Jane knelt and gave them a hug, an arm around each child.

They did not speak nor cry. "Let us get you a warm meal, children," she said. She stood and took them by the hands and led them over to the kettle where a corn and venison pottage bubbled.

Captain Smith stood watching Jane leave. "She has a generous spirit, Mrs. Peirce," he observed.

"A spirit she'll need—we'll all need one—in the coming days." I didn't meet the captain's eyes as I asked, "How ... how fared they at the ironworks?"

He didn't meet my eyes either.

"All dead. Twenty-seven souls; men, women, and children. All the tools tossed into the river. The works destroyed. All gone. Everyone and everything." He hesitated. "All but these two."

I felt all the blood drain from my face.

Captain Smith patted my shoulder. "Stay strong, Mrs. Peirce." Then he walked away.

Just then, Dr. Pott, carrying a medical chest, came into the bustling barracks.

I saw Captain Smith catch Pott's arm. "Pott, have you heard we lost Captain Berkeley up at the ironworks?"

"No!" the good doctor said. Pott shut his eyes. Berkeley was one of the most influential men in the colony and a member of council.

"Also, doctor, I ... well, I'm sorry to tell you your apothecary Fitch didn't survive up at the ironworks either."

The doctor looked pained but said nothing.

"They took it hard upriver, doctor. Terrible, tragic losses. I don't think I'll be able to sleep for weeks after seeing it," the captain said with a sigh.

"Come to see me should that be the case, Smith. I have some rose leaves which are a right good sleeping herb and will aid your melancholy, too. I'm sure ... I'm sure you may need such."

The captain gave him a grateful nod and started once more to leave.

"Roger!" Isabella cried. She'd just come back into the main room, noticing her brother there.

Captain Smith went over to Isabella and gave her a long hug.

She pulled back to look at him. "How did ye fare upriver?" she asked.

He just shook his head. He didn't seem to want to discuss it anymore. "Mrs. Peirce can tell you about it. But ... please tell your husband that his late-night row saved many. We—all the council—will have a hard time re-paying him. Most of the council who did survive owe their lives to Mr. Richard Pace," he added after a sickening pause.

"He did what he could," Isabella murmured.

Soon after, the governor led an Indian boy to the barracks. To me, Sir Francis said, "Mrs. Peirce, please care for this young man. See that he's treated well and fed."

"Aye, sir," I said. The boy had his head down. I wondered but didn't ask.

Sir Francis continued, "He tried to warn Captain Thorpe, gave him an hour's notice to escape. This young man is a Christian and knew of the plan, just like the boy at Pace's. He also tried to give a warning. Thorpe ..." Sir Francis's voice broke in grief. "Thorpe ... would not ... believe. A loss there of eleven." He clapped the boy's shoulder. "He was afraid and fled here."

The boy's dejection was powerful, his affection for Thorpe tangible.

What a terrible situation for these Christian Indians, rent in two by loyalties to their own people and to the English, I thought.

"You tried," I said to the boy. Other words failed me. "Go on up to the kettle to the woman in blue." I pointed to Elizabeth Pott. "She'll help you."

"Yes, missus," he said.

Anger? Rage? That would come for all of us, surely. But for the present, our voices were hushed, subdued, grim.

Another pair of men had come in from somewhere upriver. I only heard that an Indian friend had also warned them, and the two men had managed to ward off an attack by sixty braves on their house.

Two other men carried a litter in, seeking a place of rest for the woman on it. I recoiled a little, seeing she was still bloodied with open wounds. Her lids fluttered, but she was not truly awake.

To me, the man said, "We come from Warrisquoyak. I'm Mr. Baldwin, and this is my wife. After the Indians attacked her, she lay still, pretending to be dead. As for me, I saw 'em in time and just kept firin' my musket 'til I scared the Indians off. But as you can see, my wife needs a bed and a doctor."

"Go to the bunks in the back chamber, and I'll try to find Dr. Pott," I told him. Then I added, "We have a kettle of warm pottage. Ask the woman in front, and she'll serve you and your wife, too, if she's able to eat something."

He ducked his head. "Thank you," he mumbled.

From Bass's Choice, survivors brought in another confused little boy. John Bass was five years old. As near as we could understand the lad's story, his older brother Humphrey had told the little boy to go hide. Humphrey had tried to hide, too, but the Indians found him.

"How old was your brother?" I asked him.

He held up six fingers.

"Dear God," I murmured.

I was afraid to ask this next, but I made myself. "And where ... what about your mother and father?"

"They went away on a big ship with my little brother."

I was so relieved. "Let's get you some food, John. You've been brave today."

His eyes shone. Then he said, "If I were braver, I'd be dead and not my brother." And then he began to cry.

So did I. And I heard my mother once more as if she were standing right beside me. *Never grow so hardened to life that you cannot cry.*

On and on they came. Hours bled into one another. My feet throbbed from standing. But my ladies, oh, my ladies.

They never gave up. None of us did.

We comforted. We bandaged. We listened and directed.

We gathered blankets from our homes and started pointing the tired to the soldiers' bunks and places on the floor where they might collapse.

Mostly, we cooked and served as the slow, trudging line of exiles came one behind the other.

The Time of Our Darkness

March 28, 1622
James Town, Virginia

That since our laste letter, there cam two Indians to m[artins] Hunndred ...
one of which Called Chauco who had lived much amongst the English, and by
revealinge yt pl[ot] To divers uppon the day of Massacre, saved theire lives,
was sent by the great Kinge, wth a messuage ...
> —Governor and council of Virginia, April 1623,
> mentioning the warning Chauco, also called Chacrow,
> had given the day of the massacre

As the stars that are starry in the time of our darkness,
To the end, to the end, they remain.
> —Laurence Robert Binyon

Sir Francis and the surviving members of council sat in stunned silence in the governor's dining hall. Just inside the door stood Captain William Powell and my Will, his faithful lieutenant. These men guarded the door while other soldiers kept watch outside.

These two, the two Wills, would be privy to hearing the sensitive discussions of the leaders this day. This black, black week.

Sir Francis Wyatt, the governor, carried his shoulders as if great weights were on them. Will glanced at him. He was certain his friend wished, dearly wished, that his father George Wyatt were in Virginia and available to give him some advice. Father and son had corresponded, with the elder Wyatt offering his son wisdom concerning Virginia's issues. But no time for letters now.

The governor recognized his own inexperience in governing any place, but especially one as chaotic as Virginia. The knight sat at the head of the table as if he were quite uncertain how to even open such a meeting; his face drawn, all color blanched from it.

To the governor's left sat George Sandys, Mr. Treasurer. Sandys's face was as pale as that of his nephew. Head down, he lifted his eyes to steal a look at the governor. Concern created deep lines in the poet's face, Will saw.

The burden of governing in such straits taxed Sir Francis with his quiet demeanor. But the council stood ready to assist. That was their sworn duty to the colony.

Mr. Sandys reached out and touched the governor's arm. Sir Francis might be a knight and the highest ranking official in Virginia, but he was still Mr. Sandys's nephew, by marriage, anyway. The poet was nothing if not reassuring. He remained always certain of a broader plan, no matter the tenor of a day, the darkness of circumstance. This ability would serve Master Sandys well in the next three or four years when he would witness things he could never have imagined.

But this day, all thoughts were on the massacre, and most especially on the loss of three experienced council members. For by now, the council had learned the depth of devastation racked on the colony.

Sir George Yeardley sat at the governor's right hand. He had higher rank than Mr. Sandys as a knight and a former governor. Will saw Sir George, too, scrutinizing the governor's face. Yeardley's eyes were red. He certainly understood the challenges of the office better than anyone present.

In the massacre, Sir George had lost six tenants—five men and a woman at Flowerdieu Hundred. Will knew the knight wondered how he'd recover. Financial losses laid themselves upon the personal and emotional ones.

The carnage that each of these men had seen would stay with them the rest of their days. Will, for one, would never forget the butchered body of his friend and kinsman Tom Peirce out at his home near Mulberry Island. Captain Powell had been with Will when he found the body. Will rarely cried, but Tom's sightless eyes, the sheer sadness of it and of their situation in total had gotten the better of him.

His captain wasn't a warm man. But that day Powell had slapped Will's back, understanding that Tom Peirce was Will's kinsman. "So sorry, Peirce," he'd murmured.

As they had continued to survey this settlement, the men had seen some scalped and some stabbed and even a few shot with Tom's own musket turned on them.

Tom's wife Alice and her twelve-year-old daughter Elizabeth were missing. Perhaps the woman and girl had died in the woods. Or mayhap they'd escaped or hidden as others had ... Or perhaps the Indians had carried them away. Whatever had happened, the mother and daughter were nowhere to be found.

Nowhere to be found. And therein lay the hope.

Will could scarcely bear to think of Martin's Hundred. He'd seen over seventy men, women, and children, bodies strewn about the plantation. The Indians had scalped one woman and left her tied to a post.

Will didn't see how that plantation could survive after such a loss.

A few scattered, hiding survivors crept out when they'd seen him approach, the massacre over by more than a few hours. Will had helped one older woman to her feet. Crouching beneath a tobacco shed had saved her life.

The woman had pointed a crooked finger at Will. "I would ye to find Old Blind Margaret." Her rheumy eyes held both terror and defiance.

"I must take you onto the shallop, goodwife," Will said kindly. "Shaw!" Will called to one of his men. "Take her away?"

As the soldier led Goody off, the old woman turned about. "She be wearing a bright blue coif! Mind you keep an eye out for her. She can't see hardly at all, and her hearing ain't much better. She'll be afeared. Mind!"

Will nodded and ducked his head in deference to her age. "I promise, Goody. Now get yourself safe upon the ship."

Captain Powell had some soldiers guarding the perimeters, in case the Indians returned, while others guided the survivors to James Town.

Several children had secreted themselves in a cabinet. Will had seen that they, too, boarded the shallop with the other survivors. One of the little girls had not uttered a word since the attack and now stayed only with her older brother, who spoke for her. These little ones had gone to a home in James Cittie. Which one, Will was uncertain.

The anger he'd seen directed toward Mr. William Harwood was understandable. Harwood should be here. Harwood was not only the leading official of Martin's Hundred but also a member of council. Will didn't think the man had ever shown himself for a council meeting, as Sandys had commented once.

Harwood had not been at Martin's Hundred, either, the day of the fateful attack. Had he been, John Boyse, second in command, might have had a chance. The Indians had slain Boyse and six others at Boyse's home, just a little removed from Wolstenholme Town, the heart of Martin's Hundred. Boyse's wife and her baby were lying behind the door as if they'd been trying to force it shut. Four of Boyse's men were dead in the field. And that had been only the beginning.

Will had gone into the homes to search for survivors. The weak, injured, and dying had come forth in an unsteady march to the shallop. James Fort would be crowded this night. Will had gathered what corn he might but didn't see how the colonists anywhere would be able to plant. The cornfields would be defenseless.

Will had been fortunate. He'd lost none of his own men at Mulberry Island. The warning had made its way there, but even Will himself wasn't sure how. His man Edward Brewster, though, had died over at Warrisquoyak. Brewster had been visiting with Pountis's men there when the massacre struck.

Suddenly, Will's thoughts jerked back to the present, to the council table. He needed to remain alert despite his exhaustion.

Secretary Davison slumped in the next chair nearest Sir George. Dr. Pott sat further down the table along with Captain Roger Smith. Agitated, Smith was drumming his fingers.

The men had left three chairs empty, marking the loss of Captain Nathaniel Powell, Mr. Samuel Macock, and Mr. George Thorpe. These were three of Virginia's greatest men and councilors.

It had been a little confusing since we had in Virginia two captains named Powell, Nathaniel and William. The two men were not related. William Powell lived here at James Town and was Will's superior officer.

But Captain Nathaniel Powell lived upriver at his home called Powle-Brook. He was also a highly respected member of council. His was one of the sadder stories to emerge from the massacre.

At Powle-Brook, the Indians must have killed Nathaniel Powell first, so the council thought. Then Powell's wife Joyce, the daughter of a prominent Berkeley settler, had fallen running outside of her home. Where she was headed—perhaps for cover—no one would ever know. She had died just a month or two from giving birth.

The Indians intended that some deaths would stand as symbols, and the death of Nathaniel Powell was one. Powell had been a gentleman on the first voyage in 1607 with Captain John Smith. He'd explored the Chesapeake with Smith. Powell had traveled to the Mangoag Indians in search of the lost Roanoke colonists and had visited the great emperor Powhatan in his town. The Indians were well familiar with him. Powell's head the savages had removed to carry as a trophy to their king Opechancanough.

Will winced to think of such a man meeting so ignoble a death. His was a great loss to the governor, the council, and the colony as a whole. The baby

Joyce carried would have been the Powells' first child.

Of eighteen councilors the Virginia Company had selected just eight months ago, most were dead or missing. This didn't even include councilors sent here just before that who had already died, like Mr. Oldesworth.

Mr. Paulett, Mr. Lapworth, and Mr. Leech had also died soon upon arrival during the winter.

Mr. Davison, the secretary, had suffered much ill health although he was present today. Will admired the man's dedication and suspected it would fall to Davison to compile a list of the dead. *How many slain?* The men had papers in front of them with notes from the various settlements.

Sir William Newce, the marshal, had died early, too, just two days after Sir Francis had read his land patent to him. Thus ended Newce's dream of planting a thousand settlers within a few years.

Newce's brother Thomas, another councilor, was fortifying his home at Elizabeth Cittie, even now. He'd invited his neighbors to take refuge there. Newce and his wife were both known for their generosity. They were feeding those seeking refuge as best they could. Understandably, Mr. Newce was not present at the council meeting today.

Tom Newce was a soft spoken man. Will had visited Elizabeth Cittie as part of his rounds the day of the massacre and learned that of Newce's fifty servants, only three were still alive. *Three.* Will had heard that even as the man tried to console his neighbors, Newce himself nursed a broken spirit, one broken perhaps beyond repair.

Will realized that Mr. Sandys was offering an opening prayer for the council. All present bowed their heads. As Mr. Sandys used his poetic words to best advantage, someone was weeping.

How shall we survive this? Will thought in despair.

Our Owne Doores, Fields, and Houses

March 31 to Mid-April 1622
James Town, Virginia

Since the Massacre they have killed us in our owne doores, fields, and houses:
thus we are not safe neither at home nor abroad ...
 —Samuel Purchas

In the days following the shock of the massacre, folks came into James Town in a steady stream. They were seeking makeshift tents and shelter. Some crowded into homes. Some sought to store and protect their goods. Others led their branded cattle to the park.

I wondered how we'd feed so many mouths and bellies.

Each day we prepared big pots of gruel, made mostly with corn although we added meat if we had it available. We had little game since hunting was so dangerous and required several men to shoot and to keep watch. We could not spare many.

The last day of March, one of Sir Francis's men shot a deer, dressed it, and brought it in.

"Divide the meat into seven portions!" I said to the ladies. "One portion for today and the rest to last until weeks' end. Today's portion divided evenly amongst the four kettles." To Sir Francis's man, I said, "Please inform the governor that I'll need a key to that chamber there." I pointed to the last room. "We cannot have loose victuals lying about. And we'll need to lock the main door as well."

"Yes, mistress," he said, touching his hat. Then he smiled back at me. "Extra loblolly this evening for a task well done?"

I raised my brows but did not look severe. "No chance with that bit of sauce. But do it well anyway. And I do thank ye."

Isabella and Tempie had set about chopping the day's meat into smaller pieces for the kettle.

"What does this remind you of?" Tempie asked grimly.

I gave her a faint smile. I knew what she meant. The fall before the Starving Time, we'd gathered and rationed acorns for ourselves. We'd determined how many we'd need for the present, for the winter, and into the spring. Now the governor and council were asking us—specifically, me—to use those skills once more to keep those at James Town fed.

The Lord certainly doth work in mysterious ways, I thought, watching the ladies drop chunks of venison into the roiling pots.

The council was attempting to form a plan to prevent further loss of life.

Every hour, more colonists seemed to arrive. Those who came carried what goods they may. We believed it likely that the Indians would burn homes left empty and steal goods and cattle. This, after all, was war. Men might be able to protect their homes from burning while they were there. Once abandoned, everything was free to loot. The Indians who had attacked each settlement were keeping a watchful eye on their assigned places.

We still didn't quite understand how so many warriors from such scattered tribes had all attacked at the same time in all the settlements. Opechancanough was an impressive, if terrifying, war general.

Shallops and ships filled the riverfront at James Town. They stayed not long. Sir Francis ordered Captain Powell, lieutenant governor of James Cittie and captain of the governor's guard, to bargain with the owners. These vessels were needed to fetch other colonists and their goods immediately.

Some barks' owners were gracious and wanted to help. Others wanted only to crawl into a little hole with their families and their goods and talk to no one. Captain Powell, when necessary, ordered them to obey.

Ships making voyages to far-flung plantations often found only charred wood and smoldering fires.

Boats and sailing vessels of all sorts were in scarce supply for the great need, the many people and goods needing transport to safety. The Indians had struck a devastating and well-timed blow.

Funds and carpenters newly arrived to build James Town's first inn had already begun a palisade instead. When I asked Will about it, "Priorities," was all he had said. Virginia was likely to be in a state of war for many months.

What exactly that meant, and how we would retaliate, the governor and council had not yet decided. They were still picking up broken pieces, as dazed and confused as everyone else.

As for the Company, they may not like the change in plans, but they'd have to understand how dire was our situation.

One day stumbled into the next, and April tried to whitewash the pain of the previous month. Putting time between us was scabbing the grievous wound but not healing it.

No, never healing it. I wasn't sure it ever would fully heal.

Nearly twenty days had passed, and the leaders were emerging from their stupor.

Governor Sir Francis and his council had a map upon the table and a plan. Sir Francis the mild was now to be a military commander. We were at war.

They had called before them Captains Ralph Hamor, Will Tucker, and Roger Smith.

Captain Smith received the first commission from the governor.

Summoned by the governor's man, Smith now stood before the governor's table, hat in his hand, awaiting instruction.

"Captain Smith," the governor said stiffly, perhaps a bit uncomfortably. "As you know, we are under martial law. I am assigning each of you to one or more boroughs to command. Do you understand?"

"Aye, sir," the captain replied.

"Captain Smith," Sir Francis continued, "I'm issuing you a commission granting you absolute command in all matters of war over the people in Charles Cittie. We have great confidence in you, Smith, considering your experience as a commander in the Low Countries."

"Thank you, sir," Smith said.

The governor continued. "The people shall, upon pain of death, obey you in all occasions as you order and direct them. You must be vigilant and careful over the people, cattle, and all things there which are under your charge. Sir George Yeardley or I will give further command and instructions, which you'll observe. Do you understand?"

"Aye, sir."

From peace to war. No one had expected this as Easter approached.

"Captain Smith, I also grant you absolute power in all matters of war in Henrico and Coxendale upriver. You shall go and remove all remaining survivors. You may use force if necessary. The settlements upriver are in no wise safe or secure to hold."

The soldiers had been encountering this. Some folks had everything, their whole lives, invested in that little homestead. They were unwilling to see it and all their possessions and livestock go to the flames.

"Aye, sir," replied Captain Smith.

Smith understood the challenge: the settlements upriver were the furthest from James Town, had received heaviest slaughter, and were by far the most dangerous.

"Captain Hamor, you are to go to Martin's Hundred to survey the situation," said the governor, repeating the commands he had given to Captain Smith.

"Aye, sir!" said Captain Hamor. Hamor was a poor man but an earnest one, diligent and a hard worker. Perhaps from lack of business ability, he had not earned much from his tobacco and servants. But he'd been here many years and knew the country well.

"Captain Tucker, you are to go to Kecoughtan and remove any remaining survivors and goods. Understood?" Sir Francis gave to Captain Tucker the same authorities as to the other men before him.

Captain Tucker nodded. "Aye, sir." Another good man and dedicated to Virginia, Captain Tucker was a sharp soldier and a shrewd businessman.

"And then, Tucker, you must remove all from Warraskoyack." He meant, of course, our English settlement of Warraskoyack, named for the nearby Indian town.

Tucker's locations were hard by, hence faster and safer.

Sir George offered, "Going forward, if I may say so, gentlemen, we'll need weapons, munitions, armor, and food. Planting will be impossible. But perhaps we can trade with tribes further north, on the fringes of the Powhatan kingdom, like the Patawomecks."

Still, how would they keep the survivors safe and well fed?

"Agreed, Sir George. And as for retaliation," Sir Francis said wearily, "that needs careful consideration. Two-thirds of our survivors are women and children, and many of the men remaining are unfit for battle."

"Not enough for a successful attack," affirmed Captain Smith.

Murmurs of assent came from around the table. Within a few weeks, they would have to resolve these issues and more. They had lost so many good men, they weren't ready for war. But war had come to them.

In Despight of the Enemy

Mid-April 1622
James Town, Virginia

We have thought most fit to hold these few places—James City with Paspehegh
and certain plantations on the other side of the river over against the City,
and Kicoughtan and Newports News, Southhampton Hundred, Flowerdew
Hundred, Shirley Hundred and a plantation of Mr. Samuell Jourdes [Jordan],
all over throughout the whole colony we have been feign to abandon and to
bring the most of our cattle to James City, the Island being the securest place
for them, which we hold in all the river.
   —Council in Virginia to the Virginia Company in
   London, April 1622

Master Samuel Jorden gathered together but a few of the stragglers about him
at Beggers-bush, where he fortified and lived in despight of the enemy.
  —Capt. John Smith, *Generall Historie*

W e've decided to hold Jordan's Journey," Captain Smith told Will.
"I thought you should want to know. Jordan's will be one of the
furthest upriver where settlers may remain."
"Thank you, sir, for that great good news!" Will replied.

When Will passed this on to me, I had mixed feelings. At James Town,
Cecily and the children were bound to be safe from the Indians. But if they
abandoned their homes, the Indians would burn all Sam and Cecily had
worked for. Sam was confident, and I was confident in Sam.

"Sir Francis and the council have decided that we'll hold only a few
outlying settlements. Sam's plantation is one," Will explained. "We'll hold
Kecoughtan and Newport News near the bay. The council has deemed

Sir George's Flowerdieu protected enough to stay. So is Shirley Hundred, Southampton, and a few across the river. Paspahegh and James Cittie are secure as well. James Cittie, that is unless we decide to move permanently to the Eastern Shore where the Indians are friendly."

"Is that a possibility?" I asked.

"It is indeed. Sir George will go to scout it as a location."

"So ..." The reality of the situation was beginning to dawn on me. "So all the survivors will crowd into the few remaining settlements for a long while?"

"Aye, Joan." His gaze met mine steadily. "'Tis going to be vexing on many fronts. Overcrowded. Planting will be hard to do. What I hear from Captain Powell is that the council would prefer to hold even fewer than eight—nine if you count the little group across the river."

He brushed the rain off his doublet and then sat before the fire. "April can still be so chill," he said, more to himself than to me.

I placed some turkey and corn before him. He looked at it warily.

"What can the matter be?" I asked a little defensively.

His eyes met mine. "Feed us, all of us, little. 'Tis going to be a long, lean year."

Many of those whom the various captains brought back downriver were not happy. In fact, Captain Smith had to command Alice Proctor to leave her home upriver in Henrico. She had resisted mightily.

"Bah! I'll not go, I tell ye. You cannot make me. The Indians will destroy aught I have if I leave my home abandoned." Mrs. Proctor's narrowed eyes defied the captain to countermand her.

Mrs. Proctor was a civil gentlewoman, but times were hard. Her husband had been in England during the massacre and hadn't yet returned. He still didn't know what she was enduring here. She'd worked to hold the natives off, just herself and her servants.

"Mrs. Proctor, if you and your people go not now into the shallop, my men will fire your house themselves!" Captain Smith said. The threat hung in the air. "This is for your own safety, mistress."

"I've kept this house secure for three or four weeks, captain! I can continue to do so. I do not need those at James Town who've lived in safety to order me about."

"Once more, Mrs. Proctor. I bring orders from the governor. All survivors are to come with me back to James Cittie. No exceptions, mistress. Now come!" Smith's tone was severe. He had no time to fight with colonists who didn't understand his mission. He had too many people to round up.

Next thing, he and his men would be back up here, burying more bodies. "I remind you, I'll fire that house myself if you defy orders."

Casting a sour eye on Smith, Mrs. Proctor climbed aboard the ship. She told her servants they must come, too. And in grief she watched her lonely home grow smaller as the ship caught the downriver winds.

As soon as she left, the Indians put a torch to her home.

When the *Bona Nova* and the *Discovery* arrived in mid-April, the newcomers walked into a desperate and crowded world of James Town. We gave them a suspicious eye.

"If ye brought more mouths than food, ye can just turn around and hit the bay once more!" I heard a woman say idly to the ship. I couldn't disagree.

The ships had left England at Christmas the previous year, coming in with no idea a massacre had occurred. Not until their captains had come ashore. Secretary Davison registered the names of all on board both ships as was custom.

Mr. Sandys and Captain Smith, seeing these ships come in, urged Governor Sir Francis to send them up North on trading expeditions.

Mr. Pory set out in the *Discovery* for New England, looking to trade up there, perhaps to fish. A year and a half would pass before we saw him again.

Captain Huddleston was more than willing to go in the *Bona Nova*. He watered and reladed his ship and within a few weeks was in the bay near Plymouth.

Huddleston knew not a soul in the Northern colony. But he heard that Plymouth needed food, so he shared as much as he might.

He also sent a letter ashore, warning Governor Bradford that we'd had a terrible surprise attack down in the Southern colony.

We later heard Plymouth took the message to heart and built themselves a fort.

The Thing with Feathers

April 21 to Early May 1622
James Town, Virginia

"Hope" is the thing with feathers—
That perches in the soul—
And sings the tune without the words—
And never stops—at all—
            —Emily Dickinson

When Easter came later in April, the church felt tomblike. Easter, always a joyous time, could not be so this year. Reverend Bucke offered the service, his tone somber. His small children perched on the front pew. The loss of Maria Bucke still painful for the pastor.

I was startled when Will came into the house a few weeks later, saying, "How about a little good news?"

"Aye, I could sure use some." The long hours in the barracks, the hopelessness of the people there, the endless stories of loss were wearing me down.

"Well, the governor and council wish us to begin building our homes in New Town!"

"With all going on?" To build now seemed frivolous, and I told Will so.

He reached for my hand. "Aye, I understand your thinking. But the fort is too full. We've got to be able to move east and spread the people out some. Because we have no idea how long all those from other settlements will be with us."

"No idea?" That was all I heard. We would be serving food for much, much longer, I suspected.

"But do you see? We've already chosen our home sites," Will explained, settling into a chair. "The governor and council have had a difficult time deciding what we should do next. The carpenters are nearly done with the palisade. We'll hire them next for our homes."

I was trying to take all this in when Mr. Sandys arrived home.

Will said to him, "Mr. Sandys, please join us here. Since we're moving, we all should discuss this together."

Mr. Sandys agreed. I saw that his face, too, had the tense look that all the men seemed to carry. "Forgive my lack of a greeting, Mrs. Peirce," the treasurer said.

"You have no need of apologizing, sir," I replied. I then called up to Angelo and asked if she might fetch us some beer.

She came into the room and then went down to the cellar where the casks were. After preparing the flagons, she quietly returned. We three were so absorbed in our conversation, we scarcely noticed her.

"I thank thee, Angelo," I said as she went over to the spinning wheel.

Angelo nodded in reply.

"Mr. Sandys, I was just telling my wife about the move to New Towne," Will said to the poet. "Of course, we wish for you to continue to live with us."

"That's very gracious. I'm happy to accept," said the poet, relaxing for the first time.

"Joan, the governor and council feel we should proceed with our new plots even though Claiborne hasn't yet surveyed the land. We've certainly settled many other acres without surveys. Captain Claiborne can draw proper boundaries later, but for the moment, we have a dearth of housing and too many settlers coming in. Amongst those seeking refuge here are joiners and sawyers and other tradesmen. We can hire them to help build our new homes. That will help the tradesmen out, too, by giving them an opportunity to earn wages."

The idea, Will explained, was that the leaders had been planning a new town anyway. Already a few homes and buildings stood over there.

"The sooner it will be, the better for us all. All we need is disease from overcrowded, pestered conditions," Mr. Sandys put in.

A pestered town was an ill town.

"The island is protected enough to allow the expansion," Will said.

James Town Island wasn't truly an island. A small sliver of land joined it to the Maine. But being almost an island made it easier to protect from Indians attacking from land. This made James Town Island safer than most locations along the river, so we could spread out a little.

"We just need to endure this year. Hamor is out in the bay, trading with the Patawomecks for corn. The Patawomeck are usually friendly unless

Opechancanough has approached them. Still, they like our beads, and they have little alliance with the old chief," Will added.

I remembered. The Patawomeck chief Japazaws had traded the princess Pocahontas to Captain Argall for a copper kettle. That was how she had ended up with us so many years ago.

A pang shot through me. I missed Pocahontas Rebecca. Would we have had a massacre if she and her father had still been alive? I didn't think so. Still, who knew? We had been building far upriver. Even the old chief might have ultimately balked at so much of his homeland taken away.

"Do you?" Will was saying.

"Do I what?" I looked at him blankly.

"Do you want to come walk our plot? We'll be in our home before Christmas. Then in the spring, you may set out your kitchen garden and try your hand at Bermudian plants if you choose. Begin an orchard ... the choice is yours!"

I clapped my hands. Even in the midst of such sadness, I felt a tiny sliver of hope. "Hope be a strange thing. As they say, 'A drowning man will clutch at a straw,'" I murmured.

I could see it. Mine own kitchen garden, mine own physick garden. Could I entice Bermudian lemons, plantains, or pomegranates to grow? How about figs? These fruits, I sensed somehow, were healthful. I knew not why I thought that. I simply did.

"How much land will we have?" I asked Will.

"I'm not sure yet, not until Captain Claiborne surveys the plots. But several acres, I should think. We've already done a little sowing out there, but not enough. We need more corn than ever with so many hungry, so many who cannot plant their own for fear of the Indians."

"Can we go to see the land now?" I asked.

"Of course!"

Mr. Sandys excused himself to work on his translations of Ovid. "I think that reading the ancient myths is an escape from the modern world," he murmured, going to his small chamber upstairs.

We all, I supposed, seized whatever escapes we could.

This Sunshine and This Cloudless Day

Early May 1622
James Town and New Towne, Virginia

As long as this exists, this sunshine and this cloudless sky, and as long as I can enjoy it, how can I be sad?
—Anne Frank

A path had already formed toward the Country House, alone in the field no longer at the far end of the Back Street. The Back Street meandered east from the fort, past the park where the cattle grazed. Some lowed and stared with doleful eyes as Will and I walked past.

The park itself was overfull with the cattle we'd rescued and brought to safety here following the ... I pushed the word away as if, had the word not existed, that fateful day could not have happened. Even the word itself brought a certain horror.

We walked on; trees dotted the path. Here a cedar, there an oak. Much of the ground we'd cleared, and it rolled gently to the river.

An eagle rose from a tall pine above, sweeping the air.

Wearing his black cap, a chickadee sang from nearby. His name came from his call. *Chick-a-dee, chick-a-dee, chicka-dee-dee-dee.*

The sun was dipping deep, glinting from the river like flecks of gold. Virginia's beauty in the spring—even with the sorrow past—peeked out as if from behind some dark cloud. *I am ever splendid. Be patient,* the land seemed to say. Inklings of hope washed over me.

"I'm sorry."

I turned my head upward to Will. Lost in my own thoughts, I had missed his meaning. "What are you sorry about?"

"I'm sorry that I brought you into such a place and such a time. I ... I hope to make it up to you some with our new home." His eyes were warm and, I could see, carried genuine regret.

"You didn't know." I touched his arm. "Things looked so ... hopeful ... before the ..." I didn't need to say the word. None of us did.

He nodded with a grimace, and we walked on in silence for a few moments.

"I try not to think too much about tomorrow nor to allow the sadness of the year to overwhelm me," I told him. "The Bible says we should live but one day at a time. There's wisdom in that, I should think. Especially here." I ended with a sigh.

He agreed as we kept walking past the governor's home. Will pointed beyond it. "See the foundation of Captain Powell's house? And east of there, the doctor looks to place his home."

"I see."

"And behind Powell's house, off the street over yonder, will be ours."

"Um, Will? What about Tempie and Sir George?"

"I thought you might want to know." He grinned a little now. "No worries for your gossip!"

I wasn't sure if he meant my dear friend herself or the news we brought to each other. "Well!" I said, feigning indignation.

He smiled now. "Walk with me."

Our backs to the river, we made our way up a path which ran between the governor's home and Captain Powell's site.

"Our new home will stand just here. A full twenty by thirty feet! At least, I hope so."

Twenty by thirty was a grand house for Virginia certainly. It would be fully twice as large as our home now.

Will paced it out. "We'll have a dining hall and a chamber beside it. Brick foundation, planking, a massive chimney to warm us on cold nights. I even hope to use turn'd lead with the window panes."

Turn'd lead! I tried to imagine glass windows with runlets of lead crossing through them, joining the glass elegantly. I sucked in my breath as if the house were rising before me even now.

Will gestured upward. "Now, picture the dormers above, little Elizabeth peeking out to see the ships on the river. We'll have enough room for Jane so she can live with us until John returns. That will free our two homes in James Town for those seeking shelter anywhere they can."

"And room for Mrs. Macock as well?" I asked him.

"Aye."

"It sounds wonderful, Will," I said. It all felt so real, I thought if I squinted I might actually see the house.

"A beautiful home, I hope, Joan. Spacious. Room for Jane. A chamber for Mr. Sandys as well upstairs. And of course, Esther and Angelo until they complete their seven-year servitude soon."

"It sounds beautiful." Despite everything, a seed of hope had indeed survived the crushing massacre and seemed to be growing the more Will spoke.

Will walked off the path. Now the place he stood made a triangle between the homes of Powell and the governor. He spread his arms and said, "We'll build the house just *here!* Near the front of our lot so we'll be near Governor Sir Francis and Captain Powell. And convenient for Mr. Sandys to be so near unto his family." He pointed to the governor's house. "Gardens in the back nearer the swamp."

"True enough," I agreed. "He'll have much business with them, too." I considered my neighbors. I found Margaret Powell just a mite insufferable, but Elizabeth Pott was a kind soul. "Of course, I'll have to plant a rose hedge so that Margaret will decline to push past it."

He raised his brows. "Wryly spoken and wryly received."

"Good! 'Tis only a jest."

"All right, let's keep walking." We were almost to the Pitch and Tar Swamp. "Here to the left, Captain Smith will have his home. And over there ..." He pointed across the swamp. "Your friend Dame Temperance will continue to live just over the swamp."

I looked down at the muck, disappointed. "A primitive causeway. Just a small barrier, filled with snakes and slime."

"Well." His eyes gleamed in delight. "We'll just get you some rattlesnake root, nothing like it to heal the snake bite! A small cost to keep up with your gossip."

There was that word again. "Will!" I gave him a playful swat on the arm.

"Worry not, Joan. Sir George and I have discussed it. We'll improve the existing causeway which leads from our yard into the Yeardleys' property. The causeway is not the best as it is now. Those on this side in New Towne traveling into the island will need a better one anyway."

He took my hands in his. "Stay hopeful. Next year, next spring, all will be better."

I sighed. "I believe that, Will. I believe in good things."

We had more corn stored than some but were not as well fed as I would hope. But next spring ... How pretty this lot would be then! I was unsure how much longer I would be feeding the folks in town. By then, perhaps, food might be more plentiful, and I could think about my own gardens.

"Sailing right toward us, Will! Better times." *May God make it so.*

Trouble was, something else would soon be sailing right toward us, too. The year sixteen and twenty-two had not yet shown us all her surprises.

A Patient Crowd

Mid-June 1622
James Town, Virginia

The road is thronged with women; soldiers pass
And halt, but never see them; yet they're here—
A patient crowd along the sodden grass,
Silent, worn out with waiting, sick with fear.
  —Siegfried Sassoon

Where have all the husbands gone?
Long time passing.
Where have all the husbands gone?
Long time ago.
Where have all the husbands gone?
Gone for soldiers, every one.
Oh, when will they ever learn?
  —Peter Seeger as sung by Peter, Paul, and Mary

It looks as though we'll be having potato pottage. Lots of potato pottage," Tempie said, coming into the barracks.

"Potato pottage? The corn is near gone. Potatoes would be a great help," I said, stirring one of the kettles. Then I turned. "Wait. Do we *have* potatoes?"

"We do. The bark we sent to Bermuda before the massacre has just returned with potatoes—twenty thousand pounds of them!"

"Twenty thousand?" Relief flooded me. "The council will be sending some to all the held plantations, of course. But that should still leave us with thousands of pounds of potatoes."

"And ducks, turkeys, cassava roots ... Bermudian victuals will be a huge help to us," Tempie added.

Then her cheerful eyes clouded. "The governor and council have commissioned George chief commander, the war general. And our husbands will be off fighting again soon."

"I thought as much. I've been waiting to hear when and where. Now you and I and Margaret Powell will be back to waiting, hoping, and praying."

She agreed. "George and Sir Francis with the council are finishing their plan of attack. So the four captains will be receiving orders soon, perhaps today," Tempie added.

I continued stirring as I said, "And which four to be the war captains?" Although I could probably guess.

"My George, Captain Powell, John West, and Mr. Sandys."

She gave me a hug. "The multitudes will be here soon. Better start learning how to mix scant corn and many potatoes," she said. "Throw in a few ducks while you're at it!"

Just as Tempie had said, the captains and leaders had created a battle plan. Will brought the news home that evening.

He was surprised when I already knew. And then he wasn't.

"Your gossip is ahead of me!" Will laughed.

"Well, thank goodness for my gossip. We're soldiers, too, you know."

He was more serious when he said, "Yes, you are. I've told you that before. And you were never more soldier than now, as we try to recover from the massacre. You and the other women are in that barracks every day. Truly, you *are* soldiers."

I nodded and pretended to be patient about it. *At least he noticed*, I thought.

Will hugged me as he continued. "Joan, I'll be gone for a while. I know not how long. But you're safe here, Jane is safe, and I hear that Sam has got matters under control up at Jordan's Journey. Cecily, they say, is handling the overcrowding and those seeking shelter from nearby plantations much as you are. That is, well."

In spite of myself, I felt relieved to hear news of Cecily and Sam. Under conditions of war, only designated ships traveled upriver. "Do you know any more?"

"No, I'm sorry, Joan. All I know is they're well. Sam will be fighting, too, though whether with us or not, I don't know. He may leave Nat Causey in charge of the plantation. Nat had been injured in the massacre and wouldn't be up to fighting just yet, but should be able to tend matters there for Sam. We've scouted up and down river seeking able men to join the battle without leaving those settlements lacking."

The men, I knew were concerned. Two-thirds of the massacre survivors were women and children. The attack had left their fighting force decimated.

The leaders reckoned they needed three hundred men to fight roundly. That would be seventy-five fighting men for each expedition. But they had no more than a hundred men able to fight, another eighty who were weak but might be able to help out. These last were only strong enough to carry the captured corn. These were all the capable men remaining after the massacre.

So rather than seventy-five, each company would have twenty-five fighting men and twenty more unable to fight.

The war strategy was simple. Each captain had lands and tribes he knew best. This was actually the same method the Indians had used on us. Familiarity with customs and towns and leaders, used to best advantage.

Sir George and his men would attack the Weanocs.

Mr. Sandys would battle the Tappahannocks across the water from James Town—more than once if necessary.

Captain John West would go far upriver to the land of Tanx Powhatan. The Wests had explored there during the winter of the Starving Time. They knew it fairly well. This land on the outskirts was nearest the Powhatans' mortal enemies, the Monacans.

The Monacans didn't even speak the same language as the Powhatan. Perhaps, Captain West reasoned, he could push the Tanx Powhatans toward Monacan territory. Then let the Indian enemies fight it out.

Captain Powell gave Will his orders: they and their troops would fall upon the Chickahominy Indians.

The governor and council ordered the captains to burn the Indian towns, destroy their fishing weirs, and of course, steal their corn.

War was on.

"God be with you, Will," I said, fighting back the tears. "And with Sir George, Sam, and Mr. Sandys, too. Being so long at peace has spoiled me. Now, we travel this road once more."

This was going to be a long and brutal war. The Indians were starving us out by attacks on our fields and burning our corn, both stored and on the stalk. We were now going to starve them out in like manner.

"This is a fruitless war for us all," I said to Will. "If only we could return to how things were in early March." I looked away, knowing I was going to burst into tears.

"Joan, we can't change what we have. We just need to make the best of it."

You sound like Maggie, I thought.

I tried to be stoic and quietly said, "I know."

"Listen," Will said, taking my shoulders and looking into my eyes. "My men that are left behind will start building our new home. Captain Smith and Dr. Pott will help oversee the construction while I'm away. Their orders are to stay here and guard James Cittie. Unless of course, the council changes its mind and sends Smith and Pott off to fight, too. Then building will have to wait. Don't worry about me, Joan. This will all be over soon."

I didn't believe that, and I knew Will didn't either. But all we could do was take it one step, one battle, at a time.

"I'll fight, and you ladle gruel, and I'll meet you back here in a few months," he said with a weak smile.

The Fairest in Virginia

Mid-September to Late September 1622
New Towne, Virginia

*... to make warr, kill, spoile, and take by force or otherwise whatsoever boote
of Corne, or any thing else he can attaine unto, from any the Salvadges
or enemies.*
    —from Governor Sir Francis Wyatt's commission to Sir
    George Yeardley, 10 September 1622

*... for the planters are so busied about rebuildings & prepareing theyr grounds,
that few, at this time, ether can, or wil atend [silkworms]. Yet for my owne
part I have set 4 to do nothing else: & prepared the chamber where in I ly at
Leiftenant Perses (the fairest in Virginia) for that purpose.*
    —George Sandys, 8 April 1623

Autumn was upon us, and we had almost nothing to harvest. Some, like Dr. Pott, had enough acreage in protected areas to grow some corn, but these were only small fields compared to the vast acreages we would have planted if not for the danger from the Indians in the far fields.

We'd used the potatoes carefully, rationing them, but not keeping them so long they'd rot. Our corn situation was growing desperate. Barrels of stored corn were now all but gone. With the sowing season long past, there remained nothing for us to do but ration through the coming winter.

The Indians would rue the day they attacked us. War raged now, war without end. The Indians knew how to flee and hide and could not be surprised on the battlefield. Our men went often with armor, clanking their way through the Virginia woods.

Now Governor Sir Francis decided to send Sir George, commander of this Indian war, on an expedition of plunder. "Make war, kill, spoil, or take by force," Sir George's commission said.

Sir George was to take all the vessels riding in the river here at James Town and head up the Pamunkey River, the Rappahannock River, or any river flowing into the Chesapeake Bay and raid the Indian towns.

Come home with corn, I beg you, the governor had said to Sir George.

The gruel we made at the barracks grew thinner and thinner until it was little more than water that a chicken had run through carrying a few kernels of corn.

Meanwhile, New Towne was starting to look like a town. Not an English town, mind you, but a Virginia town. Something very different.

Captain Claiborne had laid out the roads and plats. The Great Road ran along the riverfront, and the Back Road ran behind it. So the homes formed three rows: those directly on the river, those between the Great Road and Back Road, and those on the far side of the Back Road, as we were.

Soon after the ships set off in late September, the carpenters and tradesmen finished our house. What a beautiful home compared to what we'd had before. Pride rose inside me despite the coming challenges of war. I was learning to think of just one thing at a time.

As some of Will's men carried over our table and spinning wheel, bed and blankets, chairs and pots and kettles, I could only admire my new home. My first real home since we'd been here.

Will had tried to keep all of his promises. We had clapboard siding, and he'd somehow managed to find a glazier to make turn'd lead windows. The windows were elegant over the brick foundation and clapboard siding.

Opening the lock for the first time, I walked into a large dining hall with a fireplace on the left. A door from the dining hall led to our bedchamber. I admired the large rooms and the plank floors. Will had built the house a full twenty by thirty feet as he said he would.

Masons in Melcombe Regis had built our home there of solid stone. This one was but pine planks. We made our own bricks, not enough for brick homes, just for brick foundations. But these were much sturdier than the earthfast homes of the fort, and planks a sight better than the wattle and daub of our other home.

Stairs leading down from the dining hall went to a root cellar. Steep stairs also crept upward from the dining room, making a turn halfway up. These led to four chambers connected by a small hall.

We still had a few men here from Mulberry Island. Will had also offered John Lightfoot a place to stay. John was an old planter who had lost almost everything in the massacre and was trying to regain his footing. Will said he would put Mr. Lightfoot and the other men in the hall between the two rooms, and if need be, on any other available floor space.

But not in Mr. Sandys's chamber, Will hoped. He wished for Mr. Sandys to maintain his solitude. He knew that as Treasurer, his houseguest desired to make trials with silkworms. Part of Sandys's position was to encourage commodities. But also, as a poet, Mr. Sandys somehow made time to translate more books of Ovid's *Metamorphoses*. I could scarcely believe that he was creating such an ambitious work here in our home.

We'd come far, and now after thirteen years, this house was almost as nice as the one I'd left behind. Almost.

It was a closer walk for me to Tempie's than it had been when I still lived in the fort and she either in the Country House or across the Back River. Now, we were neighbors again, this time across the Pitch and Tar Swamp. Will and Sir George had seen that the masons tossed broken bricks into the swamp, enlarging the causeway. I only had to cut across a corner of Captain Smith's yard to reach the causeway with Tempie's home just on the other side. To reach my gossip, as Will cunningly put it.

Margaret Powell had moved in without her husband, just as I had.

Governor Sir Francis Wyatt was still living in the governor's home.

Dr. Pott, too, had settled into his new home as had our other neighbor, Captain Smith. Since Isabella was living with her brother, that made us also neighbors, at least until her family could move back to Pace's.

Captain Smith was commanding the island while the other military leaders were on expeditions. One could almost feel that Smith yearned to be out with them.

That the four chief military men's homes clustered around the governor's home was not by accident. Sir Francis's neighbor to the north was Captain Smith; to the east, Captain Powell. Our home lay beside Captain Smith's and behind the Powells. Across the swamp, further north, was Sir George's home.

During the fall, we'd watched houses of various sizes bloom in the fields of New Towne. This had lessened the crowding significantly in the fort just as the leaders had hoped.

We were all healing from the massacre, and we were not giving up. Again, one could see tiny pieces of hope niggling their way through the settlement.

We had been in our new homes only a few weeks when Margaret Powell came over in a dither. "Joan, do you know I'm expecting a child?"

"Well wishes!" I said to her as enthusiastically as I could. Margaret and I should have been great friends since our husbands worked so closely in the battlefield. Should have been, but weren't. I wanted to like her, though. But I didn't.

"Now, have you heard that some of my hogs have wandered into the doctor's cornfield?"

I shook my head. These two things seemed to be related in her mind, but I wasn't sure how. "Uh, no, I hadn't heard that."

"Well, the old doctor went and butchered *my* hogs. And now I got me a craving for pork. The doctor has turned me down, but he likes you. Go and ask in your own name for some of his pork, won't you?"

"Margaret, if you've just asked him for pork, he'll know that request comes from you and not from me," I told her. I was busy trying to get the new house arranged.

Were we so soon to have problems with the neighbors?

Besides, hard times we knew were coming. Hog's flesh would be highly prized in the months to come, sure.

Bird-song at Morning and Star-shine at Night

November 21, 1622
New Towne, Virginia

A widow bird sate mourning for her Love
Upon a wintry bough;
The frozen wind crept on above
The freezing stream below.

There was no leaf upon the forest bare,
No flower upon the ground,
And little motion in the air
Except the mill-wheel's sound.
— Percy Bysshe Shelley

I will make you brooches and toys for your delight
Of bird-song at morning and star-shine at night.
I will make a palace fit for you and me
Of green days in forests and blue days at sea.
— Robert Louis Stevenson

The *James* landed her goods at James Town in mid-November, and Captain Ewens came to speak to Will and me. I told him that Will had not yet returned from the Chickahominies.

"Oh. Well, Mrs. Peirce, I have a letter for your daughter from Mr. Rolfe," he said.

I smiled and held out my hand. Then I noticed the stricken look on Captain Ewens's face.

"Uh, not from Captain John Rolfe, but from Mr. Henry Rolfe, his brother. He gave it to me in London."

My face fell as understanding dawned.

"What do you mean from Henry Rolfe?" I asked, seizing the letter impolitely from Captain Ewens. "Why didn't John write us himself?" I knew the answer, of course.

He shrugged and shook his head for he, too, had been friends with John for many years.

"I'm sorry, Mistress Peirce." He paused. "John didn't survive the voyage over. Mr. Delbridge said that Mr. Rolfe was ill from the start. A few weeks in and his condition worsened. We have his belongings on board the *James*. Lady De La Warr's goods we have left with her."

"So he never knew …" I began.

The captain surmised what I was thinking. "'Tis so, Mrs. Peirce. He never knew about the massacre. Never had the worry of it, being safely on the other shore." *God's shore.*

Then Captain Ewens reached into his pocket. "As he weakened, John gave this to Delbridge, who passed it on to me. For his wife, John said, to send her all his love and bestow good fortune on his children."

In his hand was the Spanish *reale*.

I felt faint. Another daughter a widow with a small child. I didn't think I could bear it. How would I tell Jane?

"Mother, he's gone, he's gone!" Jane was weeping, holding the unfolded letter and the *reale*.

I'd tried to tell her gently, but the hard words on paper were too much for her.

"What do I do?" she wailed.

"Janey, come here," I said, stretching my arms out to her and reverting to her childhood name. "You'll continue to live with us. Your father will tend to the estate and the lands, so you have no worries there." *Thank you, Lord, that Will is strong and healthy.*

We had, too, the widow Macock and her infant Sarah living with us. Widows and orphans, we had aplenty, sure.

When Jane pulled away from me her face was tear streaked, but her gentle look had determination laced through it.

"I'll have to get by, but I'm not alone." She was considering her own plight compared to Mrs. Macock, I thought. "What we have, we have. I'll build a future for Elizabeth, howe'er hard it be to do it. She'll have a better life here someday. I know she will. We'll *all* have a better life. She'll never even know I'm sad."

I nodded, so proud of her I couldn't speak.

"'Tis how you did it for me, isn't it, Mama? You did your best to keep me happy and not to let me know how sad you were when you thought Father lost at sea."

"Aye, 'tis so that."

"I still remember you crying that day by the river. I was so small. Do you remember?"

I did.

She went on. "You thought I didn't know your tears were real and not from the cold air, but I did know. You tried to hide your grief and fear from me, and because you did, I hid my understanding of it from you. I knew you were strong, and I knew somehow we'd be all right in the end. And we were. 'Twill be the same with little Elizabeth. I'll show her the good things so she can learn happiness. Birdsongs in early spring, noisy frogs in summer, and bright orange pumpions which ripen in fall. The stars are always bright over the water. There's that."

She seemed almost to be making an inventory.

"You do have blessings. Auntie Tempie taught me that once," I said.

"I know it to be true, too."

"I suppose I did for thee what my mother did for me. I'm sure she was afraid and alone many times when your grandfather was at sea. But she never let on to me either." I had ne'er considered that before.

When Elizabeth came toddling into the room, Jane picked her up.

Curious, the little girl wiped away a tear still upon her mother's face.

Echoing my own words from the Starving Time, Jane held her little girl close and said, "'Tis just the cold air, lovey."

Such it always is with mothers and daughters, I suppose.

One Leaf Is for Hope

Christmas Eve 1622
New Towne, Virginia

I know a place where the sun is like gold,
And the cherry blooms burst with snow,
And down underneath is the loveliest nook,
Where the four-leaf clovers grow.

One leaf is for hope, and one is for faith,
And one is for love, you know,
And God put another in for luck—
If you search, you will find where they grow.
— Ella Higginson

Whether Christmas 1622 would be worse than the one of '09 during the Starving Time, I couldn't say. Famine, that skeletal beast with sunken eyes, hovered near, but we were certain the Company would send a ship filled with corn. That is, English corn. Wheat, oats, and barley. Filled! Brimming, even. That ought to keep the beast away. The Company had learned of the massacre during the summer. By now, they'd had ample time to get the relief to us we so needed.

So we waited, and as we so often did, we watched the river.

Into the river at Christmas sailed Captain Nathaniel Butler, arriving from Bermuda. His ship contained a few chests of island victuals which Sir Francis sent over to the barracks. Food we were grateful to have, though not nearly enough for the specter of famine hanging over us. Still, we were sure the ship with English corn would be here at any time.

As for Butler, he had just resigned as governor of Bermuda, in effect abandoning his assignment. The man he left behind as governor was Captain

John Harrison, a decent man much better liked than Butler.

Harrison's promotion was glad news for Lieutenant George Harrison, who lived down at the New Towne waterfront. John Harrison was his only brother.

As for Captain Butler, he came in with a blustery spirit. *Massacre? How could that have occurred?* What we didn't know then was that over in England, two factions of the Company were still fighting. Sir Thomas Smythe had formed an unlikely partnership with the Earl of Warwick. Unlikely, because both men hated each other. But becoming allies was their best way to defeat the third faction, Sir Edwin Sandys and the Earl of Southampton.

Butler had come, in fact, as a spy. He was to learn all he could about the problems in the colony and then write a full report. But what Butler told us was that he'd come to help. Might he join Captain Powell and Lieutenant Peirce down at the Chickahominies?

Sir Francis knew something of Butler's loyalties, but he had no idea the extent of them.

"Of course," the Virginia governor said. "We appreciate all the military might we can get!"

Later, Mr. Sandys called his nephew aside. "You ill place any confidence in Butler, no matter how many cassava roots and oranges he sends from Bermuda," Mr. Sandys told Sir Francis. "He was one of my traveling companions from Cairo to Jerusalem a dozen years ago. I like him little and trust him less."

It looked as if Will weren't going to be home for Christmas. Then again, nothing this year was normal. So when Isabella came over to visit on Christmas Eve, I was glad for the company.

She was eager to tell me something, I could see.

"Well, on with it," I said to her.

"Joan, I hope this be not tactless to say, so soon after John's passing. But my brother has his eye on your daughter. If they marry, that will make us ... will make us ..." She paused. "What will it make us?"

"Will make us kin, I reckon, but I'm not sure how. Let's see, you would be the sister-in-law of my daughter."

Will and I had supposed in planning the house that Jane and John might soon move out to Mulberry Island or perhaps John would get a plot here in town.

Now that we'd learned of John's death, Jane would live with us until someone came a-courting her. She was a sweet and pretty girl, and I'd suspected this would happen presently. It was happening sooner than I'd expected, though.

Still, we'd come to like the captain, Roger Smith. He was an honest soldier and had led us well during the darkest days. Yes, it was close upon John's death. But with life in such turmoil, if love could flourish still, who to argue with it?

Meanwhile, a restlessness had taken hold of the settlement.

Isabella also told me that Richard had petitioned the governor and council, asking if they could return to Pace's Paines. They, like all in the settlements, would be on their watch for the enemy. Pace's, with the Indian boy's warning, had survived well, no loss of life, the day of the massacre. But sometime afterward, the Indians had burned Isabella's plantation as they had all the abandoned places. Now Isabella and Richard were ready to rebuild, she said.

"Others, too, have petitioned the governor," Isabella told me. "They've asked and pleaded to return to their desolate homes."

Everyone wanted to go home, and by now, many had. Back in England, the Virginia Company also wished the colonists to begin anew. So the governor and council, while a little wary of the Indian surprise, debated the question of allowing the settlers to return to their homes.

These ashes, they were their ashes.

Home to their burned-out houses and fields, home to their empty paddocks where cattle had either died or Indians had carried them off. Home to the emptiness and the loss and the graves; home also to that single fragile blossom amidst it all. That was hope. How she bloomed, I could not guess.

To Talk of Other Christmas Days

Christmas 1622
New Towne, Virginia

The wintry blast goes wailing by,
The snow is falling overhead;
I hear the lonely sentry's tread,
And distant watch-fires light the sky.

Dim forms go flitting through the gloom;
The soldiers cluster round the blaze
To talk of other Christmas days,
And softly speak of home and home.
—William Gordon McCabe

Christmas morning rose bright and cold on the river. Sir George's fleet had not arrived back yet, nor had the other expeditions. It looked like our men would be celebrating Christmas, such that it was, in the 'tween deck of a ship in the river. Or maybe locked in battle with the natives, or burning Indian homes and gathering up baskets of corn.

Or perhaps captured or injured? No! No, I wouldn't think of that.

Still, good tidings we did receive on Christmas, and a cheer went up.

True to word, the *Abigail* had arrived. Coming in on Christmas day with, surely, the corn promised us. Coming in on the holy day itself felt like a wonderful sign.

Soon after, Esther came plodding to the house, her furrowed brow indicating something was wrong.

"What ails you, Esther?" I asked. Since her hearing was poor, I had learned to look directly at her when I spoke.

"What ails me, missus?" She said in an uncharacteristically sharp tone. "I'll tell ye, I been down by the waterside. I saw me a sailor I knew from my little town in Kent. He hailed me over to tell me what news. Now I'm angered at the Company, and sure! The ship what they sent carries Lady Margaret Wyatt, the Gov'nor's wife. Ain't that somethin'? Not a grain o' corn on that ship, though. I think that's what they're saying down there. We can't eat of promised corn, missus."

It was true. I glanced at the basket of corn in the kitchen. This was it for us.

The men's fear of planting the fields because of ambush had caused many bushel baskets to be empty. Now we were in a feared position, one that had seemed all but impossible last Christmas.

How quickly our situation changes here! Only a year before, we'd had a feast—a feast!—at the Yeardleys' home. Now we were counting kernels of corn.

"They say another ship behind this one called the *Sea Flower* has a hold filled with corn." Her skeptical look said she'd believe it when she saw it.

I ticked off my fingers. I had to feed Jane, Elizabeth, Mrs. Macock, Angelo, Esther, and myself. Mrs. Macock still suckled her little daughter, born in late summer. We also still housed a few men from Mulberry Island, more mouths to feed. Now I reasoned the whole lot of those here would just have to come to the barracks' kettles like everyone else.

Esther paused. "I hope ye'll forgive me speaking my mind."

"'Tis fine, Esther. I do appreciate the news."

"Well." She pointed a finger. "Let me tell ye what else. They be all sick on that ship."

This was too much to bear. But then a new thought occurred to me. Perhaps Esther had misunderstood on all counts. Her hearing seemed to be growing ever worse. She often strained to understand.

No, I had to see for myself. I rushed from the house, leaving Esther still standing there.

Jane and Isabella were already watching the ship as I arrived.

"Corn, we hope!" Isabella said brightly. "We've seen no one disembark yet."

I scowled. "I hear the ship has no corn."

"What?" Isabella turned to me.

"Pray Esther, my near-deaf servant, hath misunderstood," I added. I didn't have heart enough to mention the illness.

Yet as passengers soon filed off ship, it was easy to see something was wrong.

"They ... they are staggering," said Isabella, watching them alight.

"Well, the sea does cause something like that," I murmured, trying to make sense of it. *No, it cannot be.*

"Not like that." Jane, too, was staring at the newcomers.

"The beer, it was bad," muttered a mariner to a man nearby unlading the ship. "I wouldn't drink of it if I were thee."

"Bad?" The servant paused.

We leaned in, too. Then I decided to make bold. Learn from those who know, Maggie had taught me.

"What do you mean, the beer was bad?" I asked as I approached the mariner.

The sailor turned to gape at me. "What I said. The beer was a-stinking from the time we got ourselves on board. If we could smell of it, I do reckon that the greedy Duppa what brewed it could smell of it, too! And then folks began dyin'. Dyin', and dyin' and dyin' and illness spreading on to the next. We lost husbands and wives and children and crew. I nearly died myself. Now do that look right to you?" He gestured to those who seemed disoriented. His sunken eyes and ghostly skin told me as much as his words that the journey had been a hard one.

"No, no, it does not."

"Blame the captain, mistress. Cap'n Each done overfilled the ship, pestered her. Too many on board, too close o' quarters, goods stowed everywhere they could be. One get sick, they all get sick."

"Corn?" I asked him weakly. I was trying to choke out the word. *Please, please. Please have corn.*

He eyed me suspiciously. "No corn, mistress. Cap'n Each was in a rush, you see. He could make more pounds on the people than on the dry goods, if you take my meanin'." The sailor obviously had no use for Each. Soon, none of us would.

Now ghoulish dread joined its kinsman, the specter of famine.

"Oh, no. No, no, no."

We Are All Undone

January 7, 1623
James Town, Virginia

Deare Sister ... [our] Shipp was so pesterd wth people & goods that we were
so full of infection that after a while we saw little but throwing folkes over
boord: ...Few els are left alive that came in that Shipp: for here have dyed
the Husband, wife, children & servants ... Our Beare [beer] stunke so I
could not endure the deck for it: This was or fortune at the Sea, and the land
little better, for as well our people as our Cattle have dyed, that we are all
undone, especially we that are new comers, and except or Freinds help us it
will goe hard wth us next Wynter ...
   —Lady Margaret Wyatt to her sister, 4 April 1623

O f the two hundred colonists who had boarded the *Abigail*, perhaps
close to half perished by the way. As folks died, the mariners could
do nothing but throw them overboard.

Many of those who made it to Virginia were already weak and sick, and
their frightening stories circled the settlement. The beer had been stinking,
fetid. We heard that over and over from those who had endured the smell.
Yet the passengers had no choice but to drink it for great thirst. And then
later, they had paid the price for their thirst when illness overtook them.

Each of the new colonists, of course, had someplace he was bound. For
many, their destinations were still abandoned, so the governor sent them
to the nearest holding settlement, be it James Cittie or Sam's plantation or
Flowerdieu or one of the others. New mouths to feed without bringing any
corn? And now these arrivals were deathly ill, too.

Whether we had a contagion was hard to say just yet. A few who hadn't
been on the ship seemed now to be falling ill.

For us already here, it was hard not to feel resentment. And great, great
fear.

Food was scarce, and game remained difficult to catch because of the danger involved in going out. We sometimes were able to procure some fish when a ship returned from a fishing voyage; sometimes by raiding or trading with Indians.

In the locked room at the barracks, we kept the two chests of food from Bermuda and the dwindling corn.

Hard conditions forced those, like my household, to go now to the barracks. Most everyone was out of their own stocks of corn, dried fish, peas.

The gruel, the loblolly, the porridge—whatever one might call such a dish—grew thinner and thinner, just as those eating it did.

To this weakened body of massacre survivors came now the contagion. Those stepping off the *Abigail* haplessly carried it to those already here.

I surveyed the women ladling gruel at the barracks. The settlers who'd been here longest were hardiest. We knew not why that was so. Of those here at the island, Isabella, Tempie, Jane, Susanna, and Elizabeth Pott were the women I trusted most. Susanna and Elizabeth were relative newcomers but had shown the warrior spirit we would surely need with low food stores.

We were now not far away from another Starving Time although the situation was not yet that dire. Unlike the Starving Time, the Virginia Company knew we needed food. During the horrid winter of '09 and '10, the Company had not known about the siege. Nor had they known that the leaders and all the victuals sent had shipwrecked in Bermuda. This time, the Company was well aware of our plight. So if the *Abigail* brought only stinking beer and sick passengers, the coming ship, the *Sea Flower,* must have its hold filled with corn.

It must. And it would surely arrive soon.

However, I had an immediate concern about safety at the barracks, so I decided to go speak with Sir Francis about it.

One of the Wyatts' servant girls opened the door for me. She invited me in to where Sir Francis sat working at his table, papers strewn over it.

Does anyone in Virginia not look weary? I thought. The governor's eyes had a haunted look, his cheeks gaunt from long illness.

"I'm sorry to interrupt you, sir," I began.

He waved me off. "I'm certain you have a sound reason, Mrs. Peirce."

I explained that I felt we needed a guard of soldiers to protect us and the food. Just as it had been in the Starving Time, having a storehouse with food was dangerous, locked or not.

Sir Francis willingly agreed. "I can spare a few men to take turns keeping watch. Consider it done."

"Thank you, sir. How fares your wife, Lady Margaret?" I asked him before I left. I had not yet met her.

"She fell sick three days after arriving and remains in a bad way. She lies with her eyes half opened and seems to see little. Her head pounds, her stomach cramps. She can eat little, and what she doth eat stays not down."

At once, he looked embarrassed, as if he'd said too much.

"Sir," I said as kindly as I was able, "I'm not delicate. I've been here too long for that."

His smile was sheepish. "I see how that could be the case."

"We can send her some loblolly from the barracks," I offered.

"I thank you for that. I'll send one of my men over for it. One who's reliable, though, lest he eat it up before he returns here!"

"True, sir!" *When did loblolly become as important as corn and tobacco?* I wondered idly.

I started to leave, then turned to face the governor.

"Sir," I said tentatively. "I've told the women who serve the gruel to treat each person the same. We do give extra to those we can see are great with child or who we know to be. We give men one and a half ladles, women one ladle. We give boys and girls a full ladle if they be three-quarters as tall as the women. Otherwise, they receive a half ladle. Once boys are taller than the women, they receive a man's full portion. However, station matters not to us." My eyes pleaded a little, I thought, that he would understand. "Only size."

The governor seemed appreciative, saying, "That's as I wish you to do it, Mrs. Peirce. I do expect you to serve all equally no matter who they be. That includes governors and doctors, commanders and councilors. Else there be mutinies and riots."

"I believe so, too. I just wanted to make sure you approved." I gestured in the direction of the barracks. "Now that we're rationing corn even further, tempers flare. Oncoming illness makes those tempers yet shorter. To make this work, I'll now only have helpers I trust most. It was ever so in the Starving Time, too," I added a bit apologetically.

"Mrs. Peirce, you have no need to be contrite. The council and I appreciate your efforts. We ask no more of you than fairness and dedication. Since you're to feed these masses, I can let you know that we think we'll begin allowing folks back to their plantations if they petition to do so. That should help the pestilence on the island here as well."

That was a little good news. "I thank you kindly. And do you remain well, sir?"

He said he did. "My sickness of the previous summer has left me, and so far, I have not yet come down with the contagion."

But it is in my house. I could almost read his thoughts.

I stood looking at him for a moment, the one question I most wanted to ask hanging in the air.

How long must I continue to watch the provisions? I had been doing so since just after the massacre, nigh a year.

I knew the answer. Until the new corn arrived and James Town had less crowding. At least, the latter.

My tour of duty was not yet over.

The next day, I let the ladies helping me know that we could expect several soldiers to watch over us.

"Wonderful idea!" Isabella said. "Especially under the circumstances."

We then considered dividing the meals into shifts but were unsure how we would know who had eaten and who hadn't. It was better, we decided, to contend with lines than to risk feeding the same person many times.

Everything we did, we did with an eye to preventing a mutiny.

We'd found some cornmeal and made as many corn biscuits as we could with it. They would see us through the next four or five days, I thought. One biscuit for each.

True to his word, Sir Francis had sent soldiers from his company, by turns, in groups of five. These men protected the servers and the stored corn all day and all night in four-hour watches.

I was now making plans in case any of my little army of women should grow ill. Would we fall sick with contagion if we'd had none of the spoiled beer? We weren't sure.

"Each of you must have someone you trust to take your place in case this contagion spreads as it seems it might do."

"I believe as long as we're not all ill at one time, we can make do," Tempie suggested. "What if we ask Mrs. Powell, Mrs. Macock, and Mrs. Hamor to stand at the ready should we need them? They can substitute for anyone here."

Jane spoke up to say that Mrs. Macock had not yet recovered from her childbirth, although it had been three months.

I said, "I also think Angelo and Esther could help if needed."

Tempie nodded and gave a sailor's salute. "Aye, aye, cap'n!"

Crosses & Miseries

January 25, 1623
James Town, Virginia

I would you could hang that villaine Dupper who with his stinking beere hath poisoned most of the passengers and spred the infection all over the Collonie wch before the Arrival of the Abigall were recovered ...
—George Sandys, 28 March 1623

To write of all crosses & miseries wch have befallen us at this tyme we are not able: The Lord hath crossed us by stricking most of us wth sicknes and death.
—Samuel Sharpe, letter from Virginia, 24 March 1623

The sword is without, and the pestilence and the famine within: he that is in the field shall die with the sword; and he that is in the city, famine and pestilence shall devour him.
—Ezekiel 7:15

Winter had fallen hard onto the settlement, onto the homes, both new and old; onto the town, both new and old; onto the settlers, new and old as well. And what a winter it had been! Besides our own lack of food and our sickness, our cattle were beginning to die in large numbers. Some murrain among the kine, but no one knew what it was.

We could expect no help from any of the other settlements as they, too, were short of provisions.

The bitter, lifelessness fell upon one and all. The mud crunched beneath our feet, and the river lay like a bitter old man, half frozen. Frost had decorated the barren tree limbs as if in a vain attempt to dress up the little colony.

Now it seemed that the *Abigail,* which we'd welcomed for bringing corn, had brought not corn but a deadly contagion instead.

A month had passed with corn barrels scraped dry, so hunger, over-crowding, and illness were taking its due toll.

The great hall teemed with refuge seekers from the settlements, elbow to elbow. Some sat at tables, some stood, some few crouched on the floor. Men, women, and children of all ages.

The hall was a roar of complaints and crying babies. I looked around the room at the anguished, the anxious, the feeble. Many had lost loved ones in the massacre. Some had barely escaped death themselves, or like Alice Proctor, had fought the Indians until they fled. Some of these same folks had suffered even more loss through the pestilence the *Abigail* had brought. Now, they were on the brink of famine, too.

How wrong I'd been to think the worst behind us! We felt as if we were living the words of Ezekiel, for we had famine and pestilence within the bounds of James Town and the sword without.

No, this was not a joyful gathering. This was a gathering of those whose bellies were hollow while the grain casks were also far too empty. Mine the task of dispensing the food.

Too reminiscent of the days when we'd starved my first year at James Town, when bones were ornaments we wore near the outside of our skin so that any could see them. In those days, we'd divided the share of cornmeal and acorn meal in our little cottage. An equal portion for Maggie, Tempie, and me, with one half-portion for little Jane.

Now I did the same, with many more hungry mouths—not all as willing to accept the lack we had. The growing number of sick had tempers flaring even more than before. Some angry. Some cursing James Town, the natives, the Virginia Company—and a few just cursing.

I was surprised to see Lady Wyatt in the hall and supposed she must have recovered from her illness.

A few moments later, my Lady approached me with a large, but not warm, smile on her face. Her servant girl, Mary Woodward, accompanied her.

I paused in serving to address her outheld bowl. "Please," she said brusquely.

I spooned in some gruel—watery, I knew, but all we could provide. One ladleful. The same as everyone else.

Lady Wyatt studied her bowl for a moment, oblivious to the growing line behind her.

"Um, Mistress Peirce. More, please." Again, the insincere smile. A touch of aggressiveness, perhaps.

I shook my head and gestured to the man behind her, a laborer named Goulding, to come forward, while I spoke flatly to Lady Wyatt. "One ladleful, M'Lady. Goodman, your bowl?"

Lady Wyatt blocked my way.

"Mistress Peirce!" She raised her voice this time. "I am Dame Margaret, the wife of the governor, a knight. He would not approve of withholding food from me. Now give it to me!"

Again, I shook my head. "'Tis not the instructions we've received, orders from your husband. Please ask him about it. Equal portions all. Else there be riots and mutinies."

"I'm just recovered illness!"

I stood unmoved and gesturing with my arm about the great hall, adding, "As have nearly all the souls in this room. All are in some stage of famine or illness."

She made to protest. "Mrs. Peirce, give me the additional ladleful. I'll not ask again. And see, I have *two* biscuits, not the one that these others have. That young woman served them to me." She pointed to Susanna.

I glanced at the young servant, who, I noticed was also watching the exchange.

"She's not supposed to give you more," I said, matter-of-factly. I would not relent. "You run the risk of getting the women in trouble for not obeying their orders, and you risk turning this great hall into a fist fight. Or worse. You risk turning the settlement into a mutiny against your husband and all who are in command. My lady, it is very dangerous not to share and share alike." This time I met her eyes, my gaze stern. I did not like this woman, nor did I care that she was a knight's wife.

She stood unmoving, but her eyes filled with anger and perhaps disdain.

Yet I continued, "Tell me, Dame Margaret, whose portion will you have? Goulding's, behind you? Or the little Mabin boy and his sister? Theirs make one full portion. They could go without today so you could have double. How about Mary's?" I nodded toward her servant. "You could have her share. Tell me which, for we'll have to choose."

Mary, standing at her dame's side, looked uncomfortable, as if the last thing she wanted me to do was to bring her into this. Lady Wyatt narrowed her eyes, and, her voice filled with venom, said, "Let's retire home, Mary."

Mary ducked her head deferentially and looked at me as if to say, "But I am hungry." I shrugged. They could eat a fair portion, or they could have none. It made no difference to me, but one thing I'd learned. James Town was no respecter of stations when it came to death, when it came to disease, when it came to surviving Indian attack. The laborer might live, and the nobleman might die. We'd left our land of princely places for one where each had a single vote in electing men to the General Assembly. The poor man's vote and the rich man's vote were equal. And the poor man's stomach rumbled as did the rich man's. Lady Wyatt, here only a month, would learn this or she wouldn't. But I couldn't in good conscience give Goulding less because Lady Wyatt wanted more.

Lady Wyatt slammed the bowl upon the table and stomped out. I looked for a moment at the abandoned bowl, then handed its contents to Goulding, who smiled gratefully.

"Thank 'ee, Mistress. Thank 'ee." He knew what I did: I only a lieutenant's wife; Dame Margaret, the wife of the governor. If she chose to demand and I chose to give his portion of food to her, there was nothing he could have done to stop it. Lowering his voice, he added, "Thank 'ee for not giving the lady my share, missus."

In the Middle of Winter

January 25, 1623
New Towne, Virginia

*Wee have, to our extreame grief, understood of the great Massacre executed
on our people in Virginia, and that in such a maner as is more miserable than
the death it self. To fall by the hands of men so contemptible; to be surprised
by treacherie in a time of known danger; to be deafe to so plaine a warning,
as we now to late understand, was last yeare given ... but to be made in
parte instruments of contriving it, and almost guiltie of the destruction by a
blindfold and stupid entertaining of it ...*

> —Virginia Company to Sir Francis Wyatt, 1 August
> 1622, blaming the colonists for their own massacre

*In the middle of winter I at last discovered that there was in me an invincible
summer.*

> —Albert Camus

After my argument with Lady Wyatt, I felt entirely discouraged.

I was doing the best I could. Had not Governor Sir Francis
himself, Lady Wyatt's husband, said I should divide the food evenly?
What else was I to do?

If I began favoring some over others, I would likely have a rebellion on
my hands in the barracks.

But then again, Lady Margaret had been sick. She'd been on that
horrifying voyage and had only fallen ill once she'd arrived. Now she was
well. Who was I to deny a knight's wife—our governor's wife—an extra meal?

Besides, I was forced to admit that she'd shown considerable courage in
sailing here at all. She hadn't known about the coming illness, but she had
come knowing we suffered under war following the massacre.

I came home from the barracks and slumped into a chair. Then braving the cold and the coming darkness, I decided to go to visit Tempie.

She opened her door in surprise.

"It'll be dark soon. You'll be staying the night if you're not careful."

"Aye, I won't stay long."

She ushered me inside where I could see she'd been spinning.

I walked over and touched the wheel. "You do enjoy spinning, don't you?" I asked her.

"I do. Susanna would spin for me if I asked, but it makes me feel rested the way planting does for you, a good thing, I think." She paused and gave me a pointed look. "Something brought you over that causeway at this hour, in the bitter cold with darkness approaching."

"Yes, something did." I wasted no time in telling her why I'd come. "I need some cheering up," I said.

"Oh, is that so? Simple as that, is it? 'Make me laugh, Tempie.' Well, certainly. For you, anything!"

Already, I found myself smiling. But then my troubles with Dame Margaret rose up inside me again.

"Did you see what happened with Lady Wyatt?" I asked her.

"I didn't see, but I heard about it."

"I don't know what I'm supposed to do."

"You do what Sir Francis asked of you. Dame Margaret will come around. Virginia is a harsh reality for her."

"Aye, I do understand that. But how will I face her tomorrow?" Before Tempie could answer, I went on. "Sometimes I feel as if I can climb from this mire we're in. Then the fight with Lady Wyatt occurs, or we hear about losing John. A contagion strikes, or corn is lacking. And the feelings of despair set in once more. It seems unfair to even keep trying. I feel like Sisyphus of old, pushing his boulder uphill, only to have it roll backward once more."

"So what will you do, you ragged old Greek? Give up? Let the boulder roll over you? By the by, you ought to be careful a-crossing the brick causeway, you know." She gave a half smile. "'Tis a bit icy and growing darker. We don't need you falling into the swamp! Everything we've endured. And then comes a muddy, frozen Joan, teeth gritted, fists clenched—and who shall she blame? Not the swamp, sure."

I chuckled in spite of myself. "And then the boulder roll flattens me. The bricks were a mite slippery. Who will I blame? I'll blame you and Sir George for putting your home in the back of Back Street near the Back River ... back of the Back in back!"

She chuckled, too. Then she sighed. "You have to laugh, Joan. If you don't find things to laugh about, you'll find nothing to make you happy. It's cold and all but hopeless, sure. No one can deny that. But one day, the sun will shine again, and the hunger and pain will be over as it was before. We don't know how we'll get through, but we will somehow."

I shrugged. "True enough. We've done it before. Many times."

"Just so. Worrying changes naught. And don't let anger best you either. Nor does being sad serve you. It helps not the ones you feel sadness for, especially not if they're in a better place. We've lost so many ..." She paused, sympathetic. A touch of wistfulness alit in her voice. "Not to mention our goods, and cattle, and estates. George and I have lost more than half of all we've worked for. Near two-thirds of it, I hear. And you as well, I'm certain."

I dropped my head. "Aye, true it is, that. Paying for servants' food and clothing and earning nothing this year. Little if any corn or tobacco grown. Very hard to bear with everything else all piled upon it."

"Aye, it is hard," she agreed. "But I believe in good things. I believe we should just put one foot down and then another, step by step, to finish the line. As the Apostle has said, *Let us lay aside every weight, and the sin which doth so easily beset us, and let us run with patience the race that is set before us.*"

I gazed at her for a long moment. "It has never been simple here, Tempie. Never for long have we been without catastrophes."

"Never once have we not come through them either. I do have a little sour news, not to add to your pile of it," she said.

"Go on then." I could feel my spirit sinking once more.

"The Virginia Company is censuring us, blaming us for the massacre."

"Tempie! No. It can't be. How can they blame us for our own grief and losses? We've worked so hard."

"They blame us for being dispersed too far upriver, for letting down our guard with the natives."

I sputtered. "But ... but they told us to move upriver, ordered us to go and to grow. Ordered us to bring the Indians into our homes."

"Aye, they did. I'm sorry to be the one to tell you about it, but you'll know soon enough. They say we dress with too much excess, that we are sinners, that God is punishing us. They implore us to do better. The governor and council are furious, enraged." She gazed up, and her eyes met mine. "Our men here didn't even attempt to be conciliatory. They fumed like a kettle of lye, who to blame them? The year here has been monstrous and likely to get worse. Easy to point a finger of blame when one is sitting secure, healthy, and fed in London."

I had no words. I sat for a moment trying to take it in. Mr. Sandys had been spending most nights lately at the glasshouse. He'd been trying to coax the Italians into continuing to make glass ever since Mr. Norton, the glass expert, had died of the summer sickness. Else I should have heard the news from our houseguest, I supposed.

"And what do you say?" I asked at last.

"I say they have no idea what life is like here, that we have only endeavored to do what they've ordered us to. That if they think they can do better, perhaps they should come here and try."

"So true that!" Then I realized that Lady Margaret probably knew that the Company blamed her husband and the council for the massacre. The blame would include also Sir George and Mr. Sandys. "Oh, my. That could explain Lady Margaret's demeanor today."

"Yes, it certainly could."

We sat in silence for a moment. I could see the sun growing ever lower. Tempie was right that I needed to get back across that causeway soon.

"Did you hear that the Paces petitioned to go back to their home?" I asked her.

"I did. Many are petitioning, and the governor and council are unhappy about it. But they must let them go as the Company wishes us to start re-building up and down river. The leaders here feel it's unwise, that we should build towns closer in."

"So the Company blames us for being dispersed and massacred, then asks us to disperse? The Company should come over and see for themselves. Do they understand how far sixty miles upriver is? How dangerous?" I asked her.

"Seems not."

"It everyone still well here?" I asked her.

"Aye, so far. It feels like the Egyptian plague, the cloud of death, I hate to say," she said. Then she reached over to pat my back consolingly. "Listen!" she said at last. "Bad news needs good news to better it, don't you think? My spirits are good for a secret reason. Would you like to hear it?" She gave a clandestine smile.

"Waste no more daylight, tell me!" *Anything good, please.*

"George has returned with a full three thousand and more bushels of corn, some by force from the Indians, some peaceably with trade."

"Hosanna! Tempie, I'm so glad. That will help feed the crowds for a while at least. Soon, maybe in the coming spring, we can plant as usually we do."

"Just so. And think of it! Three acres, lovey. Maybe four! Will's corn he can plant out at Mulberry Island, provided 'tis safe enough. You can plant an orchard of apples and plums and pears, make a trial of plantains and figs from the Bermudas perhaps, get some vines growing out there. Just think! Your own three acres to plant as you wish! The fruits and foods of the earth know not that we've had so many disasters this year. They know only that they shall work with God and you to bloom from the garden. See? Think of that. Be like unto the lilies of the field. Find summer in your heart, sweet friend, even now."

I said nothing for a few moments. Then, "Those who plant orchards intend to be around for a few years to see them prosper, to gather the fruits of their labors," I mused.

"Yes, Joan, exactly it. Think about the apples and pears and figs and plantains. Think on those and dwell not on your sadness. Next week, I'll come to you, needing you to tell me the same thing!"

I laughed and hugged her.

"Time for me to get home."

"By the by," she added, "mind your steps on the dusky causeway!"

Too Long a Sacrifice

January 26, 1623
New Towne, Virginia

Too long a sacrifice
Can make a stone of the heart.
　　　—William Butler Yeats

Furl that Banner, for 't is weary;
Round its staff 't is drooping dreary...
　　　—Father Abram Joseph Ryan

The next morning early, I was startled to see Lady Wyatt walking toward my home.

I began to tremble, fearing another confrontation with the governor's wife.

Was she coming to my door? I was in for a tongue lashing. Of this I was certain. And probably I deserved it. Dame Margaret was, after all, the governor's wife. She had been gravely ill, coming in on the ship with the contagion raging—the one which had brought the illness to us. How miserable that must have been. And her husband had been good to mine.

One thing which had been difficult was to help newcomers understand that we were English—but we were not in England. We were not *English* English. We were Virginia English.

The world was different here. It had become different from the very beginning. As far back even as when Admiral Somers and Sir Thomas Gates had bailed water alongside the laborers on the *Sea Venture*.

Class? What meant class? We all starved. We all wore rags at times. Those of us who had survived had status because we could teach others to survive. Had not young Annie Laydon, only perhaps fifteen years old, taught us that in '09? Here we were not born to rank. We sweated, suffered, and bled our way into it.

Still, how could I expect Dame Margaret to understand this? She'd not been here long, and almost the entire time, had been in an ague haze. Truly, she was fortunate to have survived at all.

Should I have given her more of the loathsome gruel? But what about the laborer, grateful to have his share? Why must he sacrifice his meal for the cries of a knight's wife?

The whole colony, it seemed, was distressed and weary, hungry and sick. Tempers were short. Including my own.

My heart was thudding with the coming harangue. She was, indeed, approaching my door.

Yes, I'd been following the governor's orders, but what if he now chose to punish me? A bodkin through the tongue or some such?

Mrs. Peirce, I asked you to treat all fairly, but you severely insulted my wife and embarrassed her before the line.

Lady Margaret reached up to knock, and I took a deep breath and opened the door. Her fist paused in mid-air. She seemed startled.

"Oh, you saw me approach, Mrs. Peirce?"

I could not read her tone. I nodded and ducked my head in deference. "Aye, my lady. I did."

We stood for a moment, each seeming to take the other in. I caught myself. "Please, will you come inside? 'Tis too cold to stand at the doorway … for either of us." *We all get cold. We all get hungry.*

She brought herself inside, and I gestured to a chair. "I have little to offer you, I suppose you know that." My tone was clipped, despite my best efforts to keep it even. I tried to remember her station; she was a lady and the governor's wife, after all.

"I do know. A brutal place, Virginia," she replied. She looked around at my home, its furnishings better than most in Virginia.

Will had done well with tobacco and still had his hopes on silk. The colony, even amidst its great sickness and massacre, was attempting to resurrect itself. Gentle hope, which seemed to grow even as a delicate flower among weeds, was a beautiful thing. Hope which, against all odds, refused to die completely.

How much I owed to this couple I now understood. If not to Dame Margaret herself, then to her uncle Mr. Sandys and to her husband at the least. And how had I repaid them? By publicly chastising Lady Wyatt—embarrassing her. *But she embarrassed me, too, and put me in a difficult position.*

Long ago, my mother had told me of a book describing two angels within a man—one enticing him to good, the other to evil. Perhaps they were warring within me? Perhaps the evil angel had already gotten the good one with a pike. I only knew I was having a hard time staying pleasant.

"Mistress Peirce ... Joan. May I call you Joan? Our husbands are respectful friends. Yours has helped mine as mine has affirmed yours his rank and privilege."

Rank, privilege, he earned!

Lady Wyatt must have seen my eyes for she quickly added, "Your husband did work into that position through many years here."

"Aye. And yours had the misfortune to be our leader during the massacre, the worst year ever we did see. Perhaps worse, even, than the Starving Time."

"So true," she replied softly. Then, "I came, Joan, to say I'm sorry for my outburst. It was unfair to you. Put you in a terrible position. I lost my temper and took it out on you."

"Oh, no, my lady. 'Tis I who should apologize to you. Your husband has done so much ... suffered ..." My voice dropped off. Sir Francis had been ill all the last summer. I remembered his haunted eyes when I'd visited.

The silence growing between us was uncomfortable.

Then she spoke up. "Did you desire to come to Virginia?"

"No, no, truly I did not." I looked down and fiddled with the ring on my finger. The carved rose ring. Mrs. Mayhew had given it to me before she died soon after we'd arrived in Virginia. Another woman who had not wanted to come here, but whose husband had persuaded her, had made her do so.

I cleared my throat. "I had a little say. But Will—Lieutenant Peirce—had already set his mind that we should come. Virginia, I should say, did seem a much more wholesome place at that time. We knew not what awaited us."

Understanding coursed through me. I lifted my head and met her eyes, which, I saw to my surprise, had tears in them. "But you did know. You did know," I finished weakly.

"Yes. I came knowing a great massacre had occurred, knowing there weren't enough victuals. Knowing I would suffer, knowing I had a pleasant home in England I loved. I came because they all insisted. First my husband, the governor, and then, too, my uncles the Company treasurer and the Virginia treasurer. 'It will be good for the Company and good for the colony if you make a presence there, Margaret,' they said. 'You shall show confidence in Virginia's ability to revive itself after the massacre.' Confidence I did not have. Confidence I *yet* do not have."

She drew a breath as if gaining courage and continued. "I sacrificed my home and my comfort and the Kentish countryside I hold dear for a place I never sought to venture. I did it for Virginia. For my husband. For my uncles." She paused. "For you. For that laborer behind me. For everyone here—for everyone but myself and my children, who remain at home in Kent. So that the Virginia Company might wave *me* as a banner saying that Virginia would survive. They have used me as a battle flag, Mrs. Peirce. It was my poor luck that the contagion took so many on my ship and then spread it to me and the settlements beyond."

Now I, too, was wiping tears. "Ah, my dame," was all I could say.

She went on, "Now everyone looks at me with suspicion. Did they not load the corn because of my presence? The banner I actually am is one showing the disease in the colony, in body and in spirit. For I am so, so tired. A near brush with death. And all I saw on ship was the mariners throwing folks overboard, entire families. I shall not truly recover from that, I think."

At once, I noticed how drawn her expression was, how pale. I saw the worry lines on her face, the fear in her eyes. She may have been a knight's wife from an affluent family, but in the end, she suffered just as I did.

In that, too, Virginia chastised us each fairly, treated us each the same.

My elbows now on the table, my face in my hands, I leaned in and listened to her words. And I understood. These words or similar I'd heard from Elizabeth Mayhew on my trip across the ocean. Elizabeth, who had never wanted to be here, who had become bitter by having Virginia forced on her. Who had preferred—and received—death over living in a land she hated. How much worse for Lady Wyatt. Her husband and father had pressed her and even used her, her sacrifice greater than I could have imagined.

I reached across the table and clasped her hand. "The laborer thanked *me*, but we both should have been thanking *you*. I see now. I see. Yes, we all do suffer alike here, and you suffer, too, but perhaps more, for you gave yourself to the cause. Please forgive me that I did not understand."

Her voice was hushed. "How could you understand? I've tried to bear up and not say it, else the banner be torn and worthless."

She squeezed my hand in return. With the other, she brushed away the tears from her eyes. We didn't need words now. My enemy of yesterday, I sensed, was now my friend.

"Could you use some help? In the great hall, I mean?" she asked gently.

"It would be an honor, my lady," I replied. "Truly, an honor. But recover your health fully first. Tax yourself not overmuch. We who have been here longer tend to be more robust. Such will come to you, too, in time."

She smiled. "As you wish, then."

Such a Pestilent Fever

February 10, 1623
New Towne, Virginia

*Such a pestilent fever rageth this winter among us; never known before
in Virginia, by the infected people that came over in ye 'abigal,' who were
poisoned with beer, and all falling sick and many dying, everywhere dispersed
the contagion ... hinc libet fugere [I'd like to fly away], which is oft in my
minde and all most in my resolution.*
> —George Sandys, finding Jamestown hard to bear,
> March 1623

*... the nature of the Country is such that it Causeth much sickness, as the
scurvie and the bloody flix ... I never at[e] anie thing but pease, and loblollie
(that is water gruell) ... but must Worke hard both earelie, and late for a
messe of water gruell, and a mouthfull of bread, and beife ... When people
crie out day, and night, Oh that they were in England without their lymbes
... Yea though they beg from doore to doore, for wee live in feare of the Enimy
... And our Leiftenant is dead, and his ffather, and his brother, and there was
some 5 or 6 of the last yeares 20 of wch there is but 3 left ... and yet wee are
but 32 to fight against 3000 if they should Come, and the nighest helpe that
Wee have is ten miles of us ...*
> —Richard Frethorne, writing from Martin's Hundred
> to his parents in England, April 1623, not long
> before he died

The *Abigail* had been in port about six weeks, and the contagion had not
struck me or my household. By now, we could see that one need not
have drunk Duppa's beer to grow ill from the *Abigail*'s sickness. Still,
my home had made it this far. I began to feel secure, immune from the beast

ravaging the colony.

Never in Virginia should one feel immune, not from anything.

As I walked home from serving supper, I wondered if something were amiss. I shivered and felt numbed, all at once. A February wind wrapped its icy arms around me as did a sense of dread. Which of them made my bones feel chilled, I could not say.

From the Back Street, I could see Dr. Pott's home. Before it stood the usual line of those seeking help for the contagion. With each passing day, I noticed, the line at Dr. Pott's seemed longer.

Mrs. Holmes rocked her babe, whose piteous crying echoed through the street. Another woman carried a small boy. The boy had draped himself over his mother's shoulder limply.

He's far too still. That isn't good, not good at all! What if this spreads through the whole settlement?

As if in answer, I felt dizzy, and the ground beneath me seemed to shake. Dr. Pott's house was moving closer and further away. I rubbed my eyes. Perhaps I was more tired than I realized. It was indeed hard work to supervise the feeding of so many, particularly with lack of food, illness, and grief intermingled. Utter discouragement and hopelessness from those who would rather be in their own homes, not standing in a line for watery pottage in the barracks. Or better still, they'd choose their homes in England. Some would prefer the grave to a home here in Virginia, sure. And many got it.

Passing Margaret Powell's house, I saw a small commotion going on there. I called to one of her servants.

"Is all well?" I had a sinking feeling as I said it.

The young man seemed forlorn. "No, mistress, not at all." He took off his cap and wiped his brow. "I'm sorry to be the one to tell you, but we've received word that our master, Cap'n Powell, has died of an arrow wound on the field.

The Chickahominies!

Did that mean Will was back now? I wondered. Yet even as much as I wished to know, I had not enough strength to ask. I needed to get myself home. I needed to rest.

My dizziness was growing, fueled by the news that Captain Powell was now with God. Powell had been the gunner of James Town, captain of the governor's company and guard, lieutenant governor of James Cittie.

The thought seemed to be as bleary as my eyes.

Powell was not always the most pleasant of men, but he was good at what he did. *I should go and comfort Margaret ... I should ... I should ...* But my feet could barely find their way to my own house. *Later,* I mumbled, *later I will go see Margaret. Bring her some pottage and a consoling word.*

In my stupor, a thought plunged through the darkness. I knew who the next gunner and captain of the guard would be—and his last name was Peirce. I would have to consider this later. Everything later.

My house was only a single door away, but it felt as if I walked all the way upriver to get there. How tired I was!

Angelo was stirring a kettle, making soap, I thought, as I pushed the door open. Esther was stoking the fire so that it roared.

I reached for the wall to steady myself, thinking I might fall.

"G'day, missus," Angelo said, then, with a touch of alarm, "*Aiué!*" she cried. "You looks so pale, missus!" She dropped her paddle and came to me, taking my arm. "Sit, sit!" She tried to guide me to a bench.

Esther came to my other side and felt my forehead. Through the fog in my head, I heard Esther saying to Angelo, "Welladay, 'tis the sickness come to the house."

"To bed. I ... I must sleep. I feel so weak." Each woman held me by one arm and walked me to my chamber. Then Angelo supported me around the waist while Esther turned down the bed. *They are so kind,* I thought.

Then I stumbled up the little stairs to the bed and let the warm quilt close around me. Such a chill I had! More than the February wind, surely ... My clothing was damp with sweat.

My head had begun to pound, a whole round of Indian drums against my temples, and my heart thumped, not quite in the normal way.

Soon, my insides began to cramp in a manner most unnatural.

Oh, God, I murmured, drifting off. *Not the contagion, no. Not the contagion.*

An Angel before Thee

February 10 to March 3, 1623
New Towne, Virginia

Behold, I send an Angel before thee, to keep thee in the way, and to bring thee into the place which I have prepared.
—Exodus 23:20

Visitors' footfalls are like medicine; they heal the sick.
—Proverb of the Bantu people of Africa

I passed an uneasy night, my whole body aching and cold.

In the morning, I found blood on the pillow. I reached up, touching my face to find that my nose had bled. My head throbbed so badly that even the touch of my own hand upon my face made it worse.

I groaned and fell back into bed. *I should take herbs,* I thought. *Should change that pillow. 'Tis not good to sleep in …* Before I could finish my own thought, I was asleep again.

I awoke and slept alternately and upon waking briefly, knew I had no idea what day it was. Perhaps I had lain there for minutes, perhaps hours, perhaps days. I had not eaten, could not eat, even as I knew I needed the nourishment to sustain me. I knew only that my head was pounding harder, my belly hurting worse. I could keep nothing down, but someone had placed a chamber pot near to the side of my bed. Had Will come home?

Oh, God, what have we done? What have we done to be so punished? I was moaning, I thought, but I wasn't sure.

Darkness had fallen somehow. Every family had its own ill, dead, or dying.

Through the darkness came a figure haloed like an angel. *I've died, I* thought, then realized I had not, for surely a soul could not hurt in heaven as I did now.

"'Allo, Missus. I bring you herbs." The figure took shape, and I saw Angelo, carrying a candle which she set upon the bedside table.

"I empty the pot now, see?"

"You ... you look like an angel in the darkness, Angelo. So Angelo must be ..." I drew a deep breath. "A good name for you."

"I going to make you well, missus. You see. You teach. I hear, and I listen. I remember." She reached a cool hand upon my head, which unlike my own did not cause a worse headache. It felt refreshing on my feverish forehead.

"You hot. Got the fever. You wait, I'll return."

I nearly laughed. Yes, I'd wait. I suspected I'd be waiting in this bed for nearly a month—*if* I were fortunate.

Else I'd be waiting down by the graveyard.

I saw the soft glow of candlelight coming through the doorway and heard the clinking of apothecary jars. Did Angelo know how to administer the herbs? With all the new words and language? I began to fret, then reminded myself that she'd said she understood.

She returned carrying a pewter tray and upon it several jars and bowls. "In Angola"—she always finished the sound of her home with a flourish—"my people, we are *Mbundu*. We use the *milongo*, as you say 'the physick.' We use the *ocingombo* or *osoma* juices for the breath, the cough. For the ague, we grind *ulembaputu* leaves or drink the *ocisekua* bark. The belly upset, we got so many—*ukua, omue, okangato, ovomomis, ucalo* ... But we no have those here, missus, no. But we got the English herbs, we got the Indian plants." I always noticed the distinctive way she said "Anglish," even while I was curious as to what she'd brought.

"Missus, you drink the hot lemon and honey. My people use to make thee well."

This was new to me. I squinted upward and said, "Well, all right." She had managed to get some Bermudian lemons and honey from the small supply remaining. Even in my weakened state, I could smell the warm honey, and it was appealing. Gratitude washed over me.

"And then, missus, I bring the fluellin. I mix her with treacle as you say. Now I got the rag, and we wash your face."

I saw now that a basin waited near me on the bed. Angelo dipped the rag and then wrung it over the water. When she daubed my face, it felt cool like dew.

"I thank thee, Angelo. I do. How ... how is everyone else?"

"Esther, she sick now, too, missus. Lieutenant, he is not returned. Jane and the Missus Macock and the little girls, they all sick. The Missus Isabella, she still well, she taking care of them in th'other house. Mr. Sandys he go to the Gov'nor's. He very sick. The Missus Macock's baby still well, and I still well. I take care of you and Esther."

"Do you know anything about my daughter at Jordan's or about the Yeardleys?"

She shook her head. "No. But the doctor he sick now, too. So we each got to take care of our house."

"Angelo, you *are* an angel. Truly you are."

"Missus," she said, her eyes bright in the candle's glow. "You take care of me after my long journey. Now I take care of you."

Over the next day, I woke and slept. While awake, I saw just how much Angelo had learned, for she brought me marigold and tormentil and drinks of butterbur roots stamped with ale. She had the distilled water of dragon, being especially good for pestilent fever or poison.

As the first week wore into the second, the ague crept higher—but not, I think, as high as some have gone. I also didn't get the rash I heard many had gotten.

Through it all, Angelo the Angel brought me remedies for fever, remedies for headache, remedies for the stomach, for the flux. She held a cup of cedar drink to my lips.

At times, I couldn't recall where I was, why I was in bed, who Angelo was. The fever climbed so high that I drifted in and out of sleep. My dreams were strange mixes of dark ships with contagion, of Indians, of St. James—and then I was a little girl running through my mother's garden. But something chased me in the garden, something ugly. I screamed and tossed, drenched in sweat. *Leave me!*

Soon, I dreamed I was at the Yeardleys' home, where great platters of ham and turkey and corn pone sat before us. But when I reached for the ham, it turned to watery gruel.

In clear-headed moments, I reminded myself that if I were to survive, the fever would soon break. *Wait it out 'til it breaks*, I thought. *Don't give up!*

Into the third week, and my belly was sore and fever still high.

And then one morning, toward the end of that week, the ague broke. Cold sweat had left me soaked, but it appeared I'd survive this. Almost everyone had gotten the contagion, and nearly half had died.

It appeared I'd be in the living half.

Again.

Life: It Goes On

Early to Mid-March 1623
New Towne, Virginia

For there is few of us that have not knockt this yeare at the gates of death.
—Treasurer George Sandys from James Cittie, 30
March 1623

In three words I can sum up everything I've learned about life: it goes on.
—Robert Frost

Will returned home, just as the cold was starting to give way to spring, a spring we needed so desperately.

"Sam was out fighting the Chickahominies with us," Will said. "He returned home briefly, then met us back on the field. When he did, he brought news you'll wish to know. He says a new baby is coming in the middle of summer. He hopes for a son this time, he said."

"What about the contagion? How did they fare?" I asked nervously.

"Fine, better than they could have expected. Only a few lives lost, and Cecily and the children all recovered."

"And you?" I asked, giving him a hug around his neck. "Did you catch the contagion out there?"

He smiled. "No, a blessing indeed, Joan."

Will also said the men thought they'd crippled the Indians enough so that we could plant corn and tobacco this spring.

But until harvest, food for this year was sparse and growing sparser.

The contagion had finally taken over so that we no longer fed people in the barracks. Most stayed in their homes and ate what they had on hand.

This was not the way I'd hoped for a reprieve in serving at the great hall.

Each day, we watched the shore for the arrival of the *Sea Flower*. Three months past, the *Abigail* had told us the *Sea Flower* would bring us the promised corn. We'd asked the Virginia Company almost a year ago to please help us stave off famine.

Everywhere in James Cittie and all over, talk was the same.

"Where's the *Sea Flower*?"

"Heard any news on the *Sea Flower*?"

"Is the *Sea Flower* coming, or is the Company lying to us, forestalling our mutiny?"

Some folks inserted curse words before the ship's name as our rations thinned and fears grew.

But slowly, folks began to emerge from their homes and to mingle again.

Then we traded stories, fearing to hear who we'd lost amongst our friends. We learned that our friends and family had fared well compared to most. But Isabella's husband Richard had died, and so had the Reverend Bucke. The Bucke children had lost their mother about two years before, so the governor dispersed the children to various friends and family.

Mrs. Macock had died as well. Like so many others, she'd survived the assault of man and the loss of her husband the pastor, but the assault of disease she could not.

Isabella had tried to care for Mrs. Macock and to nurse her back to health while also tending to Jane and the little girls. By the time Jane was feeling somewhat better, Isabella and her husband Richard had grown very ill.

Angelo had the sickness coming on about the time Esther and I were recovering. The three of us survived it.

When I finally made my way over to the Yeardleys, I learned that Susanna had not gotten sick until later. Until then, she'd cared for the family. First Sir George had fallen ill, soon behind him Tempie, and then the two older children. Little Francis had stayed well.

Mr. Sandys and Governor Sir Francis had survived. Many of those who had come over with Lady Margaret had died, though.

Observing my two daughters, Jane and Cecily, I saw that hardship had made one more compassionate, the other stronger. These were traits the girls, now women, had brought here anyway. But now these qualities were greater than before, good fruits from a bitter and twisted tree of suffering.

As for Mrs. Macock, sometimes the hand of God shows itself in the strangest of things for the tiny baby, just five months old, had not even fallen sick. Instead, little Sarah stayed pink and round.

"A miracle, lo!" said one of Roger's servants who helped tend the child's mother.

"The holiness of the father saves the child," said another in a hushed whisper.

Jane decided she would raise the orphaned baby girl as her own. "I would never leave a little child alone to suffer," she said. She had come to love the little girl, Sarah, anyway.

How strange that in Virginia, little girls and small boys became land owners. Sarah, not even crawling, would soon inherit a large piece of acreage.

Not long after Mrs. Macock passed, both of the Salters, servants on Roger's land upriver, died of contagion. Now sickness had caused another child to be orphaned, the Salters' daughter Wee Bess, as folks at Roger's hundred called her. Wee Bess, a tiny little six year old, had been sick almost her whole life.

When Captain Smith brought the small, frightened girl to his home in New Towne, Jane welcomed her with a hug. "Fear thee not, my little one," Jane said consolingly. One look at the frail child and Jane knew that she would bring Wee Bess into her fold as well.

Jane could feel the captain watching her with the little girl.

A few days later, Captain Smith asked Jane if he could speak with her alone. "Not quite alone," he added. "My sister will be with us, just to be proper, of course."

Jane studied the captain. She thought she knew what was coming. Still, it amused her that such a big man should sound a bit nervous in wanting to speak with her. After all, Jane was scarcely eighteen years old. The captain had been a commander in the Low Countries about the time she were born.

Once seated at the kitchen table, Captain Smith began. "Mrs. Rolfe, or Jane if I may so call thee?" For such a rugged war commander, Captain Smith had a surprisingly gentle side, Jane thought.

"You may call me Jane, sir," she said as she awaited what would come next.

"This might be the oddest reason ever for making a match," the captain began. "But I cannot keep bringing you—a widow yourself—other widows and orphans without offering to provide for them. The times here are as trying as perhaps they ever have been. Yet I greatly admire your courage and strength in caring for Mrs. Macock, Sarah, and now Wee Bess following the massacre. I love you, Jane, and I hope you might consider marrying me. I have a plantation across the river to leave to you and Elizabeth if something should ... should happen to me on the battlefield or with the contagion."

Jane, blushing, looked from Captain Smith to Isabella. Isabella had misty eyes but refrained from encouraging Jane to accept her brother's offer. This was, of course, Jane's decision.

"Captain Smith?"

The captain nodded. "Roger, please." Jane could see the earnestness in his eyes.

Jane continued, "I should very much wish to marry you, and we can make a home for these three little girls together. Besides," she added with a smile, "I imagine your sister will soon return to Pace's, and you'll need a woman's touch around here. If we can plant this year, you'll have to help me manage the lands John has left behind as well, out at Mulberry Island. I'll surely need the help with planting time coming."

Isabella leaped from her chair as if it had a spring in it and threw her arms around Jane. "Oh, welcome to the family!" she cried. Then she sat back down. "I'm sorry, Roger," Isabella said. "I believe a kiss best seals the bargain?"

Roger leaned forward and kissed his betrothed. They would have Pastor Haute Wyatt marry them after he announced the banns.

Strong at the Broken Places

Late March 1623
New Towne, Virginia

*What does love look like? It has the hands to help others. It has the feet to
hasten to the poor and needy. It has the eyes to see misery and want. It has the
ears to hear the sighs and sorrows of men. That is what love looks like.*
> —St. Augustine

*The world breaks everyone, and afterward, some are strong at the
broken places.*
> —Ernest Hemingway

You're taking in both girls then, lovey?" I asked Jane as I walked over
to the church together with her and her little brood. She and Roger
had married a week ago, with Roger seeming to be happy to have three
new daughters. "Oh, yes, mother, I'll raise them as my own. Roger is already
like a father to them. Wee Bess speaks little, but in time, she'll grow strong."

Still, I worried. I pulled her aside as the little girls continued to walk on.
"I fear you're taking on too much, especially with a contagion going round," I
said. "Is it not enough to keep up with your own household?"

"Mama, no." Jane gestured to the small girls. She wished to be sure they
heard not.

As my daughter's gaze followed the little ones walking on ahead, I noticed
a light in her eyes. She did love them. I could see it. "Just as you mother me
now, I'm mothering them. You care for me in my struggle, just as I care for
them in their struggle." She shrugged and smiled. "'Tis all the same truly."

She was right, and I understood. "Jane, you're the kindest soul e'er I did
meet," I said. "They'll be like unto *mine* own granddaughters, too."

Her smile didn't belie the weariness on her face. We'd all suffered so much this year. Then she said, "Pray God, mother, we do not take sick any more ourselves because others need our help. Especially the children."

So many things were happening at once, we had much confusion. I found my head dancing with images, with thoughts that came from nowhere and would not leave until the next unbidden thought arrived. Perhaps thinking to survive until fall was too much. I decided instead to face a day at a time as each marched toward us, bringing new challenges.

Will had received a new honor. Captain Powell had been one of two representing James Cittie in the General Assembly. With Powell's death, men who were able betook themselves to the church to cast votes to replace him. It came as no surprise to me that the folks elected Will in Powell's stead. He'd be one of two from James Cittie. The other was Mr. Kingsmill who owned the grand tract on the other side of James Town Island.

Mr. Sandys, back in our house, weak but well, congratulated Will warmly.

Isabella, now widowed, realized she needed to return with her son to Pace's to begin rebuilding. But before she left New Towne, Isabella came by my house to say goodbye.

As it happened, Tempie was also visiting.

Isabella joined us at the table and grasped one hand in each of ours, giving them a shake. "Well, ladies, young George and I go soon to Pace's," she said. "Merry wishes to our newly united families, Joan. I'm relieved that I don't have to leave Roger alone now that he has Jane," she said. "Besides, his house, empty but for servants, now has a lovely wife and three children."

"'Tis good for Jane and for Roger," I mused. "I fretted a little for Jane with two new little girls, but she seems content. If she is, I am. How glad it makes me as well! But we're sorry you go to an empty and charred home," I said.

"As am I. But happy am I that young George and I did survive the contagion. You and your husbands and children survived, too," Isabella said, a little wistfully. "I do now understand something." Isabella's tone turned serious. "When we have children, we can remarry, aye. But as mothers, we must learn the business ourselves. Else, how can we protect our children's estate?"

"So you will go and learn the business of planting, harvesting, and selling tobacco?" I asked her.

"I will indeed. And mayhap I'll marry again. But for this moment, I must rely on myself," Isabella said firmly.

"This is so," Tempie said. "We've proven ourselves. We understand this Virginia business, this growing and selling of tobacco, because we've lived it."

I hesitated. "I don't think I could tend to the business if Will died."

Tempie reproved me. "Yes, you could. You underestimate yourself. And it's likely that you might one day have to do just that. Death isn't the only reason. What if Will were in England for an extended time? Mr. Pace has died. My husband falls in and out of illnesses. We never know here when we may be alone. Besides, you've managed the ladies well at the barracks. No man could surpass thee."

Isabella agreed. "She speaks truth, Joan. And it behooves us, if we remarry, to marry well. To marry a man who shall respect our children, ourselves, and the estates we've accrued with our first husbands. Including acreage we ourselves have earned by planting here." Then she added, "Oh, but I do not mean Jane and Roger. He's an honest man, and he loves Jane and the girls."

"But," Tempie said, leaning in to us, "you cannot trust a second husband to take care of your children's estates as you would. *That's* why you have to learn to manage them yourselves. Marrying again is not a balm for all."

We sat in silence for a moment, each of us looking to the other. Tempie was right, and I knew it.

"I suppose we've been fortunate. Sam has been a good second husband to Cecily, and I do trust Roger as well," I said.

We changed the subject, and I told them I'd planted my fig seeds, planning for an orchard. "I may not be as wise as you two in business, but I do know a garden. I'll just rely on you both for the selling side of things."

Mr. Perry returned to Pace's the same time that Isabella did. They made a match, marrying soon after. She liked him very much, she said. Her husband and Mr. Perry had been neighbors and business partners. She assured Tempie and me that she trusted him, but had made a point to learn the tobacco business. She would keep a sharp eye on the accounts.

Isabella was only in her thirties. In less than a year, she'd give Mr. Perry a son to join her son George Pace.

Such was our life at James Town. In Virginia, we couldn't let too much time lapse before remarrying. We were in a cruel world. Children needed caretakers and someone to manage their estates. We hoped that if we should not survive, a little passel of children would.

Spring was here at last. We'd not had such a long, bleak winter since the Starving Time. We marked a year since the massacre. *A year!* I thought.

Sometimes I felt something powerful happened when a year closed. As though if a year were truly bad—just *bad*—as this one was, that we had a chance for renewal. Some years could be dark, so dark. When I remembered 1622, I remembered everything as if it were grey and black, a shroud of death overlying it.

If we could only plant this year, perhaps we could survive until the next harvest. By then, the contagion would, God willing, be past.

Those of us who lived through one more thing considered ourselves fortunate and swore it would make us stronger.

We Will Stand by Each Other

Late March 1623
New Towne, Virginia

Then come the wild weather, come sleet or come snow,
We will stand by each other, however it blow.
　　　　—Simon Dach

A few days later, a fire crackled warm and bright against the late March dampness.

A knock at the door brought my loving cousin—and son-in-law—Sam Jordan.

I threw my arms up into the air and gave him a hug, saying, "What brings you to New Towne? How are Cecily, little Temperance, and Mary? And Cecily fares well as she carries the baby?" Every childbirth gave a grandmother-to-be pause, for every childbirth could carry danger.

"She's a sturdy one, that," Sam said. "Children all well and Cecily—well, Cecily is Cecily. A mind of her own! But aye, we all fared very well at Jordan's. Few of us were sick."

I laughed, grateful for good news.

Will was coming from the bedchamber, sword already at his side, upon hearing his cousin's knock.

The men greeted each other warmly, Sam taking a moment to say that Will's Van Dyke looked foppish, and he should trim the beard a little.

At that, Will stroked his chin and laughed, knowing his cousin was joking. "I'll not take stylish advice from the likes of you! Else I should have a red beard like yours, which"—he looked Sam up and down—"clashes with your doublet."

The men shared a bond, a fondness which went back to their days at Nieuwpoort in Flanders. The Spanish *tercios* had fired around them, and yet they'd held. Cecily's father Tom, as well, as my brother had died in that same brutal battle.

Sam and Will had survived together, which gave them a bond only those who shared great anguish could understand. They had decided together to come to Virginia, then confronted the hurricane at sea together as well. Bailing, side by side.

They'd come through the massacre, the Indian wars, and the pestilence. They believed, somehow, that they shared a strength in the two together, that they were more than two when they fought side by side.

"I'm out to inspect the palisades and fortifications today. Come join," Will said to his friend, cousin, and son-in-law.

Not too dangerous a detail except for being outside the palisade at times.

And so Sam and Will set off. I watched them walking away, shoulder to shoulder.

Had I known what was to come next, I should have run after them, calling them, begging them not to go.

Where Devotion Kneels

Late March 1623
James Town Island, Virginia

All is holy where devotion kneels.
—Oliver Wendell Holmes, Sr.

… and in their death they were not divided …
—II Samuel 1:3

Will and Sam were beyond the palisade when they heard a shout coming from near the blockhouse.

"There's Sam Jordan! His carelessness caused my brother's death!" a man cried.

Sam immediately recognized the voice and the bitter look on the man's face. This man had been with him as they battled the Chickahominies in December.

Sam and some of his men from upriver had joined the Chickahominy battle. I knew the Chickahominies had put up a fierce defense although they ultimately fled. Sam's orders were to gather any abandoned corn and then burn the town, but there was trouble from within.

A few of the men assigned to Sam were to protect against a follow-up attack from the Indians. Two of the men were brothers, hungry and disheartened—bitter at being pressed into military duty. "God has forsaken this land and us in it!" Sam had heard one of them say.

The Indians had indeed struck back, launching a volley of arrows from the protection of the trees. An arrow pierced one of the brothers despite his armor, severely wounding him. Sam and his men retaliated and drove off the archers.

They were far from proper medical help. The injured brother died within a few days, a terrible and painful death. The surviving brother was grief-stricken, lashing out at Sam and anyone in authority, blaming them for his brother's death.

He was trouble the rest of the campaign, complaining to any ear that would listen. Most ignored the disgruntled soldier, but a few shared his discontent.

Now here he was again.

"Get 'em!" shouted the man, raising his matchlock as if to fire. The soldier's comrades were confused. But drawn into the emotion of the moment, they also raised their weapons.

Will and Sam saw the raised matchlocks and retreated towards a nearby tree line for cover.

Sam was a few paces in front of Will. He could hear his friend's footfalls just behind him. Suddenly, Will cried out in pain, and his racing footsteps turned into the stumbling sound of his body hitting the ground.

The bloody mutineers got Will! Sam thought. Yet he'd not heard the matchlocks' fire. He spun quickly, his only thought to reach his friend, his cousin. Will lay motionless, face to the ground and his back covered in a spreading circle of blood. An arrow's shaft protruded from just below his right shoulder.

"Will!" Sam screamed, his voice hoarse. He dropped to his knees. "I will not let you die!" Sam's eyes scanned the trees, but he saw nothing. The Indians could be anywhere. And in that instant, Sam's mind raced through images. Fighting the Spanish *tercios*. Holding up flagons in a toast to their decision to come to Virginia—all hope and promise. And the hurricane—bailing, bailing, bailing. Then on ship, the lights of St. Elmo's fire, flitting round the shrouds. Will had said that the old saint hadn't been too helpful. Sam had laughed. "Old mate, I'm glad to die with you!"

They'd been prepared to die together then. *Why not now?* Sam asked himself. *The danger in turning back matters not.* True, he could run. He saw a fallen tree and brush nearby. His best chance was to take cover there and to protect himself.

But he would not.

He lingered, wondering how to get Will to safety, how to gauge the severity of his friend's wound. Will lay far too still—that Sam could see.

He wouldn't leave Will there to be scalped while he himself lived.

In that singular motion of care, Sam found those thoughts to be his last. A volley of native arrows caught his shoulder, his stomach, his thigh—the final one piercing his great heart.

And he fell to the forest floor, shoulder to shoulder with Will once more.

The English soldiers turned quickly for the shelter of the blockhouse. Even the disgruntled brother had only meant to scare the two, not to cause their deaths. Mutiny toward someone of Will's military standing was serious indeed.

Will and Sam lay motionless, side by side, Will facing toward the woods, and Sam facing Will.

The Lions of
the Hill are Gone

Late March 1623
New Towne, Virginia

Fell, they will say, in "skirmish"!
Vanquished, my soul will know
By but a simple arrow
Sped by an archer's bow.
        —Emily Dickinson

The lions of the hill are gone,
And I am left alone—alone—
Dig the grave both wide and deep,
For I am sick, and fain would sleep!
        —Samuel Ferguson

M istress Peirce, the governor wants to see you," said Henry, one of Sir Francis's trusted servants. The man's tone was somber, his face without expression.

A dread came over me, overtook me, and left me clutching my chest. "Is it about Will? Is he back? Is he all right?"

The man shook his head. "Governor has news, mistress. It's not mine to convey."

The governor's eyes rimmed in concern, and he had no need to tell me for I had guessed.

"How ... did ... it ... happen?" I asked, forcing calmness upon myself.

The governor's eyes showed that he was near breaking down. For with Powell's death, he needed Will's soldier experience. Sir Francis answered in choppy sentences, as if putting together too many words only added to his pain.

"Three renegadoes decided to seek justice on their own. They blame Sam for the death of a fellow, the brother of one of them. Met ... Will and Sam at the blockhouse entrance. Threatened them with muskets. Gave chase to the woods. They claim they didn't mean to cause their deaths, only to frighten Sam. We'll punish them as mutineers, of course."

"They shot them!" I screamed, my voice hysterical in pitch.

Wyatt shook his head. "No. 'Twas only a threat, the men said. But once back out near the blockhouse, Lieutenant Peirce and Master Jordan must have come upon Indians. Their arrows caught the men. The mutineers, contrite, have told me the news in hopes of saving their own skins. I do not know the conditions of your husband and Jordan, mistress."

"Where ... are ... they ... now?" My voice sounded distant, as if it came from the forest itself.

"I've sent six men to fetch them. I ... I wished to ensure you knew before the men bring them in. I didn't want you to hear this in the town."

And Governor Sir Francis Wyatt and I stood staring at one another, neither knowing what to say.

Joy and Sorrow

Late March 1623
New Towne, Virginia

*Joy and sorrow are inseparable ... together they come and when one sits alone
with you ... remember that the other is asleep on your bed.*
   —Kahlil Gibran

I went straight to Jane's house, for as the governor had said to me, I did not want her to hear the news on the streets.

Roger was away. I saw that she had one of their men bringing in firewood. She was at the door, seeing me coming perhaps.

My stricken face must have told her all she needed to know.

"It's Father, isn't it? What happened, mama? What happened?" Her voice rose to a pitch, and I sighed.

This would not be easy.

At that moment, Henry burst through the door—not bothering even to knock.

"Mrs. Peirce, thought you might be at your daughter's. I got news! Straight from the governor!" he gasped, out of breath from running.

What news could he possibly have? I looked at Jane. I'd heard the worst. What now?

"They brought Lieutenant Peirce and Jordan back to the fort, except that Lieutenant Peirce is still alive! The pain caused him to pass out is all. He was in a right bad way, though. They took him to Dr. Pott, and the doctor is working on your husband now. Arrow below the shoulder, mistress."

I shouted, this time from joy. My Will was alive! How many times now had he cheated death? *Praise God.*

And then, like a topple off a mountaintop, my heart thudded and plummeted within me. For I knew what that meant about Sam.

"And … Sam?" I did not lift my eyes from my shoes.

Henry cleared his throat and shuffled the cap he held in his hands. "Jus' Lieutenant Peirce is alive, mistress. Master Jordan …" He coughed nervously. "Master Jordan, well, he turned to help your husband, mistress. Seems the Indians hit Lieutenant Peirce first. The three men saw it all."

"Sam … went back?" My eyes were filling fast with tears, and they began to drop onto my shoes as I watched.

"Yes, mistress. He went back, and that's when the Indians got him. I'm sorry, mistress. I take it they were great friends."

I nodded, one hand growing wet as it shielded my eyes, the other gripped in a fist. "Friends, soldiers together in the Low Countries, cousins, and in-laws. They were everything. Everything."

Sam's loss would devastate Will, when and if he recovered.

Medicines Out of the Earth

Late March 1623
New Towne, Virginia

The skill of the physician shall lift up his head, and in the sight of great men he shall be praised. The most High hath created medicines out of the earth, and a wise man will not abhor them ... By these he shall cure and shall allay their pains, and of these the apothecary shall make sweet confections, and shall make up ointments of health, and of his works there shall be no end. For the peace of God is over all the face of the earth.
—Ecclesiasticus 38:3–4, 7–8

We hurried to the doctor's quarters, where he had a chamber with three sickbeds and all his tools. His servant Goodman Hullaway let us in with a knowing look.

Dr. Pott barely glanced up as the two of us stumbled into the room. His apprentice Dick Townshend stood nearby and gave us a sympathetic look.

"Quiet," was all the doctor said. "Concentrating."

Nothing prepared me for the sight of Will—still encrusted with dark blood and lying on his stomach. The doctor had ripped off his doublet and shirt. The arrow and its shaft still jutted from beneath his shoulder blade.

"How is he?" I asked tentatively.

"He's lost right much blood. Arrow came nigh of protruding out the other side." Dr. Pott turned to look at me. "I'm about to try to pull it out. You may not want to stay for this."

I steeled myself. "I'll stay," I said.

The doctor was working against time. We'd learned that we had no more than half an hour to pull the arrow out. After that, a man's body heat would dissolve the glue, made of boiled deer antlers, used to hold the arrowhead to its shaft. Then the arrow point would separate from the shaft and remain in the body. I didn't know how long it had been but knew it must have been near, or past, a half hour. Arrowheads left in wounds presented more complications of removal.

As in so many other manners of warfare, the Indians, with straight shot and glue upon arrowheads, showed great skill.

"Hold him," the doctor told Townshend and Hullaway as he gave the arrow's shaft a tug. The yank caused Will to scream in pain. He seemed to be only partly awake.

The shaft pulled loose from the arrowhead and came out, and more blood poured from the wound.

Will let out a gasp and moan.

I felt utterly helpless. I reached forward and stroked his hand.

Pott cursed and tossed the shaft aside. He had expected to lose the point but still had hoped that *this* time, he might get it all out at once.

"Duck-bill forceps," the doctor mumbled to his apprentice, as he staunched the bleeding with rags.

Townshend went to the doctor's large chest in the corner. It contained all manner of compartments and drawers. We'd been fortunate to have this chest with us since 1610 when a young servant of the well-respected chirurgeon John Woodall came to the colony. Woodall now had a business preparing surgical chests for ships. Woodall had also written a book of instructions, *The Surgeon's Mate,* which, I noted, Dr. Pott had stacked atop his desk with a few other medical tomes.

Townshend knew exactly where to find the forceps from the well-organized chest, and I breathed a sigh of relief. Just seeing the array of tools and doctors' books made me feel that Will was in good hands. It was not so long ago that we'd managed without even one doctor or surgeon.

The apprentice handed the forceps to the doctor.

Dr. Pott squinted. He had been examining the wound as best he could without allowing overmuch bleeding.

"Hold tight," the doctor said to his men as he slipped the scissor-like forceps over his fingers and plunged the end into Will's back.

Will jumped and let out another scream of pain. Had the men not been holding him down, he would have writhed off the table, I thought.

I hid my eyes, not wanting to see his pain, and then uncovered just one eye—as though half a seeing might not be so terrible.

There was a *snip* sound as the forceps grabbed the arrowhead but then slipped off.

Dr. Pott tried again and again. He was speaking more to himself than to us. "Right between the ribs. Of course. Always that way. Fortunate 'tis on the right side."

I understood. Had the point entered between the ribs on his left, it would have struck near—or at—Will's heart. The right side, although the one he used for his musket and sword, was still a better choice than his heart side.

The natives were not only talented marksmen, but they had perfected their arrow craftsmanship. They knew how to align turkey or eagle feathers on the shaft in such a way that the arrowhead rotated little in flight. The braves aimed the arrow so the stone point tended to slide right between a man's ribs.

"Thank God they don't have longbows!" Dr. Pott grumbled as he tried to dig the arrow out once more. The English, the best archers in Europe, had cautiously avoided sending our Welsh longbows to Virginia. In fact, I'd heard the king was sending longbows in the next ship, the *Sea Flower,* along with its corn. All of it, we still awaited.

God help us if native marksmanship had the advantage of our superior weapon. We might have used the Welsh longbow better than any European— but we could never compete with the stealth and sharp eye of an Indian. We were desperate for weapons, yes, while sorely afraid the Indians might get hold of our longbows. The time for the longbows, we felt, had come in this desperate war where we remained short of weapons and ammunition.

"Ah!" This time the arrow slid out—a tiny, white stone triangle—and the wound began bleeding anew.

Will seemed near out of his senses from pain and blood loss, and I was fearfully worried for him.

An old country prayer for staunching blood came to me, and I whispered it three times furtively.

There were three Marys went over the flood;
The one did stand, the other stent blood
Then bespoke Mary that Jesus Christ bore,
Defend God's forbode thou shouldest bleed anymore.
But Will bled.

"More rags!" cried the doctor, and Townshend was quick to retrieve them.

The doctor took a deep breath. "Well, Mrs. Peirce, we've half the battle won. The shaft and arrow are out, and he's still alive."

"Aye," I murmured, a faint nod. I understood what the doctor meant. The arrow itself hadn't killed him—I kept myself from thinking of Sam—as it could have. But the wound would like as not fester. That was the second half of the battle, one I'd fight with Will at home.

Dr. Pott's spectacles perched low upon his nose. His treatment for

Indian wounds involved cleaning first. Townshend, who had seen his share of arrows protruding from men in the doctor's office, was a step ahead and was bringing over a jar of liquid.

"Poplar gum," the doctor said to me as if anticipating my question. "Much like turpentine. Might just be better than dragon's blood."

Dr. Bohun had been experimenting with Virginia's plants and trees. It had been he who discovered that the gum of poplar and a few other trees here served well as an astringent for wounds. We found the European red resin called dragon's blood hard to obtain in Virginia. We were learning to substitute Virginia plants for European ones where necessary.

As the doctor poured the tree gum into Will's wound, Will moaned again and began shaking his head as though trying to lift the fog.

"What the blazes ... where ... ?" His voice was groggy.

"Will, I'm here," I said soothingly, as I moved near his head where he could see me.

"Sam and I, we went down. Ran from one ambush to another." His voice took on a pleading sound—so unusual for my stoic Will. He paused, and his eyes went straight to mine. "And Sam?"

There was no concealing, no putting this off until he was better. His eyes demanded truth, and my eyes could not lie.

I shook my head and felt the tears coming.

"Oh, God," he cried, and his voice broke. "He turned around—for me ..."

"He couldn't leave you," I whispered. "You wouldn't have left him either."

He dropped his head back to the table as the doctor daubed the excess resin from his back.

Townshend was handing the doctor another apothecary jar. Pott looked up. "Puccoon root, Will, in case there's any poison."

Puccoon was the same red root the Indians smeared on their faces to keep flies away, but it also had healing powers. We had learned to use puccoon from the natives, who themselves used it on arrow wounds to remove any poison.

Arrowheads carried many threats. Besides the wounds they caused, and the festering likely to follow, the arrows could have poison on them. The Indians occasionally dipped the arrowheads in a poison root. Or, sometimes—I flinched at the thought—they would use the livers of decayed animals as a poison. *Pray to God these natives had not done that.*

The puccoon root—we called it also bloodwort—was a tincture that Pott dropped into the wound. "What else is in it?" I asked Dr. Pott.

"Self-heal and horehound."

I nodded. "Good."

He gave me an amused look over his glasses. "Glad you approve!"

I smiled and added, "And what of St. James Wort?"

"That, too. Good choice. You do know your herbs, don't you? Would you like to join Townshend as my apothecary apprentice?"

I knew he was teasing me, so I smiled faintly and said, "I'm an apothecary in my own home already, Dr. Pott. I have been since my mother died and left me a full garden of herbs and many more jars a-filled."

"Well." The doctor's tone turned serious. "A good knowledge of herbs is a savior in a land such as this."

"It's saved me and others a few times."

"It will go far in bringing this old rascal back to service! Right, Lieutenant Peirce?"

The groan that emerged from the table might have been a "yes," but it was hard to tell.

The healing tincture in the wound, Dr. Pott next reached into a larger apothecary jar and dug out white clay. "*Terra alba virginiensis,*" he said. "Another discovery of my esteemed—and greatly missed—colleague Dr. Bohun."

Dr. Bohun had found the white clay to have healing properties and packed wounds with it. "More's the pity about the sea battle that caused the good doctor's death, a great loss," he said as he wrapped rags around the arm and injury.

"Will, are you up to the walk next door, or do you want to stay here?" Dr. Pott asked.

"Home," was all he said, and the two servants helped Will to his feet.

Tales of the Herbs
and the Stars

Late March 1623
New Towne, Virginia

Excellent herbs had our fathers of old—
Excellent herbs to ease their pain—
Alexanders and Marigold,
Eyebright, Orris, and Elecampane—
Basil, Rocket, Valerian, Rue,
(Almost singing themselves they run)
Vervain, Dittany, Call-me-to-you—
Cowslip, Melilot, Rose of the Sun.
Anything green that grew out of the mould
Was an excellent herb to our fathers of old.

Wonderful tales had our fathers of old—
Wonderful tales of the herbs and the stars—
The Sun was Lord of the Marigold,
Basil and Rocket belonged to Mars ....
    —Rudyard Kipling

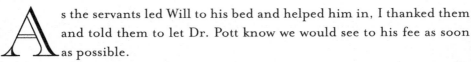s the servants led Will to his bed and helped him in, I thanked them and told them to let Dr. Pott know we would see to his fee as soon as possible.

"Ask the good doctor how much tobacco he would charge?" We used tobacco as our money in most cases.

They nodded, tipped their hats, and walked out.

I leaned over the bed and kissed the back of Will's head, for he lay on his stomach so that the wound would not press against the mattress.

Later, we could talk more about Sam, about what had happened, but right now I wanted only to see him rest.

I had long ago given thought to a compounding mixture for arrow wound. We'd been unusually fortunate that an arrow had never struck Will before. Or when an arrow had come at his body, he'd had his armor and breastplates on. Now, I went to my table book where I'd written a list of herbs for such an occasion.

Horehound—yes. For poison, should there be any in the wound. For pain and to help a fever break. Will didn't have a fever yet. But the wound would probably turn septic. If so, I'd add St. James wort. St. James again. *Well, help me, old saint,* I thought, giving the pilgrim's badge around my neck a pat. I'd been wearing it for nearly thirty years, my father's final gift to me.

St. James wort was also called ragwort or ragweed. We had plenty of that about, and I was well stocked. St. James wort happened to also be good for pain in the arms, legs, or hips, and Will's arm would be plenty sore.

And then St. John's wort was particularly good for bloody wounds. *Might as well add all the saints!* I thought.

The doctor had mentioned self-heal, also called *prunella.* Gerard's *Herball* said there was no better plant for the healing of any wound than that, so much so that some called self-heal "woundwort." A must. I hoped, in fact, that by using herbs to heal green wounds, the wound might never fester.

And of course, puccoon root. In case of any lingering poison. Sage and comfrey were always advisable. Chamomile to soothe Will's grief about Sam, to help him rest.

I got to work immediately, scooping out hog's lard to make a salve. Gerard liked the roots of narcissus mixed in honey and butter. Having only butter, I didn't see it binding enough. The lard would substitute for the honey.

If only, I thought, stirring the herbs into the grease, *if only there were some mixture 'twould bring Sam back to us again.*

I looked up as if I might see Sam walking through the door.

It's all right, Joan. Just a mishap! What did they tell you? I died? No such thing. Someone has to keep Will straight. Now tell him to get himself up. Day is nearly over!

Will's grief would be numbing. In just over a year's time, he'd lost his kinsman Tom Peirce in the massacre; his beloved friend and son-in-law, John Rolfe; his superior Captain Powell; and, now, Sam.

And Cecily—had lost her second husband, the father of her unborn child. She was barely twenty-three.

And as for Sam, I didn't think Will would even be well enough for us to see him buried.

All My Heart is Buried with You

Late March 1623
New Towne, Virginia

All my heart is buried with you,
All my thoughts go onward with you!
Come not back again to labor,
Come not back again to suffer,
Where the Famine and the Fever
Wear the heart and waste the body.
— Henry Wadsworth Longfellow

When Will began to stir, I asked Angelo to fetch him some water. Meanwhile, I made a posset of chamomile, sassafras, cream, and sack. *Calming and curing,* I thought.

Will hurt so much he had to lie very still, but he called me to his bed. I brought the flagon with the posset and suggested he try to sit up. With much straining, he was able to get himself turned and sitting upright. His eyes sparked with pain several times, and once he cried out, although I knew he didn't want to.

He took my hand. "Joan, go to Sam's burying." His eyes were serious and unyielding.

I shook my head. "I can't leave you in such condition. I have a plan for the herbs, for the cleaning of your wound with poplar gum, and I've made a hog's grease salve of healing herbs. No one can do this as well as I can. Well, except for Dr. Pott, but he has too many to care for already."

"Talk to Esther or Angelo. I'm sure one or both of them are capable of following the herbal recipe. I think it's more important that you be there for Cecily and to mourn for both of us." Will knew that Angelo had learned enough of our herbs to help heal me when I had the contagion.

To mourn for both of us. Could it be that my going might help Will? That he would feel he was doing something for Cecily? Still, the correct administering of the herbs was important to Will's recovery, and I told him so.

He shook his head. "Go for me. Sending you for Cecily and the girls is the last thing I can do for Sam." His voice choked as he said Sam's name. "He sacrificed all for me. I can sacrifice some for him."

Solemnly, I nodded, stroking his hand. "Aye, husband," was all I said.

When I talked to Esther, she seemed apprehensive about managing the herbs. Angelo looked intrigued. "You can both do it. It's good to learn. I'll leave you types and amounts and what to do. I think Dick Townshend from next door might help you as well, and I'm sure Dr. Pott wouldn't mind looking in."

Reluctantly, Esther agreed. Angelo said, "I can do it, missus. We got the healing herbs in Angola, too."

I hugged each of them and thanked them.

I ran from there to the governor's house. I hoped it was not too late to catch the next ship—the one that would be taking Sam home.

A Mother's Life

Early April 1623
New Towne and Jordan's Journey, Virginia

A mother's life, you see, is one long succession of dramas, now soft and tender, now terrible. Not an hour but has its joys and fears.
—Honoré de Balzac

Several men had put Sam's coffin on a ship, and I was able to go along as well. I wanted to be with Cecily. I was only about a day behind Jane, who had gone to bear the news.

The men, such as Sir George and Roger Smith, had no freedom for such a thing as a funeral, even if they might want to go. Soon would be another battle.

I was climbing the plank, when a voice behind me cried, "You're not going without me!"

Tempie! Beside her stood her daughter Elizabeth, who said she was coming along, too.

"Well," I said to her, "that contents me much."

I turned and embraced Elizabeth and then Tempie with thankfulness.

Tempie pulled back and looked at me with deep concern. "What happened? I only know part. How is Will? You sent Jane to give Cecily the news?" Tempie was firing questions at me rapidly.

I explained to her about the dual ambushes from the mutineers and the Indians. "And now we've lost our Sam." I finished, my voice a lament.

The trip to Jordan's Journey, some thirty miles up the river, meant a day's travel, provided we could catch the incoming tide. As the few, abandoned settlements drifted by on either side of the river, it reminded me again of the horror and bloodshed the day of the massacre. I shut my eyes tightly, as though I could blind myself to the thought. But I couldn't.

Yet this one thing I knew. Sam's final year had been valiant. Without his being able to hold his settlement after the massacre, James Town and the other held settlements would have teemed with even more people. Sam had brought many of the nearby survivors to Jordan's Journey instead. Even so, we'd still been so overcrowded that disease had ravaged us. But how much worse might it have been?

The sun had dropped low when we saw Jordan's Point. The captain eased the ship to the shore and tied it off.

I inhaled sharply. What could I say to Cecily, twice a widow at twenty-three? Expecting a child?

Dear God, give me words.

We didn't tarry near the ship but hurried for the safety of the palisade. The dangers this far upriver were rife as the war continued.

One home, larger than the others reflecting that Sam had been the master of the plantation, stood apart. A servant called out, asking who we were. "Mrs. Jordan's mother," I said, and felt the words catch in my throat. "And we bring Master Jordan home," I added.

The door swung open, and we walked inside. Behind us, a group of soldiers carried Sam's coffin up the hill towards the palisade.

My heart was heavy in my chest, and I felt very old.

Tempie and I knocked on the door of Cecily and Sam's home. Jane opened it wide, falling into the arms of both Tempie and me.

"Mother, auntie," she whispered. "Come in."

When Cecily emerged from a back chamber, I saw that she was great with child. Her face wore a mournful expression, her eyes rimmed in red.

She didn't speak, but embraced me, holding me for a long time. Another babe to be born with a father lost to war—just as Cecily herself had been.

"How will I manage?" she whispered. "This great plantation. So many people sheltering here, a new baby, the two young ones I have ..."

I started to say that Sam had died honorably—heroically even—trying to save her father. But then a damp September room in Dorset many years ago and the shadowy figures of Will Peirce and Sam Jordan came to me. They'd come to tell me how Cecily's father had died and had innocently, even proudly, said that he'd died an honorable death. My anger had flared. *Would that it had been a dishonorable life than an honorable death so soon!* I had cried out as I, too, had been great with a child who would never know her father.

No, it was cold consolation to the bereaved to know that the loss had been heroic, especially to one who carried an unborn child.

As if on cue, little Temperance, now seven, came down the stairs, holding the hand of her little sister Mary, just two.

"Father?" The smaller girl looked about the room.

Temperance wrapped her arms around her younger sister and said, "No, Mary. Father's gone."

"Gone a-fightin' Ind'ns?" The little girl's wide blue eyes gazed into those of her sister.

Little Temp turned helplessly to her mother, and Cecily beckoned them both to her. She wrapped an arm about each little girl and said, "Mary, your father won't …" She drew a deep breath. "He won't have to fight anymore. He is gone to be with the angels. Gone to heaven," she added simply.

This swept me back to Cecily trying to console me after her brother Jack had died. She'd said almost these same words all those years ago when she herself had been the small girl. I felt caught in some circle, some play where actors recited the same lines, and sadness replayed itself again and again. If I had wanted to be strong for Cecily and the girls, it was not to be. Sadness overcame me.

Life truly seemed to be one long road of meeting, loving, and letting go.

A Sweet and Virtuous Soul

Early April 1623
Jordan's Journey, Virginia

Sweet spring, full of sweet dayes and roses,
A box where sweets compacted lie;
My musick shows ye have your closes,
And all must die.
Onely a sweet and virtuous soul,
Like season'd timber, never gives ...
—George Herbert, 1633, used with the Anglican
Funeral Liturgy

Life in Virginia was hard, not least because we buried so many so quickly, and our grief stacked up. Tears upon tears while the demands of the colony fell relentlessly upon us. In England, Cecily might have had time to mourn Sam's death, to cloister herself, and to tend to her children until the grief eased away.

In Virginia, she was now the mistress of a plantation which included many smaller plantations absorbed into it from the massacre. Far from James Town, Jordan's Journey remained vulnerable to Indian attack even with its palisade and soldiers.

Sam had planned well. He'd seen to the planting and harvesting and ensured he had adequate supplies of corn, men, arms, and animals. Who would do that now? Cecily's mind was faint with the challenge, even as we prepared for Sam's funeral.

Will was right. I needed to be here, I thought. We saw that Cecily had dressed the children in their Sunday clothes. She let them each touch the beveled, gabled coffin wherein Sam lay. The coffin was in the great hall of their home, and I could swear that Sam's presence filled the room. *Perhaps,* I thought, *a stout heart such as Sam's still feels present, even when he's not.*

A little contentment I felt since Sam was here with us and not upon some foreign battlefield, where my Tom had lain. *A cold comfort.*

The next morning, a Sunday, rain pelted the ground, making the path down to the ship muddy and slippery. We were all preparing to board the ship to cross the river over to Shirley Hundred.

None of the three plantations furthest upriver—Shirley, Flowerdieu, and Jordan's Journey—had a church just yet. The three shared a pastor and church services. The pastor, a man named Greville Pooley, conducted services by turns at the largest homes in each settlement.

At Shirley, that was the home of Captain Isaac Madison, the plantation's commander, where we were all bound this grey morning.

When a death occurred near Sunday, the pastor performed the funeral liturgy after his Sabbath service.

We crossed the river in the spring downpour, which pattered the ship and the river all around us like a dirge.

As we made our way up the banks, I noticed a small crowd hurrying to what must have been Captain Madison's house. In front stood Captain Madison, ringing a bell to call the parishioners to church. The downpour drenched the cloaks of all as they splattered through the mud.

We'd lost countless souls this past year. Many had seen the deep ground without a funeral at all. But Sam had considerable respect upriver. His fortified plantation had allowed many to stay nearer their own homes, even as Cecily and Sam endured the crowding. Sam had been looking forward to them returning to their homes. His own plantation had been growing along with his family.

Muted voices fell to either side of me as I myself said nothing.

Would Sam have died if he hadn't turned back? He'd chosen Will over his own safety, and it had cost him his life.

"Good Sabbath, pastor," I heard someone say to a man near me.

"Good Sabbath," the pastor returned idly.

I glanced over at Pastor Pooley, a squat and balding man who'd arrived in Virginia just after the massacre. Then I noticed the coffin being borne off ship on the shoulders of six men.

Sam's home, I thought and then burst into tears.

Cecily had friends upriver, it was easy to see. A few came over to her to offer comfort, which lifted me a little.

Some of those bearing Sam's coffin I knew.

Nat Causey and his wife Thomasine were Starving Time survivors.

Nat had impressed many the day of the massacre. With a cruel and bloody wound, Nat had still managed to cleave a native's head with an axe. Seeing this, the other Indians had fled. Then, like so many others, the Causeys had abandoned Causey's Care for the security of Jordan's Journey. There, Nat had recovered from his injuries.

Also helping carry Sam's coffin was Mr. Farrar, an attorney who'd arrived on Lord De La Warr's ship in 1618. Mr. Farrar had survived the contagion on ship that had cost the baron his life.

I recognized also Mr. Palmer. He, his wife, and young daughter had been on Elfrith's ship, the *Tyger*, when the Turks struck near Spain. The couple had endured not one but two calamities in the span of a few months since they'd also managed to survive the massacre. Mr. Palmer had grieved the death of George Thorpe, hard, but had duly inventoried Thorpe's estate.

It was hard to be here upriver and not see the shattered dreams of those few who had managed to survive the hardest hit plantations. Assaulted but alive, they had made their way to Sam's plantation. The attack had forced all to abandon, at least for now, the dream of an English college and Indian school as well as the ironworks.

As we followed the coffin into the home, the Reverend Pooley fell into step with Cecily.

"Deepest sympathies, mistress," he said, leaning in closely and offering Cecily his arm.

Jane glanced at me. Was that appropriate?

No, it wasn't. Pastor Pooley should have met the coffin at the door and escorted it in as we followed. But Mr. Pooley was rather occupied with Cecily instead.

Cecily waved him off, saying, "I'm fine, sir. My girls will hold my hands. But I do thank you kindly." The pastor nodded politely, but he somehow made me feel uncomfortable. Something a little too forward. Something, too, in the way he stared at Cecily. *Today, sir, is Sam's day,* I wanted to say. *Have a mite of decency.*

But then, perhaps it was only my imagining things.

Sitting alongside Jane, Cecily, Tempie, and me were the four little girls. First Little Temp, then little Mary, Cecily's girls. Jane held the infant Sarah Macock on her lap. Beside them were Jane's Elizabeth and Wee Bess Salter. Jane said she now had three girls, not one. Tempie sat beside her daughter, also Elizabeth. We women made a line of strength. The thought of both my daughters widowed so young, and Cecily twice at that, caused my eyes to burn with tears. Yet, I told myself, we can overcome anything so long as we have each other.

Following the funeral, Sam's coffin returned on the ship 'cross the river to Jordan's Journey for burial. Afterward, we sat for a family meal—Cecily, Jane, Tempie, the children, and I.

"Do you need Roger to come here to help you tend things a while?" Jane was asking Cecily as she cut her ham. "To help you get the plantation's affairs in order?"

Cecily smiled appreciatively. "Jane, Roger has many duties in James Cittie, much as I appreciate the offer. I'm not sure the governor would let him slip away! Sam has written in his will that Mr. Farrar should take the mantle of Jordan's Journey should anything happen to him. Mr. Farrar has already come to me this morning and said he was glad to help. He's an attorney by training, so he'll help me with the estate as well. His plantation nearby he has abandoned since the late massacre."

"Sam must've trusted Master Farrar a great deal," I commented.

Cecily agreed. "He's a good man—fair, hardworking, and honest. Sam often left him in command when he sailed back to James Cittie. Master Farrar knows what we need to do around here and is able."

What a relief to hear this. "Good! I was worried about you. It's a large plantation."

"To tell the truth, I was worried, too, until I realized that Mr. Farrar could take charge. Sam had already thought about the eventuality of his ... death." Cecily still found this a hard word to say.

Just three days after Sam's funeral, we all headed home. I daren't leave Will too long.

Yet had I known the next ordeal awaiting Cecily, I might have stayed on.

When the Fox Preaches

Early April 1623
Jordan's Journey, Virginia

Take care of your geese when the fox preaches.
—Danish proverb

The funeral three days over, the master of the ship said he needed to return to James Cittie. We, I regretted to admit, needed to leave as well.

I gave my daughter a kiss, hugged the girls, and asked once more if Cecily would be all right. She nodded, her eyes tired.

"If I didn't have to get back to your father, I'd stay," I said, feeling the need of being in two places, as if I were not truly there for Cecily or Will. My own grief for Sam I must bury below all the other needs, for how else to get through it? This year had taken all from us that we had to give.

"I'm all right, mother. Mrs. Palmer and Mrs. Causey are nearby, and Mr. Farrar has promised to oversee the plantation. I just need time to take slow steps, I think."

I agreed.

My ship was not long downriver when Cecily heard a rap on her door. She opened it to find the commander of West and Shirley Hundred. Captain Madison shifted from foot to foot and seemed terribly uncomfortable.

Cecily opened the door fully to him as the captain held his cap in his hands.

"Is something wrong, Captain Madison?" Cecily asked. "A threat from the Indians we should know about? Should I call in Mr. Farrar?"

"Uh, might I come in, Mrs. Jordan? And no, nothing is wrong."

Cecily showed him into her home, wondering what would bring Captain Madison to see her.

"Mrs. Jordan, I'll not beat about the bush as it were. Parson Pooley has entreated me here on his behalf. He'd like to make a match with you."

Cecily stared at Captain Madison for a few moments.

At last, she said, "I covet your pardon, captain, for I do not understand. Is he proposing marriage?"

"Ah, yes. He approached me a few days ago. I told him I wouldn't meddle in such business, but he was right persuasive."

"Captain Madison, I suppose you and others at Shirley know this, but I'm with child. My husband is but three days buried. I'd as willingly have Pastor Pooley as any other, but I won't marry any man until I'm delivered."

Madison swallowed. "I see. I do understand, Mrs. Jordan. I'm sorry to have troubled you so soon after your husband's passing. My condolences to you and your family."

Cecily nodded wordlessly. What did Pooley think? That she would engage herself to him just days after Sam's passing and even worse—while great with child?

She shut the door behind Captain Madison and leaned against it.

And then she covered her face in her hands and cried.

I Sysley Take Thee Grivell

Mid-April 1623
Jordan's Journey, Virginia

"I Sysley take thee Grivell to my wedded husband, to have and to hold till death us depart."

—Greville Pooley as quoted by Capt. Isaac Madison
under oath, 4 June 1623

Cecily had to assume that her words to Captain Madison had emboldened Pastor Pooley because soon enough he came to her himself.

"Is it true what the commander says?" Mr. Pooley asked, lifting her hand in his after church the following Sunday.

"'Tis true depending on what you heard. What I did say, sir, is that I would as soon have you as any but *not* until I'm delivered. Surely you understand that."

"Oh, wonderful, wonderful news!" And the pastor's grin spread from ear to ear like a fox.

Only later did it occur to Cecily that he never did say he understood it.

A pinnace pulled ashore at Jordan's Journey a week later. Thomasine Causey saw it first and came running to Cecily's house.

"Cecily, dear, I see Captain Madison and his wife along with Mr. Pooley disembarking." Thomasine's face wrinkled a little in worry.

Cecily touched the older woman's arm. "Have no fear, Thomasine, for I've made myself clear enough. I think so, at least." This last she said to herself.

"You and Sam have made old Nat and me comfortable here after the Indians forced us out o' Causey's Care." Thomasine appreciated being able to live here in safety, and she credited Cecily and Sam their due. She was, therefore, protective of Cecily in her mourning. "I think it's disrespectful for a man of God to show himself so interested in you this soon upon your husband's death and you with child!"

"Yes, true enough. We'll see how he behaves himself."

The trio was coming into the palisade gate now, and Thomasine gave them a scowl. She, like so many of us, had a native distrust for newcomers. The land we'd worked and earned was ours. Pooley had come after the massacre. As far as Thomasine was concerned, he had no claim to the land we'd been able to hold. And no one had suffered more than those upriver.

"Good day, Mrs. Causey. Good day, Mrs. Jordan!" The parson threw a giddy wave. "We've come to pay a call."

"I got me wash to tend," Thomasine grumbled. We needed more pastors, sure. But a pastor who angered his congregation, well, that we could do without.

"I see that you're here to visit. Have you come to see me?" Cecily knew the answer but decided to pretend.

"Well, of course, who else?"

Wordlessly, Cecily turned and gestured toward her doorway.

"I ... I hope we're not intruding, Mrs. Jordan," Mary Madison said gingerly.

Mrs. Madison looked uncomfortable, Cecily noticed. "No, Mrs. Madison, come and sit for a spell."

As soon as they were inside, Mr. Pooley said to Cecily, "I should like a dram, please."

"Fine enough. Ann, please fetch a dram for Mr. Pooley."

The servant girl started for the kitchen where the wine was stored.

"Ah, no." Mr. Pooley said it forcefully enough that the young servant heard him and stopped. To Cecily, he said, "I'll have it of *your* fetching it or not at all."

The Madisons were watching the scene, and Cecily now understood they were here as witnesses.

"Very well," she said. *I am to be respectful to a preacher. This I know.*

Cecily went into the kitchen and was preparing a drink for her guest when she heard footfalls behind her. Turning, she saw that the preacher and his commander had followed her to the chamber.

"Now, Mrs. Jordan, I'll contract myself unto you. I, Greville Pooley, take thee Cecily to my wedded wife, to have and to hold till death us depart and thereto I plight thee my troth."

Cecily was so startled that she thought the room was beginning to spin. Sam's death, the two fatherless girls, a new baby ...

The crafty pastor reached for and held Cecily's hand.

What's happening? She thought. *Is this a betrothal or a wedding?*

Still holding her hand, the pastor recited, "I, Cecily, take thee Greville to my wedded husband, to have and to hold till death us depart."

Cecily gaped, hearing the pastor say what should have been her vow in a wedding ceremony. Captain Madison turned to the pastor in surprise as well.

Cecily looked down at her hand and then up at the man who had just recited her vows for her. In a wedding that was not even taking place, to a woman who had just lost her husband and was still carrying his baby.

She felt as if the floor itself were moving as she tried to make sense of these odd events.

"A toast, my dear!" Mr. Pooley lifted the jug and poured two drams, handing her one. He took a drink and said, "Well?"

She lifted the cup to her lips.

He then kissed her and crowed his toast. "I am thine and thou art mine till death us separate!"

He had not asked her permission for any of this, not even the kiss, nor had she answered anything he'd said.

Finally finding her voice, Cecily stammered, "Mr. Pooley, I do desire that you not reveal this to any. That ... that I did so soon bestow my love after my husband's death."

"My love, I promise before God that I will not reveal it until you think the time fitting."

Loose and False Ground

Mid-April 1623
New Towne, Virginia

As you know this land hath felt the affliction of Warr, sense of sicknes and death of a great nomber of men, likewise among the Cattle for doggs have eaten this winter more flesh then the men: And he that had 40 hoggs about his house hath one or two: and a hundredth henns hath now 3 or 4 ...
—Surgeon William Rowsley to his brother, 3 April 1623

I often wish little Mr. Farrar here, that to his zeale he would add knowledge of this Contrey.
—Sir Francis Wyatt, writing privately to his father,
4 April 1623

Will's wound had begun weeping, but the poplar gum poured over it seemed to help. Within a week after I'd returned from Cecily's, Will was up and moving around.

Mr. Sandys, meanwhile, was preparing to visit the glasshouse.

"The Italians called me a rascal to my face!" he said as he sat down to the morning meal. This was quite an insult. Poor Mr. Sandys was attempting to corral the Italians who would prefer to be anywhere but here.

They, of course, were far from alone in that.

Then to Will, Mr. Sandys said, "You've heard that Captain Each has died, have you not?"

Will nodded, saying, "Aye. And how will we build that fort upon the oyster shells now?" Will paused. Then Mr. Sandys and I both realized he was jesting.

"He saved his own honor by dying before he attempted it!" Sandys agreed.

Then he chuckled. Mr. Sandys had a tendency to say exactly what he thought.

The mood in the settlements was so dour, we took whatever small cheer we could. Those in Virginia blamed two people for the vast sickness in the colony—Duppa who brewed the rancid beer and Each who overfilled his ship while leaving the corn behind.

"I suppose we shouldn't speak ill of the dead. Yet I have no love lost for Captain Each," Mr. Sandys said apologetically.

"No one does," I agreed.

Yet the contagion had cost Each his own life, too. A parable against greed if there ever were one.

Each had come over, making great talk of the fort he'd build. The Company had agreed to pay him handsomely for it and even sent men and supplies with him. Captain Each and the Company expected the beleaguered settlers of Martin's Hundred and Southampton to help him build it. These folks were already barely alive on scant corn and reeling from their massacre losses.

This fort was to be over on Tindall's Shoals at Blunt Point. Anyone here, even a woman or boy, could show a better understanding of the site than Captain Each had. While it might look promising drawn upon a map, the actual grounds consisted of oyster shells which easily collapsed.

We did indeed need a fort to protect us from the Spaniards. Despite all these other disasters, no one had forgotten the Spanish attack on the *Margaret and John*. Pushed from our minds, aye; forgotten, no.

But an oyster-shell fort was not the way.

The oyster-shell fort proved what we'd long known. The Company had little idea of how things worked for us, what life was like here, even the very nature of our struggles. Of hunger, weakness, and disease in such numbers those in England had seldom seen the like.

The *Abigail's* contagion had now taken as many or more lives than the massacre. In the massacre, we lost one settler for every three, be it man, woman, or child. Now after the contagion, another one of those three had died. We'd seen nothing like this since the Starving Time. On top of that, our livestock was dying off, too, as if a curse had swept the land.

"Captain Each had a hand in both the continuing famine and the sweeping illness here, and I feel that ... well ... I suppose I should say not more." Sandys shifted in his chair.

"We're all thinking it anyway," I made bold to say.

Mr. Sandys gave me something of a wink. "If we don't say it aloud, I suppose God can't punish us. Perhaps he reckons thrusting Each on us were already punishment enough!"

I seated myself with the men. I had a question, and everyone in the colony was asking the same one. But I hoped Mr. Sandys might have some knowledge he could share.

"Mr. Sandys, does the council know anything of the *Sea Flower*? Has anyone seen her?"

This long-promised ship was carrying the corn we needed to see us to our next harvest. We were already beginning to sow corn, but we still needed to make it from the spring to the next harvest in the fall.

We knew, too, that the Company promised that the *Sea Flower* would carry gunpowder and the Welsh longbows.

Mr. Sandys swirled his beer around in the flagon and took a sip. Then he said, "No, I'm sorry to say it, Mistress Peirce, but we know nothing of the *Sea Flower*. We of the council all wonder of it as you do."

The days came and went, suns rose and dropped behind the trees, and we grew more and more hungry.

Yet the *Sea Flower* never came. Why? We could only wonder bitterly. Where was this ship?

* * *

Unknown to us, the *Sea Flower* was nearby even as I asked Mr. Sandys about her. She had stopped at the Bermudas after a trying voyage. The Company had loaded down her holds with corn, a reprieve just waiting to come to our storehouses in Virginia. Sixty barrels of corn filled to the top.

Corn, sorely needed gunpowder, and the longbows, just as promised. But the Company had gotten to discussing it and decided those longbows were as dangerous as we knew them to be in the hands of the Indians. *Leave them in Bermuda*, someone suggested. *If the Virginia colonists are desperate for them, 'tis a short voyage to the Bermudas. No Indians there!*

The *Sea Flower* had landed in Bermuda after a long and stormy voyage.

Festivities for a safe arrival on ship! The captain was delighted to entertain in the great cabin. Many guests came on board the ship from the Somers Isles to join the arriving colonists and crew.

One man, a Mr. Carter, came aboard with his wife.

Mr. Carter had lived in the Bermudas longer than anyone. He'd been on the *Sea Venture* when it shipwrecked there in '09 with Will. When the shipwrights at last finished building two rustic ships to come to Virginia, Mr. Carter had refused boarding. Instead, he had stayed behind with two others. Some said the men were holding the islands for England; some called them deserters. The men had cheerfully dubbed themselves "The Three Kings of Bermuda," its sole inhabitants.

Now, thirteen years later, Carter still lived in Bermuda as an English colony had grown up around him. He and his wife, like everyone present, welcomed the chance for a celebration.

Every man's pipe lit, and rum all around.

"Tap the firkin again, lad!" Mr. Carter cried to the ship's boy across the smoky cabin.

Those would be his last words.

A mighty *boom* echoed across the island as flames and smoke speckled with black rubble filled the night sky.

Eighteen died, and many more would carry the burned and scarred faces the rest of their lives.

Mr. Carter's days in Bermuda ended right there in the fire and smoke and drowning waters.

Later, witnesses would wonder about the cause. A spark from a pipe on all that gunpowder, many said. It had to be, sure.

Pillagers made their way to the wreck, seeking treasures of their own, some of them dying in the effort.

The gunpowder we needed to defend ourselves in Virginia, all gone in a whirlwind of red fire and black planking, flying through the air and into the sea.

But the corn? Many more than eighteen in Virginia died from lack of it.

We would study the horizon, fruitlessly, through many more months. But the *Sea Flower* lay in splinters on the ocean floor, and the corn fed the fish.

She Burns, She Frets

Late April 1623
Shirley Hundred, Virginia

She dreads the treacherous house, the double tongue;
She burns, she frets—by Juno's rancour stung ...
　　　—William Wordsworth

Nearly a month after his arrow wound, Will recovered enough to get back to the field. He wasn't one to remain inside long, injured or not. I suspected that like me, Will was using staying busy as a tonic for the sadness he felt over Sam's death.

"You're sure that Mr. Farrar has Sam's plantation well in hand? Does he need help?" Will was like a caged bird looking for a way out of his coop.

I assured him that while he might want to go see for himself, Cecily felt comfortable with matters out there.

In the end, Will rested on Sam and Cecily's belief in Mr. Farrar. He planned instead to go to Mulberry Island to see what he needed to do there, also to Martin's Hundred. He'd be taking soldiers with him in case of attack.

"Will, I don't wish you to go back to fighting right yet. Checking on the fields and servants, aye, but you've taken a bad injury, and ..."

Will put his arms around me. "I love you because you do worry about me. But Joan, I need to drill with my company. My responsibilities lie on the field. Besides, staying here only reminds me of Sam. I'd rather be out and thinking of my duties."

I nodded, but with reluctance. I'd known he would not stay inside long. That simply was not Will, who could not bear being idle.

* * *

Come the next Sabbath, Mr. Biggs took his turn hosting church in his home out at Shirley Hundred. Cecily arrived with her little girls in tow, fatigued from the rigors of being head of a large settlement.

The plantation owners upriver were in the most precarious position with the Indians, being so distant from James Cittie. Many who had sought shelter at Sam's stayed on even after the Company granted them permission to leave. The Causeys, for one, knew they'd only barely escaped death at the hands of the Indians. Stay on? Why, sure.

Sam had always gotten on with Nat, as Cecily had with Thomasine. Thomasine was older, of course, so she in her way looked after Cecily. Since I was so far away, it was comforting to have old settlers there.

Part of our resentment to newcomers was their arrogance in thinking they could have handled our trials better than we had. They were certain, too, they knew the right way to proceed; they would have done things differently had they been here. *Wait until ye hear my ideas for the ironworks! Store the salt this way. Build the house that way.*

Greville Pooley had arrived only months before he proposed to Cecily. Just his being a new arrival was enough for Thomasine to give Mr. Pooley a scowl every time she saw him. Thomasine was a Starving Time survivor. She'd earned her keep, thank you.

Services were about to begin. Mr. Biggs stood outside his home ringing the bell. *Time for church!*

Cecily was walking toward Mr. Biggs's home with Thomasine holding the little ones' hands. Mrs. Palmer had joined them alongside. At the water's edge, Nat was securing the pinnace with Mr. Farrar's help.

"G'day, Mr. Biggs!" Thomasine called out to him.

"G'day, Mrs. Causey," he said, shaking the bell again loudly.

Parson Pooley greeted each one as they came through the door, but his eyes alit on none as they did on Cecily. It was painfully obvious to both Thomasine and Mrs. Palmer, or so Cecily suspected.

Cecily understood that she herself was a prize. She'd inherited two hundred acres, both her divident and Sam's. And then her daughter Little Temp had become an heiress of another hundred acres when the child's father Tom Bailey had died. How fortunate she and little Temp had been to survive the illness which claimed Tom Bailey's life.

Then, too, she and both her daughters had survived the most recent contagion *and* the massacre. Sam's planning in well fortifying the plantation and his caution with the Indians had saved them all.

Sam had told Captain Roger Smith, before he'd courted Jane, that he could hold the savages off. Roger had believed him. Roger's assent had largely been what had swayed the governor and council to allow Sam to stay.

Now, here she was with Sam gone. Killed by an Indian arrow near James Town after fending off the surprise attack from the previous year. It didn't seem right.

Pooley's stares, even while preaching, were making her greatly uncomfortable.

She'd rather think of Sam, of the coming baby and her girls, even of her mother's knot garden far away in Melcombe Regis. Anything but the leer she was seeing.

As Reverend Pooley went through the Anglican service, Cecily caught her eyes wandering. Was it in her mind, or were folks looking sidewise at her?

As Cecily was leaving that morning, Captain Harris's wife Dorothy greeted her cautiously. Captain Harris himself was an old planter. He touched his cap to her.

"Mrs. Jordan," Mrs. Harris said slowly, "how do you fare since Mr. Jordan's death?"

Cecily sighed. "Loss is a part of life, especially *this* life. The living must keep going, and my children need me. But I thank you for asking."

Dorothy nodded approvingly. Cecily had passed the test, she supposed. Then, "Um, do you mind a question?" Dorothy asked with hesitation.

Cecily shrugged with uncertainty.

"Art thou betrothed to the pastor?" Dorothy asked cautiously.

Now Cecily gaped, widening her eyes in disbelief. "Where did you hear that?"

"From Mr. Pooley himself."

Only once in her young life had Cecily's vision ever gone completely red, and it was at this moment. Everything in front of her turned crimson. Reverend Pooley had given a promise before God not to reveal the engagement, an engagement he'd already pushed upon her. She would not have him make a fool of her before the upriver settlements—a grieving, expectant widow rematched to the pastor on the sudden.

"No, I'll not marry him!" Right that moment, right there in front of the Biggs's home, Cecily had decided.

"But did you give your word to him?" Mrs. Harris leaned in. "You cannot break the betrothal."

"I can, and I will," Cecily said with her jaw set.

At that moment, Mr. Pooley approached, his head held high as he smiled at his betrothed. "Good day, my love!"

But if the pastor had known Cecily as her sister and I did, the man would have seen her eyes afire, and not with love.

But for His Owne Words

Late April 1623
Shirley Hundred, Virginia

*John Harris Sworne and examined saith that he heard Mrs Jordan say that
Mr Pooley might thanke himself, for he might have fared the better but for his
owne words.*
  —Minutes of the Council and General Court,
  17 November 1623

D o not greet me by first name or call me 'love.' Never greet me again
except as your parishioner, Mr. Pooley. I'll not marry you, not now
or ever." Cecily's voice was even, her tone firm.

This my daughter who, when I'd asked if she could remain in England
without us, had replied, "I can, and I will!" The little girl who had believed her father dead in a hurricane and her mother and younger sister
likely starved to death. Who had walked into Dale's martial law and lived dual
widowhood by age twenty-three. Who had overseen a settlement filled with
refuge-seekers from other outlying homesteads after Sam's death. Who was
now raising two daughters, and soon another child, alone.

Surprise bemuddled the pastor's face. "Oh, my dear, I know that you've
already promised yourself unto me. Of *course*, we'll marry." His voice had a
slightly threatening tone.

Greville Pooley might have been able to impress the Virginia Company.
He might even have a prestigious position as pastor to all those upriver. But
he'd never encountered the will of the woman before him.

He was about to.

"I can, and I will break it. Who'll force me to marry you? Yourself, sir?
No, I forswear it. I'll not marry you, Mr. Pooley."

Now the pastor's voice was icy. "I conceive that you do owe me a reason,
Cecily."

"Call me Mrs. Jordan, please, and I'm delighted to give you a reason. You made a promise to me *before God* that you should not reveal our match until *I* thought the time fitting. Sir, I do not yet think the time fitting, and thou hast already spoken of it before the town, before your congregation! Think you I would not discover your perfidy?"

The pastor colored. "Uh, I conceived enough time had lapsed that ..."

A few curious eyes were on them, but Cecily no longer cared.

"I'm still great with child, sir," she said in a whisper. Then, raising her voice—let all hear, she cared not—"You might thank yourself. You would have fared the better but for your own words!"

Mr. Farrar was watching from a distance. He came forward and offered to see the upset young widow to her shallop.

She readily accepted without a single look to those staring or whispering or even to the jilted pastor.

Greville Pooley watched them depart with a frozen glare.

He was a man who didn't take the word *no* lightly. He was not yet done with Cecily.

Fleshed in Each Others Bloud

April to Late May 1623
New Towne, Virginia

They are ingaged in a mortall warre and fleshed in each others bloud ...
—Capt. John Harvey's report, speaking of the Indians
and English, after a visit to Virginia, 1625

While Cecily was struggling with the pastor upriver, the Indian war was raging on and on.

The Indians, we heard, were as weary of war as we were and just as hungry. But our men said we needed more revenge. Emperor Opechancanough had a bounty on his head.

Back in March while many were still recovering their illnesses, Captain Henry Spelman had gone a-trading. He took with him twenty-six well-armed men on the *Tyger*.

The ship came back empty but for the sailors. The governor and councilors were trying to learn what had happened.

Ambush, the sailors explained. Those on ship had known the soldiers met their fate when a head rolled down the hill.

Spelman was one of the best and most experienced interpreters in the colony. He had a longstanding friendship with the Anacostia Indians and thought they might want to trade for corn. He reckoned his friendship would carry them through.

He reckoned wrong.

The *Tyger* had sailed up to the mouth of the Anacostia's River, the sailors said. The parley went sour, and the frightened sailors hied back to James Town.

All the men were lost.

Now in our frightened, hungry, ailing state, the leaders at James Town declared no mercy, no parley, no treaties.

We were surprised when early in April, the settlers of Martin's Hundred brought us a native in chains.

"Comahum!" they said. He had helped murder their friends at Martin's that terrible day. With him was Will's friend Chacrow. Chacrow was a free man as he had not only not refused to take part in the massacre but had warned settlers of it.

Chacrow explained that his people had great famine. The burnt cornfields had created the hunger we'd expected. "Comahum is a great man. He has come on his own," Chacrow explained. Comahum, he said, had not asked permission of Opechancanough to plead for peace.

"Twenty of your women we have as captives," Chacrow said. The natives would like to use these women, who'd lived with them a year, to bargain for peace.

Most of the captives, it seems, had come from Martin's Hundred, and Tom Peirce's plantation had been between Martin's Hundred and Mulberry Island. Will reckoned there to be a fair chance the Indians were holding Alice and Elizabeth. He considered how best to help his kinsman's wife and child.

By May, we received a desperate message from Opitchapam. *I shall return the captives we have and also deliver unto you my brother Opechancanough, alive or dead.*

The men at James Town received that message, and all thought the same: sly Opechancanough was setting a trap.

They would not step into it.

Soon, the hot-tempered interpreter Robert Poole was off to Opitchapam with Chacrow and Comahum. The bags of beads he carried were to serve as pay, and the faithful Chacrow would help negotiate for the prisoners.

A week later, Chacrow brought Sara Boyse to James Town and walked her over to the governor's home. I blinked when I saw her from my window. She wore Indian jewelry made of shells and copper and had a long, deerskin mantle. The dress of an Indian queen. She was gaunt and browned from the sun. She looked almost like an Indian herself.

"We account her chief of the prisoners," Chacrow explained.

"I worked alongside the other native women in the stifling hot fields, Sir Francis," Mrs. Boyse told the governor. "We all have. Those who were with me still do. Had your man Poole the interpreter not offended the chief, all would be here today."

Soon, the Indians released the other prisoners and among them came Tom Peirce's wife Alice and her daughter Elizabeth. Thin and dark as Mrs. Boyse had been, the two told of working long hours in the Indian fields alongside the native women, long and hard work.

"I thought we'd never survive it, Joan," said Alice. "Thank you for remembering us with the beads and copper. It did make a difference." She wore a look of fear that seemed to have made its home in her eyes.

I tried to hide my tears. "Of course," I murmured. "Of course, Alice."

Elizabeth petted her mother's shoulder. I remembered the way she'd comforted her mother after her brother had died on ship.

Now I comforted both women myself, sat them down to a hearty meal, and tried to imagine what they had witnessed—the horrors of the morning massacre, being carried off far away, waiting more than a year to return home.

Soon Alice and Elizabeth regained their footing, and each married.

Fearing to look back, both looked only forward.

Despite the prisoners' return, each side continued to play dangerous tricks on the other.

It was then that either Captain Tucker or Dr. Pott came up with a plan. Perhaps they could deceive the Indians into thinking we did desire peace. Travel there and toast to friendship. What if we could lace the celebratory wine with poison? Wasn't that the plan Opechancanough himself had come up with two years ago with the water hemlock?

Dr. Pott was an expert in distilled waters with many vials, so unlike Opechancanough, he was able to create the poison.

Captain Tucker secreted the lethal mix and traveled with his company to see Opechancanough in the summer.

The Patawomeck agreed to host a trap for the Powhatan Indians.

Invited to a peace parley, the natives came.

We are also tired of war, Captain Tucker told the Indians gathered, including Opechancanough. Our men feigned more speeches of peace, offering to toast to it with sack.

Let us have peace then, Opechancanough agreed.

For Spelman's twenty-six men and the hundreds more who perished in the massacre, Captain Tucker killed two hundred Indians with poison. Opechancanough drank of the wine, and we heard that he died. Then our men killed fifty more, cutting off their heads and bringing some of these back to James Town.

So much brutality. *When,* I wondered, *oh when, will this all end?*

Weary of the Ceaseless War

Early June 1623
New Towne, Virginia

Weary of the ceaseless war
Beating down the baffled soul ...
— Sir Henry Parkes

About that time, Cecily brought herself downriver by pinnace to James Cittie. Her baby was due in September. A pinnace's underdecks were sultry this time of year, but especially for one who was expecting. So when she came up the path to my house, it surprised me.

I came around from the garden where I was tending the figs, my own orchard. I shooed Cecily into the house and out of the midday heat.

"Lovey, you've come! Sit, sit, please. Where are the girls?"

"Thomasine is watching over them for me," she said with a sigh, rivulets of perspiration on her face.

"Oh, good." I poured her some mulberry beer. "Drink. This will help cool thee."

She took a sip and said, "You make quite good beer, mother. What do you grow in your new garden?" she asked.

"My little fig orchard, still just sprouts, truly. I'm not sure when to expect the fruit to come or even if it shall. But I have high hopes. Do you know Mr. Sandys says that Alexander the Great fed his armies figs when bread was short? I hope we have no more famines. But if we did, and my fig orchard is prospering ..." I let my voice drop off. Surely, we'd have no more famines! Still, it didn't hurt to have the promise of such an orchard.

Angelo was then coming down the stairs, so I asked her to go fetch Jane.

Then I pulled up a stool and sat by Cecily. "How do ye feel?" I didn't want to say, *What would get you on a pinnace in this heat?*

She didn't answer but drank a few sips of the beer. Then she asked if she might lie down, so I ushered her to our chamber.

"Father did fine work on this home," she observed. Of course, Will wasn't Cecily's true father, but he was the only one she'd ever known.

"Aye, he did." I paused, then tried to punch the pillow a little.

"Is Mr. Sandys still living upstairs?" She shut her eyes as she said it, and I could see her relax.

"He is, but he is down at the glasshouse right now. You probably haven't heard the news. Just days ago, the governor appointed your father captain of his guard and company. He is also now lieutenant governor and commander of James Cittie and all the island and blockhouses."

She opened her eyes slowly. "Because of Captain Powell's death, I'd reckon? Father has earned it, sure. He'll be a commander against the Indians in the summer raid, then, too?"

"Aye." That last worried me a bit.

Then Cecily added, "You knew Mr. Pooley was trouble, didn't you, mother?" she said wearily.

My heart fell. "Aye, I thought as much. What happened?"

She went on to tell me about the way Mr. Pooley had recited each of their vows, about how Mr. Madison was a witness with Mrs. Madison in the other room. Finally, about how the pastor had spoken of his coming wedding to her despite his vow not to.

"I'll not marry him now. He might blame himself as I told him." She opened her eyes and sat up. "'Tis Mr. Farrar I wish to marry. We've made a match. He's a kind man and a smart one, hardworking, too. So I've come here to the court to disavow the former betrothal and signify my intent to marry William Farrar."

"How is Mr. Pooley taking this? Does he agree to the disavowal?"

She closed her eyes again. "I care not how he takes it or whether he agrees. He can't *force* me to marry him." Then she opened her eyes and said angrily, "Mr. Pooley saying my vows for me is not the same as my saying them."

I had to agree.

Jane came into the house, and I called to tell her we were in the bedchamber. She sat herself down on the bed as well.

"Something serious must have brought you here in summer in this condition, Cecily."

And so Cecily went through her story once more.

"Will God judge me for this?" Cecily asked with genuine fear in her eyes.

I hesitated. A vow was a vow. But a vow contingent upon another vow? I considered.

At last, I said, "I have to think that God Himself finds Mr. Pooley tiring."

Both girls broke into peals of laughter. "Mother! Blaspheming a man of God," Cecily said. "Shame! But true enough."

I laughed, too.

Cecily stayed three days until the court was in session. There, she stood before those she had known long like Sir George Yeardley. She bravely disavowed herself of Parson Pooley, informing the court of her intention to marry Mr. Farrar.

Several weeks later, the pastor himself came to James Cittie, so I heard from Tempie. And he had brought a witness. Mr. Isaac Madison, to be exact.

Jilted women sometimes sued for breach of promise. Those women then became the butt of many a joke when word leaked out.

Mr. Pooley, it seemed, would be that rare man to sue for breach of promise. He was going to try to force Cecily to marry him.

All the Eagle in Thee

Late July to Mid-September 1623
New Towne and Jordan's Journey, Virginia

O thou undaunted daughter of desires!
By all the dower of lights and fires;
By all the eagle in thee, all the dove;
By all thy lives and deaths of love ...
—Richard Crashaw

By late July, the governor had commissioned Will to lead another expedition to the Chickahominy. With armor and sword at the ready, Will kissed me and left in August. I paced and fretted about the house until I could stand it no longer.

I want to do something. I could not think of the fighting any longer.

I made up my mind to sail for Jordan's Journey. I would help Cecily prepare for the coming baby, the child Sam would never see. Jane's household of children kept her busy with her husband away at Warraskoyack. He was building "the castle," as we called it, a fort there. The castle was to replace Captain Each's fort on the oyster banks.

I arrived to find Cecily weary. Managing the servants and her children, the livestock and worrying about the harvest was taking a toll on her.

"You do still wish to marry Mr. Farrar and not Mr. Pooley?" I asked, knowing the answer but wishing to hear it from her.

She nodded vigorously. "Oh, aye, unquestionably. Mr. Farrar *helps* me. I could not have survived the loss of Sam while also overseeing so many people here from other settlements. Yet Mr. Pooley harasses me. He has come here *six times* to demand that I keep my vows. He knows I renounced them. Captain Madison testified in court for him but said, as I hear, nothing more than that Mr. Pooley recited my vows for me."

"Aye, I heard." While I didn't wish to tell Cecily, all of James Town seemed to be discussing the case of Mrs. Jordan and Pastor Pooley. Most thought it a scandal that he would take her to court for it. Some whispered behind my back that she should never have bestowed her love so soon upon Sam's death and while carrying a child. That was the true scandal, they said.

Truly, it was too much for a young widow expecting a child. I hoped Cecily wasn't hearing these things too, but I suspected she was. I was beginning to harbor hatred inside for Mr. Pooley. We had trouble enough without creating more.

Tempie learned the results of June's court hearing from Sir George. He explained that the court had decided to continue the case until Cecily had her child. Sir George told Tempie that privately the court wished the pastor to drop the matter and find another wife.

Tempie tried not to roll her eyes about a man of God when she said, "Aye? Do you know anyone who would desire him after such an embarrassing spectacle?"

Now it was her husband's turn to roll his eyes in amusement. "I believe you may have a prejudice. In the court, we try to forswear such bias."

She gave him an innocent smile. "Oh, I'm biased and proud of it indeed."

For now, the case lay dormant, where we hoped it would stay until the pastor dropped his cause.

"I do not think the parson will let this die, mother," Cecily said. "Mr. Pooley is particularly incensed that Mr. Farrar lives in this house. Of course, so too do various servants, both men and women. But the pastor portrays the household as scandalous, as a way to scorn me before my family and friends. Another way to prove me unfit to marry Mr. Farrar. But fit, of course, to marry him."

"That makes no sense whatsoever," I said, fuming.

Her eyes, I saw, were puffy and ringed with worry. She was not yet done grieving her husband's death. Now everyone was talking about the breach of promise suit.

"Am I flouting my Christian beliefs by disavowing a pastor?" she asked nervously. Although she had wondered this before, now she sounded genuinely fearful.

"Fie, no, child. No. Right is right and wrong is wrong. He has wronged ye and not the other way around. Besides, much can happen between now and November. Stay positive and hopeful. Try not fear," I cautioned her. Fear I understood as it had also been bettering me lately.

"I will," she sighed.

Within two weeks, the child she named Margaret was born under the watchful eye of Rebecca Gray, a midwife. Cecily had chosen Mrs. Palmer, Mrs. Causey, and me as her gossips along with several others from Shirley Hundred.

The sound of the child's squalling and the little one's pink face made my heart leap with joy. A slight edge of sadness crept in, the sadness that Sam would not see his daughter.

I stayed through Cecily's confinement, feeling confident that Mr. Pooley would walk away from Cecily.

With stunning cruelty, however, Mr. Pooley, far from giving up was gathering witnesses in his case. He was going to drag the new mother through the courts. How would a woman win against a man, a pastor at that? Especially in light of the mysterious thing occurring soon after my departure.

The Mansion of My Pilgrimage

Late September 1623
New Towne, Virginia

And (worthy George) by industry and use,
Let's see what lines Virginia will produce:
Go on with Ovid, as you have begun,
With the first five books; let your numbers run
Glib as the former, so shall it live long,
And do much honour to our English tongue ...
—Michael Drayton, from his poem to George Sandys

...yet ye wife of one of ye Italians (whom I have now sent home, haveinge
receaved many wounds from her husband at severall times, & murder not
otherwise to bee prevented, for a more damned crew hell never vomited)
reveald in her passion that Vincentio crackt it wth a crow of iron ...
—George Sandys, March 1623

Sung in the mansion of my pilgrimage.
—George Sandys

The fighting was over for the summer. Will was home, as were the other captains, and the Indians were seeking peace once more. I'd heard the men talking and knew that while we might promise the Indians peace, no peace would they have. Memories of the massacre still rankled the leaders to fury.

At least the immediate fighting had quieted, and we took what reprieve we could. The corn was bursting into ears, a happy sight to see after so much hunger the previous year.

"'Tis going to be a plentiful harvest for us this year," Will said, coming into the house. "Praise be to God!" He was actually whistling as he removed his boots.

The contagion seemed to be over; spirits broken during the massacre and the year following it were starting to lift. The evenings were cooler; the summer flies which bit and stung were abating. Even the threat of the coming winter could not dampen what was almost jubilation in Virginia.

Had I just used *jubilation* and *Virginia* in the same thought?

Mr. Sandys was cheerful as he worked on his poetry during the hours not promised to the Company. As he translated the books of Ovid, he never complained of long, late hours, his candle burning into the night. Neither did he complain of the cramped chamber up in our loft. Having no wife, the love of Mr. Sandys's life was his writing. He'd pursue it as he could.

Son of the archbishop of York, here was Mr. Sandys, a learned man and a traveled one. Perhaps the most well-traveled man ever to set foot upon our new continent. We now owned this first book of travels, a gift from him for the lodging we provided. He had published these four books perhaps six years before. Already, in a world filled with travel books, Mr. Sandys's *A Relation of a Journey* was the most popular book of its kind in England. He had written us a gracious signature inside, thanking us for the kindness.

The pleasure, it was all ours.

I found Mr. Sandys to be a polite man and a welcome guest, although he did sometimes show a temper. The glass blowers made him pull his beard in anger.

"In March, Vincentio took a crow of iron to the works!" he'd told us. "His wife has confessed. First, a tempest blew the roof off before the glasshouse was even finished. Then the Italians all fell sick of the summer sickness. After that, the massacre delayed the works and Captain Norton died. And now deliberate destruction!"

Will was quick to offer Mr. Sandys a chair in the dining hall as well as a glass of sack. "Sir," Will said kindly, "Sit and trouble yourself not over the Italians. Would you like military help to enforce your demands of them?"

Sandys sat down and smiled warmly at Will. "Which do you think would work best on the lot—a rapier, a sword, or a musket?"

Will began to chuckle and Sandys, despite his frustration, did, too.

"What about a crow of iron?" I ventured. At this, both men burst into laughter.

Then, using the colorful language of a writer, Master Sandys declared, "Fie, a more damn'd crew hell never vomited!"

But Mr. Sandys was a fair man, I discovered, even quietly criticizing the leadership of his brother Sir Edwin at times. "My brother doth think that as soon as he decrees a project, we can complete it by return ship," he had once grumbled. Sir Edwin's blaming of us for the massacre had irritated Mr. Sandys for a long time afterward.

Now, with the cooler weather, many of us who had thought we should never be well or full or happy again were all three. We could begin to dream again.

"Captain and Mistress Peirce, so nice to share a dram and a repose with you in your delightful home. 'Tis a haven against Virginia's continual surprises, certainly." Mr. Sandys lifted his cup in salute.

How, I wondered, could someone of Mr. Sandys's achievements, heritage, and education be so mild and indulgent? So willing to endure conversation with Will and me as equals?

"Pardon me, but as the light is drawing down in the sky, my muse Ovid awaits me," he said, rising from his chair.

Every evening found Sandys in his chamber, writing and devising something he called a *couplet*. These were two lines of verse rhyming, a thing he was to make popular.

Five books of Ovid's great *Metamorphoses* he had translated and published in England, two more on board ship, and now eight more awaited him. How he inspired me, that he was able to write amongst all the sickness and dying and, well, the Italians. Not to mention the French vignerons, who were perhaps less disagreeable but no more productive.

His travels fascinated me. He had climbed atop a pyramid in Egypt! He'd wandered into the crypt itself until the odor of decay pushed him backward. What was there, he said, he did not wish to see.

Mr. Sandys had stood gazing at the site of old Troy. He'd walked the footsteps of Christ in the Holy Land and another time quaked at five sail of ships. Although all on his ship believed them to be pirates, the fleet turned out to be only English. Sandys himself, he said, had been terrified and struggled to remain on board the ship.

"Pirates!" he said, with an almost palpable shudder. He could think of nothing worse than that.

He'd sailed the choppy and frightening waters of the Adriatic to Venice, to Rome, and to Sicily. "Our little ship was no bigger than a shallop on the River Thames!"

Will was rapt. We all understood the treacherous sea well enough to know how dangerous such a small craft could be. "Surely, the Greek sailors on board understood the perils of a ship so small braving such rough seas?" Will asked.

Mr. Sandys shrugged. "One would think. At last, I could bear it no more and asked the captain to put me off in Constantinople."

"Home to the Turks!" I said, as riveted as Will.

Mr. Sandys went on to describe the ancient city—Turkish women, with eyes so dark and nails so red, arrayed in colors and styles that seemed too strange to him. He'd found the home of the English ambassador and stayed with him four months, observing the Turks and the Mahometan religion.

This confused me. "That is the Turks' religion?" I asked, a little embarrassed not to know.

"Aye, they are the followers of Mohammed," Mr. Sandys explained patiently. Before he'd left Constantinople, he added, the common people had scorned and scoffed at him. "I would not wish to return to the land of the Turks," he added.

"Bold of you to go the first time!" Will exclaimed. Turks had a reputation as the pirates of the seas, their ways most foreign to Europeans.

Mr. Sandys went on to talk of the powerful Nile River, whose swelling no man understood. "Some Egyptians keep earth from the Nile's banks in a private place. Mysteriously, when the earth swells, so doth the river," he said. He'd seen the teeth of a crocodile, curved and sharp as daggers, yet watched a little bird fearlessly clean those teeth. His adventures, it seemed, were endless.

I attempted to read Sandys's *A Relation of a Journey,* the story of his travels, and then took the astounding opportunity to ask him more about them. I thanked God, while about it, that my father had been forward thinking enough to teach his daughter to read. And that Queen Bess had inspired many subjects of the kingdom to do so in that long ago age.

The next morning Mr. Sandys came down the stair, his greyhound Adonis following him. The poet, carrying his notebook, said, "God give you good morrow, mistress! A beautiful day to see more of Virginia, I'd reckon. I'll be gone upriver today with Swift and the Frenchman Poole to help me."

"Why do you go there today?" I asked him. War was still underway, after all. Mr. Sandys, on top of that, still must answer to the Virginia Company for his projects. Glass and salt and silkworms.

"We're seeking sand for the Italians to use in the glass," he said.

"Oh, I see. And do you enjoy Virginia now that 'tis cooler and more healthful?"

He shrugged. "I enjoy becoming familiar with a land I know not. Truly, these rivers, these vast forests, are as beautiful and bountiful as any. I compare them to those in France and Italy. These woods put the barren deserts of Cairo and the stony mountains of the Holy Land to shame for sheer beauty. The touch of God's hand upon Virginia is marvelous. And the mystery of its depths are alluring."

He had such a wonderful way with words as if each sentence were an opportunity to create a phrase.

But this time, as I listened, I found words escaping me that I had not meant to say. "If only I could be such a traveler! See the world as my father did. He was a mariner and always shared his adventures with me when he came home."

Master Sandys paused to study me. "My dear hostess and, may I say, friend, you are here, are you not?"

Curious, I nodded. "Of course. Many a year, here."

"Think you not that this is a journey of note? Helping to settle the New World, founding a colony for England? Because one stays in a place long makes it no less an adventure, no less a journey." And then he added something which sent a thrilling cold over me. "Think it not that 'tis less of a pilgrimage?"

Suddenly, I wanted to share with him.

"See, sir, what I carry with me each day." I reached for the chain around my neck and retrieved the old pilgrim's badge.

"What is this?" he asked, intrigued. "An old pilgrim's badge! Spared from the Thames, mistress?" Few of these badges still existed since most pilgrims had thrown them into the Thames for luck.

"No, sir. Not at all. My ancient grandfather decided to keep his badge as a remembrance of his journey to Compostela rather than to make a wish. 'He decided he should rather have the badge than the wish' is how my mother explained it to me." Without knowing why, I continued, "I do think of myself as a pilgrim sometimes."

Sandys mused for a moment and then said, "*All life is pilgrimage*. Have you heard that? 'Tis from the writings of the revered St. Augustine in the fourth century after Christ."

We stood in silence for a moment, and then, thinking I had seen the most of the day's surprises from Master Sandys, he surprised me once more. "Have you considered, Mrs. Peirce, writing the story of your own pilgrimage, a pilgrimage to Virginia? Your own journeys, your own travels? To some, traveling to Virginia is as exotic as traveling to Egypt. And a journey through life a journey still is."

My voice was completely gone. It came out, instead, as a squeak. "Me? But ... I am only a woman and not a very educated one at that! Lady Temperance Yeardley, there is one to write. But I, sir, well, no. It cannot be." I ducked my head and felt my face flush red as the dogwood leaves in autumn.

He smiled kindly at me as if reading my expression. "An artist's soul, a poet's soul, a writer's soul ... These need not be only traits of men, nor even, I do say, of the highly educated. One learns from a country's vernacular sometimes the more. I believe, in fact, that some women see more deeply than e'er a man does. Consider the pilgrimage, consider the ... remembering of it. The learning from it. The learning from it that *others* may do," he added with a meaningful emphasis. "The journey once over is forgotten unless one survives to tell of it. Is it not so? And one can never speak indefinitely. But the written word? Ah, there's the rub, as Mr. Shakespeare said. The written word survives us. A little life becomes a great life with the perspective of time, you see."

He then sipped his mulberry beer as if he had said nothing more than, "What a lovely sunrise!"

But something had happened. A bolt of inspiration coursed me like the ripples of a river when the wind blows west. Here was one of the greatest poets and travel writers of my century. The first published poet in the New World, too. He had sat before me in my little home on the edge of this abyss called James Town. And this man had told me to write.

Blockheaded Parson

November 13 – 19, 1623
James Town, Virginia

*Then Mr Pooley told Mr Pawlett that he lied. Then Mr Pawlett called him
blockheaded parson, with some other the like words that passed between them
on both sides and taxed Mr. Pooley with speaking false latten and teaching
false doctrines and charged him with Symony and bribery.*
—Minutes of the Council and General Court

I'd already heard from Tempie that the parson was incensed that Mr.
Farrar was living in Cecily's home. "Mr. Pooley presses his cause with
George and the council. The court will hear this case on the seventeenth
of November," Tempie said. "They've summoned Cecily to the island, so
expect her here shortly."

"How shameful to bring a widowed new mother into court on such a
thing!" I cried.

I truly had believed—perhaps forced myself to believe—that the case
would never return to court. As long as Pooley was suing and the case open,
Cecily couldn't marry Mr. Farrar or anyone else, for that matter.

As for Mr. Farrar, would he wait for Cecily? I knew she loved him, and
from all appearances, he loved her, too.

About a week afterward, Elizabeth Pott came to my door.

"He's here. I've seen him," she whispered.

"Oh, *him*?" I asked, knowing who she meant. "The blockheaded parson?"

Elizabeth tittered. Word was that Mr. Pawlett, a friend of Mr. Farrar's
who had been with him on arrival in the *Neptune*, was feuding with the parson.
Mr. Pawlett privately referred to Pooley as "that blockheaded parson," and
the name had stuck. Whether Pooley knew that his parishioners referred to
him that way, I knew not. But I suspected that he didn't know. Perhaps if

the feud boiled over, Mr. Pawlett might just let the preacher know what he thought of him!

Anyway, the nickname had made its way downriver with Pooley's case against Cecily.

Cecily arrived on the shallop, cradling the baby.

"I suppose you've heard," she said, her mouth taut and rings beneath her eyes.

"Aye, indeed. Come on in, lovey."

Will was home this time. He stood and greeted his stepdaughter with a hug.

Cecily turned to give me a hug as well. Then she said, "Mr. Farrar would have come with me as well. But we thought it best not to give Mr. Pooley any more gunpowder with which to fire upon us," she said gloomily. "But since Mr. Farrar is helping me settle Sam's estate, he'll have to appear in court for that. But he'll arrive on another ship."

"A sound idea," Will said, musing.

"Who is he calling as witnesses?" I asked, pouring her a dram as she dropped into the chair.

"Thank you kindly, mother." She took a sip, then said, "I know he asked Captain Harris to testify against me as well as Mrs. Madison. "Mrs. Madison was in the next room when Mr. Pooley repeated *our* vows. I understand she heard not what we said but that Captain Madison told her about it afterward. They both heard me say later that Mr. Pooley would have fared better if he'd not revealed our betrothal. He broke his promise and proved himself untrustworthy. I'll have no part of marrying him. Ever."

"Did I hear that Captain Madison passed?" I asked her.

She said that he had. Captain Madison had been the primary witness against Cecily. His death would certainly hurt Mr. Pooley's case.

The governor called court at his home soon after. Sir George, Mr. Sandys, Dr. Pott, Roger Smith, as well as Captain Hamor and Mr. Pountis, comprised the attending court. Also, Mr. Davison was present as secretary, although he seemed quite ill.

All but Mr. Pountis and Mr. Davison were friends of our family. Even though Mr. Farrar's staying in Cecily's home was illegal, she maintained that as long as others were living with her, no harm was done.

Now the question, after the continuance, presented itself. Mr. Pooley had broken his promise; could Cecily not break hers?

I had a hard time believing that these men would rule against Cecily between our friendship and the fact that she herself was an Ancient Planter and had been here in Virginia since just after the Starving Time. Outside of personal quarrels, the council—acting as the court—accorded the old settlers much respect. But the court also must respect a man of the cloth. For the governor and councilors, the problem would be vexing, certainly.

Will asked Sir Francis if he and I might sit in on the proceedings with Cecily, and the governor agreed.

Mr. Pooley glared at Cecily as we came through the room. We found three chairs against the wall and sat near the dining table. Cecily put herself as far from the pastor as possible. Will and I and other witnesses sat between them.

Governor Sir Francis first called Mary Madison to testify. She pledged the oath, her face inscrutable. She seemed a bit nervous, I thought.

Sir Francis said, "Mrs. Madison, you were present at Mrs. Jordan's home the night Mrs. Jordan and Mr. Pooley were engaged, is that so?"

Mrs. Madison wriggled in her discomfort. "Well, sirs, I was there but in the other room when the contract took place. I did hear Mrs. Jordan say, 'If Mr. Pooley had not revealed it, he might have fared the better.' My husband Isaac did tell me that night that Mrs. Jordan made herself sure to Mr. Pooley. He said they drank to each other, and Mr. Pooley saluted her with a toast."

"Thank you, Mrs. Madison. Gentlemen, any other questions for our witness?" Sir Francis asked, turning to the rest at the table.

They all shook their heads, and a few murmured, "No."

They excused Mrs. Madison and then brought John Harris to testify.

His only comment was that he, too, had heard Cecily say that Mr. Pooley might thank himself for he might have fared the better but for his own words.

Secretary Davison was scribbling furiously.

The governor dismissed the witnesses and those attending with no word as to what he was thinking.

Later that day, Tempie crossed the causeway to come see me. By then, Mr. Farrar had also arrived from Jordan's.

"Good news?" I asked hopefully.

"'Tis not good news but not truly bad either," she said. "George says they know not how to decide so nice a difference, as they put it. Our divines are not in a position to settle this, a church matter, and know not whether it be a formal and legal contract. They are sending it to the Company and asking civil lawyers in England to consider the case."

"Oh!" Cecily wailed. "That could take a year or more, and they could still force me to marry that man in the end." She turned to Mr. Farrar. "William, I don't know why you would wait for me all that time."

Of course, Mr. Farrar was betrothed to Cecily. He could no more leave his vow than she could hers to the pastor.

"Cecily, I'll wait for you, howe'er long it take." he said. "Worry not."

"Oh, will you? Thank you!" she said. "But still, who is this man to be so unforgiving, so determined to win his point at all costs?" she asked in frustration. "Is he not bound as a man of God to forgive as Christ did?"

"There, there," Tempie said, taking a seat by Cecily and giving her a hug. "What do you expect from a ... a ... blockheaded parson?"

Cecily laughed a little in spite of herself, and William Farrar grinned.

There Came a Tyrant

January 1624
New Towne, Virginia

There came a tyrant ...
—William Wordsworth

When Mr. John Harvey stepped off the *Southampton* and into our lives for the first time, he was fighting with the ship's master, mate, *and* crew. One thing we had learned was squabbling with the men who see you safely across the ocean was never wise. Most accorded them respect and treated them well.

Not Mr. Harvey, who happened to own the ship.

"See here, you shall *not* sail onward to New England and Canada to fish! I own this ship, and *I forbid it*." His face reddened and his fists clenched.

"Mr. Harvey, you signed on as a passenger, so you'll not be ordering us about," the captain said calmly.

The sound of shouting had brought me from my home where Tempie was visiting. "Who is he, and why is he here?" I asked Tempie.

She shrugged. "I suppose we'll find out. Perhaps just another person who believes that he understands the rules of Virginia ..."

"When he doesn't?"

"When he doesn't."

Tempie came back across the causeway the next day. She'd learned about the man we'd seen remonstrating the captain. I could not then have known how this man—this singular man—would come to haunt my days.

"As I hear it from George, 'tis a complicated thing. Sir Thomas Smythe's allies, now including my Lord of Warwick, are battling against the allies of my Lord of Southampton and Sir Edwin Sandys. The two halves of the Virginia Company quarrel as does Harvey with his ship's captain."

Sir Thomas Smythe had completed his term as Company Treasurer a few years before. He'd been the leader from the time of Captain John Smith until that time. Sir Edwin was now the leader, the present treasurer. The two sides hated one another, each blaming the other for Virginia's failures.

Will and I and the Yeardleys all sided with Sir Edwin. After all, Sir George Yeardley was one matter both sides fought about. Was he an able governor or not? Sir Edwin stood staunchly by his friend.

As for us, living with George Sandys influenced our opinion of his brother Sir Edwin, of course, but not entirely.

No one who'd lived through it could ever, ever forget Sir Thomas Dale's martial law. Those days of brutally harsh discipline when the leaders had censored our letters home, forced us to work long hours, and forbidden us to leave the colony for ten years.

These had been Sir Thomas Smythe's commands, an attempt to keep the colony going. The Virginia Company had hoped that by suppressing us and forcing us to stay, word wouldn't reach England about the miserable conditions in Virginia. No wonder those who'd been here then now favored Sir Edwin Sandys!

"I see," I said wearily to Tempie. "And so the fruitless battle continues. And what has this to do with Harvey? Whose side does he favor?"

"He favors the Smythe faction. But that isn't why he's here. Smythe's allies have demanded that the king call for an investigation. For this, the king has created a commission of four men. Harvey is one." She paused. "He could be troublesome. He's come with a 'list of queries.' The man is unpleasant but well-connected. The king recently knighted his brother, Sir Simon, and bestowed on him the honor of procuring food and wine for his majesty's household. So this Harvey fellow went to the king and offered to gather intelligence on us. He's here as a … a spy. A spy who came to determine why so many have died over the past five years."

I almost laughed bitterly. "The king needs a commission to tell him that? I'm a woman, and I can tell him. We trusted the natives when we shouldn't have. The *Abigail* brought us great sickness overtopping a famine because we couldn't plant corn. The hordes of people coming in before that overfilled James Town, causing more illness. Lord De La Warr's ship brought in an earlier contagion. We've had seasons of great drought. They send too many ships in summer when the seasoning strikes the new arrivals the worst."

"I know, I know, Joan. We all know who've lived it." Tempie looked thoughtful. "You don't think the Virginia Company could split apart and collapse, do you? And what would that mean for us here in Virginia?"

That was the first time anyone had asked such a thing in my hearing. But sometimes women perceive well the unsaid.

John Harvey, we learned soon, liked to settle things with violence and tantrums when no other method would work. His servant Mutch learned that the hard way. Mutch dared to ask for his freedom dues which Harvey owed him. Harvey not only refused to give them to Mutch but punctuated it by slamming his truncheon onto the man's head.

No doubt about it. Harvey would be trouble. Just how much trouble, we wouldn't know until later. He would one day affect me personally in ways I could never have imagined even possible.

The Duty of a Patriot

January 1624
James Town, Virginia

Nearly all men can stand adversity, but if you want to test a man's character, give him power.
—Abraham Lincoln

The duty of a patriot is to protect his country from its government.
—Thomas Paine

When we understood that Mr. Harvey had come as part of a commission to examine us, we were rightly offended. The Smythe faction had taken its grievances to the king and Privy Council, bolstered by incoming letters impounded from a ship.

Now Mr. Sandys's private musings to his brother were fodder for the Company, Lady Margaret's report of all the deaths on ship, servants complaining of illness and lack of food—all these letters fell into the hands of Sir Thomas Smythe and my Lord of Warwick. These letters all written in March or April when things were at their worst.

Reading the passel of letters in alarm, the Privy Council ordered four commissioners to report back to them—John Harvey and Mr. Pory arrived on ship. Mr. Peirsey and Sam Mathews were already here.

Yes, Mr. Pory was back—this time in a position of greater authority.

The Yeardleys invited him over to dinner, which pleased him very much, he said.

"Right after the massacre, you took the *Discovery* up to New England, seeking to trade and fish for us, and then you sailed home? We hadn't expected that of you," Sir George said, lighting a pipe and trying to keep any accusation from his voice.

"I went a little further than the north coast, I'm sorry to tell you. Did you not hear?"

Both the Yeardleys shook their heads.

Now Mr. Pory shared in Sir George's tobacco with another pipe. He drank deeply of the pipe, let the breath go, and then said, "We ended up back in England—ultimately—after quite a terrible adventure. Contrary winds blew us off course."

"Do tell?" Tempie asked, eyes wide. "Where to?"

"East off of New England, out to sea. Toward the Azores. Too close to these Portuguese islands, I fear me. The Portuguese thought so, too. They captured our little *Discovery* and ferried us back to the Azores. The same islands which feasted our Lord La Warr right before he died. But we received no such hearty welcome, I assure you."

The Yeardleys met one another's eyes. They had not expected this.

Mr. Pory continued before his speechless hosts. "There the Portuguese arraigned us as pirates! They threw us all in prison for a time, nearly hanged us. 'Til at last we managed to convince the Azorean governor we had no ill intent. We were simply lost. They returned us to our ship, and we made for England."

Tempie nearly dropped her spoon. Every time she convinced herself she'd heard every possible sea story ...

We'd known the factions of the Virginia Company were in deep war, a war that was like firing a hole into one's own ship. The quarrelers might make their points, but we were going to sink. And we were the ones in the ship.

In his possession, Mr. Harvey had a paper he wished Governor Sir Francis to endorse. "It tells the Privy Council how thankful you—representing Virginia—are for the king's proposed change in government. That you're delighted he is revoking the Virginia Company's letters patent."

In less than a month's time in Virginia, Harvey had managed to get just about every person he crossed to hate him. He was coarse and foul, ill-tempered and belittling.

Now Mr. Harvey held the paper out to Sir Francis. "As a commissioner of his majesty's Privy Council, I order you to sign." He didn't bother with the pleasantries. He didn't see the need.

"That, sir, is not for me to sign. That must go to the people of Virginia, our General Assembly. Only they can endorse your paper," Sir Francis said as evenly as he could.

"You're the governor, you sign it!" Harvey pressed, irritated.

"No." Sir Francis was a man rarely terse, but he sensed Harvey was drawing him into a trap. Besides, the governor's wife, Lady Margaret, had just set sail. Here she was, great with child, and Sir Francis had been obliged to send her off alone on ship. The governor hoped to follow the next year when his term was over.

So as Harvey attempted to bully him, Sir Francis was unusually bellicose.

Harvey snatched the document away from Sir Francis. "The king will hear of your impertinence to one of his commissioners!"

The threat hung in the air. Neither man spoke.

"Fine, then," the governor replied evenly. "Tell his majesty that Governor Sir Francis Wyatt stands not on his own authority but on the authority of the people through their elected representatives."

As it happened, the General Assembly had been sitting when these commissioners arrived.

Sir Francis would present Harvey's proposal to the General Assembly directly. And the governor thought to himself, he'd wager a gold crown that the representatives would *not* sign that paper.

That Precious Jewel

February to Late March 1624
James Town, Virginia

*The governor shall not lay any taxes or impositions upon the colony, their
lands or commodities, otherwise than by the authority of the General
Assembly, to be levied and employed as the said Assembly shall appoint.*
—Act of the Virginia General Assembly, March 1624

*Liberty, the greatest of all earthly blessings—give us that precious jewel, and
you may take every thing else! ... Guard with jealous attention the public
liberty. Suspect everyone who approaches that jewel.*
—Patrick Henry of Virginia, 1788

Sitting in the James Town church on a cold day in February, Will
surveyed the room. Around him sat fellow members of the General
Assembly. Seated in the chancel were the governor and council. Will
saw men who were battle weary, thin, and survivors of long illness.

Will also saw a glint of steel in the other men's eyes. They weren't giving
up. Let Mr. Harvey and his fellows present the petitions.

They had much business to attend to, but they knew Harvey's paper was
one reason they were here.

Governor Sir Francis presided over the meeting of the General Assembly
with aid from the council. Mr. Sandys and Mr. Pountis were present, so
were Dr. Pott, Ralph Hamer, and Roger Smith, all members of the council.
Yeardley must be at his plantation, Will thought.

The General Assembly met once or twice a year as needed.

Nat Causey was down from Jordan's. Will swallowed, wishing it were Sam
here instead as it surely would have been. Sam had been part of the General

Assembly from its start in 1619.

Will recognized Captain Madison and Mr. Biggs from Shirley. Mr. Blaney the merchant, now married to the widow Powell, was present.

Lieutenant Uty was here. Will didn't know the large man well but found him engaging. Uty had been a musician in England and had recently won a court battle for being slandered as "a fiddling rogue and rascal." Will liked him. Fiddler? Yes. Rogue and rascal—no.

Captain Martiau, the engineer, sat near the window. He was in charge of building a fort at York. Desperately needed, Will thought.

He recognized Mr. Chew, Mr. Southern, and Henry Watkins. Also Captain Jabez Whitaker, brother of the late Pastor Whitaker who'd baptized Pocahontas. Reverend Whitaker had a second brother, Isaac, in Virginia as well. Will was glad that despite the pastor's early death, his brothers seemed to be doing well.

In all, twenty-four representatives had come from up and down river to this General Assembly.

So the Smythe-Warwick faction were trying to get the king to give the Company back over to them? Or perhaps they just wished to bring down the Company all together?

Each faction blamed the other. But most of the Ancient Planters who'd lived it blamed Smythe for those first horrible twelve years. And the Earl of Warwick had caused the old planters all sorts of problems with his piratical exploits. The earl had schemed with Governor Argall to send our ship the *Treasurer* out to prey on Spanish ships in the West Indies a half dozen years before. The *Treasurer* had looted a Spanish ship, and we still feared they might attack us here as revenge.

On the other hand, Sir Edwin Sandys had shown compassion for the settlers. True, some of his policies might have caused them overcrowding, might have been too ambitious. And he had unfairly laid blame on them for the massacre. Yet Sir Edwin had strongly supported their release from martial law and had given them a voice in their laws with a General Assembly. Sir Edwin believed in the headright system, too.

Now the delegates listened as the governor read the letter to the Privy Council Harvey wished them to sign.

"Will ye sign and endorse this?" Sir Francis asked the General Assembly.

One by one, the men responded.

"No, sir!"

"No."

"Never!"

"No, sir."

"No!"

"No, sir!" Will said firmly when the vote came to him.

Our battered survivors would not cower to anyone, not to these commissioners, not to the king or Privy Council, not even to the Virginia Company—except for what loyalty they owed to Sir Edwin.

They refused to sign away all their rights to the king. The little Virginia band was sturdily in agreement on this.

Suppose the king forced them back into martial law? Suppose his majesty took away their voice, the General Assembly? Suppose he overtaxed their tobacco and refused to renew their lands? No, sir. They'd had calamities under Sir Edwin, 'twas true, but he was an ally of many there. Even a friend and family member to some.

No one would force their hand.

Instead, they would plead their case directly to the king and Privy Council. These Virginia men wanted their land grants to stay ratified, fair tobacco trade, and a General Assembly.

Together, the men composed their response.

They determined not to send their answer through the commissioners, whom they didn't trust. Instead, Mr. Pountis would escort the letter directly to the Privy Council in London.

When our consent to the surrender of the patents shall be required, will be the most proper time to make reply. In the meantime, we conceive his majesty's intention of changing the government hath proceeded from much misinformation, they wrote, bravely countering both the king and Privy Council's wishes.

Mr. Edward Sharples was busily writing. He was filling in since Mr. Davison had died. Sharples wasn't full secretary, but with Davison's death, Sharples would have to do. Later, Mr. Sharples would take all the notes and changes to rewrite a clean copy.

These men desired under all costs to keep their General Assembly. To make sure that point was clear, the Assembly made a resolution which Sir Francis signed: only the General Assembly could tax the people, not the governor or council. Only by the people's will could the government tax the people.

Brilliant! Sir Francis agreed heartily and signed this into law. "This shall protect you indeed from future greedy governors."

And past ones. The men looked around, but no one said anything.

Governors like Argall? Who imposed fines to enrich himself!

These men also now knew that while Captain Butler had come under pretense of helping them fight the Indians, he had instead been spying on them.

Now the General Assembly, council, and governor had all learned of Butler's scathing report, part of the reason the king had stepped in. *The Unmasked Face of our Colony in Virginia,* Butler called his account. So Butler had come as a rat from the Smythe-Warwick faction. His report insulted everything they stood for, everything they'd worked for. More than that, it insulted the condition they'd been in these past few years.

Butler had been here as they struggled with the aftermath of the massacre, with being unable to plant, with the winter's illness. Butler? The former governor of the colony of Bermuda? The colony without Indians? How hard was *that* to run?

These men sat for days, answering Butler's petition with angry retorts supported by facts. They could testify from personal blood spent and tears mopped that Smythe's policies hadn't worked.

Sir Thomas Smythe's man Alderman Johnson had written another unflattering report. They answered that one, too, with plenty of detail to show they knew of what they spoke. In fact, they were speaking for the many, many who would never speak again because they were dead.

The men in Virginia might support Sandys over Smythe, they might be the king's subjects, but they were learning something. Virginia was its own being. We were not English, not Virginia Company pawns, and far from within the king's ready grasp.

We would fight for ourselves. Because, it seemed, we could trust no one in England to fight for us.

To the shadowy home of Edward Sharples came John Pory late one evening. Sharples had but a single candle burning as he created copies of the secret document. Mr. Pountis was to carry the document in a locked shipboard trunk to the Privy Council.

The two men spoke few words as Sharples handed Pory copies for each of the commissioners.

"Keep the pact of silence and remember my fee. The governor and General Assembly will harangue me if they learn of this," Sharples muttered.

Mr. Pory laughed acidly. "Harangue you? Man, they shall pillory you and cut your ears off and mayhap your tongue, too!"

"And you?" Sharples asked Pory. "What will the governor or Sir George do to you?"

"I'm under the protection of my Lord of Warwick as I've always been. I care not for Sir George's wrath." Pory laughed again. Lord Warwick would repay him far more than he'd just given this simpleton clerk. Pory had enjoyed the Yeardleys' food and hospitality, sure, but he was a Warwick man. Always had been.

Sharples wasn't laughing as he repeated, "My fee, our pact."

Pory placed the folded copies into his coat. "I'll remember."

Sharples watched the commissioner leave his home, knowing he had broken his oath of trust to the governor, council, General Assembly, and the entire Virginia Company.

Oh, well.

But Pory was right. When the General Assembly discovered Sharples had violated both his word and oath, they ordered both his ears cut off.

Sharples was contrite, he begged. So the governor and council reduced the sentence and only cut off part of one ear. A light sentence, sure.

The ship sailed off with a locked trunk in Councilor Pountis's capable hands. The Virginia leaders would not deal with two-faced, irascible commissioners. They'd come too far for that. They would take their requests, particularly their desire to keep their General Assembly, directly to the king and Privy Council.

When Mr. Pountis died ere reaching England, Mr. Harvey and Mr. Pory had little trouble finding his trunk. They carried this straight away to the Earl of Warwick. The king would never see these Virginia petitions, they'd see to that.

Locks, after all, could be forced.

An Injurious, Passionate Speech

Late March 1624
James Town, Virginia

A man's blood for an injurious, passionate speech—for a disdainful look?
—William Chillingworth

The Assembly was still meeting in the church when a crowd gathered down by the bridge. Lieutenant Harrison claimed Mr. Richard Stephens the merchant had cheated him in an invoice sent him by his brother, John Harrison.

Mr. Stephens said Lieutenant Harrison had a head filled with sawdust and that the invoice was fair.

Lieutenant Harrison raised his voice and accused Mr. Stephens of being a greedy merchant.

Now their voices rose a pitch. By the time they were screaming, I came from my house to see what the matter be. I wasn't the only one, as a crowd had gathered down by the waterfront.

Jane called over to me, and I stood by her as we watched the show.

We didn't have theatre, but we did have hotheaded men.

"You speak untruly. I give the lie to you, sir!" cried Mr. Stephens, stepping closer to Lieutenant Harrison and leaning in. Calling Lieutenant Harrison a liar was surely escalating the argument.

Several down by the dock had now grabbed the men's arms and were holding them off each other. Still, nothing could calm the men down until at last, they agreed on the only reasonable way for gentlemen to settle their dispute.

They would duel.

"You've offended my name and my honor, sir!" Lieutenant Harrison puffed his chest out, his face flushed. "Apologize at once, or I challenge ye to a duel!"

Dick Stephens wasn't known for mollifying situations. Now his face purpled, too. "I'll not apologize, sir, and I accept your challenge!"

"George, you ain't well. Don't do it," a man near to Harrison said.

Harrison shook it off, not hearing, his ears filled with anger.

"I'll see ye at dawn right here on the field of honor in one week!" said Harrison, looking piqued and winded. He pointed to the field where the men drilled on holy days.

Stephens spat and narrowed his eyes. "One week."

When the day came, we wondered if the duel would happen, but the crowd gathering at the field told us it would. Duels were illegal, but much a curiosity.

Each man had chosen his second and third man, who would act as witnesses.

"Mr. Menefie!" I said sharply and improperly. "You're not his second?" Mr. Menefie, a merchant who ran the town forge, was one of Will's friends.

Mr. Menefie looked embarrassed. "Not by choice, mistress," was all he said. Mr. Menefie was a calm man, not one prone to fighting.

Each man would also typically have chosen his own doctor, but we had only Dr. Pott, so he stood at the ready.

Someone had marked the drilling field to twenty paces square with handkerchiefs. The men started at opposite ends. Neither could leave the square else he be branded a coward.

Now the men marched toward one another, rapiers poised to battle.

"This is ridiculous."

I turned to see Tempie.

"Yes," I agreed.

The clack of rapiers caused us to turn our attention back to the men. Each was skilled, but I adjudged Stephens to be a bit faster.

"Harrison was terrible ill this morning. He ought not to have come," said a man near me.

"That be why he lost his temper, I say me," said another.

Just then, a flash of red and a cry from Harrison. Stephens had managed to slice a deep cut to Harrison's knee, and Harrison went down. His breeches bloodying more as he lay there.

"Halt!" cried someone. "Halt the duel!"

Just two weeks later, Lieutenant Harrison was dead. The governor and council ordered Dr. Pott to perform an inquest. He determined that the cut had not caused Harrison's death but the disease already overtaking his body. Mr. Stephens faced no charges for causing the lieutenant's death.

The Wind is Wild To-night

Late July 1624
New Towne and on the Pamunkey's River, Virginia

*The Indyans were never knowne to shew soe great resolutione, either
encoraged by the paucytie of ours, or theire owne great numbers, There
beinge of the Pomuckeys eight hundred bowmen, besides divers nationes that
cam to asiste them, fightinge nott only for safegarde of theire howses and
such a huge quantetie of Corne, but for theire reputatione with ye rest of
the Salvages ... The Pomunckeys havinge made great braggs, of what they
would doe, Amonge the Northerne nationes: of whom the kinge of Potuxsone
[Patuxent] sent an Indyan vnto us expressly to be an eye witnes of the evente ...*
—Letter from the Governor's Council, 2 December
1624

The wind is wild to-night, there's battle in the air ...
—Emily Lawless

When Will told me of the battle before him, I felt my heart turn to stone.

At first, he tried not to tell me. But I'd been a military wife too long; I knew when they don't want to tell you, you must know. Those are the worst battles.

As he was preparing to meet Governor Sir Francis to sail out, Will kissed me and said, "Never worry, Joan. We can handle the natives."

"How many men will you have?" I asked.

He looked down and adjusted his belt. Then he looked up and said, "We'll win, no matter what the Pamunkey say."

"Will, how many English?" I was not letting him go without telling me.

His eyes met mine. "Sixty. Twenty-four to cut corn and thirty-six to cover them while they do so." The long contagion coupled with the massacre had decimated our fighting men.

"What force will the Indians have?"

He reached for his sword and put it in its scabbard. He said nothing.

"Will!" His not telling me told me everything.

"Eight hundred, Joan," he said quietly.

"Thirty ... thirty-six? To eight hundred bowmen?" I dropped into a chair. "Oh, Will." But I knew nothing I could say would dissuade him from his duty.

And then he set off, Governor Sir Francis leading the expedition.

The Pamunkeys were resolved to conquer the English this summer when we came a-cutting down their corn. So great a belief did the Pamunkeys have in their warring ability that they planted more corn than usual to help the other hungry tribes nearby, those unable to plant for fear of being ambushed in the fields.

They'd boasted to other tribes that this would be the summer the English could never vanquish them. Not like the previous two summers.

In fact, word of how great this battle would be spread so that other Indian nations sent bowmen to join the eight hundred Pamunkey. The Patuxent chief, far up the bay, even sent a brave to witness it.

Never had there been such a battle in Virginia in all our years here. Never had we seen such determination.

This was the fight Sir Francis, Will, and his five dozen men were willingly sailing into.

On the River of the Pamunkeys, the corn fields were vast, blowing in a sweltering July wind. Perspiration poured down the men's faces behind their hot armor. The war cries penetrated the air all about.

Opitchapam, now called Otiotan, took to the field of battle since the poisoning of his brother Opechancanough.

When arrows began flying, the men fired their muskets again and again, their swords at the ready for Indians coming close upon them. If the soldiers did their tasks correctly, the natives wouldn't get that close, Will thought. But their powder, too, was limited. Something else he hadn't wanted to tell me.

Stalk by green stalk, the corn fell. Acre upon acre upon acre, as the battle thundered on for the whole day and into dusk and again the next day. The Indians were so sure of victory that they were willing to fight in open fields, a most unusual thing as they preferred to fight from stealthy places.

Our men began to fall from arrows. One, two, three down. Six down.

Eight, nine down. In the end, sixteen English fell, nine of them being the best shot we had.

Yet the remaining men kept on fighting. Some tended to wounded while others continued cutting corn. In the end, none of them died.

The Indians rarely fought for extended times and never in the open. Still, they held their ground as the first day wore into the second day, two full days fighting in open country.

But the corn kept hitting the ground, sword stroke by sword stroke. And as the corn fell, so did the Indians.

At last, the Pamunkey knew they were defeated.

Then they stood, disheartened, just watching the green stalks topple. Enough corn to have fed four thousand Indians for a year. This would be another hungry winter for them.

Had the Indians known our powder was now completely exhausted in all the plantations, they might have pressed their advantage. All we could do was wait and hope we'd discouraged them enough not to do that.

The Border of the Widow

January 3, 1625
New Towne, Virginia

Nathaniell Causey gent sworen and Examined sayeth that Mrs. Palmer
Cominge to his house said to this Examinant and his wiefe that there was a
farefull thinge falen to Mrs. Jurden & being demanded by this examinant what
it was, shee said that Mrs. Jurden being uppon her bed, she sawe two hands,
the one hande uppon her head the other hand uppon her Childs head and
harde A voyce which cried. Judgment, Judgment. To which Mrs. Causey said it
may be it was A dreame, noe sayeth Mrs. Palmer she was as broad Awake as I
am now.

> —Records of the Council and General Court, 3 January
> 1625

The Lord will destroy the house of the proud: but he will establish the border
of the widow.

> —Proverbs 15:25

Early in January, Cecily had returned to the island. With her, she
brought baby Margaret but left Mary with Little Temp.

Heaving a big sigh, a sigh that said, *This has dragged on too long,* she
told me, "He—Mr. Pooley—is growing most impatient. He demands an answer to his lawsuit. He has lashed out at me several times. How he thinks this
helps his case *with me* I know not! William checked into it for me, and the
Company has as yet sent no reply."

No, I reckoned not. The Virginia Company had been teetering on the
brink of collapse from warring factions and commissioners who took sides.
Each faction was plying the king with their side of the case.

"They've been a little busy," I said wryly. I doubted that the case of a breach of promise was all that important to them when so many other troubles brewed. Howe'er hard it might be on Cecily or the pastor.

Cecily went on. "Now Mr. Pooley is bringing more witnesses, still claiming it to be 'scandalous' for William to live with me."

I put my arm around her. "How are you holding up?"

She shrugged. "'Tis a long time to wait for marriage."

The council had sent the case transcripts to the Virginia Company over a year ago. Cecily and Mr. Farrar still couldn't wed, not until the case resolved.

"Do you know which witnesses he has against you this time?" I asked her.

"Just Mr. Causey, I think."

"Well, that's good! The Causeys are your friends. They have nothing harmful to say, do they?"

Her eyes met mine steadily. At last, she said, "I did have a vision, mother. Perhaps God judges me for promising myself to Mr. Pooley or perhaps for William living in my home."

I felt my heart drop. *A vision?* "Tell me about it before we head over to the governor's house for the testimony," I said, trying to sound unconcerned.

"Well, I was sitting upon the bed with the baby when I saw two great hands, one upon my head and the other upon little Margie's head. A voice cried, 'Judgment, judgment!'"

"I know not what it means," I said slowly. "Did you tell anyone?"

She nodded. "I did, mother. I was so shocked. I told Mrs. Palmer." She paused. "Pastor Pooley could not induce Mrs. Palmer to come today. She said she could remember nothing of what I'd seen!" Cecily smiled for the first since she'd arrived. She truly was a beautiful young woman.

"So why is Mr. Causey coming?" I pressed.

"Mrs. Palmer had told the Causeys about the vision. I think Nat will testify as to what Mrs. Palmer told him I saw."

Jane was aware of the proceedings today and met us at my home. I huddled beneath my cloak. Together, we walked over to the governor's house. All our breaths filled the air with white clouds in the January bitterness.

"How are the girls?" Cecily asked idly. Then, again, she smiled. "We certainly have our share of girls! My three and your three."

Jane said they were well, that one of the servants was watching them for her. "Roger will be at the court today," she said with a foxlike wink.

Again, Cecily gave a half-hearted grin. "Well, there's one vote for me!"

"Is Tempie coming?" Jane asked me.

I told her that I thought she would.

"If Sir George is there, that's two votes!" Cecily said.

Indeed, the council consisted of Sir Francis, Sir George, Dr. Pott, Roger, and Ralph Hamor. These were all friends or relatives. That boded well, I thought.

A number of cases went before. Enough, in fact, that we walked back to my house for an hour or two of gossip and then returned because the Country House was rather full.

By the time we returned, the court was discussing a Mr. Julian who said he was due damages in tobacco. He'd cleared a house and grounds at Kecoughtan, and no one had paid him. That case went on for a bit longer as we waited impatiently.

I saw the governor glance at little Margie in Cecily's arms. Bringing her today was a wise idea, I thought. It reminded the court that Cecily was a mother and twice widowed. Compassion might be in order.

Mr. Pooley was there, sitting, shaking his leg nervously. He kept glancing at Cecily, who pretended not to notice.

I studied those who I felt must be here for Cecily's case. Mr. Causey was here, of course, as was Mr. Biggs, who lived at West and Shirley and had some authority there.

"The case of Mr. Pooley and Mrs. Jordan," said a weary Sir Francis. "Mr. Causey, can you come forward?"

He did, and the governor swore him in.

"Now, Mr. Causey, Mr. Pooley here claims scandalous behavior between Mrs. Jordan and Mr. Farrar. Can you tell us what you've witnessed?"

Nat Causey had known Cecily since she'd first arrived. Since he and his wife were fond of her, he found himself in a precarious position. He carefully repeated the story Mrs. Palmer had told him of the two hands and the pronouncement of judgment.

Mr. Causey continued, "My wife said to Mrs. Palmer, 'Maybe it was a dream.' No, sayeth Mrs. Palmer. 'She was as broad awake as I am now.'" He looked embarrassed that Mr. Pooley had forced him to testify.

He doesn't wish to do this, I thought.

"Mr. Causey, hast thou seen any overfamiliarity between Mrs. Jordan and Mr. Farrar?" Sir Francis asked.

The soldier shook his head. "No, I've not seen any unfitting or suspicious behavior between them. Uh, I've seen Mr. Farrar kiss her. Only that."

"Thank you, Mr. Causey," said the governor.

The council and governor took a moment to confer among themselves. Few were still present since the end of day was nearing.

Now Sir Francis stood and spoke formally. "Whereas Mr. Greville Pooley, minister, hath given forth speech that Mr. Farrar and Mrs. Jordan lived scandalously together. Whereas Mr. Pooley being in court and willed to produce witness, he produced *none* but Mr. Causey."

For the first time, I saw something of defeat in Mr. Pooley.

Sir Francis continued, "But Mr. Pooley says that he conceiveth it scandalous for Mr. Farrar to break the order in court." Mr. Pooley felt that Cecily and William Farrar were flagrantly violating the court order. After all, Mr. Farrar lived each day at Cecily's and was often in her company alone.

Then Sir Francis looked around the room. "The council and I have decided to respite the determination of this business." They would decide nothing today, the governor said. Instead, they'd wait until the next ship out of England. They felt, surely, an answer would come from the Company then.

"In the meantime, things to remain in the state they are," Sir Francis said. The governor also ordered Mr. Farrar to behave himself without scandal during this time.

However, Sir Francis added, eyeing Mr. Pooley, the court did not see a problem with Mr. Farrar continuing his living situation. They'd seen no evidence of any familiarity between Cecily and William Farrar, no just cause of scandal. The court felt in both important points and less material ones, they might just dispense with all of it, he said sternly.

My heart leapt, but we all made an effort not to show any emotion. If Mr. Pooley were to dismiss the case, we must not goad him.

The court heard a few more depositions, while Mr. Causey signaled to Mr. Pooley to meet him outside.

When the pair returned, Mr. Pooley said, "Governor Sir Francis, I shall drop my case. To that end, I've written out and signed a release. This paper says that I do absolutely acquit and discharge Mrs. Jordan from all former contracts." The pastor said this included all promises or conditions, any that Cecily had made to him concerning marriage.

Nat Causey stealthily met Cecily's eyes. She knew then that he'd encouraged the pastor to drop the case.

Without further evidence of anything improper between Cecily and Mr. Farrar, Sir Francis declared the case over. However, the court pressed Pooley further for a bond. Mr. Pooley then added a note to the bottom of the release. As he did so, he said loudly, "I do bind myself in five hundred pound sterling never to have any claim, right, or title to her that way."

Delighted but trying not to show it, lest Mr. Pooley change his mind, Cecily approached the pastor and thanked him.

Mr. Pooley said little, then walked out with Mr. Causey and Mr. Biggs.

As soon as we were out of earshot of the court, Cecily said, "Now William and I can at last marry!" The court and Mr. Pooley had finally lifted the weight of a useless lawsuit from her shoulders. It had taken over a year and a half to settle it.

We could not hug her enough after her long ordeal.

A few years later, we heard that fate had perhaps caught up with Mr. Pooley. He had married and had several children. But one balmy day at their house, the Indians came and killed all of them as well as several other men visiting.

My thoughts on hearing it were selfish. *That could have been Cecily and my grandchildren!* But by then, the Farrars were all still secure at Jordan's, as we continued to call it, and Will and Cecily had several children of their own.

Promis'd to the Old World

May 9 – 10, 1625
New Towne and Kecoughtan, Virginia

My knees, affections, teares, verse, here place I:
My inlarged soule to her heavenly home doth flie.
O promis'd to the Old world, to the New;
That gavest blest lawes of freedome to ensue ...
     —George Sandys

Al that wil be paid in smoak.
     —Edward Bennett, London merchant and Virginia
     Company member, 1620

Margaret Powell, now Blaney, was suing Dr. Pott. She claimed that when food had been scarce after the massacre, the doctor had butchered one of her hogs.

Dr. Pott, for his part, said the hog had trespassed and trampled his corn. That had been the year of the scarce corn crops, after all. He'd taken the hog in payment.

Now Margaret accused the doctor of causing her miscarriage, saying she'd been with child and craving pork. The doctor had refused to give her any, and because of this, she had lost the child, she said.

I vaguely remembered Margaret coming to me about it. She'd proposed I ask Dr. Pott for the pork as if it were for me. Then I'd pass the pork on to her.

Margaret reminded me a little of the prickly pear from Bermuda.

I hadn't gone to Dr. Pott that day because I didn't care for the idea of deceiving him. He'd always treated me well. I couldn't even remember if Margaret had lost her child before or after the pork incident, all of it being two or three years ago.

The court was meeting this day and called on me to testify regarding the case.

Governor Sir Francis placed me under oath and asked me about the pork. Adding little to the discussion, I departed.

I must tell Tempie about this!

I made my way across the brick causeway and over the marshlands to the Yeardleys' home. But as soon as I saw Tempie, I forgot my annoyance with Margaret Blaney. Tempie had been crying.

"Why, whatever is the matter?" I asked.

She dropped into a chair. "He's leaving again."

"Do you mean Sir George is leaving?" I asked, afraid to hear the answer, but all the while a-knowing it.

"Certainly, who else does the council rely on time and again? And he isn't well. You know that."

I did.

Tempie then related to me what had occurred the previous night.

* * *

After the children were in bed, Sir George pulled a chair close to Tempie's. He handed her a goblet of sack, the best he had from Tuscany.

She smiled in surprise as he lifted his goblet. Slyly, Tempie said, "The last time you were this attentive, I believe you told me we were coming to a charming little place called Virginia."

"Ah, has it been that long? I just wanted to give a toast to you, who is the true reason Virginia runs so smoothly," he said, his eyes sparkling.

Tempie laughed. "Powhatan's hounds are lively tonight," she said. This is what we called Virginia's bullfrogs as they loudly yelped on summer evenings. The little flies with blinking yellow tails danced outside the window. Virginia was presenting her usual summer theatre of music and lights.

The Yeardleys' goblets touched, but then Tempie's smiled faded. At once, she realized bad news was in the corner of the chamber, like a presence, awaiting its entrance. She set the goblet down quickly, shakily. "What is it, George? What's happening this time?"

He dropped his eyes, then swigged some sack as if for courage. "I mean it sincerely, Tempie. When shipwreck stranded me in the Somers Isles, you had no idea I lived. Yet you carried on."

She nodded, unsure why he was remembering Bermuda this evening.

Sir George swirled the sack in his goblet. "So many times, I've been out fighting Indians or working late on Virginia Company business. You were the one who kept our household a home. And when I was sick a few years ago, you were truly the one who kept my—*our*—business moving. When I could barely keep apace with Company business, you read for me the Company letters when they were a-blear. I had little education compared to most of these men in the council. Will Peirce and I both have risen well beyond our station." He shrugged. "I'm just a merchant tailor's son. No Oxford training, no time at the Inns of Court. My only travel abroad has been with a sword in a man-of-war filled with soldiers. Again, the same it is with Will. But Will never had the weight of the whole colony on him. Knowing that Sir Thomas Smythe and my Lord of Warwick have plotted against me, that Smythe has resented my knighthood. These have been troublesome. Even your cousin Pory has been part of that. You never doubted, though. You've always believed in me."

Tempie held up her hand to stop him. "Darling, the king granted you that knighthood. Smythe is just an old rich—" She smiled. "Well, an old rich something. I won't sound like a lady if I say it."

He smiled despite himself.

"What's troubling you, George? Oh, I don't mind you bragging on me ..." Tempie, as usual, was trying to break the tension with humor.

Sir George sighed deeply, and his eyes met hers.

"I'm going back. I know I'm not long over my last illness, but I must return."

She swallowed hard around the lump in her throat. She thought she knew what *back* meant.

At that moment, young Argall came down the stairs to say he was thirsty. Susanna was right behind him. "I have him, my dame," the young girl said.

"Thank you, dear." *What would I do without her?* Tempie thought.

In tacit agreement, neither husband nor wife spoke until the pair was back upstairs. The Yeardleys listened for the door to shut.

Then Sir George continued, "To England, Tempie. The governor, council, and General Assembly believe I'm the one to approach the king about the tobacco contract. The Company is dead, and we're directly under King James now. We must make ourselves heard, our desires known. We must keep our General Assembly and have our land ratified along with fair tobacco trade."

Tempie gasped, "The Company? Gone?"

"Aye, ripped apart by strife and fighting, I fear me," Sir George replied.

"This petition is critical now that we're formally under the king. Mr. Pountis carried a similar petition, but he died on ship. We believe that petition fell into the hands of our enemies, the Smythe-Warwick faction. I'll also bring a second attempt to petition the king and Privy Council concerning these important matters. We believe someone who has governed the country will have the most sway with them. His majesty has made choice of me for governor once more, and Sir Francis and the council approve."

He said this last gingerly. Tempie suspected he'd known much longer, not wanting, she supposed, to break this news to her.

Tempie's eyes flared in anger. "Why you? Again? George, you are not well. We have three small children, thousands of acres, dozens of servants, tobacco ripening in the fields. *We need you here.* And then, too, once you become governor, we'll have to open our home once more as Virginia's inn."

She saw the lines etching his face as if her words drew them tight. So she softened and said, "I'm sorry, George. I know it's neither your choice nor your preference." She felt the tears welling and said, "Please, my love. Please, don't go. Please, let them send ... let them send ..." She paused as the depth of the situation dawned on her. Someone else? Except for Governor Sir Francis himself, no one was better suited—although George Sandys was close.

"And Master Sandys? Why not him?"

"Sandys is departing with me. He thinks he may have an appointment awaiting him as a gentleman of the king's Privy chamber. In that position, he can influence the king as well, of course. But that's a different type of influence than one coming from a former governor of Virginia. Trust me that I'd rather do anything but voyage there again, but the king's proposed tobacco contract will be disastrous for all in the colony. Every settler will suffer. We have so little except tobacco." His voice had taken on a pleading tone. "Sandys and I have to help his majesty understand that we do seek other commodities. But at this moment, tobacco and tobacco only pays our accounts. We trade corn and tobacco, even while the king doesn't prefer his colony to be built on ... smoke. And we—the governor and council—believe the General Assembly is critical for Virginia and her future. We won't give it up."

Tempie sighed, a sigh that said she knew she would not win this discussion. He was going. Virginia always seemed to come first. And yet she loved him for his dedication to their cause. "God be with you on your journey," she said, trying to keep the sullenness from her voice. Then added in a whisper, "Every Virginian owes you, George. I don't even think they know it."

He patted her hand. "Some do." His voice trailed off. Some also criticized him harshly. No matter now. "Meanwhile, 'tis I owe you, my lady. And I'm sorry to leave you and the children. But the dangers of the sea ..." He hesitated.

Tempie understood. "I know."

The ship would be departing in late June or early July, Tempie learned. The two Georges would be going—her George and Mr. George Sandys.

Mr. Sandys was ready to return to England although he'd be back, he assured us.

The council agreed that Sandys might be able to help the king understand the challenges in the push for commodities. Glass, iron, sassafras, silk, salt, wine ... The only commodity that seemed to be successful was, well, *smoke*.

But about this voyage, Tempie felt especially troubled. Something dark hung over the doorway or lay in wait on board the ship. *Something.*

By the Ann, Whom God Conduct

May 10 to July 1, 1625
New Towne and Kecoughtan, Virginia

To avoide the oppression of Governors there; that their liberty of Generall Assemblyes may be continued and confirmed, and that they may have a voice in the election of officers as in other corporations.

> — from "The petition of the Governor Counsell and Colony of Virginia assembled together," 25 June 1625, which Yeardley was to present to the king. In his possession was a similar petition he was to present to the Privy Council.

July 1, 1625. Kiccowtan. Geo. Menefie to John Harrison. Account of the surrender of the estate of his late brother, Geo. Harrison, to Mr. Carter, according to his authority. Endorsed, "By the Ann, whom God conduct."
> —Calendar of State Papers, Colonial Series

Tempie was still crying as she recounted why Sir George would be leaving.

"Why do I weep, Joan? I know this is who he is, and I know his devotion to Virginia. Something just feels wrong to me, something I cannot explain. I feel it, Joan. I feel it." Her eyes were shadowed in fear. "Mayhap I'm anxious about him leaving the children and me, but he's already survived a hurricane and a shipwreck when every chance was against it. At what point are you asking fate—and God—for too much, too many favors?"

'Twas true, to be sure. This I could not deny. But neither would I let her know that I, too, had an uneasy feeling about Sir George's departure.

"Pray, Joan? Pray for him to return safely to me."

I promised. "We'll both pray. *For where two or three are gathered together in my name, there am I in the midst of them*, saith the Lord. Now wipe your tears, lovey. We'll await Sir George's return together."

He that will learn to pray, let him go to sea, some said. Tempie and I knew that proverb to be true, but we might have altered it. She *that will learn to pray, let her* husband *go to sea.*

The first day of July burned as hot as a smithy's forge. For all our time in Virginia, we sometimes forgot how humid and damp the heat could be, how languid we should feel each summer. But Sir George and Mr. Sandys would have to bear this heat, so much worse in the sweltering ship's decks on the ocean.

As the *Anne* docked at Kecoughtan before moving into the bay and open sea, Mr. George Menefie approached the ship with a smile.

"Good day, Sir George, and I pray thee fair winds and a safe voyage."

Sir George gave a weary nod. "Fair winds in safety would be welcome indeed. Thank you."

"Aye. See here, sir, I have a letter for Mr. John Harrison of London, only brother to that Lieutenant Harrison lately deceased following the duel with Stephens. It concerns Harrison's estate. Would you be so kind as to deliver it to him, sir?" Menefie handed it to the former governor.

Sir George knew that Menefie and Harrison had become friends here in Virginia. "Of course! That is, if I can find Mr. Harrison. The same John Harrison who formerly governed Bermuda?"

Menefie nodded. "And a Company member."

Sir George studied the outside of the folded letter. Menefie had written, "By the *Ann*, whom God conduct."

Mr. Menefie added, "I'd hoped to sail with you myself, but that will have to wait for a future voyage. I pray you, God does conduct your journey and your critical mission to the king and Privy Council, sir," said Menefie, a tip of his hat to the knight.

"I covet any prayers I can receive, Mr. Menefie." Sir George thanked Menefie once more, even as a sense of dread washed over him. He wasn't sure why. Maybe Tempie's fears were getting the better of him, too.

The bosun was ringing the bell, signaling all aboard. Sir George climbed onto the ship with only one backward glance at Virginia.

The Sailor's Star

August 3 – 4, 1625
On board the *Anne of Poole* at sea

See, there she stands an' waves her hands, upon the quay,
An' ev'ry day when I'm away, she'll watch for me ...

The sailor's wife the sailor's star shall be,
Yeo-ho! we go across the sea ...
        —Frederic Edward Weatherly

But no intreatie could get me aboord; choosing rather to undergo all hazards
and hardnesse whatsoever, then so long a voyage by sea, to my nature so
irksome.

        —George Sandys, in *A Relation of a Journey*

The *Anne* rocked as the winds surged. George Sandys's greyhound paced restlessly.

"By God, you are a timid dog!" Sandys said sharply, but his tone betrayed a hint of affection. The dog was utterly useless, yet a good companion nonetheless. "Down!" he commanded, and the dog dutifully obeyed although its beseeching look seemed to say, *We won't be doing this again, will we?*

"Good boy. And I hope not." Sandys couldn't blame the dog for its agitations as he, too, found storms at sea frightening.

He went over to Sir George's cabin door and knocked.

The door opened, and Sandys asked the former governor if he'd like to take some tobacco. Sir George agreed that he would, so the two found a table and sat, each with his pipe.

"I'm not a voyager, Sir George," Sandys said. "People suppose me to be, but it's the foreign lands I prefer. The endless water, the storms? Bah!"

Sir George Yeardley looked up in surprise. "Indeed? With all your sea miles, Sandys?"

The poet shook his head. "'Tis a necessary evil to embark upon one of these things."

"Storm's coming in," Sir George said casually. 'Twas a studied casualness, to be sure. Anyone who had seen the power of the sea, the fury of an ocean storm, could never forget one.

"If the ship sinks, my work bubbles to the ocean bottom for the fish to read," Sandys mumbled. All his translations were complete—all fifteen books of Ovid. He'd finished the last eight between prolonged sickness and the Italians in Virginia. Now he gave a crooked smile. *The Italians.*

"Your work!" Sir George laughed. "Man, if the ship goes down 'tis *we* that will go to the bottom for the fishes."

Sandys stroked his dark beard and chuckled. "You're not a writer then. The work is the child of the father. My children, such as they are, lie nestled within a trunk in my cabin. But pray, save us all from deep watery graves."

Both men understood the dangers of the sea. If they could laugh a little, well, what of it?

My wife awaits me. Pray, God, carry me home to her and the children, Sir George thought but did not say aloud.

The winds were now howling, the waves crashing loudly against the ship's sides. The two men paused when they heard the ship's bell ringing wildly.

Sandys shuddered. Soon rain would lash the decks, and the sailors would batten the hatch closed above their heads. He sighed. *To England. And speedily at that!*

"*Speedily*" being, of course, a relative term. Many more days lay before them.

Hours passed. The waves towered above the ship, dashing it and knocking it about and all those inside it, too. At times, the ocean even seemed to be growling at them. *In the horns of the beast!* Sandys thought. "Truly, 'I saw a beast rise up out of the sea,'" Sandys recited, more to himself than to Sir George.

"'Tis biblical? From Revelations, aye?" asked Sir George.

Sandys nodded.

Sir George continued to pray. He implored the Lord that he stay well and strong, that the ship would hold sound, and that fair winds might bring him home to those who awaited him.

And Sandys? Well, Sandys just prayed. Both men were deeply religious.

If they needed to address their God, each man knew He could hear them—even in the uttermost parts of the sea.

After the storm raged and ended, Mr. Sandys betook himself above board to speak with the ship's master.

Nick Nurrey had long experience at sea. Born in Wiltshire, Nurrey now made his home in the coastal town of Poole in Dorset when he wasn't on the ocean. His sailors, too, had been with Nurrey on many a voyage.

The *Anne of Poole* was sturdy, Nurrey assured Sandys, and well kept, too. "'Tis my ship, Master Sandys. Named for my wife. I keep her as well as I keep my wife, too! You know, 'tis as they say, *A woman and a ship ever want mending!*" He laughed and patted the bulwark. "These are the two ladies in my life." He winked. Then he gave the wood a knock. "Can't hear it when rapping this deck—one needs to do it on the hull—but my *Anne*, she's solid, not a worm nor rot here, y'see. She's ship shape, she is. And while we're touching the wood, let's wish ourselves a peaceful end to our voyage." He rubbed the wood again for good measure, a sailor's assurance of fair luck.

Sandys grinned at Nurrey's superstitions, but not with disdain. The poet enjoyed learning the way folks trod the path of the world—be they English or Egyptians and Italians and Turks abroad. He'd heard Nurrey earlier upbraid the ship's boy for whistling, for sailors believed that whistling caused storms at sea. When a storm had indeed arisen a few hours later, Nurrey had slapped the boy across the ear. "That's for whistling up a storm, lad!"

As for the ship's sturdiness and Nurrey's expertise, Sandys had sought to assure himself of all these things early on. One thing his travels had taught him: when a foreigner, rely on guides to save you for it's often not possible to save yourself. Sandys was, to his mind, a foreigner on the sea.

True to his word, Nurrey had guided his second lady *Anne* through the tempest. One reason Sandys had come topside was to shake the master's hand when it was over.

"Grateful to you, sir, for you handled your ship well."

"Sir, no needs to thank me. 'Tis my duty to get you all safe to Plymouth and on to London." The old salt stroked his beard, and his eyes clouded. "Now, see, the worst that ought to befall a ship comes when a ship's bell rings itself. That were as if the ship itself sees the misfortune a-coming. And that bell did ring itself this morning."

"I did hear it pealing during the storm. But the wind could have caused that, could it not?" Sandys asked logically. "A strong wind before a storm?"

"We go through many such winds. What causeth my bell to ring this time?

No, sir, 'twas not the wind rung that bell." A few lines of worry carved the sailor's craggy face.

The *Anne of Poole* had weathered, the two Georges hoped, the worst that the Atlantic had to offer. As for Nurrey and the sailors, they weren't so sure.

The *Anne*, her crew and the two Georges, had traveled now perhaps a thousand leagues of ocean and were well into the Narrow Seas off the coast of Cornwall. Just eight or nine leagues more, and they'd be docking at Plymouth on the sweet Devon soil.

Dawn was creeping upon the ship, and George Sandys could scarcely sleep in his excitement. He'd loved Virginia despite its trials but was eager to return to his home, to have his new works published, and to see his dear friends at court once more.

Sir George was also awake early, still lying abed, but he was not so calm. He must arrange two audiences, one with the king and one with the Privy Council. His duty was to present the objections and pleas of the governor, council, and Assembly about the tobacco contract. For a man in his mid-thirties, he still felt aged. His bones creaked, his mind raced, and while English soil would be a fairer sight than the ocean, Virginia soil was best of all.

At least, the ship neared land. A steady wind already filled the sails and should bring Plymouth Hoe into sight soon. *A day or two more*, Sir George told himself.

A tumult up top roused each man from his respective thoughts—sailors' voices raised in alarm and a bell ringing with great urgency.

At first, Sir George thought he had drifted to sleep and dreamed the sounds. But now his soldier's instincts caused him to yank on his breeches, stockings, and boots as fast as e'er he might.

One cabin over, George Sandys, too, trembled as he reached for his boots.

A commotion at dawn. Either the ship was sinking or pirates were making their way to the *Anne*, dawn being their customary hour of attack. Pirates struck their sails to render themselves near invisible in the half-light while they scanned the horizon for prey on the seas nearby.

But there could not be pirates here in the Narrow Seas off Devon. Could there be?

All thoughts of his translations gone, George Sandys, for one, preferred to hope the ship was sinking.

I Will Reign King at Sea

August 4, 1625
On board the *Anne of Poole* off the English Coast

Go tell the king of England,
Go tell him thus from me,
If he reign king of all the land,
I will reign king at sea.

> —Early seventeenth-century English ballad about the
> pirate captain, Jack Ward

After scrambling up the scuttle, Sir George in front, the two Georges saw a fearsome sight—one they could never have imagined. Three sail of ships, moving rapidly across the waves, were making their way to the *Anne* much faster than she herself could escape.

Pirates.

Sandys looked up the mainmast and rigging where a sailor held a Dutch perspective glass to his eye. This was a new device, Sandys knew, allowing a man to see much further than by his own sight. The glass had apparently given the ship earlier warning than she might have had. This, and this alone, gave the *Anne* some slight chance. But she was facing skilled pirates. Few ships ever escaped through either guns or flight.

Captain Nurrey directed his men to set the sails for speed and away. Others he ordered to prepare the saker and falconets in case the English needed them.

"Take courage, men!" Nurrey cried, tapping a half firkin of rum. He held up the West Indian drink. "Salute, ye lads."

The sailors consoled themselves as they threw back the rum, for soon they might be slaves. If they didn't die upon the voyage, didn't anger the Turks and suffer a gruesome punishment first. Drink rum they might.

The three ships closed in on the *Anne* like sharks circling prey. Two, Sandys could see, were xebecs. These were the sleek, low, slippery, and agile ships of the Moors. Neither of the Georges had ever seen a xebec before, but the triangular lateen sails gave the ships away. The Turks polished the bottoms of these ships so that they glided through the water like greased fish.

Barbary pirates in the Narrow Seas off Plymouth? Those traveling in the Mediterranean knew they took their chances with pirates; but here, just off the coast of England? Sandys stood astounded, speechless.

Several of the *Anne's* sailors now manned the saker and falconets. They blasted several shots toward these closest ships with a deafening noise and acrid smoke.

Horror struck the men anew when they understood the English ordnance could only hit taller ships. The *Anne's* shots missed the xebecs altogether.

Traveling behind these small, lightweight ships was a larger vessel. Dutch, Sir George guessed. Its make differed slightly from an English ship and greatly from a Spanish one. Then, too, it flew Dutch colors.

For a moment, Sir George hoped that the Dutch ship had captured the two xebecs. But as one of the swift xebecs drew nearer the *Anne*, certainty dawned that the vessels were capturing, not captured.

The second xebec drew alongside the *Anne*. Now all could see the many men on board—men with shaved heads and bare arms, dressed in red vests and baggy pants.

Some brandished curved swords. Sandys knew they were scimitars, as he'd seen them before in his travels to Arabia.

Other pirates waved knives.

Some were preparing to fire muskets at the *Anne* while others manned the big guns on the top deck. These guns, Sandys saw, had wooden planks to give those firing protection from small arms.

The pirates began screaming in a strange tongue, threatening, daring, cursing.

Terror, see, was a weapon, too. Brandishing scimitars while hurling insults gave the pirates an advantage. Shaved heads and blood-colored clothing added to the intimidation. The Turks' prey might surrender without e'en a fight. So every good pirate hoped, anyway.

Now, on the larger ship, the Dutch colors came down, and a distinctive green flag with a skull shot up the pole. These were not Turkish colors, but that of some other enemy altogether—an enemy these men would soon know all too much about. Moroccan, they guessed, for Morocco was another land of Turkish pirates.

Outrunning the ships was not possible. The pirates had concealed themselves long enough. Now they were close—too close—to the *Anne*. The Turks knew how to make captured ships light and fast. They removed timber which strengthened the hull and many of the structures above the main deck. Turks were not only adept at sailing but often used European ships as throwaways. Alter the ship to make it light, catch another ship filled with booty and human cargo.

Slaves.

When Turks came upon a hapless ship, all on that ship feared the Turks carrying them away to a Moroccan slave market in Algiers or Tunis.

Nothing in Christendom more dreaded or dreadful. *Dear God.*

But little time to consider that, even while fear gripped its cold, dead hand upon the Virginians' necks and throttled their hearts.

The two xebecs, propelled by a galley of Christian slaves as well as sails, grew e'er closer.

Sandys felt ill, more ill than during the great sickness at James Town. The xebec now hailed musket fire at those on the quarterdeck, blasting the hand off one sailor.

Nonsensically, a song came to Sandys's mind. The old refrain recounted the exploits of Captain Jack Ward, the infamous pirate, and his fight with the *Rainbow*.

> *Go tell the king of England,*
> *Go tell him thus from me,*
> *If he reign king of all the land,*
> *I will reign king at sea.*

Musket fire quickly turned the top deck of the *Anne* into a battlefield, forcing the men below and inside.

Sandys and Yeardley, with instincts to fight, had been on the quarterdeck and now entered the roundhouse. The roundhouse was up on the stern, the highest cabin. From there, they scurried to the cabin beneath it which had loopholes allowing them to fire back. Nurrey and one sailor were with them. The Turks had driven the others below, Sir George guessed.

"Turks prefer to keep the ships whole if they can!" cried Nurrey as loudly as he could above the din. "But they'll do as necessary to win the battle." And just as Nurrey said it, a large ordnance shot plowed into the stern and rained the splintered wood down upon them. Sir George was knocked to the floor with blood upon his doublet, a gash in his head. Sandys rushed over, grabbing a rag, and tried to staunch the flow before returning to the loops.

Through the loops, Nurrey and Sandys could see that the pirates had grappled the ships to fasten them together on the starboard side. Only a moment now before the surging, crying, terrifying men swarmed the ship.

And then they were there, everywhere.

In their midst now a figure, clothed in a blazing red Moroccan vest, strode calmly as though he never doubted his victory.

The piratical captain, Sandys thought, and his blood coursed gelid as the James River in February ice. He felt faint but willed himself to breathe.

More and more Turks climbed aboard, creating a fearsome noise.

The sailor and Captain Nurrey fired and saw one, two, six Turks go down. But so many others covered the deck, the battle was hopeless.

Nurrey knew it. "Quarter!" he cried. "Quarter!" *Take us prisoners* meant the word. "No quarter" meant no prisoners—meant death. Quartering was their only hope of survival.

But the captain, mariners, Sandys, and Yeardley were valuable to the Turks. They'd merit either a fine ransom or a fine sale price as slaves in the marketplace. Sir George and George Sandys would fetch the highest prices of all. And most slaves were never seen nor heard from again.

The poet could hear Adonis barking helplessly back in his cabin. *Good try, old fellow.* Then, *Quarter. Dear God, we are going to Morocco,* Sandys thought, dropping to push the rag once more against Sir George's head as crimson stained his hands.

And Ships that Never Came Back Again

August 4, 1625
On board the *Anne of Poole* off the coast of England;
and at New Towne in Virginia

The father sat, and told them tales
Of wrecks in the great September gales,
Of pirates coasting the Spanish Main,
And ships that never came back again ...
—Henry Wadsworth Longfellow

Below decks, Captain Nurrey signaled Sandys and Yeardley in a whisper, "Keep ye quiet about yourselves. The Turks will see you as golden booty, sure."

They both understood.

And then suddenly, the Turks burst in, shoving them and ushering them back topside.

A fine drizzle now fell.

Sir George still held the rag to his head. A glance down showed that his blood and the blood of others now shone upon the deck. The dark, brooding red spread beneath them as the rain threatened to wash it into the sea. Much of the bloodstain came from the mariner who'd lost his hand. He had collapsed on the deck where he first fell, Sir George saw.

The multitude of Turks thrust weapons—scimitars, muskets, knives. The picaroons outnumbered the Englishmen perhaps ten to one. There was, Sir George thought, no escape. None.

Before them stood the pirate captain in the blazing doublet that Sandys and Nurrey had seen earlier. The captain of the Turks had come on board to speak with the English ship's master. Rather than *lingua franca*, this man, to the captives' astonishment, greeted them in English.

The pirate's tone, cunning but cordial, betrayed an accent that Sir

George recognized immediately. It carried him back to his many years of fighting in the Low Countries, a lifetime ago.

Dutch.

A renegado, a Dutchman who had sided with the Turks and Moors. *I have fought beside your countrymen on the field of battle!* thought Sir George angrily.

The pirate captain lifted his scimitar menacingly in a signal the others seemed to understand.

The Turks then set upon the English. In a moment, the pirates stripped the captives' clothes from them, yanking off stockings and shoes, doublets and breeches and shirts. The several wounded men, including Sir George, received no different treatment.

One of the English sailors whose arm bled profusely screamed in pain, "Mercy! Mercy upon the injured, I beg you!"

The Turks paid him no mind. Yet they separated two mariners and Nurrey for reasons unknown.

Straining to understand the *lingua franca*, Sandys thought the pirates were saying they'd send the trio away on a smaller vessel. Sandys could make out words in a few languages and understood the Turks were referring to the men's infirmities—not worth feeding. One had lost so much blood he couldn't stand, one was lame, and Nurrey was older than the rest.

Sandys somehow realized, through his haze, that while he had heard Adonis barking as the men boarded, the dog was quiet now. The Mahometans hated dogs, believing them filthy. Sandys knew somehow, without knowing why, that the dog was dead.

The oddest thoughts go through one's mind in such circumstances. *I should have left him in Virginia,* Sandys thought. *But Adonis will fare better than I, for I know not what my own fate shall be.*

The yank upon his clothes sent Sir George's wound bleeding anew and caused his head to pound. But he refused to beg for mercy. He represented Virginia—whether these men knew it or not. He had faced down a hurricane at sea and a shipwreck. His wife had starved near to death. They'd both survived an Indian massacre ... Sir George was now a rock of will and determination, created in the iron forge of Virginia. Yet even such will could not prevent him staggering.

Sandys, standing nearby, reached out a hand to steady the knight. A fruitless gesture in the wild flinging and pulling and shoving going on about them.

I've seen wolves fight over meat that were not so ravenous, thought George Sandys. *And those indeed seemed more reasonable.* Sandys himself was fighting the rising dread. He stood now, naked, while one Turkish Moor grabbed his hands and bound them behind him, doing the same to all the prisoners.

Now the captain addressed the English. "I'm your *new* captain! I'll thank ye to remember who is now in charge."

This crazed Dutchman has turned Turk, Sir George thought with disgust. *Given up his Christian religion to become Mahometan.*

The Dutchman-turned-Turk continued. "A fine ship! I thank ye for sharing it with us. Now, onward to what is to be your new home in Salé once we have you gentlemen secure below decks. Truly, you shall *love* Morocco as I do," he said, a reptilian smile upon his face, his dark eyes reflecting no light at all. "And do we have any men of fine breeding on board?" he asked in an almost hospitable tone.

No one spoke.

"No? We'll ask later when ye might be of more, uh, accommodating demeanor."

Sandys's sense of debasement, his humiliation, as he stood like an animal, unclothed and bound, was complete.

Or so he thought. Now another Turk grabbed a sponge rope—as wide as Sandys's arm—and began beating the prisoners as hard as ever he could. Blood wept through the red welts.

And then the pirates kicked all the men one by one down to the 'tween deck where they lay in a pile of aching, bruised, bloody hopelessness.

* * *

Back in Virginia, Tempie startled from a terrifying dream of darkness. She saw George's ship. At least, it appeared to be his ship. She knew somehow that George was on board, though she could not see him. A storm flashed—the sky scarlet—and the ship shook violently. Something was wrong with the ship—something red, red, red. Fire? Blood? Was it sinking? What was she seeing? Everything colored ghastly crimson. She heard men howling and guns blasting.

She shot up in bed as though someone had fired her through a saker. Sweat covered her, a colder one than any sweat in a Virginia August ought to be.

Dressing quickly and ensuring the children were in Susanna's hands, Tempie raced across the swamp causeway to my house. She tried the door—latched—and rattled it, crying, "Joan! Joan! 'Tis I. Hurry!"

Will had stayed at Mulberry Island, and so only Angelo, Esther, and I were in the house. I had just stepped out of bed myself.

Tempie's tone made my heart race. I could *feel* her fright through the door. I rushed over to it, unlocked and opened it. There stood Tempie, hurriedly dressed, her face drained of color. Tears streaked her cheeks.

Sobbing, she fell into my arms.

"What, lovey? What frightens you? Is it the children?" My heart was now in my throat. *Dear God.* What had happened during the night? Could Indians have attacked the Yeardley home over the swamp?

Instinctively, I reached for the scallop shell around my neck and gripped it. I had known Tempie many a year through famine and attack, but I had never seen her like this.

"A spirit or angel has given me a warning." She choked out the words. "Perhaps it comes from God Himself. Maybe even from a demon who might cause such things. A mare of the night has come upon me!" Her voice quivered, and her hands trembled. "'Tis George. Something's wrong. I'm sure of it. I feel it over my whole body. A dream! Red, bloody red. Pray, Joan! Please pray." She shuddered and murmured, "He should not have gone! I tried to tell him so." And she continued to weep for what could be happening away on the sea.

I cried, too. Pray God, it wasn't another hurricane. The sky was eerie red, the sailors said, when that storm it did approach.

Red?

The Endurance of the Human Soul

August 5, 1625
On board the *Anne of Poole* en route to Salé, Morocco

Not in the achievement, but in the endurance of the human soul, does it show
its divine grandeur and its alliance with the infinite God.
—Edwin Hubbell Chapin

I n the gun deck of the ship, the two Virginians had managed to push
themselves apart from the mariners. They wished to be able to plan without the sailors hearing their talk—hard as that was in such close quarters.

Whenever the pirates appeared below decks, as the corsairs did at that
moment, both men ceased conversation.

A little light penetrated the 'tween deck. It must be morning, Sir George
reckoned. His night had been, not surprisingly, fitful and restless. He awoke
to learn that his tormented dreams were real.

The Turks now brought ragged clothing down to the captives, no one to
have more than one piece. Sir George received breeches and Mr. Sandys, a
doublet—Portuguese, he thought.

The pirates unexpectedly threw Sir George some canvas drawers, too.
He guessed he was getting them because of his injury. But as the pirates made
their way through the hold, Sir George whispered to Sandys, "Take them. I
at least have breeches."

Sandys gave a grateful nod.

Trying to don the clothing while bound was a challenge, but at least their
nakedness was somewhat covered.

The corsairs then beat them once more with a rope for good measure.
Sandys could feel more welts and bruises rising, but with his hands thus tied,
he could not touch the sores. As it were, the two Georges were near to each
other, feeling helpless as babes.

A few hours later, the Moorish pirates came down and inspected all hands. Sir George's hands hadn't given him away as anything but a soldier. Sandys they had pegged for a writer. Ink smudges.

It became increasingly clear that these men, these barbarians, were quite good at the business of plundering and slavery.

Now, huddled in the hold of the ship, the two Georges looked askance at one another. Friendly but never great friends in Virginia, the men were embarking upon an unsought adventure together.

Sandys, as far as he was concerned, had lived a fair and fruitful life. The writings in his trunk he hoped to publish. But he was aware that God's timing, God's plans, were not his own. He had jested earlier about his manuscripts, and true enough, he would protect them with all he had. Still, he realized that his fellow from Virginia had much more at stake. A still-young wife and three small children awaited his companionship and protection at home.

Sandys reached with his elbow and nudged Yeardley's arm in what he hoped was an encouraging gesture. Now that the sun was rising, he could see that his friend's wound was no longer bleeding, and for that, he was glad.

Above the clamor of the wild-eyed Moors, the crashing of the wood above, and the screams in an unfamiliar tongue came a voice to Sir George Yeardley.

Son, you are not done yet.

Sir George looked around. Sandys had managed to get himself upright and onto a nearby bench.

Catching Sir George's stare, Sandys gave a half-hearted smile to the knight. *We will get through this somehow,* Sandys hoped his expression said.

Yet the voice Sir George heard had not been Sandys's, and it seemed too calm to be anyone else on board.

Once, in the Yeardley home back at Henricus, Sir George had teased me a little about hearing and seeing things. *Do you 'see' things often, Joan?* Sir George had asked. How could it be that in a time he most needed the encouragement, Sir George himself had received it? He'd just heard a voice he could not explain.

Son, you are not done yet.

Sir George now managed to get himself upward to the same bench as Sandys. The knight's body throbbed with the effort. Deprivation and injury were taking their due toll upon him. He then bowed his head anyway, still grateful for the encouraging words, and George Sandys, seeing the gesture, bowed his as well.

They were in their own silence for a moment, praying or thinking or planning—it was hard to tell which. Neither was sure what he was doing.

Finally, Sandys leaned toward Sir George as close as he might. He said in an undertone, "Yeardley—I'll forbear calling you 'Sir,' sir, if that be all right," he added. "We need to keep your knighthood secret."

In England, one always called a knight "Sir." But they were not in England and may never see England *or* Virginia again. Sir George swallowed hard as fear threatened to overtake him. But the knight simply said, "Good thought."

"We need a miracle, Yeardley," Sandys continued, louder above the din. He leaned toward the knight, hoping Sir George could hear him.

At this, a memory came rushing to the former governor. Sir George remembered Tempie telling him how the women had sought a miracle during the Starving Time. How they had tried to believe in life and hope despite overwhelming odds of ever seeing their husbands again. The husbands who had been on board the lost *Sea Venture*. Another time, another doomed ship that was not, after all, doomed. Sir George could hear Tempie's voice as if she stood beside him. *You know as well as I do that miracles happen every day. If it takes a miracle, a miracle it will be.* The hope that had sustained his wife during the worst of the starving.

And Sir George lifted his eyes to meet those of his friend. "Sandys, you know as well as I do that miracles happen *every day*. If it takes a miracle, a miracle it will be." And then he added, echoing the voice he had just heard, "Friend, we are not done yet!" Sir George said it with all the conviction he could muster. But inside, his doubts flogged and kicked his courage as the pirates had beaten him.

Well, they had beaten him physically. But if bear this he must, bear it he would.

He looked down at the ropes binding his wrists. He was aware that, though he might beg for a miracle, a miracle was still a dim possibility.

He sighed, and the weight of all his family, all his trials, all his striving to make something of himself in Virginia seemed to bear down on him.

"Courage, old man. Courage," whispered Sandys next to him.

The corsairs gave the men only bread and water twice a day. Now, Sir George's doubts grew with his hunger, as his thirst burned his throat.

The ship headed away from England and southward, Sir George was certain, to the North African coast. The knight began to question the voice he'd heard. Yet he continued to repeat the words to himself. *Son, you are not done yet.*

Say them, though you believe them not! You need not believe them. Just say them, say them, he told himself.

But escape by ship was impossible; escape once enslaved in Morocco stretched credulity. Sir George knew that few slaves ever escaped the Turks because, he reminded himself once more, these Moors were very, very good at what they did. Talented, even.

The only conceivable way out, Sir George reckoned, would be if someone ransomed him. How would he obtain the ransom if the opportunity presented? His brother Ralph would never be able to raise a princely sum, especially if the Turks discovered how valuable he, Sir George, was to them.

The knight rolled his eyes. He'd be better off a poor peddler. Of course, none of the Turks knew who he was yet. At least, he thought they didn't. How could he be sure? Might one of the captured mariners talk in hopes of better treatment?

Still, Sir George considered. From Morocco, he could perhaps write to Ralph in England. If Ralph received his letter, he could send it on to Tempie with instructions of how to raise the needed money. Tempie could then sell land and tobacco, all of it if need be.

And then what have I worked for all these years if all my estate be gone to the Turks? Despair threatened to overtake him once more. He turned his attention away from that thought.

Tempie! Praise God, he had married the most capable woman in Virginia. She had shown that she could manage as well as any man. And he had allowed her to. How grateful he was for that! For she knew how. When he was ill or away with Company business, circumstance had forced her to manage. Now, she would have to do so alone once more. She could sell tobacco … send it back to England where Ralph could handle its sale. Ralph could then send the needed sum on to Morocco.

Morocco. North Africa. How? How often did English ships brave these pirate-infested waters? Was there anyone who made trips to Morocco just to ransom slaves? How many months would it take for him to be able to write a letter, send it on to England, and thence to Virginia? Tempie or his men would have to ready the tobacco, then ship and sell it. And then someone must carry the ransom overseas again. Then the money shipped from England to Morocco. The knight's head began to swim with the chain of connections needed. If he even had enough tobacco and perhaps land. He had no idea how large the ransom would be, but he'd heard that even servants required grand sums. How much more his if the Turks found him out?

Despair grew in the knight's heart. Even as Sir George made his plan, he realized that the likelihood of failure was high. He had not been well when he left Virginia, and he now had a festering gash on his head. He was not receiving enough to eat or drink. He was weak.

Whatever voice had attempted to encourage him surely knew nothing of the hopelessness of his situation.

Still Some Solace

August 5, 1625
On board the *Anne of Poole* en route to Salé, Morocco

They chain'd us each to a column stone,
And we were three—yet, each alone;
We could not move a single pace,
We could not see each other's face,
But with that pale and livid light
That made us strangers in our sight:
And thus together—yet apart,
Fetter'd in hand, but join'd in heart,
'Twas still some solace, in the dearth
Of the pure elements of earth,
To hearken to each other's speech,
And each in turn comforter to each ...
                    —Lord Byron

As the knight sat in his dark and brooding thoughts, so Sandys sat in his.

Sandys spoke first. "See here. I've been thinking. You have no real holdings in England, do you?"

Sir George shook his head miserably and said weakly, "All I have is in Virginia. My lands, my cattle, my tobacco." *My wife, my children, my home.*

"Just so, then. I'll attempt to write my brother Sir Edwin. *Edwin,*" he corrected. It wouldn't do for the Turks to overhear that Sandys's brother was a knight, too. "I know how fond Edwin is of you—Virginia Company or no. You've done so much to keep the colony going. He and I and all the former Company stockholders owe you. Now, I have a large family, many brothers. Lady Marg—I mean, Margaret Wyatt, my niece—has some means, although my nephew Francis is yet in Virginia. Let us seek both our ransoms together from them. I shall ask. It's not charity, you understand. You may repay us once you are safely back home—in Virginia."

Sir George felt tears well in his eyes. He never cried in hardship, but something about the kindness of this man in such a circumstance touched him. "The sums for even poor men are great. If they know who we are, the sum needed may be more than we both own together," said Sir George in a lowered tone.

"But we shall try, Yeardley." Sandys felt sure he could procure the ransom—if it were even possible for his family to raise it—more quickly than Sir George. And he could not envision leaving this man, his friend now, behind. Besides, Virginia needed its former and future governor.

The two sat in silence, broken only by Sir George with a fit of coughing. The coughing, in turn, caused his head gash to throb. He wished he could hold his head in his hands. He was brutally uncomfortable. His mind roamed back to happier times—to Tempie; to the boys pretending to be soldiers; to Elizabeth, bestowed with such charm like her mother.

If he died in this endeavor, Sir George thought, he hoped at least his family would know the cause was a just one. In his trunk, he carried the petition to the king about tobacco and the liberty of a General Assembly. All critical to the colony's sustainability and survival.

Idly, he remembered, too, that letter from Menefie to John Harrison, wherever Harrison may be. "*By the* Ann, *whom God conduct,*" Menefie had written upon it. Sir George felt sure God had not conducted *this* voyage.

"You holding up?" Sir George heard Sandys say in the near darkness. The concern in his voice was touching.

"Aye, I suppose." Another cough. Then, "While you were living with the Peirces, did Mrs. Peirce ever tell you of how she and my wife survived the Starving Time together?" Sir George asked.

Sandys shook his head. "She refrained entirely from speaking of it. No, I cannot think that she did."

"The two women created a bond. There was at one time a third woman involved, too, in their pact, but she died during the Starving Time. First the three—then just the two—prayed and wished for a miracle and strove in all ways together. Such a bond they still share to this day. That is how they made it through the blackness and bleakness alive." His voice wavered upon the word "alive." It still pained him to think of Tempie's sufferings during that time he himself had been a castaway in Bermuda in relative comfort.

Sandys was quiet for a moment, and at first, Sir George thought the poet had not heard him.

At last, Sandys said, "Great wisdom they demonstrated in that." His tone turned thoughtful. "Perhaps God has placed us in this unfortunate position together for a purpose. I have the means, the knowledge of other cultures and languages. You have the military experience and the valor needed to get us home." Then Sandys's voice broke, too, on the word *home*. "*For where two or three are gathered in my name ...*" he recited.

"*... there am I in the midst of them,*" Sir George finished. "A pact, then?"

"A pact, brother," Sandys said.

Unknowingly, the two men had just claimed for themselves the same verse that Tempie and I had prayed for their safety before they set sail.

And then Sandys began to regale Sir George with stories of his travels. How quick witted and pleasant the Sicilians were! "Epicharmus of that nation was the first inventor of comedies." Sandys nearly bellowed this out as though such a great truth could never hide. As though it were actually important in the hold of this dark, smelly 'tween deck. Sandys went on to tell of great pyramids "shaped like unto diamonds. The old Egyptians created them for their own vainglory." He described an ancient bridge over the great Nile River and of seeing Solomon's cisterns in the Holy Land, even of a man eaten by a leopard.

Sir George knew that Sandys feigned enthusiasm trying to keep him heartened. And somehow, incredibly, it was working. Sandys hated the sea, and here were the poet's worst fears realized. Yet even so, Sandys was more concerned about the sick and injured Yeardley than himself. The man's generosity of spirit impressed the knight. As well, he noticed that Sandys avoided mentioning any tales of Turks or Moors or pirates just yet. For the moment, it seemed that Sandys, as well as Sir George, would rather think of Egypt, Sicily, the Holy Land, and Greece. Not that place to which they were surely going.

After a while, Sandys noticed that Yeardley's head had dropped. He had nodded off to sleep, Sandys realized. *It is well then,* he thought with satisfaction. *Storytelling is a great potion.*

Neither man was certain what awaited him in Salé. Could they expect more beatings, near starvation, and chains? They knew the Turks would pressure them to convert to their religion as well as force them into slavery.

But at least they were together, not alone.

This Dungeon Stone

August 14, 1625
In the *Mazmorra* at Salé, Morocco

Plunged in night, I sit alone
Eyeless on this dungeon stone,
Naked, shaggy and unkempt,
Dreaming dreams no soul hath dreamt.

Rats and vermin round my feet
Play unharmed, companions sweet;
Spiders weave me overhead
Silken curtains for my bed.
—Frederick George Scott

Within ten days, pushed along by fair winds, the *Anne* approached the entrance to the Bouregreg River. "Known for its sandbar," said Sandys. "Only experienced pilots may make their way up it."

Salé, or Sallee as the English often called it, had never been a pirate haven like Tunis or Algiers. But Salé, it seemed, had suddenly become something of a pirate republic.

The ship once up the Bouregreg dropped anchor.

"We're here," Sir George whispered.

"Indeed," said a frightened George Sandys.

Within an hour, the Turks were herding the prisoners up the scuttle to the main deck and marching them off ship.

Sir George, the soldier, studied everything he could of the landscape, the people, the possible routes of escape.

George Sandys, the traveler, did as well. Sandys knew the world, and he knew that Old Salé was across the Bouregreg River from this town. This town contained an ancient, abandoned fortress these pirates were calling "New Salé."

In fact, New Salé was a town called Rabat.

The oppressive heat and stark sun caused each man to feel lightheaded. Here they stood on the coast of Africa with their fellow captives. All were pale, quivering, and dressed in tattered parts of clothing. Sir George still had on only his breeches and Sandys just the Portuguese doublet with the drawers. The other men looked much the same.

Not for the first time, Sir George thanked God he had not brought Tempie along on this trip. The price of a woman ... Well, he dared not think.

Buildings the color of sand crawled over a hill above the harbor. The two Englishmen saw a large entrance gate. Each realized, to his disgust, that townspeople had clustered near to get their first look at the new captives.

And then a memory came back to Mr. Sandys, distant but still troubling. He was back in Constantinople and the common folks, the Turks, were taunting him. Now, here he was once more. Except this time was worse. Much, much worse.

This time he was enslaved.

Like watching sheep pass as you choose one to purchase, Sandys thought. It made him sick.

As the Turks ushered the *Anne's* men through the streets, the people pointed and jeered. Even children joined in. Mr. Sandys could make out Arabic words: *Dogs! Christian dogs!*

Sir George, while not understanding the words, had no doubt of the meaning.

They passed through the mocking throng, half walking, half stumbling.

Before long, a great building rose before them.

"In, in!" cried the Turks, giving a lash and a kick to the men as they could.

Inside were many other captives—a hundred or more, Sandys reckoned. The Turks had chained the slaves to the walls and shackled great iron balls to their legs. The prison reeked of human waste and human misery. This place, Sandys would soon learn, the natives called the *mazmorra,* the dungeon house.

The Turks, smirking at their captives, chained them to a wall with the others. The two Georges were fairly close together. Thank God. The Turks then removed the manacles on their wrists.

Now what? wondered Sir George. He didn't have to wonder long as some of the townsfolk had followed them in.

They are viewing us as future purchases. We are merchandise! Sir George thought.

Yes, this was plain to see. Some of the folks walked closer to one or the other newcomers. One Turk with dark eyes and rotten teeth mumbled something in Arabic as another lifted Sandys's doublet to study his chest. The man gave it a poke then clucked his tongue at Sandys. He waved his finger as if saying *no, not you* in disapproval.

Sandys saw another man rubbing Sir George's arms, checking for strength, Sandys thought. A companion pointed at the knight's crusted head gash.

Both Englishmen were so, so hungry they felt relief when victuals came out. The food was unfamiliar, at least to Sir George, but victuals nonetheless.

They are fattening us up now! Sandys thought. Indeed they were, but Sandys could not care just then. He was famished.

The hours passed, and Sandys tried to converse with a fellow, a Frenchman, next to him to help pass the time. *I should rather talk than think,* Sandys said to himself. Sandys spoke fluent French, and for this he was grateful. The man knew no English.

The Frenchman, whose name was Honoré, had a wizened face and dirty grey hair. His bright blue eyes shown outward, the last bit of light left on his face. Sandys learned that the Turks had captured Honoré from a fishing boat off the coast of Britanny in France. Honoré had an old wife at home, but they were poor, he said. He had no hopes she could ransom him unless the church contributed money.

The older man shrugged helplessly. There were many such as him from Concarneau, his little town. The church could not pay for all, could not raise that many gold or silver ducats. He would not further impoverish his wife—who had no means of support with him enslaved—for a ransom that may or may not bring him home. Honoré's eyes demonstrated a sort of woebegone acceptance of his own plight, Sandys thought.

The poet listened then nodded sympathetically. He understood.

George, he said to himself, *no matter the circumstances, someone always has it worse than you. A man would do well to remember that.* How fortunate he was that even if his ransom were ten times—no, a hundred times!—that of the poor man beside him, the Sandys and Wyatt families could pay it. It would be painful, no doubt. But they could raise the sum. The devastating effect on the Frenchman's family was obvious.

The Englishman was Anglican, the Frenchman probably Catholic. The two had nothing in common—nothing except that the Turks had reduced their humanity and value down to a matter of ducats and labor.

Honoré gestured to the many men, women, and children shackled as the two men were. He explained that the Moors would hold these captives for about one week and then march them to the *Souk el-Ghezel,* the wool market square.

Their keepers would then parade the naked slaves for an hour or two. The Turks wrote on each prisoner's chest how many gold or silver ducats each captive cost. Strong or skilled workers brought the best prices along with merchants or high ranking officials. The Saletins, or people of Salé, purchased these last for the fat ransom they hope to gain from them. It was a bit of a gamble: would the bidder pay less for the prisoner than the prisoner brought in ransom? If not, the Saletin kept the prisoner as a slave, perhaps allowing the captive to write a letter home begging for money.

The townsfolk would bid on the prisoners, and the prisoners could only hope for a good master. The Frenchman then rattled off the names of a few of the best of the worst and a few of the worst of the worst. Truly, their only hope was a kind master.

"*N'est-ce pas?*" Honoré asked. *Is it not so?*

Sandys nodded.

Honoré had seen many of all ages and stations brought through. They had marched him over to the *Souk el-Ghezel* twice, but no one had yet bought him. He pointed at his protruding ribs. The keepers were trying to plump him up for a better price, he thought. They had not yet succeeded. As well, Honoré said, he had a rash on his legs that deterred potential buyers. He suspected his keepers were hoping the pustules would go away.

Sandys asked what price the Turks had placed on the Frenchman?

Honoré shrugged. "*Seulement quarante ducats.*"

Only forty ducats. At eight shillings per ducat, Sandys reckoned that to be about sixteen English pounds sterling.

But Honoré went on to say that his was a poor price. He had seen others sold for many times that—three hundred or five hundred ducats, much more than that even for men of quality.

Now Sandys understood the gravity of Yeardley and himself remaining undiscovered. The Turks had chained here one knighted Virginia governor and one son of an archbishop, friend to the English prince. He and Yeardley would probably garner the highest price of anyone here.

Trying to push his fears deep inside, Sandys prodded for more answers. "When did Salé become a pirate port?" Sandys asked in French.

His new friend answered that the Spanish king had banned the Moors—called here *Moriscos*—from Andalusia in Spain. So these outcasts had come here, angry and ready to battle Christians. All Christians. Some had been Christians themselves but were now reconverting to the Mahometan religion.

Also, renegadoes of European countries had found their way here, and the native Berbers were also involved. New Salé lived and thrived on the sale of its captives, the selling of booty and captured ships, and slave labor. *"Nous sommes leurs produits." We are their goods.*

Old Salé across the river does not want these exiles, so they have come to inhabit this abandoned town, Rabat. They now call it New Salé, the Frenchman explained.

Understanding glimmered in the poet's eyes. Probably, the Old Saletins considered the New Saletins beneath them. These exiles were not truly wanted anywhere. And so they burned with rage. An opportunist like the Dutch pirate captain came in and capitalized on such anger.

Honoré explained that once night fell, their captors would usher them down to the dungeon. There they were again locked up and made to sleep on the cold ground. In fact, all the *patroonas*—the slaves' owners—brought their Christian slaves back to the *mazmorra* each night.

Sandys was beginning to understand why some would "turn Turk." Those who converted to the Mahometan religion were still enslaved but treated much better.

Sandys's spirit was leaving him, and Yeardley looked much the same. *Utter defeat.*

Then, *if it takes a miracle, a miracle it will be!* A miracle, and only a miracle, could free them now. Even ransoms were slow business. If they could raise the needed amounts, if the monies made it to New Salé at all, if they were even given a chance to write home for it.

But if two starving women could believe in a miracle, so could he, Sandys realized. At least, he could try.

Star of Faith the Dark Adorning

August 14 – 15, 1625
In the *Mazmorra* at Salé, Morocco

We shall have a bon voyago.
　　—Corsair Captain Jan Jansz, alias Murat Reïs

Angels watching ever round thee, all through the night;
In thy slumbers close surround thee, all through the night.
They should of all fears disarm thee, no forebodings should alarm thee,
They will let no peril harm thee, all through the night.

Star of faith the dark adorning, all through the night,
Leads us fearless t'wards the morning, all through the night.
Though our hearts be wrapt in sorrow, from the hope of dawn we borrow,
Promise of a glad tomorrow, all through the night.
　　—English translations of a Welsh folk song

Just as the Frenchman had said, come nightfall, the Turks shuffled the captives down to the dungeon. This dank, windowless place was, impossibly, worse than the *mazmorra*. The darkness lay thick and heavy. Sandys could see nothing.

Instead, he felt the rats crawl across his bare feet, the tickling of cockroaches.

His weary body snatched some sleep as it could, yet his overwrought mind refused to rest. Thoughts merged into dreams of blackness, fear surrounding him like a ghoul. Tears trickled down his cheeks.

What would morning bring? Sandys could only rely on his faith. Being all he had, it would have to be enough.

He could see nothing, not one roach, not one star. Yet just as the vermin were, the stars were. He could see neither, but both were there. And that thought was his solace.

If only an angel could chase his demons from him. Sandys imagined the Archangel Michael standing watch nearby, wielding a sword, ready to fight for him and Sir George and even Honoré.

And then he fell into a merciful, dreamless sleep.

The next morning, the Turks ushered Sandys and Yeardley back upstairs where the populace gawked. While he dreaded that, Sir George had also felt rats crawling past in the dungeon, and he preferred the human variety to the rodents.

Sir George and Sandys had declared they'd seek a miracle, but Yeardley's hope was ebbing. The dampness of the dungeon had caused him to cough much of the night, and he suspected the wound on his head might be septic. He felt dazed and sore besides.

The Turks again chained Sandys not too far away from Sir George, close enough for the two Georges to converse if they raised their voices.

Sir George could see that Sandys' Frenchman friend was near to Sandys again. Good. Sandys was learning a great deal from the man, Sir George reckoned, if the intensity on Sandys's face was any hint.

Now, Yeardley listened as the Christian slaves loudly recited Bible verses they knew, many of them Psalms. As someone shouted a verse, Sir George listened and repeated it to himself. Then he reminded God—not irreverently, he hoped—that his wife once had a great miracle. Now he needed one, too. Another one, he corrected. He'd already escaped the hurricane.

"Come, and behold the works of the Lord, what desolations he hath made in the earth!" cried a woman's voice. Psalm 46?

Someone else recited in Dutch; another in what sounded like Italian.

"He maketh wars to cease unto the ends of the world: he breaketh the bow and cutteth the spear and burneth the chariots with fire!" This sounded like a boy. A brave boy, certainly, Sir George thought. How old? The lad's voice had not yet changed.

And then the verse that perhaps resonated the most with the imprisoned Christians. A man's words, faltering. *"Be still and know that I am God: I will be exalted among the heathen, I will be exalted in the earth!"*

I will be exalted in the earth. All the earth. Even Morocco! You, God, shall be exalted in the land of the Turks! Somehow. Oh, God. Somehow. Sir George was trying to repeat what he heard. He was growing too ill to remember any verses on his own.

Tempie, if I go, you are the strongest woman and the best wife, and you shall endure and make me proud. Water was sliding from his eyes again. What was happening to him? His sons would take care of their mother, someday. They were too young just yet. Tempie was still young, too. Surely, she'd remarry. Who would his children's stepfather be? *No! I'll return somehow.*

The Northwestern African heat was blistering, searing, unbearable as the sun rose higher. Sir George's vision swam before him.

Just then an aged Moorish man came around to give the prisoners water from a ladle, which helped a little.

A miracle it will be. Was he being greedy, expecting God to save his life twice by miracles? Perhaps. The sun speckled the grey floor through openings and seemed to dance and fly. *I think I am becoming faint.* The sun dappled through the shadows looked, for a moment, like light angels. *I shall die here and see true angels, I suppose.* He heaved a sigh which came from the bottom of his soul rather than the bottom of his distress.

Into this holding pen walked a man, a native who, by his dress, was someone of importance.

"Ah," Honoré said to Sandys in French, "They call him the Saint of Salé." A *marabout*, a holy man, and the chief of the town. His name, the Frenchman said, was Sidi al-Ayachi. With the *marabout* came two others, one a man of square shoulders with fairer hair but the creased face of a seaman. He was discussing something with the holy man.

"And who is that?" Sandys indicated the one with broad shoulders. "He appears to be a European runagate."

Oui, Honoré said. In fact, the most famous and powerful renegado in all of Salé. His given name was Jan Jansz of the Netherlands. He'd turned Turk and taken the Arabic name of Murat Reïs—Captain Murat, Admiral of the Saletin pirate fleet, ceremonial governor here, and now a very wealthy man. With a grimace, Honoré referred to him as *un corsaire extraordinaire*—an accomplished pirate. Murat, Honoré said, was one reason the Sallee rovers were now terrorizing the Atlantic so far from their usual Mediterranean lair.

Honoré's knowledge impressed Sandys, and Sandys said so.

His French friend pointed to his ears and said, *"Ah, l'homme attentif echappé peut-être."* The attentive man perhaps escapes! And then he gave a bitter laugh. No one ever escaped from the *mazmorra*.

Jansz barely seemed to notice the wretched prisoners as he walked through.

Sandys felt hatred welling within himself, an emotion he rarely experienced. He estimated that close to a thousand helpless souls were imprisoned here. This man—this renegado Dutchman—was enriching himself. He was doing so on the backs of his fellow Dutchmen, not to mention the English, Irish, Portuguese, Italians, Spanish ...

Sandys drew a deep breath. He must keep his head and learn all he could just as the wise Honoré had. This was merely another traveling adventure, he told himself. Albeit, an unhappy and miserable one. But perhaps if he were ever ransomed, he could help others.

"And the third man? Also a renegado, no doubt?" asked Sandys in French.

Honoré shrugged, saying he'd never seen him before.

This third man, thin and blackened from the sun, listened to the conversation of the holy man and the pirate Jansz respectfully. As he did so, he cast his eyes about the room.

Sir George was also watching with interest through bleary vision. He must stay alert, awake, aware. As a military leader, he understood the importance of studying his captors, particularly those who appeared to be of highest rank.

These last two looked to be European. *Renegadoes,* Sir George thought with disgust. All three were wearing traditional Moroccan clothing and seemed all too comfortable in it. *While we wear sparse rags.* Sir George's helpless bitterness and anger did him no good. Men like these were the reason he and Sandys were here to begin with. *I'd like to see all three swing from a yardarm!* he thought, though he suspected hanging was too good for them.

Now, to Sir George's surprise, the thin, swarthy man leaned over and whispered to one of the mariners from the *Anne*.

The mariner said something in return, which over the din neither Sandys nor Yeardley could hear. *That man is so darkened from the sun, he must have been here many a year,* Sir George said to himself.

Meanwhile, Sandys took it all in. He would, he hoped, be able to explain to Sir George all that Honoré had told him at some point. But for now, both Georges had their eyes on the three men as they strode through. What were they after? Sir George wondered. Why were they here?

Then, to Sir George's astonishment, the thin European walked directly over to him and gazed down at him with kind eyes. In a crisp English accent, this man said, "Sir George Yeardley? We're acquainted through reputation though not by face. My name is Captain John Harrison, former governor of Bermuda and special secret envoy to Sallee from his majesty, the king of England. I've traversed the desert from Tétouan in pilgrim's dress to meet with these gentlemen." He indicated the two men who awaited him. "And I have been here well received. What great fortune I was present when they brought you in! Despite the fabulous ransom these men must forego ... I hope to set you and Mr. Sandys free."

Sir George's eyes widened, and he could not even stutter a reply. He apparently was hallucinating. Or was he?

Captain Harrison, seeing Sir George's confusion, said, "The sailors talked. They thought to save their own hides by telling the Dutch captain about you. One of them has just now pointed you out to me."

Sir George blinked hard, but his mind refused to clear. *This man says he's John Harrison?* Lieutenant Harrison's only brother? Sir George must be faint from the heat, the hunger, and the injury, he reckoned. He could not believe what he was hearing. "I ... I have a letter to you in my trunk about your brother's Virginia estate," he said stupidly.

Harrison smiled warmly and said, "Truly, you did not have to bring it all the way here."

A Most Desperate Journey

August 15, 1625
Salé, Morocco

*I undertook a most desperate journey by land from Tetuan to Sallie in a
disguized Morish habite ... and the greatest parte on foote, barelegged and
pilgrime-like ...*
> —Capt. John Harrison, writing about his Moroccan
> journey in the summer of 1625

*Within a few daies after, [the Turkish leaders] caused a pregon or
proclamation to bee made that noe Englishman heareafter should bee bought
or sould, as hearetofore, by the Turkes, or made captives, but freelie trade, as
in times past; and that under a great penaltie.*
> —31 July 1625, letter from John Harrison, King
> Charles's agent in Morocco, reporting on his success
> in getting the Moroccans to agree to a piracy truce

John Harrison escorted the two prisoners to his quarters in Salé as soon
as the guard freed the pair.

As the men walked, Captain Harrison placed a finger on his lips.
Say nothing of importance until we are alone, his face said.

In tacit agreement, Sir George expressed his sympathy to Mr. Harrison
about his brother's death in Virginia.

Harrison sighed and regret filled his voice. "Ah, my younger brother.
Why did he go a-dueling? He had a hot temper, I fear me. It has finished
him."

Sir George assured the envoy that while his brother had indeed dueled
at James Town, the rapier cut the younger Harrison received on his knee
had not caused his death. The doctor and several surgeons had examined

Harrison's body, determining that he had a grave illness. "They believe he would have died shortly of his malady regardless," Sir George finished.

"Cold comfort, I'm sure," Mr. Sandys added.

"Indeed. Well, I thank those in Virginia for establishing that," said Harrison. "At least, my mind is at peace."

When they arrived at Harrison's chambers, they spoke freely.

Harrison could see that the Virginians were famished and thirsty, so he found them food and drink and fresh clothes.

Sir George thought it would amuse Tempie if she could see him in a tunic. Unfamiliar Moroccan attire would have to do until they could retrieve other clothing from the ship. Besides, the less conspicuous they looked, the better.

"We're so grateful to you, Mr. Harrison," Sandys said, stirring his coffé and sitting on a cushion as all did here. Sandys had seen coffé before in Arabia, even visiting a coffé house.

But Sir George stared at the bitter, midnight-black drink and wished for a glass of sack or a pint of ale. Still, he could only say 'twas better than bread and water!

The stew before them had strange flavorings, but Sir George was hungry and ate without hesitation.

"Beef you'll recognize," said Harrison. "The wheat the Moroccans call *couscous*." Then Harrison added, "Sir George, I assure you that before you leave, we'll find a Turkish doctor to see to your head wound."

Freedom and a warm meal were doing wonders for him already, Sir George assured his host.

As they ate in privacy, Harrison explained the secret mission of his work in Morocco. He made both men swear to say and write nothing of their experiences until all the negotiations and the war incident with Cadiz, Spain, were long past.

The whole point of his presence, Harrison said, was the king's hope that the Spanish outcasts here would fight with him against Spain. "Our new king, Charles, is not so forgiving of the Spanish as was his father!" Harrison said. "And of course, his majesty hopes fair dealings will free as many English slaves as possible. I'll be able to use your release as a show of good faith between the two nations."

So the new king—Charles—was not the pacifist his father had been. Sitting there in Salé, Morocco—of all places!—the two Georges learned for the first time that King James had died in March.

"His majesty James is dead then?" Sandys asked. "The new king, Charles, is a childhood friend of mine. *The king is dead. Long live the king!*" he said, holding up his coffé as if in salute.

Sir George had believed he'd be presenting a petition to King James. Now he wondered if the new king would be amenable to Virginia's elected body, its General Assembly.

Harrison went on to promise that he himself would let the new king know of the Turkish leaders' generosity to these leaders of Virginia.

"And when did you arrive here, Harrison?" Mr. Sandys asked, savoring the warm stew.

"I sailed into Tétouan early in June," Harrison said. Tétouan was in Northeast Morocco on the Mediterranean, he explained. He'd begun negotiations with several *marabouts*, including al-Ayachi of Salé, while there.

Traveling from Tétouan to Salé across the breadth of Morocco would be dangerous, the Saletin leaders had told him. But journeying overland, rather than by ship, allowed him to arrive in Salé stealthily. "All along the way were *revueltas*, and the people acknowledge no king," Harrison added.

"*Revueltas?* Do you mean 'revolts'?" asked Mr. Sandys.

Harrison nodded.

Moreover, Harrison had learned that the Spaniards were looking to betray him by way of an ambush along his way. So the diplomat had changed his route, crossing the high mountains near Fez to avoid those dangers. He'd walked most of the way, bare-legged and pretending to be a pilgrim.

At Alcazar, some had recognized him for the thousand-ducat bounty on his head. These men had nearly captured him to carry him to Mamora or Larache—dangerous outposts. But Harrison had befriended two *sheiks*, desert wanderers, he said, and these men had helped him cross the desert to Salé. This was why his skin was so dark. He'd left Tétouan in late July and so had only just arrived himself when the pirates brought the *Anne* into the harbor.

The fortuitous timing—the miracle—still awed both Georges.

"I've been to Morocco many times. I traveled here for Queen Elizabeth and King James—long before I was governor of Bermuda," Harrison said. So when the new king was seeking a secret envoy, Harrison seemed a first choice. He was familiar with the customs of the people and knew something of the language.

"My heart, I must admit, is yet with the Moroccans. I feel that I do more good here than I do in Bermuda, much as I loved the place. But here, I sense the displaced Moriscos and the Jews in Salé are ready to become

Christians. Perhaps?"

I do not see it, Sir George thought. He exchanged glances with Sandys and suspected the poet felt the same way. But Harrison's kindness, his acting as their savior, meant that they were not going to disagree.

Harrison told them that upon ascending the throne, King Charles had decided immediately to go to war with Spain. Who better to support his war efforts than the displaced and angry Moriscos? Not to mention, the Moriscos possessed a port strategically opposite Cadiz, Spain.

Charles envisioned an alliance with Salé and a treaty. The Saletins would fight for him against their mutual enemy, Spain. As part of the treaty, the pirate Admiral Jan Jansz would cease attacking ships off the English coast and release English slaves.

"Late in July, we reached an accord whereby they do agree to stop attacking English ships. Of course, the Dutch captain captured you before he knew of the treaty. Sidi al-Ayachi and Captain Murat were most gracious in letting you go. I hope to free others, but these men are liberating you as a goodwill gesture to his highness in England. I do not reckon to get many more out of the country." He shrugged. "But perhaps. They hope releasing a Virginia governor will win favor with our king."

Good-hearted Sandys asked what the chances were of the Turks freeing Honoré.

Harrison shook his head. "He's French and beyond my reach," he said apologetically. "As I say, I'm still unsure I can get any more English released, much less a poor Frenchman."

As he sipped his coffé, Sandys recalled the pleading look in the Frenchman's eyes as the Turks had unfettered the two Georges. Sandys had called back to Honoré in French asking his surname.

"Despret!" the old fisherman had cried. *"Je suis Honoré Despret!"* I am Honoré Despret.

Perhaps I can be the vessel of a miracle for Mr. Despret just as Mr. Harrison hath been for me, Sandys thought.

The Pilgrim to His Home

May 11, 1626
New Towne, Virginia

Sir George Yeardley left Northborn suffering from loss of appetite and goes to seek physic in London.
—Sir Edwin Sandys to John Farrar, 23 December 1625

Shine on her sweetly-scented road,
Thou star of evening's purple dome,
That lead'st the nightingale abroad,
And guid'st the pilgrim to his home.
—Thomas Campbell

The evening star glowed over the James River, shimmering and reflecting May's full moon off the water. The sun was setting, and the late spring skies in Virginia glowed their lilac hues, making the James seem dusky purple and tranquil.

Does the sky reflect the sea or the sea reflect the sky? Sir George thought idly. No matter. 'Twas all beautiful to him this night.

Sir George had been home three days. He could smell the forests and the wildflowers. At least, so he imagined. He had left the desert behind him, pray God, forever. He was here at last. Virginia seemed so peaceful to him, he vowed he'd never again leave his home or his family.

And Sandys? Good Mr. Sandys had departed Virginia the previous July with plans to return here. But if Sir George adjudged correctly, the itinerant poet's traveling days were over.

Sir George felt much the same. God had spared him from not one but *two* ship catastrophes. Such good fortune and the smile of God upon him he would not ask a third time.

She was so delighted to see him that Sir George couldn't bring himself to tell Tempie at first what had happened to him. Of course, she noticed the weight he'd lost and the scars from the gash. Shipboard incidents, he'd said. Tossed in a violent storm. She'd believed him as she had no reason to distrust his answer. He would tell her later, but he was reliving it already in his dreams night after night. He could not bring himself to speak of it just yet.

But this much he could tell her. He had conducted his business with King Charles posthaste. He'd presented the letter and the pleas to the king and Privy Council and then waited for the king to ratify him as new governor of Virginia.

The plague had been rampant in London at the time, and he understood it had ravaged Morocco just before the Turks brought him there. Little plague remained by the time the pirates had brought Sandys and himself into the English capital.

Perhaps God does indeed look out for this old Virginia soldier. He had narrowly missed plague in not one but two places. And he doubted not that had he stayed in Salé's dank dungeon longer, he should not have survived the experience.

Sir Thomas Smythe had died in September from plague, Sir George heard. So passed another of Virginia's champions—even though he and Yeardley had not agreed on much. Smythe had died just weeks before Sir George had, at last, reached London in October. He and Sandys had stayed in Morocco long enough to regain their strengths.

After conducting his business, Sir George had traveled to Northbourne, Kent. He relished a chance to visit his friend Sir Edwin Sandys. Sir George had found there Sir Edwin's brother, George Sandys. The two erstwhile captives had formed a friendship that, Sir George thought, would last until the end of their lives.

Sir George was thirty-seven. George Sandys a decade older. And Sir Edwin almost thirty years older than the young Sir George. Yet the two men, Sir Edwin and Sir George, found they enjoyed one another's company very much. Too, the older knight was always eager to hear of life in Virginia. He and the Ferrar brothers had devoted much of their lives trying to make Virginia a success.

"Ah, if I'd only been a younger man ..." Sir Edwin had said, tamping his pipe upon the table.

Sir George had smiled knowingly. Virginia was so much easier in the telling of it than the living in it. Yet he appreciated the two Sandys brothers for they treated him as an equal for his accomplishments.

A stay among the two brothers with little pressure on him was just what he needed, he thought. Sir George spent about a month at Northbourne recovering from his ordeal at sea and in the *mazmorra*. Mr. Sandys stayed a fortnight, but then returned to his home in London.

Sir George found that the poet had already described the ordeal to Sir Edwin. "Write it not into any letters nor share it on the street," Mr. Sandys cautioned his brother. "For Mr. Harrison's mission is the king's most secret diplomacy. We've sworn an oath that we'll forbear discussing it."

Sir Edwin's cook prepared bountiful meals for the beleaguered once-and-future governor. Mutton, pork, shred pies, cheese, apples, nuts, and puddings.

"Can't you eat?" Sir Edwin's wife Katherine had asked him with concern.

Sir George had shaken his head. He knew the victuals before him to be delectable, but he could not eat them. And he had no idea why.

At last, with Christmas coming on, Sir George thanked his hosts. With Sir Edwin's good wishes, he rode to his brother Ralph's home away in London. Ralph, the apothecary, should be able to provide him some physick for his appetite loss. The gash was healing well.

Christmas in London with Ralph and Rose and their children would be almost as delightful as being with his own wife and children. Almost.

Come spring, he expected the king to sign his commission to be the incoming governor. And then ... the loathsome thought of boarding a ship to pass through those Narrow Seas. But a ship would take him home to his family. So he would do it somehow, no matter how much he feared it.

And then his appetite left him all over again.

Now, he was finally home. The voyage had brought nothing more unsettling than storms.

Just then, Tempie came up behind him and rubbed his shoulders. "George, you're as thin as a tuckahoe reed in the marsh." She smiled at her own allusion. Even their proverbs were becoming Virginian. "You still aren't eating well. I can feel the bones in your shoulders."

"I, uh, haven't had any appetite since before Christmas. I'm unsure why," Sir George stammered.

The concern shone in her eyes. "We'll butcher a beef just for you."

He tried to appear eager. "That would be splendid, Tempie." Ralph's physick had helped a little. Perhaps he could eat better now that he was home.

He knew that the present governor, Sir Francis, wanted to get back to his own wife and children. Sir Francis had a child he'd never seen. And the present governor also must settle his father's estate. So Sir George would take the governor's oath soon.

Sir George intended to pull Sir Francis aside before the departing governor boarded ship. First, to warn him of the dangers he and Sandys had encountered. Second, to let him know that he and his uncle had arrived back to London safely in a most providential manner. Harrison's mission was secret, but Sir George would have to share it quietly for Sir Francis's own safety.

Sir George also wanted to apprise the outgoing governor, as this might be his last chance, of how much Sandys had done for him. He wanted to tell him what a kind and generous soul Mr. Sandys was. And how they had supported each other in the midst of a living torment.

Within days after Sir Francis sailed, for better or for worse, he would be governor again.

Tempie was talking, and Sir George realized that his mind had been wandering. She smiled at him and said, "You seem to be far away."

He nodded. "I'm sorry. Indeed, very far in my mind, but with you now." How far away, she could not have imagined!

He couldn't bring himself to mar her joy with what might have been. But he would tell her soon. Because from what Tempie had said, dark dreams had plagued her while he was away at sea. Even when she supposed him to be in England—when he, in fact, stood chained to a dungeon wall.

"I prayed—well, Joan and I and even Susanna prayed for you, George. We prayed for you and for Master Sandys from, oh, I suppose the fourth of August until early October. Until my bad dreams subsided."

"I have seen prayers at work myself," he said mysteriously.

"Now," she continued, not noticing his wry expression, "I feel rather foolish. Alarming my friend and my sweet servant girl for naught. Of course, perchance the prayers prevented something horrible from happening? Who can know?"

He smiled wanly. "Perchance, indeed. A man at sea covets all the prayers he might receive." She still looked to him like the young girl he'd married, even after all the hardship. He wondered if she knew that.

She squeezed his hand. "Never leave me again, George."

To her surprise, tears appeared in her husband's eyes. "No. Never."

The Earliest Fruit on the Fig Tree

August 24, 1626
New Towne, Virginia

Here [in Virginia] grow as good Figgs, as there do in Spain, but there are few planted as yet.
—Thomas Glover, 1676

I saw your forefathers as the earliest fruit on the fig tree in its first season.
—Hosea 9:10

Our son Tom, no longer a child but a young man of fourteen, had completed his schooling in the spring and—at long last—had returned to Virginia. Our Virginia-born son. Tom was small and fair and of a slighter build than his father, but eager to become a soldier in Virginia. Will reminded him that soldiering went with farming here, though.

I sighed. *Soldiers and soldiers and soldiers.* My life had been from camp to camp, it seemed.

I tried not to think of Tom fighting. But Will was delighted. He nearly strutted to know that his son had returned and would be taking over some of the family work out at Mulberry Island. He would also be able to help with the lands on the Maine and across the water from James Town.

Jane and Roger Smith made their home at Mulberry Island now, and so Tom would live with his sister out there.

Cecily, meanwhile, had married William Farrar, and they made their home still at Jordan's Journey. Just a few months before, the king had placed Mr. Farrar on the council, just as Roger had been. Both men had much-respected roles.

Now Tom was home and would start learning his father's tobacco business.

And for me, healthy rains this year had made our gardens prosperous all over. Everything felt right in my world as if all the stars smiled down on me.

Standing behind my home, I surveyed the fig orchard. The early evening August sun, dropping low, swept away some of the heat making it bearable to be out of doors. But then emerged the little biting flies the Spanish called *mosquitoes* which were such a nuisance. Heat or biting flies? I chose the coolness and withstood the flies.

In England, we never had such heat or these mosquitoes either.

Still, nothing could make me unhappy this evening. The fig bushes were green and the branches filled with blossoming figs.

So far as I knew, no one had planted any figs except for me. Will was proud of my success, and I was a mite proud, too. Here was proof that a Bermudian and Mediterranean fruit could flourish in Virginia. As for the plantains, they had never come up from the ground.

This would only be my second fig harvest. The first two summers, the trees were not mature enough to produce fruit.

Now, the long wait was paying off. Last year's harvest, my first, had been no more than perhaps twelve or thirteen dozen figs. This year looked to be triple that!

Figs, I was learning, required patience to cultivate, but paid handsomely in rich, sweet fruit. Many figs had already fallen to the ground, and more were dropping each day.

I picked one up and studied it. A fig was small, a purple-brown color with a bulbous base. The top rose into a dainty spire. One could eat the skin as well as all the fruit and seeds.

Taking a bite, I marveled again at the tiny seeds, the rich sweetness. Eating a fig was like eating a pudding.

Delicious as all that, and good physick as well. Gerard said that various treatments of figs made them good healers. One could dry them or powder them. They made a fine remedy boiled with nuts or soaked in wormwood wine.

Gerard praised figs, especially when dried. He said they were good for the throat and lungs, for coughing, and for preventing the effects of poison. Figs could cure tumors behind the ears, dropsy, boils and stomach cluttering. Gerard claimed, too, that figs could relieve stones of the kidneys, toothaches, and rough skin. Even throat swellings and pustules.

Altogether, figs may have been a better curer than sassafras. Imagine that, better than sassafras!

Here was I, with a garden abounding in figs already. And if I understood growing figs properly, a greater harvest each year for the next six years. Aye, a crop of patience, certainly.

Angelo or Esther could gather the figs for me, and sometimes they did, but I enjoyed seeing the fruit fill my basket. A simple pleasure in a complicated settlement.

Just then, Tempie crossed the causeway which led from her orchard, through Roger and Jane's land, into my own fig grove. She and Sir George, though entitled to use the Country House, had decided to let it out instead. "We're done with moving," Tempie had told me.

Now as she walked toward me, she admired the plump bushes, weighted down with fruit.

"Figs!" she said happily. "You've done well."

"Thank you," I said with pride. "Have some, and take you a bushel home. The figs' goodness has made my efforts worthwhile, I think."

Tempie gathered a few from the ground.

Will had built for me a bench in the garden, and my friend sat with a sigh, still holding her figs. She took a bite. "Delicious indeed."

I spread my arms wide to show the bounty. "Look how many, Tempie! I may harvest thirty bushels this year. And more to come in the next half dozen years. But since I can't dry them, what shall I do with them?"

The year before, I'd tried drying some of the figs as they do in Spain or Italy. I'd spread the figs in the sun, but I quickly learned that the air was too damp here. The figs had rotted. Then, too, as the fruit lay on the ground in the sun, birds would steal them. I'd even had one of Will's men throw a fishing net over the figs to discourage the birds.

Now, here I had more figs even than last year. Such good physick, but this fruit spoiled quickly.

"Well, marmalade is usually made with quinces. Why not try it with figs? Then you could have the healthfulness of figs stewed and preserved in sugar," Tempie said, eating another one.

Marmalade had been around in the Mediterranean world since a time no man could remember. For a century or so, wealthy Englishmen had imported marmalade shaped into bricks from Portugal. These made a sweetmeat and a physick, both. Some were now making marmalade in England.

"Hm, marmalade? I could try. Still, I have more figs than even that. But I could preserve some, certainly."

"You could also try making some fig beer or fig wine," Tempie added. Then she exclaimed, "I have an idea, Joan! Why don't you see if Dr. Pott would buy them? He's talented in distilling waters. He could surely use them to create a cordial somehow."

"Of course! If Dr. Pott will buy my figs, I can make my own provision. Provide for myself at least a little," I said, thinking aloud. "I'll approach him tomorrow."

Tempie agreed, musing. "We here are different women than those in England. We've learned to be self-sufficient more than they, I think. We've lost so many men and faced strange events, too. We women have had to think for ourselves, just as Cecily confronted the pastor. Some are managing plantations. Mary Bailey here in James Cittie hath done it. Isabella is learning, as am I." Then she paused. "That's actually what I came to talk with you about."

I gave her a curious look, encouraging her to continue.

She wasted no time before saying, "First, I must tell you what happened to George—both our Georges!—while they were away at sea. And 'tis a secret," she added conspiratorially. She glanced around to make sure no one else could hear.

Secret? Now she had my interest!

And the Stars of the Sky
Fell to the Earth

August 24, 1626
New Towne, Virginia

Kelinet [Kililet] Hitchcock sworne & examined sayth that about Aprill last past John Upton ... desired that he might have the house & ground at Blacke point of my Lady Yeardley, gieveing unto her a reasonable rent because of ye repairing of the house & ye fense, & agreed to pay one hundred waight of Tobacco, & repair ye house & ye ffense.
> —Minutes of the Council and General Court,
> 13 January 1627

And the stars of the sky fell to the earth, as a fig tree casts its unripe figs when shaken by a great wind.
> —Revelation 6:13

I sat beside Tempie after I gathered a few more figs. We enjoyed our treat as the shadows of the day grew longer.

Tempie explained that Sir George had finally admitted to an encounter with Turkish pirates. The freebooters had captured his ship, taking him and most on board to Morocco. She told me about John Harrison and the two Georges' providential release.

"Joan, word reached his majesty that the Turkish leader released George and Mr. Sandys. Our men's good treatment impressed the king, so his majesty decided to parley with the Turkish ambassador. This could be the beginning of peace and the end of the Turks' piracy, the release of many more captives. George believes the new king will not tolerate as much as did our late king, James."

She added, "George says he never truly understood how you and I felt during the Starving Time. Now he appreciates what it means to be completely helpless and hopeless, how this created an unbreakable bond between us. He drew hope from *us!* From us, Joan. Imagine that," she said with wonderment. Then her tone darkened. "It terrifies me to even think of the Turks capturing him, imprisoning him in such a place," Tempie whispered. "God surely was with them. I'm just glad I didn't know at the time."

This news left me near speechless. "Welladay, Tempie! Truly? Sir George and Mr. Sandys? The Turks, you say? And Lieutenant Harrison's brother, the one who dueled Dick Stephens, secured their release?" This was a great amount to take in. Then I remembered Tempie's terrifying dreams. "But ... 'tis as if you *did* know. Somehow."

"Oh, bah, Joan. Beware the words from thy mouth, lest they brand me a witch!"

"Aye, true is that," I said. "But none more likely to come to trial on it than Mistress Wright."

We'd been hearing tales from those who lived near our old midwife across the river and from her former neighbors down at Kecoughtan. Neighbors spoke of the bewitchment and curses Goody brought upon them. Such gossip wasn't new; folks had been whispering about Goody Wright for seven or eight years. So far, though, the accusers had not taken the step of having the court try Mrs. Wright. And we were glad.

Goody Wright had delivered our babies and blessed us with healthy children, all. And even those, like Maria Bucke, whose children had been infirm, blamed not our midwife.

"Do you remember what happened when Isabella's son Henry was born a few years ago?" Tempie asked, taking a bite of another fig.

I did. As Isabella had labored, the midwife crowed, "Your baby is a boy, and ye have no worries of tonight. He'll grow to be a man of Virginia, a councilor he be!"

Not that the baby had even been born yet.

"Her predictions make me so uncomfortable," Isabella had whispered to me later. "She needs to be careful lest someone call her 'witch!'"

"I'm not a witch, though I do understand conjuring a little," the midwife had fired back from the next room. How was it even possible she'd heard?

"Good Lord," I'd whispered in return.

"Goody Wright's problem is her harshness, her unbridled tongue," Tempie said to me now on my little bench. "She never could abide a fool!" Then her voice sobered. "About George, though, this journey was hard on him. Now he can sometimes eat and sometimes not. He's growing quite meager, I'm sure you've noticed."

Actually, I hadn't. Sir George spent larger amounts of time in his home in New Towne and less roaming the settlements since his return to the colony.

"George struggles to keep our houses and fences repaired. A few months past, Goodman Upton approached Mr. Hitchcock asking if I might lease one of the smaller houses on the property here. I'm so grateful to have Hitchcock's help with such matters."

Kililet Hitchcock, once a servant of the Yeardleys, had since earned his freedom, and now Tempie paid him to help her manage her properties. Sir George was doing less of that as his health confined him more.

Tempie went on, "Of course, George was in England when Mr. Upton approached us. Still, Upton is aware of how many repairs that property needs, so he asked if I might give him a lesser rate." Her shoulders slumped a little. "Once George is well ...," she said wistfully, her voice trailing off.

"How does Sir George manage the business of the government?" I asked her. "Not that I distrust his ability, even though he's ill," I hastened to add.

She hesitated. "He doesn't fare too well, I'm afraid to say. So I'm starting to help by taking on more of our family's business. Land sales, tobacco, and corn, overseeing the servants at all the properties."

Tempie's face let slip the strain she was feeling. Beyond trying to manage the plantations' business, she feared her husband's health wasn't improving. Even if she tried to say otherwise.

Sir George had bouts of illness going back probably six years. Added to that, he had endured losses in the massacre and commanded the Indian war. His imprisonment would have caused him further physical and emotional distress. Then he had confronted a new king with our General Assembly petition, endured two sea voyages, and returned to the governorship. All these things had exacted their due toll, I was certain.

Suddenly a knot of worry was in my own belly, too.

Tempie went on. "We've discussed it. George believes in me, that I can take care of these things."

"And how will you manage with the little ones?" I asked, but even as the words came from me, I knew the answer. Susanna was a tremendous help to Tempie.

"Susanna is an angel. She's like my own daughter." When Susanna's indenture had ended last year, Tempie had offered to pay the young girl to stay on to help with the children. The Yeardley brood was as attached to Susanna as she seemed to be to them.

Tempie mused. "As for George, if I can remove some strain from him, I believe he can recover. And no more trips at sea!" she said firmly.

"Do you think you could stop him from going?" I asked, skepticism creeping into my voice.

"He has promised me, and I believe him. But then again, if duty calls him …"

How well I knew that.

As for me, after learning of the real danger of the Turks and the Spanish sea fight, my ocean fears threatened to strangle me. These fears had remained as a remnant of my father's death at sea and the hurricane but now bolted through me anew like lightning over the river. I had been here near twenty years without a single voyage home. A reason to stay had always stopped me from sailing, most especially that the Company had not allowed colonists to leave Virginia until 1617.

Will had returned to England once but had asked me to remain behind and make sure our affairs were well tended. I had done that with John Rolfe's help. Now, I could not see myself ever returning to England, much as I missed some things there.

"I pray for your sake that it be so, never more to sea," I said. "I don't know if I'll ever go over sea again myself either. Pirates and Spaniards and hurricanes …" My voice trailed off. I tossed my head as if I could remove the thoughts of such beasties. "Fie, if Virginia don't kill us, the sea will, sure!" I laughed, but a touch of bitterness edged it.

"But you'll want to return to England at least once?" Tempie asked, surprised. "Just to visit and to remember how it was? See the old sights?" She sighed. "Oh, sweet London. Sweet as this fig!" Tempie considered the luscious blue fruit in her hand.

"Sweet as a fig? London? I remember it as crowded, noisy, and dirty."

She laughed. "Oh, Joan, London would enchant you anew if you only endured the ocean voyage. Then feel the joys of the thriving city for what they are. Small things can be delightful if you but seek them and see them."

I couldn't imagine anything pressing enough to best my fears and make me board a ship. "My brothers and parents are all gone. Nothing but sepulchers there be now." I felt a twinge at the thought of my little son's grave in the old churchyard. Even that could not make me desire to go. "No, I won't be going back," I said firmly.

"I predict something will be important enough one day. Something greater than your fears," Tempie said. "The fates have their own ideas, I fear me. May they use you well!"

I chuckled. "Oh, eat your fig."

She tittered, too. "We'll leave it lie for now."

As we sat there that day, a rare August breeze tickled past. A few mosquitoes nipped our arms as the day drew to a close.

Still, there might be truth in what Tempie had said. To declare I'd never again sail was, perhaps, to lure the fates to find a way to force my hand. Could the fates be so tempted? Just the thought made me uneasy.

Most Delightfully Sweet

August 25 to September 9, 1626
New Towne, Virginia

But they shall sit every man under his vine and under his fig tree; and none shall make them afraid ...
—Micah 4:4

Patience is exceeding bitter; but its fruits are most delightfully sweet.
—Jean-Jacques Rousseau

As the morning sun climbed above the water, I had betaken myself to the Potts' home. With me, I'd brought a basket of figs.

"Well, to what do I owe this pleasure, Mrs. Peirce?" Dr. Pott asked. He eyed the figs. "My, my, no Spanish fig could look more luscious than those, I'll say! For us?"

"Aye, indeed they are. Dr. Pott, I wondered if ..." I hesitated, feeling at once a bit flustered. Would he truly want to buy the figs? I was his neighbor. Should I not just give them to him? But we had paid for *his* services when he healed Will's shoulder.

"Yes, Mrs. Peirce?" Dr. Pott was already eating a fig. "Delicious! Truly delicious. My compliments."

I gathered my courage. "Could I interest you in purchasing fresh figs for your distilled waters? Gerard says figs have many healing qualities. I can provide them to you by the bushel. Or by the peck, as you wish.

The doctor picked up another fig and held it to the light, turning it around.

"Not a bad idea, Mrs. Peirce, but how much distilled water would I need?"

"Could you sell the distilled waters to others besides making it just for your own use? How about to ships' masters and plantation commanders?" I suggested. My own bravery amused me.

He bit his lip. "Brandy burnt onto figs cures a cough. There's that. And cordials? Could make a wonderful cordial at that. A cordial of figs with raisins remedies surfeits caused by eating too much and cures plagues as well. How many contagions have we had here?" he said as if speaking to himself.

"Too many," I mumbled. Then, more brightly, I said, "I can't dry the figs in the damp Virginia air. I'd have to bring them to you fresh. But I might be able to stew them into marmalade."

"No, no, fresh would be best."

We stood for a moment, the doctor and the fig lady.

I made bold. "We have but one doctor and one fig orchard. And we are neighbors. I'll grow them, and you distill them into physick. And then we'll each help the other and help the sick besides."

He looked to the rafters as if doing figures.

At last, his face broke into a broad grin. "Bring me a bushel, and I'll get started!" he said. "I'll give you seventeen pounds of tobacco per bushel. That would be about three pounds sterling."

I gaped. "Three pounds? For a bushel?" I looked down at the basket, still in my hands. I couldn't believe that something growing freely in my orchard could earn so much.

"Well, Mrs. Peirce, you know how to make the bargain, sure. Fine then. Four pounds sterling."

Shielding my surprise at his price, I agreed.

When I left the doctor's door, a spring of joy had come into my step.

I returned home, filled another basket, and then walked over to the brewing house, newly built.

Gingerly, I walked in. I saw barrels, several large wooden mashing tubs, a kiln, and covered copper keelers. The brewer stirred a keeler's contents with a bunch of broomstraw.

Wiping his hands on his apron, the brewer came over to me with a look of annoyance.

I explained my proposal and my price. Could I interest the men there in purchasing figs for brewing beer, stout, or ale? Then I handed the basket to the brewer, a gift for him and his men to share.

Despite the brewer's gruff demeanor, he agreed to take two bushels as a trial.

After that, things happened quickly.

During the last days of August and into September, folks began knocking on my door. Many were not long off ship.

On my threshold, I'd find a ragged sailor or a mother holding a young child's hand. Sometimes there stood others from New Towne or settlements downriver.

The question was almost always the same. "Are you Mrs. Peirce, the fig lady?"

"Aye, that I am."

I'd show them in. My best figs were six pounds sterling or thirty-four pounds of tobacco per bushel. Lesser quality figs for physick or brewing were four pounds sterling or twenty-three pounds of tobacco a bushel. The poorest quality figs, I sold for two pounds sterling. For a quarter of the bushel price, folks could purchase figs by the peck. Four pecks to a bushel, of course.

Meanwhile, Angelo and Esther were refining their marmalade of figs with help from me.

First, the women pricked the figs so that the water could seep in well. Then the ladies put the figs into a pan of fair water with sugar. We discovered that the amount of sugar must match that of the figs.

Since quinces were more sour than figs, we added some lemon juice to the marmalade if we had any from Bermuda. The juice seemed to help the bricks of marmalade hold together better, although we knew not why.

The pan warmed beneath a soft fire. A pewter plate partially covering the pan kept most of the steam in, letting just a little out.

From time to time, Angelo or Esther turned the mix with a spoon to prevent burning or mashed the figs into the syrup.

After the figs and sugar boiled and simmered for hours, the women poured the brown marmalade into chests. Once cooled, the marmalade formed bricks, which we could cut and serve. The sugar should preserve the figs through the winter and into the next year, we hoped.

A few of these chests of marmalade I also sold, once word got about that I had some. I estimated the number of figs in a chest of marmalade and trebled the price to include the sugar and work required to produce it.

Will and his men who tried our marmalade of fig approved. We ate the marmalade as a sweetmeat after dinner, since both sugar and figs were healthful for digestion.

How glad I was that although the trees had blossomed with no figs those first two years, I had continued to tend them. Of the fifteen trees I'd planted, three died early leaving me a dozen.

Yet I had kept watering and protecting the trees, hoping they would bloom.

Last year, I'd harvested less than one bushel per tree, only ten bushels total for the dozen trees. This summer, I'd tripled that, and next summer, the number of figs harvested would perhaps double. Even after that, the harvests would continue to grow. This orchard wouldn't reach its peak harvest for six more years.

Will had an empty account book. I began to note the names and dates of those who bought figs, as well as how many figs and at what price.

Perhaps next year, I'd seek out these same souls to see if they might buy again. After all, I'd need to be more clever to unload the greater harvest I expected.

I felt so pleased with myself that I had to go tell Tempie that the fig lady was earning enough to help the household.

With the vines and fig trees in my orchard, I was living the Bible verse that said each man would sit in safety under his own vine and fig tree. For those newcomers who had no such trees, they could sit under mine.

My Ladys Com̃and

September 9, 1626
New Towne, Virginia

Clement Dilke gent sworne and examnd sayeth, that uppon the weyinge over of
my La: yardleys Tobacco at hog Islande he founde the Tobacco to be Contrary
to my ladys Com̃and and directions ...
　　　　—Minutes of the Council and General Court,
　　　　3 January 1626

As proud as I was of my little fig business, it was nothing compared to
what Tempie bore on her thin shoulders.

The Yeardleys had a great many thousands of acres to oversee.
First was Flowerdieu Hundred, which Sir George had named for Tempie's
father, Anthony Flowerdieu. Then Stanley Hundred out on Mulberry Island.
Sir George had named that after Tempie's mother, the former Martha Stanley.

Not a one had he called Yeardley's Yearning or some such name, as many
of the other men had done. Chaplain's Choice, Jordan's Journey, Pace's Paines,
Causey's Care ...

No, Sir George had decided to name the land for his wife's family. Sir
George seemed to love honoring Tempie in the naming of his plantations. He
was, in fact, the only man I could think of to do so. And Will? Practical Will
simply called it his land on Mulberry Island!

The Yeardleys also owned Weyanoke, the former seat of the Weanoc tribe.
Soon after he had come to power, Opechancanough had given Sir George over
two thousand acres there. The Yeardleys also owned land on the Eastern Shore.

Will, too, was amassing acreage, but his was on the Maine near James Town,
on Mulberry Island, and across the river from James Town Island. Tempie's
land sprawled up and down the river and even across the bay.

Having so many plantations required great work and diligence with
planting tobacco and corn, clothing and feeding servants, and keeping the

plantations stocked.

Several weeks had passed since Tempie and I had sat in my orchard, and yet Sir George's health had not returned. Tempie, as she saw it, had no choice but to continue her work.

She had taken on quite a bit when Sir George sailed for England this last time. Now that he was back, it sounded as if Tempie had never ceased that work. How could she? Still, it was a wonder to me how she did it.

Susanna let me in, and I found Tempie at a desk in their bedchamber.

"I've been watching, Joan. I've had ample education for a woman. I can reckon numbers and count tobacco as well as a man. I know more about tobacco than *any man* who sets foot first time on the soil here."

She was right. We'd come to believe that our long experience here, even as women, gave us an advantage over new arrivals, be they even men. To live here was to learn. But to understand the reckoning as well as she, that seemed above me.

Tempie looked over the figures and determined when her servants were handling land well or when they were not. She tallied tobacco harvested and sold, determined fair prices, decided when selling land was wise. She instructed her servants to bring her tobacco to the inspectors so they could duly discard that of poor quality. She paid the mariners for their services. She understood, too, that tobacco was hard on land and her men must plant other crops in those fields after a few years. She saw to the servants' clothing and victuals and knew when the time came to release servants from indenture.

Sir George had said once that Tempie was the most capable woman in Virginia, and I, for one, was certain of it. Tempie's reasons for taking on what she could were sound. She hoped to spare George some of the worry—"Lord knows Virginia frets him aplenty!"

As I came into the chamber, I saw that Tempie had a fire crackling in the fireplace, a little smudge of ink on her face, and papers pushed hither and thither.

"I'm glad you came, Joan. I want to show you some of what I'm doing," she said to me.

"I don't wish to slow your work," I replied. But I thought, *To understand such work, I am not capable.*

As if reading my mind, she said, "Fear it not, Joan. Should Will be … ill or taken from you, you may need to know this, too." She tapped the papers before her with her finger. "You can do this if you have to."

"Will Sir George mind me looking on your figures, his private business?"

She shook her head. "*My* private business. And I do not mind." She shrugged. "If 'tis mine to tend, 'tis mine to discuss as I choose. The more

I grasp, the more I see that if we women don't learn for ourselves, we leave ourselves to the mercy of forces ..."

"Maggie would be proud of you. Remember how she used to say that?"

Tempie smiled, a thoughtful look on her face. "Thinking of Maggie makes me happy. How much she's missed here."

I counted on my fingers. "What she's missed? Contagions, fluxes, Indian wars, to start. Overcrowding, gruel in the barracks, childbirth in poverty, martial law ... So much she's missed!"

Somehow, we both laughed.

"Flowerdieu Hundred, Stanley Hundred, Weyanoke, the land on the Eastern Shore. The men have reported the tobacco harvests from each plantation to me. I've determined how much I need to sell to feed and clothe the servants. I've made arrangements on ship to send tobacco back to England for sale and arranged for more servants from England if any be willing to come."

She showed me how she did her reckoning in the account books and tallied her costs.

My head began to spin with so many numbers.

"By the by," she said, pushing the papers back. "I nearly forgot to tell you! I've some news. George and the council will indeed try Goody Wright for witchcraft."

"Oh, no." Temperamental though the midwife was, I hated to think of folks humiliating her at trial. "When?" I asked.

"In two days, the hearing will be here in my house," Tempie explained. As the governor's wife once more, Tempie must entertain and host guests, the court, the General Assembly, and the council. "So come! Let us hear what the witnesses have to say about our old midwife."

Even Tempie would lay aside her account book and quill for this.

Tempie and I hoped Joan Wright was not a witch. Was she one? The trial would determine that.

If the court found possible evidence of witchcraft, the council would have no choice but to duck the midwife in the river. All knew this to be the only sure way to find innocence or guilt.

A ducking stool was a long sturdy plank balanced on wheels so that soldiers could push it down to the river. At one end of the plank, a chair was affixed. The soldiers would bind Mrs. Wright onto the chair, raise that end of the plank high, and let it fall into the water.

If Goody Wright could unbind herself and float, she was a witch and would face execution.

And if she sank and drowned, she was innocent.

Witches Are Moon-Birds

September 11, 1626
New Towne, Virginia

A witch is one that woorketh by the Devill, or by some develish or curious art,
either hurting or healing, revealing thinges secrete, or foretelling thinges to
come, which the devil hath devised to entangle and snare mens soules withal
unto damnation. The conjurer, the enchaunter, the sorcerer, the deviner ...
are indeede compassed within this circle.
　　　　—George Gifford, 1587

Witches are moon-birds,
Witches are the women of the false, beautiful moon.
　　　　—Amy Lowell

From across the river, the witnesses came. Those who had seen Mistress Wright do supposed witchcraft, create curses and spells. And then came her poor husband Robert, who swore he'd never seen such things.

I was at the Yeardleys' home early. Sir George greeted me warmly if a little absently. Each time I saw him, he seemed to have more lines on his face than the time before.

Tempie and I chose chairs beneath a window at the dining hall's far end. We were not here to testify.

"Good mornin', my Lady Yeardley," said the first person to enter. This was Rebecca Gray, another midwife from upriver.

Behind Goody Gray, Goodwife Wright knocked on the door and asked to enter. She seemed determined to look indifferent, but the fear showed itself in her eyes.

"Goody Wright," I said, as warmly as I could, standing. "I'm glad to see thee." Then I realized why she was here and fumbled with my next words. Fortunately, Mrs. Wright had her gaze boring into Goodwife Gray standing in front of her.

A few others entered whom I had seen but knew not well. Lieutenant Allington, another man and woman I knew not by name, and finally Isabella.

Isabella turned her eyes to Tempie and me. We met them. She shook her head ever so slightly. *I do not wish to be here*, the gesture said. Then she shrugged. *But perhaps I can help the midwife.*

Joan Wright's husband, wearing a grim frown, was just behind Isabella. With a hawkish but not unkind face, he seemed rattled and embarrassed by the proceedings.

Dr. Pott entered with a grin and a tip of his red hat to all. He seemed to love a party, no matter the reason. It was hard not to like him, I decided.

He leaned over and whispered to me, "Fig cordials going well, quite well. Brandied figs, too!"

Before I could respond, the door opened once more.

In came Captain Francis West, brother of my Lord La Warr. He smiled broadly to Tempie and gave Sir George a firm handshake.

The court then assembled itself around the Yeardleys' table. Susanna brought ale in for all. The witnesses sat at the edges of the room, awaiting their turn to be sworn in and to testify.

Thomas Jones was the last to enter. Susanna let him in quietly, and he took a seat.

Mistress Wright fixed those about her with a stare. Her accusers would have her ducked in the river, she was sure.

First called to give his oath was Lieutenant Allington. He raised his right hand and placed his left on the Yeardleys' Bible. Sir George administered the oath, and then the lieutenant sat down at the table.

"What say you about Goodwife Joan Wright in the matter of witchcraft?" Sir George asked sternly.

The room stilled as Allington said, "A woman put a spell on Sergeant Booth." He went on to explain that a woman had argued with the sergeant. After that, no matter how good a shot Booth had, he could never kill any flesh, the lieutenant testified. "Booth claimed himself cursed for a full year."

A murmur went through the room. Mistress Wright shifted uncomfortably.

"But whether it was Goody Wright who cast that spell, I cannot say."

"Thank you, Allington. Anything else to add?"

"Aye, sir."

"Proceed then."

"When my wife, who was with child, took to bed, I called for Goody Wright, a midwife. But my wife knew Goody to have the left-handedness and said she'd rather have Rebecca Gray."

"Is that all?"

"No, sir. Then the accused here became angry the next morning as she departed my house. She'd learned that Goody Gray would be bringing my wife to the childbirth bed."

Goody Wright was an old settler; Rebecca Gray a newer one. Probably, I thought, Joan Wright was as we all were—a bit jealous of newcomers causing us loss. If we had survived this far, we were protective of what belonged to us. Goody Wright would have lost her midwifery fee to Goody Gray.

"Do you have anything further to add?" Sir George asked, making a few notes.

"Aye. I do. My wife's breast soon developed a pustule, and she was ill with it for four or five weeks. After that, I myself became very ill for three weeks. And then the child ..."

He paused. The room was rapt.

"My child took ill after his birth and stayed ill for two months. He then recovered and was well for another month. After that, he fell into great pain which continued for another five weeks ..." He hesitated. 'Twas never easy to speak of one's own child in such a state. "And so departed this life."

Death of a child! I turned to Tempie. Her eyes were on the witness. I knew she must be thinking what I was. We'd been in the lying-in chamber with Mistress Wright, and she would never harm a babe. No, that could not be. Yet here was the testimony of it.

I stole a look at the midwife. She had pursed her lips and appeared stung. Jealous of the other midwife? Perhaps. She needed the tobacco given her for a baby's birth to help support her own family. Anger didn't mean she'd harm the mother or child, though.

Sir George thanked the lieutenant and asked if he had anything further to say.

The military man shook his head. "No, sir."

"Fine, then. Again, thank you, Allington."

"Am I needed here, sir? I should like to get back to the fort at Pace's Paines."

Sir George looked at Dr. Pott and Captain West. "Do you gentlemen have any other questions for our first deponent?"

Captain West spoke up. "You know nothing further, then? You're certain?"

"Aye, quite certain, captain."

"Let him go," West added with a dismissive wave of his hand.

I felt my skin crawl. I had never cared for Captain West. Not since the Starving Time when he and his men had taken our last ship and only corn, sailing for England. He had claimed mutiny. It certainly was a convenient mutiny, I thought.

Next, the governor called Rebecca Gray, the midwife. She took the oath and then seated herself. Goody Gray had the look of Irish heritage. I could see red hair peeking out beneath her coif. She had a quiet way and seemed uncomfortable at the questioning.

Still, when Sir George asked her to testify regarding Goody Wright being a witch, Goody Gray was firm. She pointed to her temple and said, "Goodwife Wright knew, she did. She did tell me that I should bury my husband. Further, she told Mr. Felgate that he should bury his wife, which came to pass." Goody Gray eyed Goody Wright as if she might cast a spell and kill her right there at the table.

For her part, Goody Wright was now studying the floor.

Rebecca Gray cleared her throat. "And further, Goodwife Wright told me that she told Thomas Harris he should bury his first wife, who was then betrothed to him. That, also, came to pass."

The room rumbled as those present felt their shock at the charges.

Dr. Pott spoke up. "Anything else, Goody Gray?"

"Aye. Goody Wright also told me of a woman. This woman said, 'I have a cross man for my husband!' Goodwife Wright told her, 'Be content, for thou shalt shortly bury him.' That too came to pass."

The evidence was damaging. Trying to be subtle, I stole a glance at the midwife. Her stiff demeanor had crumbled some under the weight of the words spoken against her. I had never seen Mistress Wright look small in all the time I'd known her, but she was shrinking into her chair.

More hurtful testimony was to come, however.

Ile Tell No More

September 11 – 18, 1626
New Towne, Virginia

*Also the changing of witches into hares, cats, and the like shapes, is so common
as late testimonies and confessions approve unto us, that none but the stupidly
incredulous can wrong the credit of the reporters, or doubt of the certainty.*
—Edward Fairfax, witchcraft victim, 1621

*I can tell you if I would, but I am exclaimde against for such thinges and Ile
tell no more.*
—Goodwife Joan Wright, 11 September 1626, when
asked to predict a death, according to testimony

Sir George called Thomas Jones to take the oath.

Jones confirmed that Goody Wright had indeed been the one who
had argued with Sergeant Booth. The midwife had wanted something—perhaps a piece of flesh?—from Sergeant Booth, but Booth either
would not or could not give it to her. "Afterward, the sergeant went forth
with his piece and came to good game with a fair shot at it. But for a long
time afterward, he could never kill anything."

Next, the governor swore in Robert Wright, Mistress Wright's husband.
As he was pulling the chair in, a memory came to me. I saw Annie Laydon
and Mistress Wright with a whip lashing them during the time of Sir Thomas
Dale. I remembered sweet Annie, how she had lost her child. And I could see
the glint of defiance in Mistress Wright's eyes. She had refused to cry then.
She did now, too.

Goodman Wright explained that he had married his wife sixteen years
ago. He opened his hands helplessly. "Sirs, I know nothing touching the
crime she is here accused of."

"Nothing? You have no more to say?" Dr. Pott asked kindly.

"No, sir. Nothing more."

Next was a Daniel Watkins explaining how Goodwife Wright had foretold another death. "I was visiting Pace's Paines about January last. Robert Thresher was there."

Watkins went on to say that Robert Thresher had a couple of hens he had separated from the flock to send to Elizabeth Arundel.

"Goodwife Wright was in that place. She said to Thresher, 'Why do you keep those hens here tied up? The maid you mean to send them to will be dead before the hens come to her.'"

I remembered Bessie Arundel. A servant, she'd been part of the Yeardley household for about a year before her death. Had the old midwife caused the death of one of Tempie's own servants?

Tempie's face betrayed nothing of what she was thinking. I turned my attention back to the proceedings.

The other witnesses nodded knowingly. Goody Wright predicting another death? This they could believe.

Finally, Isabella came forth. She gave a serious glance toward Tempie and me. Would Isabella turn on the midwife who had delivered both her sons, or would she stand up for her? How damaging would her testimony be?

Isabella took the oath and then cleared her throat.

"Someone stole lightwood out of the fort, so Goodwife Wright railed upon a girl of Goodwife Yates for stealing it. Whereupon Goody Yates charged Goody Wright with witchcraft. She said Goody Wright had done many, uh, bad things at Kecoughtan."

Isabella paused.

"And then what happened?" Sir George asked her.

"I chided Goodwife Wright and said unto her, 'If thou knowest thyself clear of what she charged thee, why dost thou not complain? And clear thyself of the same?'"

I could see Isabella's frustration with our midwife for not declaring herself innocent of witchcraft, even from where I sat.

"Goodwife Wright replied, 'God forgive them' and made light of it. Then Goodwife Wright threatened the Yates's girl and told her that if she didn't bring the kindling back, she'd make her dance stark naked. And the next morning we found the lightwood in the fort."

The crowd mumbled and whispered.

Why does Goodwife Wright say such things? I wondered.

"Anything else?" Sir George prodded.

"Well, Dorothy Beheathland asked me why I suffered Goodwife to be at my house. 'Why would you allow her inside? She's a very bad woman. Don't you know that all at Kecoughtan accounted her a witch?'"

Isabella sighed as if wondering if she had to tell everything. "Goodwife Wright told me a story from when she lived at Hull in Yorkshire. One day, while she was churning butter for her mistress, a woman came by who all believed to be a witch. Goody's dame told her to thrust the churn staff to the bottom of the churn. The dame then clapped her hands across the top of it. By these means, the witch was not able to stir out of that home for six hours. After that, Goodwife Wright desired her dame to ask why the witch had stayed so long? Then the witch fell down upon her knees and asked for forgiveness. The witch said her hand was in the churn, and she could not stir until Goody Wright lifted up the staff of the churn. Goodwife Wright did so, and the witch went away. Goody said it seemed to her that both the witch's hands looked to be free, and she affirms this to be a true story."

The governor and council looked among themselves.

"Does she have other knowledge of the dark arts?" Dr. Pott was tapping his finger as if thinking.

Isabella went on to explain. Goody Wright's mistress had instructed her to keep a known witch away by using a hot horseshoe flung into her dame's urine. While the horseshoe stayed hot, the witch would be sick at heart. When the horseshoe cooled, the witch would be well again. In this way, one could determine who was a witch and control the sorceress at the same time.

As Isabella finished her testimony, she looked drained, I saw. She did seem to be sympathetic to Mrs. Wright.

Alice Bailey was the last witness of the day.

"I did ask Goodwife whether I should bury my husband first or he should bury me," she testified.

"How did she respond?" Sir George asked wearily.

"She said, 'I can tell you if I would, but I'm exclaimed against for such things, and I'll tell no more.'"

A few other cases came before the council, one involving a calf the deponent had killed which did not belong to him. Also, someone owed someone else corn.

Finally, the court adjourned for the day.

After all had left, including the other councilors and Isabella, I prepared to excuse myself. Tempie said, "Stay, please, Joan. A moment."

Sir George was rubbing his eyes in fatigue.

Tempie spoke up. "George, I have something to say, and I wish Joan to back me up."

I lifted my brows.

"Goody Wright is not a witch. She's crusty, aye. She can be difficult, 'tis true. She does seem to know things before they may happen, or perhaps she simply guesses. But she's not a witch. She's a fine midwife and has delivered all three of my babies as well as Joan's son and Isabella's sons by Perry and Pace. Also, she delivered Maria Bucke's children and others. Many young Virginians here owe their birth to that woman. Except for Isabella Perry, those testifying are just old gossips, all of them, stirring trouble. Let Goody Wright be. Leave her be. Please."

Tempie turned her eyes toward me, a silent prompting.

"Governor Sir George, I agree with all your wife says. Please don't put our midwife to the ducking stool."

Sir George looked from one of us to the other.

"Even if she cursed your own servant, Tempie?" Sir George asked. He seemed genuinely perplexed.

"Oh, fie, George. Bessie was a sickly lass from the time she entered our household from Buck Roe. Of course, I felt sorry for her, but her death was not a shock nor a curse either."

"Just so, then. Well, I'm sorry to disappoint you two ladies, but we have several other deponents to come to next week's court. We're going to have to follow up with Robert Thresher and Elizabeth Yates to see how their stories match with what we've heard today. We can make no decision yet, under Common Law, until we hear all witnesses."

And that was that until the following Monday.

The next court, Captain West wasn't present. However, Roger and his nephew Captain Claiborne were. Captain Claiborne was now secretary of the council.

Tempie could influence her husband and Captain Claiborne. I also had influence with Captain Claiborne and, of course, Roger. This court, Jane also attended.

First were several testimonies on a different case. Sergeant Sharpe and Richard Taylor had disliked one of Sir George's proclamations about ship trading. A Mr. Phillips testified that at Jordan's Journey, he heard Sharpe and Taylor swear many violent oaths. "They said, 'We're freemen and as free as Sir George Yeardley *himself*,' that they would not be bound by the governor's proclamation."

Sir George rested his cheek upon his fist. "Thank you, Mr. Phillips," he said dryly.

A few more witnesses, one being Nat Causey who agreed with Mr. Phillips. "Sharp and Taylor were under drink when they spoke these words," he added.

To speak against the governor was a serious offense. Still, we wanted to get to the testimony against Goodwife Wright. We waited impatiently through several other testimonies. One regarded a home in Martin's Hundred, and another was a proclamation about trade.

At last, Goodman Thresher took the oath.

"She came to me asking for plants," he said, indicating Mrs. Wright. "I told her that when I'd served my own turn, she could have some. She went away, and that night, all my plants drowned."

He went on to talk about Elizabeth Arundel's death. "I had two good hens that I left with Goodwife Wright. Goody was to send them to Elizabeth Arundel, either by the provost marshal or some other manner."

"And what happened then?" Sir George asked with a steady gaze upon the deponent.

"Well, the goodwife, she told Daniel Watkins that Elizabeth would be dead before we could send the hens over."

Next up came a woman, Elizabeth Yates, that I knew not. She took the oath and said that Goodwife Wright had come to Mr. Moore's at Kecoughtan to buy some chickens. "But Mr. Moore would sell Goody none," she said flatly.

I suspected these chickens were going to die.

They did. First the chickens, then the hen. "I affirm that I heard this from others."

"Did she threaten your maid, goodwife?" asked Dr. Pott.

Goodwife Yates gave the midwife a disdainful sneer. "She did. Told me she'd make her dance naked and stand before the tree. That's what she said!"

"Councilors, any other questions?" Sir George asked.

The men shook their heads.

The governor and council heard one more testimony on a separate case, then began to file out of the house.

"You work on your husband and his nephew Claiborne, and I'll do the same to my husband and Captain West," Tempie whispered to Jane. "Joan, you have a kind word with the good doctor and his wife, will ye?"

Jane smiled slyly. "Of course, auntie!"

"I'll visit them today," I replied.

The midwife had her head hanging low as she made her way to the Yeardley door.

I tapped her on the arm from behind. She gave me a wary look.

I held out a small basket of figs to her. "In case you have a laboring mother to see to. Gerard says figs help a woman to deliver her child. And if you have none to deliver, then you and your husband might enjoy them."

She considered me for a moment, then said cautiously, "'Tis grateful I am for your kindness, Mistress Peirce."

Goody Wright should have sat the ducking stool based on the testimony, probably. Yet the council never brought charges against her.

Tempie, Jane, and I thought it might have been our private persuasions that made the difference. The men would never admit it if that were so, but we had our suspicions. Roger did tell Jane that Goody Wright was fortunate to have us as friends. That was all we were going to learn.

A few months later, a beleaguered Goodman Wright asked to move once more, this time to James Town Island, a property he would call "Labor in Vain."

As for Mistress Wright, as she said herself, she'd tell no more.

And she didn't.

My Seale Ring of Gould

January 10 to Late March 1627
New Towne, Virginia

*I bequeath to Edmund Rossingham my grandson all my messuages and lands
in Scottow or elsewhere in the county of Norfolk, and to his heirs forever. I
give unto my daughter Temporaunce Yeardle alias Flowerdewe my seale ring of
gould ...*
—From Martha [Flowerdieu] Garrett's will, Scottow,
County Norfolk, 3 February 1626, proved 4 Dec 1626

The new king had not decided whether we could keep our General Assembly, despite Sir George's petition and pleas in England. Our formal permission to hold a General Assembly had ended in May 1624 when the Virginia Company dissolved.

Now almost three years had passed. King James had not ruled on the General Assembly before his death, and now King Charles had not done so either.

Yet the governors Wyatt and Yeardley had each avowed they'd keep the Assembly anyway. They and the councilors let settlements vote and then called the elected representatives to an Assembly. Just as though the General Assembly still had the king's approval.

Both governors had agreed to sign letters to the king "The governor, council, and colony of Virginia assembled together."

That was what we ladies might have called a strong hint.

Without a General Assembly, Sir George and Sir Francis had an opportunity to snare more power for themselves. They chose not to do so. This simple but important matter made the two knights more favored than ever amongst the settlers.

When Sir George's Stanley Hundred on Mulberry Island seemed to overlay part of Will and Roger's lands, both parties agreed on what they would do.

In January, Will and Roger presented themselves to the court and renounced their claim to any land overlying Sir George's plot. They'd be happy to choose the same acreage nearby, they said.

"It's the least we can do," Roger said to Will. This land had once belonged to Jane's first husband, John Rolfe, and Roger now managed it for Jane and his stepdaughter, young Elizabeth Rolfe.

These words, from Roger, showed a change of heart. Some years back, he'd signed a Virginia Company petition which insisted a nobleman should lead Virginia. Now, time and experience in Virginia had shown Roger differently.

Besides that, Will and Roger wished to help Sir George because he still ailed. As a colony, we appreciated that he had given all—truly all—for Virginia. He seemed still unable to recover from his voyage to England on the colony's behalf, although few knew about Morocco.

Tempie and I rejoiced about Sir George's new land grant at Mulberry Island. One day, we promised, we'd be neighbors again on Mulberry Island as we had been for so many years here at James Town. At Mulberry Island, our homes would be just across Morrison's Creek from one another.

"And then we'll make our husbands build us another causeway," I said gleefully.

By March, though, Tempie reeled from more news.

"Joan, she's gone! See what I have." Tempie's tear-streaked face made me know that my friend was, still and again, suffering far too much.

"Lovey, who's gone?"

She fell into my arms, a letter in one hand, her fist clasping something in the other.

She drew back. Pain brushed through her eyes like a sorrowful water-color painting. "He writes, 'I do not know if you've heard of her passing. She went peacefully.' My mother. Oh, Joan! I wasn't with her. She died alone."

I helped Tempie into a chair, my eyes never leaving hers.

"I'm sorry, Tempie." Words failed me, so I simply let her talk.

Just the previous year, my last surviving brother Tom had died. I'd heard in a letter from his wife that had arrived months after his passing. News such as this, being from so far away, was particularly devastating. We could not be present to console, to grieve, to watch the burying. We felt sometimes like haunts ourselves. Our families could write us, but not see us. We could listen but not see. And so I understood something of how Tempie felt.

Tempie tried to gather herself as she said, "My sister died so young. Then my brother died young as well. Only I survived, but here am I an ocean—" She began to sniffle and gasp. "An ... an ocean betwixt us. So none of her children were present to hold her hand at the end ..."

"May I see the letter?" I asked gently.

She nodded, still wiping tears with the back of her hand, and gave me the two pages.

I turned to the second one and looked to see who had signed it. *Your loveing nephewe Edmund,* it read. *Edmund Rossingham.*

Rossingham had come to Virginia with the Yeardleys when they returned from England perhaps eight years ago. Tempie had always felt some suspicion to Rossingham's motives as she had, too, with her cousin John Pory. She did much prefer Rossingham to Pory, though, as Pory had schemed against Sir George more than once. *I am my Lady Yeardley's cousin German,* Pory would say, a mixture of elegance and contempt for the word "Yeardley."

Besides overseeing the Yeardley lands, Rossingham would accompany Sir George's tobacco to various ports. During the contagion after the massacre, Rossingham had shipped some of Sir George's tobacco to the Netherlands. From there, he'd sailed on to England, never to return. He'd been gone about four years now.

Edmund's presence with her mother left Tempie feeling bereft, a pointed reminder of her own absence. "At least, he was with her. Edmund, I mean."

Tempie buried her face in her hands. *How much more must she bear?*

Tempie had managed to mend the rift with her mother on her voyage to England some years back. She had known, of course—as we all did when leaving loved ones ashore—that she might never see her mother again. Mrs. Garrett had at last accepted, somewhat anyway, her daughter's life in the primitive Virginia backwoods. In the nearly twenty years since Tempie had left Scottow, she had made only the single visit to England, had seen her mother only that one time.

It had not been Tempie's fault, of course. We'd not been able to leave at all, by law, until 1617, eight years after Tempie had arrived here.

Soon thereafter, Tempie had gone home with Sir George. Sir George had been governor from the time of their return in 1619 until late 1621. Then had come the massacre of '22, followed by the great contagion of '23. And what if she *had* gone home with Sir George in 1625? Might the Turks have captured and imprisoned her? I shuddered. Such a thought I could not bear.

Now Mrs. Garrett was gone, and the memory of that single visit was all Tempie had to cling to.

Child, show them how a Flowerdieu conquers the wilderness! Mrs. Garrett had said to her daughter. Still, Tempie knew that her mother had never cared for her husband, knight or no. His breeding was not what a Stanley-Flowerdieu should marry into. *It made me feel sorrow for Sir George, who loved his wife so much.*

Now the Wests, like the Captains Francis or John West, relatives of Tempie's family and Baron De La Warr's brothers. These would have earned Mrs. Garrett's approval, I thought.

An idle daydream, but one I would come to rue.

Tempie retrieved a kerchief and then daubed her eyes, one fist still clenched about something. She tucked the kerchief back into her dress pocket and then opened her hand. On her outstretched palm, she held a seal ring of gold. "All I have," she murmured.

Now my eyes narrowed suspiciously. Edmund wrote—was he crowing?—that he was to be his grandmother's executor and that she had left all her lands to him as well as all her other goods. For her daughter and her daughter's children, she left nothing but one gold ring.

I read on. Mrs. Garrett had left a kinswoman her black cloak and a fan of white feathers. She'd bequeathed twenty shillings to her goddaughter as well as forty shillings to the poor of Scottow. Ten shillings more to the minister to preach her funeral, and a few bequests to servants.

See, grandmother, I am all your flesh and blood now, with the Yeardley children in remotest Virginia. I could almost see Edmund wheedling his grandmother.

Anger welled within me, anger I just as quickly pushed deep within. Tempie would not need me criticizing her nephew just now. Even if she might—probably would—consider such criticism justified. Had Rossingham influenced his grandmother as she wrote her will?

No, just now, I had little to offer her but an ear, a piece of warm buttered corn pone, and a dram of mulberry beer. I brought them out to her and bade her to have some.

Dear God, prithee, let her eat of this bread for now Tempie, like her husband, is far too haggard from worry.

Putting the Stars Back in Their Skies

August 10 to November 13, 1627
James Town and New Towne, Virginia

There is a deafening alleluia
rising from the souls
of those who weep,
and of those who weep with those who weep.
If you watch, you will see
the hand of God
putting the stars back in their skies
one by one.

—Ann Weems

Figs were hanging low and plump in my orchard. Although both Esther and Angelo had completed their indentures by summertime, I paid them to stay on a bit longer. They were helping me harvest the orchard and make marmalade once more.

By the fall, Angelo had married Anthony, one of Sir George's African servants. Anthony had once lived at Flowerdieu but had been living at the Yeardleys' home here in New Towne for several years. Angelo and Anthony each received fifty acres for completing their indenture.

As for Angelo, she told me she enjoyed being able to remember her Angolan village, her language, her people, together with Anthony.

"Missus, he say to me, '*Muene ua-ngi-zola*,'" she told me, eyes shining.

"What does it mean? Although I think I can guess," I said with a smile.

"He love me, missus."

Despite the great hardships she'd endured, Angelo yet showed a great will to survive and to forge a new home here in Virginia. For what other choice did she have?

Esther had married Goodman Clariet and was doing well despite being now almost deaf. She and her husband, too, had each received fifty acres.

Now Esther and Angelo were able to work their own land, sell tobacco, and grow their own corn. When they had earned enough, they could also pay the passage to Virginia of others willing to be servants, thus earning themselves more acreage.

In this way, the headright system brought prosperity both to those who paid their own passages to Virginia like Will and me and to those who needed to work off payment of their passage.

I couldn't deny I missed the two women. We'd endured much and seen a lot through the windows of my home in New Towne.

Together Angelo, Esther, and I harvested my best crop yet, almost seventy bushels of figs.

We sold as many fresh as we could. I was finding that folks up and down the river now sought me out even more as word spread about the fig lady. Dr. Pott remained loyal to my figs year after year as well. Between those using the figs for physick, beer, sweetmeat and marmalade, I sold forty bushels. As we always did, we used the remaining thirty bushels to make chests of marmalade which continued to sell through the year, even to ships' masters for their voyages.

To Tempie, of course, I gave both fresh figs and marmalade. I'd brought her some just as the leaves were turning their colors once more.

"He grows weaker, Joan," was all Tempie said as she accepted the fresh figs. I also brought her favorite mulberry beer.

"Is there aught I can do?"

She shook her head forlornly. "Dr. Pott has been over every day for the past month. I keep hoping George will recover soon ..." Her words trailed off.

By the time the forest turned brown and bare, Sir George closed his eyes and never opened them again. He was but thirty-nine years old, the first governor to choose Virginia as his permanent home. The only one who desired to be buried in his new land and not in England.

He was now what many of us wished to be—a Virginian even after death.

Tempie, still mourning her mother's loss, now must bury her husband.

The sadness on the island hung like a pall the day of his funeral. The air breathed heavy. Even the dark foreboding skies seemed to grieve with us.

Sitting in the church that cold day, I heard Councilor Dr. Pott say, "Sir George has been a main pillar on this our body of Virginia. To lose him, I say, shall weaken our whole structure."

Our two most capable and sincere governors were now gone, first Sir Francis to England and now Sir George to the grave. We all recognized that we needed another strong governor behind these two. I was then able to see that Sir George's loss not only devastated Tempie but created uncertainty for us all.

I wished Will were home, but he'd been spending a great deal of time at Mulberry Island recently. He'd decided to build the island's first church for his family out there on Bakers Neck—for Jane and Roger and Tom, as well as his servants and men there. Did Will know Sir George had died? I felt sure he'd want to attend the funeral.

As the service was beginning, I saw Will, Roger, and Jane slip in and sit near the back of the church. Their shallop must have just arrived from Mulberry Island.

Sir George's children huddled in the front pew of the James Town church, the boys hardly understanding the proceeding. Elizabeth leaned on her mother's shoulder. Tempie had an arm draped around her daughter and one around Francis. My friend wore all black and stared, as near as I could tell, straight ahead. I could almost feel the pain coming from her and the children.

Tempie, I'll help you get through this.

Isabella and I sat together. She grasped my hand and I hers. Life in Virginia would never be the same without Sir George as governor. And even more painful, life for Tempie would never be the same at all.

Annie and Jack Laydon had come up from Elizabeth Cittie and sat further back in the church. Annie waved sadly.

Captain Francis West assumed the reins of governorship while awaiting the king's formal decision for a new governor. Will said that the council's feeling was that no loss in Virginia could have been as great, none as keen, as that of Sir George. "They say in the council that his loss shall weaken the whole body of us still here," Will remarked.

I watched as it certainly weakened Tempie's body.

Time heals, though. It must, I told myself.

They buried the knight in our church's little chancel, a place of honor.

I stood at a distance as Tempie talked to her children at her husband's grave, and the November skies wept a cold downpour of loss.

In the Yeardley home gathered Isabella and Annie, Elizabeth Pott, Jane and even Cecily had caught a shallop on hearing the news.

Margaret West, new wife of Captain Francis West, patted Tempie's shoulder. Margaret understood Tempie's pain, having been widowed from Captain Powell a few years before. Now her second husband Mr. Blaney had died as well. Margaret had then married Captain West. But Margaret was resilient. She knew Tempie could be, too.

While Margaret wasn't one of my favorite people, I saw her steadying and encouraging Tempie. "I survived it, and you can as well, dear," she said.

Isabella understood, too, having married Mr. Perry after Mr. Pace had died.

My daughters also had each outlived their husbands, Cecily twice and Jane once.

Even I had been a widow long ago when Tom Reynolds died in battle.

Somehow, we each had endured the loss and kept going. We were here to show Tempie that she, too, would get through, that life goes on despite it all.

We brought out the best victuals and pudding, pumpion and corn dishes we could. On the table sat also jugs of mulberry beer I'd made as well as pumpion beer and distilled corn.

Virginia food and drinks to mark the loss of a man who embodied all that was Virginia.

When Tempie came through the door with Susanna and the children, Tempie's eyes brightened with tears.

"You are loved, Dame Temperance," said Elizabeth Pott in her soft voice.

"You are loved, sweet auntie," Jane chimed in.

"You are loved, my friend," I added. "We remain here for you always."

Over and again, each of her friends told her how much they loved her. By their presence, they said, *You will get through this, and we shall surround you to see that you do.*

Tempie seemed to take it all in—the food, the company, and the bright fire crackling against the autumn chill even as rain beat upon the glass.

"I thank you all," she said in a whisper.

Pale for Weariness

February 10, 1628
New Towne, Virginia

Art thou pale for weariness
Of climbing heaven, and gazing on the earth,
Wandering companionless
Among the stars that have a different birth ...
—Percy Bysshe Shelley

Tempie's brow had furrows, and she was shaking her head and mumbling. She hunched over the papers at George's escritoire, surrounded by columns of numbers and scrawls, an inkwell and quill nearby. She had inadvertently wiped ink on her forehead, and I couldn't help but laugh.

"Well, don't you look the scribe?" I asked.

She returned a half smile. "Come in, Joan. Susanna let you in?"

I nodded. "What are you doing?"

"'Tis accounts I've been at for nigh five hours."

Suddenly I was sympathetic. "Five hours, Tempie!"

"Five hours." She gestured at the papers and said, "It is endless." She had sold so much land that the actual account management wasn't as difficult as it might have been. Planting and reaping schedules, Indian safety, weaponry, shipping .... Still, she said, even transferring these things to others, left many tasks. The tallying of books and accounts, determining fair value, and so many other things.

"Seems every time the court sits, either they call me or I present myself. I must testify about this captain using our goods improperly or that dispute amongst servants here or there. Land to sell, poor quality tobacco. On and on." Her voice trailed off.

I saw, to my dismay, that her face was pale, her eyes shadowed. "Tempie,"

I said, walking closer and taking her shoulders in my hands. "You mustn't overdo. I'm concerned about the strain you're under since Sir George died. Why, the circles beneath your eyes are as dark as ashes. Are you sleeping at all?"

Three months had passed since Sir George's illness had finally stolen him away, leaving Tempie a widow and Captain West as governor. Despite her encouraging words to Tempie at the funeral, Margaret West hadn't long survived her marriage to Governor West. She had died just after Sir George's funeral.

I didn't care for West, but perhaps I had misjudged him. I knew not.

Sir George had shown the faith and trust he had in Tempie by making her executor of his estate. He had recovered his financial losses from the massacre and remained the wealthiest man in Virginia. He had traded broadly to England, the Bermudas, the Dutch colony in North Virginia, and the Low Countries of Holland.

"Two days ago, Susanna and Captain Claiborne gave their oaths in court that George's will was authentic and that they had witnessed it. Now 'tis my duty to try to settle the will," Tempie said as she rubbed her temples. "I sent George's brother Ralph a letter asking his help with the formalities in England. I'm sure he will. He's good that way."

She had taken it all on bravely. She'd learned to settle accounts and bargain the price of tobacco. She knew, too, that tobacco was hard on the land, and so she ensured that her men sometimes planted wheat or flax instead.

Tempie sued to collect from those who owed her money and cared for the servants' clothing, food, and housing. When servants died, she had to ensure word went back to England, usually, to next of kin.

In the twisting ways of Virginia, she'd asked Captain Claiborne to help her. He, of course, was the nephew of our son-in-law Roger. More often lately, the older settlers were banding together. Perhaps because of a shared bond of enduring great hardship. Captain Claiborne—now the colony's well-respected secretary—said he'd be delighted to help.

Tempie sighed, a look of resignation on her face. "Your concern is justified, Joan. I think I cannot do this ..." She pushed the chair back and rested her cheek on her fist.

"Let's have some perry, Tempie. You could use a respite, and the day is so cold."

She nodded. "Aye, then. Yes, I will."

She rose from her chair, with one backward frown at the papers, and tossed her head in dismay. She called to Susanna. "Do we have any perry in the cellar?" she asked.

Susanna curtsied politely, replying, "Indeed, my dame."

When Susanna returned, she also brought us some cornpone. Tempie, though, did not take even one bite. It was then that I noticed she was thinner, haggard, with a weariness that suggested it lay very deep within.

"Eat, lovey," I said, pushing the plate closer to her.

She didn't seem to hear me as she stared into the fire, her chin upon her hand. "'Tis not to be, Joan," she said suddenly.

"What do you mean?" I asked, letting the warm butter melt over the steaming pone.

"Mulberry Island, Stanley Hundred. I had to sell it and other lands as George requested me to do."

Our plantations adjoined on the little peninsula jutting into the James at Mulberry Island. On that good, hardy, and fruitful land, we'd planned to make our future homes. We'd hoped to convince our husbands to move a distance from their duties, away and downriver from the politics of James Town.

Now, with Sir George's passing, the dream of being island neighbors had vanished like morning fog.

I took Tempie's hand. "Selling Stanley is not something to fret upon. Dreams change as times change, but new dreams alight. They always do. One bird flies away, and a new one comes to sing for you. Look for the new bird, not after the one which has flown."

Of course, inside I felt deep disappointment, but I would not show Tempie that. She already looked so weary and sad.

Tempie smiled, the first glimpse of cheer I'd seen from her in a while. "Mismatched Virginia birds! Aye. And plenty of them, all colors. The spring will bring them, sure!" She looked down at her bread, and when she looked up, she had tears in her eyes. "Thank you for understanding what I must do."

I patted her hand. "Always."

"How did it go at court yesterday?" I asked brightly, hoping this would be a better thing to discuss. "You did go?"

She nodded again. "Aye. It went fine. I brought back the communion silver cup and two little chalices, done up in a beautiful black leather. I also brought the damask carpet, the communion cloth, and the surplice. Lovely items, all. These were gifts for the college before the ..."

She stopped with a grimace. It had become customary in Virginia to make such a gesture and omit the word *massacre*. It was still too painful for our ears.

"I'm trying to close all of George's business. I returned seven cows and five young heifers to the governor and council. George had received them as incoming governor, and now they must go to Governor West. I've been selling land. I made formal the sale of Stanley Hundred's thousand acres yesterday at court. These all according to George's wishes. He thought I should sell the land and collect tobacco for the sales. I've shipped *hundreds* of pounds of tobacco to England!"

I beamed at her in admiration. "You're a wonder! You're conducting Sir George's affairs as well as he could."

She shrugged. "He was sick or absent for years. He taught me much of what he did. I completed more of his business these last three years than anyone knows."

She was being modest, I saw, but she had a head for figures, and I was proud of her. And also worried.

"But, Tempie, must you push so hard? 'Tis not healthful ..."

"Aye, but time is critical," she said cryptically.

I wrinkled my nose. "Why?"

She stood and looked around the corner to make sure no servants were about. They were not.

"Because, Joan," she said, her voice hushed, "Governor West has asked me to marry him."

He Inspired Uneasiness

February 10, 1628
New Towne, Virginia

He was obeyed, yet he inspired neither love nor fear, nor even respect. He inspired uneasiness. That was it!
—Joseph Conrad

A shocked look must have crossed my face, because Tempie added, "It's not *that* bad!"

How could I say what I felt? I didn't like our new governor, and neither did Will. Surely West could have tried harder to stay his ship's mutiny during the Starving Time. His men had revolted against him, he said, forcing him back to England with the only corn we had. The last corn we'd see that terrible, hungry winter. Devastating.

An instinct about Governor West ruffled my opinion of him. He was Lord La Warr's brother, it was true, but he lacked something of the baron's honor. I couldn't in the least understand exactly what made me think that. It was just ... just a feeling.

"And ..." I made an effort to keep my voice level, pushing the judgment out of it. "You're going to make a match?"

She nodded, but it was not the playful nod of the happy bride, but the resigned nod of a woman who has fought hard for a long, long time. "Aye, 'tis a good match. He's a distant cousin, you know."

I understood. One gave special consideration to marrying cousins. These strengthened family alliances. West's bloodline was noble, nobler even than Tempie's Flowerdieus and Stanleys. By all accounts, this should have been a good match. *Should have been,* I thought as a twinge worked its way through me.

Tempie, oblivious to my own conflict, went on. "He's been after me since January, and I've put him off. I've done about all of that I can do. Except ..." Here she lowered her voice. "Except I'm bound to protect the children's inheritance if something should happen to me. I'll continue to manage the sales of tobacco and land with Captain Claiborne's help even after I marry. I have the captain working on a covenant which will offer my husband, the governor, only one thousand pounds should I die before he does. He'll not receive my full dower, which would be three or four times that."

"Well, one thousand pounds is no small sum in itself! That sounds wise." I thought, *I would protect everything I had from that man!* But I tried to feign a smile before adding. "You seem thin, Tempie. Have you been eating?"

Again, she nodded, a tad frustrated. "I'm eating, Joan. No need for concern, truly! I'm just tired, and my children's welfare is of utmost importance. Speaking of that ..." She stopped. "Wait."

She went to the doorway and called, "Susanna!"

Within a moment, the tall, sweet girl emerged at her mistress's beckon. "Yes, my dame?"

"Run and get yourself a glass of perry and then join us. Now is as good a time as any to talk before my nuptials with the governor."

Susanna didn't seem surprised, so she apparently was aware of West's attentions. But why had Tempie called Susanna in?

I raised my brows at Tempie, but she said only, "You'll see."

When Susanna returned, holding her perry, she asked permission to sit. Tempie indicated a chair.

Susanna was about twenty. She'd grown up with the Yeardley children. At once I had an inkling of what was to come.

"If anything should happen to me, before or after my marriage to the governor, I'd like the children to return to England. George's brother Ralph will be their guardian. He's an apothecary in London. You remember, Joan, I told you that George took me to his home when we were in London? George was fond of Ralph and his wife Rose, and so am I. 'Tis Ralph who'll oversee the children's inheritance and any remaining lands. This way, there's no chance of them coming into the care of Francis and a new wife. Ralph will raise and educate the children in London if ..." She looked up and away, and a knife cut me.

If.

Keeping my gaze steady, I nodded, as did Susanna.

"Do you remember, Joan, long ago in the Starving Time ..." Strange how that singular time lived so deeply in Tempie's and my memories. "You asked me to care for Jane should anything happen to you."

"Aye, I remember."

"If something should happen to me, would you escort the children to

Ralph's? I do not want them on the ocean alone." She paused, sympathetic. "I know 'tis your last wish to go aboard a ship. I could ask Isabella or Elizabeth Pott ..."

The sea. All my fears held nothing to me now; not pirates nor Spanish nor tempests could have kept me back. "No, lovey. My *last* wish is for your children to lose you." My voice cracked. "But, aye, I'll be the one to see them to England. You know they're like unto my own niece and nephews." I thought it best to clarify. "You're saying that under *no* circumstances are the children to stay with the governor?"

"That is correct. They are not his flesh and blood. I feel that if I should pass, they'd be better with their aunt and uncle and a clutch of cousins who love them. George would have wanted that, too. He *did* want that, in fact."

I agreed firmly. With the number of parents dying and remarrying, stepmothers and stepfathers were always at issue. A child might pass to a stepmother, who then died, and then onto a stepfather. He might remarry, and then he and his new wife would raise the children. This couple would have no blood connection, no interest in the children's welfare whatsoever. Multiple marriages were common—and Will and I the exception because we'd both lived so long.

Margaret Powell Blaney West was a good example, having three husbands before she died. Now Captain West would take his second wife. And here she was—sitting before me. Tempie was right; there were no guarantees in James Cittie. "It is as you say."

Tempie seemed relieved. "Good. And Susanna, I would wish for you, too, to return to England as the children's caretaker, only should you choose to do so. You'll have a nice home with the Yeardleys—the *other* Yeardleys," she added with a smile. To me, Tempie explained, "Susanna's parents, before she was orphaned, were friends of Ralph and Rose."

She continued to Susanna, "There would be little for you here. You'll be well cared for and all your expenses covered. We'll pay your passage there and back, if should you ever desire to return to Virginia. If the children lose both their father and me, then losing you as well would be so hard for them, for you are like their elder sister. It would mean so much to me if you would do that, Susanna. And Mrs. Peirce will be with you along the way."

Tempie lifted her eyes toward me, and I nodded assent.

Susanna's eyes shone. "My dame! You've been like a mother to me. I've been with you all these years. If that is what you wish, I'll surely do it. And besides," she added, "I'd miss the children so much, too."

"But this is just for prudence," I chided Tempie. "Nothing will happen."

Tempie looked solemn. "Perhaps. But 'tis wise to plan ahead."

I agreed, and she reached over and grabbed each of our free hands and clasped them. "Oh, thank you both."

I realized then that she had never taken a bite of her bread, and her perry remained on the table untouched.

In Fowler's Snare

March 31, 1628
James Town, Virginia

If birds could weep, then would my tears
Let others know what are my fears
Lest this my brood some harm should catch,
And be surprised for want of watch,
Whilst pecking corn and void of care,
They fall un'wares in fowler's snare ...
                                    —Anne Bradstreet, 1659

The bridegroom looked thrilled to see that the day for which he longed had come. The match between cousins, he and Tempie, just made sense.

My uneasiness was growing. It was odd that Tempie seemed so tired and distressed. Did she know she was making a mistake? Or was she?

Tempie's smile was faint, her eyes wan. She glanced at her three children, sitting proudly in the front pew beside Susanna and me. She truly loved them, I knew. She also no doubt felt that having a stepfather served her children's present interests best. That is, if she could protect their future from—dare I say—plundering.

Then Tempie's eyes met mine. I saw panic in them. *Am I doing the right thing?* she seemed to ask. This was not the happy bride, no.

I forced a smile and an encouraging nod. *Aye, you are. You are.* All the while, my heart told me it was *not* the right thing, not at all. But Tempie was at this moment caught in a hunter's snare. There was no stopping the wedding, no turning about and walking out.

Being married was the holy state, the will of God. Governor West was right for Tempie and yet wrong for her at the same time. I felt suddenly ill. *Joan, your worries do get the better of you. He is my Lord La Warr's brother, after all!*

I looked around. Folks had filled the church. The governor marrying Temperance, Lady Yeardley, the former governor's wife, was a grand day at James Cittie.

West was cheerful. Obviously, no second thought had entered *his* mind. *And why should it?* I thought. *He's marrying the wealthiest, most prestigious woman in all Virginia! Tempie had shown herself hardy, too. Few settlers from those first years still lived. Beyond that, she was intelligent with strong wits.*

Sir George had done well for himself, acquiring land and marketing tobacco with finesse. He'd built the first windmill here. It was he who had presided over the first General Assembly, too. He'd steered the colony to recovery from Argall's piracy. And guided it after Sir Francis Wyatt had departed. He had done so much for the colony. His death left a wide gap, a maw, I feared, that Governor West could never fill.

Aye, for our little city, a Yeardley marrying a West was the closest thing to a melding of dynasties the colony was ever likely to see.

As the pastor read from *The Book of Common Prayer*, I found myself only partially listening. I wanted to scream, "Don't do it!" Yet it was not my choice but Tempie's, and she'd made it. She couldn't back out now, anyway. The truth was that Governor West *was* a fine match for her. He was, of course, a baron's son and a baron's brother. The brothers West, sons of the 2nd Baron De La Warr, had made quite the name for themselves in Virginia. An elder brother, Sir Robert, had died before receiving the baron's title, which then passed to our Lord La Warr, second son. Captain Nathaniel West had died in Virginia a decade before. Captain John West, whom Will liked best, still lived. And, of course, Captain Francis, who stood before us at the altar.

But why did I feel that Governor West's eyes were like a weasel surveying the henhouse?

Joan, truly. Tempie's right—you are such a worrier.

Return unto Thy Rest, My Soul

Mid-April 1628
New Towne, Virginia

Return unto thy rest, my soul,
From all the wanderings of thy thought,
From sickness unto death made whole,
Safe through a thousand perils brought.
—James Montgomery

The first sickness came upon her almost immediately after the wedding. "Joan, I swear I make my body sick by vexing mine own self! And, here I've told you not to worry," Tempie was saying from her bed. She had lost more weight, and a cough had overtaken her. Worse, she was having trouble with nausea. Her belly had never been the same after eating those berries during the starving winter, it seemed. Now, bouts of stomach illness came and went with her regularly.

Dr. Pott, she said, had come to visit her and to offer his remedies.

I'd come to bring parsnip pottage, warm herbs of wormwood, mint, comfrey, and balm along with marmalade. Susanna was tending her well, but I'd been stopping in to visit once or twice a day.

"I have the accounts set up separately. I am not blending my tobacco and lands with those of Francis. The covenant is in place. But, as I've been sick, Francis has been helping me with the management. Captain Claiborne, whom I trust, still has authority, too."

The words "whom I trust" hung in the air. The message was clear: Tempie did not trust Captain West not to mismanage her children's money.

Feeling helpless—and frustrated that I'd been able to do nothing to stop this—I bent and kissed her forehead. "Get better, Tempie. All is well and will be well."

As we left Tempie's chamber together, Susanna leaned closer to me and whispered, "I do not trust him either, mistress. He's taking some of her tobacco and using the sales for himself. He seems to feel that since he's her husband, 'tis his right."

We kept our voices low. I didn't want other, less trusty, servants to overhear. "You're sure? Does your dame know?"

"No, ma'am. I'm helpless!" Her frustration was evident. "But I do watch him carefully. I witnessed Governor Yeardley's last will and his expression of his wishes, and I know also what my dame desires. So I watch and listen and pray that my dame suffers not in this."

I thought of Tempie, fretting and forced to leave much of her business dealings to West.

"She suffers already, I'm afraid." The young woman showed considerable wisdom for her age, and I hugged her. No wonder Tempie loved and trusted her so. "You're a treasure, do you know that? Your dame is blessed to have you nearby at all times."

"I'll tend her and never leave her side," she vowed. And I believed her.

Like Ghosts in a Tale of Long Ago

November 1, 1628
James Town Island, Virginia

The russet leaves of the sycamore
Lie at last on the valley floor—
By the autumn wind swept to and fro
Like ghosts in a tale of long ago ....

Days departing linger and sigh:
Stars come soon to the quiet sky;
Buried voices, intimate, strange,
Cry to body and soul of change;
Beauty, eternal fugitive,
Seeks the home that we cannot give.
——George Sterling

Today is All Saints', tomorrow All Souls' Day," Tempie said as we walked among the blazing oak and maple upon the edge of New Towne. "A time to remember those who passed on before us." I turned to look at her and saw that her eyes were damp. "We've buried so many, but here we are. Still here."

I echoed, "Still here. Just so! How hard to believe that seven years, but only seven years, have passed since the *George* came in bearing such good fruits. Will, Sir Francis, Mr. Sandys, and so many others. On this very day. We had so much hope then." My voice faded wistfully.

"But now we have hope again, don't we?" Tempie asked, more to herself than to me. "Of course, Virginia without George is a little empty. Still, what a beautiful day it is." Then to me, she added, "We've never truly given over our hope, have we? Despite the many strange hands old fate has dealt us."

"Hope? I think we've misplaced it at times," I said with a smile. "But we've always found it again."

"That's what matters in the end I suppose. I don't know what I should have done without you all these years, Joan. You've kept my spirits up when all seemed at its worst. I wouldn't even be alive today without you."

Now tears sprang into my own eyes as a great lump filled my throat. "I love you, Tempie. I cherish our friendship. 'Tis you, not I, who have kept our spirits lifted. You kept *me* alive."

"I love you, too. I reckon we've each kept the other alive. It might be that all the times we hoped, even when things went awry, those times are what truly kept us in spirit. We found hope in so many things."

It was true. "We had hope in our families, hope in our friends, hope in laughter," I began.

"Hope in the goodness of those even in the worst of times," Tempie put in.

"Remember when Walter and the other soldier buried Maggie for us?" I asked, remembering those kind men as if it were just yesterday and not nearly twenty years before. "I wonder what happened to Walter? I suppose he died."

"No, I think he has land in Charles Cittie and lives out there," Tempie said slowly. "Yes, that day they buried Maggie? I remember it well."

Somehow, hearing that Walter might still be alive made me happy. Those of us who came here twenty years ago and still lived were few.

"They loved Maggie's singing, remember?" I asked. "We had hope in music and the Psalms, too. And we always hoped in God and even in miracles, like when God gave us the little chickadee to make pottage." As I said it, I felt hope rising in me, as if remembering moments of hope could sprout hope anew.

"Remember when the Lord ransomed George and Mr. Sandys from the Turks?" Tempie asked, kicking a stone from our path.

"That *was* a miracle," I replied still awed by it. "And hope in compassion, like your compassion for old Grace. You took her in when I would not have."

"You would have come round to it. You just weren't there yet." Tempie laughed good-naturedly.

We began to count. Friends and family, laughter, God, music, compassion, a stranger's good nature. We had six hopes, but then Tempie said, "I would add hope in hard work and perseverance."

"Well, that's so. I think hard work saved us after the massacre and during the contagion," I said. Something deep within me knew this to be true.

"Hard work saved our spirits *and* our bodies when we ground acorns, too. It kept our hands busy, sure. All right then. *The Seven Hopes.* That's what we should call them," Tempie said triumphantly.

We walked on a bit further, considering that.

Then Tempie ventured, "Joan, have you thought any more about writing as Mr. Sandys suggested?"

I'd told her how the poet encouraged me—or any of us here—to write our own travel story. As if this whole twenty years were but a journey, a pilgrimage. "No, I don't think I'm able to do it well." Each time someone brought it up, I tried to change the talk to something else. I was a little unsure of myself. Actually, *a lot* unsure of myself.

Tempie gave me a critical eye. "Silly. Write it all, write it for both of us! Business keeps me too busy. I wish you'd write these hopes down, that I could later teach it to my children and my grandchildren. *The Seven Hopes*," she announced. "No. Our *Seven Hopes*," she corrected with emphasis.

"Seven years and seven hopes. It seems ... providential somehow," I said thoughtfully. How that could be, I knew not.

We linked arms as we made our way into the forests away from New Towne, deeper into the island. Tempie had recovered well from her spring sickness, but she had developed, again, a small cough.

She coughed a little as we were walking, and I told her when we returned I'd prepare some comfrey and honey to help the cough. "And marmalade of fig after every meal!"

"Well, so be it, fig lady. Thank you, Joan. I do have a confession. I've brought you away from the house to confide my troubles." She gave a deep sigh and with it came a cough. "I cannot prove it, but I feel that Francis is somehow directing some of our money—the children's and mine—to his own use. I feel it in my bones!"

Tempie had done all she could do. She had regained her health by late spring and returned to shipping and managing her own tobacco. Captain Claiborne was, she said, fair and honest. She scowled, and the pain in her eyes was deep. "I cannot say the same about my husband. He may be so, but I cannot tell."

In that lay a sad statement. Sir George had organized his will to give a third share to Tempie, a third to their eldest son Argall, and one-sixth each to Elizabeth and Francis.

Tempie had deliberately secured a covenant before her marriage to West. She would have use of her third share during her lifetime. But if she should die, West received a much smaller amount than the full third. Yet the amount was still generous by the standards of most planters due to the Yeardley wealth. The balance of her dower share would revert to her children's fund. "I am adamant about keeping my money separate because the children's future is at stake."

"Hm." My eyes were upon my shoes, which pushed wayward, brilliant leaves to this side or that. Since Susanna had suspected the same thing as Tempie did, I felt there must be something to it. "Is there anything you can do?" I glanced up to gauge her reaction.

Her expression was wry. "Take it to the governor?"

"I see your point." The governor led the council, and the council determined whether someone had broken the law. And Captain West was himself, of course, the governor in question.

"It would be scandalous, at any rate. And if we couldn't prove it—and right now I can't—it would cause bad blood between Francis and me and embarrass him as well. The whole town would talk. No, but I have Captain Claiborne keeping a tight rein on all my accounts and assets." She frowned. "'Tis the best I can do now until I find a better means." Pausing, she added, "But it reinforces that I want the children to be with their uncle should anything happen to me."

I nodded solemnly. "Aye, I have promised."

A sudden chill rushed through me, and I shivered. The autumn was beautiful, but I didn't look forward to the bitter winter whose presence hovered so near these dying leaves.

The Music of Rustling Leaves

November 1, 1628
James Town Island, Virginia

... I wander'd Virginia's woods,
To the music of rustling leaves ...
       —Walt Whitman

Earth's crammed with heaven,
And every common bush afire with God ...
       —Elizabeth Barrett Browning

Now, we found ourselves walking further than usual—to the portion of the island called the Uplands. Tempie's house was behind mine across the Pitch and Tar Swamp. We had Tempie's home to our backs and approached Mr. Kingsmill's Island House.

The day was mild for the first of November, and the trees were showering us with leaves in vivid colors.

"We just received a gift, Tempie," I said, not knowing why I said it exactly. The words and thought sprang from my lips.

She cocked her head at me. "Why do you say that?" Then added, "Not that I doubt it's true."

"Just that it's a glorious fall day, and you're well enough to be outside again. The leaves are splendid, and I don't fear your being out to enjoy them with the weather so warm."

We could forget winter if we tried. We could imagine it should not come this year.

She laughed. "Virginia weather is a mystery, isn't it? Some winter days are warm, some spring days are cold. And this one I shall *always* remember."

Each leaf, still wet with morning dew, reflected the sun, and the effect was brilliant. We walked in silence for some moments, just taking it all in.

The loveliness of the trees, singing their colors against the rich, smoky blue sky, drew us deeper into the island. Tempie stooped to pick up a maple leaf, a brilliant scarlet. The cedars tenaciously held their deep green color. All the while, some little bush, seeming unable to make up its mind, had only its leaves' edges trimmed in gold. From afar, it gave a sandy green effect—until one looked closer.

"Look at the dogwood trees!" I said. Everyone used to call them "dog trees," but now the name "dogwood" had caught on. Tempie and I both loved them. These were our Virginia trees. The leaves were green at the base but speckled a burnt orange as they went further up. Come spring, they'd brighten the forest with white flowers and red berries.

"Ah, the *pokahicharies!*" We'd eaten of the nut the natives called *pokahichary* during the Starving Time. The leaves were slender and rich yellow—as yellow as a Bermuda lemon!—stunning against the black bark. Sometimes we just called them the 'hickories.

Smaller bushes were the color of fire, while the sassafras, we saw, blushed golden yellow. Sweet gum trees seemed to be unsure which color to turn with leaves of green, orange, brown, and red. We saw shrubs were dotted in russet and still others a deep vermilion. Some were pure red, speckled with tiny black dots. A bush had dainty crimson leaves with folded orange berries.

A marvelous rainbow of color flashed all around, as far into the woods as we could see. As far back and as high as we could see, and beneath our feet as well. And while we walked, all about us the leaves tumbled upon the breeze, spinning until they touched the ground. The earth grew speckled with the brown of older leaves and the brilliant yellows and reds of those just fallen. The whole forest shimmered in a mystical way.

It was hard to walk past the acorns, sprawled about, without remembering that first fall nineteen years before. "This reminds me of when we first saw Virginia," I murmured. "Do you remember? I said to you, 'Virginia is alive,' and you remarked that you only hoped we stayed alive in it!"

We both laughed at the memory, and then I said, "We did, you know. We did. Tempie, we've done well."

She reached for my hand and held it. "Together, I think. Together we did what neither could have done alone."

"Aye."

Tempie seemed wistful. She still had the scarlet maple leaf in her hand and held it out to admire it. While gazing at it, she said, "Did you ever think, Joan, that we are like these leaves?"

"We're probably somewhat like the *oak* leaves, as we've eaten so many acorns, seeds of the oak, in our day!" I said, chuckling at my own humor.

She smiled but persisted. "That's so. We're probably something like oak leaves and something like squirrels, for we fought them off that winter, didn't we?" She made a shoving motion. "'Give me that acorn, you!'" She laughed too, and something magical lingered—the warmth of an old friend, the wonderland of color. It felt as if we were walking into a forest painting and the artist had used every color.

As we drew deeper into the woods, we seemed to be unto a world all our own, and the brilliant leaves welcomed us in. A secret place, a holy place. Sacred, as if God were doing a great work all around us and only we were here to see it.

James Town Island, I thought, had never been more alluring than this.

"I think," said Tempie, kicking a few nuts from the path and then looking heavenward at the trees and beyond the trees. "I think that we should learn from them—the leaves, I mean. They don't face death with fear, do they? They send a fiery message to God. *We are here, and we are coming. We are not afraid!*"

I studied her curiously. It was unlike Tempie to be pensive, but she had something on her mind. I allowed her to finish.

"Dying leaves are beautiful because death is beautiful in a way, don't you think? God is telling us so, showing us that. Look around." She swept her arms, taking in the forest, the river beyond, the cornfields and the homes past our sight. All lit as if from some heavenly gold and red flame. The trees as torches against the sky, the bushes burning around our feet, the yellow forest floor. "We should be so bold to depart as a leaf—fiery, proud, vibrant! Who would know these leaves are dying? With their death, they fall, how? Do they scream in pain as they drop to the ground?"

I laughed at the image of the woods filled with screaming leaves. For a moment, I imagined the sound of leaves nearby, louder, and those further away, more softly, but all echoing a yowling protest. And I imagined a *snap!* as other leaves fell and they, too, began complaining. The whole forest drowned in a cacophony of distressed leaves …. I draped my arm around her waist. "Tempie, you always could make me laugh."

She laughed too, then added, "No, Joan. The leaves fall silently, and yet they *dance* to the ground. Pirouetting, swirling, turning … catching a breeze and floating back upward." I watched with new wonder as the leaves around us spun in playful circles to the earth. "They *enjoy* the ride down!" She reached out and let a falling oak leaf alight on her outstretched hand. Speaking more to herself than to me, she said, "They do, don't they? They aren't dying, but living in their death."

And then, silence, except for the rustle and crackling of the leaves. Those which had gone before, the first to fall, as we picked our way through the cathedral forest.

So True in Sorrow

December 1, 1628
New Towne, Virginia

Women are so gentle, so affectionate, so true in sorrow, so untired and untiring! but the leaf withers not sooner, and tropic light fades not more abruptly.
—Barry Cornwall

I headed with a basket over to Tempie's home, much as I did every day. She had developed a sore cough—from a slight cough at All Saints' Day to a chesty one, and one which caused her throat and ears to hurt. Her head pounded ceaselessly, and she had coughed up phlegm, a sure sign the humors were out of balance, cold and wet.

My mother had taught me well, although I had pulled *Gerard's Herball* from the shelf to make sure I remembered correctly. My mother, in fact, had suffered from much the same ailment just before she ... I brushed that away. Just because my mother hadn't pulled through a similar illness didn't mean Tempie ...

Thinking was too painful. Instead, I made myself look at the contents of the basket once more, although I knew perfectly well what it contained. *Lemon balm and marshmallow for the ague, comfrey and licorice for the lungs, and syrup of horehound. Also, more marmalade.*

I felt we—Susanna and I—could bring her back to health. And Elizabeth. Mustn't forget her loving daughter who tried so hard to soothe her mother.

Today I brought a special surprise for Tempie, hidden in my basket.

Susanna met me at the door, wearing a look of deep concern. She reached for me and drew me into a hug. "Mrs. Peirce, I was going to call for you. And Dr. Pott will be here soon. My dame has taken a turn during the night. She has a fearsome pain in her chest and back, and ague wracks her.

Oh, welladay!" Susanna's face was nearly frozen with fear.

"Dear God." I rushed past Susanna to Tempie's chamber. There I found Tempie's face, far too pallid, the circles under her eyes too dark while her cheeks flushed crimson. The contrast was altogether frightening.

Tempie, being as it appeared mostly asleep, had not seen me come up. I drew a heavy breath and steadied myself. It would not do to let her know that I was afraid—indeed, weak with fear.

I walked to the side of her bed, and deciding not to wake her, sat instead in a chair nearby.

Glancing around at the finery, I was proud of Tempie. Around me were Chinese porcelain, Dutch Delftware, and fine candlesticks on either side of the mantle. All reminded me of how far Tempie had fallen in our early days here, yet how boldly she had returned.

We had lived in poverty during those first years. We'd struggled even to find lightwood from abandoned houses nearby, and I mean breaking off parts of the houses. We had pulled out our finery—the little we had—only once. We'd toasted to spring, the final death of winter, late in April 1610.

And we'd pulled through that disheartening winter. Time had passed, and now near twenty years had blustered by. We'd recovered our health, and our minds had been able to push away the horrors we'd seen. Yet thoughts from that earlier time seemed to flash before me every day. One, I supposed, never forgot. Not truly.

These thoughts I cannot forget. What do I do with them? I mused as I watched Tempie sleeping. Her sleep pierced sometimes by the ragged cough, she murmured as though in distress without ever waking.

Rest you, just rest. The time is nigh when you'll recover as you always do.

Lost in my thoughts, I startled when a young Tempie appeared in the doorway. It was Elizabeth, now thirteen. Seeing me, she whispered, "How fares my mother?"

What to say? Elizabeth came to embrace me and I stood, wrapping my arms about her and whispering, "She rests mostly comfortable." The girl drew back, and her alarmed eyes met mine as I continued, "Where are your brothers?"

"Oh, Argall and Young Francis have sailed with Captain Claiborne on a shallop toward the bay. They set off yesterday afternoon." Argall was now eleven, his brother eight. We had taken to calling the boy Little Francis to differentiate him from his stepfather.

We were whispering, but Tempie soon stirred and called us over. Elizabeth kissed her mother's cheek. "Mama, in the spring, you'll be well, and I'm going to bring you flowers—all the prettiest flowers of New Town! I can't wait to fill your room with them although you won't be sick then, will you, Mother? You'll be all well again."

The girl had such hope in her voice that I silently prayed, *Dear God, make it so.* Elizabeth and I both held the same hope. If we prayed enough, if we nurtured Tempie enough, she'd make it through. She always did; she always had. Yet I could not help gripping my own hands in fear—wringing, them, I supposed.

Tempie's face was wistful. She gave her daughter a hug, a long one, and said, "My Bess, how I love you." The words set off the coughing, a deep and menacing sound. I felt my heart sink. This was not good. Clearing her throat, she tried to speak normally, although her voice was uncharacteristically raspy. As Tempie held her daughter, my mind was racing. *Chamomile, comfrey, hyssop* ... In a few minutes, I would bring the herbs. But the preciousness of this moment, I felt, should linger.

"Let me visit with Aunt Joan and then we'll spend some time together, aye?"

Elizabeth's smile was sad. "Aye!" she said, with a brightness that didn't sound wholly genuine.

As Elizabeth departed, Tempie looked after her. "My little darling. And the boys, my little men." Coughing, hacking. In a voice strained by the sickness, she said, "We are fortunate, aren't we, Joan, to have survived childbirth and the children to have survived this far. I feel blessed." And then more coughing.

She felt blessed, even as she suffered. Water filled my eyes suddenly. "Such a true heart, you are," I whispered.

I made to pull up a chair, but Tempie patted the bed and said, "Come up here with me. I want to see you." I cautiously climbed the little steps beside the bed, and once settled, took her hand.

"What are you doing so sick?" I said, as though scolding her. I was trying to hide the tears I could feel coming—tears of panic. *Comfrey, chamomile, burdock. Be you calm,* I scolded myself.

"I can't seem to shake this cough, and my back and chest are afire! I continue to cough and cough, never seeming to get all the bad humors out when I do. A bitter taste in my mouth." She made a face.

"Aye, bad humors will do that, they will." I touched her forehead. "And you're burning up with the ague."

She gave a weak bob of her head. Her eyes, I saw, were glassy, her cheeks flushed around the ghastly whiteness of her skin.

"How are the girls? Jane, you know, came to see her 'Auntie Tempie' just yesterday. She's a lovely young woman. I feel privileged to have had a hand in her raising, to have her call me 'auntie.'"

Tempie took long pauses between some words, trying to catch her breath. Then she said, "Remember our Starving Time, Joan?" She had, I saw, a faraway look in her eyes. "I'm glad for the last twenty years, grateful even. They were a gift, a gift of time, which allowed me to bear these three beautiful children. God is good, e'en when we suffer. He is good. I know it." She set her mouth in determination.

I nodded. "Twenty years, nearly so. 'Twas just thinking of it. In fact ..." I squeezed her hand and tried to smile. "See what I've brought? Remember these?"

From out of the basket, I withdrew two bundles. Ceremoniously, I unwrapped the first, revealing the Chinese wine cup.

"Oh," she said huskily, and a round of coughing began. "Are they the same ones? From our toast to friendship, all those years ago?"

"The same. Never broken." I looked at her, and my voice was soft. "Just like us. Never broken. Like the scallop shells. Whole and surviving despite it all. I thought we could toast once more—except now we'll have the joy of a true warm beverage and not a spoonful of aqua vitae!"

She smiled, and her eyes twinkled like stars. "I'm much obliged," she said in near whisper.

"I'm only sorry that our little purple and blue flowers won't bloom for months." That made me sad for some reason I could not explain. "Remember how I brought them to you? A wee bit of spring after such a winter."

"I remember those little flowers! You picked them down by the riverside. Never worry, Joan," Tempie said. "We'll see them in the spring! They'll encourage us all over again," she added dreamily. "Maybe e'en when we need it most."

"Then let me fetch Susanna," I said, rising.

Moving from the bed to the kitchen, I found Susanna at work on the midday meal. "Susanna, might we have some sack?"

She nodded courteously. "Of course, mistress." As she pulled a jug down from a shelf, she looked back at me and said in a troubled voice, "She's in a right bad way, isn't she, mistress?"

I could neither lie nor actually say the words. I nodded. "Aye." My voice was barely a whisper. "Yet we won't give up hope."

"Prayers be powerful things," she murmured as she filled the little Chinese wine cups with golden drink.

As Angels in Some Brighter Dreams

December 1, 1628
New Towne, Virginia

As angels in some brighter dreams
Call to the soul when man doth sleep ...
—Henry Vaughan

Tempie had nearly fallen asleep in those short moments, but hearing me return, she opened her eyes. Her smile was weak but nonetheless warm and grateful.

"A toast, my friend," I said, trying to keep my voice hearty, though it wanted to choke.

She held the cup, her hands shaking.

"Gently," I whispered.

"A toast," she said. Feeling the need to cough once more, she handed me the cup, spilling a little of it as she did so. Coughing, round upon round, she caught her breath and said, "Good Lord, my chest hurts."

This had not been so easy as I imagined. I could not have known how she would falter in one night. Her coughing kept her from saying too much or doing too much, and she was clearly weakening. Something had gone wrong during the night—very wrong.

She breathed in resolve, forcing herself to sit up straight. She wanted to toast with dignity, I knew. I saw her will arise from the midst of her sickness.

"The wine cup, Joan," she said. "Why have we waited so long to reminisce over this old toast?"

I handed the little delftware cup back to her. Seeing her desire to do this simple but, for her, strenuous act, made me remember how much I loved her.

"Now, what was it we said?" I struggled to remember that faraway morning, the exact words. "*To friendship*," I quoted, my voice atremble. "*To things which never change, howe'er mean the circumstance."*

"To friendship," she echoed and clinked the little wine cup against mine. In that simple sound, memories flooded past, half a lifetime's commitments to one another. We had not hoarded food from the other even as we starved. We had forged our bond on that if nothing else. We had helped one another's babies come into the world. We had not fallen nor given up. It was all there, in the quiet sound of two fragile cups touching.

We each turned up our cups and drank.

When Tempie finished, I reached for her cup. I saw that the sack had warmed her complexion just a bit.

Tempie was wistful. "I think about Maggie sometimes. The most willful little nightingale in heaven's choir!" she said and chuckled.

I smiled too, loving Tempie's spirit that could still emerge even as sick as she was.

A day never passed without Maggie's voice running through my mind. She seemed always nearby. "We both thought we heard her that Christmas some years back, remember?" I said, my voice distant.

"Aye, I do. I wonder what her life would have been like had she lived? Would she and Hugh have had children? She'd have been a good mother, think you not, Joan?"

"Yes, a fine mother. We both miss her, I know. But I think she never truly left us."

"And soon, one of us to be with her," Tempie murmured, and her smile was sad.

I knew to what she alluded and would not accept it. "No, you will overcome this," I said, forcing the words. "You must believe it!"

She shook her head. "I cannot hide it from you, Joan. I know I'm weak and growing weaker. I know the cough and ague overtake me greater each hour. And ..." She hesitated, giving me a look of deep feeling. "I have seen them," she said, her voice hushed. "Two of them. All golden, shimmering ... at the foot of my bed. They smiled at me." Her face glowed in remembrance.

"Seen who?" I was afraid to hear her answer.

"Angels," she said simply. "And, Joan, I ... I do swear one resembled *Grace!* Do you remember Grace from that awful winter?"

"You saw two angels, and one looked like Grace?" I tried not to sound skeptical. I knew she was speaking from the heart. Grace, whom we'd taken in that starving winter. Grace who had been so ragged, and yet had such wondrous eyes. Grace, who had seemed to know more than she should, and who had offered a curious blessing upon us just before her death. *That* Grace?

Tempie nodded in wide-eyed innocence, then laughed a little. "I know it sounds strange. But ..." She gazed into the distance. "This angel looked like Grace, but she was beautiful and strong and ... and clean. Younger. Not infirm, not starving. She wore a shimmering white gown. Do you think Grace was an angel somehow? Did she *become* an angel to us because we took her in?"

In a heaven above us, no one is starving. That's what we'd said when we touched our little cups in toast all those years ago. And now Tempie had seen proof that may be so.

A chill passed through me. Tempie had seen angels, and one looked like Grace? I remembered back to when I had not wanted to bring the dirty old woman into our home. *She will only die anyway,* I'd thought. *Why should she eat our corn and yet have but the same end result?*

But Tempie had insisted. Could it be that on the other side of heaven, Grace remembered? And came to bring assurance to Tempie now that Tempie herself was so ill? What if Grace had always been an angel? A Bible verse ran through my mind about entertaining angels unawares. I shuddered as my mind tipped and turned in so many directions I could not make sense of any of it.

I clenched shut my eyes against too many unbidden thoughts, too much I could not understand. And against fear. Great, great fear.

The Spirits of the Blest

December 1, 1628
New Towne, Virginia

The stars are mansions built by Nature's hand,
And, haply, there the spirits of the blest
Dwell, clothed in radiance, their immortal vest ...
—William Wordsworth

I tried to push away the fear.

Yea, though I walk through the valley of the shadow of death, I will fear no evil, for Thou art with me. Psalm 23 had comforted me during the hurricane. But nothing, I saw, could comfort me now.

"Are you well, Joan?" Tempie asked with sudden concern. "You look ill yourself."

I opened my eyes once more and pushed every thought but one away. Tempie was going to be all right. If I thought nothing else, nothing else could happen.

"I ... I'm well, Tempie. Just the thought of you seeing Grace has moved me." I stroked her hand. This vision obviously meant a great deal to her. If it meant so much to her, I must believe it.

Then I said, "Grace did bless us, Tempie. Before she died. She said something like, 'A blessing be upon you both and upon your families.' I didn't tell you at the time. I did not take her meaning. Could she have been an angel?" I shrugged. "Stranger things have happened. Perhaps many angels surrounded the suffering and dying at James Town. Could it be so odd that Grace was one?"

At once, the true implication of Tempie's vision of angels struck me. "You saw them, you say? They were solid, real? At the foot of your bed?"

She nodded, seeming grateful that I validated her vision. "Aye, right about there." She indicated the center and right of the foot of her bed. "I thought they were telling me 'twould soon be time." Her voice trailed off, and her eyes sought mine. She knew this would be hard for me.

"Maybe you were just dreaming?" My voice had an edge of desperation to it.

It all reminded me of the day we'd had much the same conversation, near the end of the Starving Time. Tempie had known she was closer to death than I. She insisted I sing the 91st Psalm for her since we had no formal churches or liturgy during the worst of it.

"If ... if such should occur, I still want you to sing the 91st Psalm for me," she said again, as though reading my mind. "Sing it, perhaps, over my grave, and I'll be there with you. I promise. I'll miss you—God only knows how much!—but we've fared better than most. Through the Starving Time, through childbirth and the massacre. Through our separation when I was in England, and you were all so sick here." Her voice trailed off. "Through the famine and contagion of '23 and so much else. Truly, we can't be sorry, can we? We've been blessed many times."

She was asking me to be grateful for the time we'd had, and I was—oh, I was. But it was still not long enough, still too soon. I could not let go! There were things we should say, so many things we still needed to share together. Yet I knew the sound of angels had such finality to it. It was crushing, devastating.

"Temperance, please!" I was crying now. "Don't say these things! I'm forty-eight—I'm the old woman. You are but thirty-eight ..." But my words lay buried beneath the sound of Tempie's coughing and wheezing.

I felt my heart plummet, far and deep, leaving a trail of sadness through my body. I knew she was right this time, and I didn't know how I knew. I felt it, a wrenching certainty that seemed to weigh my whole body down with it.

I leaned over and gave her a hug where she sat, propped on pillows. The heat from her body told me how severe the ague was.

"You'll take the children back to England, to Ralph and Rose, as you promised?" Her face had a haunted expression, betraying how much she hated to let them go.

"If ... " My voice croaked. "If ... just if ... aye." I reached toward her to clasp her hand.

She forced herself to sit upright, not leaning against pillows. The sack had, I noticed, quelled the coughing for now.

As I pulled back and looked into her pale face, I saw my friend gather strength. *Where does it come from?* I thought. Now Tempie's tone became suddenly, strangely, strong, her eyes burning, intense. "You must love them for me, Joan. Love them as I cannot. Love them for me, and help them ... help them to remember George and me. For they are so very young."

Sensing the greatness of the commission she gave me, I nodded. "Always, my friend."

I wrapped my arms around her and she around me. How thin she felt. Her body trembled, and her breathing whistled in my ear, as breathing never should do. The strength she had summoned had left once more.

In my ear, she whispered, "I want to go as the leaves do."

Unable to speak, I only nodded.

"Fiery, aglow, brilliant as a flame," she mumbled. Then she gave a slight laugh and said, "Heaven, prepare! I'm on my way."

I laughed and burst into tears at the same time, like sunshine in the rain—a rainbow of feelings rushing through me.

"The children?" She seemed to need the reassurance.

I kissed her ear before whispering, "You will survive this, but if … if …." I paused. "I promise you, my sweet friend, they are ever under mine eye. All the days of my life will I love them for you. I will see them to Rose across a whole ocean myself. Fear won't stop me, I promise you. I am always here for them." Well I knew, nothing comforted a dying mother more than to know someone would love her children.

She'll come through this, too, said some hopeful part of my heart. Our words were naught but precaution.

She heaved a sigh, her body seeming to relax.

"I love you, Joan," she whispered.

Within me, the battle raged. The part that understood the truth before me and the part that could never admit it. *It does not hurt to say the words although she'll be well soon.*

"And I love you, Tempie. I'll always love you. I'll never forget you. You live always … my heart." I patted my chest. I had tried to make my voice strong, but could not get all the words out.

Her eyes shone as she took my hands within her own and squeezed them. "Remember how it felt to see the stars after the hurricane? The mighty storm was over. Do you remember? We had been reborn! I'll live in the stars. Look up on any bright night and see me. For I am there." She weakly pointed a finger to the ceiling as if the stars were right before us and we could see them even then.

She looked at me a long time, and I looked at her. I was trying to remember her eyes. What I would give for another week, another month, another year. *Pray, God, do the ones we love always pass so quickly? Life is but a candle. How did I never know that before?*

In a voice of greatest sincerity, she said, "And, my old companion, I'll never forget you. I'll bring Maggie, and together we'll watch over you. In fact, you won't be able to escape us if you try!" Her face creased into a gentle smile. "Your very own haunts."

I wanted to tell her to forbear speaking of death as if its presence hovered in this chamber, and she were drawing it to us, to her.

At the same time, I understood that she was, even now, trying to help me recover from the loss of herself. It was perhaps the most unselfish act I'd ever witnessed.

"But don't be sad, lovey. Do you promise? Mourning doesn't become you," she said with as much force as she could muster.

I had no voice at all. I felt like an old sack with a tight rope around it.

She spoke deliberately as if determined to see this thought out. "A time will come when you feel happy again, and then guilt will seep in there, too. I'm telling you, lovey, to keep the happiness and discard the guilt. For me. Don't mourn forever. Cry for a week, but that's enough." She laughed a little. "Promise me?"

I managed to nod despite the great lump in my throat.

Tears sprang from my eyes and this time, I knew, she would not recover as she had before, all those years ago. A Virginia without Tempie I could not imagine. Pain seemed to tear at both edges of my heart, threatening to pull apart and shatter it. As hard as I had tried to believe that this time, too, she would recover, a knowing had pushed through instead. And I felt I could not breathe anymore.

Susanna had come quietly to the doorway with an arm about Elizabeth. I turned to look at the maid, and her kind eyes said, *We have come to sit awhile.*

The children needed their time. Tempie's eyes were drooping with sleep, sleep which was more powerful than she. Still, she fought it in her Tempie way.

Perhaps I should not have taken so much of her time. Then I realized that she had needed me there, had needed to hear me promise about the children if nothing else.

I bade her goodbye, almost backing out of the room so that I could keep my eyes locked on hers.

At the doorway, I bowed my head. I silently prayed this would not be our last conversation. Then I whispered, "Godspeed to you in all your journeys, sweet friend."

She blew me a kiss before dropping onto the bed once more. As I walked out the entrance hall, her coughing echoed in my ears.

In One of Those Stars

December 2, 1628
New Towne, Virginia

*In one of those stars I shall be living. In one of them, I shall be laughing. And
so it will be as if all the stars were laughing, when you look at the sky at night.
And when your sorrow is comforted (time soothes all sorrows) you will be
content that you have known me. You will always be my friend ... I shall not
leave you.*
>—Antoine de Saint-Exupéry

Say not "Good-night" but in some brighter clime, bid me "Good-morning."
>—Anna Laetitia Barbauld

The December morning dawned bright and clear.

I arrived at Tempie's just after sunrise, wanting to see her but being afraid to, just the same.

Governor West greeted me, busy at his desk. "Good morning, Mrs. Peirce. Your friend is sleeping soundly."

"Thank you, sir." My voice sounded far away, hollow.

I let myself into the chamber. There I found Susanna already sitting by the bedside, holding her dame's hand.

"Good morning, lovey," I said to her, and she rose and fell into my arms. Her eyes brimmed with tears, and then so did mine. "We'll take turns sitting with her, how about it?" I asked. "A new day, new hope?"

She nodded and slipped from the room.

The day wore on, but Tempie was awake little and even then seemed to be unaware of her surroundings. And so the tide of Providence swept in, a little at a time, just as the river tide eased up to shore.

All the herbs, all the healing, all the knowledge of the English and Indians in the forests were not bringing her back to us. But I still hoped tomorrow would be better.

She awakened for a little while as the evening was coming on. It surprised me when her eyes opened. Her voice was clear and even strong. "See you in the new light, Joanie," she said. Her eyes sparkled with fever and love, bright as any starlight. The crackling fire and glittering candles cast a warm rosiness in the room, such a contrast to her fairness. Her cheeks blushed red, her face so ashen.

It was as if she'd awakened to say only that, then she fell into a peaceful sleep.

I smiled. "Aye, see you in the morning, lovey."

She never calls me Joanie, I thought. I pressed her hand with my own, but she had already drifted back off to sleep. So I sat for just a little while more, holding her hand as she slept.

I stood to leave but looked back from the doorway. *She looks so small.* All the spirit, the ardor that was Tempie, contained in a tiny, huddled form on the bed.

Fear like a demon reared its head, but I pushed it down. *No!*

As I walked from the chamber, I saw Susanna there with all three in her fold.

I gave each of them a hug and a kiss, saying I'd be back at dawn.

Then I paused. Susanna, too, was afraid. I could see it. "Would you like me to stay the night here?"

"Oh, would you, Miss Joan? Please. Governor West is little help, and the servants are … I mean, I can't …"

"I know," I said consolingly. There was an extra bed upstairs in Susanna's room.

"Stay a-vigil with me," she pleaded.

"Sure, and I will," I said softly.

Susanna then led the children into the room, and I gave them the time they needed. I walked into the dining hall and sat at Tempie's spinning wheel, the last yard still on the wheel.

She'll finish it next week when she has come through this ague, I told myself.

Susanna and I decided to take shifts at Tempie's bedside overnight, hoping Governor West would be staying at one of the plantations. But that plan came to naught when Governor West did indeed return home that night, looking to retire. So Susanna left her dame's bedside after all.

To me, Governor West said, "Stay the night if you would, Mrs. Peirce. I'll not chase ye out after the darkness has fallen."

How very generous! I thought bitterly.

So Susanna and I settled ourselves in for the night, waiting for the dawn when we could return and hold Tempie's hand.

Tomorrow, I thought as I tried to drift off. *Tomorrow.* Tomorrow, I would sit all the day long, ministering as I could as I prayed for the ague to break. I would take a quiet spot in the corner of the chamber.

Tomorrow.

My sleep was fitful in the cold, damp December darkness. The night was still deep black when a knock at the door awoke Susanna and me. My heart thundered.

"No, no," I sobbed as Susanna opened the door gingerly.

Governor West stood in the doorway in a nightshirt, holding a candle. In the ruddy shadows, I could just make out his expression. Compassion I saw on his face.

I knew. I knew before Susanna wailed. I knew before I crept down to the bedchamber. My head spun in a dizzying array of images. I felt I might faint. I grabbed my eyes, my head. The pain made it hard to breathe.

Make it go away, dear God. Make it go away!

And Sweet to Remember

December 3 – 4, 1628
New Towne, Virginia

I heard a bird sing
In the dark of December.
A magical thing
And sweet to remember.
"We are nearer to Spring
Than we were in September,"
I heard a bird sing
In the dark of December.
　　　　　　—Oliver Hereford

The sun rose over a household in mourning.

At least, Susanna and the children and I were mourning. I could not be certain about Governor West although I thought his eyes were red.

Susanna and I had not slept anymore, although we had tried to.

The grey December air was still, but bitter. The leaves on the trees all dead. For a moment, I was carried away to that November day, some twenty years past, when Janey had cried with me, at the edge of the woods. At the edge of the earth. At the edge of my courage.

Now, I felt the same. A world without Tempie, I could not imagine.

Strangely, over the next few days, I found Tempie's vision of angels comforting, as I had found it terrifying before. She had slipped her hand into one of theirs—they had lifted her up. She had flown away. Flown with the angels, as little Cecily had said when her baby brother died so long ago.

Afterward, I remembered only snatches of the funeral. Elizabeth trying to be brave and Argall acting every bit the man of the family. Each of them wrapping an arm around Little Francis as they stood on either side of him. Elizabeth and Argall, now needing to be mother and father to their young brother.

Sweet little orphans.

The lump that had been in my throat for a day rose up again at the sight of the children, bringing tears to my eyes just as it prevented me from eating anything. I felt weak and light-headed and hopeless.

Captain West did cry, for I saw him. Now I thought perhaps he had loved Tempie after all, despite such a brief marriage. Still, I resented the fear he had caused her. I felt some part of Tempie had died with Sir George, anyway.

I sat in the church with the children, with Susanna and Will. Captain Claiborne sat there, too, sturdy as a post. Gratitude washed over me that he had helped Tempie in her last days. I would make sure to tell him.

Behind us were Jane and Cecily with their children, William Farrar and Roger next to them. Isabella and Captain Perry were in a pew behind my daughters.

Annie and Jack Laydon had come. Even Goody Wright was here with her husband.

I caught Goody's eye. She put her hands together. *I'm praying for you,* the gesture said.

She knows what Tempie did for her, how she asked Sir George not to duck her as a witch. My heart warmed.

Thank you. I mouthed the words to the midwife, who nodded gracefully.

Mr. Menefie was here with his wife, and I noticed Captain Mathews and Lieutenant Uty. Dr. Pott and his wife Elizabeth sniffled together. How sweet that was.

See how many people love you, Tempie? I asked my friend as if she could hear my thoughts.

The whole settlement, it seemed, had turned out as it had for Sir George just a short year before. The ringing in my ears prevented me from hearing the pastor, and so I sat, instead, dreamlike.

This has not happened. I'll go by her home today and bring her some bread. Oh, warm cornbread and mulberry beer. And we'll talk about the old days, about the days to come, about the children, about the ...

No, she's dead.

To weep so hard at a service and yet to feel as if I were not even there. As if I floated above myself. I must do that, I guessed, because it was too painful to be me, to be inside myself.

They buried her in the church at James Town beneath the floor, near Sir

George's tomb with the brass crest. The knight's tomb. And she, forever, his lady. If our little church had a chancel of honor, this was it.

I could not imagine how I'd survive the strange, wild world of Virginia without her.

All had left Tempie's gravesite now, 'til just I remained. I let them all go before me, though some beckoned, "Come, 'tis time for warm pottage and ham."

Isabella tried to encourage me to come in from the cold, as did my daughters.

I nodded but made no move to retreat. Will stretched his hand out. I shook my head. Knowingly, he nodded, too, and left.

There, in the quiet of the church, with no one for company but the other graves, I slowly sang the Psalm from St. Augustine's book as I'd promised.

> *For why? Unto his Angels all*
> *with charge commanded he,*
> *That still in all thy ways they shall*
> *preserve and prosper thee.*
> *And in their hands shall bear thee up,*
> *still waiting thee upon*
> *So that thy foote shall never chance*
> *to spurn at any stone,*
> *Upon the lion thou shalt go,*
> *the adder fell and long:*
> *And tread upon the Lion's young*
> *with Dragons stout and strong*

My voice strained through parts of it, but I continued on. A farewell hymn for my Tempie.

With trudging steps, I started to walk toward the Yeardley home where all had gathered.

The ground is cold. No! She is not there.

And then, looking back just once, I heard—by my leave—a cardinal cheering from the bush. Just as one had done all those years ago when I'd said goodbye to Maggie at her grave.

Maggie, I thought, was singing for her, too.

I don't know why, but the sound of that little bird, while causing me to cry anew, also gave me hope. Just as Tempie and I had said a month before.

Hope always comes from somewhere. *We found hope in so many things*, Tempie had mused.

Now, here it was, singing from the bushes. *Cheer, cheer, cheer, cheer.*

The minstrel hopped forth as if to introduce himself. His tiny red cloak, brighter than every grey thing in late fall at James Town. A beacon as if to say that color still was, even on a dark, grief-filled December day. A day when every spirit was also filled with grey.

Tempie was part of the natural world, just like this little bird. Somewhere, she was whole and healed with no more starving, no more sickness. No more grief.

Standing before me, this little red bird sang and sang and sang, as if saying, *Spring is coming one day soon. Cheer, cheer, cheer!* And I felt the faintest tremor of renewal, of an understanding that everything, somehow, was as it should be in God's world.

It was—because this little bird said it was. And by his cloak, he showed me.

I Am the Leaf that Quivers

December 4, 1628
At the Back River in New Towne, Virginia

*Two women shall be grinding at the mill; the one shall be taken, and the
other left.*
> —Matthew 24:41

I am the leaf that quivers,
You, the unshaken tree;
You are the stars that are steadfast,
I am the sea.

You are the light eternal—
Like a torch I shall die.
You are the surge of deep music,
I but a cry!
> —Zoë Akins

Will would worry.

I had gone to the Yeardley home where much food awaited and all gathered.

Had I eaten? Maybe I had. I wasn't sure.

Then I quietly stole away to the Back River once more, a quiet and secret place. The sun was rocking itself lower into the sky behind the clouds.

My fears were many and dark as the coming satin night. The night of no stars.

I will never see Tempie again.

I will, oh, I will. I'm sure I will for I have heard Maggie. She lives, and so does Tempie. Even old Grace lives.

Somewhere.

Somewhere, but not here.

I wanted to picture Tempie's smile, imagine her laugh, but it hurt too much. I pushed the smile of my sister away from me, but it would not leave.

Face this, the image seemed to say. *For face it, you must.*

Twenty years!

Twenty years at James Town with her. Almost, anyway.

How many years would I have to live without her? How *would* I live without her at all? I had so many questions and no answers.

The voice in reply was gentle, startling even. I'd heard it before so many years ago at the harbor in Melcombe Regis. *Count yourself fortunate you've had her so long. Remember the Starving Time. She was thin as a shadow, nearer to death than to life,* the voice chided.

Yes, I'd had her for many more years after that terrible spring.

"Count your blessings," Tempie had suggested during martial law when I felt I could bear this place no longer. And later, she'd asked me if it helped. *I am going to think. To pray. Perhaps to list my own blessings,* she had said then.

She lifted me up, and then I lifted her up. It had always been so.

Counting blessings *had* helped, I remembered. I'd had blessings aplenty even when I thought I had none.

I sighed. A deep and piteous sound, even to mine own ears. I had blessings, even now. I knew that. But I did not want to think about blessings in the midst of such loss.

Pages of blessings could not o'ercome this! I thought in despair. *Tempie is gone, Tempie is gone.* And I sobbed again as if I might never be comforted.

One thought intruded above all others, a deep cry of the heart. *Did I do enough? Could I have saved her?* One herb different might have been the one that kept her here. One forgotten plant deep in the Virginia woods. Some flower I knew not at all could have been the one. Some plant that grew just over the next hill. Or the next. Or in the great blue mountains west that the Indians described.

A chill of fear stabbed me with its icy blade. I might have done something different, something better, something ... something that I had not.

You did all you could, the voice in my heart said.

I tried, I did, Lord.

My grief might have been getting the better of me, but I felt as if the woods and the water and the land were speaking to me. *She knows.* Gentle, reassuring.

Does she? Did she hurt? Was it hard to die?

A patient reply, engraved in the clouds and the sky. Surrounding me. *Death is beautiful, as beautiful as life and even more so because where Tempie is there is no pain, no suffering. 'Twas Grace led her away.*

Grace! I'd wanted to deny a home to the old woman. But Tempie had been kinder than I, had shown grace in the midst of unbearable suffering. She had forced me to show it, too.

You are being so hard on yourself when there is nothing to fear, no judgment to be made.

But no words could console me. My arms I wrapped around myself and rocked as if that could soothe the desperate ache, the searing loss.

The leaves, the leaves. She knew. I think she knew. Was she afraid?

And then I remembered.

See you in the new light, Joanie, she'd said. She had awakened for just that moment, these her last words to me. *The new light.* Not morning. A sudden dawning realization ... She had known she was dying and had been saying goodbye. But gently, so as not to be hard on me. *She was still thinking of me, even at the end.*

Compassionately, the voice replied, *She died as she lived ... with great courage.*

Courage. I had none left. I wondered if courage were like a little pitcher of cream, if every day one poured some out. One day, like today, would there then be none left?

Maybe that was why I felt so empty.

How does courage become refilled then?

Tempie always gave me courage, heartened me when times were worst. Now, how would I go on?

My vision blurred with tears as the rich blue river blended with the grey of the trees.

If Tempie were here, she'd make me laugh. But if Tempie were here, I'd not be crying.

My thoughts were a muddled mess, whirling and swirling like the little eddy near the riverbed.

For a while, I just watched the water moving past. Dark and dense. I felt like that—as if my life were the darkness beneath the water. And yet ...

The sun caught the water and reflected light back at me.

See you in the new light, Joanie!

Somehow, that light comforted me. But only for a moment.

I knew that in the morning, I would open my eyes and everything would be fine. Until the first thought of the day struck me.

Tempie was gone. She was gone.

James Town would never be the same.

A lone leaf caught the wind and blew from the oak above into the water, into the eddy, and it danced.

A lone leaf dancing in the great blue river in the too sorrowful land called Virginia. Did the leaf not know that all was sad in this world today?

And yet the leaf danced and danced and danced.

In my heart, I heard Tempie say once more, *The leaves fall silently, and yet they* dance *to the ground. Pirouetting, swirling, turning ... catching a breeze and floating back upward.*

And at once, I understood that Tempie would be all right.

I looked into the blue of the sky, colors sinking just a little with the sun. I remembered that inside a home in New Towne, inside the darkness, were three tiny candles of light. Three desolate children who had only just lost their father and now their mama, too.

Love them for me, Tempie had said, had implored.

The voice concurred. *Go to them,* it whispered.

And so I did.

The East Winds Blow

Christmas 1628
James Town, Virginia

Above that grave the east winds blow
And from the marsh-lands drifting slow
The sea-fog comes, with evermore
The wave wash of a lonely shore,
And sea-bird's melancholy cry,
As Nature fain would typify
The sadness of a closing scene,
The loss of that which should have been.
　　　　　—John Greenleaf Whittier

I went back to the gravesite several days before Christmas, letting myself in the church.

Kneeling beside her grave, touching the brick beneath which she lay. Irrationally, patting it as though somehow that would make her more comfortable. I said, "I came to wish you a happy Christmas, our first without you. Susanna and I are trying to make your home cheerful for the holy day."

Then I sat in the silence, just listening. Listening to nothing.

"I ... I know you aren't truly here, Tempie."

More silence.

"I won't be here this spring. I'll be in England with your children. But the next spring I'm here, I'll bring you flowers. Little purple and blue ones like we had that day we toasted during the Starving Time. Remember?" And my voice trailed off. I could not say more.

A few more moments passed, and I gathered myself.

Finally, strengthening my voice, I said, "'Tis fine to sing memorial hymns, but love must move forward. This I do, howe'er hard it be. I'll carry your children across the sea, as I promised."

At that, the wind whistled and whispered and hummed around the church, though it had been a quiet hush all the day. Now I stood upright, letting the cold wind, an eerie singing, whip about me.

"I hear you, my friend."

I walked stiffly back home to New Towne. Knowing that things would never be the same, feeling an actual aching in my heart as though it were wringing itself.

And then I wondered how the children would like London.

It pained me to admit it, but having something to do would help me. *Hope in hard work*, Tempie had said. True it was. Hard work had saved me more than once. And leaving Virginia—where Tempie had been part of everything—must help heal me by sheer distraction.

Tempie had charged me with getting the children across the sea. By the time we arrived in London, it would be near June. June of 1629. Exactly twenty years since I'd last seen the port of Devon.

The house had a deep chill within it, only partly due to the December cold. I sat in a chair next to the fire, knotting thread to make a lace collar. The little knots were comforting somehow. As though with my mind absorbed in their intricacies, I could not think of the thing that consumed me each day. The thing I could not get past.

Tempie is gone.

Each time the thought went through my mind, my heart sank anew, as though a fresh grieving. Each morning I woke up feeling joyful until the first thought occurred. "She's gone. 'Tis not a dream."

Susanna and I had placed sprigs of holly and cedar hoping to lift the children's spirits. When that failed, I reminded them that soon we'd be sailing to England.

That perked them up a little, the boys, at least.

"This was like losing your mother all over again for you, wasn't it, Susanna?" I asked her as we placed sprigs of holly about.

"I was so young when I came over. My parents were long gone, but they'd been friends of Mr. Yeardley, the apothecary. 'Twas he who suggested I come here as a servant. I'm glad I did because Sir George and Dame Temperance were my new family." Her expression was desolate.

I gave her a hug. "'Tis a good thing, Susanna, that you're going with the children. And it helps that you already know Ralph and Rose."

"It does, mistress."

The children and Susanna had come to eat with us for Christmas dinner. I had little appetite for the holidays—for the fine food or the celebration. But for the sake of the little ones, I pretended I did. So did Susanna, I noticed.

A servant had brought in two fat turkeys shot at Mulberry Island. We would have fresh corn pone and corn pudding as well as figgy pudding. We'd decorated with sprigs of holly. The candles burned, casting a glow as evening wore on. It would soon be time to retire to our chamber.

I felt tears welling up once more. I began sniffling, trying to stop them, until at last, I put my hand upon my eyes. It was no use. I knew I would attract Will's attention, and my grief, I felt, was private. He would tell me not to worry. We'd lost many friends and loved ones, hadn't we? Cecily had lost two husbands, Tom and Sam. Jane had lost John. We'd lost Maggie and Pocahontas and Maria, Sir George and ...

Tempie.

I Will See You Again

Early January 1629
New Towne, Virginia

*And ye now therefore have sorrow: but I will see you again, and your heart
shall rejoice, and your joy no man taketh from you.*
—John 16:22

What saved me was the practical matter at hand. We must get the
Yeardley children and Susanna to England.

This meant that we needed to begin planning immediately.
Governor West understood the need to remove the children—was not at all
opposed to the idea.

As for Will, he, too, had business to attend to in England, and affairs had
detained him here for too many years now. This season, we'd both go. Will
began cleaning up his accounts and asked Roger, with young Tom's help, to
supervise his business while he was away.

Will had been writing to Henry Rolfe, John's brother, since Will was executor of John's estate. Henry said that John and Pocahontas's son Thomas
hoped to return to his mother's home, Virginia. Thomas had inherited a
considerable plot of land across from James Town which his grandfather
Powhatan had given to his father. Henry wrote that Thomas longed to see
the Virginia hardwoods and rivers that were somehow in his blood. He'd
been just a small child when he had left, so 'twas not as though he could
remember it.

Captain Claiborne had written a letter to Ralph Yeardley within days of
Tempie's death and sent it on the next ship. I prepared a trunk of clothes,
then went to the Yeardley children to ensure that they, too, had their packing
well underway. Susanna, enjoying helping her departed mistress, assured me
that she had the children moving along.

"When are we coming back?" Little Francis had asked me.

I placed a hand on his shoulder. "You may come back whenever you please! Once your uncle decides you're old enough."

He seemed relieved, for he had friends at New Towne, and England seemed to him a strange and foreign land.

How odd, I thought, *that Virginia seems exactly to us as England does to these Virginia-born children.* It had started—the children born here who felt England more foreign and exotic than Virginia! I sensed that this was the beginning, right in front of me, of a new way of thinking in the colony. Virginia was English and not English, of England and not of England. We called the Indians Virginians and ourselves English. Yet we weren't exactly English either. In fact, more often lately we called ourselves Virginians, too.

The one I was most concerned about was Elizabeth. She'd been so close to her mother and was a sensitive child. She was just at the age when a girl most needs her mother.

"Elizabeth, I know how devastating it is to lose a mother and a father so young." I took her hands in mine, hoping it would be soothing. "I was about your age when my father died, and shortly thereafter, my mother did, too. I was fortunate. I had a loving stepmother, but it's still hard. But soon you'll see London—'tis a whole new world for you!"

"But I'll never forget my mother." Her face shadowed in deep grief.

"Nor will I," I said quietly, and the two of us embraced. "Going there was her wish for you," I whispered.

"Her grave, auntie. How can I leave her behind?" Elizabeth's voice was suddenly a quiet wail.

I understood. "Your mama isn't in that grave, sweet girl. I know it seems like she is." I stroked her hair. "But she'll always be where you are."

Elizabeth nodded, her beautiful eyes wide and filled with tears.

But she did not cry. Instead, she set her chin in what I thought to be determination. In that instant, I saw again a glimpse of a young Tempie in Elizabeth. And that thought filled me with joy.

Tempie is not dead! She lives in this beautiful daughter and in her two enthusiastic sons.

Susanna was also taking this hard, but she threw herself into easing the transition for the children. "I would make my dame proud," she told me.

"And so you do."

Turning her attention to the children, Susanna said to them, "Oh, wait 'til you see the ocean swells! And we'll play cards and drafts and Nine Men's Morris." Susanna had been just a child herself when she made the journey. "Mayhap we'll tell stories, too."

"Do you think we'll see Spanish pirates? Maybe get into a sea battle?" Argall asked eagerly.

"Shush, child! I should hope not." Yet I couldn't help smiling at the boy.

If Elizabeth were much like Tempie, Argall, it was plain to see, was every bit Sir George. "He'll do great things one day like his father," I told Will privately, and he agreed.

"He'll return to be a future leader of Virginia. I know it." High praise from Will.

After leaving the Yeardley children, I walked over to Tempie's grave and assured her that she could rest easy. "We'll see that they get safely to England—God willing! Sleep well, dear friend."

Leaving the church, I paused and looked into the heavens, into the rich, deep blue clouds of winter. "Or fly joyously!"

After that, the next months we spent finishing preparations. I'd come to realize that returning to England could be an exciting adventure if I let not my fears best me. So many years had passed since I came here. I'd crossed the *Blessing's* threshold almost twenty years before, and that had been my last look at my old home.

I'd kept my mind moving on something, anything, other than my loss. Tending the children was something I loved, and it kept my mind occupied— a sure, if temporary, cure for grief, I'd learned by hard experience.

The Wind a Hawk,
and the Fields in Snow

February 12, 1629
New Towne, Virginia

... that the Governer [West] should give into the Cort [Court] an account of
the estate belonging unto the Children and Orphants of Sr Georg Yeardley
deceased ... The governor made answer that hee conceaved that the Cort
[Court] had nothing to doe to require anything from him and therefore hee
would not delyver in an acc° of the Childrens estate neyther give in bond
to the Cort [Court] to bee any waie accountable for the same, but will bee
ready to bee accountable to them that have power and authority to Call him
thereunto in England.
> —Minutes of the Council and General Court,
> 11 February 1629

Oh, what a night for a soul to go!
The wind a hawk, and the fields in snow;
No screening cover of leaves in the wood,
Nor a star abroad the way to show.
> —Arthur Sherburne Hardy

About a month before Will and I planned to board ship, I saw Dr. Pott through the frosty window. He seemed to be coming toward my home. It was near suppertime; the sun was dropping low, especially since the sky hung so heavy with clouds.

I opened the door. The doctor's shoes crunched across the frozen ground.

"Looks like snow, Mrs. Peirce!" he said genially.

The bitter February winds cut through us and whipped around the side of the house. The doctor blew on his hands.

"I think it may snow at that! But if 'tis Will you're seeking, he isn't home, doctor," I apologized. "Will has gone across the water, over to the lands Powhatan gave John Rolfe."

"No, 'tis you I wish to see, mistress, to speak confidentially. May I come in?"

"Of course, you may," I replied, ushering him into the dining hall. "Come in and warm yourself!"

"I can only stay for a moment." He walked straight over to the fire and held out his hands, then turned his backside to the flames.

I gave him a curious stare. He obviously had something he considered important to discuss. Else, why brave the winter day?

"Are there servants about?" His eyes roamed the chamber, his expression guarded.

"No, doctor."

"Good. I wish to tell you something from the council, something I should not be repeating. But I desire the best for the young Yeardley children. My devotion to Sir George, may he rest in peace, is steadfast. My loyalty to our present governor is, uh, weak."

My heart started to race. When Dr. Pott mentioned Tempie's children and Governor West together, I knew it should not be good.

"What is West about?" I said with a touch of sarcasm. I should not speak so disrespectfully of a governor and captain. Yet I wanted to add, *the scoundrel!* But the court could prosecute us for harsh words about an acting governor. So I used more restraint than I felt.

"You are taking the children to England, is that correct?" He asked, seeming to read my thoughts about Governor West. I suspected my face betrayed more than my words had.

"Aye, as soon as we might. In the early spring, we hope."

"It is well, then. I need you to let Ralph Yeardley know something. Yesterday we, the council, demanded an accounting of the Yeardley children's estate. As you know, this is the proper course since the governor has not reported to us regarding the children's property. But this Captain West has refused to perform. He waits for someone in authority in England to request it, saith he. Let Mr. Yeardley know that he must carefully account for the children's inheritance, for I fear me West is seeking more than his share." The doctor's eyes were troubled. "The council, for the sake of unity, has not overridden the governor's refusal. But Ralph Yeardley hath it in his power to settle Sir George's estate. I believe that Mr. Yeardley is taking over the settling of Sir George's will from Dame Temperance?" he asked.

I nodded wordlessly. Now my trembling heart sank low and withered. *We knew it!* Susanna and I—and even Tempie—had suspected as much.

"One other thing, Mrs. Peirce. I know for a certainty Governor West prepares to sail as soon as possible to approach the courts himself. Do not dally! Get the children and this message to Mr. Yeardley in London soon. Mr. Yeardley needs to prepare, for I suspect he shall have a court battle on his hands."

Oh, no. Tempie had tried to prevent that, but West was a stubborn man.

"Who ... who will the next governor be if West leaves?" I asked stupidly.

"The council has selected me."

"Good," I breathed.

An acting governor for an acting governor? This was a strange turn of events, meaning Captain West was in a rush. We needed to be, too.

"Thank you so much, Dr. Pott," I said, taking the man's hand in my own. "Thank you for watching out for the Yeardley children." I was so touched that he had chanced his reputation and braved the cold to share all this.

"We must look out for each other should ill winds blow," he replied. "Which they'll soon do if it snows. So let me get home to Mrs. Pott." His smile was kind. "My hearty wishes and sincere sympathies to the Yeardleys. And Mrs. Peirce? Do let your husband know he can count on me if he needs someone to watch over his property here."

"I thank thee, sincerely, I do, doctor."

By the time the doctor eased down the icy steps, snow coated the ground.

Dr. Pott walked across our yard, huddled against the cold, his breath coming in white clouds. Soon he was a grey figure in the distance.

The snow looked to be fierce. It had already dressed the land in a shroud of white. Will would not be returning home tonight, sure. And no ships would be sailing anytime soon.

I shut the door and cursed West beneath my breath.

Little Blue Flower

March 1 – 20, 1629
In New Towne, and on board the *William and John* at sea

Little blue flower
wagging with a bee,
before the sun strikes shoal
tell me why the night's more sweet
than the day is honey,
as the sea too with all its salt
blossoms.
    —Edward Wright Haile

Isabel the wife of William Perry a merchant of Virginia, 40 years. 26 Aug.,
1629. About Christmas last one John Riley of London, merchant who lodged
in the house of her husband in Virginia there died ...
    —High Court of Admiralty Examinations

After the February snowstorm, the weather changed abruptly and turned warm. Musical Virginia, with birdsong returning, said the countryside was thawing and reviving.

Yet even an early spring couldn't lift my anxiety as time approached to board ship. The *William and John* would be weighing anchor soon.

Coming by our home to arrange our passage, ship's master Tobias Felgate sensed my fear and tried to reassure me. "I've made this voyage more than a half dozen times and back again, Mrs. Peirce. If any man can see you safe across the ocean, I am he."

I appreciated his confidence and his bravado, even.

Toby Felgate was well known and liked here. He'd married a girl in

Virginia, but his wife died after Goody Wright predicted it as we'd learned in the witch trial.

I wondered if he himself believed Goody Wright to have cursed his wife. Sailors were the most superstitious of us all. Still, I didn't ask.

Mr. Felgate was now married to the widow Hamor for we'd lost Captain Hamor a few years ago, too.

Besides his loyalty to Virginia, Felgate was reputed a stout mariner. He'd grown up on the English coast and brought much sailing experience, even before the Berkeley Hundred Society had hired him a decade ago. As well, he was a trusted sea partner of Captain Ewens.

All this, I knew.

However, what charmed me most was when Master Felgate held his cap over his heart when speaking of the Yeardleys. He felt honored to carry the children to England, he said.

It seemed only yesterday that Felgate's men had delivered the letters to Tempie, the day we'd sat before the fire drinking perry.

Life and Virginia weather were much alike. All that one knew was how little he knew. Changes blew in, sudden as a snowstorm, unexpected as spring sunshine melting a snowdrift.

Now the day had come, and the ship in the river greeted me. Even the cheerfully painted wood, bright colors of blue and red and yellow, couldn't allay my fears.

The children had eagerly climbed on board earlier. To them, this was all adventure. Even Elizabeth seemed excited, which gladdened me.

But for me? I walked toward the vessel as if I were marching to my own execution.

Strange how one supposes she's forgotten something, something fierce ... and yet she hasn't.

Confidence in Toby Felgate? Indeed, I had it. But the ship's voyage still frightened me.

Courage, oh, courage, Joan, I told myself. I would do this for Tempie somehow even as my heart throbbed into my throat with the old demon, fear.

Just before I stepped from the muddy shore, I looked down. "Oh, my! Oh, oh," I cried aloud, and several nearby gave me searching looks as if I'd lost my senses.

But, no, my senses hadn't departed. Instead, they'd saved me.

Down near the bridge, a row of little purple and blue flowers smiled up at me.

"You're up early!" I said to them in surprised delight. A sailor nearby rolled his eyes. I paid him no mind. This was important to me.

I could almost hear Tempie, could feel her beside me. She'd spoken of these little flowers ere she died. *Never worry, Joan. We'll see them in the spring! They'll encourage us all over again. Maybe e'en when we need it most.*

"See that you were right," I whispered to Tempie. "You were always right somehow." I reached down to gather a few flowers to press in my daybook. Surely, having them with me would give me heart.

Now the looks I'd gotten before turned more sour. I was holding up the line.

"Joan!" A voice from behind me made me turn around.

Isabella waved. "I'm coming, too!"

I left the line completely. "You are? On Mr. Felgate's ship?"

"Yes. Look see."

She pulled out a folded paper. "A man died at our home in December. The same sickness as Tempie, I think. He was a merchant, passing through. Now I must testify regarding his estate. I thought I might as well go along with you now."

"Testify?"

She flipped the letter open. On it was printed boldly *High Court of Admiralty: Summons to Appear for Deposition.*

"Are you frightened to appear before such a court?" I asked her, forgetting my own fears for a time.

"Well, I suppose not. What can I say? Whatever they wish to know, I'll tell them. I didn't know the man well. He was a houseguest."

True. In Virginia, these things happened all the time—houseguests arriving, houseguests dying.

I hugged her. "I'm *so* glad you'll be along."

"This notice just came to me. I'm packing quickly, won't stay too long there. But it will give me a chance to visit my family in Surrey, too. Also, I've been shipping quite a bit of tobacco from the Pace fields. I'd like to visit the Tobacco Exchange while I'm there, learn a little more." She paused. "And besides, Tempie asked me to look after you."

"Did she now?" I said slyly. "Missus, I can take care of myself."

"Joan, you're scared to death. I saw the line and you pretending you wanted to pick flowers so you didn't have to get on ship."

"Well, yes." I laughed. "I did want those flowers. But come along and take care of me then."

What Seas Shall Be Thy Fate

March 20, 1629

On board the *William and John* in the James River

I do not know beneath what sky
Nor on what seas shall be thy fate;
I only know it shall be high,
I only know it shall be great.
        —Richard Hovey

When I climbed down the scuttle down into the 'tween deck, my mind raced.

The last time I was at sea, a hurricane had shaken and thrown us for days. Even now when I shut my eyes, I could still feel the darkness. The battering wind and rain, the trembling of the *Blessing,* Jane wrenched from my arms. I could still feel my cries drowned by howling wind and roaring sea, screaming into nothingness.

No hurricanes will fright ye, I told myself. It could not, would not, happen again. I hadn't even known I carried so much fear. It must have lain hidden in the dim corners of my mind. It only now crept out, peering over to say that fear never truly goes away. It only hides itself in darkness.

Beastie, go! Go. *I am not afeared.*

Hurricanes? Spanish warships? Pirates! Turkish rogues with scimitars, screaming commands in a language none—but possibly George Sandys— could understand. *A treaty. Will says to rest easy, that our king did sign a treaty with the Sallee rovers. But could such a thing prevent picaroons from raiding?* More than for myself, more than for Will, I worried about Tempie's children. How could I ever forgive myself if anything happened to them or to Susanna?

I shut my eyes to push the terrifying sounds and images far, far away. *Beasties! Please.*

"Are you all right, mistress?" Susanna asked, taking my hand in concern.

I nodded with as much enthusiasm as I could muster. "Oh, I am. Indeed. Just a few memories of coming into Virginia."

Susanna had heard Tempie speak of the hurricane. She gave an understanding smile but said nothing. We would not scare the children. Then she whispered, "Such a storm is rare. We saw none on our voyage, and I've never heard of another expedition having such as that."

I understood and appreciated her trying. Fear, though, had its own sort of logic.

Isabella came and plopped herself down beside me. "Stretch your worrying out some. Don't do all of it today. You'll use it all up!" Then she lowered her voice. "That's from Tempie. I was supposed to tell you that before you got on ship. Figured since I was coming along, I could do it on board."

Now I laughed some. "All right then. I'll ration it. I'm good at that, so they tell me. I did it with acorns and with venison."

The *William and John* was a small ship, only about fifty tons burthen. It was able to carry just a dozen or so of us in the 'tween deck.

God, do get us safely across. The children were all I had left of Tempie. To give them up would be so hard. Meanwhile, I'd left my own children behind as I traveled. That was a little frightening, too.

Will came over and sat down.

"How are you?" he asked, patting my arm.

I shrugged.

Oceans were wide, mysterious things. Why was the great Atlantic always the barrier between myself and those I loved?

Joan. George tells me 'tis time, time to return … to England, Tempie had said to me some eleven years past. It had felt the worst thing in the world to me then when she'd left. Now that she was truly gone—how glad I was that she'd seen her home, England, a final time before she died. Once more to see her mother, to make her peace.

And she'd spent time with Ralph and Rose Yeardley, now to be the guardians of these children. She'd stayed with them and grown to love them. She knew they would do right by the children. That was a comfort, sure.

How many times have I wished for England? How many times have I made myself as content as possible in a place I thought I could never love? Yet here am I and would trade the voyage home for the friend lost. As these thoughts roved my mind, I heaved a long sigh.

Wishing for home? So many years had I done that. *I had me a wish once, but I wished awry.* Now I would have to make myself content once more while the reason for the journey made it anything but joyous. *I'd trade the return to England for one more flagon of mulberry beer with Tempie. The whole return home for one more moment with her, once more to hear her pealing laughter. That is what I'd truly wish if I could choose again.*

As my mind meandered, I realized that Will was talking.

"So between Captain Claiborne and Roger, our affairs in Virginia should be in fine hands. Also, Dr. Pott will mind our New Towne home."

"He and his wife will gather the figs, too," I put in. "He'll keep an accounting of how many he reaps. He'll sell some back to himself at a lower rate for his time."

"You're paying our doctor *wages* now?" Will asked playfully.

"My figs, my fees," I said in mock seriousness. "That's why I'm the fig lady."

Will went on to say that he'd left those in charge of our goods and harvest the name of our inn as well as Ralph Yeardley's street. "Cecily and William Farrar know how to reach us both places as well. I sent them a letter upriver on Mr. Menefie's shallop," he finished.

If something happened in Virginia, it would take us a full two months and more to know of it. But if no one knew where we stayed, we might be a year and a half without knowing. I was glad Will was thinking ahead, as he ever did.

"'Tis a good thing," I said before my mind wandered again to the voyage. "Pray God, no one will need it."

Sooner than we knew, the bosun cast off our lines, and the *William and John* eased into the gentle river tide and away into the unknown.

Sacred Storytelling

March 20 to April 7, 1629
On board the *William and John* at sea

So if storytelling is a journey, sacred storytelling is a pilgrimage—a pilgrimage to a place called Hope.
    —Andy Fraenkel

Slowly the days passed in the 'tween deck and cabins of the *William and John*. I offered the children, Susanna, Will, and myself gum dragon cakes and ginger.

"Pardon, but what's in them?" asked Argall curiously, looking at the little cakes.

"Cinnamon and gum dragon and sugar. 'Twill help thee when the ship's rocking makes thee feel sick," I explained. "Ginger we add to our beer for the same reason."

Francis held the cake up. "Is it made from dragons?"

I smiled. "No, dear. From the gum of trees."

He tasted it. "I'm going to pretend I'm eating dragon meat."

The herbs did seem to help as we suffered little except in one frightening storm, a storm which passed as storms are wont to do. The choppiness of the waves and howling wind scared us all for a small while.

"My mother wrote about the whales when we came to England before," Elizabeth said. She'd brought her mother's daybook.

I laughed. "She would!" If only she were here with us, traveling with the children back to England. I took a deep breath and tried to push the thoughts away.

The children and I played a game to pass the time.

"I love my love with an *A* because he's *Artistic*. I hate him with an *A* because he's *Annoying*. His name is ..." I searched for a biblical name. "*Adam*, and the best part about him is his *Arm*. I invited him to the sign of the *Artichoke*, and I gave him a dish of ... *Acorns!*" The children laughed, and so did I. "No, truly. How about *Apricots?*"

Elizabeth gave it a try. "I love my love with a *B* because he is ..." She hesitated. "*Bashful!* I hate him with a *B* because he's *boring*. His name is *Ben*, and the best part about him is his *Bacon!*" The two boys laughed. "And I invited him to *Berkeley* and gave him a dish of *Beans!*"

And on it went.

About a fortnight into our journey, the boys were putting pegs into a game board of Nine Men's Morris. Argall was trying to teach his brother the game. The older boy gave me a withered look. *These children!* his eyes seemed to say. I reached over and patted his back fondly.

Elizabeth, watching the boys and me, said tentatively, "Auntie Joan, you knew my mama best, didn't you?"

"I suppose, child. Many a year in the colony we endured together. Many a trial, many a fond memory, too." It would hurt to talk about those times although I sensed Elizabeth longed for stories. I'd avoided speaking to Elizabeth about her parents, both for her sake and perhaps even more, for my own.

The boys had stopped playing to listen. They, I saw, were curious too, and after all, what had we but time? Elizabeth's pleading eyes and the boys' curious ones, drew me in. To them, Sir George's death already seemed long ago. *What will they remember of their parents?* I wondered.

Susanna brought herself over and draped an arm around each of the little boys. "May I listen?" she asked. Again, I saw Susanna's own grief and uncertainty. Sometimes I overlooked that her life faced drastic change, too.

"Of course, lovey!" I said, warming to the idea. The crucible of that terrible night had forged Susanna and me together. That night where everything changed.

Stories, I chided myself. I brushed a tear and began.

Isabella came from her cabin and sat, tucking up her knees. She nodded encouragement. I smiled at her.

Memories, once I opened the gate, came flooding in. The children's father Sir George, who had come to Virginia bringing only his sword and a share of the Company. He'd risen to be three times a governor of Virginia. Sir George, as an Indian fighter. Their mother and I making it through the Starving Time. Sir George, trying to arrest the rogue Governor Argall. Tempie saying her farewells to the children's grandmother back in England.

These were the stories, the fabric, of their souls, these little Virginia-born children. Still, I chose not to tell them, now at least, of the hurricane at sea or how the Turks captured and imprisoned their father. Stories I must choose with care, else the children would be afraid. And I hastened to admit to myself, I should fear also to think of those things.

Elizabeth was still gazing at me hopefully, her eyes wide, their expression Tempie's.

My friend, I am still with you, after all, Tempie seemed to say through them.

"Well, your mother was able to make me laugh, even during the worst of times, the time of our starving. We ate acorns ..."

"Acorns!" Argall piped up skeptically. "Squirrels eat acorns, Auntie Joan."

At this, I burst out laughing. "Now, that's just what your mother said. She said she had to fight the squirrels off the acorns, wrestle them to the ground, and tear the nuts from their little paws.

All six of us laughed now.

So I began to tell the stories, whiling away the time at sea. As many as I could remember, and more came to me just when I thought I'd told them all.

And as I did, a strange thing happened. Tempie came back alive to me. So did Maggie and old Grace, e'en my mother and father. Why, it was as if they'd never left! And maybe they hadn't. They lived on in my memories; they lived in my stories. I'd thought the past would make me sad, like ghostly shadows no longer part of my world.

Instead, remembering the past made me happy, even when sometimes a tear or two slipped down my cheeks. Tempie, I saw, could live on for her children through me.

We talked through the suppers of salted cod and sea biscuits when the dim light of the ship grew yet dimmer. We even enjoyed marmalade on our sea biscuits from the chest I'd brought. We talked until those around us began to crawl beneath their blankets.

All the while, I felt Tempie there.

You're doing it, she seemed to say. *Doing what the doctor could not. Keeping me alive for my children.*

Remembrance of Things Past

April 7, 1629
On board the *William and John* at sea

When to the sessions of sweet silent thought
I summon up remembrance of things past,
I sigh the lack of many a thing I sought,
And with old woes new wail my dear time's waste ...

—But if the while I think on thee, dear friend,
All losses are restored, and sorrows end.
 —William Shakespeare

Lying in our bunk that night, I heard the gentle rhythm of Will's breathing. He was already asleep, but my mind still paced. The stories, once I let them come, were so many. *The children are asleep, and so is Will. Why am I still awake? I'm missing something. Something.*

And then I understood. *What if God had spared me so long so that I could be the ... the rememberer? What if He hadn't forgotten me after all? Perhaps a purpose for me remained, not in spite of, but because of my losses.*

George Sandys's words came rushing back: *Think you not that this is a journey of note? Helping to settle the New World, founding a colony for England? Because one stays in a place long makes it no less an adventure, no less a journey. Think 'tis less of a pilgrimage?*

I remembered Argall's face as he tried to teach his brother. And even as I did, I realized that Argall was growing up a little each day. His young memories of Tempie would fade with each bit he grew as would those of his brother and sister. Elizabeth was all but a young woman. In Virginia, she was nearly old enough to marry. Would she be able to tell her own children stories of her mother and father? Of our early days in Virginia?

Elizabeth's children would never know their grandmother Tempie. A pang shot through me. Nor would they know their grandfather Sir George, who had striven so hard to keep Virginia alive. These children would rely on what Elizabeth recalled of her mother and father and on Captain Smith's history books.

With all due respect to the captain's history, he'd not been here for much of it. We'd lived it, had seen it ourselves. Captain Smith could write of Dale's martial law, but could he see Annie's tear-streaked face? Good and bad, hard and touching, these stories were all a part of who we were, who *they* were.

Tempie's children, and even mine, would not know and be able to impart these stories to their own children unless someone like me passed them on.

Maybe the boys would become councilors or a governor like their father. Important tasks would fill their days. Or maybe they'd be explorers, the ones to find the Northwest Passage.

Mayhap they'd live out their lives in England; mayhap Virginia.

What would they remember of these days? The older ones, like me, by then long gone.

What if our little colony actually does *survive?* It had never seemed more likely.

What if the settlement goes west as far as the eye can see, just like the vision I'd had long ago in the time of Sir Thomas Dale?

What if these early days truly mattered to anyone besides us who lived them?

Suddenly, I grasped it as I had not before. *The stories are important.* The days long past would seem distant, perhaps even forgotten completely.

Of course, others could also tell their stories. It might be that a man could tell the story better. I still thought so. But Mr. Sandys's encouraging words stayed with me. What if a woman *could* see things a man couldn't?

Of Indian wars and the soldiers' confronting warriors in the field, I knew only what Will had told me. But I did know. I'd heard; I'd watched and listened. I'd sat with the men when they came to my table, even perhaps when I shouldn't have. I'd paid mind while stirring the pot or churning or spinning. We women had shared with one another whatever we heard happening.

Will had said it: I was a soldier, too, in my own way. So were Tempie and Maggie, Annie and Maria Bucke, Pocahontas, Jane and Cecily, Isabella and so many others. We'd fought right alongside the men, just not with weapons—not usually, anyway. We had been here, too.

"If I am to be the rememberer, then let me embrace it," I whispered into the darkness as the ship rocked gently in response. The water lapped onto the sides as if to say, *Sure, Joan, sure, Joan.*

"Ah, you old ocean. You near killed me coming over here. Now, traveling way back yonder, you're my friend? Well, all right then. Sure, yourself!" I smiled as I rolled over onto the straw pillow.

My Courage Is Reborn

April 8, 1629
On board the *William and John* at sea

I can shake off everything if I write; my sorrows disappear, my courage is reborn!

—Anne Frank

The next day, I found my daybook in our trunk, the same where I'd written a list of blessings many years before. Now that I'd decided to do this, I wanted to start right away. I began to scrawl the dates, the names, the places—the times of our first years in Virginia.

I propped myself upon the little bunk in our cabin and wrote. I wrote of my mother and father and of my father's ship, the *Seawynd*. The journeys took me to places that made me laugh and made me cry even while I strained to remember. *Was I eighteen or nineteen when I married Tom Reynolds? I was newly nineteen. Which ship had Annie come in on? The* Mary and Margaret? *Or the* Margaret and John? I would ask her when we returned. I saw once again Pocahontas sitting, lit by the sun, and her grief at her betrayal. What had John said about Pocahontas's death in England? *Gravesend at the fisherman's cottage.*

I struggled to remember Maggie's poem, when she had written about hope being a flame in the midst of despair.

Elizabeth offered for me to borrow her mother's daybook. Tempie had kept something of a short diary. Having Tempie's thoughts, I decided, would add to my remembrances.

Now I worked up my courage to open the daybook. There in Tempie's neat script, I read:

What a lonely feeling, to be caught somewhere on an ocean, partway between Europe and the New World, Africa off ahead in the distance. I can almost imagine the Dark Continent, the tribal songs of eventide. And If I could but see them, I know whales and porpoises swim below the keel of the ship, lonely beneath the deep as I am above.

Tears swam in my eyes as I copied her words.

Oh, Tempie. Why did you feel you couldn't write? I should have encouraged you *to write when you were instead encouraging* me! *How beautiful this is. You left us too soon. Far too soon, lovey.*

Remembering the sad times felt a little like cauterizing a wound. First, it hurt in a searing way. Then somehow the worst of the pain subsided, and I knew, without knowing how I knew, that healing was beginning.

The rememberer. Or perhaps *the remembrancer* as I scrawled my remembrances for my children and for Tempie's and for any others who wished to know. It gave me hope and purpose. And so I wrote as if, somehow, I could preserve those things that were no more.

I mentioned it to Will, and he smiled approvingly.

"John Smith has his history of Virginia events. Mine is a remembrance of people," I proclaimed, perhaps a little self-importantly. I'd lived it, so why not?

The voyage proved blessedly uneventful. Long and tedious, as any such would be. But no dragons appeared—no hurricanes bearing down on us. No Turks firing on the ship. No Spanish lying in wait.

Still, all my fears, just as Tempie had said years before, had come to nothing. *What will worry gain you? Fight the battle when the battle it is,* she had said.

I did it, Tempie! I said to the salt air and the oak planking.

Traveling in March and April was so much cooler than our voyage over when we'd departed in early June. The chill of an early spring night in the 'tween deck we could abide with blankets—but no remedy existed for the sultriness of August.

The northern route, too, was so much better. When we'd sailed in '09, the Virginia Company had wished to try the Azores route, sailing past the Azores and the Bermudas. Such a route was truly sweltering. Shorter than the early voyages, which went well south and stopped to water in the Caribbean, but the heat had been oppressive.

On this voyage, as we headed north, we wouldn't be stopping at the Plymouth colony, which hadn't existed twenty years before. Some ships did make port there, but ours was full and no room for any more. Then near Newfoundland and the English fishing grounds. Finally, entering open ocean as we made for the Narrow Seas off England. Our first brief port would be at the original Plymouth, Plymouth in Devon.

We'd disembark while the ship resupplied and then climb back on board for the final leg of our journey to London.

The ship leaving just before ours had carried Captain West and our letter to the Yeardleys. If all went well and that ship had fared well on the sea, the Yeardleys would know we were bringing the children to them.

Ralph and Rose Yeardley would soon have their hands full. They would add to their household three orphans while also battling West in court, I supposed. Susanna and Tempie's suspicions had been well founded. The man who rushed to England as soon as possible after Tempie's death would not be giving up Tempie's dower share easily.

The Sun Was Chasing the Moon

Late May 1629
At the Sign of the Artichoke, Wood Street, Cheapside, London

The children were shouting together
And racing along the sands,
A glimmer of dancing shadows,
A dovelike flutter of hands.

The stars were shouting in heaven,
The sun was chasing the moon:
The game was the same as the children's,
They danced to the self-same tune.
                    —A. E. Russell

How strange it felt to see the great Thames, the bustling docks, the street vendors, and stone buildings.

We'd said our farewells to Isabella. Having Isabella, writing, playing games, and storytelling had made the voyage pass much quicker than I'd expected.

Tempie had said coming back to England would feel shocking and odd. It did.

We'd grown used to tall trees and endless forests. None of that would we find here. Not many, anyway.

Down the street called Wood, we walked.

I held the smaller boy's hand while Susanna guided Elizabeth and Argall. The shops and homes of Cheapside rose up before us, signs swinging in the approaching spring storm. The skies darkened to an angry grey and rain threatened.

We passed old St. Alban's church, its growths of weeds and broken gravestones looking as bereft as I, too, felt. I gripped Francis's hand a bit tighter. I thought, *These three are my last link with Tempie.*

My heart wrenched each time her memory came to me. Tempie! How would I ever recover from her loss? I'd helped Susanna care for the children these past few months in James Town. That had given me something—some thin thread to Tempie, something I could *do* to forget the aching emptiness. And I'd confronted many memories worth the telling, painful and freeing at once.

Tempie is in a better place, a holy place. I had thought that so many times. Aye, and no doubt of that! No suffering, no Indian wars. And yet ... and yet ... She would never see these children grow up, would never be a grandmother. I tried to imagine Tempie an old woman, cradling Elizabeth's babe in her arms.

But I could see her only at thirty-eight. That was the age she would ever be.

The smell of rain came just moments before a few drops fell.

I looked down at little Francis, reaching out his hand to catch the rain. His innocence warmed me even as my cloak became damp.

He'll grow up in comfortable England. He won't have Captain West raising him with a new stepmother soon married to his old stepfather.

At that, relief washed over me like the rain. These children would be secure here. Master Yeardley, the apothecary, would care for the little ones as his own. Elizabeth would marry when the time seemed fitting, rather than finding an unwelcome suitor pursuing her.

They will know England! That thought did bring me momentary joy. *But will they remember Virginia?*

I swallowed a lump. More importantly, would they remember Tempie and Sir George? How glad I was I'd used the time on ship to tell them stories.

After a few moments, a gale blew through. We shielded the children as brickbats and tiles rattled onto the streets from the roofs overhead, damage from the wind. At the same time, we tried to avoid the mud and dross and water runlets below.

The clicking of our heels on the scattered, cobbled stones marked the passing of streets. We were now drenched and wind tossed.

"Just there!" Will called out, pointing ahead. "The sign of the artichoke."

A warm and dry home offered a welcome reprieve from the weather. I was eager to meet the Yeardleys.

Then, unexpectedly, a bit of nervousness took hold of me. I knew Tempie had liked the Yeardleys, but would I? How hard would it be to leave the children so far away? From habit, I touched the little pilgrim's badge around my neck. *I can do this.*

Will rapped the door knocker, and sure enough, Ralph Yeardley threw open the door. At least, I supposed, it must be him for he resembled Sir George.

"Well," Mr. Yeardley said, looking at his niece and nephews who stood shyly with us. "Well." I saw tears enter his eyes. "The boys do look like George," he murmured. "Little George. Such an adventurer, even as a young man. Stay home and grind the herbs, that life suited me. But George wanted to be a soldier. Always."

We nodded politely, my soldier and I. And then Ralph shook himself and said, "Where are my manners?" He ducked his head. "This must be Susanna. My! You were just a tiny thing when you sailed for Virginia. And Captain and Mrs. Peirce? Please come inside. A storm has surprised us!"

"Good day, uncle. Good day, auntie," said Elizabeth, extending her hand with as much courage as she could muster to her aunt.

Rose Yeardley ignored Elizabeth's hand and reached out to hug the girl instead. "Let me call down your cousins! Welcome to your new home."

At that, Elizabeth frowned, but just a little. I could read her thoughts. What would her new home be without her mother? And then I felt very, very selfish. For all this time, I had thought of *my* loss. But these children had suffered the greatest loss of all.

Tempie, we've done it, I said to myself in the habit I now had of speaking to her as if she were right beside me. *We're here. No sore voyage, albeit a trying one. But no hurricanes! No great wind or rain, save for one storm. Just the tedious ship, and that passed soon enough. The children well. Yes, we've done it.*

"And you must be Mrs. Peirce," a small woman with a bright smile said to me. "I'm Rose Yeardley. Please call me Rose."

"Aye, and prithee call me Joan."

We grasped hands, and her gaze met mine. Suddenly, her smile faded not, but her eyes teared. She drew a deep breath and whispered to me, "For the children's sake, I'll not cry, but oh, how I wish Tempie were here."

I nodded and my eyes welled, too. "For the children," I whispered in return. *We won't let the little ones see us cry.*

A small brood of Yeardley children came bustling down the stairs at the sounds of commotion.

There I saw a boy with Sir George's grin as well as two other boys and two girls. Rose ushered her children over and introduced the cousins to one another.

The elder Yeardleys invited us to sit.

The fire crackled, bright and warm against the late spring dampness. The Virginia children brought themselves before it, all the while looking up at the old beams, the ancient oak floors, the high ceilings. *England.* The Yeardley home was hundreds of years old. How odd to them it all was.

Tempie had stood here, one autumn's day more than ten years before. She'd seen this home; had made peace with her mother across the sea; had come back, somehow, to our wild and strange land.

After a while, Rose put her arm around her older daughter and said to Elizabeth. "Rosie is eleven years old, just a little younger than you are, Elizabeth. And Anne is ten." To her daughters, Rose said, "Why don't you girls go find some dolls upstairs and show Elizabeth where she'll sleep?"

Elizabeth's eyes lit for the first time since December. I could see she was warming to the situation. Although she was a bit old for dolls, she seemed happy to be with her cousins and to explore the old house.

Anne shyly took Elizabeth's hand, and up the stairs they all tumbled.

"And here we have John, Andrew, and Young Ralph." Ralph looked to be just a little older than Argall.

"Ralph?" said the elder Ralph to his son. "Perhaps you could take your cousins to your chamber and find them a game."

"I can play Nine Men's Morris!" Francis volunteered bravely.

His brother grinned and shook his head at his cousin.

The older boys sat to talk with us while Young Ralph scampered away with his two cousins.

"*Not* the apothecary shop, Ralph!" the father called after them, then turned to us. "He loves the jars. I think he'll be an apothecary himself if he learns not to bobble them." He laughed indulgently.

"What age is your oldest?" I asked Rose.

"John is sixteen," she said.

"Then you'll have eight children between the ages of eight and sixteen, Rose!"

Her eyes brightened. "A privilege," was all she said.

Then the Yeardleys reminisced over the visit with Tempie and Sir George. They spoke of how the comet with the blood-red tail had traveled the night sky that evening.

"Then, too, George came by the Christmas after his, uh, adventure in Morocco. He was seeking physick for a poor appetite. I could see he wasn't feeling well." Ralph's face clouded as if he wondered if he might have done more for his brother.

"He was a good governor and an able soldier, a right sound commander after the ... during the Indian wars," Will put in.

"A well-loved governor," I added.

Ralph broke into a smile, and the mood lifted once more.

Before the evening was over, we'd discuss the estate and Captain West. But now? Let the pair enjoy seeing their niece and nephews.

I liked the Yeardleys. I, too, began to feel comfortable in leaving Tempie's children behind. How glad I was I'd braved the ocean to bring them here myself, to see the loving home that would now be theirs. The children would flourish here, and the warmth I felt was only partly due to the great fireplace.

Understanding dawned on me. I saw that Tempie had here found the warmth and loyalty lacking within her own family. Neither Tempie nor her brother or sister had liked their stepfather Garrett. And their mother's expectations had been hard to fulfill. Tempie's own nephew, as well as her cousin Pory, had both been untrustworthy. Her sister had died young; her brother was now gone.

But here? Here, Tempie had not been Dame Temperance, Lady Yeardley, a Flowerdieu-Stanley-Appleyard. No, here she'd just been Tempie, welcomed into Ralph's simple apothecary shop. It said so much about Ralph and Rose, but it said even more, I thought, about Tempie herself.

As these thoughts settled upon me, so did something else: peace. Like a little bird, it first alighted on my shoulder and then fluttered within my chest. I'd said to Tempie to wait for a new bird to come, not to look back. Now this one had come to me, just as I'd said. And I remembered this little bird. I'd not felt it restful for a long while.

I knew the children would thrive here. I just felt it. And with that knowledge, I could let them go.

Rose fetched us a glass of sherry, and we all sat together, including Susanna and Ralph's older sons. Missing only were Sir George and Tempie. Now that we'd brought the children here, the last tie to the Yeardleys in Virginia had passed.

Come back someday, I thought hopefully as if the little ones could hear me. *Please come back to the lands of your father and mother. Come back,* I thought at last, *to Virginia and to us.*

Rose turned to nod at me, for rather than a thought, I'd said that last softly. She took my hand and said, "Pray, tell us all about Sir George and Tempie, these last ten years ... and Virginia."

Tulips Are Tripping down the Path

June 1, 1629
London

In spite of war, in spite of death,
In spite of all man's sufferings,
Something within me laughs and sings
And I must praise with all my breath.
In spite of war, in spite of hate
Lilacs are blooming at my gate,
Tulips are tripping down the path
In spite of war, in spite of wrath.
"Courage!" the morning-glory saith;
"Rejoice!" the daisy murmureth,
And just to live is so divine
When pansies lift their eyes to mine.
  —Angela Morgan

A comedy, Will!"

Will grinned. "Then a comedy it will be."

We were discussing seeing a play—a real play. We'd left theatre behind when we'd sailed away from port all those years ago. In Virginia, we had no public houses, no theatres. Entertainment was much what we could make of it.

Now here in London, we were going to take ourselves out, indulge ourselves so much it felt reckless.

"I haven't any need of tragedy. I've seen enough in two decades at James Town to last me the rest of my life, thank you very much." I spoke as I gazed onto the little knot garden in back of the inn. Summer here. Summer in England. *Home.*

Will's warmth toward me was palpable. He'd never intended for us to suffer so much in Virginia. This day marked exactly twenty years since our ship had departed Plymouth Hoe in Devon. Then, I'd looked at the Narrow Sea and the western waters, a much younger woman with little idea of what lay ahead. Sailing west, sailing west.

Does one ever know what will come? Life itself was both tragedy and comedy, and we swung between the two like actors confused as to what part we were to play.

A line from Mr. Shakespeare's *As You Like It* came to mind. *All the world's a stage, and all the men and women merely players. They have their exits and their entrances, and one man in his time plays many parts.*

That was the play Will had taken me to when we were courting. How true Shakespeare's line would prove to be, I couldn't have then known.

And yet, here we were ... back in London and with enough means to see a play. Will, I thought, would have taken me to a playhouse—a most expensive indulgence—rather than simply a theatre. But talk around the market was that Mr. James Shirley's *The Wedding* was a lighthearted comedy of manners. *The Wedding* was playing at a theatre, the Phoenix, in Drury Lane. The players called themselves "Queen Henrietta's Men" to honor our queen, Will said. He assured me we'd have tickets.

"I'll talk to Mr. Beeston down at the theatre and arrange the purchase," he said. "And you'll have these as well," Will said slyly. He went to the door and opened it. Outside sat a bouquet of four tulips in a clear glass vase with brilliant blue threading. Sunlight danced across the glassware invitingly. Dutch tulips, the colors of a rainbow of red and purple and yellow and orange.

I gasped. "Will!"

He lifted the vase and brought it inside, setting it on the mantle.

At once, the tulips carried me back too many years, to the time when Will and Sam had come to tell me that my first husband Tom died in the war. And the two had rambled about the beautiful flowers they'd seen while fighting in the Low Countries. *Tulips*, they'd called them. The Dutch had been making trials and had learned to create the flowers in vivid and cheerful colors. And now, all these years later—a lifetime, a world, an ocean between—and yet Will had remembered.

"I had to travel down to Leadenhall Market to find the tulips as well as the Venetian vase," he said, almost apologetically. "'Tis why I left you this morning. And before we sail, we'll find some bulbs to take back to Virginia."

I knew tulips had a dear cost. Yet here they were and for me.

My heart lightened and lifted. For the first time since Tempie died, I felt perhaps I could be happy again.

But is it wrong? A pang of guilt shot through me. Then I caught myself. Tempie had predicted this, had asked me to discard the guilt when it came marring joy.

Live your life, Joan. Your sadness does nothing for me, Tempie seemed to say. *Do not cry for me, my friend. For I am in a place far more grand than London!*

Suddenly a weight, heavy as a Thames barge, seemed to lift itself from my shoulders.

You did go like the leaves, Tempie. Brilliant and graceful to the end.

And now a new season was upon us. The long bitter winter lifted, and warmth returned to the earth and to me.

The sun beamed bright as Will held open the door of the hackney carriage. Gone the clouds of the last few weeks. London, it seemed, was favoring us with her prettiest face. *Welcome back,* she seemed to say.

As we made our way from our inn down the winding streets toward Drury Lane, the street vendors cried their wares. The children played, and sounds of a noisy—I could imagine, happy—London greeted us.

A carriage, a new dress and shoes—gone the ragged clothing I'd worn for so many years. And as the horses trotted us down the streets of old London, I laughed.

I laughed with the joy of it all. I felt like a dashing soldier was courting me once again. My Will.

The carriage meandered the streets, approaching the theatre. The building had first been a round barn for cockfighting before becoming the Cockpit Theatre. But when the Cockpit burned in 1617, its owners had rebuilt and renamed it, a name appropriate to its history. A theatre which died in flames and then rose from the ashes: the Phoenix.

At last, the Phoenix stood before us.

Carriages were dropping giddy and well-dressed folk in front. The sheer excitement of the play!

Now I, too, felt like a phoenix. Rising from the ashes of James Town.

Mistress Pearce,
a Honest Industrious Woman

Mid-June 1629
Sir Samuel Saltonstall's home, St. Sepulchre's Parish, Newgate, London

Mistress Pearce, a honest industrious woman, hath beene there [in Virginia]
neere twentie yeares, and now returned, saith, shee hath a garden at James
Town containing three or four acres, where in one yeare shee hath gathered
neere an hundred bushels of excellent figges, and that of her own provision
she can keepe a better house in Virginia, than here in London, for 3. or 400
pounds a yeare, yet [she] went thither with little or nothing.
  —Capt. John Smith, *Generall Historie*

... Of five hundred within six months after Capt. Smith's departure, there
remained not past sixty men, women and children, most miserable and poore
creatures; and those were preserved for the most part, by roots, herbes, acorns,
walnuts, berries, now and then a little fish.
  —Capt. John Smith, *Generall Historie*

No, it's *you* he wants to meet," Will was saying, as we approached the home of Sir Samuel Saltonstall. Sir Samuel had offered the redoubtable Captain John Smith a chamber here, and it was Captain Smith who wished to speak with me.

I looked at Will skeptically. "Why on earth would he want to meet *me?* I am but a woman."

Will raised his eyebrows. "You are far from 'but a woman.'" His smile was genuine. I brushed him with my fan playfully.

"No, seriously, Will. What could he possibly want to talk with me about?"

"He wants to hear about your ... experience at James Town. You are, after all, an Ancient Planter. Only a few women alive have been there as long as you have. Oh," he said quickly. "I did not mean ..." He had realized how that sounded in light of Tempie's recent passing.

I nodded, indicating I understood. "You speak truly," I said simply. Annie had been there nearly a year longer than I had. Thomasine Causey had traveled to England a few years back, although she had since returned. Jane was now an adult but had come as a child. With Tempie's passing ...

"My word!" It had never occurred to me until just that moment.

"Will, of the women and children, only Annie, Ginny Laydon, Thomasine, Jane, and I remain from the Starving Time!" So far as I knew, anyway. We had been ninety women and children that fall of 1609. Now we were but five. I felt some dizzying little realization and grabbed Will's doublet suddenly. "Wait, please."

He nodded. "Of course." He gestured to a bench in the garden plot. "Take a moment, Joan. Gather yourself."

As I sat, I felt all the charm of an English June. "'Tis a lovely place, St. Sepulchre's," I said idly.

"Indeed." Will was silent for a moment. When he spoke, his voice was more serious. "Joan, 'tis important that you be cautious in what you say to Captain Smith."

I glanced at him without understanding.

"He's writing a book, a history of Virginia. He's at odds with the Company—or was, before the Company fell apart. He may be, uh, looking for something in your words."

I felt slightly alarmed. "Do you think I shouldn't speak with him, then?"

"No, no," he said quickly. "I think it *very* important that you speak with him—that you be heard. You have a woman's perspective on this venture, and soon enough all of us 'Ancient Planters' will be gone."

I hit him with my fan again. "Speak for yourself!"

He smiled. "Aye, as you wish. We shall live twenty more years then. But twenty-one years from now ..."

I saw his point. "This is something for ... for ..." I groped for the right word. "Posterity?"

"Aye, yes." His voice was firmer. "So be heard! State your case and your memories. I'm only saying to be wary that you choose those words carefully so no one can misconstrue them."

"I see." I was starting to tremble just a little. I hadn't been nervous before, but now I was growing so. "Let us go, then." I was ready. The longer I waited, the more my heart raced.

Meeting the famous Captain John Smith again after all these years! How would it be? Would he still be, as I remembered him, all red—beard, hair, and face?

The servant at the door greeted us warmly. "Good day. Might you be the Peirces? Captain Smith is awaiting you."

I nodded politely as he escorted us through the house, past a few trifles and paintings of places I didn't recognize. Emblems of war somehow, I thought. Yet the captain's portion of the house was somewhat modest by English standards.

As the servant led us into a chamber, a gentleman I recognized, despite the twenty years since I'd seen him, stood and shook Will's hand. Indicating chairs, Captain Smith offered us a seat.

"Captain and Mistress Peirce. 'Tis a pleasure!" he said warmly, and the enthusiasm in his voice was genuine.

"Pleased to meet you, sir!" Will said.

"Captain Smith, the pleasure is ours," I offered, somewhat shyly. "The last I saw of you ..."

"I was being loaded onto the *Blessing,* near bereft of my senses?" He laughed. "Talking out of my head, I suppose. What secrets did I reveal, I wonder?"

I was feeling more at ease. "Yes," I said, returning the smile. "We were so very worried about you! But you have pulled through, a most remarkable recovery, sir." I wondered if I were being too forward, but he seemed to take no offense.

He shook his head. "I'm only sorry I was not there for those next months. Maybe I could have helped ..." His voice trailed off.

My stomach fell at the memory. "Our Starving Time," I said quietly. "Aye, perhaps you could have prevented ..."

I stopped as Captain Smith nodded gravely. "Indeed. When I left, there were enough provisions. A lean winter it would have been, yes, but, should not have been utter starvation. It all went wrong ...." He was speaking more to himself than to me. Bad memories for both of us, I gathered.

"And how many of those first women are still surviving today?" He scrawled a quick note on his sheath as he said it. "Pardon, mistress. May I write your words?"

"Aye, sir."

As he wrote, my mind wandered—so many faces. I could see Elizabeth that first fall, stretching a gaunt hand out to me. *Do you have any herbs that will help me, Mistress Peirce?* And then her sudden realization. *And I won't see the month* out. *This heat, these flies...* Offering me the ring off her bony finger. *Take it! I do not want to have to fuss at you. I have done so much of that.* I looked down at the ring, still on my finger, the carved rose had been with me all these years.

And Grace. Old and dying. *A blessing to you and Tempie for helping me!* Grace the angel.

Maggie. I felt my throat tighten. Maggie and Tempie. We had all striven together, so many of us. All with an eye on the future. Now that future was here. Twenty years gone by. And of those first women only a handful of us remaining to tell the story.

Strange how life was like that. It meandered like the James River, turning and twisting back upon itself until one was not quite sure which way it was flowing. Whether, indeed, one was on its north or south bank! In places, the James's north bank was south of its south bank. Such an odd river. Such an odd life ... Things which appeared good—like our prospects—turned suddenly bad. Things which appeared bad—like the *Sea Venture's* loss—turned suddenly good when we learned of its survivors.

The James River wove from foothills to sea, making giant bows in the process. And then sometimes one simply made a cut—a gap—and connected things and the way appeared much shorter. The connection was neither so hard nor so helpful as imagined.

"What about the Causeys?" Captain Smith was saying. "Nat was always a fine old soldier. I met with them when he was here, recently."

I caught myself and returned to the conversation at hand. "You probably know, then, that the Causeys abandoned their plantation after the ... the bloodshed. They moved to my daughter's plantation, Jordan's Journey. Thomasine was a great help to my daughter there."

Smith nodded. He was lighting his pipe and offered another pipe and tobacco to Will, who accepted. "Mr. Sam Jordan's place," the captain continued. "One of the few plantations held after the massacre. I never met Jordan, though. Just heard about his plantation being well fortified enough for the commander to hold it open."

He puffed. "Now, old Nat. He was a trusty soldier. Glad to see he's survived these many years. And his wife, too. Another hardy Starving Time survivor?"

"And do you recall the young girl, Annie Laydon, you sent to us that first night?" I went on. "She was expecting, newly married to Jack Laydon?"

His eyes lit up. "Of course! Our first English marriage in Virginia, the Laydons. I had no idea what to do with so many women—women whose husbands appeared to be lost at sea." He glanced at Will. "No offense, sir."

Will chuckled. "None taken. *That* was a sure mistake to make."

"Had I known your large expedition was due to land that August ..." Captain Smith began.

"You wouldn't have pointed the ordnance and guns at us on our arrival?" I sensed he was up to the challenge and that I would not offend him.

He threw his head back and laughed. "Not quite a gentleman's greeting to the ninety women and children entering his fort!"

"Besides Thomasine, few women and children remain from the Starving Time." I ticked them off on my fingers. "Annie Laydon, her daughter Virginia, my daughter Jane, and I. We lost many in the ... in the ..." I stopped, and Will took my hand.

"Massacre," Will said quietly, and Smith pursed his lips.

For a moment, none of us spoke. What was there to say? The wound remained raw, both for those of us who had lived it and for those here in England as well. "And of course, many perished in the contagion following it," Will added.

I wanted to change the subject. My voice caught, but I kept going and added brightly, "Of course, there are many more—hundreds more—women now. Maybe a thousand." I glanced at Will for verification.

He agreed. "Aye, there probably are close to a thousand women in Virginia."

Smith was scribbling.

I was pleasantly surprised that no tension passed between us. Instead, I felt as if I'd always known the captain. Perhaps something in our shared experience, but I wasn't sure.

"And have you been back to Virginia?" I asked, before remembering. No, no, of course, he hadn't. Will had told me that the Virginia Company rejected several of Smith's offers to return to Virginia as a commander.

Smith's face clouded for a moment, the same memory apparently flashing through his mind, before he added cheerfully, "Not to James Town, but up to the area we've called 'Northern Virginia,' but which I dub 'New England' in my history. The charter has since confirmed that name." Pride shone in his eyes. "I've surveyed it, made maps, as I did for your part of Virginia. New England! A great hope for the English in Virginia." For it was all Virginia, of course.

"How wonderful!" I said politely.

One of Sir Samuel's servants came through carrying a tray with three glasses. We each helped ourselves to a goblet of sack.

Captain Smith leaned back in his chair. He said matter-of-factly,

"Mistress Peirce, I assume you know I'm writing a history of Virginia?"

"Yes, I've heard about it."

"You are part of that history. I would like to hear something of your experiences there, and ... I promise to scribe your words fairly!" He winked at Will. How strange! He seemed to know what we had discussed.

I believed him, and I told him so.

"Many years, sir. I've been there, as you know, nigh twenty years. Some of them better than others, not surprisingly."

Smith cradled his sheath of paper, placing his quill upon his chin.

"Mistress Peirce," he said with conviction. "How *did* you survive? When the provisions ran out?"

I laughed. "Do you truly want to know?" The answer wasn't exotic, to be sure. But Smith was looking at me intently, and I sensed he *did* want to know.

"It was the acorns. A mast year! We collected walnuts, roots, herbs, and acorns. Sometimes berries if we could find them. The acorns provided our best sustenance, for they kept well. We made bread with the acorn flour."

"Acorns, you say? Walnuts, roots, herbs ..." he was muttering as he wrote. "Fish?" he asked.

"Now and again, thanks mainly to Captain Tucker. He built a ship when we had none," I said by way of explanation.

"Aye, I do recall hearing of Captain Tucker's boat through Mr. George Percy." He paused to write. "And how do the women fare in the birthing of children?" He almost blushed, but I sensed he truly wanted to hear.

"We have scarce one miscarriage in ten births," I said matter-of-factly. Almost proudly.

"This is true, captain. Blame not the land for the troubles we've had. The land is good. Solid and fruitful," Will put in.

"I see," Smith muttered, still scribbling. "Good to hear, Peirce." He then looked at me. "And your life in Virginia this present day?" His quill was poised.

I smiled. "And today, I have a fine garden at James Town. I'm so pleased with it! We've imported Bermudian fruits of all kinds and made trials of growing them. Of these, potatoes and figs have been most successful." I told him that my New Towne garden consisted of three or four acres and that figs prospered well there. "Last year, I gathered near a hundred bushels of excellent figs."

He raised his brows. "A hundred, you say?"

I nodded and went on to explain that I sold the fresh figs for physick and foods. "We make marmalade of fig with the rest. We tried to dry the figs, but they rot that way. Our air is too humid, I think," I added. Few in Virginia were growing figs just yet, I told him. "Therefore, my figs fetch a handsome price."

"You're able to provide for yourself then?"

"I am. For the three or four hundred pounds I earn, I can keep a better house, much better than I'd be able to in London on that amount. Yet I went there with little or nothing."

He seemed impressed. "Truly?"

"Yes. We'll soon be planting gardens at Mulberry Island as well," I continued. "One reason we chose land there is that the James River surrounds it on three sides. We thought the climate there might be more like the climate in Bermuda, surrounded on so many sides by water as the Somers Isles are."

"A strong natural fortification as well," Will put in. I could tell Will was trying to allow me to talk but couldn't resist adding a few of his own thoughts. "We also reckoned that with the acres of mulberry trees, silkworm seed would thrive there."

"Ah, of course," murmured the captain, still scribbling. He understood that mulberry leaves were food for the little silkworms, certainly.

I studied him as he wrote and wondered how much of what we were saying would make it into his history. These things seemed only trifles to me.

When he looked up once more, I told Captain Smith how well English and some Bermudian plants grew in the Virginia soil along with so many native ones.

Smith showed keen interest in the fruits we'd imported, the success of the herbs—and the fact that the Virginia land was, indeed, as fertile as he'd thought. He seemed excited that many of his predictions of so many years ago had come to fruition. The Virginia Company might not see that, but Smith himself did and that pleased him, I thought. We spoke for the better part of an hour.

When we were all done, I reached for Will's hand.

"Captain Smith, we appreciate the hospitality. I do thank you kindly for thinking that my poor thoughts deserve a plea in a book of Virginia history." It wasn't false modesty. He had the words of the great men of Virginia—Percy, De La Warr, Strachey, Dale, Gates, even himself. Mine were surely humble by comparison.

"But you, Mistress Peirce, have lived it all. You've been there longer than the rest of us, who have come and gone. Or, as in the case of Sir Edwin Sandys, who have never been there at all. Frankly," he said, putting down his quill and stretching his fingers, "I can obtain very little of value from the *leaders*." There was a tinge of judgment in his voice. "Their words are so politically weighted. I attempt to understand the details of Virginia today—how *many* horses and cattle there are, what you do for beverages, how crops fare. But they instead prattle and dance and talk to me about the *correct* things and not the actual ones. So I've turned to settlers such as you and your husband and Nat Causey," he added.

"Oh." I hadn't thought of it that way. "I thank you kindly once more, sir. 'Twas a pleasure to speak with you before we turn homeward." Will reached out to shake Captain Smith's hand once more. I began walking to the door.

Smith smiled. "Home is Dorset?"

I glanced over my shoulder at him. There were tears in my eyes. I shook my head. "Virginia," was all I said.

These Motley Pilgrims

Mid-August 1629
At George Sandys's home, London

Gone are the sensuous stars, and manifold,
Clear sunbeams burst upon the front of night;
Ten thousand swords of azure and of gold
Give darkness to the dark and welcome light;
Across the night of ages strike the gleams,
And leading on the gilded host appears
An old man writing in a book of dreams,
And telling tales of lovers for the years;
Still Troilus hears a voice that whispers, Stay;
In Nature's garden what a mad rout sings!
Let's hear these motley pilgrims wile away
The tedious hours with stories of old things ...
—Benjamin Brawley

ill had hired a coach from our inn in London. The driver came around front, pulling back on his horse. The carriage drew to a halt, and we climbed in. We were going to visit our old friend and houseguest, Mr. Sandys.

As we traveled by the Palace of Westminster, Will pointed out the old Hall, nearly six hundred years old and built by William the Conqueror's son. "'Twas probably the largest building in Europe when 'twas built," Will said with a touch of English pride. "Inside houses the Star Chamber." Will lowered his voice from the driver although the pitted roads made the carriage noisy. "The king has begun using the Chamber as a substitute for parliament, letting it make decisions best handled by elected members. Some here say the august old court now makes a mockery of justice, a frightening position for us all."

The grand palace gave little impression that such a court could be inside it, I decided.

Around Westminster Hall, newer buildings sprawled, lazily but importantly, at the Thames's edge.

As the carriage driver made his way across the London Bridge, I averted my eyes. The king's men had mounted several heads on the bridge as staring reminders that the price for high treason was steep.

Even that gruesome sight couldn't spoil my day, though. Instead, I took in the Thames from above, so majestic and ancient, yet so tame compared to the wild James, still hugged by wilderness.

Now, just over the Thames from Westminster, the driver stopped the hackney. He alit, placing some steps by the carriage door for us, and then politely took my hand to help me out.

Will climbed out next, thanked the driver, and then reached into his satchel to pay him.

We believed this to be the London home of Mr. George Sandys, the rooms he kept near Lambeth Palace. Will had sent Mr. Sandys a letter, so he was expecting us. He had, in fact, offered to send us his own carriage. "Hackney carriages do not have the best reputation for cleanliness," he'd written. But we wished not to be a bother and were perfectly content in an old carriage for hire.

We appreciated the opportunity to hire one at all. So many things were ever changing in the city. These public carriages had not been around many years. They came about when inns concluded they might as well use their carriages for more than just their own guests. Despite the carriages' reputation as being neither clean nor gentle, we'd traveled in a ship for months. This little journey was nothing to us.

"Sit, my dear guests," Mr. Sandys said warmly after his servant swung the door wide. He called for his man to prepare us two goblets of canary wine and some marzipan, charming almond cakes shaped like fruits.

"I'm delighted to still be holding forth in London to entertain you now in *my* home after all your hospitality in New Towne. In a few days, I leave for Northbourne, in Kent, to visit my brother Sir Edwin," Mr. Sandys said.

Having lived with the poet for so long, I caught the note of concern.

"Is all well with your brother, sir?" I asked him, reaching for a cake.

"No, I'm afraid not. His wife Katherine sent me a letter saying he is ill due to over-study, she fears. She worries enough to think his brothers should come if they can."

"Should something happen to my brother, I'll endeavor to help my sister with any business affairs I might." Mr. Sandys continued with a forced note of brightness, "Fortunately, I'm here today to see you, friends.

"How has your brother fared since the Company's dissolution?" asked Will. Will always asked many questions, an old soldiers' habit of learning as much as he could about his surroundings.

"He fares well, particularly since his majesty King Charles does not have the old king's distaste for him. His majesty and I have ever been close, too. So Sir Edwin remains a Member of Parliament and focuses more of his time on the East India Company. Some of the upheaval in parliament distresses him, I'm sure." Everywhere we went, it seemed, folks were discussing the contention between the king and his parliament. It unsettled us a mite.

As for Mr. Sandys himself, he told us that as a Gentleman of the Privy chamber, he would have to make arrangements with the king before leaving London. With all this on his mind, Mr. Sandys seemed actually glad for the company and the distraction.

Will presented Mr. Sandys with a gift of an Indian pipe and tobacco.

Sandys thanked him and asked, "And the glassworks? How are those blasted Italians?"

Will laughed. "Not faring so well, as you might suspect. The project is all but dead, I fear me."

Mr. Sandys furrowed his brow in dismay.

Then he said, "Mrs. Peirce, I know you do love a garden. Come, then, and see mine."

We strolled into the knot garden behind the home and seated ourselves in several chairs overlooking the late summer blooms.

Mr. Sandys turned to me as we walked among his cornflowers and coneflowers, asters and goldenrod. Some were blooming, some soon to be.

"And how is that fig orchard?" he asked me.

"Bursting with figs!" Will answered for me. Pride brightened Will's face. "In fact, she's created her own commodity by selling to Dr. Pott and others."

"Fine, fine! Well done, Mrs. Peirce," said the poet warmly.

The afternoon whiled away in conversation as Mr. Sandys's natural curiosity rose. He wanted to know Will's opinion of the present state of Virginia.

"Well, I prepared a report about that for his majesty, a brief report. We do well, about four or five thousand people there now," Will said.

Mr. Sandys then confirmed that Mr. Harvey, now knighted Sir John, would be the incoming governor of Virginia. Will had met Sir John when he came as part of the commission to examine Virginia some seven years past.

Upon Will's first impression then, he didn't like the man nor his violent temper. Neither did Mr. Sandys or I. The king, however, did.

"I hope Sir John won't cause us trouble. I do not think he ..." Will groped for the right word. "I do not think he *understands* us in Virginia."

"Sir John will consider Virginia his kingdom, I suspect," Mr. Sandys said bluntly. He dropped his voice to a whisper as if hoping it didn't sound like criticism of the king. "Captain Peirce, you know I've recommended you for the council for the past half dozen or more years. I believe you should have a place there. I continue to recommend you to the king."

Will ducked his head sheepishly, but smiled. "I do thank you for the compliment. I should be delighted to be part of the public service on council should it arise." Will believed his first seat on the General Assembly was largely due to Mr. Sandys's good opinion of him.

After a few moments, Will spoke up. "I mean not to be impertinent, Mr. Sandys," he said tentatively.

"Speak your mind, sir," Mr. Sandys said. "We've endured much together."

"Thank you. Upon your going away from Virginia, you spoke of returning. You remain interested in the Virginia Company, but we've seen you not these four years."

Sandys sighed. "'Tis true I'd planned to return. And then ..." His face darkened. The words hung in the summer air.

"You do not like the sea, of this I'm aware," Will said mildly.

"I do not. Never have. After the ... Well, Sir George told you about the pirates?"

"We did hear, but spoke nothing of it because of the nature of Harrison's secret mission," Will said. "Sir George didn't even tell his wife immediately."

I nodded. This was so.

"I know that none put anything in writing," Will emphasized. "But word gets about a settlement, you understand."

Mr. Sandys gave a knowing smile. "Indeed. 'Tis ever thus amongst the nature of men!"

We all laughed gently.

Then Mr. Sandys sounded a somber note. He added, "My greatest sympathies on the losses of Sir George and Lady Yeardley, Mistress Peirce. Lest I neglect to say so. I know you and she were close. Word of her death reached me here just a month ago." He had the sensitive eyes of a poet, and I could see that he truly mourned my loss with me. "Sir George and I became close during our capture. An ordeal of that nature is wont to create lasting bonds. The Turks tested our mettle, sure; Sir George was wonderfully courageous."

"Aye?" I was eager to hear Mr. Sandys's version of the story. The Yeardley children would surely wish to know more about it someday.

"Sir George said as much of you," Will put in.

Mr. Sandys shrugged. "Courage borne on the high seas is apt to be feigned for one such as I. I'm but a traveler and an observer. Not so, Sir George. When the Turks chained us to the wall in the *mazmorra*..."

"*Mazmorra?*" I said blankly.

"A dungeon. A terrible prison where many slaves awaited their fates. 'Tis probably not a fit subject for a woman to hear."

"Were women chained there? And children?"

He nodded, casting his eyes downward.

"Then if they can live it, I can hear it," I said firmly.

"Fair enough, and true enough. Just so then. Truly, Mrs. Peirce, you helped me in that dungeon as did Dame Temperance."

I sat very still. Will turned to me, looking as confused as I felt.

Unto the Morning Stars

Mid-August 1629
At George Sandys's home, London

The uncreated joy in you
Hath lifted up my heart unto
The morning stars in their first pride,
And the angelic joys that glide
High upon heaven-lifted wings.
—A. E. Russell

I helped you?" I blinked.

"Soon after the pirates captured us, Sir George told me the story of you and Dame Temperance during the Starving Time, the pact you made, the faith you had."

I felt my heart warm to a memory and to the words of the man before me. "Mr. Sandys, with all respect, I'm not sure I understand how a James Town famine can compare to a slave dungeon in Morocco."

"But it can. Both are terrible, hopeless situations where fate has wrested all control from your hands. Yet you two dared confront fate, to say, 'We're not done yet.' You said to fate, 'You may control our circumstance but not what we think, not who we are, not how we react.' Fate gives to those who challenge it. It must. To be so bold is remarkable, whether you know it or not."

No, I hadn't known it, had never considered it that way. I blushed and dropped my eyes to my lap. "Thank you, Mr. Sandys. You're very kind."

"And you're most inspirational, and I should rather be inspirational than kind. You and Lady Yeardley were inspirational in the truest sense of the word. To *in-spire*, to fill with the Spirit. You did this for Sir George and me. We thought of you and Lady Yeardley, of your strength and fortitude. We remembered your work and your survival, your belief in a miracle when a miracle seemed impossible. Everything familiar was taken from you and from us. And so Sir George and I pledged the same bond as you two had. We called for a miracle, believed even that angels might be with us on our journey. Your story sustained us. We said that if you could do it, we could do it, too." Now my surprise peaked as the poet's voice trembled. "I can never repay you for what you gave me in those bleak days. I thank thee, mistress. I thank thee from all that I am."

And then he began to talk. He told of the Turkish dress, their language, the way the Turks deftly captured the *Anne.* He told us about his prison companion, the Frenchman Honoré, and the surprise meeting with the envoy Harrison. The story spilled out as if, now safely home, Mr. Sandys did not mind recounting it.

Will listened with muted response, worrying, I suppose, that a tale like this would frighten me. We had, after all, to board a ship to return home. But I listened, too, more with fascination than with fear. I'd heard about it from Sir George, by way of Tempie, and now from Mr. Sandys. I reconfirmed to myself that I would continue trying to write these stories down. Besides, this, too, was part of the Yeardley children's history.

"What a shame Mr. Harrison could not rescue Honoré, too," I mused.

The poet's eyes lit. "He's home, mistress. He's home."

We gazed at him curiously. With a bit of embarrassment, Mr. Sandys continued, "'Twas a pittance to me, a fortune to his wife."

The buzzing of bees in the garden, the occasional robin or lark flitting among the blooms, the sweet scents of field poppy and lilac filling the knot garden. These seemed a world away from the sordid and dank dungeon. Mr. Sandys apparently felt that way too. And liked it that way.

Will explained to Mr. Sandys that Captain Claiborne had given him some Virginia stones and shells for Mr. Tradescant's museum.

I turned to Will in surprise. "You have those?"

"I didn't tell you because I wanted to take you to the museum as a gift," Will said, almost shyly.

"Then you must go!" Mr. Sandys said. "And, Mrs. Peirce, see every exhibit. The museum won't disappoint you, this I promise. While his name is *Tradescant,* around here, folks often call him Mr. Tradeskin. He's a trader of animals, of captain's toys, of plants ... Well, you'll see! He's lately named Gardener to the king."

Mr. Sandys was, in fact, a friend of the Tradescants. This no surprise, since Mr. Sandys had traveled to Africa and the Holy Land as well as to parts of Europe. Mr. Sandys reminded us to look for the treasures he himself had brought from Ancient Egypt. A thrill of excitement raced through me. These would be just a small part of the many pieces we'd be able to see for ourselves.

"His many friends have urged him to charge a few pence to those wishing to see his collection, but as of yet, Mr. Tradescant declines. He feels that many have generously donated to him; he should be generous in return."

Before we departed, Mr. Sandys brought forth a volume of his translated *Metamorphoses*. "Printed not long after I returned from Virginia and dedicated to his majesty, King Charles. This is some of what I translated while a guest in your home. Please have this as a gift from me."

It was such a beautiful volume, and I thrilled to think he'd written much of it in our home in New Towne.

Mr. Sandys apologized that he couldn't offer us his coach to travel over the Thames to Lambeth as he'd need it to visit his brother in Kent.

"Send Sir Edwin and his wife our best wishes, Mr. Sandys. Tell him we're doing well in Virginia. We're growing and learning how to be a colony, and much that we've accomplished, we owe to him and to his ideals. The death of the Company does not mean the death of that we've held dear."

"Do you think there be any interest in reviving the old Company?" Mr. Sandys asked.

"It depends," Will said. "The king finally agreed to our keeping the General Assembly. His majesty's purpose was to have the settlements voice their approval of his tobacco contract. Being unfavorable to them, I don't know why his majesty expected they would. But we still need the king to ratify our land. Else, what have we toiled for all these years? If the king will not approve the land previously granted us, then the colonists will accept a new Company. Whatever course we must take to keep our lands. But if the king confirms our previous dividents, I don't think you'll find much support for a new Company, no." Will spoke in his typical straightforward manner. "We're learning that we like to deal directly with the king where possible so that investors in England are not earning gold on our endeavors."

Then Will added, "We succeeded in keeping the General Assembly. Our land, our General Assembly, and low taxes on tobacco. These three things we'll fight for."

"I understand. Once you've been in Virginia, you appreciate what those here cannot," Mr. Sandys agreed.

"A constant battle it is, too," said Will.

"Do you think you'll ever return to Virginia, Mr. Sandys?" I asked him. I knew he still had financial interests in projects there.

The poet paused. "Mistress, I don't see myself ever boarding a ship again. I never was much for the sea, and that last 'adventure' near finished me off. I should like to be buried here in my native land," he finished wistfully.

That a bold traveler like Mr. Sandys feared the sea made me feel as if perhaps I were not such a coward. Or at least, I was in good company!

We thanked Mr. Sandys for his many kindnesses and bade him farewell.

When frost laced the Kentish fens, we heard that Sir Edwin Sandys had died. The old treasurer joined his Virginia Company predecessor and opponent, Sir Thomas Smythe, in death. Admiral Sir George Somers and Captain Christopher Newport had died long ago. The noblemen, Baron De La Warr and the Earl of Southampton; Governors Sir Thomas Gates, Sir Thomas Dale, and Sir Samuel Argall—all dead by this time, too.

And with that, another chapter of the old Company closed.

Apple Holy and Bright

Late August 1629
London

For the western sun and the western star,
And the low west-wind, breathing afar,
The end of day and beginning of night
Make the apple holy and bright ...

Golden-kernelled, golden-cored,
Sunset ripened above on the tree.
The world is wasted with fire and sword
But the apples of gold hang over the sea.
        —Alfred, Lord Tennyson

H ot sheep's feet!"
        "Come buy my singing birds?"
        "Oranges or lemons, missus?"
"Come buy my beans, right Windsor beans."
"Here's dainty poplin pears!"
"Buy my hood to cover your head?"
"Plum pudding! A groat a pound."
"Two bunches a penny, turnips, ho!"
"Come buy my sand, fine silver sand."
"Mackerel, oh, mackerel!"
"Diddle, diddle, diddle dumplin', ho! With walnuts nice and brown."
"Have you any work for a tinker, missus? Old brass, old pots, or kettles?"

The London street criers sang of wares and fares. So many filled the
narrow streets, the city seemed more crowded than I remembered it.
One man reached toward me, his aged eyes pleading, "Salmon, oh!

Salmon of Newport, mistress? Salmon, oh!" He reeked of old fish, and I drew away.

Will and I kept walking toward the home of Tradescant, collector of all things unusual from around the world. In a hurry and a little annoyed, we wove around the vendors who sometimes blocked our way, seeking our attention. Will grasped my arm and guided me amid the throng.

"Hot codlins hot, oh! Hot codlins hot!"

Still, as we moved along, a gentle and strangely pretty song somehow rose above the crowd, singing the praises of her fruit. The voice reminded me, as all melodic singers always would, of Maggie.

Despite myself, I paused to see her.

> *Hot codlins hot,*
> *The best that e'er you see,*
> *Who buys these dainty hot codlins of me?*

The woman, with shoes ragged and clothing tattered, looked pitifully back at me. Her words were more song than cry as she held the basket filled with roasted apples toward me.

Clinging to her skirts, a boy of not more than three watched the street commotion with great and confused eyes.

The young woman, sensing my interest, persevered hopefully. "Hot codlins, missus, hot codlins! Fire roasted, rolled in caraway. Ye'll find *none* better on any London street!"

I couldn't remember the last time I'd eaten a warm apple. I glanced at Will. "Don't we have time to buy us each a codlin? 'Twould help her a little." My voice trailed off hopefully.

He shook his head, reading my thoughts. "Many's the sad story you'll see here, Joan."

"William Peirce!" I said, not even attempting to hide my reproval. "Not long ago *I* looked like that poor woman. My children looked just the same, too. Remember all the rags, the holey shoes, the dresses all torn?"

Will smiled, relenting. "Aye, I do. As you wish then. Good fortune ought to be shared, I reckon," he said to me. He turned to the woman. "We'll take six, goodwife. Four for my wife and me, and you and your child have one, too."

The woman's eyes shown, "I'm grateful to ye. God be blessing ye! Bless you He will, I say. Ye won't be sorry, no ye won't, sir!" she said, as Will dropped the coins in her hand.

"You bought extra apples, but did you also give her some few more coins than needed?" I asked. We were doing well. A little generosity and perhaps God smiled somewhere. It felt wonderful to have something to give again.

"I did. Mr. Sandys said it well. It was a pittance to me, a fortune to that young mother. And I could see it meant something to you, too." Then he handed the codlin to me. *"I'll give my love an apple,"* he said with a lilt and sweet affection in his voice.

"Ah! I haven't thought of that old song in years." For the song came from Dorset, my home. And I began to hum with the happiness of being with Will.

When had I last heard Will almost singing? Ever? Yet there he was.

> *I'll give my love an apple without e'er a core.*
> *I'll give my love a house without e'er a door.*
> *I'll give my love a palace wherein she may be,*
> *And she may unlock it without e'er a key.*

I joined him on the last verse, singing too.

Then, "A house without a door, a lock without a key," I said, musing and taking another bite of the juicy apple. "Will, I once worried about keys at James Town, whether we would have any keys. How silly of me! How young I was ..." My voice trailed off. Keys had been the very least of our worries. Had I only known then what I now did.

Yet so much to be grateful for! I remembered the day I'd sat by the river, mourning Tempie, and long before that when she'd told me to count my blessings.

Sometimes, I realized, blessings spring up like little wildflowers where one seeks them not, like the flowers by the river. Despite every winter storm or gust, despite every spring torrent. You turn, and there they are. That was how I felt this day. As if I had just stumbled upon a field of flowers in the turbulent city.

I saw that the little woman gripped the coins tightly. A smile lit her face as she plied her wares once more, a lilt of joy now in her voice. *"Hot codlins hot oh!"*

"Such a small thing, Will. But those few pence will help her. Time was I never thought I'd understand being poor. Now I do."

"But you're poor no more. Our fortunes have turned. Hard times, I believe, are over for Virginia and for us. Our home and our lands secure— once ratified by the king, anyway. Our tobacco and corn growing well!"

Can it be? I marveled, as I enjoyed the warm, sour apple.

"More joy to come, my love, because soon we'll see an ark! Tradescant's

Ark, as they call it here. The wonders of the world open to the public. For you, plants and flowers and even, I hear, Henry VI's cradle! A mermaid hand, a mummy. And for me, a little business. Tradescant knows silkworms, and I'll seek his advice on them." He winked. "But I might have time for a mermaid hand or two."

I chuckled and took his arm once more.

How could I feel fortunate after all I'd been through? How was there still happiness?

Ah, just that. I'd been through so much that now small wonders and joys thrilled me. My entire being had changed as to what made me happy.

A warm apple and a mermaid hand? Yes, indeed.

A Door of Hope

Late August 1629
At Tradescant's Ark, Lambeth, Surrey, England

I am almost perswaded a Man might in one daye behold and collecte into one place more Curiosities then hee should see if hee spent all his life in Travell.
—Peter Mundy, 1634, visitor to Tradescant's Ark

There I will give back her vineyards to her, and transform her Valley of Troubles into a Door of Hope. She will respond to me there, singing with joy as in days long ago in her youth, after I had freed her from captivity in Egypt.
—Hosea 2:15

The Museum Tradescantianum!" Will said. "I believe that's it."

He pointed to a large but plain home, a court in front, made of stone and ancient wood. Behind it, we knew, the Tradescants had a large physick garden and collection of trees from their travels. Beyond that, the Thames.

A great iron gate stood open, awaiting visitors.

Will had the same fervor as I to see the curiosities within. Mr. Tradescant, see, had a new idea. Why should only friends of wealthy collectors be able to see such marvels, to be able to learn from the many wonders of the world? Why should not anyone be able to do so?

The Tradescants, we knew, were Dutch. John Tradescant the Elder had lived in England many years, and his son John the Younger had been born here. When John the Elder greeted us, he spoke melodious English with his Dutch accent.

Mr. Tradescant reached out to shake Will's hand. "Captain Peirce. My thanks for your service to the Virginia Company, to keeping the venture going." He had, it turned out, invested in the Company a dozen years before.

"Sir Samuel Argall, then the governor, was an acquaintance of mine. I'd been present to meet the princess Pocahontas and her husband Rolfe. The princess, she ... well, she stirred me to adventure for a Company share."

It comforted me to hear how Pocahontas had charmed those she met here. "She was my friend," I offered. "They both were, John and Rebecca."

"And so you met Mr. Rolfe?" Will asked. "He was, you see, our son-in-law, having married our daughter after the Indian princess died."

"Ah, I see we have many friends in common!" the collector said with delight.

Before the journey through the museum began, he offered us a seat in his hall. Will then gave him Claiborne's gift, retrieved from his satchel.

John Tradescant the Elder was an affable man. He accepted the gifts from Virginia with something approaching glee. Again I saw that Virginia was both exotic and fascinating to those here in England.

Will also seized the opportunity to thank Mr. Tradescant for his son's advice sent to Virginia regarding growing silkworms.

"Any success?" Mr. Tradescant raised a brow.

"Not too much," Will replied. "But we continue to strive."

"Striving is good, too."

We all sat for a few moments with Will asking if Mr. Tradescant knew how to keep the seeds alive crossing the ocean. How could Will tell when the silkworms were prospering?

I tapped my foot impatiently. *Silkworms, silkworms. I want to see a mermaid hand.* Sometimes Will could be so maddeningly practical!

At last, the conversation was over.

Mr. Tradescant stood, saying, "Now you truly must see what we have from Virginia. Come, come!" said the curator with enthusiasm. "But we'll start with the chambers closest and work our way there."

We walked toward a shadowed hall as Mr. Tradescant asked, "Were you in Virginia to meet Captain John Smith?"

"My wife was," Will replied.

Mr. Tradescant looked intrigued. "Oh?"

"I sailed on the *Sea Venture*. When I, at last, arrived in Virginia after my Bermuda stranding, Captain Smith had already returned to England with a grave injury," Will explained.

"I see. What a place, as I hear it, the Somers Isles! Well, Smith is a friend of mine. Such a keen adventurer. He says he'll bequeath me a third of his books stored here in Lambeth."

Mr. Tradescant's dog Shem walked by his side, ever obedient.

"Shem?" Will asked.

"Noah's son." He placed his hands on his chest. "See, I am Noah! And this is my ark." And then he laughed at a jest I supposed he made each time his dog was about, but it made me laugh, too.

I also wondered, were there biblical curiosities within? My heart raced in excitement.

Along the way, Mr. Tradescant explained that he'd once been a gardener and friend to Lord Cecil at Hatfield House. "I journeyed through Europe, gathering new plants for Hatfield. Along the way, I began to see what a wonderful world we live in. So many curiosities! I spent sixteen weeks just in Russia collecting and learning, many a storm and much fog I encountered. Wonderful. Miraculous, strange as well."

Before we could respond asking how storms and fog could be wonderful, something had caught the old gardener's attention. "See here?" He indicated an ancient cradle. "The cradle of our infant king, Henry VI! Perhaps my greatest treasure."

I tried to envision the babe, the heavy crown that awaited his young head. He had slept here, just right here in this tiny bed, not knowing he was the most important person in England, what God had ordained for his future. Thanks to Mr. Tradescant, I could see and touch the present, the past, the world.

"Wondrous!" I breathed the word. "Simply marvelous."

"Are the stories true that you once joined a privateer fighting the Barbary pirates?" Will asked.

Mr. Tradescant shrugged. "Indeed I did. Apricot trees, you know. One then had to go to Algiers to procure them."

Will and I exchanged glances, our eyes wide. Here was someone who thought battling Turks a fair exchange for the right sort of trees. We doubted Mr. Sandys would agree!

While glass cases lined the chamber, Mr. Tradescant had also hung many curiosities on walls. Other items were on shelves attached to the walls and even upon the ceilings.

Imagine living here! I thought, catching glimpses of filled chambers and hallways as far as I could see.

"Joan!" Will said eagerly, pointing to the two largest turtle shells I'd ever seen. "We ate turtles such as these in Bermuda. Much larger than those in Virginia."

Mr. Tradescant adjusted his glasses. "They *are* from Bermuda, sent by a governor there."

Each case had so much to see, I wondered how there could be any more. Yet always another case followed. Ancient coins, eighty faces carved on a cherry stone, medals, feathers and shells, beasts and serpents.

Outlandish purses wrought in gold and silver. Turkish boots made my skin shiver. I studied the portraits of two French kings sitting on mirrors to appear lifelike and admired all kinds of brightly colored birds of the East Indies.

"Our birds in Virginia are bright, but nothing like these," I murmured to Will.

Nearby was cloth woven from bright yellow bird feathers.

"And these come from the legendary phoenix!" Mr. Tradescant gestured toward several large and colorful feathers. "Here, a dragon egg." The large egg rested innocently in its case.

"Dragon ...?" Will said. "My, certainly the things we've always wondered about, you have."

All the while, Mr. Tradescant regaled us with stories. "I sailed to the Indies myself to fetch these birds," he said, admiring them as if for the first time. His collections evidently brought him as much pleasure daily as they did to us.

Mr. Tradescant lifted a cup from the shelf. "Not just any cup, mistress," he said, sensing my anticipation. "Fifty-two paper-thin cups are within this one cup!"

I was able to see the rich blue of sapphires and the wonderful purple amethysts, a wheel and spindle made of amber. We gasped to see a unicorn's horn and the famous mermaid's hand, gray and strange but with five fingers.

We discovered living things turned to stone and the passion of Christ carved into a plum stone. We saw a white partridge and a goose which had grown into a tree.

We marveled at things familiar to us, if odd to those in England. The cape of King Powhatan and an Indian canoe. Next to these, a picture of an Indian with his bow and dart. We recognized also Virginia animals: skunks, 'possums, beavers, and raccoons.

"This mantle of Powhatan? I have seen the like in Indian towns, though not this grand," Will commented.

That caught Mr. Tradescant's attention. "Aye, have you? Captain Newport donated it to my collection." He adjusted his glasses to study the piece. "I recall Newport traded King Powhatan a copper crown for Powhatan's old shoes and cloak. The crown bestowed King James's blessing on the Indian as another king."

Before I could consider that, almost immediately new things drew my attention.

"My, my!" I exclaimed upon seeing an ape's head. "So much larger than e'er I imagined. The face 'twould frighten me if I should encounter one in Virginia." We had never seen apes in Virginia, but we heard that in the Caribbean were monkeys.

"You're a friend of Mr. Sandys, I hear?" said Mr. Tradescant with interest.

"Aye, indeed!" Will said. "In fact, he sends you well wishes. Mr. Sandys lived with us for several years in Virginia. We recently visited him here at his Lambeth home. We're bound to see what he brought you from Egypt!"

Mr. Tradescant smiled. "Ah, of course, you'll want to see them." He led us through several rooms over to yet another large glass-encased cabinet. "See here then." He pointed. "He brought me the idol Osiris and Anubis the sheep, along with the beetle and the dog which the ancient Egyptians worshipped."

Here then was the proof of the many stories Mr. Sandys had told us.

At once, I remembered joy, the kind of joy that made a body want to laugh at the wonder and beauty of God's world. The kind of joy that the woman who wove the yellow-feather cloth and the man who carved the plum stone understood. As if they and I were joined in something greater than any of us knew.

Now I saw that joy had never left me, not truly. It had hidden itself, secreted itself deep inside, just as fear had. It only awaited the darkness lifting so light could shine for me to see more than I ever had.

I felt reborn, reborn to a place where no death, massacre, or plague could touch me. On this day, I was happy. Should times grow difficult again, I knew that I'd lived a hardy and adventuresome life. I could hold onto this joy, this day.

Many years ago, I'd counted my paltry blessings and found them not wanting, even then. How many more blessings to come?

When we stopped for a farewell visit with Ralph Yeardley, I'd insist—*insist*—that he and Rose bring the children here. Tempie, somewhere, approved. Of this, I felt sure.

Perhaps one day, I'd bring my own grandchildren here to Mr. Tradescant's. Or perhaps the children would risk that ocean voyage and come to see it for themselves. Because only when you risk, can you find the reward, just as my father had taught me. One can stay home and avoid the pirates, or get on the ocean and experience life.

That's what Tempie had been trying to tell me that day we sat in my fig orchard. *London would enchant you anew if you only endured the ocean voyage,* she'd said.

Will clasped my hand as if reading my thoughts.

"It's been a good life, Will," I whispered, as a servant led us back through the labyrinth of corridors. "Truly, never apologize for it again."

Mr. Tradescant's man held the door for us, but lost in our own quiet conversation, we scarcely noticed.

Will's eyes widened at my words. He hadn't been expecting that, only that I'd enjoyed the dragon egg!

"Why so surprised?" I asked in amusement. "While we struggled through poverty, darkness, and discouragement, still we never wanted for richness. Not richness of means, but richness of purpose."

The Turning of the Tide

Late March 1630
London

Oh, the moon shines bright, and we sail to-night,
And we're bound for Sourabaya!
So it's 'Farewell, Jane!' for we're off again
With the turning of the tide!
— Charles Henry Souter

R alph Yeardley had come to find us at our inn. He brought word that Tempie's former servant Susanna would have to testify as to her dame's intentions in her will. "Captain West does claim his wife's dower share," Ralph explained. Just as we had known West would do.

Susanna was afraid, Ralph said, of speaking against such a powerful man.

"I thought so!" I snapped. I stamped my foot. "How can he? He knows Tempie strove to have the assets of her husband preserved for her children."

"Not so quickly, Joan," Will said reassuringly. "I must settle Rolfe's will, also at the Prerogative Court of Canterbury. You and I shall go with young Susanna and encourage her, bolster her courage before she testifies. At the same time, I can settle John's estate. Tell her," Will said kindly to Ralph, "not to fear. A West is but a West. The Yeardleys and Susanna might not possess such high means, but the court shall wish to do right by Sir George, who gave all to Virginia."

Ralph sighed. "Thank you, Will. I shall bring Susanna around in a few weeks so that we may all go. I shall go, too, of course. But she feels safe with both of you. Particularly with you, Joan."

I sometimes felt guilty that I'd survived while Tempie had not. Yet I also saw that being able to look after the children and their interests gave me a chance to rise above the sadness, to do for Tempie's children what she could not.

"Of course, I shall be there, too," I said. "Tempie would have it no other way. She loved Susanna and would not wish her to be afraid while defending her children."

Ralph looked relieved. "Thank you both."

After the door closed behind Ralph, I said to Will, "Our duty is to the children. All four. Thomas Rolfe, too." My eyes burned with tears. "Tempie and Sir George, John Rolfe and Pocahontas, all gone too young. But this we can do. Take care of the children left behind, make sure they have what they need. You'll pay Thomas Rolfe's passage should he desire to return to Virginia, as we hear he does?"

Will nodded. "I'd have it no other way. Then he wrapped his arm around me. "Aye, it does give one purpose, doesn't it?"

Will also needed to visit the Tobacco Exchange and oversee incoming arrivals of tobacco shipments. The exchange was nearby, and Will planned to go there this afternoon.

However, before he could leave the inn, a knock at the door startled us.

Reckoning it to be the innkeeper, Will opened the door and drew back in shock.

Before him stood Captain Claiborne, holding his hat, and looking as if someone had died.

"Oh, God." I reached for a chair and sat down. I suspected I'd need to.

News from a Foreign Country Came

Late March to Early May 1630
London

News from a foreign country came ...
—Thomas Traherne

Will ushered Captain Claiborne in without a word as if he, too, knew Claiborne bore ill tidings.

"Captain Claiborne, are my daughters and grandchildren all right?" I blurted the words without even greeting the man who'd come so far.

He nodded. "They're well, Mrs. Peirce." He gestured for me to remain sitting. "No need to rise," he said gently. He turned and shook Will's hand.

"Won't you have a seat, sir?" Will gestured to a chair. Then Will walked over to prepare our visitor a glass of wine.

After handing the drink to Captain Claiborne, Will himself dropped into another chair. His face, I saw, was pale. He also suspected sore news was afoot.

Captain Claiborne took a sip, and his eyes were sad. "Well, I must get right to it. I'm sorry to tell you that my uncle Roger has died of a sudden."

"What?" Will rose abruptly. "How be it? He was in perfect health when we departed."

Captain Claiborne agreed. "Indeed he was. In fact, the General Assembly had ordered my uncle to lead another force against the Indians in November and again now in March. Even the last of November, Uncle sat on council to sign a petition to the king. He died soon after, though, in the early part of January."

I choked a sob, and Will, I could see, was also upset.

"Was he injured while attacking the Indians?" I asked, hushed.

Will Claiborne shook his head. "No, Mrs. Peirce. He seemed healthy. But when Jane arrived back to the house after asking her maid to churn the butter, she found my uncle. His head back in a chair as if sleeping and ... Well, he was already gone." Captain Claiborne gripped the glass in his hands tighter, and his knuckles whitened. He shook his head then as if still in disbelief.

"And Jane? How is she?"

"She's fine, Mrs. Peirce. She's stalwart, that one. She does what she needs to do. Your son Tom has supported his sister, and we have other relatives who live near the island as well. They've offered their immediate help."

"Thanks be for family and friends! I'm so relieved Jane has company."

Captain Claiborne assured us. "Jane and the children are in good hands. And we sent the shallop to Jordan's Journey to let Cecily know." Then he smiled. "Your daughter upriver is great with child! A little happy news."

I touched my heart. "Is she! And she, too, is healthy?"

Captain Claiborne nodded and beamed, delighted he could tell us something cheerful. Then he pulled folded papers from his satchel. "Captain Peirce, the governor and council appointed me to execute Uncle's estate. I'll have to visit the Prerogative Court of Canterbury to have Uncle Roger's sisters Gertrude and Audrey appointed. They'll handle the probate here in England. I've spoken with my Aunt Isabella to tell her the news. She agrees that her sisters are well suited for such."

He turned to me. "That reminds me, Mrs. Peirce. I have a message for you from Aunt Isabella. She is already home safely. She says to tell you that testifying before the high court wasn't too difficult, and she'll see you when you're home." Then to Will, he said, "Also, the prerogative court has called on me to testify concerning my Lady Yeardley's estate and wishes."

I sucked in my breath, trying to take in the mix of good and bad news. "The battle rages with West, does it?" I felt something like hatred, which I tried to push down.

"It does. But don't fret, Mrs. Peirce. Dame Temperance's wishes were clear. We just need to show the court that."

"He speaks truly, Joan," Will said. Then he turned to Captain Claiborne. "As it stands, I myself need to settle John's estate. Jane's first husband, John Rolfe. I'm to be the executor," Will said. "And we've talked with Ralph Yeardley about Susanna Hall's testimony. We'll escort her to the court to testify."

"Aye. Let's go to Canterbury together, then," Captain Claiborne said. He hesitated. "I should attempt to settle Uncle's estate myself, but I have an important task ahead of me as Secretary of State. And this, sir, is the next news I bear if you haven't heard. Lord Baltimore, the old Catholic, has forgone his colony in Avalon on a Canadian island. 'Too cold,' he says." Captain Claiborne's eyes said he didn't believe him.

"And such is not true?" I asked. I certainly made myself comfortable with men's business, I realized. And then again, why shouldn't I? I might need to run Will's tobacco trade myself one day, as both Tempie and Isabella had been forced to do with their crops. In case that should happen, I needed to pay attention.

"Oh, I believe the winters were desolate there. No doubt," the captain replied. "But I also believe he has his eye on a piece of our beautiful, mild Virginia for his Catholic colony. He's looking to settle between the land granted to Sir Robert Heath for Carolana and our James River. *Both* colonies—Carolana and Baltimore's proposed one—are within our bounds, bounds his majesty King Charles promised us to uphold. The baron refused to take the oath of supremacy, so he has departed. As of now, his wife and children remain at James Town."

Captain Claiborne's eyes were grim as he continued. "But the old Catholic has ideas, of this I'm sure. And so I shall be busy at the king's court. I'll also be bringing a hundred colonists and supplies to Kent Island. The king only grants unsettled land. This should ensure the upper Chesapeake Bay remains in Virginia hands as it should. The way past tobacco is with furs. I firmly believe that." The surveyor set his jaw in determination.

"Lord Baltimore seeks his own territory, not to be part of Virginia?" Will asked. His tone was somber.

"That's so," Captain Claiborne said. "My Lord Baltimore desires to carve off some of our fairest lands for his own. These lands our former king granted to us by law, and our present king confirmed this grant. I'm here to watch Lord Baltimore's actions at court."

"Suppose my Lord Baltimore attempts to proceed?" I asked, eyes wide.

Claiborne grimaced. "Then, Mrs. Peirce, we shall have trouble."

In early May, Will and I arranged a hackney to Ralph Yeardley's home, and we gathered Susanna and Ralph for Susanna's court appearance in Kent. The young girl was obviously affrighted.

"I do not wish to cross Captain West," she said as the carriage hobbled along. "But I'll tell the truth. I'll do it for my dame." Her voice quivered.

When called to give her deposition, she spoke strong and clear.

Your dame would be proud, I thought, watching her.

Within a few years, the case would end when Captain West, having remarried, drowned.

But our surprises in London were not yet past. Will received word from the Privy Council. *Mr. George Sandys recommends you for a position on the council of Virginia to which we give our most hearty approbation.*

And just like that, Will was a councilor, the most prestigious position in Virginia behind the governor. He followed three of his sons-in-law who had been councilors—John Rolfe, William Farrar, and Roger Smith.

Most of the time, becoming a councilor was a position one held until he left Virginia or died. We both realized, with mild horror, that the seat he was filling belonged to his own daughter's husband, Roger Smith.

That letter and his new honor would take Will places he couldn't have imagined, not all of them good.

Fare-well, Sweet Guiding Star

Late June to Early July 1630
Plymouth Hoe, Devon, and Melcombe Regis, Dorset, England

O, bright though years how many! fare-well, sweet guiding star—
The wild wind blows me seaward over the harbor-bar!
    —George Edward Woodberry

Plymouth Hoe came into view, a row of merchant's houses veiled in fog. We could see the homes beyond another ship, trying to make port as well. Gulls dipped into the water, seeking scraps of bread or fish, reminding us that while we were still in the Narrow Seas, the ocean lay not far beyond.

Here, Will and I would disembark to spend a month in the West Country before departing on the long adventure, the one home. Here, too, young Thomas Rolfe would meet us.

Soon enough, we'd be in my old home, Melcombe Regis in Dorset.

With my brothers gone as well as my parents and stepmother Lattie, little was left for me there. But I'd asked Will if we could go to Melcombe anyway.

Later from Dorset, we'd travel to Somerset where Will had been born. Like me, Will's family had died or moved away.

We explored Plymouth, and Will pointed out the lawn where Sir Walter Ralegh was said to have bowled while waiting for the Armada.

The West Country. How I love it! So familiar and so foreign, all at once.

Less than a week later, we set out for Melcombe. I was going home. Or was it home? My heart was in my throat. I didn't know how to feel.

An old innkeeper in Melcombe Regis welcomed us in. The musty paneling and ancient oak beams declared this inn to be many hundreds of years old.

I looked up and down, around at the portraits and burning sconces on the walls.

Aye, the light would be dropping soon. "I should ... I should like to walk to the harbor," I said to Will from our chamber.

Will moved to accompany me. "I appreciate that, Will, but the harbor was a friend to me as a girl. I feel I should speak to it alone."

My husband nodded with a curious expression. "As you wish, Joan."

Down the rutted street, around the bend until I saw it, as peaceful and marvelous as ever it had been.

"I've missed you," I said to the old harbor.

I stooped to pick up a shell. A scallop shell, in fact. Similar to the one I'd found here twenty years before, the one Cecily and I had broken in two, each of us keeping half until we reunited.

A burning went through my chest, a sense of time passing too quickly, my life sliding by like a ship out to sea.

The harbor waters chopped in the wind, the same wind which tickled my cheek.

Then, "You're not nearly so strong or so powerful as you shall think," I said mysteriously.

The brisk lapping seemed to say, *Why, what do you mean?*

"I mean, I've crossed an ocean twice and seen a great river five miles wide and a mighty bay as well." But then, almost apologetically, I added, "I do miss your peace at times, though."

The water glinted in the late afternoon sun.

"You pushed that scallop shell right to me, the one I shared with Cecily. You helped me decide what to do when I thought my world might come to an end. In fact, it nearly did."

The lapping of the water seemed thoughtful.

Was it right to go? the water seemed to ask.

I paused. I looked up the street at the old familiar homes, the tavern signs, and boys playing skittles on the green. I thought of the years missed with my brothers; of the quiet, forlorn graves of my mother and infant son; of the wonderfulness and staidness of old England. How nothing ever seemed to truly change except for the folks in it, who were dying while I was far away. The faces I'd left behind were not the ones I saw now.

I thought of the ancient castles and gentle Thames; such an old man was he, surveying London as it had grown from Roman town to English city. The old man had never left nor interfered. Just watched it all happen. Another thousand years or two, he'd still be watching, I reckoned.

In my mind, I saw the ruins of King Arthur's castle dotting the hills overlooking the Narrow Seas; Cornish piskies living amid the high moorlands; the ancient walls still visible in Exeter and old Stonehenge the rock ruins, in Salisbury. The memories washed over me as if it were all a dream, a life I no longer lived or belonged to.

Was it right to go? The water asked once more, but not impatiently. The harbor had been here a millennium, or two, or ten. It was, I supposed, in no hurry.

"Yes," I said to myself or to the harbor, I knew not which, and even my own ears surprised to my answer. "I've missed you, longed for you, even begged for you. I desired so many times to return to you. But now that I'm here, I see this world is no longer my home nor can ever be again." The light dropped e'er lower in the sky. "I don't belong here anymore, but in Virginia."

I told you, I told you, the lapping water seemed to say.

A Grain of Mustard-Seed

Late July 1630
Plymouth Hoe, Devon, England

*Thirdly, This kingdom [of England] now first in his majesty's times hath
gotten a lot or portion in the new world by the plantation of Virginia and the
Summer Islands. And certainly it is with the kingdoms on earth as it is in the
kingdom of heaven: sometimes a grain of mustard-seed proves a great tree.
Who can tell?*
—Sir Francis Bacon, 1621

As we prepared to board the Virginia-bound ship, I looked back at Plymouth Hoe, the English buildings so grand. The welcoming pubs, the winding streets leading to the countryside and beyond.

We brought with us now Thomas Rolfe, seventeen years old. Will had paid for Thomas's passage and had helped Henry Rolfe cover some of the expenses incurred over the years Thomas had been with him. That had come from John's estate.

"You cannot remember Virginia, Thomas?" I asked Pocahontas's son, handsome with his dark eyes and hair.

"No, mistress," he'd said politely. "Not my mother, nor my father."

"Your father was ill and returning to see you and also to settle some business when he died eight years past. He would have brought you home had he survived the voyage."

"Oh. I'm curious about my mother's people. I can't deny it. And I'm ready to see my mother's homeland once more."

I tried to hide my thoughts. How hard it would have been on John and his son to have witnessed the massacre. It lay behind us now, even though the war lingered. Still, I hoped his mother's people would likely—maybe?—welcome Thomas.

As for me, how different from when I'd set sail twenty-one years before.

The ship was still frightening in its way. Soon it would be at sea and us within it.

But before, the other side had represented the unknown. A land filled, we'd heard, with Indians and dark, impenetrable forests of bear, lions, 'possums and raccoons. So strange it had all seemed.

All this time, I'd asked Will when we could go home. In 1611, I'd begged him. *No,* he'd replied. *The leaders will never allow us to leave.* In fact, not until 1617 had the Company given us permission to sail from Virginia at all.

How I had longed for home—this home—back then. Someday, I'd promised myself, someday I would return home to England and live out my years here.

Now I stood on the wharf and surveyed Plymouth and the Narrow Sea. I pictured the sweeping Armada attack when I was little. The centuries of family stones in the Dorset churches and the lead casket holding my father in the sea. This abundant island my family's home since I could never have guessed when. Some ancestors would have come during the Norman invasion of 1066, surely. Other ancestors would have been here to greet them. Tribes with my family members who would have met the Vikings at the shores. Who would have fought and protected this island, the land of the Saxons, at all costs.

How I had loved the harbor at Melcombe, the little churchyard, the winding roads leading from the church to my parents' home.

I'd loved the theatre and Tradescant's Ark, the visits with Captain Smith and the Yeardleys. The street vendor calls of London and the tulip bulbs. The return to London and the West Country. I had drunk it all in like one starved for English culture, for city life.

Yet I came as a stranger. England I no longer understood, and it no longer understood me. I was English and not English.

How can that be? I wondered. *Where do I belong?*

Being that I cannot be in two places at once, I must choose where my days end, where my body shall lie one day. And the choice is a simple one because I've made it already. I made it when I fell in love with the Virginia rivers. With the tall oaks and hickory and smaller chinquapin trees. The teeming fish of the river and the enormous eagles overhead.

I made it and did not know it sometime in the past. Sometime as my family grew and married and grandchildren came along, little Virginia grandchildren who knew of England only in stories.

My home was in Virginia. Even though we had the means to stay, we could not leave Virginia bereft of us. We could not leave ourselves bereft of it. We could not abandon her.

She was our home now and always would be.

Behind me, a bewildered throng of men, women, and children checked their possessions and kissed loved ones. All the while, they laughed, cried, and fretted.

"What'll she be like, Amelie?" I heard one man ask his wife.

"Big trees, I hear. Biggest trees you ever like to see. I can't imagine!"

"The opportunities are ours, love. All ours."

I turned to look back at them and smiled.

Opportunities and big trees. This couple was not so different from me twenty years ago. Wild, exotic, strange. *Our home.*

"Have ye been there, missus?" The wife asked me.

How did one answer that? I simply nodded and smiled. My voice had gone.

Just then, Will stepped up behind me and pointed to the ship.

"She's a fine one, Joan, and a captain I trust. Are you prepared for another voyage?"

"Yes," I said simply. "Yes." How to explain the feelings within? I only knew that I missed home, and home wasn't England. I'd miss my Dorset harbor, I suspected, but I would never again long for her until it hurt.

As we stepped aboard the plank and onto the ship, I thought, *Now, pray, Virginia has given us all the surprises she has to offer!*

But, I had been in Virginia many a year. I should have known that could not be true.

Beauteous as the Silver Moon

Late September 1630
New Towne, Virginia

White she is as lily of June,
And beauteous as the silver moon
When out of sight the clouds are driven
And she is left alone in heaven;
Or like a ship some gentle day
In sunshine sailing far away ...

And she hath wandered, long and far,
Beneath the light of sun and star;
Hath roamed in trouble and in grief,
Driven forward like a withered leaf,
Yea like a Ship at random blown
To distant places and unknown.
—William Wordsworth

Sir John Harvey, this new governor, was going to be trouble. That much was apparent from the time our ship anchored at James Town. So the rumors were true.

The governor had come to welcome the ship, despite the threat of rain, with a company of halberdiers in flaming red silk. This was undoubtedly designed to impress incoming settlers with Harvey's majesty.

Will's look showed what he was thinking. I, however, said it.

"Did we get an emperor while we were away?" I whispered to Will. He gave me a little prod that said, *I have to get along with this man if I am to succeed in Virginia.*

"Does he know he's in the wilds of Virginia and not at Whitehall Palace?"

I whispered once more.

Will grimaced.

The king had commissioned Sir John as our new governor upon the death of Sir George. But Sir John had spent two years in England angling for more pay, more commissions. Virginia was now his empire, he'd decided.

Sir John's brother was well connected with the king, but for Sir John himself the king seemed to have limited tolerance. Sir John, we were soon to learn, would test the patience of all with whom he came in contact. That is, except for his fat cronies.

When we arrived, the new governor had been in Virginia six months, the formal replacement for Governor Pott, whose position had been temporary.

We'd already learned of Sir John's reputation for being arrogant and irascible, vain and greedy. Now, seeing such a display, we reckoned at least some of those things to be true.

Will took a shallop to see how Jane was managing after Roger's death. I went home to unpack and to inspect the house. Then I, too, would go over to Mulberry Island.

I'd hoped time away from Virginia would dull the pain of losing Tempie. English distractions had filled my life with something akin to whimsy.

But now, here I was, surveying the palisades and marshes and the homes I could see in New Towne, knowing that Tempie was nowhere on this island. Tempie, Sir George, their children, and Susanna. Nowhere in Virginia. Tempie's home across the swamp would stand empty until Ralph Yeardley saw it all sold.

I drew a deep breath and determined to stay content, all the while knowing that without the Yeardleys, Virginia would never be the same for me.

Thanks to the doctor, our home in New Towne stood as we'd left it, if empty of children and friends. Almost desolate, as I myself was starting to feel.

A slow and steady autumn rain fell onto the settlement so that it was awash in grey. The earth, it seemed, felt as deep a sadness as did I.

I came in and sat down in my chair, wondering how I would make it now that I were home and Tempie's loss, oh, so vivid. In my mind, while away, I could almost imagine her steps greeting my return.

As the gentle tapping of the rain kept me company, I glanced at the empty chair beside me. I pretended Tempie was sitting there, leaning forward, so eager to hear about England.

"Would you like some mulberry beer?" I said quietly to the empty chair.

I heard Tempie say, *Lovey, I need no mulberry beer where I am now. But how I've missed you! You must know it, sure. Now, how was the voyage? Did ye go to Melcombe Regis to see the harbor? Captain John Smith wanted to talk about us? Tell me, please! Did you tell him we fought the squirrels for acorns? Were the children happy and healthy on the voyage? How do Ralph and Rose prosper? They didn't seem to mind caring for the children, did they? And tell me about Tradescant's Ark. What was in it? What did you see?*

And so I began to talk, silly as it may have been. I told her about the voyage and Tradescant's museum, Will and the tulips and the play. I was only talking to myself, but somehow it made me feel better.

"Tempie," I said at last. "I have to go on. I hope you don't mind?"

Lovey, I don't mind at all. You cannot grieve forever, nor should you.

"It will be lonely without you here."

Don't let it be.

A tingle passed through me. I'd just take things for the best.

The Winds That Brood

Late September 1630
New Towne, Virginia

But all things, my lord, in this world pass away ... wife, children, honour,
wealth, friends, and what else is dear to flesh and blood; they are but lent us
till God please to call for them back again ...
— Sir George Calvert, 1ˢᵗ Baron Baltimore, writing
after the loss of his wife and children in a shipwreck
returning from Virginia

I feel no shadow of the winds that brood,
I hear no whisper of a tide that veers,
I weave no thought of passion, nor of tears ...
— John Spencer Muirhead

Just then, I espied a face in the window. Isabella! She cupped her hands, looking in to see if I were home. Quite literally keeping an eye on me, which caused me to smile a little.

She broke into a grin and waved, rushing over to the door, as I wiped away tears with my hand. I hoped my eyes didn't look too red.

Isabella Perry, however, wasn't fooled. Not even a little.

She gave me a hug and said, "And why dost thou cry? Oh, I forget. Virginia makes us all cry."

In spite of myself, I laughed a little.

"Well, true that. No, I'm crying because of coming home and Tempie not being here." Then, how careless of me to forget! "Isabella, I'm sorry about your brother Roger, sorry for you and sorry for Jane. I know she's heartbroken. I'm going over to Mulberry Island as soon as I can pack once more," I told her.

As I said it, I considered that others had suffered far more losses than I had. Besides Roger, Isabella had lost her first husband, Mr. Pace. She'd accepted it and married Will Perry. A son by each marriage had survived.

"I'm being selfish, I know," I added.

She pulled back, grabbing my hands in hers and giving them a squeeze.

"No, you're not," she said in a soft tone. "I understand. I do. We lost Roger eight months ago, so the pain is mending. May I come inside? I've made my way over despite the rain to see you."

"Well!" I forced some brightness. "What have I missed? I saw our new governor in grand glory." I rolled my eyes, and Isabella smiled. One thing I knew, men might not say what they were thinking ... but fireside, my friends would.

"Oh, so much you've missed! You saw Sir John then, Virginia's Caesar?"

I couldn't help but chuckle. In spite of myself, Isabella was cheering me up. "Why, that's what I said, but Will shushed me. Like an emperor, our governor appears."

"Oh, aye. And there's more."

Just a few months before, Governor Sir John had placed Dr. Pott under arrest at the doctor's home for a strange litany of crimes, Isabella said. Dr. Pott had failed to prosecute several servants for murder and had stolen some cattle, the governor said.

"The truth is, Joan, Sir John just doesn't like the good doctor and wishes to embarrass him in a show of power. To carry on this way to his predecessor, the previous governor, is truly shameful."

"Poor Elizabeth!" Dr. Pott's wife was a good and quiet woman.

"Elizabeth Pott? She'd make a body proud. She's taken ship to England to tell the king and Privy Council that Sir John hath treated her husband unfairly and to beg for his release."

My eyes widened. "No! Shy Elizabeth Pott?"

Isabella gestured with both hands for effect. "And ill she was, too, Joan."

"The poor family. On the wrong side of a tyrant."

"Aye." Isabella paused. "Sir John seems to hate the doctor's brother Francis Pott, too. An ill-boding I have of Sir John," she said somberly. "Pray he stays not long."

Isabella went on to tell me that I'd but missed a baroness, Dame Joane Baltimore, who'd come on a surprise to James Town with her husband, Baron Baltimore.

"She departed Virginia, too?" I asked. "Her husband was in England, but I heard his wife and children had remained in Virginia. Captain Claiborne met us in England and told us that the leaders made him leave since he refused to take the oath of supremacy.

Of course, the baron would refuse the oath, and we knew why: the oath pledged one's highest allegiance to King Charles. For a Catholic, the Pope would be a higher authority than an English monarch. This, in part, made Catholics a frightening and unpredictable presence to us. "We are bound to offer the oath!" I said. I knew that this was part of what the councilors had pledged to offer all new arrivals. Those who refused to take the oath must leave the colony. This had always been true.

Isabella went on, "He offered to take an amended oath, but my nephew Claiborne declined to give it to him. It must be the oath as we are pledged to administer it or none at all," Isabella went on, relishing her story. "Well, why's this baron here?" she asked pointedly. "You know why," she said, answering her own question. "Codfish and cold don't agree with Lord Baltimore. The king has granted him land in Newfoundland, but he suffered." She laughed. "Suffered! As if we know not that."

I had to agree. While we had milder winters than Newfoundland, the heat of the summers was when we suffered much. Will said that Lord Baltimore's Avalon settlement was founded on an isle off Newfoundland, halfway between Greenland and Virginia. Sure it was cold. So now the old baron eyed his most Southern neighbors.

"Lord Baltimore is hoping to slice off a piece of Virginia. So my nephew Claiborne went back to England when Baltimore did, to keep an eye on him." Isabella pointed to her eye. "What I hear from the men is that the king did indeed grant Lord Baltimore some land south of the James River. But my nephew is working to have that patent revoked. He'll explain that the acreage is part of our Virginia grant, which both kings promised to keep intact after the Virginia Company loss."

"If the Lady Baltimore wasn't welcome, where did she tarry while in Virginia?" I asked Isabella.

Now Isabella's knowing look turned dark. "Why, she stayed with our Governor Sir John Harvey! Our new little king. He is *nothing* like Sir George or Dr. Pott or Sir Francis or any of them. Lord Baltimore, who would have a part of Virginia to reign, I suspect Sir John might give to him with both hands open!"

"But you say the baroness has since departed?" I asked.

Isabella nodded. "A Catholic ship came for them. Lord Baltimore sent it, so I heard." A French prize ship called the *St. Claude* had come to fetch them this past summer, Isabella said.

She went on to tell me about the French Huguenots who had come with dreams of settling in Carolana, a new territory to the south granted to Sir

Robert Heath. This I had heard of while in London. "A French baron, they said of this newcomer. Name of Ridouet or some such. But these French, they landed in Virginia, and here they've stayed. They found themselves some other tract of land and hope to plant vines and olives and to make silk and salt.

Early the next winter, word reached James Town that the *St. Claude* had foundered and crashed upon the English coast. All on board had perished, including Lady Baltimore and her children.

The Bible said that God made the rain to fall upon the just and the unjust. It seemed true that we all, as colonists and seafarers, Catholic or Protestant, suffered under the rains.

While the 1st Lord Baltimore would never again return to Virginia and died soon after his wife, the baron's son, the 2nd Lord Baltimore, would not be giving up on Virginia so readily.

I should have known my Will would fight for Virginia, even against the royal favorite Baltimore or the king's own substitute, Governor Sir John, should those winds blow our way. A tiptoe into treason, that.

But that rainy day, I only knew that I felt sorry for the doctor who had removed Will's arrow, prayed Mrs. Pott a safe return, and wished I could have glimpsed Lady Baltimore. And the only winds I felt tousled the falling fig leaves on the orchard out back, spattering rain onto the rich island soil.

Those other winds, though, were whipping up in England and coming sooner than I might have guessed.

Calling Him Jackanapes

January 1631 to April 1635
New Towne, Virginia

*...[I,] who may be as well called the hoste as gouvernor of Virginia, all the
country affayres being prosecuted at my house in James [Town] Island where
is no other hospitalitie for all commers, and if some speedie remedie and
reliefe be not found for me, not onlie my creditt but my hart will breake ...*
> —Sir John Harvey on the difficulties of there not being
> a State House, 1632

*Mr. Panton abuses Mr. Sec'y Rich. Kemp by calling him Jackanapes & saying
ye King was misinform'd of him, that he was unfit for his place would be
shortly turned out as ye other Secr'y was, that he was poor and proud and
that he'd preach ag't his pride of a Lock he had tyed up with a ribbon as old as
Pauls.*
> —Council and General Court Records, 6 December
> 1634

By the time we received a copy of Captain John Smith's *Generall Historie*,
we learned that the old captain had died.

I remembered him fondly and eagerly flipped the leaves to see if
he'd published any of my words. How surprised I was to find my name in the
print of the book! The only woman except for Pocahontas that I saw quoted.
My heart warmed to the faith he had in what I'd said. It seemed largely because of my success with figs that he'd chosen to write about me. Figs! Who
could have known how far they'd take me?

Captain Smith's loss marked the end of most of the old Company.

The old leaders may have been gone, but the colony was growing well
without them.

Mr. Benjamin Syms left money and cattle to establish a free school, the first school in our colony. The dream of the college had died in the massacre.

Corn had been so plentiful that we'd sent five thousand bushels up to New England to help relieve their hunger. I couldn't recall New England ever helping us, but then again, they'd been hungry themselves the year of our massacre. Perhaps I shouldn't judge.

Peace reigned in Virginia once more. The Indian war had endured for ten years following the massacre, but we had a truce now.

We'd built a palisade across the forest, the land between the James and York Rivers. Feeling safe now that the Indian war had ended, and protected by the palisade, settlers began to inhabit the York River.

Now if only we could survive the reign of our irate and unreasonable governor, Sir John Harvey. The years were passing, and we were tolerating the man as best we could.

The council found that the governor constantly undermined their authority, treating them as servants rather than as trusted advisors in the running of Virginia. He also placed his own interests above those of the colony.

"Anything to enrich himself or to curry favor with his betters," the council grumbled.

Governor Sir John grew more entitled as time went by, hard as that was for us to believe.

He also complained about having to host visitors in his home, although every governor before him had done the same thing. The man never seemed to have enough money and owed everyone. He declared that if he received no relief of additional money, his heart—as well as his credit—would break.

He was rather dramatic, we learned, and sometimes liked to pretend he was an actor in one of Mr. Shakespeare's plays. All we could do was to endure his capers until the king replaced him, while having no idea when that would be.

After arresting Dr. Pott, Governor Sir John ceremoniously released him as if to show that what Sir John gaveth, Sir John could take away. And also the other way around.

The governor also petitioned the king to dismiss Claiborne and appoint his own friend and ally, Richard Kemp. This was twice a blow to the colony as we loved Claiborne and hated Kemp.

Like the governor, Kemp had a reputation for getting into quarrels. At the moment, he and the pastor at York, Parson Panton, were feuding. Panton, a friend of Dr. Pott's, couldn't abide either the governor or Secretary Kemp.

Kemp flew into the governor's home one morning.

"Sir! You should be aware of the mutinous actions of the pastor at York. Parson Panton has called me a jackanapes. Has said the king was certainly misinformed to make me secretary, that I am unfit being both poor and proud. Preached a sermon about pride, using me as the lesson. And proceeded to tell me that I tie my hair back with a ribbon as old as the Apostle Paul's!"

Governor Harvey's face burned red with rage. He ordered Pastor Panton to apologize publicly in every parish in Virginia and fined him £500. Harvey then banished the parson for being riotous and mutinous and forbade him ever to return to Virginia. In the process, the governor confiscated Panton's goods and saw Panton back in the colony to execute him on sight. Nowhere did the governor have such authority—not to banish or fine, seize property or make any man an executioner. This was why he had courts.

Now Panton would take his case to the king, and so the division in the colony continued to grow.

At the same time, wearily, we realized we might soon be fighting with fellow Englishmen.

True to his word, Claiborne had brought in a ship with one hundred settlers to Kent Island in the Bay. Kent, named for his home in England. Captain Claiborne would never give up his claim to this island, along with another island the Susquehannock had given him—both strategic sites for fur trading.

Not ever, the captain vowed. A vow that would follow him even while the Virginia councilors stood behind him, even as Governor Harvey openly supported Lord Baltimore. Harvey liked wealthy, influential friends. Preferred them that way.

By the spring of 1634, our fears came to be. We learned that although Lord Baltimore had died, his son had inherited his grant from the king for land already granted to Virginia. Baltimore had arrived in two ships, the great *Ark* and the little *Dove*, with nearly two hundred colonists.

They settled north of us just across the River of the Patawomechs on the bay and gave their city a Catholic name—St. Mary's Cittie. They held mass in honor of their arrival.

Their colony was squarely between Kent Island and us.

The one thing we still didn't have was clear title to our land patents. The king had not yet ratified the old Virginia Company grants. He had promised to do so nine years before, after the Company had collapsed and his father had died.

Still, we waited and waited, even while we settled more along the York River.

Finally, late in 1634, the king declared that we could keep our land, that he had ratified all our old patents and the individual grants within it. This was wonderful news to us all, the result of many petitions and much patience on our part. This meant that Will and many others would collect on eleven years of headrights, for it had taken that long since the Virginia Company fell for the king to decide the matters.

Will enlarged his patent out at Mulberry Island and suggested we move out there. I was happy to be there. A fresh start for me would be a good thing.

"But what about my fig orchard?" I asked Will.

"Never worry. I'll lease our house here at New Towne, and part of the rent shall be the harvesting and sale of your figs. You may be as involved as you like. And you can finally start your new orchard out on the island."

"And our home?"

"A larger one, a better one, we'll build there. Just wait, Joan!" Despite the ongoing problems with Sir John, his unfair taxes and edicts, Will's optimism bloomed.

All finally seemed well for us, many disasters behind us. This was the largest stretch of pleasant times I could ever remember.

But then came the April when everything changed for us once again. I should have expected it, but I didn't.

A Vaine Headded Man

April 26, 1635
York and James Town, Virginia

*[Sir John Harvey was] of [Spanish Ambassador] Goundamars procuringe
sent thether [to Virginia] at the Desolvinge of the company to ruine the Poor
plantation as he well nighe did ... longe before beinge a Vaine headded man
always and a Fantasticke fit for any impression of gaine ...*
                —John Ferrar, written in the margin of a 1649 report
                about Virginia

We'd had enemies of many Indian tribes in Virginia. We knew the
Spanish were always a danger to us. The Dutch were eyeing our
success in the New World—with all its trade possibilities—with envy
and perhaps some hostility. The French disputed our claims to Canada in
North Virginia. Those up in Plymouth, also in Virginia but not as far north
as the French, had tried to keep us from the fishing grounds we'd used since
many years before their founding.

And now we confronted some new enemy from within and much closer
by: the Catholic Marylanders. It would be this group which would cause us
the harshest grief of all. The Marylanders would be part of the day Will would
turn king's prisoner.

Our people were here and had been here, and we won Virginia for
England upon the deaths of many of our own. This claim we wouldn't give
over easily, especially if we felt it unjust.

Our governor and Lord Baltimore seemed to be great friends, and so
Sir John sided with the Maryland trespassers against us. That was just one of
many reasons the colonists in Virginia decided they'd had enough of Harvey.

Councilor Richard Stephens learned that no one disagrees with our little
emperor, Sir John Harvey. Stephens learned it when he received a mouthful

of broken teeth from the cudgel that Sir John Harvey swung at his face.

"I told you never to speak back to me!" Harvey had said as he delivered the blow to one of the dozen highest men in his government.

The blow had left Stephens staggering and the other councilors enraged at Harvey's lack of respect, at his violence.

"That is most improper!" Sam Mathews groused to Sir John when he heard about it.

Sir John shrugged. "Your friend Stephens spoke ill words to me, his governor. *The king's substitute.*" His tone was haughty, self-important. "Besides," he said with a grin, "we were not *in* council when I knocked out the teeth."

Milder councilors, like Will, were losing all patience with the man who seemed to favor the Marylanders over the Virginians, whose temper was terrifying, whose self-interest and greed made even old Governor Argall look generous.

Others in Virginia were taking notice, too, particularly those in the General Assembly.

Will explained their frustration to me.

"Members of the General Assembly are angry about letters they wrote, intended for the king and lords of the Privy Council." Will looked weary. "Sir John has held the letters here, refusing to send them. The General Assembly has learned about his treachery. They feel this to be an attempt to override the colonists' will. These letters—two letters—are causing a big embroilment."

"Sir John believes the colonists dislike him because they think he wishes to give our Point Comfort fort to the Catholic Marylanders! A Catholic plot. But no. They hate Sir John for being oppressive, for being violent, for not listening to their concerns, for outrageously high taxes he imposes without any ear to the council. The letters are the spark to a much larger powder keg."

All the councilors and the General Assembly were aware of that law they'd signed the first time Sir John had come around, the one that said only the Assembly could impose taxes.

To protect you from future greedy governors, Sir Francis had said. Indeed! Yet Sir John didn't feel compelled to follow the law.

Members of the General Assembly, elected to listen to the colonists in their settlements, were hearing complaints against the governor daily. Meetings were taking place up and down the river, in secret since they were illegal.

"Trouble in York," Will said one morning.

York was north of the James River and across the forest. The parish bordered what we used to call the Pamunkey River, now named the York River.

"What kind of trouble?" I asked as I laid some hot buttered hominy porridge before him along with fried saltfish. I placed a second plate down for myself and took a seat.

"Ah, wonderful," he said at the sight of the meal.

Will took a bite and then said, "You must keep this to yourself, Joan. Tell no one."

I nodded. Without Tempie, I usually kept my secrets close, although I trusted Isabella and Annie.

"Oh, 'tis another meeting. This meeting is fraught with a little danger as it's near the governor's property on the York, and he has some allies there. Martiau the engineer is in charge of it. Captain Uty sends word that he shall attend himself. He tells me that the settlers of York are as disgruntled as all others." For a councilor to attend such a meeting was dangerous business, abetting those attending illegally.

Sam Mathews had held some meetings at Newport News as well. This had now reached the level of mutiny.

The councilors seethed as Harvey treated them as little more than his footmen, not advisors, as the king had intended.

"All want to thrust out the governor. He's the king's man, and that's not something we can do lightly," Will said. "Thought I might go to this one myself."

"Will, no! You know that if Sir John finds out, he'll be furious," I said in a hushed tone.

"Yes," Will replied simply.

In the end, Will didn't attend, which was a good thing. The governor would be angry enough if he learned of this without having his councilors involved, too.

That night in York, two of Harvey's spies stood with their ear to the door of Mr. Warren's house.

"The governor will wish to know of this seditious meeting!" whispered one to the other. And they set off on horseback to New Towne as the evening turned to night.

The door pounding awoke Sir John from his slumbers.

When he heard of yet another meeting—this one with a location and colonists he could identify—he determined to arrest the leaders.

By morning, Captains English and Martiau and Dr. Pott's brother—all members of the General Assembly—were in chains in the fort's dungeon.

Forgetting English law and our rights as freemen, the governor had decided he'd impose martial law at his whim.

"I shall execute these treasonous men to teach others!" he said. "They will learn by the hangman's noose."

If This Be Treason

April 27, 1635
New Towne, Virginia

Caesar had his Brutus—Charles the first, his Cromwell—and George the third—may profit by their example. If this be treason, make the most of it!
—Patrick Henry, responding mid-speech to cries of
"Treason!" from the Speaker and other members of
the Virginia House of Burgesses, 1765

Will came in with hardly a word, and strain showed itself in every tightened line on his face. He walked to the chamber, sat on the bed, and was pulling off his overshoes.

"Will, what troubles you?" I asked, taking a seat beside him on the bed.

He paused, one shoe on and one off, dropped his head into his hands, and ran fingers through his hair.

Rarely had I ever seen Will look so tortured, and it frightened me. He was a planner, a thinker, a man whose firm belief in God carried him far.

I rested what I hoped was a comforting hand on his arm. He lifted his head and smiled at me, and his eyes gazed deeply into mine. He sighed, shook his head, looked upward. But still I had no idea what was distressing him so.

"Will?"

He drew another deep breath and at last said, "I'm sorry, Joan. Governor Harvey could threaten everything we have. Everything we've worked for. But I stand with Virginia, or I stand against her by remaining silent."

The flutter in my chest had started upon the word *everything* and was still fluttering on, a bird in a cage panicked and unable to free itself. Will was not one to exaggerate, not one to say such strong words lightly. Knowing this, I suspected all might be even worse than he said.

"I have my musketeers at the ready—ready to surround the governor's home, ready to send the man back to England with charges from us, the council."

I gasped, and my mouth hung open awkwardly. Now the little bird was banging itself against the walls of the cage. I thought I might cry.

"Can't someone else do this? Why must it be you?" Even as I said it, I knew the answer.

"Joan, that someone else *is* me," he said. "Most of the other councilors believe that we must depose Harvey—after first offering him one more chance to listen to our counsel. If he will not hear us, will not work with us, the situation calls for military strength."

Will was still the lieutenant governor of James Cittie, still the captain of the Fort, the fort's gunner. All these positions had he held for twelve years. He was the leading military man behind the governor, perhaps in all Virginia. He wielded the power to beckon more men, especially here on the island, than anyone besides the governor himself.

Now Will was suggesting he use that power against the governor—the king's substitute. What if the king sided with Harvey as he was likely to do? Opposing the governor was opposing the king. Overthrowing the governor was overthrowing the king himself. Proving that Harvey had violated the charter was taking a deep risk.

"But, Will, that's ... that's ..."

"High treason," he said mildly. "I know."

Devilish Plots

April 28, 1635
New Towne, Virginia

Gloucester: I pray you all, tell me what they deserve
That do conspire my death with devilish plots ...
    —William Shakespeare, from *Richard III*

We must, indeed, all hang together or, most assuredly, we shall all hang
separately.
    —Attributed to Benjamin Franklin, responding to John
    Hancock's assertion that signing the Declaration of
    Independence must be unanimous

The morning dawned with a touch of chill from the river winds, the sound of crows calling from treetops, the breath of spring winnowing over the fields and roofs.

The council, though, could enjoy none of that. This was to be a day of reckoning, they themselves reckoned.

The men walked uneasily to the governor's home. The midnight arrests and threats to put their fellows to death meant that the governor was effectively now at war with the members of the General Assembly and the council. Some knew of the arrests, and some did not.

Secretary Richard Kemp, the governor's only ally on council, opened the door to each man wordlessly. The gentlemen nodded to Kemp politely but also without speaking, nor did they smile.

One by one, as they entered, the councilors milled about the entrance to the room: Cecily's husband Captain William Farrar, Mr. Menefie, Captain Uty, Captain Mathews, Captain John West, and Dr. Pott.

Will was not among them this day, something that escaped the governor's notice. Not all councilors could sit all meetings, after all.

Sir John's eyes met not one of the assembled council.

He paced the floor of his dining hall, then dropped to a chair with a frown upon his face. "Sit!" he ordered his council without greeting or pleasantries.

The time for niceties was over, it seemed.

Still without words, the men found chairs and pulled them to the table.

The governor looked at each of the men, still frowning. Tension hung from the rafters of the room.

Sir John then drew a paper from his pocket and read it over to himself.

Each councilor lost in his own thoughts.

This won't end well.

Oh, for the days of Sir Francis or Sir George!

The price of a grasping, violent, and arbitrary governor—a price too steep for the colony to afford.

"I am to propound a question to you," the governor announced grandly. "I require every man, in his majesty's name, to deliver his opinion in writing under his own hand. No man to advise or counsel any other, but simply write a direct answer to this question."

The councilors met one another's eyes stealthily. What manner of proceeding was this?

The governor continued. "What do you think they deserve that have tried to persuade the people from their obedience to his majesty's substitute? And to this, I do require you to make your present answer. No man to advise or interrupt with the other."

Brows lifted in surprise about the table. The governor was quoting Mr. Shakespeare's Richard III. Certain it is that every man recognized the passage. The men exchanged incredulous looks at the pomposity before them. Did Sir John consider himself *a king*?

"And I begin with you, Mr. George Menefie."

Small, dark, intelligent, and hardworking, Mr. Menefie nearly jumped when he heard his name. He looked as if he were about to receive a beating from the schoolmaster. Then, reaching for his voice, Mr. Menefie ventured, "I'm but a young lawyer and dare not upon the sudden deliver my opinion."

"That shall be your answer then. Write it under your own hand!" ordered the governor.

"I say, sir, but that is a strong command!" said William Farrar bravely. "I durst not ..."

"In his majesty's name, I command you *not* to speak till your turn!" Sir

John yelled, cutting off William Farrar's speech entirely. Mr. Farrar looked about helplessly.

Now Captain Mathews spoke up. "I conceive this a strange kind of proceeding."

"In his majesty's name, *silence!*"

Mathews would not be so quickly quieted. "There's not precedent for such a command!"

Sir John glowered. "I give you leave to speak further," he said. But before Captain Mathews could do that, the governor launched into a passage from Richard III, the tyrant's speech. As he finished reciting, hand on his chest as if he were on stage, he then began to curse them all.

The men turned to one another in confusion.

This council meeting was strange, Sir John stranger, and meanwhile, men imprisoned in the dungeon might end up hanged by the tyrant before them.

The governor adjourned until the next day, and the men departed quickly to mull their next actions.

Would they be the king's traitors and lose their own skin or stay silent and lose the country?

A Pox upon Maryland

April 28 – 30, 1635
New Towne, Virginia

*They [some Virginia colonists] would rather knock their cattell on the heads
then sell them to Maryland ... This faction I find great cause to suspect is
nourished from England, for this summer came letters to Capt. Mathewes,
who is the patron of disorder ... upon the reading whereof hee threw his hatt
upon the ground, scratching his head, and in a fury, stamping, cryed a pox
upon Maryland.*

—Governor Sir John Harvey, making his case against
colonist Samuel Mathews, 16 December 1634

*Mr. Manifie [Menefie] did absolutely refuse his aide in arresting him [Sir
John Harvey] alleadging reasons that it was not fitt to deale soe with his
Majesty's substitute; hee went not home as hee said, but to the back river
where hee debated with himselfe, desiringe of God to confirme his resolucon
or abolish it, but the losse of the Country sticking in his stomacke at last hee
came, resolved as the rest ...*

—Sir John Zouch's son writing from Virginia to his
father in England, 1635

At the next day's meeting, open hostility had replaced the previous
day's tension.

"What reason do you conceive the country's petition against me?"
Sir John bellowed, anger evident in his coloring.

Calmly, Mr. Menefie said, "The chiefest cause was the detaining of the
letters to his majesty and the lords."

Harvey flew to his feet, now purple with rage. "And do you say so?" he
cried.

Mr. Menefie, refusing to let the governor bait him, replied simply, "Yes."

Now Sir John walked over to the smaller man, who still sat before the table. The governor unexpectedly drew back his fist, striking Mr. Menefie's shoulder as hard as ever he could. Mr. Menefie cried out in pain as his chest flew forward.

"I arrest you on suspicion of treason to his majesty!" The governor's voice echoed through the chamber as this day would echo across the Atlantic soon.

Captain Uty, sitting nearby and furious at the blow to his friend, snapped, "And we the like to you, sir!"

Harvey's rage rose from him as he lunged toward Uty.

Sam Mathews was already on his feet. He grasped the governor from behind, holding him off Uty and Menefie.

"Sir!" shouted Sam Mathews. Mathews was the governor's greatest enemy, but the situation was growing far too volatile. "There's no harm intended against you, save only to acquaint you with the grievances of the inhabitants. And to that end, I desire you to sit down in your chair."

Harvey grabbed for the chair, nearly toppling it, and sat. He glared about the room. Mathews explained the colony's objections to Sir John's behavior and practices. "Their complaints are just, sir. We desire only that they might receive some satisfaction."

"Never!" said the governor nastily. "I say, *never!*"

The time had come.

Dr. Pott moved to the window and waved his hand—a prearranged signal to Will, who waited nearby with his men.

Was Will's heart thundering more than the boots of thirty men marching to the governor's house? Marching right into treason for the leaders of such a tumult.

The men beset the governor in his house, surrounding it and preparing to fire if needed.

Harvey swung his head to see out the window—the fury building outside his home.

Standing at our window where I could just see the governor's house, I gasped and a lethal mix of dizziness and fear pushed me to the floor.

"What's happening, mistress?" cried Phoebe, my young maid servant from Cornwall.

I waved her low. "Down, down!"

She, too, dropped to the floor.

The sound of musketeers approaching the governor's house was terrifying. The rattle of guns, the clattering swords, the *thud-thud-thud* of sixty boots in the dust ...

Governor Sir John Harvey jumped from his chair once more and went to the door. His face had suddenly gone a pasty grey. "What means this? Betrayal? By mine own soldiers! Mine own council?"

Sir John swung around to his assembled council—Mr. Menefie, Captain Mathews, Dr. Pott, Captain Uty, and Captain John West, brother to the late Baron De La Warr.

Standing outside the governor's home, Will threw open the door. He stood, feet planted firmly, hand on his musket, eyes narrowed. Behind him stood his men.

The governor growled, "What is the meaning of this? I am the king's substitute! Handle me, and you handle the king himself!"

Will was unmoving and relented not. Inside his chest, his heart still hammered. The walk to the governor's house might end in a walk to the gallows. But when forced to choose whether to fight for Virginia or not, he'd chosen to fight.

Sam Mathews stood, too, pointing a finger at the governor. "You, sir, are a traitor to the colony of Virginia. Your heart and interests have always been with the Marylanders, the land properly belonging to us."

Now two and three more councilors stood.

Harvey edged himself back into his seat as if he couldn't believe his own men had turned on him.

"Captain Peirce," said Dr. Pott coolly, "Please send some men to release those prisoners, including my brother."

The councilors held Harvey at Menefie's house until they could find a ship to send him home. Once on ship, the captain held Harvey prisoner on it at Point Comfort. Soon enough, the prisoner was bound for England.

The councilors elected John West to be their governor until the king could rule. West would be the third West brother to become governor, the youngest.

The councilors could only hope the king would understand their side of things, that Harvey was hurting his majesty's Virginia colony.

But no one could know how the king might feel about the councilors countermanding his decision of governor and placing one of their own in charge.

The councilors also hoped to make truce with Maryland. Sea battles in the Chesapeake between countrymen were not in anyone's best interests.

* * *

Unknown to the other councilors, but just as they'd feared, things had already gotten bloody with the Marylanders.

It had started when a Maryland ship seized Captain Claiborne's shallop, the *Cockatrice*, crying "illegal trading." Tensions had escalated from there.

Claiborne considered Kent Island rightfully his and part of Virginia, something his fellow councilors knew to be true. King James's much earlier letters patent to Virginia had included Kent Island. King Charles had assured them he ratified all former patents.

Now here was the king, taking this land from Virginia and giving it to a Catholic!

Lord Baltimore's patent stated that any land he claimed must be unsettled.

Captain Claiborne had settled it the year before Lord Baltimore had received his own letters patent, the Virginians said. Go and see the homes and hundred settlers for yourselves!

In the councilors' eyes, Lord Baltimore was now trespassing on their property until further notice from the king, and our governor had encouraged him to do so. By doing so, Harvey had committed treason, the councilors claimed.

Fur trading would be the next successful commodity along with tobacco. That little island, Kent Island, was a critical waypoint to the best Indian fur traders, the Susquehannock. No, the Virginians wouldn't give that island over to those Catholic Marylanders. The king and Lord Baltimore would have to pry it away from them.

As a councilor himself, Captain Claiborne had the men's full support and respect. All the councilors and the General Assembly detested the idea of their Virginia governor siding with Maryland against his own councilor. The other Virginia leaders could only suppose that Harvey hoped to curry favor with the king and Lord Baltimore. His loyalties were only to himself, not to Virginia. That much was clear.

Besides, Captain Claiborne's connections with other councilors ran deep. As Isabella's nephew, Councilor Claiborne rightfully called Councilor Perry "uncle." Claiborne's Uncle Roger Smith, another former councilor, had been Will's former son-in-law, and Jane was now married to one of Captain Claiborne's cousins.

Virginia connections were strong, solid, complicated. And Virginians were loyal to other Virginians if that person deserved their loyalty. Captain Claiborne, they knew, did.

Another Claiborne kinsman had commanded the *Cockatrice*. In the end, the *Cockatrice* had done battle with two large Marylanders.

Now flames rose from the *Cockatrice*, and Smith himself lay dead. A dozen men more were dead or wounded upon the decks.

Come Once Again

May 1635 to February 1636
Mulberry Island, Virginia

*... Capt: Clayborne two days since repayred unto us for redress against
the oppressions of the Marylanders who have slaine three and hurt
others of the Inhabitants of the Ile of Kent. Notwithstanding their
knowledge of his Majesty's late express Letter to command freedome
of Trade ... I doe believe that they would not have committed such
Outrages without Sir John Harvie's instigation however in conformity to
his Majesty's command wee have entreated Capt: Utie and Capt: Peirce
to sayle for Maryland with Instructions and Letters from the governor
and Councell desiring them to desist their violent proceedings promising
them all fayre correspondencie on the behalfe of the Inhabitants of the
Ile of Kent ...*
      —Samuel Mathews, 25 May 1635

Ah, Greensleeves, now farewell, adieu,
To God I pray to prosper thee,
For I am still thy lover true,
Come once again and love me.
      —English folk song

In May, Governor West asked Will and Captain Uty to sail to Maryland
carrying letters and instructions from the governor and council. *Please
desist your violent proceedings, and we shall do likewise. We speak on behalf of the inhabitants
of the Isle of Kent. Let us await his majesty's further pleasure.*

Will returned in June with news that the negotiations had been successful with Lord Baltimore. "We shall not attack you if you do not attack us."
Calvert, the Lord Baltimore, agreed to allow those on Kent Island some

freedom to trade. At least, for now.

Months passed. All was quiet, and no word came from England about Harvey's arrest. I could almost believe that the worst was behind us, trying not to consider how Sir John would present the matter to the king and Privy Council.

I consoled myself that my gardens at Mulberry Island were flourishing. I'd planted a whole new orchard of fig trees here but also considered planting pears and apples, and of course, vines. The land was beautiful and rich, more peaceful than James Town had been.

The councilors went about the business of Virginia and their own plantations. How serene matters felt with a governor we respected, one who worked in harmony with the councilors and not against them.

The harvest came, tobacco ripened. Corn stalks stood like rows of green soldiers in the fields up and down the river.

Will went on about his work as if nothing had happened, but I caught him at times staring into the air. He worried, I thought, but tried to conceal it from me.

At last, in the fall, Will announced he was sailing to England—this time, to determine how things stood with the king.

"And to conduct other business, of course. To sign on new servants as the old ones complete their indenture. You're settled at Mulberry Island, away from the turbulence of James Town," he said to me. "Jane is nearby with grandchildren to keep you occupied. Please don't worry about me. Enjoy the gardening here and the family." His voice was almost begging. He must have guessed my response. "Please, Joan."

"Will, I've sent thee away more times than I can count." Anger was welling within me, anger I knew I might regret if I never saw him again. "I have sent thee away to the Lowlands to fight the Spanish how many times? Sent thee on a separate ship which foundered near Bermuda. Sent thee away to England when we first received our land. Sent thee just recently to Maryland. Sent thee out after the massacre, many times. Sent thee out to fight Indians countless times."

I knew this hurt, but not as much as what I was about to say, and which I said with all the emphasis I could. "One of these days, Will Peirce, when you return, I won't *be* here. *I'll be dead.*"

Will's eyes brimmed with pain. "I'm sorry. Truly, I'm sorry," he said. "This is our livelihood, our living." His shoulders slumped.

A silence between us turned into a ringing in my ears, a ringing that somehow formed an old song with my mother's voice singing it. *Greensleeves.*

> *Alas, my love, you do me wrong,*
> *To cast me off discourteously.*
> *For I have loved you well and long,*
> *Delighting in your company.*

You do me wrong. It had hurt each time my father left my mother for the sea. Was it wrong for him to have left even though he had to do so for his trade? How many times had my mother watched my father's ship hoist sails to catch an offshore wind? How many times had she said farewell to him?

Then the last verse sang itself to me.

> *Ah, Greensleeves, now farewell, adieu,*
> *To God I pray to prosper thee,*
> *For I am still thy lover true,*
> *Come once again and love me.*
> *For I am still thy lover true.*
> *Come once again and love me.*

My mother had never given up hope of my father's return. If she despaired, she never let on to me, the only child remaining at home. She'd shown me a strength I only now was beginning to understand.

Strange how so many years had passed and still she could teach me.

Will broke into my thoughts to say something he never had before. "I promise you, Joan, for all our many years of marriage—near forty—when I return this time, I'll never leave you again. To fight in Virginia, perhaps," he hastened to add. "But I'll never sail away again across the ocean. I believe a man knows when he's pressed the patience of fate too long."

Tears were now in my eyes. "You do promise? An oath before God?"

"I vow an oath before God," he said firmly. I knew that he wanted to add, "Unless ..." But he didn't.

Jane came the day the shallop left for James Town where Will would catch an outgoing ship. Her blue cloak framed bright, earnest eyes.

"Your eyes remind me of your grandfather," I said for no particular reason. Something about all this made me wish my parents were standing nearby, offering advice and love.

And maybe they are.

Jane put her arms around me and whispered, "I'm here, mother. Lean on me now. All will be well in the morrow."

Without words, I nodded and tucked my face into her cloak to hide the tears. Then I turned back for one last look as Will climbed onto the shallop.

I have loved you well and long.

I knew I could not stop him, knew when his duty called he answered it. My mother's long-stilled voice sang on.

Ah, Greensleeves, now farewell, adieu,
To God I pray to prosper thee,
For I am still thy lover true,
Come once again and love me.

To his departing back, I whispered, "God travel with you, Will. Pray our last words are not harsh ones."

Then, "Will!"

Amongst the bustling of the mariners working with the ropes and sails, Will couldn't hear me. He was speaking with the captain on the far side of the ship and pointing upriver toward James Town. Suddenly, Will hearing me became the most important thing in the world.

"Will!"

One of the sailors saw me, left his work, and walked over to Will. Taking him by the arm, the sailor turned him around and pointed him toward me.

Will came over to the side of the foredeck, beaming even if a sad smile.

I waved him back to me. I saw him approach the captain, asking for a moment perhaps. Then Will came back down off the plank.

"I don't want us to part on harsh words. I only ask that you be safe, and 'come once again and love me.' Please, do that."

He gave me a hug, a kiss, and a promise. "As soon as I may."

And then I felt better, for I knew it might be a year before I saw him again. Could I have known? In truth, it would be much more than that.

The Charming Gardeners

February to Early April 1636
Mulberry Island and at Littleton on Archer's Hope Creek, Virginia

*Let us be grateful to people who make us happy; they are the charming
gardeners who make our souls blossom.*
        —Marcel Proust

*At noon, we came to Littleton, where we landed, and where there resided a
great merchant, named Mr. Menifit [Menefie], who kept us to dinner, and
treated us very well. The river is half as wide as before. Here was a garden
of one morgen, full of Provence roses, apple, pear, and cherry trees, the
various fruits of Holland, with different kinds of sweet-smelling herbs, such
as rosemary, sage, marjoram, and thyme. Around the house were plenty of
peach-trees, which were hardly in blossom. I was astonished to see this kind of
tree, which I had never seen before on this coast.*
        —David Peterson DeVries, Dutch traveler, 1633

During the coldest of the winter, while alone, I busied myself with
writing pages for my remembrance book. As memories came to me,
I wrote details and dates as best I could. Then I ordered them, pages
of events from longer ago on top with most recent on the bottom.

One day, I told myself, I might collect them into a notebook, rewriting
while correcting the many errors.

As for the writing itself, I knew not what I was doing, and so I tried not
to dwell on it too much. I need never show it to anyone, I considered. That
helped.

When spring began to warm the air once more, I forsook writing for
gardening, which at least I knew how to do well.

In gardening, I understood that my only task was to plan where the plants might best go. Then I sowed the seeds or cuttings, watered the ground, and pruned as needed. I trusted God for the rest, the creations of blooms and the fullness of the vines and trees and shrubs.

Then the harvest, be they herbs or flowers or fruits, came as fully as God ordained. What withered on the vine, I tried to learn from, seeking to do better next time.

I never did consider that writing might be much the same.

Well, perhaps I did wonder of it once curiously. Then I realized that to be a silly notion.

Enough time had passed that Will's ship ought to have landed in London. It was still too soon to receive a letter, of course. That required a return voyage by some wandering sea captain.

Worries crept to the corners of my mind, try as I might to turn them out. Not worrying was something I was actually working quite hard at. So I tried to think of my gardens and orchards instead. Figs and mulberries and herbs and perhaps trials of new plants.

The fig trees here at Mulberry Island were too young to yield figs yet, but the harvest should be plentiful at the old orchard in New Towne.

When we'd moved to Mulberry Island, Will had let the house to a tenant, a relative of the Harwoods here on Mulberry Island. Harvesting the fig orchard was part of their rent. My orchard there was producing by my estimate four thousand figs a year, two hundred and forty bushels. Will had a store now at New Towne and come fall, one of the goods sold were my figs. The Harwoods kept the store well stocked of these for me.

Come later in the summer, my servants and I would use the excess figs to make more chests of marmalade. And so went another season. As yet, no one else was growing figs, so those who wanted them bought mine.

Once my orchard here at Mulberry Island matured, I expected to have perhaps twelve thousand figs a year to sell.

When the mulberries were ripe—here at Mulberry Island were plenty—I'd make mulberry beer once more and salute Tempie as I drank it.

Tempie had cautioned me about worry, too. *What was it she said?* I asked myself as I tilled a garden near the house. *What will worry gain you? Fight the battle when the battle it is.*

"Fight the battle when the battle it is," I said to myself as if it were the refrain of a hymn. "Thank you, Tempie." I looked around as if I might just see her, peeking around the house. Then I resumed gardening.

Without Will, the days were long, but I determined not to wish my life away awaiting his return. I couldn't change his absence, after all.

My grandchildren were growing up. Little Temp, now called Temperance was a young lady of twenty. Her husband John Brown had died and left her with two children by the time she was seventeen. She had since married a Mr. Cocke. They lived at a plantation he called Malvern Hill, named for his Shropshire home.

Cecily's three children by Mr. Farrar were young yet, her two daughters from her marriage to Sam just reaching marriageable age.

Our son Tom had married and was living on the island, and Jane was content with her husband Francis James, a relative of Roger and Captain Claiborne. Jane and Francis now had a son and a daughter.

Jane's daughter Elizabeth had married a Mr. Milner. The baby Sarah Macock was herself nearly old enough to marry, but Wee Bess had died of a summer ague a few years ago.

And so went the seasons of life, like the seasons of a garden.

A shallop coming downriver from James Town brought me a letter. *Mrs. Joane Peerce at her home at Mulburie Iland*, it read on the outside. I opened it to find a note from Isabella. There would be, she wrote, a council meeting at Mr. Menefie's home Littleton. Isabella's husband, Captain Perry, was a councilman as my Will was.

"We council wives are also meeting there as we used to do when the meetings were at James Town. Please come," I read aloud. "I imagine Captain Farrar and Cecily will be there, too. My husband is now in England like Captain Peirce. So I'll be coming alone, and we can be chamber mates! I'll come on my shallop to pick you up."

My heart leapt. *This is how to be happy. Just be content. All right then, aye!*

I wondered which wives would come? The meeting would take place in two weeks. I packed a small satchel and waited for Isabella to come.

When she did, she brought her son George with her, now grown into a handsome young man. Isabella's siblings had intermarried with the James family, so Jane's husband Francis was George Pace's cousin. Isabella thought George might like to visit with Jane's family here while she went on to Littleton, a little further downriver. Yes, indeed, they did.

Here at Mulberry Island, the younger people would have their own time to socialize. Francis and Jane, George and his gaggle of cousins along with Sarah Macock, were friends and relatives both.

What twisted roots and branches our Virginia tree had. But how big it also grew!

I was so excited to see Isabella again. She came off the shallop and gave me a warm hug. Then she and I both climbed aboard to sail over to Littleton on Archer's Hope Creek.

Now Virginia was truly showing her spring finery. White dogwood blossoms sprinkled through the forests along the river. Cornfields worked and planted. Then I understood something I hadn't before grasped.

I'd held myself to a low standard. I only desired not to worry. Why could I not go further and be full of cheer? Just the idea lifted me up.

Tempie, I thought, would approve.

The shallop came to the landing at Littleton and anchored alongside Mr. Menefie's ship, named for himself and his wife, the *George and Elizabeth*.

Once we were safely tied off, Elizabeth Menefie came down to the wharf to greet Isabella and me.

Already present were Governor John West and his wife Ann. Dr. Pott and Elizabeth were also here. They'd come down from the Potts' plantation, Harrop. Sam Mathews had arrived as well.

Captain and Mary Ann Uty would be coming from Utimaria, the Uty plantation at the mouth of King's Creek in York.

William Farrar's shallop came down carrying word that he was ill. He and Cecily would remain at Jordan's Journey rather than hazarding the river voyage, his man told us. I was disappointed, of course, but glad he was caring for his health.

Tomorrow, the men would hold their council meeting. 'Twas true some anxiety lingered over Harvey's deposing, but each of us silently chose not to mention it.

Mr. Menefie was a gracious host, welcoming us inside for dinner after we strolled through his garden.

His fruit trees were in bloom. "Come in the late summer, and I'll show you Provence roses and serve you peaches!" Mr. Menefie said proudly. As a merchant, Mr. Menefie had prospered well in Virginia. It was heartening to see.

"Mr. Menefie, can we discuss growing peaches sometime?" I asked him.

He leaned in. "Aye, if we can also discuss figs, 'fig lady'!" He grinned, and so did I.

"That's a bargain for me," I replied.

Mr. Menefie's servants laid before us pork and turkey and corn pudding. Then a servant brought out a tray holding crystal glasses filled with perry.

"How lovely," murmured Ann West, turning the glass carefully once the servant had handed her one. It caught the light in sparkles.

"I thank you," Mrs. Menefie replied. "The glassware comes from Sir Robert Mansell's company in London."

As soon as each person had perry, Captain Uty brought out his fiddle. As he rosined the bow and tuned the strings, the captain turned to me. "Mrs. Peirce, I'm greatly glad you've graced our presence even though your rascal husband be in England!"

Far from being the brusque man who had arrested the governor, John Uty was most of the time a boisterous and fun-loving gentleman, the only violinist in the colony.

I laughed. "To tell the truth, I'd rather Will be home. But I'm glad to be here myself, just the same!"

"Tomorrow will be dull council," said Captain Uty good-naturedly. "This evening, let's enjoy some music. 'Turkeylony,' my wife's favorite country dance!"

"Mine, too!" cried Elizabeth Pott enthusiastically.

Captain Uty put the violin up to his chin, and lively strains filled the refreshing night air.

As he played, Mrs. Menefie worked to sing along with Captain Uty:

If ever I marry, I'll marry a maid:
To marry a widow, I'm sore afraid.
For maids they are simple, and never will grudge,
But widows full oft, as they say, know too much!

The old song went on for a few more verses as other cheery voices joined in.

A maid is so modest, she seemeth a rose,
When first it beginneth the bud to unclose;
But a widow full blown, full often deceives,
And the next wind that bloweth shakes down all her leaves.

Then Isabella laughed and said she should bet a pretty farthing any man present would marry a widow if need be—and most here had!

More laughter went up around the table and for a moment, I forgot that Will was so far away, that troubles unresolved were brewing in England. *Forgetting is a kind of gift sometimes,* I thought.

The air was light, the tune merry, the company lively. Another cold winter past and sweet scents of spring filled Littleton.

A raised crystal glass of perry, a salute to the lovely wives, be they once widows or maids, offered gracious Mr. Menefie. The ringing of glasses touching made music as well.

How nice for us all to be together once more, the old Virginia council and wives, most of us Virginians now for many a year, I thought. We truly were the survivors, survivors of so many things.

As the sun set over Littleton, dark shadows lengthened and colored the water of the river.

An Angel Rides in the Whirlwind

Early April 1636
At Littleton, Virginia

We know the Race is not to the swift nor the Battle to the Strong. Do you think an Angel rides in the Whirlwind and directs this Storm?
—1776 letter to Thomas Jefferson from Virginia
statesman John Page, born at Rosewell Plantation a
hundred years after George Menefie owned the land

If there must be trouble, let it be in my day, that my child may have peace.
—Thomas Paine

A shallop not expected tied off at Littleton early the next morning, and someone pounded impatiently on Mr. Menefie's door.

Isabella and I shared an upstairs chamber overnight, and we awoke with the sun. Hearing the knock, she looked from the little window down to the river and said, "I see Merchant Menefie has a guest, perhaps bringing goods to sell. We might have a first look!"

I laughed and felt almost like a young girl. Our good humor from the previous evening hadn't left us. How glad I was to be with friends.

"Ah, Joan!" Isabella feigned severity. "You may laugh but not sing, for you know the proverb, 'Sing before breakfast, cry before night,'" she said with a grin.

"No singing then, as I'd rather keep the mood as 'tis," I responded lightly.

We made our way downstairs, just as the merchant opened the door to see a man he didn't recognize.

We took our seats about the table where several servants were pouring cider for the first meal. The crystal glasses were once more festively on the table.

"Well!" said the man at the door. Bushy brows studied the guests he could see behind Mr. Menefie. "Are the council meeting here?"

Mr. Menefie confirmed that they were. "What can I do for you, then?" asked Mr. Menefie courteously.

The man held out a letter. "From the governor, sir," he said.

"I'm afraid the governor is inside, goodman. It cannot be he who sent the letter," replied Mr. Menefie, bemused.

"No." The stranger's face crinkled into a catlike smile. He shoved the paper into Mr. Menefie's startled hand. "The governor, *Sir John Harvey*, is at James Town. The man inside, Captain West? He's the governor no more."

The stranger turned to leave but not before muttering impudently beneath his breath, "And next'll come his arrest."

Mr. Menefie gasped, then shut his eyes. "See yourself back to your shallop and wait. We'll read the letter and prepare a response for ... for you," he said, trying to keep his voice calm. He couldn't bear to say "Governor Sir John," apparently.

The man grunted assent.

Mr. Menefie's stricken look caused those in the next room to pause their chatter. Every laugh faded. Every smile dropped.

"Well, what's the news?" asked Captain Uty. He had a large piece of cornpone buttered and ready to eat. Seeing the expression on his friend's face, the captain put it back down.

I had a lifted spoonful of milk hominy, which I fumbled back to the bowl with a clatter.

"'Tis a letter addressed to Governor West and the council from ... from Sir John Harvey, who is now at James Town. Our new governor."

I realized that I had stopped breathing.

Ringing silence greeted the sound of Captain West opening the letter. All eyes fastened themselves onto the man we believed—we hoped—still to be governor.

As Captain West looked down the letter, his face went ashen.

He sucked in his breath. "I should not say this before ladies, but it does involve you all, too."

His eyes went around the table. Then he continued, "Sir John is back to be our governor. Indeed, 'tis true." Captain West's voice was tremulous as he began to read aloud. "To the below mentioned: take heed and hear ye. To Captain John West. To Captain Uty for arresting the governor. To Captain Mathews for laying violent hands on the governor. To Captain Peirce, for bringing thirty armed men to James Town to beset the governor. And to Mr.

George Menefie who took possession of the governor's instructions."

Captain West set the paper down. His hands, I saw, were shaking. He continued, "Gentlemen, his majesty commands us to England at once. The next ship outward bound to England will carry us in close quarters as prisoners. We must present ourselves before the Star Chamber for high treason. Sir John has authority to seize all our property as well."

Elizabeth Menefie dropped her crystal glass. It shattered onto the pine, and cider ran below the table and into the cracks.

Dark Enough to See the Stars

Mid-July 1637
At the Court of the Star Chamber, Palace of Westminster, London

This place is called the Star Chamber, at the first all the roofe thereof was
decked with images of starres gilted.
    —John Stow, 1598

When it is dark enough, you can see the stars.
    —Ralph Waldo Emerson

The king had summoned Will to the imposing room, the Court of the Star Chamber, where His Majesty meted out justice without regard to parliament. The Chamber was quickly gaining a reputation as a place of inquisition, of harsh interrogation.

The Crown attorney had already ordered Will to his offices. There the attorney had handed Will a document comprised of thirty-five pages of questions.

So Will had sat, late into the night many nights in a row, trying to answer truthfully, trying not to implicate his friends and fellow councilors. Wondering if his memory were true. Hoping not to offend the king and yet hoping to be fair to his fellows of Virginia. Hoping to be fair to Virginia herself.

The other councilors had come to London as prisoners, all except himself—only because he was already in the country. Now, all were on bail.

Mr. Menefie had come, protesting his innocence. Menefie's treasonous role had been minor compared to the other men, and the court had released him after holding him but two months. One man saved.

But Will, bringing armed soldiers to beset the governor's home? That was much more serious. Taking over the government as Captain West had, or laying violent hands on the governor as Captain Uty and Sam Mathews had? Those acts any court would frown upon, were undoubtedly treasonous.

Will and the other gentlemen had hired their own London attorney, who pledged to plead their cases and to keep the councilors from having to appear in that chamber. *That* chamber.

Yet still the summons had come. And here Will was, about to face the lords and reverend judges and the lord keeper himself. The notorious Star Chamber.

A member of the guard bearing a halberd escorted Will. The guard had Will lightly by the arm, but by the arm nonetheless.

Will was, in fact, a prisoner, accused of high treason. The king might sentence him to feel the rope about his neck, to have horses pull him through the town, drawing and quartering his body into pieces. The king's father had hanged Sir Walter Ralegh for little more than these, the accusations against Will and his fellow councilors.

The two men's heels clicked upon the tile floor and echoed around them.

Will understood that each step brought him nearer to the inquiry. He must explain why he felt he had the right to lead armed men against the king's governor of Virginia.

What right? Did twenty-five years of battling to keep the Virginia colony alive count? Battling threats within, like mutineers, and threats without such as Indians and Spaniards? Trying to keep order when the people had not enough to eat. When their habitations had broken down and illness raged dire. When the hopes of the colonies floundered like a drowning man in the river?

What right, indeed?

His majesty, King Charles, had a reputation for not being decisive, for not heeding parliament. Not unlike Sir John Harvey's own behavior. How would a king with the same attitude understand the damage Sir John was doing to Virginia? A governor who considered himself above the councilors even though the king had appointed the councilors, too.

A legion of inconsistencies.

Click, click, click. The sprawling hallways and chambers showed the antiquity of the buildings. Ornate carvings graced the walls imposingly.

Then there were issues with the Star Chamber trials themselves. Secret accusers causing the court to issue writs based on hearsay and rumor, verdicts not subject to English Common Law.

Archbishop Laud had become infamous for placing spies in churches.

His agents listened to sermons for signs of pastors saying anything against the king or his policies. The past half dozen years, between Laud and the king, the power of the Star Chamber had been growing, its recklessness growing, too.

Witnesses? No witnesses allowed.

Squelching all opposition to the king.

Will would have to take the Star Chamber oath, hand on a Bible, as Uty had described to him.

You shall swear that this is your one act and deed. And to answer all such questions as shall be drawn out of it—what you know or believe concerning yourself or any others.

Would the king take him and the other men from Virginia to Newgate and hold them as close prisoners? That would be a fortunate outcome. *Heads on the bridge. No!*

Click, click, click. The great wooden doors rose before Will.

Sooner than he knew, sooner than he wished, these doors were open. The tiers of Privy Councilors and common-law judges rose before him, eyes bearing down on him.

The great central hall wherein he would stand alone beckoned him, forced itself upon him. He, Captain William Peirce. Captain of the governor's guard, lieutenant governor and commander of James Cittie. Former member of the General Assembly and now councilor. He, Will Peirce, would have to answer the interrogations, hoping that all his work, all his efforts—and mine—had not been in vain.

He, Will Peirce, stepped into the room, where the guard released his arm.

Where eyes bored into him like a cooper's drills.

Where the scent of ancient mahogany and stale tobacco assaulted him ....

He, Will, struggled for reason, struggled for courage, and momentarily looked up—where he saw the stars. The gilded stars engraved into the Chamber's ceiling, the stars which shone golden above him, gazing at him below. And he knew that life was now dark enough, just dark enough, that he must keep his eyes on those golden, terrifying, wondrous stars.

He gasped, breathed as evenly as he could, and awaited the inevitable. One eye, dear God, on those stars.

The Ability To Do
and the Patience To Wait

Late Summer 1638
Mulberry Island, Virginia

Someone has defined genius as intensity of purpose: the ability to do, the patience to wait. Put these together and you have genius and you have achievement.

—Leo J. Muir

Will was in the battle of his life, the battle for his life, too. Gone to England to face the wrath of a furious king, a king who felt betrayed on all sides. King Charles was having trouble with the Irish and with parliament and was, in a word, besieged. On this king's whim and mercies hung Will's fate.

'Til now, everyone said the king held his kingdom through Divine Right. God Himself had bestowed the kingdom upon him. But what if that were wrong? What if rebels could overthrow the king? How would God react to our England? We heard that a revolution might overthrow the king's realm.

Were we secure in Virginia? Now a threat seemed to be coming from England itself!

I tried desperately to keep myself busy after learning that Will and the other councilors were under arrest for high treason. The king could do anything with Will, anything with the other councilors. Anything with all the lands, the entire country.

Everything we held, we held because the king said we did.

Now the council, hand-picked by the king, had risen up against the governor, the king's chosen substitute for himself in Virginia.

The king had also been showing that he favored Maryland in disputes. Might he give all our Virginia lands over to Maryland?

I heard the king was angry and not holding parliament. He seemed to desire unlimited authority. That thought alone was terrifying.

These thoughts kept me awake at night in the long and lonely blackness. Owls screeched outside my window, telling of death as owls always did.

High treason. High treason? My Will? A more honorable man I did not know. Staying busy, it seemed, was easier to say than to do.

Will had written me, assuring me with an assurance he himself didn't feel but tried to pretend he did. I knew he was trying to secure his release. But right now, nothing was certain. Not our lands, not our income or servants, not Virginia itself.

I have testified in the Star Chamber, he'd written. *I have answered every question put to me. Why did I do it? What were my ulterior reasons for doing so? Why did I think I had the right to overthrow his majesty's substitute?*

The Chamber councilors and judges had questioned Will at length. The verdict hung in the air, unknown. Waiting was the only thing he, or I, could do. He had been gone now almost three years.

The king might imprison Will for the rest of his life and I, here, would lose him and everything we'd worked for.

All snuffed like a single candle.

Of course that other penalty for high treason, those ghoulish heads on the bridge. That I could not, would not, think about. At least, as little as I could.

When Will stood up to Harvey, we'd known there would be repercussions. How could there not be? But somehow, when it did happen, it had seemed like nothing more than a dark dream.

Should I take the next ship to England? What would I do there? Could I fight for Will the way Mrs. Pott had fought for her husband? What if I wrote a letter pleading his case? Suppose that made matters worse? Pacing and fretting were not helping me, and I could find no answers except those that might bring more troubles.

A year and a half had gone by with my husband and my friends' husbands still under arrest in England. Only Mr. Menefie had returned. In the meantime, Elizabeth Menefie had died as had Captain Perry. Both now widowed, Mr. Menefie and Isabella had married late last year.

William Farrar had died last year, too, leaving Cecily for the third time a widow at the age of thirty-seven. Cecily had remarried and was keeping herself busy. Like the rest of us, she'd learned to manage lands and estates to protect her children's properties. Cecily had now a daughter by Tom Bailey, two daughters with Sam Jordan, and a daughter and two sons by Mr. Farrar.

We were the survivors—Jane, Cecily, Isabella, Annie, and I. We just carried on and on.

For me, with Will gone, time passed exceeding slow.

In late summer of 1637, I heard from Will that the Privy Council had ordered all the councilors' land and property released. Yet he himself and the other men were not yet free to come home.

We petitioned them to consider what hardships we'd endured to obtain and to work the land. We explained to them, too, that holding our land and goods had created hardships for us and our families overseas. The Privy Council decided that we had behaved ourselves quietly and peaceably, Will had written. For that reason, the Privy Council had agreed to honor the petition. For now. Nothing at all was certain for the months ahead, no verdict rendered.

Tom along with Jane's husband Francis now managed the lands as best as they could. They assured me that no matter what, they would have a place for me in their homes and would use any money earned on tobacco to care for me.

"I appreciate it kindly, I do," I told them. "But I like my own home. I hope to keep it."

The other council wives who were also alone came to see me sometimes, staying for a week or two at a time. I'd go to visit them as well.

We kept up with the news. More European countries were surveying our home in Virginia with an eye to taking pieces from us. This made us resentful for we'd given all to learn how to live here. Now, these foreigners would benefit from our deadly mistakes.

Swedes coming to James Town. *Swedes?* Indeed, a Dutch ship carrying Swedes, the *Kalmar Nyckel*, had come up the James River. Oh, they didn't plan to stay right here, but would instead squat in Virginia on Lord La Warr's river, they said. Well, perhaps they didn't phrase it that way. That was what we said.

Now as Isabella and Tempie had suggested, I was indeed in a position to care for myself. I trusted my son and daughters but still asked if I might look over the accounts. They were happy to let me do so. I would never be as good at this as I knew Tempie had been, no, not ever. But I could at least become involved.

Life and fortune were too chancy here to do otherwise. My friends' words, all those years ago, had been sage, and I now knew it.

Still, at our home in Mulberry Island, I felt like a bird in a cage. I needed a distraction. *I'll go visit my Annie!* I thought one bright September morning.

Laughter in the Diamond Air

Late Summer 1638
Mulberry Island and on Fisher's Creek, Virginia

But Ann Burras, lady's maid, to John Laydon, a laborer
After some six weeks' courtship—a full wedding
When the leaves were turning and the wild air sweet ...
    —Stephen Vincent Benet

A laughter in the diamond air, a music in the trembling grass;
And one by one the words of light as joydrops through my being pass:
"I am the sunlight in the heart, the silver moon-glow in the mind;
My laughter runs and ripples through the wavy tresses of the wind."
    —A. E. Russell

D raper, who captained Will's bark, was down by the tobacco barn.
        "Captain Draper, would you ferry me downriver, just across the
Warwick River to the Laydons'?"

He nodded and tapped his cap. "Of course, missus."

I needed to be away from the island, away from the empty house. Annie,
I knew, would welcome me with warm arms and a refreshing cup of beer.

She did.

"I'm sorry I didn't write ... I ...," I began.

"Nonsense, dear! Oh, nonsense, sweet Joanie!" she cried as she envel-
oped me in the loving arms of an old friend. Annie was my last surviving
friend from the early days, from the Starving Time, the days of Smith and
Percy and De La Warr. Isabella had come just after that.

"Come in, come, come!" she cried. "Ain't you a sight? Jack! Come on in
here. Sit, sit!"

Jack came out from a back chamber, wiping his hands upon his jerkin. "Good day, Mistress Joan. How be you?"

"Fine, fine!" I tried to sound bright, but then the words stuck in my mouth and my voice choked.

Annie's eyes clouded. "Oh, dearie, welladay! Tell me your troubles. I got a good listenin' ear," She said warmly. "It's Will, ain't it?"

I nodded. Of course, she knew of the arrest.

I poured out my story—the loneliness, the fear, the waiting for a letter.

"What if ..." I began. "What if ..." And I suddenly burst into tears. I finished in a whisper. "What if he doesn't *come* home? What if he goes to the Tower?" Images of the executed Sir Walter Ralegh flooded into my mind, whether I wanted them to or not.

Annie squeezed my hand. "Oh, dear, 'twon't happen. 'Twon't. I swear it. I swear up ... Well, I got nothing to swear upon, but I swear it still!"

In spite of myself, I smiled. We had a special friendship, she and I. Even with Jack, I felt unusually comfortable. He and I had formed our bond over a baby boy, his son. Dale's whipping had caused Annie to miscarry, and I had tried to help her through that long night. Jack had shown unusual skill in making a tiny coffin for the child. Together with Reverend Whitaker, we'd buried the little stillborn child.

"Joan, what can I do for you?" Jack's eyes were charming and gracious.

My heart warmed. Home is where your friends are, those who will bring you in and love you, no matter what.

I shook my head. "Nothing, Jack. Just thank ye both for the welcome. Means so much," I said, still choking on my words.

A servant girl brought us beer. I felt myself relax as I hadn't since Will left. Annie had managed to make me feel at home and welcome and ... safe.

As the night wore on, Annie and I talked over old times—the times we'd visited Pocahontas at the Reverend Whitaker's parsonage, times when we'd seen savages in the fort, times spent with Tempie and Maria Bucke. We never spoke of the night her baby had died, but then, we didn't need to.

"So many years, Joan," she said, shaking her head. Her home was comfortable. Jack, she said, had well over a thousand acres of land, many servants, was prosperous with his tobacco. He had come only as a carpenter. "He don't spend much time at the lathe these days," she added, grinning. "And did you hear, I'm to be a granny, *again!*"

"You are a young one!" The price of our girls marrying so young, and Annie had been the first, a fourteen-year-old bride. Ginny, Anne's daughter, had married just as young. Not unlike Cecily, Annie had become a grandmother for the first time at thirty. She was, even now, only in her early forties.

"You were just a girl when we met, Annie. Now look at you, friend, a grandmother thrice over," I said to her. A memory of her as a young girl, barely fifteen years old and expecting a baby, flooded back to me. How she'd come into our home the night we arrived and helped us understand what we were facing.

Which reminded me ... I had brought my daybook. "This I wish to tell you, Annie. See, I've been writing these old times down. The folks who remember them are dwindlin'."

Annie's eyes shrouded, chary. "We've lost so many ... many a friend and not a few foes. Not that we wasn't sad to see the foes go, 'course." Her eyes crinkled around the edges just a little, and then she laughed, a light laugh like tinkling bells.

"How I miss living near you!" I said to her.

"As do I."

In the silence, the fire crackled. Neither of us spoke. The memories danced through the room before and between us like ghosts.

Jack, I noticed, had slipped from the room.

"And still we live," I said. "At times, I've felt forgotten, left to travel the world on a lonely road like an old pilgrim. The daybook, see, it makes me feel better. It makes me feel ... useful. And so I write the memories. Wherefore? I know not. Who will ever care what *I* write? So I write for myself and for the trees and the stars. They watch and listen as I write."

"Well, you never know," Annie said in a sacred hush. "You never know. A blessing those words might be to someone someday. Maybe after we're gone and naught but ashes and dust. God might use you yet. He might use ..." She tapped the book. "That."

Then Annie's eyes clouded with pain. "Did you write about my baby, my wee boy, Joan?"

I wasn't sure what to say. Should I memorialize such a painful day? I considered my own son, long dead of plague. *Aye,* I understood at once, *aye.* I would have to hope Annie didn't mind.

I nodded. "Yes, lovey. I've written about him and about Jack's pine coffin and the pastor's prayers upon the child. I did remember. I *do* remember. In fact, I shall never forget." *Pray, God, is it well if it makes her so sad?*

She dropped her eyes, now speckled with tears. "Good," she whispered. And smiled. "It makes me happy that you remember him."

Annie tapped her foot as the fire kept us company. "Being here, though,

- 486 -CONNIE LAPALLO

Joan? Wouldn't trade it. Nay, not a whit would I trade."

"No?"

"Oh, some things could've been *easier*, sure. But Jack and me, we've made ourselves a good life here. My girls have made me proud. I'm going to have to get my littlest granddaughter over here in the morning. Did you know she can play the tambourine?"

"Like Maggie!" I cried with delight. "Oh, please do."

"And she can sing ... Wait 'til you hear her sing 'Barbara Allen.'"

For some reason, that thought made me laugh and cry at the same time.

I stayed for five days, and Annie and I never ran out of conversation. Even though I saw her less than I wished to, it always seemed as though we'd never been apart. Besides, we had so much news to catch up on.

"The good Lord blessed us, Joan. How many have lost husbands and wives? But we haven't, even being here all these years."

"True," I said. Then a sinking feeling came to me that I pushed away. Will wasn't home yet.

Finally, I reluctantly said I must take my leave, that the island called me home. I'd have to catch a ship going upriver.

"Well, make sure it has a mite of cargo room," Jack said slyly. "Come outside."

He walked me around to a small outbuilding on his property, where he did his carpentry, I saw. In the back stood a most unusual piece, about the height of a table and several feet wide.

"For you, a writing desk."

I gasped. "Jack, no! Your hard work, your time."

"I remember when you sat up all night with my Annie. After the baby," he mumbled. "'Tis my sorrow I've never thanked you properly. Hearing you tell about your daybook made me think you might need a writing desk."

"It's lovely, just lovely," I said shyly. "But having a writing desk gives my writing an importance it lacks." Still, I felt a thrill run through me. "Imagine, my own writing desk!" I said. It was oak, very solid and simple, yet elegant in a strange way.

Jack explained that he'd had a large oak tree recently fallen. This desk had a pedestal which appeared to be solid oak, with short, sturdy, slightly turned legs to support it. The top slanted for writing and also lifted to hold a pen and daybook in a shallow well inside. He showed me how he had crafted its rather surprising construction.

In the end, I was elated, touched, and charmed all at once.

The time spent there had allowed me to forget, at least for a while, that Will remained the king's prisoner.

* * *

As we sat in Annie's warm little home, enjoying our time, how little we understood the changes going on in the larger world across the ocean.

Once upon a time, yes, only nine years before, I'd pitied a market woman on the London streets. Under my urging, we'd bought her apples and Will had even stealthily paid her more for them. I remembered her still. I remembered her eyes and her song, which reminded me of Maggie.

Something had drawn me to her, to desire to help her. I hadn't known why then and still didn't know now. Unless it were that I'd seen in her eyes the same desperation I'd felt as a poor and ragged mother upon an island in a faraway land, a hungry little girl at my side.

What I did know was that the women who peddled all the day had children to feed at home, would work into the night to mend clothing so to be on the streets in the new morn. Some, like the codlin seller, brought their little ones along perforce. These women, the poor and the dirty, who hawked their wares 'til their feet bled, who bandaged their feet to cover the weeping wounds, who wearily carted that which they could not sell back to their hovels. These women ... Who noticed them? What mattered their lives?

Buying an apple to help someone is such a small thing that it cannot matter. Can it?

All the world spins on good done in secret, mysterious old Grace had said before she died. Almost thirty years had passed, but I could still see her bony, extended finger drawing a circle in the air.

Maybe to God there are no small things; maybe such things do cause the world to spin, just as Grace had said. And so perhaps God does take notice—He *must* notice—and in the irony of His humor, He brings it yet around. *Spinning the world.*

I cannot know and do not know. And yet I could never have imagined that somewhere in a church in Scotland, an old peddler woman would soon start something that would reach into the chambers of his majesty's London palace. Something that would even affect Will as he waited for prison or for release.

One little peddler woman. What mattered she?

All would soon find out.

What Stars Give Light

Christmas 1638
Mulberry Island, Virginia

Hope can disperse the thickest clouds of night,
That fear hath overspread the soul withal,
And make the darkest shadows shine as bright,
As the sunbeams spread on a silver wall.
   —George Herbert

Who are exiles? As for me
Where beneath the diamond dome
Lies the light on hill or tree,
There my palace is and home ....

Captive? See what stars give light
In the hidden heart of clay:
At their radiance dark and bright
Fades the dreamy king of day ....
   —A. E. Russell

Can a hungry stranger get a spoonful of pottage?"

The words startled me, and I thought I might be having a day-dream. The voice sounded just like Will.

Turning in my chair, I saw him in the doorway. Tall but too lean, his time in prison and weight of treason exacting its toll on him. He had a satchel slung over his shoulder, his trunks and chests undoubtedly still on board ship until the daylight. Many lines drawn in his face since he'd crossed the sea back to England.

He dropped the satchel to the floor and spread his arms. I fell into them, and relief flooded me like a great river after a too hard rain.

"You're home! You didn't write me. I did not know ..."

He laughed. "Oh, Joan, love, when they released me, I sent you not a letter. I sent you me instead."

The sound of his laughter, the genuine relief brightening his face, made me swoon. How quickly things changed in Virginia!

He held me wordlessly for what seemed a long time until at last I pulled back and asked, "So is it over? Is it all over? Are you free now and forever? What about our land and servants ... all we have worked for? Is the king still angry, is Sir John ..." I was rambling, and Will placed a finger gently on my lips.

"Easy, my darling wife, we have time, all the time we need, to talk.

I drew a long deep breath. "Can it be that our long, dark night is over?" My voice shook.

"It may not be over, but only over for now. Of course, Sir John remains governor, for how long, I know not."

He was right. Sir John had been serving as governor for ten years now, a very long term. Our governors usually only served three years. As long as Sir John was the leader, he would keep Virginia his empire and fill its council with men who would tell him, *aye, aye, aye, sir!*

"And the others? Captain Uty, Captain Mathews, Captain West ...?"

"All home with me."

I sighed, deep and long, the kind of sigh that fills your lungs with air and your body with hope, the kind that says, *everything will be all right. Worry not!*

"If the king summons me back, I must go at any time before the Star Chamber again. Sir John has loud, loyal friends like the poet's son, Mr. Donne, at court. But for now, I'm home."

And then Will sat in a chair and drew me onto his lap. We sat that way for a long time until I realized he must be famished.

"I'll fetch you a dram and a bowl of venison and potato pottage, some corn pone and beans. Tomorrow, we'll butcher a beef as a special meal. But I must hear what happened!" I cried at last impatiently.

Will sat at the end of the table and chuckled. Long, low, and slow; at once gentle and merry. He'd filled his pipe and drew it in as if he had never tasted aught before. And then he shook his head. "The king is busy in Scotland. He's had little time to be concerned about our band of mutineers. I believe he'd like the support of our planters here in Virginia."

With a crinkled brow, I placed the bowl in front of him. I did not understand. "Why is that amusing to you?"

He reached out and touched my arm. Then pointed to a little folding stool by the fire. "Because I owe my release to a stool such as that."

This conversation was so unlike Will that I thought perhaps he'd become ill on board ship. I raised my eyebrows. "Did an ague strike you at sea?"

He chuckled again. "No, Joan. It happened just as I said. The king has lost his sense of how to rule his people, so he orders his subjects about and ignores parliament. So his majesty decreed that all churches must use the *Book of Common Prayer*—all churches. That includes the Puritans and Calvinists, who would never touch such a book, believing it to be too Catholic, too ceremonial."

I nodded and then, realizing his pottage was growing cold, I whispered, "Eat, eat."

Will filled his spoon with the steaming meal and savored it. "In England, they have no idea how large and tasty our raccoons and 'possums and beavers are. And best of all, venison!"

"And ... a stool? What of it?" My curiosity was getting the better of me, and at once, I felt like a child listening to my father's strange tales from other lands.

"As I heard it in London, the strife began outside of the great St. Giles church in Edinburgh. This is the church where Presbyterianism was founded," he added. "There a little woman named Janet Geddes has a stall and sells cabbages each day. Jenny, the townsfolk call her, is well known about Edinburgh as her husband is a deacon in the church and her face a familiar one at market. One Sunday in July, the Dean of all of Edinburgh entered St. Giles to an unruly congregation. The women sat on stools to the right while the men sat in the pews as is their tradition. All were aware that their service had been changed by order of King Charles. The good dean prepared to preach as the king had ordered him to. So he pulled out the Anglican prayer book. 'Let us read our Collect,' he announced. Well, Presbyterians do no such thing. And from the back, the little market woman named Jenny stood up and threw her stool at him!"

I gasped. "At the preacher?"

"At her preacher. And as she threw it, she cried out, '*De'il gie you colic, the wame o' ye, fause thief. Dare ye say Mass in my lug?*'"

Will was using his best Scottish brogue. Which wasn't too good. Now he had me laughing. I countered, "I take it that meant, 'Put the *Book of Common Prayer* away, you dolt! *We are Presbyterians.*'"

"Near enough! It means, 'Devil give you colic in your stomach, false thief! Dare you say the Mass in *my* ear?' At that, the whole of the church began throwing stools and books, some even sticks and stones—whate'er was near at hand. One man who seemed too eager threw a Bible at the pastor, which knocked him out to the floor."

"They say, 'A little pot is soon hot.' I suppose that is so," I said, unsure whether to be horrified or amused. "Jenny Geddes sounds like a little pot, sure. But, Will, one little cathedral in the south of Scotland, albeit the capital. What matters it?"

"It matters much, Joan. After the service, riots began in the streets of Edinburgh and then spread to other parts of Scotland. Soon enough, the king had a full Scottish insurrection on his hands."

"All because of Mistress Geddes, an old peddler woman?" I said, amazed.

"Indeed. And thanks to her, the king is otherwise occupied. He received my petition and allowed me to come home." Will sobered and then added, "War, Joan. It looks very much to me like Scotland is but the beginning of a larger Civil War, with the king foisting Anglicism onto those who want it not. The Puritans side with the Presbyterians. The Catholics lurk, always hoping England will return to the Pope. And then all the parliamentarians are angry that his majesty disregards their motions. The Londoners support parliament; the loyal West Country supports the king. And the powder 'neath the keg ..." He pointed again. "A stool."

"Oh, fie, Will! And which side shall you support? The king or the parliament?"

Will's eyes met mine directly. "Whichever side supports *Virginia* most. This is our country."

I squeezed his hand. "I'm glad you're home. Thankful. To Mrs. Jenny Geddes or the king, whoever I should thank!"

Will smiled appreciatively. He continued to eat his pottage. "Corn pone and beans. I've missed our Virginia fare, Joan. I have missed Virginia. And most of all, I've missed you. Oh!"

Suddenly, a memory seemed to come to him. He stood and went to his satchel. From it, he pulled a small book of prayers and poems. "Reverend Herbert gave these to Nicholas Ferrar ere he died, and Mr. Ferrar had them printed. 'Tis making the rounds among some of the old Company." This last he said sentimentally. The old Company. Gone, but its first subscribers still planting themselves here in Virginia.

"The good reverend has a way of making the sullen seem bright. I read his book over many times while on board ship. In the end, I felt ... hope. Hope that all would mend. *Hope can disperse the thickest clouds of night,* Mr. Herbert writes. Indeed, night came upon me most hard while I awaited my hearing in the Star Chamber. Somehow, I believe it will all be well. At last."

Will's eyes shown. Gone was the old Indian fighter, the sage councilor, the farmer, trader, and landowner. All I could see in these eyes were the young soldier I had first met in Dorset, who had taken my baby and me into his family, who had brought such earnest belief to this Virginia venture, who had never truly given up hope. Perhaps he'd needed to experience the loss of his beloved Virginny, the loss of all he had striven for, and then to return.

Hope. I said a silent prayer of thanks to the old reverend for putting those words before Will's heart on a long voyage home when he'd needed them most.

All may not have been right with Virginia, or with the many lands we owned, or with our troubled king or governor.

But this night, in this home, on the little river that ran through the great land of Virginia, all was right with those who mattered.

All was well with us.

My Prevayling Enemies

Late November 1639
Mulberry Island, Virginia

*I groan under the oppression of my prevayling enemies [who] have soe far
already proceeded against me as to teare from me my estate by an unusual
way of inviting my creditors to clamor and not so content but I am denyed my
passage for England notwithstanding my many infirmities & weaknesses of
Body ...*

—Sir John Harvey, writing to the king from Point
Comfort, Virginia, 6 May 1640

Still, the sea voyages had been hard on the men, as sea voyages always
are. After a few months, Will recovered the weight he'd lost from his
confinement and the voyages.

When Mr. Menefie sailed to Mulberry Island to discuss their situation,
Isabella was with him. She said her new husband was worried, but she had
managed to get him to eat. "He's trying to put the Harvey business out of his
mind and recover his business. The color has at last returned to his cheeks."

"Same here," I told her conspiratorially.

Isabella continued, "I saw Ann West at James Town, and she's worried
about her husband as well. But the Wests have friends at court, of course.
Captain West is writing letters to encourage them to come forth on the
councilor's behalf."

How has Will gotten tied up into this business and with a baron's son? I wondered.

"Do you know anything about how Captain Uty fares?" I asked her.

"I hear his strength has left him and that Mary Ann is concerned for him."

My heart fell. Friendly Captain Uty. These men had given everything
they had to protect Virginia from Harvey.

I could still see Captain Uty rosining his bow at Littleton, could hear
his cheery words: *Tomorrow will be dull council. This evening, let's enjoy some music.*

- 493 -

'Turkeylony,' my wife's favorite country dance.

By the time the buds were on the mulberry trees, we heard that Captain Uty had died at his home, his fiddle by his bed and treason charges still hanging above him.

It was with great relief, then, that we learned that Sir Francis Wyatt had returned to Virginia as new governor. Will was eager to invite Sir Francis to our home at Mulberry Island.

Relief and joy replaced the fear and frustration we'd experienced under Harvey's two governments. At last, Sir Francis! A man who understood the planters and Virginia. A man who believed in the voice of the people, our General Assembly, and who heeded his councilors.

Will stuck out his hand, a great grin on his face.

"An honor to have you here, sir. Have we not appreciated you? We do so now!" He said.

After being under the government of Sir John for eleven years—with only a slight intermission while Captain John West held the office—we felt the most powerful relief.

I put the best meal I could before our new governor—venison and ham, sweet potatoes, beets, rhubarb, and buttery spoonbread.

"To tell the truth, I missed Virginia meats," Sir Francis said warmly. "No squirrel? No 'possum or raccoon or beaver?"

I laughed. We still used the Indian names for these animals, once strange to us. The meat was hearty indeed. "Next time, surely."

As we ate, the two men exchanged stories and shared news.

Sir Francis was sorry to learn of Captain Uty's death. He was to have been on Sir Francis's council, and Sir Francis said he remembered him fondly.

Then to happier news. Yes, yes, Sir Francis said, his wife was just fine! She hadn't wanted to cross back over the ocean again, understandably. She sent her regards. And Mr. Sandys? Healthy, as well. He'd been living with Sir Francis and Lady Margaret out in Bexley, the Kentish parish where the Wyatts made their home.

"Mr. Sandys was a delight to have living with us," Will said.

"And is a delight for us, too." Sir Francis confided, "My wife is, I think, his favorite relative. And he ours."

The dinner over, Will brought out pipes for the gentlemen to have a smoke. "Mr. Sandys still doesn't care to return here?" Will asked, tamping his tobacco.

"No, Will, I fear not. The pirate adventure hath put quite a damper on any sea travels for Uncle. Such a chilling experience that was."

Will agreed.

Sir Francis went on to tell him how Harvey's many enemies—a list which seemed to grow daily—had managed to oust Harvey as governor at long last. These same men had put forth Sir Francis as governor, and he was delighted to return to Virginia for another term, he said.

"Not as delighted as we are to have you!" I put in.

The fire crackled in the fireplace, and the November wind howled outside. A feeling warmed me that all was yet right with the world.

I marveled at the closeness the two men shared. Had it not been for Sir Francis and Mr. Sandys, Will might never have been a councilor. Then my heart fell. *A councilor who probably must return to answer to the king!* I pushed the thought away hastily.

With pipes lit and tobacco burning, the two men continued to discuss the embroilments of Sir John Harvey.

"He still fights to have you arrested and returned to England," Sir Francis said. "Will, I know you. I know the men of the council. Most of them, anyway. I doubt not that if half a dozen or more of you say he's at fault, then he's indeed at fault."

"What happens to him now?" I asked as I set pumpion and apple pies before the men and joined them at the table.

"Well." Sir Francis drew on the pipe and considered. "He has many debts here, so I understand. As the incoming governor, I'll not allow him to depart Virginia until he pays these off. His debts so great, I expect he'll have to sell off his land and property before he can leave us." Sir Francis gave Will a meaningful look that said, *Since you know we can't trust him to repay the debts, and he'll do more harm than good in England anyway.*

"Thank you, sir. Truly," Will replied. "We have so needed your leadership."

Miracles and Mystery

Late November 1640
Mulberry Island and New Towne, Virginia; and London

[The king] to the governor and Council of Virginia. Requires them by the first shipping to cause John West, Sam. Mathews, Wil. Peirce, and Geo. Menefie, to be sent to England, in safe custody, to answer an information in the Star Chamber at the king's suit.
—Calendar of State Papers, 27 August 1640

And pointed to the stars and to the sea,
And taught him miracles and mystery ...
—Walt Whitman

A year passed.

During the summer, Will went out one day to find his skiff gone and six of his indentured servants gone with it. As well, the men had brazenly raided his guns, powder, shot, and corn, and then stolen away under cover of darkness.

A young servant from Devon told Will of the plot. Christopher Miller, a Dutchman, had planned to make for the Dutch plantation up north. He'd convinced a fellow Dutch servant, a chirurgeon, to come along with him. Four English servants had decided to flee with them. All six broke their indentured agreements. One of our neighbor's African servants also joined the renegades.

The seven men set off down the James River and made it as far as the Elizabeth River. There, a friend of Will's recognized the two Dutchmen as Will's servants. Questioned as to why they were down at the Elizabeth, the men could come up with no good explanation. Will's friend held them and sent a messenger to Will asking what he should do with them. "Hold them there until I can come," Will had replied.

Will and our neighbor then brought the seven men before the General Court, where the court ruled that servants flaunting their indentures could set a dangerous precedent.

The court sentenced the men according to their involvement. Miller, the leader, received the harshest punishments. He would receive thirty stripes and have an "R" for "runaway" branded into his cheek. He must also serve Will in shackles for one year and serve the colony for seven additional years after his indenture expired.

The General Court made it clear that servants must respect their indentures.

Soon, more pressing matters were at hand.

In late November, Sir Francis sent a servant to the homes of the four councilors who had previously been prisoners.

Come at once, please, on the thirtieth of November to my home in James Cittie. A matter of great importance.

As instructed, the men gathered at Sir Francis's home in New Towne to hear the news they'd dreaded.

"I'm sorry to inform you that you must all return to the Star Chamber. Sir John swears never to surrender the fight to imprison you. His allies petition on his behalf. His majesty hereby orders your return to answer an information in the Star Chamber." Sir Francis's eyes showed the sorrow he felt. "I know not what I shall do without you," he said, folding the parchment and laying it upon his table.

The men looked one to another, concern lining their faces.

The first to speak was Sam Mathews, who hated Sir John more than he hated the devil himself. "Bah on that old bag of air!" cried Mathews.

"Can this not be over?" Mr. Menefie said, distress creeping into his voice.

"Is there any way to delay this?" Captain West put in hopefully. Stalling seemed a good strategy. Perhaps.

"I need you here, that much is certain. Let's delay a little while, gentlemen," said Sir Francis.

Will sighed. "But after that, we shall have to go once more." The thought sickened him. "What choice do we have? It will take a miracle to overturn Harvey's suit."

Every man in the room knew he might not escape with his head this time. At best, they might return with pieces of their ears missing, all their property seized. At what point did they truly own what they had worked for *so many years*? When?

The governor and councilors sat, lost in their own dark thoughts. Candles on the table caught wisps of sighs and flickered.

Candles and light. Will's mind grasped for a single bit of flint to light the darkness.

And then it came.

Once, not so many years ago, Sir George had needed a miracle as he lay nearly naked and chained in the bowels of a ship. The knight had seized upon Tempie's long ago Starving Time words: *Joan, you know as well as I do that miracles happen* every day. *If it takes a miracle, a miracle it will be.*

Will had heard this story from Mr. Sandys himself.

Now those same words came rushing at Will. Two starving women had dared to hope and believe in the impossible: the return of their husbands' ship, lost at sea for an incredible ten months.

Maybe sometimes daring to believe was enough. *Fate gives to those who challenge it*, Mr. Sandys had said.

"Gentlemen," Will said suddenly and, inexplicably, brightly. "The saving of the *Sea Venture* was a miracle, was it not? And Sir George and Mr. Sandys received a miracle when they least expected it at the hands of the Turks. You know as well as I do that miracles happen ever day. If it takes a miracle, a miracle it will be! Let us believe that."

Sam Mathews drew a puff of tobacco and said tartly, "Well, Will ..." He paused as if altering the words he had been about to say. "Why not?"

* * *

Unknown to these men, in England, a very unhappy parliament was meeting. A parliament standing at a crossroads with the king himself. Dismayed with the arbitrary orders of a king who ran reckless with authority just as his man Sir John Harvey had. A king who spied on his pastors, who denied prisoners their most basic rights under English Common Law. *Why? Because I said so.* Sir John had modeled his behavior after none other than the king himself.

The king had at last called the elected representatives of parliament, after forbidding it to meet for a dozen years. Just as his majesty had allowed us our General Assembly only hoping it would support the hated tobacco contract, the king had called parliament for his financial needs as well. He needed money to send an army to deal with Scotland, troubles brewing since old Jenny Geddes threw her stool.

By summer, the Long Parliament had made their decision.

"Well," one of the parliamentarians said, shutting his notes for the day. "I think we're in agreement then. Though the court is venerable and once served a noble purpose, of late the king has abused it. So we have no choice but to abolish the ancient Court of the Star Chamber."

A court which had ruled since the late fifteenth century died with a pen stroke. And in an instant, Will was no longer a traitor.

This Miraculous Premonition

Winter 1642 to April 13, 1644
At Fisher's Creek, Virginia

A light like the moon arose about the N. E. point in Boston, and met the former at Nottles Island, and there they closed in one, and then parted, and closed and parted divers times, and so went over the hill in the island and vanished. Sometimes they shot out flames and sometimes sparkles. This was about eight of the clock in the evening, and was seen by many. About the same time a voice was heard upon the water between Boston and Dorchester, calling out in a most dreadful manner, boy, boy, come away, come away.
—Governor John Winthrop's Journal, Massachusetts
Bay Colony, 18 January 1644

Upon the first day of April my wife was washing a bucke[t] of clothes, and of a sudden her clothes were all besprinkled with blood from the first beginning to the rincing of them, at last in such abundance as if an hand should invisibly take handfuls of gore blood and throw it upon the linnen. ... Upon this miraculous premonition and warning from God having some kinde of intimation of some designe of the Indians (though nothing appeared till that day) I provided for defence, and though we were but five men and mistrusted not any villiany towards us before: yet we secured our selves against 20 savages which were three houres that day about my house. Blessed be the name of God.
—Anonymous account, April 1644 in *News from Virginny*

The winter of '42 was the coldest I could ever remember. The snow was very deep, and all our rivers froze into long, winding, white blocks. Some of the boys took flat pieces of board and slid down the solid sloping banks onto the Warwick River.

Will's shallop was frozen right where he'd left it down at the James, and the vessel looked to be staying there for weeks.

Even the Chesapeake Bay was mostly frozen over, and the Indians told us they'd not seen a winter this cold in forty years.

Our cattle died from want of hay, and most of our swine did as well. As they died, we butchered the meat and salted it. At least we were well fed through the cattle and swine's starving winter.

Older and slower now, Will stoked the fire and rattled around the house as if it were much too small for him. He wished he could talk to his men at other lands. He managed to get out to some of the smaller cabins on our property where his servants lived.

He vowed that once this long winter ended, he'd sell some of that property further out.

"I never did understand until now why Sir George started selling off his lands." He sighed. He held up his fingers, crooked now with age, but broad from all the work and soldiering he'd done. "Look at that, Joan. Do your fingers cramp when you write?"

During this bitter winter, with the snow well over our door sill, there was little for me to do. I sat by the fire with a flagon of warm perry and wrote about the things I could remember. I read over much of what I'd already written, pulling the leaves out of daybooks and reordering them by date with the oldest on the top.

Gone was my own arrogance of being a remembrancer, someone, I reckoned, who wrote remembrances. Now the page became an intimate, a friend, and I felt that we shared the past, the page and I. Like my garden, I just let the words sprout and grow. I'd finally learned to do that.

I touched the page with my father's death as if I might be comforting him, as if the cold sea weren't going to swallow him up. Could I but write a different ending.

And I found there something precious between the lines of ink. Something a great book could never give to me.

I found my life on those pages.

In the midst of this bitter February, our new governor had arrived. We were wary at first, having had so much trouble under Governor Harvey. But Governor Sir William Berkeley won us over.

Sir William had attended Oxford. He was a soldier, diplomat, and playwright, a genial man with a talent for compromise. He believed Virginia could have limitless prosperity and planned to begin his own trials with diverse commodities.

He also came bearing news that England was almost certainly going to war with itself—a civil war was coming and soon. The situation between the king and parliament had turned white hot like iron in a forge.

While Sir William was a friend of the king and a royalist at heart, he tried to steer a middle course in Virginia. We in Virginia wished to stay as removed from any more war as we could.

Will came home from his first meeting with the new governor, saying simply, "I like him."

By the time the buds were opening, Annie had invited me to come visit on the other side of the Warwick River. We were enjoying the talk of everything and nothing before the fire, evening giving way to night. Seeing Annie brought back so many memories, and as always, it felt like no time at all had passed.

She was quite good at lace tatting and worked a needle to keep her fingers busy.

She asked if I still enjoyed the desk Jack had built me, and I assured her I did.

"And do ye yet write?" She cocked an eye at me as if verifying that I was telling the truth.

"Oh, aye. Some, that is." I stammered, hoping to downplay my writing.

She pointed a finger at me. "You do that. I can write not, but you can. Write about us. Write about it. All of it, even the sad and wearying parts." She looked back down at her work. "I want someone to remember we were here and how trying it was." She squinted. "My eyes struggle to see the needle anymore, Joan."

I was grateful that she seemed to have forgotten what we'd been talking about, distracted by the low lighting and her tatting.

As for the writing I did, I talked about it to only a few, Annie being one, because I knew that I was a poor storyteller. A poor *woman* storyteller.

In fact, I had all but decided to throw the daybooks onto the fire at some point. *But not yet*, I thought. *Soon, though.*

As the hour was growing late, we found ourselves telling strange tales. True tales, at that.

"I heard me the most astounding story out of a ship from Boston!" Annie announced. "Did ye hear about the lights?" she asked in wonderment.

I shook my head.

"Do ye remember the man supposed to have killed his master down at Kecoughtan?" she asked suddenly. "I forget his name, but he went on Captain Chaddock's ship up to Boston. Chaddock is son of a Bermuda governor and uncle to the Earl of Warwick."

The old earl! Who could forget his piracy scheming with Captain Argall? That had caused the first fractures in the Virginia Company and been the start of Sir George Yeardley's health worries. The earl had angered the Spanish and caused us to be left with the Africans stolen from the Spanish ship. Now Warwick was the hero of the Northern colonies, or so I heard. Did the colonists there know that he liked to have ruined us?

"The old rascal still lives, fie, Annie! The Earl of Warwick. *He* is not an easy one to forget. So Captain Chaddock is the earl's uncle?

"Aye. Chaddock *was* his uncle. This man fleeing on Chaddock's ship caused it to blow up, killing himself, Captain Chaddock, and three others on board," Annie went on.

"A pity." I, for one, was glad my sailing days were over. "I'll take a shallop to your house and to James Town and upriver, but that's as far as this old woman goes!" I said to her.

"Ha!" She laughed. "This old woman will join ye in that. Well, on Chaddock's ship was a man who claimed to be a necromancer! Told 'em he could speak to the dead." Annie's voice dropped to a hush. "After the fire, three men survived to row to shore. They told the townsfolk about the necromancer, which curdled the blood of the townsfolk there just in the hearing of it."

I paused and looked up. "Aye?"

"But that isn't the tale's end. Just a fortnight later, the town seen lights rising up out of the water—" Annie had put her lacework down and now lifted her arms over her head. "Sometimes sparkling and sometimes flaming! And then it become the shape of a man. They say 'tis the old conjurer rising up from the water. And many saw it all at once. Two days later, the lights come up again from a point of land in the harbor. And they heard a voice over all the water, saying, *Boy, boy, come away!* And listen to this, they found all the other bodies, whether they died by fire or drowning. But never found the necromancer's body! I think the devil took him."

She dropped her voice, and the fire shadows danced in the corners of the room.

"Aye," I said to Annie. "Strange things are happening in Virginia as well, over the other side of the river. Did you hear about the goodwife, I know not her name, who saw blood in her laundry?"

"No." Annie breathed the word, and her eyes widened. She leaned in expectantly.

"Goodwife was washing a bucket of clothes when suddenly her clothes were besprinkled with blood. From the time she began to wash them until she rinsed them. More and more blood she found like some invisible hand was throwing gore blood onto the clothes. She called to her husband to come and see the linen in the washing tub. He himself lifted a gob of blood as big as the end of his finger. Yet when he stirred it in his hand, it didn't stain his fingers or the linen."

Annie's mouth was agape. "And what means all these frightful things, do you reckon, Joan?"

I shrugged. "Mr. Sandys liked to quote from Mr. Shakespeare's plays. 'There are more things in heaven and earth than are dreamt of in your philosophy.'"

"More indeed!" Annie whispered.

The goodman on the other side of the river believed God had warned him that the Indians were about to commit some treachery. Despite there being peace with the Indians, he secured his home against attack.

The sound of ordnance firing in the river made us forget our gossip's talk.

The king's war with parliament had made its way to the very banks of Mulberry Island.

The Clash of Resounding Arms

April 13, 1644
On Fisher's Creek, Virginia

Gentlemen may cry, Peace, Peace—but there is no peace. The war is actually begun! The next gale that sweeps from the north will bring to our ears the clash of resounding arms.
> —Patrick Henry, 1775, at St. John's Church in the old Henrico parish where Rev. Alexander Whitaker had baptized Pocahontas

The blasts sounded as if they were coming from the mouth of the Warwick River.

Were these warning shots? Had the Spanish come? The French or Dutch? Could these ships be pirates?

Annie and I hastened over to the riverbank where we could see what was happening. The Warwick River divided Mulberry Island from the banks where I now stood, so this ordnance fire—whatever its cause—was occurring between our two homes.

What we witnessed was the English Civil War, come right to our own little river.

We saw three English ships, two larger ones pursuing a smaller one.

The smaller ship flew the royal standard flag. We counted six guns on one side, so we reckoned there to be twelve in all. This ship, we discovered later, came from Bristol in the loyal West Country.

The larger London ships fought for parliament, the so-called Roundheads, and flew a new English flag we'd never seen before.

Having less draft, the smaller loyalist ship was trying to use the Warwick River for escape, a river too shallow for the larger ships.

Boom! Boom! The parliament ships still had their guns trained on the small ship, even though they could not give chase. Red smoke and fire and the smell of gunpowder filled the air.

"Welladay, Joan! We don't need no more war here. We don't." Annie's voice was almost a wail.

We later learned that one of Will's friends had been killed on the Bristol ship, having only gone on board to purchase goods. This didn't endear us to the parliament's cause in Virginia.

Since Governor Sir William Berkeley's sympathies were wholly with his friend the king, he was a confirmed cavalier. But he also wished to keep Virginia as independent as possible of the war.

The New England colony had sent some Puritan preachers down to save our sinful colony. At first, we welcomed them, but then Sir William thought that might just turn Virginia on its ear. After all, Puritans backed parliament; Anglicans in Virginia backed the king.

We did have Puritans here. The General Assembly had asked them to worship quietly, hoping not to bring the warfare here to Virginia. But, here it was—come to us.

In Virginia, we had little time to consider the Civil War; within days we would enter a war of our own. A war that, as we later learned, eleven London warships sporting twenty guns each didn't stay to help us fight. They fled Point Comfort at first word of our other war.

All these London parliament ships were under the new lord high admiral, fighter for parliament's side, the Earl of Warwick.

Our old friend, the earl, was back. As before, he turned his guns on us.

Old Soldiers

April 19, 1644
Mulberry Island and James Town, Virginia

Is not old wine wholesomest, old pippins toothsomest, old wood burns brightest, old linen wash whitest? Old soldiers, sweetheart, are surest, and old lovers are soundest.
—John Webster

Six days passed after the ships' confrontation in the river. I'd hurried home as soon as the battle ended.

I'd almost forgotten about these strange incidents—the river battle, the mysterious Bay Colony voice, and laundry blood—when I heard a trumpet blast coming from a shallop.

Will stuck his head out the door, knowing the sound of alarm. "Now what?" he muttered. His hair and beard, neatly trimmed, were now well-salted grey and a little old fashioned in style. Yet he still moved deftly, grabbing his musket and launching himself to the doorway.

"I hope we'll have no more of the English warring in our rivers!" he said, more to himself than to me. "We're Virginians. What care we for such civil battles? For we have our own battles and challenges, this much is true." He paused to look at me. "If we have ships from diverse parts of England continuing to fire on one another here, we have a great trouble. The council will meet soon to discuss our actions. But what matter causes alarm now? Another river fight?"

I stood and watched and wondered when, if ever, my husband would rest from the many wars.

"Will!" I called. "You're not as able to fight as you once were."

But he'd made his way down to the shallop, and my words were lost on the wind.

Will soon returned after hailing the shallop from his skiff. He told me that he'd be leaving on the shallop with Captain Mathews over to a hastily called council meeting. His eyes were weary, his face drawn.

"The Indians have attacked up and down river, mostly to the south. Yesterday, we had a second massacre," he said breathlessly. "We know not yet how many lives were lost. I may have to lead an expedition, but first I'll alert the other settlers here on the island and have men posted to secure the edges of our home site."

I dropped to a chair. "Oh, fie, Will, fie." *Another massacre?* We'd had a truce for twelve years with the natives. *A new war? Another one?*

Another Indian war and Will off fighting it at his age, and my age, I could not bear. I was now in my mid-sixties and had been watching my husbands— first Tom, then Will—go off to war for nearly half a century.

"I am far too old for this nonsense anymore," I said to the table and the fireplace.

Will and I were among the last of the early settlers. Because of this, the Grand Assembly had granted us certain privileges, among them that Will no longer needed to serve in the wars.

But for Will, his heart and his sense of duty would never let him rest.

Should I have told him not to go fight? Should I have reminded him that his old arrow wound bothers him more than it used to and his knees creaked when he arose from the chair? Should I have said to him that a slow soldier was often a dead one?

No, I knew it would not have made any difference.

"Will!" I called out the door, and this time he heard me and turned back.

"Take me with you. I'd rather be with you at James Cittie than here."

He nodded apologetically. "I should have thought of that."

When the shallop dropped anchor at the James Town wharf, we learned more of what had happened.

Sir Francis had been a young governor when the first massacre occurred. This time, young Sir William would have to confront one.

For many years, we'd believed the Indian war chief Opechancanough to be dead from poisoned wine. The old chief had surely drunk some; Captain Tucker had seen it himself and had sworn the acting chief died right then, twenty years before.

But Opechancanough hadn't died that day. Instead, the king had taken himself to some remote Indian town and had recovered. Recovered from a lethal poison? This man, whom the Indians claimed was a hundred years old, was astounding. His brother Opitchapam had died a dozen years before, and Opechancanough had finally inherited the title of *werowance*.

It seems that the old king had come through the wars following the massacre, ended for a dozen years now. But the old Indian had not given up the fight for his nation.

The English were spreading settlements upriver and across the river and over to the York River, too. Homes lay dotted in the forest, the narrow peninsula between the York and James Rivers. This middle land, between these two rivers and still protected by a palisade, we simply called the Middle Plantation.

Now we learned that Opechancanough had observed his land eroding into English hands. The old emperor still lived, still ruled his people, and still hadn't given up. No, not yet.

Will sighed. "I reckon we're both just old soldiers, Joan—Opechancanough and I."

One Lamp

April 19, 1644
Along the James River, Virginia

A ship coming from Virginia certified us of a great massacre lately committed by the natives upon the English there, to the number of 300 at least ... It was very observable that this massacre came upon them soon after they had driven out the godly ministers we had sent to them ...
—Governor John Winthop's Journal, Massachusetts Bay
Colony, 20 May 1644, blaming the Virginia settlers
for the second massacre as the Virginia Company had
blamed them for the first one

One lamp—thy mother's love—amid the stars ...
—Nathaniel Parker Willis

It was the final desperate attempt of an elderly king, Governor Sir William said.

The spring attack occurred on Holy Thursday, which happened to fall on the eighteenth of April this year. But we were so many and so spread afield that the old chief mostly attacked south of the river. The Indians killed five hundred—perhaps six hundred—colonists. Even though this was many more lives than we lost in '22, we were never truly in danger of toppling as we had been then.

Someone had captured and brought to James Town an Indian who confessed what he knew of the attack.

The great *werowance* Opechancanough had seen the fighting among the English, the ships firing in the river. This, he said, would be a good time to run these English out of his land. He was alarmed that the newcomers were building on so much of his land. *Soon we shall have no land left,* the captured native said.

"The Indians saw that we were firing ordnance on each other—they saw the Warwick River battle. They thought, perhaps rightly, that this was the season to drive us from our country for good," Sir William was saying to his council. "We shall, of course, have to lead retaliatory raids. Else, they'll be emboldened to surprise us again. In other words, gentleman, we are once more at war."

The men made plans as to who would lead which raid. The governor and council voted Captain Claiborne commander.

Will watched the proceedings of the council, voted for Captain Claiborne. Claiborne was young, at least to Will, who was now in his mid-sixties. Will had absolute confidence that Captain Claiborne was the right choice.

But, oh, how Will wished he could still do it.

The Indians had crept and hidden near the homes just before dawn and awaited the first person to leave the house to strike and kill. Then they entered the home to kill the rest, burning the house down on leaving.

As with the first massacre, no one expected an Indian attack to occur after this long peace.

Now, stories were beginning to filter back to us.

At the Edloe place, the Indians carried off a son.

Captives were valuable for treaty negotiations, and women and children tended to survive their captivities until ransomed. We'd all learned that from the first massacre.

Out at Old Town Creek in Henrico, Mr. and Mrs. Cookney managed to escape the massacre with a musket pointed out a window.

After Cookney and his wife had run off the Indians, they rushed to their daughter's home next door. To their horror, they saw that Mary and her husband Godfrey hadn't been as fortunate. The Ragsdale farm was in disarray and with the dead scattered about, inside and out of the house.

Flames licked the house and burst from the windows.

"Where is my grandson? My grandson?" Mrs. Cookney shrieked.

John Cookney tried to comfort his wife. Either Mary had been able to hide the infant, little Godfrey, or the Indians had taken him as a captive. The child was only three months old and could not survive long if his mother had hidden him.

After a frantic search, Mr. Cookney found the baby wrapped in a blanket and tucked in a corner of the cellar. Even though Mrs. Cookney couldn't stop crying into the baby's blanket, she knew at least this part of her daughter and son-in-law had survived.

Dr. Woodson had helped Tempie on the *George* long ago when she'd suffered from stomach illness. He'd made a good life for himself in Virginia. He and his wife Sarah had two sons and lived out in Charles Cittie on the old Flowerdieu property—it had changed hands a few times since Tempie had sold it so many years past.

Dawn came to the Woodson home, and Dr. Woodson had set off soon after.

He opened the door with no hint that Indians were lying in wait, hidden behind trees and bushes. A half dozen set upon the doctor, striking his head so swiftly that he still carried the look of confusion as he died.

Mr. Ligon had spent the night at the Woodson home and would have gone with the doctor. But he'd paused to collect his belongings. Those few steps saved Ligon's life.

Seeing the commotion out the door, Ligon slammed the door and dropped the bolt.

"Indians!" he cried.

Sarah grabbed her husband's musket and thrust it to Ligon. She couldn't go see to her husband, even to try to save him. If she ventured out, her children would be orphans, sure.

Sarah heard Ligon fire the musket through the window.

She turned to her sons and thinking as quickly as possible, said first to John, who was almost twelve. "Make yourself small upon the floor in a ball, John! I'll turn the washtub over your head. Stay still, no matter what you hear! Only come out when I tell you to," she whispered. John trembled but obeyed as she turned the tub over him.

Ligon fired the musket again.

"Robert, climb down into this potato pit! Do the same as your brother. Still and silent! Understand?" He was two years younger than his brother but was trying to be brave. Frozen in fear, he still managed to nod.

A third musket blast.

When two Indians tried to climb down the chimney, Sarah grabbed a pot of boiling water and scalded one of them. The second one, she struck over the head with a roasting spit.

In the end, Sarah and Mr. Ligon saved the home and the boys' lives as well as their own, though nothing they could do for Dr. Woodson.

Sarah Woodson had done what so many mothers had done before her, be they Indian or English. Fight for the children with strength they never knew they had.

Our Countrymen in Virginia

Early February to April 6, 1645
Bay Colony, New England

*[The house of the surveyor general of the ammunition] fell on fire in the day
time ... and there being in it seventeen barrels of the country's powder and
many arms, all was suddenly burnt and blown up, to the value of 4 or 500
pounds ... This loss of our powder was the more observable ... in that, at the
court before, they had refused to help our countrymen in Virginia, who had
written to us for some for their defence against the Indians ...*
  —John Winthrop's Journal, Massachusetts Bay Colony,
    6 April 1645

A ship from Virginia anchored at the Bay Colony, a younger colony
than Plymouth. This captain carried a letter from Governor Sir
William Berkeley. *We are desperate for munitions! The Indian war has started
once more,* the letter said. *We have lost five or six hundred settlers to a massacre.*

Governor Dudley studied the letter handed to him by the captain.

"We'll take it to our court, but no, I don't think so, sir. You in Virginia
have created a law against public worship by Puritans. You've turned out
our godly preachers, sent by us in good faith. We believe that your colony is
sinful and that God is punishing you for your darkness and evil ways."

The Virginian standing before the New England governor blinked. He
blinked again. "Are you saying you leave us to our own fates with the Indians?"

"I am, but I'll give you final word after court."

The Virginian returned to ship, taking stock. We'd warned Plymouth
after our first massacre, we'd sent New England the five thousand bushels of
corn when they were starving a few years ago, and now they'd turned us down
in our time of need? Who were the godly men?

The court indeed rejected the Virginians in their plea for help. They also

THE SUN IS BUT A MORNING STAR

turned down their rival colony, Plymouth.

Before the Bay Colony held its next court, the ground shook so furiously, an earthquake seemed to rattle Boston and Cambridge. Fire, smoke billowing, wood planks thrown across town, rags and small items thrown even further away. This was no earthquake; the munitions house had blown up.

John Winthrop, now deputy governor of the Bay Colony, heard the explosion, saw the red sky, heard his china rattle.

When he understood that now no one would have use of those munitions denied the Virginians, Winthrop was left musing. And he wondered who indeed God was punishing?

Perhaps we should have helped our countrymen after all.

The Sun and Moon

August 1646 to February 1647
James Town and Mulberry Island, Virginia

[Opechancanough] continued brave to the last Moment of his Life, and show'd not the least Dejection at his Captivity. He heard one Day a great Noise of the Treading of People about him; upon which he caused his Eye-lids to be lifted up; and finding that a Crowd of People were let in to see him, he call'd in high Indignation for the Governour; who being come, Opechancanouigh scornfully told him, That had it been his Fortune to take Sir William Berkeley Prisoner, he should not meanly have exposed him as a Show to the People.

　　—Robert Beverley, describing events of 1646 fifty
　　years later

... the Emperor Nichotawance came to Sir William Berckley, attended with five petty Kings, to doe Homage, and bring Tribute to King Charles. With his solemne Protestation, that the Sun and Moon should lose their Lights, before he (or his people in that Country) should prove disloyall, but ever to keepe Faith and Allegiance to King Charles.

　　—An observer describes the new Indian emperor's
　　tribute of twenty beaver skins, part of the 1646 treaty.
　　The Mattaponi and Pamunkey tribes still present
　　tributes to the Virginia governor annually

The Indian wars raged on, but this time, we had many more settlers than before and were able to strike down the Indians. Shooting to kill, burning homes, stealing corn—just as we'd done before.

Will set off by ship to the Northern Neck to visit a far group of settlers who had escaped from St. Mary's Cittie. These colonists had crossed the

River of the Patawomecks to come settle a new home they called *Chickacoan* for the tribe there. Although far distant from our other plantations, those in Chickacoan would have to pay their share to support the war.

At last, we had plenty of horses. Will saddled up with his lieutenant and a company of thirty men.

By early in the year, 1646, word came back to Sir William Berkeley that Opechancanough was far from his home and near the headwaters of the River of the Appomattocks.

Governor Sir William went himself with his company on horseback. The Indians here had never seen horses, so these presented a new and powerful way for us to attack them.

Firing and dying, one by one the Indian king and his warriors fell. At last, one of the Indian wives led Sir William to an Indian roundhouse.

And there he was. Sir William had never seen Opechancanough before, but several generations of English had known, respected, trusted, hated, or feared this man, now older than perhaps anyone else in our colony.

Sir William found the emperor, decrepit and with deeply crinkled skin, in one of the Indian homes.

The governor's men captured the old chief and brought him to the gaol at James Town. The soldiers carried Opechancanough on his litter—too weak to stand or walk—and when he wished to see, one of his braves held his eyelids open. Sir William brought a few other natives along with the king.

Incredibly, peace surrounded the old man. He was not upset, not afraid. No one had ever met anyone like him.

After a few days, the emperor heard the tread of feet around him, felt the eyes boring into him.

"Hold open my eyes," he said to one of his warriors in their language. This the warrior did.

Now Opechancanough, unable to stand, turned his head to see the English come to view him. Boys pointed. Women whispered to one another, their gaze never leaving this great Indian. Men narrowed their eyes at him.

In all the years we'd been in Virginia, we'd never captured a high king, neither had one ever come of his own will to our towns—certainly not to James Cittie. Being here was new to Opechancanough and new to the settlers.

This old emperor was famous and strange to us, but he was rightfully affronted and shouted for the governor.

When Governor Sir William came to see all the commotion,

Opechancanough, frail but still fiery, berated the knight. *Had it been my fortune to take you prisoner, I should not meanly have exposed you as a show to my people*, the old chief said with defiance and dignity in his language.

A man fluent in the Indian tongue explained the chief's words. But Sir William already understood by the chief's indignation and gestures to those staring at him.

"You're right, sir," the governor said to the emperor, chastened at his oversight. "I'm sorry, truly." Sir William then ordered the crowd dispersed.

As for Sir William, he wondered. Should he carry the chief to England? This man was so impressive, so ancient. Look at how long the Indians could live! This proved more than anything that Virginia was healthful. The king could beckon ten times more warriors than we had English in the entire country. He could order a large attack to occur at the same hour all across Virginia. This still astounded the English.

But Sir William had no time to decide what to do.

Within a fortnight of his capture, a guard aimed his musket at the old man's back and fired. Soon after, the force, the mystery, the fire that was Opechancanough extinguished.

Despite the two massacres and the many times war had taken Will away, I felt some sorrow for Opechancanough's death.

It seemed even Will did, too. To me privately, he mused, "For all the grief, the many years of fighting and war, I must say Opechancanough was a worthy opponent. He led his warriors well. His power, his authority, even at his incredible age, is something we've never seen before. How many thousands of warriors over the last twenty-five years have drawn their bows at his command?"

From Will, that was high praise.

By autumn, Will no longer had the strength to get on horseback, to roam the riverbanks and battlefields and cornfields.

After a while, his weakness forced him to stop attending council meetings.

But when time for the spring planting came, I found him milling around outside, studying the fields and kicking at the soil. He picked up a few branches and tossed them off. *He loves this land*, I thought. *He loves his home.*

He stood there for a while. The sun dropping lower cast its golden glow onto the man who had never once broken his word to me, who had tried to make up for the hard times.

Then I saw him look up at the sky, over to the forest and to the river beyond, then down at the rich earth of Mulberry Island.

To no one in particular, he nodded.

As I watched him out the window, an old Bible verse came to me.

His lord said unto him, Well done, thou good and faithful servant: thou hast been faithful over a few things, I will make thee ruler over many things: enter thou into the joy of thy lord.

And just four months later, he did.

Under the Morning Star

August 1649
Mulberry Island, Virginia

Not long did we lie on the torn, red field of pain.
We fell, we lay, we slumbered, we took rest,
With the wild nerves quiet at last, and the vexed brain
Cleared of the wingèd nightmares, and the breast
Freed of the heavy dreams of hearts afar.
We rose at last under the morning star.
    —Hermann Hagedorn

Let her alone; why trouble ye her? She hath wrought a good work for Me ...
She hath done what she could ...
    —Mark 14:6-8

I'm awaiting the arrival of a young visitor. Rachel is my kinswoman from over on the Eastern Shore. I know that Rachel's grandmother's mother was a Phippen from Dorset, so perhaps we are cousins. She was born not long after the first ... the first time the Indians rose against us in surprise. I heard Rachel was intelligent and inquisitive.

As for me, I'm glad for the company. A body my age often hears such noises that I wonder if it be the creaking of my bones or the creaking of the rafters?

I've been writing since that voyage with the Yeardley children. Now, here are Argall and Francis returned to Virginia, grown men and married, Argall on the council.

Still when I hear someone say, "Captain Yeardley," my heart does a thud. And then I remember that Sir George is long dead, and they speak of the new and present Captain Yeardley, Francis Yeardley, commander of Accomack on the Eastern Shore.

Or they might mean Captain Argall Yeardley of the council. He and Will were even on the council together before Will died just two years ago.

I wish me that Tempie could see her sons and be proud of the Virginia men they became. I hear that Argall has a child, Rose. I felt a pang when I understood that having a daughter, he chose not to name her after her mother but for the woman who raised him in England.

"It's good, Tempie, it's good," I said to the sky when I heard. "It ... it seems hurtful at first. Until you remember that it means Argall loved Rose. Rose told me herself she'd raise the children as her own, and she must have done so. It doesn't mean he'll forget his mama," I added as if Spirit Tempie needed assurance.

No, living Joan needs reassurance, I realize. Spirit Tempie is quite happy with the world, I say to myself. Spirit Tempie can see everything now, all of this world, all the next. Over the horizon. Under the sea like the whales she wrote about so long ago on ship.

Now I look back over the two books I've filled and realize that I have no idea what I'm doing. I fancied myself a writer, a chronicler, a remembrancer, but the story is large, and who am I to think I can tell it? The last time Elizabeth, Tempie's daughter, came through, I considered the books. Should I give them to her? But I felt embarrassed.

My thoughts now are that while the writing may have been good physick for me, the writing itself is poor. I decided to destroy the two books at the time I write my final will, when my body is giving out on me, when I'm going back.

Yet I have no understanding of when that may be.

I'm nearly seventy, and all in all, I feel right well. I know not how, but I do.

Meanwhile, I love taking a walk from my home to peer downriver, even though it's early, early morn. I squint into the sky, past the mulberry trees and the oaks and ash leaves and branches. I see the morning star still arisen, not yet abed with his brother stars.

Brother stars. I roll my eyes at my own thoughts. *Bah, Joan, you're getting old.*

I do love stars. I've loved stars ever since they came out that night at sea. The night we knew we would survive the unthinkable: a hurricane. *Good Lord.*

Yes, I do love stars.

I still see no ship's mast.

Looking downriver. Looking upriver. Looking to the sea. I've spent almost my whole life doing just that. First for my father, then for Tom Reynolds returning from war in the Lowlands. Then for Will, returning from battles in places not England. Then for Will or Tempie or so many folks, sailing and traveling, while we here just wait.

Where can that ship be? Today is the third, the day the ship from Eastern Shore was coming by. I hope Rachel, my young visitor, comes soon.

No ship.

I wonder if my young visitor will like hearing stories? I should love to tell some. But not too eagerly. For I'll chase her off with stories of wars and starving and my little son Jack, who died. Of Cecily being away from me in Dorset and Tempie's good humor. Of Duppa's stinking beer and the two Georges and the pirates.

I'll scare her away, sure.

Still no ships on the river today.

I walk back to my little home and appreciate Will's thoughtfulness in planning it where it could overlook the water. I surely miss Will and Tempie. Maggie and Isabella, my mother and father, John Rolfe and Sam Jordan, and even old Goody Wright.

I miss 'em all.

The mothering, the friending, the surviving, the travels and travails of many years? One thing I know is I'm at peace.

I've done what I could.

Epilogue:
I Have Loved the Stars Too Fondly

August 1649
Mulberry Island, Virginia

A poor old widow in her weeds,
Sowed her garden with wild-flower seeds,
Not too shallow, and not too deep,
And down came April drip-drip-drip.
Up shone May, like gold, and soon
Green as an arbour grew leafy June.
And now all Summer she sits and sews
Where willow herb, comfrey, bugloss blows,
Teasle and tansy, meadowsweet,
Campion, toadflax, and rough hawksbit,
Brown bee orchid, and Peals of Bells,
Clover, burnet, and thyme she smells,
Like Oberon's meadows her garden is
Drowsy from dawn till dusk with bees.
Weeps she never, but sometimes sighs,
And peeps at her garden with bright brown eyes,
A poor old Widow in her weeds.
          —Walter De La Mare

Though my soul may set in darkness, it will rise in perfect light;
I have loved the stars too fondly to be fearful of the night.
          —Sarah Williams

R achel has been a good listener indeed. I cast her a fond look from the sides of my eyes. She catches it, ah, and returns a smile.

I was born to the water, and to the water I'll die. But a harbor sits safely, never venturing, and here's what my father knew. He knew he had to go to the big water, to the land beyond. And when I asked him to stay, he told me gently, *no*.

The river is like that. It flows down from the hills in the land of the Monacans, through the lands of the Arrohattocs and the Appomattocs, to the Weanocs and Paspahegh. The old lands. The lands of the Indians being now some our lands, some their lands. We share, in a manner of speaking.

Virginia is, for all we know, boundless. Around every bend of the river lies another bend. And we can watch the eagles and peregrines, alight and aloft, flying westward, and we do not know what these birds see—but we wish we could.

We'll always move westward. And in a generation or two, we'll know what lies beyond the next hill and the next. And perhaps one day, we'll see those Western tribes the Powhatans speak of and the deserts they say lie there. The great rock mountains, far to the west. "We have never ourselves been that far, but we talk to warriors of other tribes who speak to warriors of further tribes, who live in the sacred Black Hills. And even they speak to warriors beyond that."

Now I wonder, how do these Indians know so many other Indians and how do they send these messages? I have lived here forty years, and still I cannot fathom all the native ways.

Are the hills truly black? I'll never know, and my children may never know, and my grandchildren may not either—but someday, someone will know.

And as for me now, I expect to rest in the churchyard at Bakers Neck, content to lie near the great and wide river that rolls to the bay. Near the church, an orchard of figs and crab apples, peaches and mulberries, which in the springtime smell so sweetly. The blossoms of the orchard trees dance to the ground, as I, too, will dance to the ground. As Will did, as Tempie and Maggie did, as Sam and John and young Tom Reynolds did so long ago. As my son did, God rest his little soul.

I am not afraid of the dancing downward, spiraling from the tree, for I know that blossoms fall and people fall, and it is all the same. Tempie saw it, too, as she grew near to her passing.

I think, somehow, that as one grows nearer death, God allows a glimpse into the beyond. My mother was wistful, and Tempie was wistful, and now I, too, am wistful.

"Miss Joan, what about it all? The starving and the poverty and the illness? The hard, hard work of creating a colony on the very soil where we sit?" Rachel speaks, and lo, have I near forgotten I was not alone.

I pause and look into the sky as I consider. I am old, and with age should come wisdom, but I do not feel wise. I have, in fact, never felt wise. But wise I must have been and knew it not.

"Now, see," I say slowly, letting the words comprise my rambling thoughts, "I know that I was never alone. Never was I without hope for long. 'Our Seven Hopes,' Tempie and I called them.

"Whenever I felt as if I were drowning in a deep, sunless pool, hope ever arrived in the strangest of ways. Oh, not always at that moment. But it never did fail me in the end. Like a chickadee when we were starving or Will and Sam's tulips after my first husband died. Angelo's herbs when death's shadow stood over me or Tempie's leaf dancing in the river. The soldiers who buried Maggie for us. The mysterious rescue of our two Georges from the pirates, and then Sir George's mercy to Goody Wright. The love between Pocahontas and Annie even after so much war between our people, and the way Tempie nursed little Peleg Bucke after his mother died. How I tried to encourage Jack Laydon when his son died, and then he tried to encourage me in return by building me mine own desk. The old sailor Harrison's kindness to Maggie and me in the hurricane, and Sam turning back to save Will. Cecily standing up to a cruel preacher, and Jane loving those orphan children even despite her own losses ..."

What blessings I've lived! Just as Tempie told me so long ago. *We do have blessings. Count them and see.*

"I've seen miracles light the fearful black darkness. Hope is like a small, silent pinnace. Your ship seems without rudder or sail, and you feel alone. Then you turn a bend, and there you find the brilliant ship to aid you—on it be friends, or family, or God's mercy, even the loving-kindness of strangers or compassion where you should least expect it to be. As the *Tyger* sat, barren of sails and food, and the *Concord* appeared and saved her. 'Tis just like that."

I know that I've never truly been alone. That hope always carried me to the next bend and to the next. And now, here am I. I'm just an old pilgrim, but I'm not unhappy to be old nor to be a pilgrim either. Just like any ancient pilgrim, you must keep walking. Just keep walking. Never give up. God knows your ends and your beginnings, and He shall let you know when the trail ends. Do you see?"

Her eyes light, and she smiles. "I do see. Thank you kindly for sharing."

I came in with the spring, and I hope to depart with the spring, too.

Of course, in autumn comes the harvest. Indian pumpions and Indian squash; all the acorns fall, and some do take root. Maybe I'll go like Tempie, like a leaf which knows God has called it to perish.

The fall, I decide, would also be a fine time to pass on.

The season shall come when I'm not the one planting but the one planted—for I've been an Ancient Planter and my mother, in her way, was an ancient planter. For folks like us, no more comfortable place can be than to be planted next to the tulip bulbs and the buried acorns—the ancestor of the oaks that tower in the forest.

One day, we who came first will prove to be the acorns of a mighty oak of colony. I think we already are. Sometimes, I can almost see it.

"I must write my will in the coming weeks, and on that day, I might burn the books I've written. These contain much of my story, memories I've been writing these many years. I first conceived to write when Mr. Sandys encouraged me, and I determined to do it while outward bound to England with the Yeardley children. The writing is poor. Of this, I'm sure.

"Will said we must tell our stories for posterity. I think posterity will not so much care about an old woman's ramblings. They're not lyrical as Mr. Sandys would compose, no fine history such as Captain Smith wrote. A history? Fie! I'd not know where to begin.

"But my life—that I remember; memories have I many. *Those* I can scribble down. You see," I whisper conspiratorially, "I am the remembrancer. And these days I have more to remember than ever. When my memory seems to fail, I place a little pouch of rosemary upon my writing desk. Rosemary is for remembrance, don't you know?"

My visitor, Rachel, nods. "I'm glad you've written it, Mistress Peirce. I pray you not destroy it, that it survives beyond us both."

If only I could have been a better writer, to more admirably have performed the task before me. I did try, though. Perhaps I was arrogant to think I could capture it all.

Rachel now asks, "Remember you told me about the vision you had in the church? And this," says my young visitor suddenly, "is this what you saw?" She throws her arm and hand outward in a gentle arc. It encompasses the fields at Mulberry Island, the corn, the grove of fig trees, the peaches, the tobacco. The vast forests and the shushing river. And the manor house—a story and a half, plank, elegant, in fact, compared to those first James Town cottages. "All the settlements—the one at Kecoughtan, the plantations spreading west to Fort Royall, way up the Pamunkey. Bristol Parish over on the river of the Appomattock? This is what you saw that day, isn't it?"

"No, child," I say quietly. "This is not it."

She gazes at me, through long lashes, eyes brown and innocent as a doe. "What then?"

"I will not live to see it. *You* may not live to see it, either. But Virginia will spread far and wide one day. This I know. This I feel. This I can tell you because *I've seen it.*"

The sun has risen eagerly in the sky but hasn't yet come close to crossing its peak. It will rise further to warm the day, to cast its light on the fields we can see and those we cannot, the forests in our vision and the forests far north by the Patawomecks. And then farther north still to Northern Virginia called "Newfoundland," where our fishing vessels are hauling in their catches. And also south to the graves of the Roanoke Island settlers, and more southern even than that to the land of old La Florida.

Moving west as the morning wears on, the sun will rise above the Monacan lands and then to the mountains the Indians say are west even of them, the ones Sir William Berkeley says he shall go explore; far, far up the James River.

And to the deserts beyond. The Indians say there are deserts, and greater mountains, and plains, and greater mountains still.

The sun is rising, moving westward 'cross the sky, and not all our blunders nor all our bravado can alter what will be, where the sun will go, where it casts its light this day.

All the land that the eye can see, the sun will shine upon.

Before the sunset, the sun will rest for a moment upon the South Sea—the Pacific. The sun will soothe its broad, expansive water, touching it, caressing it, shining in a gaping triangle, pulling the ocean down to it, sinking below it, further and further, until like a candle at dusk, a snuff of air shall extinguish its last light.

Sable the night at long last. Deep and rich and blue-black.

The darkness should affright me, this I know.

And yet it does not.

I shall never be afraid of the darkness again.

I've learned that every dark night has one star or many stars or a whole colony of stars—even when the clouds do cover them. Never have these stars left me, however much it seemed they did. So how can I be afraid? 'Twas the learning that they were still there that was most difficult.

Stars light our way across a whole ocean, and when you cannot see the stars, brother moon can help guide, does help. The moon, silver like an old grandfather. Kindly, but powerful. Pulling the tides. Sunrise comes, and the morning star is the last to depart.

And then, when the night seems impossibly long, when the blackness engulfs like an old Indian blanket, when the owl's dreadful cries go on and on and on …

Only then, the sun.

How broad the sun's rays—those we can see and those we cannot.

I look up at the rising sun, and say, "My cousin, it will be a long and glorious day, I think, before *this* sun shall set, far away in the South Seas."

Rachel looks at me curiously. "Yes, ma'am. I think so, too."

And taking hands, we rise from the bench, sun to our backs, and together stroll to the manor at Mulberry Island, the island sitting in the James River, the river reaching into the deepest parts of the colony of Virginia. And far, far beyond.

It is so good to be home.

> *Sunset and evening star,*
> *And one clear call for me!*
> *And may there be no moaning of the bar,*
> *When I put out to sea,*
>
> *But such a tide as moving seems asleep,*
> *Too full for sound and foam,*
> *When that which drew from out the boundless deep*
> *Turns again home.*
>
> *Twilight and evening bell,*
> *And after that the dark!*
> *And may there be no sadness of farewell,*
> *When I embark …*
>   —Alfred, Lord Tennyson

Afterword:
With Shells from the River Cover Me

Once in a while a curious weed unknown to me,
Needing a name from my books;
Once in a while a letter from Yeomans.
Out of the mussel-shells gathered along the shore
Sometimes a pearl with a glint like meadow rue ...
I, lover of Nature, beloved for my love of her,
Held such converse afar with the great
Who knew her better than I.
Oh, there is neither lesser nor greater,
Save as we make her greater and win from her keener delight.
With shells from the river cover me, cover me.
I lived in wonder, worshipping earth and heaven.
I have passed on the march eternal of endless life.
        —Edgar Lee Masters

Rachel Finch, Her Owne Remembrance of Miss Joan

I stand in the old cemetery at Bakers Neck Church. The breeze off the river is refreshing. I know that 'tis not the reason Captain Peirce chose Mulberry Island to be his home. He chose it for its military strength and its rich earth. But the breeze is nice too.

I was born in Virginia and have grown up in the heat of its summers. I've run the length of fields and ambled along the blackberry ridges. But for the Peirces, this land was unique and wild, and—after the baptism by so much blood—holy in a way.

Aye, 'tis true. The blood of many an English wife, many a mother, many a child, many a soldier, and many a warrior, mother and Indian child, bathes the land and gives it some feel, something I cannot define.

Miss Joan's stone is before me, cocked just a little but bearing the words I trace with my finger.

MRS. JOAN PEIRCE
WIFFE OF CAPT. WLLM
DYED OCTOBER YE 3ᴿᴰ, 1649
SHE HATH ENDURED MUCH
& HATH REMAINED FAITHFUL.
Thy Sun shall never go down,
Neither shall thy Moon be hid:
For the Lord shall be thine everlasting light,
And the days of thy sorrow shall be ended.
—Isaiah 60:30

Someone has taken shells from the river and placed them lovingly on the grave. They are, I see, mostly mussel shells but also scallop shells. These last, the marks of a pilgrim, as her son Tom had told me. Symbolic of her pilgrimage, the end of her journey and beginning of the next. He knew she had loved cockleshells since the day she parted one in two betwixt Cecily and herself.

I reach down and pick up one of the shells and think about Miss Joan, about what I learned from her.

"Thank you, cousin, for sharing so much with me," I whisper. No one is about to hear, but a chill comes on me.

"The soldiers are fighting for Virginia," I continue.

This past month, above a thousand of our men gathered at James Cittie, making a stand against the English Commonwealth.

Virginia, see, she stands alone.

Barbados has fallen, the last dominion of the king's supporters, next to old Virginia.

But Virginia will not give up unless we, its settlers, can keep our land, can receive protection despite having stood with the deposed king and can trade as we wish with the Dutch and any other country in the world.

We also desire and demand, always and ever, to have our Grand Assembly.

Virginia, see, she thinks for herself.

"True is that, Miss Joan?" I say to the old stone.

"Maryland went right along with the traitors who overthrew the king." I knew Miss Joan's thoughts on the Marylanders! Maryland was part of the reason the king had imprisoned her Will in the '30s. Well, the Maryland governor said he stood by the king, but the council behind him said no. Our governor, our council, our Grand Assembly—they all agree to stand with the king until this day—this day that the English ships shall force us to yield.

We're too small to fight the English, but still and aye, the king should not push us too hard.

Virginia, see, she treasures her independence, her freedom. She has already fought so hard for it, all these years, all the years Miss Joan remembered.

"Fifteen ships from England sent, Miss Joan. But only four made it here in December! Storms at sea destroyed the rest. You know of that!" Contrary winds had foiled the Armada when Miss Joan was a girl, and now, sixty years later, winds were protecting us from invaders again. Invaders from our own home country.

The wind tickles past me.

Yes, she knows.

I'm here on Mulberry Island because Miss Joan's son Tom says that his mother has left me an escritoire, a writing desk. Why me and why this piece, I wondered as I looked it over last evening. I know only that Miss Joan's instructions are that I will appreciate it. Well, I do appreciate the thought, Miss Joan. I do indeed.

Perhaps she wants me to write. She told me that she herself had been writing her stories. Did she destroy them as she said she might? I wonder.

The desk is oak, I believe. It has a tilt top for a Bible, or it can be used for writing. The tilt top opens, and inside are places for papers or pens. It has two drawers and then lovely carved oak beneath it and four turned legs. The piece is Virginia-made, Tom says. At least, he thinks so. So do I.

Last evening, he and I studied the piece.

"You know, I believe your mother told me about this desk. I think Jack Laydon made it for her as a gift." I said.

Tom nodded, his eyes shining. "Ah, could be. The Laydons are good folk. I'm so proud of my mother. You could be right, aye, you could be. I remember that whipping. My mother tried to shield me from it—she would—but I knew. I heard."

He turned to look at the desk, and I ran my hand across its surface. Some such pieces have long, turned legs, very delicate. This one is almost homely and squat, with short, simple legs and a whole, turned piece of oak below the central space. So much oak made it very heavy, Tom said. Solid and sure it was. Jack Laydon the carpenter, the artisan, created it to last the years, 'twas plain to see.

It wasn't pretty, but it was unique.

"I feel I should not take this from your family, Tom. It belongs to you."

Tom demurred. "We have many a marvelous piece my mother has left behind," he assured me. "We—my sisters and I—have treasures here. She left her Geneva Bible, a chest from Dorset, two Chinese wine cups she'd brought from England ..."

"The wine cups!" I cried. "She toasted to your Aunt Tempie during the Starving Time with them. Might I see them?"

"Of course."

He led me into the kitchen where on a shelf sat the two old cups. Each was perhaps two inches high and two across, but delicately featured so that the mouths fanned outward. Each was white with a blue crosshatching traced on it.

"She loved that you listened to her stories for so long, cousin," Tom said to me, with his smile every bit that of his mother. A small man, he hasn't the power his father once had, but what he lacks in size, he makes up for in spirit. Tom ... he is the new and present Captain Peirce. "I'm sorry we have known so little of one another. Cousins on the Phippen side in Dorset, is that right?" he asked. He was, I saw, letting me know that as family, it is fine to ask such things. "Are you a Jordan as well?" He used the ancient French pronunciation, *Jerr-don*.

"Yes. From Dorset," I echoed. "My grandmother's mother was a Phippen, and her brother married a Jordan. And I enjoyed the stories, Tom," I said, almost embarrassed. I still have wondered if Miss Joan minded my curiosity. Perhaps, by this desk, she is telling me that all is well.

You remind me of no one more than myself, she'd said. She, too, had been curious. 'Twas, after all, her curiosity that brought her the old scallop badge.

"Cousin, if I might not be too forward, what of the old pilgrim's badge from her father? The one she always wore?"

Tom looked down. "She took it on her journey, Rachel. She told me once that it had been with her all these years. It must be with her on her pilgrimage. Her final one."

"Oh ..." I felt, once more, that I was delving into personal matters. My cheeks burned. "I'm sorry, Tom. I'm impertinent. Everyone tells me so."

"Nonsense!" Tom was suddenly impassioned. "Someone must ask. You ask because you cared for my mother." His voice softened. "I appreciate that myself." That was when he told me to look upon her grave for the marks of a pilgrim. I hadn't taken his meaning at the time but hesitated to ask.

Silence passed between us for a moment, but I sensed Tom's kindness, his willingness—even eagerness—to talk about his mother. And so I made bold once more.

"She said she'd written some of her memories, Tom. What of them? On my visit, she said she'd decided to burn them. Surely she didn't."

Tom shrugged, a helpless look upon his face. He shook his head. "I know not, cousin. We think perhaps she did destroy them. They were not among her belongings nor anywhere to be found. Perhaps she gave the pages away before she died. No one seems to know their whereabouts or how many papers or notebooks there were. She said little about them, and ..." He flushed. "Well, one always believes there shall be more time to ask on such things."

"So she ... she passed on quickly then?" Was I asking too much? But Tom seemed only to mind about what he perceived as his own failings in the matter.

He sighed. "Aye, but too quickly. One morning, the sun rose like all the other days before it, the many days of my mother's life ... But yon day, when the sun rose, my mother did not. Her servant girl went in after a while to see if all were well." He paused, and his eyes filled with tears. In the light of them, I saw Miss Joan.

Tom gathered himself, and with the courage I had come to recognize in Miss Joan, he said, "Well, cousin, she did pass peacefully in her bed as a woman of her stature should, I suppose. Seemingly, she knew not that death was upon her. She had suffered much in life. She should suffer not in death. I reckon that to be God's thinking, anyway. That, it seems, is only fair." His eyes were still misty yet filled with pride. "I was to visit with her the following week. How sorry I am I did not come sooner," he added.

I nodded sympathetically, words failing me. At last, I said, "None know the day nor hour, sir." *How many tears might we avoid if we did!* I thought. "Your mother suffered, but suffering did not defeat her," I said. "She was like a rose, pruned to become stronger and bloom more. Or perhaps a tulip. I know she loved the Dutch flowers."

Tom smiled, his affection for his mother obvious. "'My father wooed her with tulips twice—once upon their courtship and once upon their return to London. So we unearthed one of the tulip bulbs from around the house, the ones my father had bought, and planted it betwixt her stone and his."

"How sweet," I murmured. "She joins your father, your little infant brother, her parents, and of course, Tempie and Maggie." I blurt these words before I realize they may not be appropriate.

But Tom, every bit his mother, smiled knowingly. "Oh, yes. Aunt Maggie died, of course, before I was born. Still, I heard of her often. Auntie Tempie was close to my mother as e'er a sister. I suppose Maggie was like a sister as well. I owe them, cousin, because I am certain they, Maggie and Tempie, are the reason she survived to birth me."

I nodded. "Miss Joan certainly thought so." She had outlived Tempie by more than twenty years, Miss Maggie by nearly forty. "She lived long enough to honor their memories and to pass these onward in the telling, to the future, to the young, such as me. So I suppose even if she destroyed her writing, she still has shared these stories to those like me."

Now, standing before her grave, remembering my visit with Tom, Miss Joan's words come back to me.

I am the remembrancer, Miss Joan said to me a few years ago. *I write the memories because what other reason can there be for living so long? I thought once God had forgotten me. I must believe now that this is not so. The older you live, the more you see that God knows what He's about. He hasn't forgotten me, child. He's simply given me a new purpose. That purpose is to remember and to pass along as I have to you. We—Annie Laydon and I—are the last of our kind. We are the ones who were here nigh at the beginning of the colony, who watched it almost die over and again, and who stood with it until it were sure ... She, our Virginia, would live, even as so many of us would not. I suppose Virginia, she did grow upon our backs, upon our tears and stubbornness. Our not knowing when yielding would make the most sense.*

Annie Laydon is gone now, too, I realize, although she died after Miss Joan.

"I hope you threw not those pages upon the fire, Miss Joan. I pray it so. Perhaps Tom will yet find them. I fear me you took that secret to your grave, dear kinswoman. I enjoyed meeting Tom, Miss Joan. And you were a good remembrancer. I thank you for that. And I thank you for the escritoire, the old secretary, as well. I shall treasure it! Time for me to go now," I say softly.

I touch the stone and turn, preparing to stand.

But I gasp, startled. I see something, lo, an apparition? It cannot be. I rub my eyes, and still, I see it. A white form in the meadow by the cemetery. I blink. I look for light from the trees. Still, I see the whiteness which slowly takes shape. Three women dressed in white, leaning upon one another.

Miss Joan stands in the middle, smiling. Holding her right shoulder is a thin woman with a determined smile ... This must be Miss Maggie. And with an arm about her waist, a thin and also smiling woman ... Miss Tempie. *We had been as three legs of a stool,* Miss Joan told me.

I know they are not truly here. I tell myself that anyway.

But still kneeling, I see them most clearly. And then the vision fades, leaving me to wonder.

As I walk away from the stone and towards the river, a cardinal calls, crisp and bright.

Cheer cheer what what what what. Cheer cheer what what what what.

And I smile. The same cardinal who cried over Maggie's grave, who called before Tempie's grave. And who now sings above Miss Joan's.

I look back toward the grave and see that it's not alone. It has, of course, Captain Peirce's grave beside it. But more than that, it has the river whispering nearby. A mulberry tree gives it shade, and someone, perhaps a child, has circled it in shells from the river and added a cross made of little scallop and mussel shells on it.

A squirrel climbs over the grave's walnut bench. A deer grazes at the edge of the forest. A fox darts away, leaving just a flash of orange tail as it goes. The rich, red, singing cardinal hails a new spring.

And above it all, a peregrine falcon—the great pilgrim bird—soars sunward on winds sweeping off the river, far and away.

Miss Joan is with all of Virginia now.

Postscript:
That Beautiful Old Parchment

The sky
Is that beautiful old parchment
In which the sun
And the moon
Keep their diary.
                    —Alfred Kreymbord

The Story of the Desk

Rachel Finch returned with the old desk to Charles City, Virginia. She loved it because it reminded her of the old woman, Mrs. Joan Peirce, who'd given it to her.

Many years passed before Audrey Mason of Hanover County inherited the little writing desk. That was in the 1750s, more than a hundred years after Mrs. Peirce had died.

Audrey had come upon the old desk while cleaning out her grandmother's small clapboard house down in Charles City. Someone, probably Audrey's father, had cleaned out most of the other furnishings years before. Now with him gone as well, Audrey was sorting through the small home in which her grandparents had once lived. She knew, too, that her great-grandmother Rachel had once owned the house, very long ago.

Among the items Audrey's father had left behind was the writing desk. It had sat, forgotten, in the Finch home in Charles City. After the Finches' deaths, the house lay abandoned for some time. Later, Audrey found the dusty old piece and decided to clean it up and keep it as a memento of her grandmother. The heavy and solid little desk moved with Audrey down the King's Highway to Edenton in Carolina. The piece was quaint, not in terribly good shape, but Audrey loved it nonetheless.

A contagion was hard on the family, and only Audrey's son survived it. He moved away leaving the Masons' home after a family adopted him. A few of his parents' belongings he entrusted to a spinster friend of his mother he called Miss Johnny. He loved Miss Johnny for she'd cared for him immediately following his parents' deaths.

The writing table was among these few possessions. Miss Johnny placed it in a corner of her bedroom, and there it sat for twenty more years. It was, all had discovered, too heavy to move often.

Before Miss Johnny died, she left a will bequeathing her few belongings, including the table, to her brother's children. In the will, she included a note about the secretary. She also wrote a note and placed it in the piece: *Once owned by Audrey Mason, whose friend I was ere the contagion took her. Her boy moved away, further west, leaving me the old secretary wherein this note lies. The chest once belonged to Audrey's great grandmother Rachel from Virginia, so Audrey once told me. Audrey was a Miss Finch before her marriage, so I reckon it might have belonged to a Rachel Finch.* The note was signed, *Miss Johnny White.*

That was how the desk came into the possession of Miss Johnny's grand-nephew, Jacob.

During the Great War for Independence, the old table was sitting in Jacob's house in South Carolina, mostly forgotten except by the dust and spiders once again. Somehow, the table got moved to an old outbuilding and stayed there many more years. Forlorn and blending in with other unused pieces.

Jacob, a foot soldier for the colonies, was killed in the fighting at Camden, South Carolina, a miserable death of heat and dysentery. Jacob's wife Lucy kept the secretary after she remarried, tucking Miss Johnny's note in the top space. The piece was now almost impossible to open, a victim of the high humidity, so Lucy more or less forgot about it. The desk had long ago ceased to be used for writing or even as a Bible table. Or anything at all really.

While the piece remained as solid as ever, its parts had become fragile, and pulling too hard on the oak top made an unsettling cracking sound. So the desk sat as a whole, not opened but not an eyesore, either. Funny how one can see a thing for so long and then not see it at all. That was kind of what happened with Lucy and the desk.

So the piece continued to age as the years rushed by. Miss Joan and Rachel and Audrey and even Miss Johnny, all long since forgotten.

Years later, Lucy died with the yellow fever in Charleston. She bequeathed the old writing table as an afterthought to her daughter. Her son received the important pieces, but Carrie Anna always liked old things. Carrie took it with her when she moved to Georgia.

She kept Miss Johnny's note with it, along with her own mother's note saying the secretary wasn't much, but she knew her daughter loved it. Carrie's father's war papers were also left in the writing compartment after he procured his pension. But still the top stuck, more and more it seemed, and so no one thought of using the desk. After a while, even the notes within were forgotten as such things sometimes are.

Not long after, Carrie was taken with the diphtheria, and the table went on to her granddaughter, Anna. Anna's husband became a corporal in the War of Northern Aggression, and he returned to her with one leg missing but his heart intact. Anna stored his war letters in the top drawer with the pension papers, which were still there. The drawer didn't open fully by then.

When the Yankees came through Rome, Georgia, where Anna lived, they burned much around them, even the fields, and so many hopes and memories went up in flames as well. Even furniture, sometimes raided and used as firewood. Beautiful old pieces like the rosewood piano and the William and Mary chest-on-chest, to the flames, warming Yankee hands and breaking Southern hearts.

The Yankees did seem to take especial pride in destroying those things which Southerners loved most.

Anna had Yankees on her farm, too, and they terrified her. Taking valuables and some silver, throwing a few chairs which had belonged to her husband's family atop a blazing fire in Anna's own yard. One soldier reached for the archaic desk, struggled and grunted. "Heavier than it looks," he grumbled. And so the piece once again, by its own strangeness and bulkiness, was saved.

A few years later, Anna's own granddaughter, given the family name Carrie, admired the desk, and Miss Anna said she might have it. Anna told her that it had passed from a Carrie Anna to an Anna and then to a Carrie. That just seemed right to Miss Anna somehow. "The Yankees tried to burn it, but they could lift it nary an inch!" old Anna said proudly. "Of course, I reckon a Southern soldier boy wouldn't have struggled none with it."

At this point, any victory from the Yankees, howsoever small, seemed a good one.

And right then, although no one knew it, the Yankees were pillaging their way across old Warwick County, Virginia, ripping out pages from the county court books and General Assembly meeting notes, some going as far back as the seventeenth century. Some the only records of entire families, obliterated just like their homes and possessions and family Bibles.

Some county court records were going on the fires, and others were traveling back up north as souvenirs and trophies. And into the ashes and into Northern attics went many old family legacies. The will of one Captain William Peirce was tossed onto the fire. With it burned the record of his final possessions and home as well as the names of his children and wife, Joan. Ashes to ashes.

The old desk, though, it kept moving. Or being moved, as it were.

Carrie married and made her new home across the Mississippi, taking Miss Johnny's old desk, which also still held the war papers in an upper drawer as well as Miss Johnny's note. Once in a while, someone visiting asked her about the piece. "It dates from about the mid-1700s, so I believe. It has been passed down in my family many years. And the Yankees couldn't lift it!"

After that, it became the little desk the Yankees couldn't lift. This one legacy assured the odd little desk would never see the rubbish pile, at least.

When the century turned once more and the nineteen hundreds began, Carrie's first husband died of the cholera, a most miserable and sad time for her. A few years later, she met and married a man from Virginia who dealt in cotton on one of the Mississippi steamboats. They lived out there a few years, but the river trade wasn't what it used to be. He decided it was time to move back to his family homestead outside Williamsburg, Virginia, the Middle Plantation, it was once called.

By then, the old desk had traveled from Virginia to North Carolina to South Carolina, Georgia, Missouri, and finally had returned home to Virginia. No one knew at the time that the desk was Virginia-made or much else about it except that some in the family now called it the Yankee desk. It was old and simple and still quirky, quirky and old enough that no one considered throwing it out, and simple enough that it never received much notice from anyone.

Carrie's daughter Etha felt intrigued by the old piece, and so once, her mother had tugged open the drawers and shown her Miss Johnny's note and the war papers, as well as Carrie's grandfather's war letters.

When Etha's beau died in World War I, Etha cried and declared she'd never marry. But one day she did, to a man named Wicker. The old secretary went with her after her mother's death and in an old Tidewater Virginia house, that heavy solid old escritoire remained many years, biding its time.

By now the piece was so old, no one lifted the top at all anymore.

During the 1940's, Etha explained to her granddaughter that the Yankee desk was an old writing table, that it had spent the last century passing from mother to daughter or from grandmother to granddaughter, moving through several states.

"Was it made by the Yankees, grandma?" Maria had asked once.

"Oh, heavens, *no*, child!" Etha had replied as if Maria had insulted both her *and* the desk.

Etha remembered that years later and left her granddaughter Maria the old desk. Maria was thrilled to own the desk, which was beginning to look worn all over. Too many moves, humidity, storage in the wrong places. Sometimes, folks just get busy.

Maria kept it in a corner of her small house overlooking the James River in a crossroads east of Williamsburg. Again, it sat for many more years, the days and years trudging by like foot soldiers on a lonely path into the unknown.

By now, unknown by those who touched its old wood as they walked by it, the lonely desk had quietly witnessed more than one hundred thousand sunrises. Those like Joan and Rachel, Miss Johnny and Miss Anna, who had owned it, loved it, and carried it all across the country were but shadows, shades from the past.

Until one day, one that was different from the many thousands which had come before it for the forlorn Yankee desk.

Maybe it was the magic of the old river. Maybe the desk had longed to be home again in Virginia. Whatever the reason, Maria—my mother—decided to clean the desk thoroughly one day. She took out the polish and orange oil and lovingly buffed the top, the sides, the back, the underside, and all the legs.

The desk was old and quaint, primitive but not ugly. Somehow, she suspected the desk knew more than it was telling, but the desk, biding its secrets, remained silent.

Maria loved it, she said, because she knew that it had belonged to her grandmother Etha, and she'd heard the Carrie and Anna story. She figured that meant the secretary had belonged to her grandmother—maybe her sixth great-grandmother, if she understood the legacy properly. With the table had come stories of Miss Johnny—Miss Johnny had a pipe and smoked it. She was a gritty Southern pioneer woman. She was, somehow, a great aunt. Well, there were lots of greats in there somewhere.

Maria sat for a moment with her hand on the desk, feeling it. All was silent in the house, and Maria might have thought for a moment that Miss Johnny heard, that she were even there. Surely, her presence was strong about this desk—once someone paid a mind to it.

All kinds of presences, in fact, seemed to hover about the desk.

Maria might have thought that was creepy had she not been so fascinated with the piece. She tugged at the top drawer.

Stuck.

She worked it carefully, gently, a little at a time. How many years since anyone had tried to open it?

When the drawer finally was out far enough, she could see some papers inside. She eased them out, and there were those old Revolutionary War pension papers! *A country was built on the men who earned pensions such as this,* she thought. She held Miss Johnny's note and squinted to make out the faded writing on the war papers. The note itself was now so old, it probably belonged in a museum somewhere itself, Maria thought.

So while cleaning the desk, Maria got the top open and read over the old war papers. Tucked further back was Miss Johnny's note. Intrigued, Maria read, *Rachel Finch from Virginia.* Where in Virginia, Maria wondered.

She took the old note to the Library of Virginia and showed it to the librarian, who helped Maria find a will from 1710 in which Rachel's name appeared. Rachel had lived in Charles City.

Rachel. Audrey. Johnny White. With some help from the librarian, Maria sorted out the family line. Johnny White had been the aunt of her seventh great-grandfather, Jacob, who had been killed in the Revolution. They were his papers in the old secretary. Her seventh great-grandmother had remarried after the war, leaving the secretary to her sixth great-grandmother. She did indeed find proof of Carrie Anna, Anna, and Carrie, names just as she'd always heard them. And then, of course, Etha was her grandmother.

Now Maria looked at the Bible desk with new respect. She rubbed her hand along the edge of the secretary and said, "Miss Rachel, I promise to take good care of this chest you loved, home in Virginia now after all its travels. It has come back, you see."

But is anything of Miss Rachel's still here? She didn't see how there could be.

Why did she feel such a pull to this woman? She had no idea.

Maria's hand then felt a loose piece—intentionally loose. She was sure of it. She lifted it off and then tried the opposite side which also lifted off.

Drawers. Four secret drawers! Maria gasped. She'd never heard anyone mention them to her before.

They were stuck fast, swollen from the heat perhaps, but at last she opened one enough to see a yellowed paper inside. Gently, she pulled it out and read the faded writing.

Sometime in the early 1700's, Rachel Finch must have left a note in the desk.

This escritoire originally belonged to Mrs Joane Peirce, wiffe of Capt. Wllm Peirce. She left it to me ere she dyed October ye 3rd 1649. Rachel Finch, 1712. I have left two letters I wrote about Mrs Peirce, my cozen. Since this table was hers, I have placed these letters with the desk.

All those years ago, Rachel had discovered a false front and four small drawers which were empty. In these drawers, Rachel had left these as well as a mourning ring she'd inherited after another cousin had died. In the top, Rachel had kept her pen and inkwell and a sheath of writing paper. She had loved the smell of the old desk. It never failed to remind her of the old woman who had left it to her. All these things, Rachel included in her note that stayed in the desk until it yellowed, until the dust threatened to reclaim it.

"1712? 1649?" Maria cried in whispered astonishment. No one had thought the desk that old.

Two more of the drawers were empty. But the third held the best surprise yet. Not one but *two* letters from Miss Rachel herself!

Carefully, Maria picked up one and opened it, the creaking of the old paper, folded for so long, reminded her of its age.

At the top, Rachel had written, *Auguste anno. 1649.*

Then Maria read:

The sunne is stille low, a candel in Virginnea's dustey blue skye, as it peekes over thee river. The moone has hidden itself; thee morning starre has nearly vanished. But thee sunne breaks thee daye, changing thee colors of thee river as if to saye, "See, I am thee sunne. I can do this".

Miss Joane is sitting beside mee, her weathered hande tucked into mine. Her once dark hair has whitened to thee colour of dogwoode tree blossomes.

"She's writing about meeting Mrs. Joan Peirce, whose desk this was," Maria said to herself, her voice reverent. The aura about the letters felt hushed, sacred.

She was nearly frightened to open the second letter.

Aprile anno. 1652—I stande in ye olde cemetery at Bakers Neck Church. The breeze off thee river is refreshing. I know that 'tis notte thee reasone Captaine Peeirce chose Mulberry Island to be his home. He chose it for its military strength and its riche earthe. But thee breeze is nice too. I was borne in Virginia and have growne up in thee heat of its sommers. I've runne thee length of fieldes and ambled along thee blackberry ridges. But for the Peeirces, this land was unique and wilde, and—after the baptism by soe much bloude—holy in a waye.

Maria read the letter as best as she could, wondering if she should even be holding it. Hadn't she heard something about oils in hands damaging old paper? But her suspense was too great. She had to know what the letter said. She read on, feeling Rachel's surprise at inheriting the old desk.

Maria was the sort of person who was rarely speechless, but this time, words failed her. Completely.

She had found a secret, a secret hidden for centuries. *Yes, 1960 to 1711 is almost two hundred fifty years.*

Somehow, she did not want to share this with anyone, not yet. She felt as if she might be communing with two long-dead women, the owner of the desk and the writer of the letter. The letter in her hand felt hallowed as a Bible.

She sat in the silence so long that her ears began to ring.

Sometimes I sits and thinks, and sometimes I just sits, she thought absurdly, although she wasn't sure who had originally written those words.

Finally, she tentatively said, "Rachel? Are you here?" Silence in the house. *Silly.*

But she couldn't help herself. "Miss Joan?" She looked about as if a spirit might pop out at her. What a tantalizing find. It was 1960, and the writing table was just over three hundred years old.

"Amazing," she said aloud again.

Now she addressed the desk directly. "Tell me your secrets, sir. Who built you? Do you have anything more to share with me besides these two mysterious old letters?"

If a desk could look like a quizzical and bemused old man, she felt certain this one did.

She really should call someone, call out the door about it. But something inside said, *Wait.* The moment felt almost holy. This carefully penned note had sat hidden all these many years, and she—*she*—had been the one to find it.

"Thank you," she said as she lovingly touched the edges of the desk. "I don't mean to be greedy. I just want to ensure there's nothing else overlooked these many years."

She lifted the lid again and gently caressed the inside. She would clean it more. It amazed her that dust could even make its way into hidden old drawers if they stayed closed long enough. She polished the inside of the drawers with something of reverence, almost love. *See Miss Rachel, I've cleaned them for you. Miss Joan, I've cleaned it for you, too.*

The old wood began to come alive under her touch, her effort. It soaked the oil as if it had been thirsty for years, maybe for centuries.

She paused to admire her work and thought a few crevices might need polishing, too.

And then it happened.

Her finger caught in an uneven edge. The bottom jerked out slightly with a loud *creak*.

Oh no! she thought. *Now I've broken it. I should know when to leave well enough alone.*

She knew she should push the bottom back in place, but something, something indefinable, made her pull as if to lift it more. She cringed. Why was she doing this?

She lifted a bit more.

"Why, this is *meant* to be opened!" It lifted upward, but not all the way off.

She grabbed a flashlight and shone it inside. The center was not a solid pedestal as it appeared but partially hollowed out.

She might have been Dr. Carter finding King Tut.

She might have found the Rosetta Stone.

What she found instead was what appeared to be some type of notebook, very old by the looks of it. Brittle to the touch and wedged so tightly that it had never moved.

"Holy cow! No wonder everyone thought this was solid oak," she gasped. Her mouth hung open in a way that her grandmother would surely have scolded her for. She couldn't help it.

Gently, she slipped her fingers to the edges of the book, but the book was lodged tightly.

She stopped, unsure. What to do?

She reached inside again, so eager to see the contents of the notebook that she did not trust herself. Suppose she damaged it? Suppose it crumbled?

She shone the flashlight inside once more. This time, she noticed that the builder of this piece had created finger-sized ridges within in the back.

"Ah!" Maria said aloud, delighted and awed. "You were meant to be stored here but also to be retrieved."

Now she reached in again, her own fingers sliding carefully down into the ridges until she felt the bottom of one notebook and, she thought, the top of another.

"Two!" She gasped. "Two. *My Lord.*"

Gingerly, she slipped her fingers beneath the top notebook and lifted.

With a puff of dust and hint of mold, the notebook was free.

"Thank you, Rachel!" she cried. These were, she reasoned, Rachel's notebooks. She could not yet see the second one, but this top one looked to be about five or six hundred pages and perhaps four inches thick. Its design was ancient. How old? Maria trembled with excitement as she lifted the cover. What she saw atop the first page astounded her. These were not Rachel's notebooks at all, but those, seemingly, of a seventeenth-century woman. Maria read:

Joane Peirce, her daybookes. I do hereby leave these, my written memories, to my daughter Jane James to do with as she pleese and to destroye if shee so choose.

All these yeares have I kept my writing secreted within this deske. This day have I decided to preeserve these two bookes and to let Jane deecide their fates.

Mayhap my grandchildren might learn from them. I aske Jane to share, if shee choose, these writeings with her brothere and sister and the children and grandchildren of Dame Temperance Yeardley, thee friende of my hearte.

As to thee remembering, this have I compleated.

Thee writing deske where I have stored these pages, John Laydon made for me, anno. 1638 at Fisher's Creek on Warwicke River. Hee saide hee made it so that I might keep my dayebookes safe and secure deepe inside. This have I donne, but ere I dye, I shall remove the dayebookes and give to my daughter Jane.

I praye that all my children and grandchildren and perhaps those e'en that follow might remembere mee and what life 'twas like, when Virginnea were too wilde and I too younge to understand what I had done by cominge here. I wishe that the children of Ly. Temperance Yeardley (I say not West), my friende, and her grandchildren and all those who inhabit these shoares might reade and understande what wee yet endurred but how in the ende, we loved old Virginny, a beautiful and abundant lande she was. Tragedy could not stay us long.

This noate written by mee ye 29th of September, be it Holy Michaelmas (sainte of ye sea and ye shippes), 1649, at Mulberrie Islande on James his River, and fourtie years since I arrived here in this Countrie.

Signed Mrs. Joane Peirce, wiffe of Capt. Willm Peirce, of Mulbery Iland in Virginnea. September ye 29th, anno 1649.

On the top page Maria read, "*Joane Peeirce, her storye & memmories, remembering a long liffe in Virginnea and her liffe first in Englande.*"

Maria wasn't sure she was breathing at all. She gently lifted the first page and struggled to make out the ancient yet neat handwriting.

"May 1592?" Her heart pounded as if she were viewing an old secret not meant for her eyes. She was going to pass out right here and someone would find her with a burned-out flashlight and an old opened desk.

"*Thee spring*," she read, pausing. The spelling was archaic, the writing tidy although still occasionally difficult to decipher, and the musty smell almost unbearable. She read aloud slowly as each word's meaning came clear. "*Thee spring I turned twelfe in 1592, I learned my father would not bee returning from sea one daye. I knew because hee told mee.*"

Maria dropped the flashlight. It hit the floor and rolled away. She sat frozen to the chair. *1592. 1592?*

The personality of the long gone and forgotten woman, Joan Peirce, seemed to fill the room around her. As if she, Maria, had summoned her. As if Joan were right here with Maria, all these many years later.

Carefully, Maria turned the pages of the notebook. She was now convinced that these had been in the secret central compartment since Mrs. Peirce placed them there.

Centuries ago, Rachel had inherited the desk. Why had Joan not removed the notebooks? Had she changed her mind and decided to leave them to Rachel rather than to Jane?

No, Maria didn't think so. Rachel's notes suggested a reason: Joan had died quietly in her sleep, had not known death were upon her. Joan had only decided, it seemed, at the end of September to share her writing and to preserve it. Rachel had said the gravestone gave the date of Joan's death as the third of October. Joan hadn't had time to remove her notebooks from the writing desk, had not suspected her heart would cease so suddenly. And Tom, Jane, and Rachel had no hint of the secret compartment. No one, in fact, had all these many years.

"John Laydon did his work well," Maria murmured. "Perhaps too well."

Holy cow! Maria said again. How were the notebooks still here? Why had no one found them?

Because you were curious, child. Just as I was curious, curious to hear a story. Curious to know the truth. Curious and patient.

Maria knew Miss Rachel—or was it Joan?—one or both of these women weren't actually speaking to her. Or were they? For this one moment, Maria felt suspended ... suspended between the past and present, between reality and fantasy.

She reached once more into the finger grooves and gently lifted out another similar-sized notebook. She turned to the back of that one. What was the latest date? *1649*, the year of Miss Joan's death.

On a final page, in the same handwriting, Mrs. Peirce had written:

How broad the sunne's rays—those wee can see and those wee cannot.

I look up at thee rising sunne, and say, "My childe, it will bee a long & glorious day, I think, before this sunne shall set, farre away in thee Southe Seas."

Rachel looks at mee curiously. "Yes, ma'am. I thinke soe, too."

And taking hands, wee rise from thee benche, sunne to oure backes, and together stroll to thee manor at Mulberie Islande, the island sitting in thee James River, the river reaching into thee deepest partes of thee coloney of Virginnea. And farre, farre beyond.

It is so good to bee home.

"It is so good to be home," Maria read aloud. Yes, the diaries were home, back in Virginia in Maria's home overlooking the expansive James River. No one had found them during the wars and fighting they'd seen, hadn't been found as they crisscrossed the country.

The daybooks had watched the sun come up, surely. Had seen the struggles and the wars and the colony of Virginia join with its friends and sometimes enemies—the Marylanders, the Plymouth colony, the Dutch colony. Who had put aside their differences, at last, to form one great country spreading from one sea to the other.

But only when these books had come back to the soil and the place of their birth had they arisen, giving voice to themselves.

Now Maria went to rock on her porch. She sat alone and quietly. A peregrine perched nearby on a large limb, a cardinal cheered nearby. The river whispered its way down to the sea. *So much has changed and yet nothing has.*

This night, this very night, Maria determined to take her find and, page by gentle page, to transcribe it. How long it would take, she didn't know. Years? She would tell no one. She would simply open and read and attempt to make out the writing.

Rachel and Joan would approve, she thought. Yes, they would.

Three curious women, all.

Author's Note

As I write this, I've been working to research, compile, and complete these three books for almost nineteen years.

Leaving behind Joan, Tempie, Maggie, Janey, Cecily, Will, Sam, Sir George, John Rolfe, Annie, Isabella, Pocahontas Rebecca, Maria, George Sandys, Angelo and Esther, Walter the soldier, Harrison the sailor, and so many others won't be easy. They've been a part of my life in a way I'll never be able to explain.

Joan speaks to me (sometimes more and sometimes less), and I often hear her remind me to keep going with words like *The road to Compostela is always rocky.*

Two empaths have told me that Maggie was an actual person that I have somehow "tuned in" to and that she comes to me to encourage me when I need her "much as she did with her friends in real life when she was alive."

Many times, I've wanted to abandon the books and series as too hard, too stressful, over my head, beyond my abilities ... but what always pulls me back is the desire to tell the stories of these women and the devotion of thousands of readers who have taken the time to write, call, email, text, and approach me in person.

Thank you to all who have encouraged me, but most especially to my husband Chris and to my children Sarah, Michael, Kerry, Adam, and to my son-in-law Dale Beck.

My family has made many sacrifices to allow me to make these books a reality. They've done everything from being website designer, book designer, administrator, photographer, editor and critiquer, but also travel companions for research trips as well as for speaking engagements and conferences, a marketing advisor, bookkeeper, shipping clerk and sales personnel. Remarkable, right?

When I began researching and writing in the summer of 1998, my children ranged in age from two to eight years old. I was in my mid-thirties and am now in my mid-fifties.

That also happened to be just after my first year of homeschooling the four, which we completed after a total of seventeen school years.

Since then, three of my children have graduated college and the fourth graduates soon. My oldest daughter has married, and I'm now a grandmother.

It's no exaggeration to say that my children have grown up with Joan and Tempie, Cecily and Janey.

If I'd known this kitchen table project would take nearly two decades to complete, it would have terrified me, and I'd probably never have started. Had I known it would require three books (not the one I initially envisioned) as well as half a million words; 320 chapters; 450 quotations; and 500 speaking engagements along with ten thousand emails, I would have run away in terror. Fortunately, sometimes ignorance really *is* bliss.

Just take it one step at a time, and I'll get you the rest of the way, God seems to say. And so I do.

While Joan is a real person and did live these events (with a few embellishments), Joan's desk and her notebooks are a fiction.

I like to imagine that somewhere in a crowded attic, tucked behind the old blender and Grandpop's violin, is a trunk, locked and with a lost key. And no one wants to break that lock. If only they would, inside they'd find Joan's notebooks or Tempie's diary or Maggie's poems. Or maybe Isabella Pace saved all the letters she received from home. Or Cecily recorded her feelings about Pastor Pooley. I like to think that somewhere is a quirky old desk with a secret compartment, and one of the women at Jamestown has left her writing hidden inside.

Well, maybe someday.

Folks have approached me, written and called me, to tell me how remembering the women of Jamestown helped them in trying times.

"Don't worry about me. If those women at Jamestown can do it, I can do it, too." So a young woman, who'd just learned she had breast cancer, assured her older friend. The friend is the one who told me the story.

One widow went a year without crying after her husband died. Her daughter told me that she read *Dark Enough to See the Stars in a Jamestown Sky* and cried all the way through. "Then the healing began."

A sweet woman from Puerto Rico said that Joan came to her in a cardinal on her windowsill. Facing difficult times, she heard Joan say to her, *I did it, and you can, too.*

Mike Tanner, a courageous man in Greenville, South Carolina, upon learning that he had one year to live, listed three items on his bucket list. Reading *The Sun Is But a Morning Star*, about sixteen months away from publication, was one. "I might need an advance copy," he wrote.

A mom from Philadelphia wrote that she and her husband had spent Christmas alone. Her son was in Afghanistan, a paratrooper for the 82nd Airborne, and her daughter was teaching in Korea. She described them as her pilgrim and her adventurer, like the young girls in the book. "Your novel kept my mind focused on things other than missing and worrying about our children."

A widow in Oklahoma wrote of having to care for a large and remote ranch alone. "When days get tough, I say to myself, 'acorn flour,' and I get on with it."

Perhaps the most remarkable story came from a woman in Minnesota who told me about her mother. Her mom found herself alone and trapped in rising floodwaters in Baton Rouge in August 2016. She worked all day, all night, and the next day, trying to save her belongings while the water continued to rise. Her daughter wrote, "She told me that what kept her going to work so hard to save things and to make decisions and to survive the experience was her memory of your books and the women in your books, the women who settled our land ... their strength and fortitude. She remembered their work and their survival!" After being rescued, she wrote, her mom "kept her strength through the spirit of the women you wrote and included in your books. She still draws on the strength of the women as the cleanup and rebuilding is now happening."

The courage of the women in early Virginia was real. It must have been because like these folks above, when times were tough, these women had no choice but to keep going. They understood that, in the end, they were fighting for something greater than themselves. And that helped them along when times were bleakest.

These early women and children little knew that their strong efforts and weak results would be a cornerstone of our great nation. They only knew life here was hard, it often felt fruitless, at times even defeating. And yet, they were never defeated, not for long.

During all the calamities, the Virginia settlers still managed to create in the future United States of America: the first free public school, the first representative government (the model for the U.S. Senate), the first private ownership of land, the first bourbon whiskey (thank you, Mr. Thorpe), and many other remarkable firsts.

These women have shown an enterprising spirit remarkable for the time, and it emerges in the records.

Anne Laydon and Joan Wright did survive a whipping for sewing shirts too short. And Anne miscarried because of it. Yet she carried on.

Pocahontas did survive betrayal and kidnapping to make the best of what she had, courageously meeting the English king himself.

Maria Bucke did name her children for the events going on around her in Virginia, a gift to us by sharing her emotions through the children's names. She managed to raise three special needs children on the Virginia frontier.

Elizabeth Pott did indeed sail to England, even while being ill, to petition the Privy Council for her husband's release.

Isabella Smith Pace Perry Menefie did testify before the High Court of Admiralty and ship tobacco in her own name from her Pace assets after marrying William Perry.

Sarah Woodson did fight to save her two boys by hiding them during the 1644 Indian attack. Descendants of the two boys still refer to themselves today as "Washtub Woodsons" or "Potato Hole Woodsons," depending on where their ancestor hid.

Jane Peirce Rolfe Smith did take in orphans after the massacre, and Cecily did fight the pastor because he broke his vow to her.

Lady Temperance Yeardley did indeed spend the last year of her life working to protect her children's assets. She was a savvy businesswoman who also oversaw her husband's land and property while he was ill or overseas.

Captain John Smith did learn from Joan about her success with figs and wrote about it in his *Generall Historie*. Joan made something of horticultural history since she had the first recorded fig orchard in the New World. Little fig seeds, hard work, and patience. Could she have known?

I hope you'll remember these women. I hope you'll remember that founding a colony is hard work and sometimes no one—not even your own Virginia Company—gives you credit for what you've done. But yet you do it anyway, and you let history do the rest.

Thank you to all for the warm welcome, the continuing encouragement, the opportunities, and the faith you've had in these remarkable women and in me.

I used to tell myself when I wrote *Dark Enough* that if this book helped or changed just one person, it would have been worth all the effort and research, the eight years I'd put into it.

When the book was complete, I looked at it and realized it had changed someone. It had changed me.

Finally, as Joan would say and as I myself have handwritten in about twenty thousand copies of my books and counting ...

Godspeed to you in all your journeys.

Acknowledgements

With deep gratitude to my husband, Christopher Lapallo, who has read, re-read, and re-re-read this manuscript, offered advice with both editing and storylines, digitized maps, talked me down from ledges, and provided dark chocolate and coffee in times of crisis.

My children have made numerous sacrifices, especially during the past year, so that I could sequester myself and finish this novel: Sarah Lapallo Beck and her husband Dale, Michael Lapallo, Kerry Anna Lapallo, and Adam Lapallo. They've cheered me up and cheered me on. My sons (both novelists themselves) have also been my writing buddies.

Special thanks to my daughter Sarah Lapallo Beck and her company, Inkwell Book Co., for providing the cover artwork and interior book design, corrections, advice, and much time, all with a new baby.

Also, heartfelt appreciation to my friend and colleague, Edward Wright Haile, author of *Jamestown Narratives* and *John Smith in the Chesapeake* (as well as Jamestown maps and volumes of poetry). Thanks for carefully reading the manuscript and for offering historical, literary, and editing advice as well as resources. Thanks, too, for the opportunity to explore many original seventeenth-century sites, both English and Native American, in Virginia, Maryland, and Delaware along the Chesapeake Bay and its rivers.

Thanks so much to the following people and organizations:

To those who read the manuscript and offered their thoughts: Kimberly Colgin, Sally Fraser, and Therese Silberman.

Joan has her friends of the heart, and I have mine. For the love and encouragement beginning when these books were just a dream and all along the way: Kimberly Colgin, Kathy Lowry, Janet Lee, Stephen Leftwich, Becky Shermer, Holly Boyle, Donna Chesson, Denise Del Prete, Nancy Blackburn, Beth Goldsmith, Sally Fraser, Therese Silberman, Sharon Baldacci, and Lois Badey.

Also thanks to dear friends Fara Caldwell, Rhonda Germain, Traci Haden, Bess Haile, Elaine Feltrin Knight, Kim Kremer, Jeanine Moore, Parrish Mort, Joann Robinson, and Jean Weller.

To Kristi Tuck Austin for providing advice regarding book marketing, lots of ideas, uplifting words, and hard work. Also for providing tulips as needed! Likewise to Ashley Powell for toiling away with a smile regardless the task.

To my cousin Richard and his wife Tracey for showing me around England, particularly London and the West Country.

To Bill Young, who portrayed Capt. Gabriel Archer at Historic Jamestowne and all across the country, sincere thanks for the enthusiasm and generosity, opportunities for us to speak and sign together, and especially the friendship.

To Dick Cheatham, Founder and Director of Living History Associates, Ltd., for advice regarding John Rolfe and for being a great friend in so many ways. I look forward to future collaborations.

To the interpreters, genealogists, and historians who have so willingly offered research and ideas, including: David Canada (the Bass family), Freda Daniel (John Brown, Temperance Bailey's first husband), Mark Greenough (Historian at the Virginia State Capitol and Virginia General Assembly), Lisa Kirkham (lacemaking), Frankie Liles (genealogy and English probate), Kerry McClure (Lady Margaret Wyatt), Randy Pace (Richard and Isabella Pace), Rebecca Suerdieck (Marye/Maria Bucke and seventeenth-century cooking), and Nancy Jamerson Weiland (Elizabeth Rolfe).

To the late and great Rev. Clayton Custalow of the Mattaponi Reservation for his kindness, encouragement, and friendship over many years. I'm better for having known you.

To John Haile and Ben Rennolds for opening their families' seventeenth and eighteenth-century homes for me to explore while learning about Joan's home.

To all those individuals and organizations across the country who have invited me to speak, thanks for your confidence and your incredible hospitality. With particular thanks to the Jamestowne Society, Daughters of the American Revolution, National Society of the Colonial Dames of America, the National Society Colonial Dames XVII Century, the Genealogical Research Institute of Virginia, and many local historical societies.

Special love to the wonderful ladies of Houston, who have hosted me for dozens of events. Most especially to Sarah Elizabeth (Beth) Leney, now a very dear friend.

Thanks to Toni Wirth and Dr. Shirley Godsey for hosting me in Dallas and Gulfport, Mississippi, respectively.

To more than a hundred book clubs who have invited me to speak over the past ten years, it's been an indescribable pleasure to discuss the books with you and to hear your thoughts and questions. You've helped guide the books and given me valuable insights as readers.

To readers across the country for taking the time to send me your thoughts and encouragement in thousands of emails, texts, Facebook messages, and phone calls. How nice to have a cheerful word when this series has felt daunting!

To Historic Jamestowne, Jamestown Settlement, Henricus Historical Park, the Yorktown Custom House, and Colonial Williamsburg for the many readers you've pointed my way and all the hospitality in hosting book signings.

To the Chesapeake Conservancy, thanks for the opportunity to become involved in a fascinating project, the John Smith Chesapeake Trail Cross Markers as part of the Captain John Smith Chesapeake National Historic Trail.

Character List

Key

(1) = 1st spouse   (2) = 2nd spouse   (3) = 3rd spouse
> = Children with listed spouse

Characters represent real people in the series unless otherwise noted. There are more fictional characters in the first book because so few names survive from that period. It's a way of representing those who died and whose names we'll never know.

I caution against using this series for genealogy. Although I never change known history or family relationships, many gaps in our knowledge remain. Writing fiction forces me to fill these in. (A character has to know the name of her mother or her husband, for example.) I do seek to solve some of these puzzles along the way. But we've lost so many records, especially in the Civil War, that I have to make leaps where necessary. That includes some spouses, children, and birthplaces, among other things. The lines below are as I've written them in the book unless otherwise noted.

Joan Peirce

The narrator. Joan was born in Melcombe Regis in Dorset, the daughter of Capt. William Phippen and Jane Jordaine. Her stepmother was Lattie.
(1) Tom Reynolds > Cecily
(2) Will Peirce > Jack (who died in England), Jane, Tom (Young Tom)

Joan's Daughters

Cecily Bailey Jordan Farrar

Joan's older daughter, daughter of Tom Reynolds. She lived upriver all of her adult life.

(1) Tom Bailey > Temperance (Little Temp)
(2) Sam Jordan > Mary, Margaret (Margie)
(3) William Farrar > Cecily, William, John

Jane (Janey) Peirce Rolfe Smith

Joan's younger daughter, daughter of William Peirce.
(1) John Rolfe > Elizabeth Rolfe
(2) Capt. Roger Smith > Sarah Macock (adopted), Elizabeth (Wee Bess) Salter (adopted), Possibly a son John Smith
(3) Francis James: Circumstantially, appears to be her third husband, and it appears that she had children with him, too. He would have been a relative of her second husband.

Joan's Closest Friends

Anne (Annie) Burras Laydon

One of the first two women to arrive, 1608. Married to John (Jack) Laydon, the first English wedding in the New World. She had four surviving daughters, including Virginia (Ginny) Laydon, the first English child born in today's Virginia. The desk that Annie's husband Jack built for Joan is fictional.

Isabella Smith Pace Perry Menefie

A close friend of Joan and Tempie, an early settler who probably arrived in 1611.
(1) Richard Pace > George Pace
(2) William Perry > Henry Perry
(3) George Menefie

Maggie Deale (Fictional)

A fictional friend of Joan's who was with her on the Blessing in 1609 and who died during the Starving Time. Maggie represents the many women whose names we'll never know who perished during that time. She was married to Will's friend Hugh, also fictional.

Lady Temperance (Tempie) Flowerdieu Yeardley West

Joan's closest friend and Starving Time partner. She arrived in 1609 on the Falcon.

(1) Sir George Yeardley > Elizabeth, Argall, Francis (Young Francis)

(2) Capt. Francis West

Tempie's other relatives:

1. Her mother, Martha Flowerdieu Garrett

2. Her stepfather, Capt. Garrett

3. Her brother, Stanley Flowerdieu

4. Her sister, Marie Rossingham

5. Marie's son, Edmund Rossingham

6. Her 1st cousin, John Pory

7. The Wests were her cousins.

Joan's Other Friends & Relatives

Alice Peirce

Alice was married to Thomas Peirce, a kinsman of Will Peirce, who was sergeant-at-arms at the first General Assembly in 1619. During the massacre, Indians captured Alice and her daughter Elizabeth. Both married after their ransom: Alice to Thomas Bennett and Elizabeth to Anthony Barham. Anthony bequeathed Joan Peirce a mourning ring in his 1641 will.

Elizabeth Mayhew (Fictional)

Joan's acquaintance on her voyage over on the Blessing. She gave Joan a ring when she died soon on arrival in 1609.

Grace Fleetwood (Fictional)

An old woman that Joan and Tempie took into their home during the Starving Time. She died in the midst of the starving.

Harrison the sailor (Fictional)

Helped Joan and Maggie during the hurricane at sea on the voyage over and gave Jane (Janey) a Spanish *reale* for luck.

Joan Wright

An old settler, a midwife who some thought was a witch. The court tried her in September 1626, but she seems to have been acquitted or the case dropped. That the ladies sprang to her aid is fictional although no one knows why no ruling occurred. She probably did deliver the children of the first women as she is the only known midwife in that earliest period. She was married to Robert Wright.

Mrs. Macock

(First name unknown or unproven.) Married to the Rev. Samuel Macock. Their only child was Sarah Macock, orphaned when both parents died within a year of her birth. Rev. Macock was killed in the massacre, and Mrs. Macock died soon after, probably in the 1623 contagion. Jane Peirce Rolfe Smith became guardian of the infant Sarah.

Margaret Powell Blaney West

A resident of New Towne, neighbor of the Peirces, and wife of Capt. William Powell, commander of James Cittie and Lieutenant Peirce's superior officer. After Powell died, she married first Edward Blaney. Upon his death, she married Capt. Francis West. She died soon after this marriage. Capt. West then married Tempie. That her personality was difficult is fiction although she did bicker with her other neighbor, Dr. Pott.

Lady Margaret Wyatt

Wife to Sir Francis Wyatt, the governor, who arrived at Christmas 1622 on the ship *Abigail*, which brought contagion. She returned to England early in 1624 while expecting a child. Her arguing for more food is fictitious. Her coming over in a time of dire need is real. Her possibly being encouraged to do so by her husband and uncles is speculation.

Maria Bucke

An old settler married to the Rev. Richard Bucke. She had four children: Mara, Gershom, Benomi (or Benoni), and Peleg. Maria died around 1620 and her husband a few years later. Benomi is believed to have had Down's Syndrome, the first reported case in the New World.

Pocahontas (Rebecca) Rolfe

Daughter of the great *werowance* Powhatan. She first had a Powhatan husband, Kokoum. She was a friend to the settlers even before being kidnapped by Capt. Argall in 1613 in exchange for a copper kettle. She thereupon converted to Christianity and acquired the Christian name Rebecca, married John Rolfe in 1614, and bore him a son, Thomas. She sailed for England in 1616 and visited the English court. She died at Gravesend as her ship was departing for Virginia in 1617 in her twenty-first year. She has thousands of descendants today through her son Thomas Rolfe.

Rachel Finch (Fictional)

Joan calls her "my young visitor." Rachel comes to visit Joan on Mulberry Island during the summer of 1649 and asks about Joan's life, prompting Joan to tell her stories.

Sam Jordan

Sam is Joan's cousin and a more distant relation of Will's. He married Joan's daughter Cecily. The story of his plantation, Jordan's Journey, is real. His death by arrow is fictionalized although this is the period in which he died, leading to Cecily's troubles with Pastor Pooley.

Thomasine Causey

A Starving Time survivor who arrived on the *Lyon* in 1609. Her husband Nathaniel (Nat) Causey came in 1608. Thomasine lived upriver at Causey's Care until the massacre when she and her husband moved to Jordan's Journey.

Walter The Soldier

He buried Maggie during the Starving Time and warned Joan about the dangers of Henricus. (Fictional.)

Servants

Angelo

Joan's African servant who came to Virginia in 1620 aboard the *Treasurer*, a ship Gov. Argall was illegally using for piracy. The Portuguese had captured the Africans and sold them to the Spanish, who were transporting them to Mexico as slaves. The *Treasurer* then captured the Spanish ship. In Virginia, the first Africans were indentured servants in the years before the laws changed. We know nothing of Angelo after the 1624/25 Muster, but presumably she was released after an indenture term. While Anthony was a real African servant of Sir George, I created their marriage. They would have been neighbors at New Towne, and their indentures would have ended at the same time. It's certainly possible they married.

Esther Everett

Joan's servant who arrived on the *Jonathan*, 1620. She later married Goodman Clariet. That she was losing her hearing is fiction.

Susanna Hall

Tempie's servant who also witnessed her will and testified on her behalf in England. She was born c. 1608 and arrived in 1619. She seems to have accompanied the children back to England after their mother's death. She testified at the Prerogative Court of Canterbury the same day that Capt. Peirce settled John Rolfe's will (21 May 1630) in the same court, so it's a possibility the Peirces accompanied Susanna to court. That she was an orphan whose parents were friends with Ralph Yeardley is fiction.

Governors During Joan's Time in Virginia (1609-1649):

1608 – 1609	Capt. John Smith (president of the council)
1609 – 1610	George Percy (provisional president of the council)
1610 – 1610	Sir Thomas Gates
1610 – 1611	Thomas West, Lord De La Warr
1611 – 1611	George Percy
1611 – 1611	Sir Thomas Dale
1611 – 1614	Sir Thomas Gates
1614 – 1616	Sir Thomas Dale
1616 – 1617	Sir George Yeardley
1617 – 1619	Capt. Samuel Argall (later knighted)
1619 – 1621	Sir George Yeardley
1621 – 1626	Sir Francis Wyatt
1626 – 1627	Sir George Yeardley (died in office)
1627 – 1629	Capt. Francis West
1629 – 1630	Dr. John Pott
1630 – 1635	Sir John Harvey (officially starting in 1628, arrival 1630)
1635 – 1636	Capt. John West
1636 – 1639	Sir John Harvey
1639 – 1642	Sir Francis Wyatt
1642 – 1652	Sir William Berkeley

Gov. Sir William Berkeley

Virginia's longest-serving governor, skilled at compromise and well liked. His challenges included the 1644 Indian assault, the English Civil War, and later, Bacon's Rebellion.

Gov. Sir John Harvey

An unpopular Virginia governor thrust from office by his councilors in April 1635. Capt. Peirce was part of this action by bringing 30 armed musketeers to beset the governor's home. Harvey tended to favor the new colony of Maryland and his personal interests over supporting the Virginia colonists. His violent temper and arbitrary policies are well documented. (He did knock out Councilor Richard Stephens's teeth with his cudgel.)

Dr. John Pott

Physician general of the colony after Dr. Bohun died. Pott lived at New Towne, was married to Elizabeth, and often involved in controversy. He was interim governor when Gov. Francis West sailed for England in 1629. The king charged Pott with treason in the deposing of Governor Harvey, his enemy. His brother was Francis Pott.

Gov. Francis West

One of Baron De La Warr's brothers. He was Tempie's last husband and engaged in a lawsuit with Ralph Yeardley regarding the Yeardley estate after Tempie's death. He remarried and died by drowning in the early 1630s.

Gov. John West

Lord De La Warr's youngest brother, took part in the thrusting out of Harvey. The council selected him governor to replace Harvey. West was called to England to answer for treason for his actions but was never prosecuted.

Gov. Sir Francis Wyatt

A popular and mild-mannered governor. The 1622 massacre occurred early in Wyatt's first administration. He was governor when the king dissolved the Virginia Company, but the king commissioned him to remain in office. He continued to allow the Virginia General Assembly to meet although the king had not formally approved it. Married to Lady Margaret Wyatt, who joined him in Virginia at Christmas, 1622. He returned in 1639 to replace Gov. Harvey, a welcome relief to the old settlers.

Gov. Sir George Yeardley

Tempie's husband. Yeardley was a popular governor (for the most part). In his administration, the Company authorized land grants for the settlers, the right to a General Assembly, and freedom from martial law. That Yeardley endured pirate capture is my discovery. In his 1626-27 term, Yeardley followed Wyatt's example and allowed the Virginia General Assembly to meet without the king's formal approval. The king granted that approval immediately before Yeardley died in office in 1627. The records indicate that Yeardley suffered from a recurrent sickness as far back as six years prior to his death. We believe he's buried in the Jamestown church in the knight's tomb. Whether Tempie is buried with him is unknown but seems likely.

Other Leaders in Virginia and Bermuda

Dr. Lawrence Bohun

Member of governor's council and physician general, also Lord La Warr's personal physician. Performed experiments with Virginia plants. Killed in the Spanish sea battle on the *Margaret and John* in 1621.

Capt. Nathaniel Butler

Bermuda governor and ally of the Earl of Warwick. He wrote a report, "The Unmasking of Virginia," criticizing Virginia to the Privy Council at a time when the colony was struggling with contagion and famine following the massacre. Capt. Peirce and many others signed a document rebutting the charges. Butler's report was part of the reason the Virginia Company collapsed.

Capt. William Claiborne

First surveyor of Virginia, councilor, secretary of state, fur trader, and founder of the Kent Island settlement. He was embroiled in Virginia's issues with Maryland because he settled Kent Island, which the king then gave to Maryland. He was military commander in the Indian war following the second massacre of 1644. In 1677, forty-two years after the troubles with Harvey and long after the councilors who ousted Harvey were dead, Claiborne was still attempting to secure Kent Island for Virginia. At that time, he petitioned King Charles II, saying he was "now in his old age" and "a poor old servant of your Majesty's father and grandfather."

Virginia officially claimed Kent Island until 1776, a hundred years after that. He was the nephew of Isabella Pace and Capt. Roger Smith.

Richard Kemp

Virginia secretary and councilor. Ally of Gov. Sir John Harvey. His argument with Pastor Anthony Panton is historic. Kemp was a later governor of Virginia.

Capt. Isaac Madison

Commander of West and Shirley Hundred. Rev. Greville Pooley wanted Madison and his wife Mary to be witnesses to his engagement to Cecily.

George Menefie

A successful merchant and council member. Arrested for the ouster of Sir John Harvey.
(1) Elizabeth > Elizabeth
(2) Isabella Pace Perry
(3) Mary

Rev. Greville Pooley

Pastor of Shirley Hundred, Flowerdieu Hundred, Chaplain's Choice, and Jordan's Journey following the 1622 massacre. Pooley sued Cecily Jordan for breach of promise, the first such suit in the New World.

John Pory

First cousin of Lady Temperance Yeardley, Virginia secretary, an explorer, and an avid "newsletter" writer. Considered to be the first English-language news correspondent. Pory was in northern waters seeking food after the massacre, captured by the Portuguese, and carried to the Azores. His alliance with the Earl of Warwick conflicted with his relationship with Temperance Yeardley's husband, Sir George.

George Sandys

Colony treasurer, poet, translator, and author, who lived with the Peirces in New Towne. Youngest brother of Sir Edwin Sandys. Encountered pirates in 1625 on his return to England with Sir George Yeardley. His translation of Ovid's *Metamorphoses*, substantially completed in the Peirce home at Jamestown, stands as a work of genius. His *Metamorphoses* is also a significant first: the first published work written in the New World.

Sandys did have a greyhound, but its name, Adonis, is fictional and taken from *Metamorphoses*.

Edward Sharples

Disgraced assistant secretary of the colony. He clandestinely and illegally provided copies of important Virginia documents to John Pory. The governor and council sentenced him to being pilloried and having his ears cut off. The governor and council reduced his sentence so that he lost only part of one ear.

Capt. John Uty

Councilor and York County justice. He lived at Utimaria and was married to Mary Ann. He died while charges of treason for ousting Harvey were still active. He made musical history on his arrival in 1620 by being the first known fiddler on American soil. William Tyler testified in 1624 that he called Mr. Uty a fiddler "because he saw him play upon a Violl at sea" and heard others say that "he was a musitione in England."

Native Americans

Chacrow (Chauco)

A friend of the English since at least the time of Sir Thomas Dale (1611-1616). Chacrow (or Chauco) lived in the barracks with Lieut. John Sharpe, William Powell, and William Peirce, where he learned firearms. He warned the settlers on the *Elizabeth* of the coming massacre in 1622. Chacrow's name is often mistakenly given as the Indian boy who lived with Richard Pace and William Perry and warned Pace of the massacre. A Christian Indian did live with Pace and Perry and give this important warning, but his name is unknown.

Esmy Shichans (The Laughing King)

A long-time ally of the English who lived on the Eastern Shore and was *werowance* of the Accomack.

Nemattanew (Jack of the Feather)

A great warrior and one of Opechancanough's right-hand men. He wore large birds' wings on his shoulders, hence among the settlers his cognomen "Jack of the Feather." Some natives believed he had magical powers. When he killed a settler named Morgan, he was in turn killed by the settlers. There's some indication his death was a trigger for the 1622 massacre.

Opechancanough

Paramount chief who followed Opitchapam, a shrewd and powerful war leader. Powhatan's brother and Pocahontas's uncle. He led both the 1622 and 1644 massacres. A soldier murdered him while he was an aged captive in the Jamestown jail in 1646.

Opitchapam (Otiotan, Sasawpen)

Paramount Chief who succeeded the *werowance* Powhatan beginning in 1618. His war chief brother, Opechancanough, overshadowed him during his rule. However, he led a massive battle to protect the Pamunkey cornfields in July 1624. He died around 1630, and Opechancanough officially became the paramount chief of the Powhatan natives.

Powhatan

Paramount chief of the alliance of Native Americans in Central and Eastern Virginia when the English arrived in 1607 and until his death in 1618. Pocahontas's father.

Sea Captains & Ships' Masters

Capt. Anthony Chester

Captain of the *Margaret and John*, memorable for its 1621 sea fight with the Spanish.

Mr. Richard Delbridge

Mariner from a well known Devon mercantile and political family. Owner of the *Concord*, which towed the *Tyger* in after pirates stripped it.

Capt. Daniel Elfrith

An ally of the Earl of Warwick. Captain of the *Treasurer* when it captured the Spanish slave ship. Captain of the *Tyger*, in consort with the *Warwick*, when pirates stripped the smaller ship.

Capt. Tobias (Toby) Felgate

An experienced mariner with land in Virginia. Captain of the *William and John* which transported the Yeardley children back to England in

1629, following Lady Temperance Yeardley's death.

Capt. Nicholas (Nick) Nurrey

Captain of the *Anne of Poole* when pirates captured it.

Pirates & Others in Morocco

Sidi Al-Ayachi

Holy man (*marabout*) of Salé, Morocco. He worked with John Harrison to create a treaty with England.

Honoré Despret (Fictional)

A Frenchman from Concarneau, France, chained in the *mazmorra* with George Sandys. While fictional, he represents the many unnamed prisoners from various European countries held in Salé.

Capt. John Harrison

A former governor of Bermuda and special envoy to Salé, Morocco, for King Charles. Brother to George Harrison, who died following a duel in Virginia.

Jan Jansz Or Janszoon (alias Murat Reïs—Captain Murat)

Dutch renegade who became a notorious leader of the Moroccan pirates and grand admiral of the Republic of Salé, Morocco. Notable raid includes a nighttime sack of Baltimore, Ireland, capturing many citizens. His son moved to New Netherland (New York) and became an ancestor of Jacqueline Kennedy, the Vanderbilts, and Humphrey Bogart.

Virginia Company Leaders

Sandys Faction

The Earl Of Southampton (Henry Wriothesley)

Officially the treasurer of the Virginia Company. The Virginia Company put forth Southampton to be treasurer because the king vehemently opposed Sir Edwin Sandys as treasurer. In practice, Sandys remained the treasurer. Southampton and Sandys were leaders of the liberal, anti-royalist faction of the Virginia Company.

Sir Edwin Sandys

King James refused to approve Sir Edwin Sandys as treasurer, but he was effectively treasurer of the Virginia Company from 1619 until the Company's dissolution in 1624. He was the leader of the Company's liberal faction accused of harboring democratical sentiments. He was better liked by the old settlers than the previous treasurer, Sir Thomas Smythe, although his administration had its dissenters as well.

John & Nicholas Ferrar

Two brothers who were heavily involved in the Virginia Company and assisted Sir Edwin Sandys.

Smythe Faction

Sir Thomas Smythe

First Virginia Company treasurer (1606-1619) and leader of the king's faction opposed to the leadership of Sandys. His tenure as treasurer included the Starving Time and a period of martial law, which caused much resentment in Virginia. Smythe was one of the most prominent merchants in England.

Warwick Faction

The Earl of Warwick (Robert Rich)

A staunch and powerful Puritan. The leader of another Virginia Company faction which ultimately joined with Smythe to defeat Sandys. In 1618, Warwick encouraged his ally, Gov. Samuel Argall, to send their jointly owned ship, the *Treasurer*, from Virginia to raid Spanish ships. The *Treasurer* successfully attacked the *São João Bautista* and stole its cargo of slaves. The settlers feared Spanish reprisals upon them for this action.

Other People the Peirces Visited in England

Capt. John Smith

Famous for his early days in the colony as president, he is known for his exploration and maps of the Chesapeake Bay and his *Generall History of Virginia, New England, and the Somers Isles* (Bermuda). He wrote about Pocahontas saving his life.

John Tradescant

A famous collector of curiosities from around the world. He lived at "The Ark," the first public museum in England.

Ralph & Rose Yeardley

Sir George Yeardley's older brother, an apothecary who lived in London. Married to Rose and had five children: John, Andrew, Ralph, Rose, and Anne. He helped Tempie settle her husband's estate and took the children in after their parents' death. Capt. Francis West sued him over Lady Yeardley's estate trying to obtain a larger portion of her dower.

Brief Timeline of Virginia Events

1590   Roanoke Island becomes the Lost Colony when John White discovers the settlers missing. Searching for the colonists is a goal the Virginia settlers don't abandon until 1621.

1607   First landing in Virginia.

1609   Joan's expedition arrives.

1609 – 1610   The Starving Time winter. When help finally arrives, Sir Thomas Gates institutes brutal martial law, which will stay in effect until 1619.

1610   First English/Indian war begins in retaliation for native siege during Starving Time.

1613 – 1614   Pocahontas kidnapped and brought to Henricus. In 1614, she marries John Rolfe, leading to peace with natives until 1622.

1616   Pocahontas sails to England with Sir Thomas Dale. Settlers arriving by this time are called "Ancient Planters" and receive certain privileges.

1617   Pocahontas dies in England.

1617   The Virginia Company allows settlers to leave Virginia for the first time since colony founded in 1607.

1618   Chief Powhatan dies. Opitchapam and Opechancanough come into power. Opitchapam is formally the paramount chief and Opechancanough the war chief, but Opechancanough wields much authority.

1618   The Spaniard, Don Diego de Molina, receives permission from his king to attack Virginia. His crew mutinies and kills him en route.

1618 – 1620   Gov. Argall illegally sends out the *Treasurer* to look for Spanish booty. She captures a Spanish ship with Africans on board. Yeardley tries to seize the *Treasurer* and her captured Africans, but the ship flees to a friendlier port, Bermuda. Some of the Africans (including

Angelo) end up in Virginia in 1620. The settlers worry for years that the Spanish will attack them due to Argall's reckless actions under the Earl of Warwick.

1619   In London, Sir Thomas Smythe, the first Virginia Company treasurer, leaves office and Sir Edwin Sandys replaces him. These are the only two treasurers of the Virginia Company, and members choose sides around them. Those supporting the Earl of Warwick create another faction, which ultimately aligns with Smythe. These troubles lead to a rupture and the end of the Company in 1624.

1619   The Company gives Yeardley authority to repeal hated martial law (in effect 1610-1619), to grant land, and to call a General Assembly.

1622   The first massacre, leading to second English/Indian war.

1624   The Virginia Company dissolved. Virginia becomes a royal colony.

1625   King James dies, and Charles takes the throne.

1632   Second English/Indian war ends.

1634   Founding of the Maryland colony leads to territorial settlement disputes with Virginia due to grants King James had given to Virginia and King Charles had promised to ratify.

1635   The Council ousts Harvey for siding with Marylanders and for his violent temper and arbitrary policies.

1635   Chesapeake sea battle between Marylanders and Virginians.

1644   A ship supporting the king battles with two ships supporting Oliver Cromwell at the mouth of the Warwick River. Seeing the English fighting among themselves, Opechancanough seizes an opportunity to strike once more. The second massacre occurs soon after, leading to the third English/Indian war.

1646   Opechancanough captured and brought to Jamestown, where a soldier (without authority) shoots him in the back. Necotowance becomes the new paramount chief.

1646   An Indian treaty with Necotowance, still in effect today, ends the third English/Indian war.

What's Fact and What's Fiction?

The Spanish Attack the *Margaret and John*

This exchange happened pretty much the way I wrote it based on eyewitness accounts. It brought well-deserved attention to the settlers who were braving such threats to come to Virginia and Bermuda. There was nothing the English liked better than besting the Spanish, particularly in a David and Goliath encounter!

Young Abraham Wood was indeed on the *Margaret and John*. Wood later became a major general, an Indian trader, an explorer, and commander of Fort Henry at the falls of the Appomattox River, the site of today's Petersburg, Virginia. Petersburg is named for Abraham Wood's son-in-law Peter Jones.

Mr. Mennes, one of the three who rowed over to the Spanish ship, was later knighted Sir John Mennes. He became the noted poet, Comptroller of the English Navy; and superior of Samuel Pepys, the diarist.

Joan's Home in New Towne: "The fairest in Virginia" according to House Guest George Sandys

Joan's home and those of her neighbors were where I locate them. Twentieth-century archaeology along with surviving land patents have established the boundary lines of seventeenth-century homeowners.

After excavating the foundations of the New Towne homes, archaeologists reburied them to preserve them. However, they placed new brick to mark where the old brick foundations are located.

I described Joan's home based on various archaeological finds regarding New Towne homes. The size of her home is from measurements of its foundations.

Did you know you can see the foundation of the Peirce house at Historic Jamestowne? (See map on the following page.)

The Peirce home is just behind and to the east of the Ambler mansion ruins (a much later structure). The road running in front of the Ambler mansion ruins is the old Back Street.

You can just make out a path between the Ambler ruins and a New Towne foundation, the home of Capt. William Powell and his wife, Margaret. The Peirce home (marked with a pointer) is just behind the Powell foundations and to the north.

Source: Google Maps

The Brutal Years of 1622-1623

Based on reports of the illness, the epidemic of 1623 sounds like typhoid. All first-hand accounts point to "Duppa's [or Dupper's] stinking beer" as the culprit. The Duppas had held the royal brewing contract since the time of Queen Elizabeth.

The combination of typhoid and famine was an especially lethal one for the settlers. More lives were lost that year than in the Indian attack of March 1622.

The starting population in March 1622 was about 1,400 men, women, and children. Three hundred forty-seven perished in the Indian attack or about one in every four.

The estimates of deaths to illness and famine the following year was another 500 settlers, including deaths among the 1,430 new arrivals.

The *Sea Flower* Explosion

Desperate for corn in a time of plague and famine, the settlers placed all their hopes on the relief ship *Sea Flower*.

She exploded and was lost in Bermuda when a spark from a tobacco pipe ignited gunpowder bound for Virginia defense.

Celebrating the arrival of the ship there, several Bermuda residents died in the explosion. The loss of life occurred as I tell it in the story, as did the looting of the wreck in the water, where some of the looters lost their lives as well.

The Strange Case of Cecily and the Overzealous Pastor

When I first started researching Cecily, I found a persistent reputation associated with her, that of a flirt. Passages commonly read something like, "The young widow Cecily Jordan introduced the fine art of flirting into the New World."

The original documents don't read that way at all. I'd like to address the issue.

First, a bit of background.

At this time, breach of promise suits were rare and usually initiated by women. These suits often amused the community, which heaped scorn, laughter, or pity on the woman bringing the suit. A man bringing such a suit would have attracted even more.

Enter Reverend Pooley, by all indications a stubborn man unable or unwilling to read signals. He was a relative newcomer to the colony.

Cecily, an Ancient Planter, had earned and inherited hundreds of acres for her own passage and that of her husbands. Pooley doubtless had his eye on all of it.

By her early twenties, Cecily had been widowed twice. She had two young daughters and was expecting a third child.

Samuel Jordan's death left her to oversee a large plantation, Jordan's Journey. Jordan's was one of the few settlements the governor and council held and did not order abandoned following the massacre. Neighbors from surrounding, less safe, plantations crowded inside the palisade for a year or more. Being far upriver, it was an easier potential target in the ongoing Indian war, a nerve-racking living situation.

Meanwhile, the colony was still reeling from the previous year's massacre followed by famine and epidemic contagion. Imagine the cumulative effect of all these conditions on this young woman.

Just a few days after Cecily's second husband died, Pooley pleaded with Captain Isaac Madison, commander of West and Shirley Hundred, to ask if the new widow might be interested in marrying him. Madison testified that he reluctantly approached Cecily on Pooley's behalf.

Cecily told Madison that she'd as willingly have Pooley as any other man but that she wouldn't marry anyone until she had delivered her baby. (The records don't indicate how far along she was in her pregnancy.)

Feeling emboldened, Pooley then came to Cecily's home bringing the Madisons as witnesses.

The pastor asked Cecily for "a dram" (a small drink). She agreed and asked a servant to fetch it for her. Pooley protested, telling her he "wold have it of her fetching, or not at all."

Remember that Cecily was a new widow; imagine the level of physical, mental, and emotional exhaustion she must have been feeling. Still, Cecily obligingly got up to get it for him.

At this point, Pooley followed Cecily and unexpectedly performed the marriage ceremony, reciting both parts, bride and groom. According to Madison's testimony, Pooley declared:

> I Grivell Pooley, take thee Sysley, to my wedded wife, to have, and to hold, till death us depart, and thereto I plight thee my troth. Then (holding her by the hand) he spake these words: I Sysley, take thee Grivell, to my wedded husband, to have, and to hold, till death us depart.
> —Minutes of the Council and General Court,
>   4 June 1623

Pooley's actions were strange and presumptuous even for the time. Madison said he didn't know whether Cecily understood Pooley's intentions when he'd followed her. She didn't repeat any vows, he added.

> ... but [Madison] heard not her say any of those words, neither doth he remember that Mr. Pooley asked her whether she did consent to those words or that shee did answer any thinge which he understood, then Mr. Pooley and she drank each to other, and he kissed her, and spake these words, I am thine and thou art mine till death us seperate. Mrs. Jordan then desired that it might not be revealed that she did so soone bestow her love, after her husbands death;

whereupon Mr. Pooley promised before God that he wold not reveale it, till she thought the time fittinge.
—Minutes of the Council and General Court,
4 June 1623

Contrary to his vow "before God," Pooley did tell the community. Here, Cecily reached the end of her patience and disavowed her engagement. Pooley decided to force the issue by suing for breach of promise, the first such case in North America.

The governor and councilors (who comprised the general court) likely had opinions about the pastor's actions. Still, the law was on Pooley's side. Being betrothed in this period was serious church business, and pastors were an important part of the community. But the court didn't rule, probably hoping he'd tire of the suit.

The leaders in Virginia asked the Virginia Company in London for their opinion in the matter. They needed advice because "wee not knowinge how to decide so nice a difference, our devines not takinge upon them presisely to determine, whether it be a formall and legall contract desire the resolution of the Civill Lawiers, and a speedy return thereof."

In London, a year into the lawsuit, the Company scratched its heads as well, asking Samuel Purchas, a cleric, to "conferr with some Civilians and advise what answer was fit to be returned in such a case." However, on the brink of collapse, the Company took no further action.

Pooley's suit dragged on for almost two years. By then, his key witness, Isaac Madison, was dead. Anglicans of the time considered marriage the proper, holy state, yet neither could marry with the suit pending. At last, Pooley relented.

In the meantime, the attorney (and future councilor) William Farrar was helping Cecily settle her husband's estate. That Cecily decided to marry Mr. Farrar instead isn't surprising, then. All the very many descendants of Cecily and William Farrar undoubtedly feel she made the right choice. Now onto the charges of flirting.

In the mid-nineteenth century came a rise in patriotism and glamorizing of the country's colonial origins.

Edward D. Neill, the assistant secretary to President Lincoln, seems to have been the first to unearth Cecily's case from Virginia court records. Neill published his version of the story in an 1867 history. (At that time, the records were still in manuscript form. It wasn't until 1924 that Henry Read MacIlwaine first transcribed and published them.)

William W. Henry, a grandson of Patrick Henry, seems to have first used the term "flirt" in connection with Cecily. In 1895, he wrote:

Within a few weeks after [Samuel Jordan's] death, in 1623, his widow, Cicely, distinguished herself greatly by introducing into the Colony the art of flirting, an art which has been practiced somewhat in Virginia ever since. It was alleged that she had accepted two suitors, the Rev. Greville Pooley, and Mr. William Ferrar. Each claimed her hand. Their hot dispute was carried before the Council.

—Hon. W.W. Henry, *The Virginia Magazine of History and Biography*, June 1895

To be fair, Henry had likely not seen the records as Neill had, so he simply drew his own conclusions from Neill's account.

By 1921, Cecily's case made it into The Constitutional Review with this comment: "As the men greatly outnumbered the women [in Virginia], every woman was a belle, and the opportunities for flirtation were boundless."

This story might have been amusing, even quaint, to two 19th century attorneys.

Indeed, the title of "flirt" has attached itself to Cecily for more than 120 years, causing injury to her reputation while simultaneously blaming her for it. Yet I'm certain nothing about the case was humorous to this young woman facing so many challenges.

Sir George Yeardley, George Sandys, and the Moroccan Pirates

While I don't have space to discuss this event thoroughly here, I can give an overview.

Dr. Richard Beale Davis is the only person who seems to have gleaned a clue that George Sandys may have been the victim of a pirate attack. Davis's sixty-year-old biography of Sandys mentions the possibility, winnowed from Sandys's autobiographical poem.

Fascinated and stunned by this speculation, I took Davis's idea to the next level and accumulated what I consider fair proof that Davis is right.

I was able to piece together many tantalizing details about the event. These include Sir George Yeardley being on the ship with Sandys, the ship's name and captain, where and when the pirates captured them, why the pirates were there, and why I believe the two men were able to secure their release through John Harrison. Harrison was on a secret mission for King Charles.

Significantly, Yeardley carried an important plea to the king to preserve the Virginia General Assembly. I discovered that, unbelievably, Yeardley also carried a letter to none other than John Harrison. (Harrison's brother had just died following a duel in Virginia.)

All this required intensive research, not in my original planning for the book since this find was a complete surprise. I went through Dr. Davis's papers at the University of Virginia and familiarized myself with the Moroccan pirates. I even read Harrison's letters in the French archives, a repository of Moroccan history. (For a good time, try reading archaic English about old Morocco, translated into French!)

When you read these parts, you might at first think I've fallen into a wild and contrived story line regarding Moroccan pirates. Just remember that truth continues to be stranger than fiction. Especially, it seems, where early Virginia is concerned.

The details of the pirate capture scenes, the treatment of captives in the mazmorra, even the specific Bible verses sung out, come from an old account. I drew them from Stephen T. Riley's paper, "Abraham Browne's Captivity by the Barbary Pirates, 1655."

Browne wrote in incredible detail about his capture. I blended the capture details of Browne's ship and experiences in Salé with what I knew of Yeardley and Sandys's capture.

To write a novel, I have to create some details.

Sir George Yeardley's injury is plausible but my creation. His loss of appetite at Sir Edwin Sandys's home and his seeking help in London following the attack are real. (His previous illnesses and later ones are also real.)

The Frenchman Honoré Despret is fictitious, but he represents the men, women, and children from many European countries who were captives during that brutal period. Most were never heard from again. I came to like Honoré very much. He was very real to me.

Even in fictionalized parts, I still aim for authenticity. Coastal waters near towns like Concarneau, Honoré's home, fell frequent victims to pirate attacks.

I already had the period French name, Honoré. When I discovered that Despret is a surname in Concarneau today, I liked it. It sounded to me like "Desperate Honor."

Joan's Fig Orchard

I spent longer than I probably should have doing what I called "fig math."

If Joan's garden had three or four acres, and she gathered close to 100 bushels of figs by the harvest of 1628 (she sailed in spring 1629), and she first planted her garden around the spring of 1623 … How many trees did she have? How long did it take those trees to begin producing figs? How many figs might one expect to harvest in, say, the fifth year of production? How many figs fill a bushel? How much more would the orchard produce in the coming years?

Complicating the calculations, the trees don't produce any figs the first two years. But once production starts, it will increase until the tenth year when production levels off.

Fig math. You heard it here!

Well, I can give you impressive spreadsheets to show my logic, but suffice it to say that what I've written of her orchard agrees with the facts she gave Capt. John Smith. I believe she had twelve trees in New Towne.

What did Joan do with what I estimate to be 240 bushels of figs by the 10th year in 1632?

She couldn't dry the figs due to Tidewater Virginia humidity, but I found enticing proof of fig marmalade being produced a century ago in the Deep South. So it's possible Joan also pioneered this treat, a combination of the English love of marmalade and the exotic figs filling up Joan's home in New Towne!

As a neighbor of Dr. Pott, an expert in distilled waters, Joan may have sold him some figs as well.

Capt. Smith reports that "of her own provision," Joan can keep a better house in Virginia than in London "for 3. or 400 pounds a yeare …"

Joan is here saying that she can support herself! What is she supporting herself with? The figs. So part of my "fig math" was to determine how many figs she'd have to sell to earn 300 or 400 pounds per year. Based on the value of tobacco, of course.

Her fig gardens give Joan Peirce an interesting place in horticultural history—one that probably would have astounded her. Her fig orchards are the first recorded in the New World.

Joan and Tempie and Mulberry Island

Captain Peirce had first patented land on Mulberry Island in 1619. He subsequently increased his land patents there.

In 1626, Sir George Yeardley also patented land on Mulberry Island next to the Peirce property. At the time, Yeardley had a great deal of land in various places in Virginia.

By 1635, the Peirces were living at Mulberry Island in a home on Morrison's Creek near the James River. The Yeardley tract was just over Morrison's Creek from Joan's home. Were they hoping to be neighbors once more? We'll never know.

In his will, Yeardley's instructions to his wife were to divest herself of the land and convert it to tobacco, which Tempie did. She died the next year.

By the way, Captain Peirce had a good eye for strategic property. His Mulberry Island tract became the site of Felker Army Airfield, the world's first military heliport!

The heliport opened in 1954, three hundred years after Capt. Peirce's death. It's near the boundary of the old Rolfe parcel and the 1619 Peirce tract.

The two men, Rolfe and Peirce, were business partners out at Mulberry Island.

Fort Eustis has encompassed the island for a hundred years, part of the military build-up for World War I.

Susanna Hall, the Peirces, and the Yeardley Children

Evidently Joan, on her visit to England, sailed on the same ship as the Yeardley children, the *William and John*, in March 1629.

Were the Peirces tasked with escorting the young Yeardley children to England?

A further clue emerges on May 21, 1630, the day William Peirce settled John Rolfe's will and the same day Susanna Hall testified on Lady Temperance Yeardley's behalf. Same day, same court—the Prerogative Court of Canterbury. This seems beyond chance to me, and when I happened to notice one date was the same as the other, I was very excited.

Simultaneous dates suggest the Peirces may have been protective of Susanna Hall and the Yeardley estate. It also suggests Susanna had traveled back to England with her dame's children in 1629.

Susanna was still a young woman, about twenty-two years old. It's not hard to imagine that she might have found the whole event daunting—a former servant confronting the lawsuit of Capt. Francis West, testifying to her dame's wishes, not to mention having to ferry the three children across the ocean and to their uncle's home in London.

Perhaps the Peirces saw an opportunity to support Susanna—and therefore Tempie—which suggests some familiarity with Tempie's wishes and the Yeardley estate. (Another possible indicator of some closeness between the two families is that Lady Temperance Yeardley had been a witness to John Rolfe's will. Rolfe's father-in-law William Peirce had been made executor.)

Capt. John Smith interviews Joan Peirce

Capt. Smith either interviewed Joan personally or spoke with someone who had talked with her. However, Capt. Peirce was in England about the time John Smith finished his history, and according to Smith, Joan had returned at that time with her husband.

Outside of Pocahontas, I can't think of any other woman Captain Smith quotes in his histories besides Joan Peirce.

The Peirces Take a Holiday!

The Peirces were in England for a year or more. What did they do during that time? I enjoyed planning a little vacation for Joan as I felt she'd earned one.

The play and Tradescant's Museum are fictional visits, but entirely possible as both were popular amusements at the time.

James Shirley's "The Wedding" was indeed playing at the Phoenix on Drury Lane that summer just as I wrote it. The theatre, formerly the Cockpit, had burned and was renamed the Phoenix.

The unusual and fascinating items of Mr. Tradescant were quite real and on display.

Capt. Peirce and the Overthrow of Gov. Sir John Harvey

These events happened much as I report them, based on surviving documents and accounts, including Mr. Menefie's soul searching at the Back River.

Captain Peirce was already in England when his fellow councilors were arrested in 1636 and sent to England as prisoners.

Peirce answered the charges in the Court of the Star Chamber and was then forced to remain in England on something similar to parole.

When he sailed, he left a large sum behind as a bond to ensure his return when or if called. He arrived in Virginia late in 1638.

Around November 1640, the men received word that the king was summoning them back to answer the charges.

However, on July 5, 1641, the Privy Council dissolved the Star Chamber.

Considering the Star Chamber is first documented to 1398 and had been around for 243 years, the timing of the end of that hated institution was nearly a godsend for these men.

It doesn't appear that the councilors ever returned for these charges, perhaps stalling as they understood their king was in great trouble with Parliament and the people.

Thus the 1635 mutiny is, to me, a critical step in Virginia's history. These men risked severe punishment (perhaps even execution) for overthrowing Governor Sir John Harvey. At this time, royal governors were "the king's substitute," meaning anything one did to this man was done to the king himself.

They took matters in hand in response to Harvey's misrule and his efforts to surrender to Maryland interests at the expense of Virginia planters. Peirce, Menefie, Pott, and the others had risked all to create the Virginia they knew. They'd endured hardships along the way—drought, mutiny, siege, shipwreck, famine, massacre, Indian wars, contagions, murrains. (Captain Peirce had been in Virginia longer than any of the others. He and Joan could list each one of these catastrophes and more

You can almost feel the men's impatience, their sense that they would not allow one incompetent, irascible, conniving, royal appointee governor to destroy all they'd worked for.

Were the ideals, the seeds of the American Revolution, in this event?

I think so.

1644 Massacre

Few records survive from the 1644 massacre, but some stories are preserved. The ones I told are fact. Historian Robert Beverley (*History and Present State of Virginia*, 1705) provided the information concerning Opechancanough's capture, his age and state of health, and murder.

A Final Glimpse of New Towne's Ruins, 185 Years Later

... [Of Jamestown] nothing was left standing but yon broken steeple, which has continued to be the land mark of centuries, and the aged sentinel over the dust of departed generations. The town was afterwards partially rebuilt, and many of its houses remained during my early novitiate at William and Mary College. They stood in a connected street, running east and west, from near the present dwelling house [the Ambler house ruins] to the ruins of the church.

—Former President John Tyler, 1857, at the 250th Jamestown Anniversary, recalling all that was left of New Towne, 1802-1807, then the remains of a very old town!

A Selection of English Settlements
along the James River

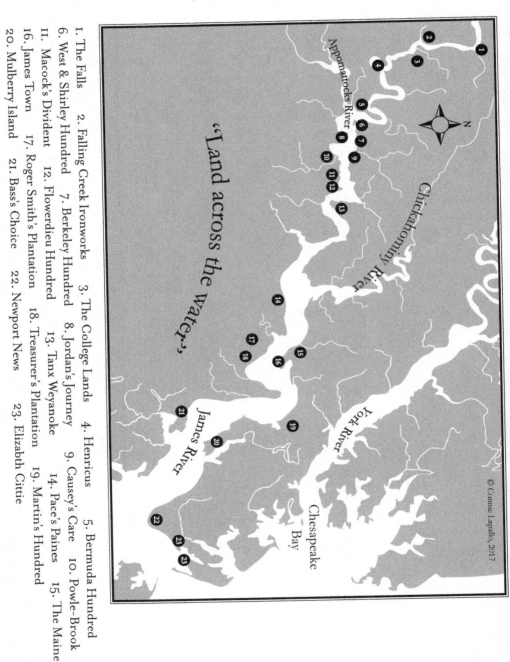

1. The Falls   2. Falling Creek Ironworks   3. The College Lands   4. Henricus   5. Bermuda Hundred
6. West & Shirley Hundred   7. Berkeley Hundred   8. Jordan's Journey   9. Causey's Care   10. Powle-Brook
11. Macock's Dividend   12. Flowerdieu Hundred   13. Tanx Weyanoke   14. Pace's Paines   15. The Maine
16. James Town   17. Roger Smith's Plantation   18. Treasurer's Plantation   19. Martin's Hundred
20. Mulberry Island   21. Bass's Choice   22. Newport News   23. Elizabth Cittie

World Map & Atlantic Sea Routes

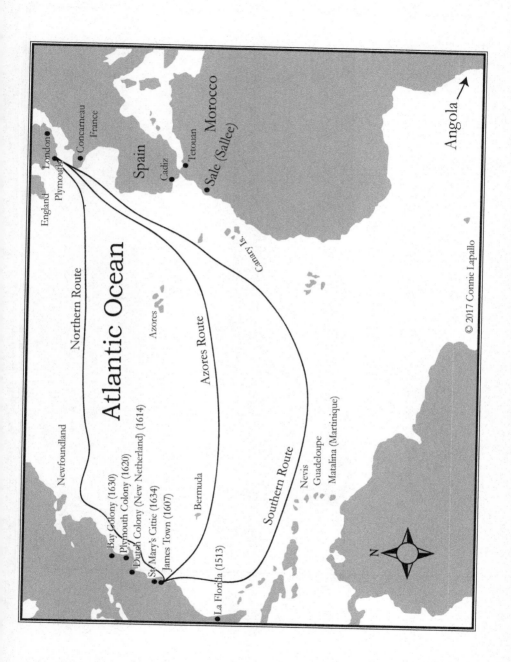

© 2017 Connie Lapallo

James Town Island

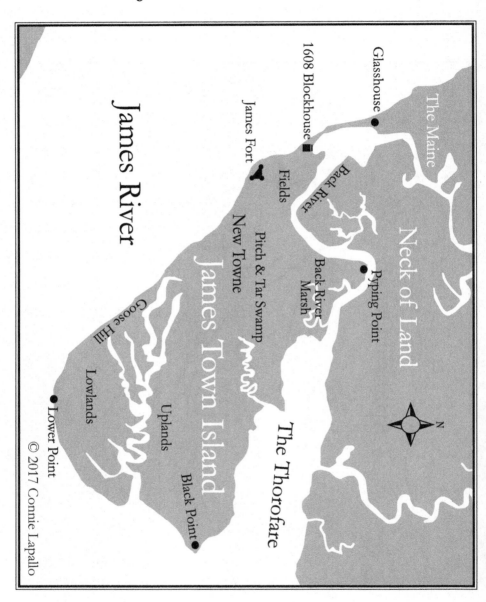

1608 Blockhouse

Glasshouse

James Fort

Fields

James River

Back River

The Maine

Neck of Land

Back River Marsh

Pyping Point

Pitch & Tar Swamp

New Towne

James Town Island

Goose Hill

Lowlands

Uplands

Black Point

The Thorofare

Lower Point

© 2017 Connie Lapallo

N

New Towne

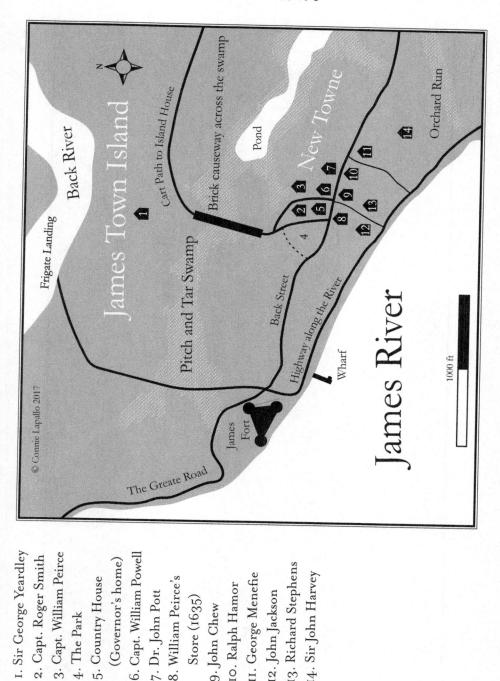

1. Sir George Yeardley
2. Capt. Roger Smith
3. Capt. William Peirce
4. The Park
5. Country House (Governor's home)
6. Capt. William Powell
7. Dr. John Pott
8. William Peirce's Store (1635)
9. John Chew
10. Ralph Hamor
11. George Menefie
12. John Jackson
13. Richard Stephens
14. Sir John Harvey

Mulberry Island

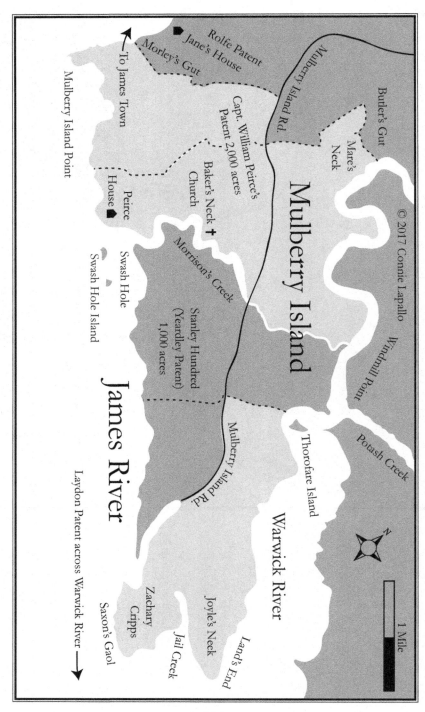

Rolfe Patent
Jane's House
Morley's Gut
To James Town
Mulberry Island Rd.
Mulberry Island Point
Capt. William Peirce's
Patent 2,000 acres
Baker's Neck
Church
House
Peirce
Butler's Gut
Mare's
Neck
© 2017 Connie Lapallo
Mulberry Island
Swash Hole
Swash Hole Island
Morrison's Creek
Stanley Hundred
(Yeardley Patent)
1,000 acres
Mulberry Island Rd.
Windmill Point
Thorofare Island
Potash Creek
James River
Warwick River
Laydon Patent across Warwick River ⟶
Zachary
Cripps
Jail Creek
Saxon's Gaol
Joyle's Neck
Land's End
N
1 Mile

Chesapeake Bay

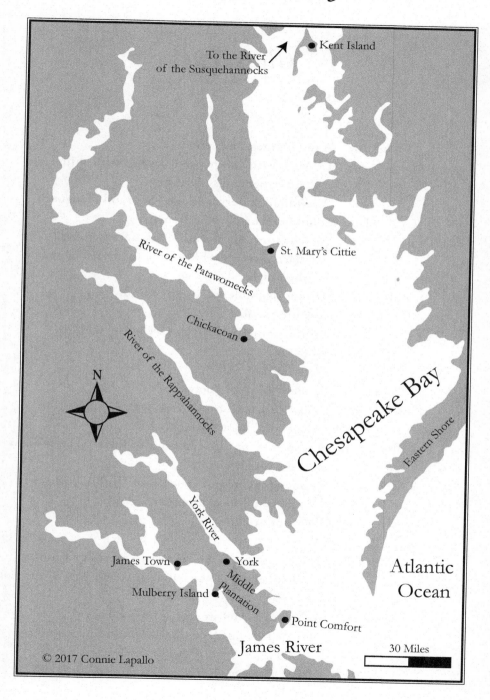

To the River
of the Susquehannocks

Kent Island

River of the Patawomecks

St. Mary's Cittie

Chickacoan

River of the Rappahannocks

N

Chesapeake Bay

Eastern Shore

York River

Atlantic
Ocean

James Town

York

Middle
Plantation

Mulberry Island

Point Comfort

James River

30 Miles

© 2017 Connie Lapallo

Glossary

Adam's Ale	A phrase meaning "water."
Ague	(Rhymes with "plague you.") Fever with chills, shivering, and sweating.
Aiué	A sound of suffering in the Kimbundu language.
Alack	A mild exclamation of despair.
Alarum	Archaic form of "alarm." The alternate form, "alarm," was just beginning to make its way into the English language.
Aqua Vitae	Strong alcoholic spirit, often brandy.
Aught	Anything at all.
Banns	Proclamation in church of a coming wedding.
Betaken	Gone to.
Betook	Went to.
Betwixt	Archaic word for "between."
Blockhouse	A structure used for defense with loopholes for guns to shoot through.
Bloodwort	A type of plant with red roots or leaves. The Indians called it "puccoon."
Bosun	Phonetic spelling of "boatswain," a ship's officer in charge of the equipment and crew.
Brickbats	Pieces of brick.
Bridge	Wharf.
Búfalo	The English used the Portuguese word for animals they believed to be buffalo, actually American bison.
Bulwark	An upward extension of a ship's sides.
Burthen	Archaic for "burden," the weight in tons a ship can carry.
Bushel	A unit of dry measure equal to 4 pecks or 8 U.S. gallons.

Calenture	Feverish delirium believed to be caused by tropical heat.
Chamay, wingapo	"Greetings, friend" in the Powhatan language.
Chinquapin	A shrubby chestnut native to Virginia, which keeps its Powhatan name.
Chirurgeon	Old form of the word "surgeon."
Coffé	Early version of the word "coffee."
Coif	A woman's close-fitting cap.
Collect	In its religious sense, a short, structured prayer.
Coneys	British term for "rabbits."
Cousin German	First cousin.
Crow of Iron	Crowbar.
Dame	The mistress of a household.
Delftware	A style of blue and white glazed pottery from the town of Delft in the Netherlands.
Diverse	Also spelled divers. Various, several, or assorted, as in "diverse ships going to Virginia."
Divident	Dividend or division, a share of a public company. The Virginia Company granted dividents of land since it had little money.
Dost	Does.
Doublet	A man's short close-fitting cropped jacket.
Dower	A widow's share of her husband's estate.
Dragon's blood	A bright red gum derived from certain palm trees. In Medieval times, originally thought to actually come from dragons or elephants.
Ducats	Gold or silver Venetian coins used for trading.
Falconet	A light cannon.
Fardels	Parcels, packages.
Fain	Pleased to; with pleasure; gladly.
Fens	A mineral-rich mire or bog found in Eastern England.
Firebrand	A piece of burning wood.
Firkin	A small cask.
Flagon	A large drinking glass or mug.
Flux	Dysentery.
Foredeck	The deck toward the front of a ship.
Fortnight	Fourteen nights, two weeks.
Gaol	British spelling of "jail."

Grapple	To use iron hooks with claws, a type of anchor.
Gum dragon	A natural gum from the sap of certain types of trees.
Hackney	A hired horse-drawn carriage.
Halberd	Effectively an ax mounted at the end of a long spear.
Halberdiers	Someone who wields a halberd.
Hard by	Nearby.
Headrights	A right to a certain amount of acreage for paying someone's passage to Virginia.
Helm	A tiller or wheel to steer a ship.
Hie	Go quickly.
Horehound	A member of the mint family.
Humors	From ancient times, people believed the body had four humors which must stay in balance for good health.
Hurricano	Early modification of Spanish word for "hurricane."
Jackanapes	A conceited, rude, and annoying person.
Jerkin	A sleeveless jacket.
Keeler	A large copper pot used in brewing beer.
Kine	A group of cows.
Knot Garden	An herb or flower garden with plants arranged in patterns to give a woven effect.
Lateen	An ancient type of triangular sail coming from the word for "Latin rig."
League (nautical)	Three nautical miles.
Letters Patent	An open document from a monarch conferring a patent or other right.
Lightwood	Kindling.
Lingua franca	A blended common language created by speakers whose languages are different.
Loblolly	English seafaring term for a thick porridge sometimes including meat or vegetables.
Mahometan	In the seventeenth century, the English referred to Muslims as Mahometans, followers of
Mahometan Religion	Mohammed.
Marabout	Islam, or "the religion of Mohammed."
Mare of the night	A Muslim religious leader or holy man.
	At this time, the idea of a "night mare" was of a supernatural and evil creature which caused such dreams, not the bad dreams themselves.

Matalina	Probably today's Martinique.
Matchcoat	A Native American garment, effectively a woolen blanket fastened around the shoulders.
Mayhap	It may happen, it may be.
Mazmorra	Dungeon.
Morisco	A Moor in Spain that had accepted Christianity.
Morrow	The following day.
Murrain	A plague or epidemic.
Narrow Seas or Sea	The English Channel.
Ordnance	Cannon.
Parley	Negotiate.
Patroonas	Moroccan slave owners.
Peck	A unit of dry measurement, about 2 U.S. gallons.
Perspective Glass	Early term for "telescope."
Pestered	During this period, to be so crowded as to bring pestilence or disease.
Physick	Medicinal herbs and remedies.
Physick garden	An herb garden with medicinal plants.
Picaroons	Rogues or scoundrels.
Pike	A weapon comprised of a long spear with a spike on one side.
Pinnace	A small ship.
Piskies	Pixies.
Pokahichary	Indian name for hickory trees. The English shortened this to "hickory."
Posset	A hot drink of milk curdled with wine or ale, often spiced.
Prithee	Shortened form of "I pray thee."
Puccoon	A type of plant with red roots or leaves called by the English bloodroot. The Native Americans used it on their skin to repel insects.
Pumpion	Pumpkin.
Quarterdeck	A ship's open deck at the stern.
Renegado	A renegade, also at the time called a runagate. "Runagate" initially meant a vagabond, while "renegado" meant someone who had given up their religion, as the Dutch and English became Muslims when they became Moroccan pirates.

Roundhouse	On a ship, the uppermost cabin, located on the stern.
Runagate	Another word for renegade, also called a renegado.
Runlet	A small stream.
Sack	An old term for white wine from Spain or the Canary Islands.
Saker	A medium cannon.
Saletin	Of or relating to Salé, Morocco, or a resident of Salé.
Saltfish	Fish, especially cod, preserved in salt.
Scimitar	A short sword with a curved blade used in Eastern countries.
Scupper	A hole in a ship's deck where water can drain to the sea.
Scuttle	A small hatchlike opening in the deck of a ship large enough for a person to fit through.
Seasoning	New arrivals had difficulty adapting to Virginia's hot summers. The settlers referred to this as "the seasoning." Often, once immigrants survived the first summer, their harshest adjustment was over. The colonists referred to this as being "seasoned."
Self-heal	A member of the mint family, also called prunella or woundwort.
Shallop	A light boat used for shallow waters.
Shrouds	Rigging which runs from a ship's mast to the sides of the ship to support the mast sideways.
Snaphaunce	The earliest form of flintlock firearm.
Souk el-Ghezel	The old Wool Market Square in Rabat, Morocco.
St. Elmo's Fire	A weather phenomenon causing sparks of light. St. Elmo was the patron saint of sailors, and sailors often believed St. Elmo's fire to be a supernatural indicator of good luck.
Surfeit	A condition caused by overeating.
Sweetmeat	Sweet foods.
'Swounds	An archaic oath.
Tercios	Elite infantry forces of the Spanish military during the sixteenth and seventeenth centuries, combining firepower with pikes.

Terra alba Virginiensis	A white earth from Virginia which the Indians used for healing. Today, we call it "kaolin."
Thence	From that place.
Truck	Barter.
Truncheon	A short, thick stick carried as a weapon.
Tuckahoe	A wetlands plant with arrow-shaped leaves and an edible root.
Turn'd Lead	Slender grooved lead used to hold pieces of glass in place as in a stained-glass window.
'Tween deck	The deck or space between decks.
Twelvemonth	Year in length.
Vignerons	Grapevine grower, tends a vineyard.
Wattle and Daub	Building material made of woven sticks and mud, used to fill in a wood frame.
Welladay	Woe, alas!
Werowance	Powhatan word for chief.
Xebecs	Small, sleek Mediterranean sailing vessels, typically with lateen (triangular) sails.
Yardarm	A "yard" is a horizontal spar on a mast from which sails hang. The yardarm is half a yard.
Yonder	Over there, in the distance.

About the Author

Connie Lapallo grew up in Mechanicsville, Virginia, surrounded by history and only fifty miles from where her ancestors landed at Jamestown. Her childhood home included four generations where she loved listening to her grandparents' and great-grandmother's stories of old Virginia as well as her father's memories of growing up impoverished in war-torn Sicily.

Today, Lapallo enjoys traveling the country speaking to book clubs, schools and colleges, lineage and historical societies, conferences, clubs, churches, and symposiums about the women and children in her novels. She's also a volunteer historian for the Chesapeake Conservancy.

She still lives in Mechanicsville with her husband Chris and their two rescue dogs who help them keep the household under control.

Lapallo spent nineteen years researching and writing her trilogy, which overlapped seventeen years of homeschooling her four children. She has no idea what she'll do with her time now that the novels and the children have all flown the coop.

CPSIA information can be obtained
at www.ICGtesting.com
Printed in the USA
BVOW03s0507120417

480489BV00004B/3/P